SINISTER

SINISTER

A NOVEL

VERONICA LANCET

ATRIA PAPERBACK
New York Amsterdam/Antwerp London
Toronto Sydney/Melbourne New Delhi

ATRIA
PAPERBACK
An Imprint of Simon & Schuster, LLC
1230 Avenue of the Americas
New York, NY 10020

This Atria Paperback edition August 2026

ATRIA PAPERBACK and colophon
are registered trademarks of Simon & Schuster, LLC

Interior design by Davina Mock-Maniscalco

Printed and bound in the UK using 100% renewable electricity at CPI Group (UK) Ltd

1 3 5 7 9 10 8 6 4 2

Library of Congress Cataloging-in-Publication Data has been applied for.

ISBN 978-1-6682-4250-6 (pbk)

The authorised representative in the EEA is Simon & Schuster Netherlands BV, Herculesplein 96, 3584 AA Utrecht, Netherlands.
info@simonandschuster.nl

AUTHOR'S NOTE

Warning: This is not your regular romance story.

This is dark and entirely morally ambiguous. The plot will take you to some wild heights, but bear with me, okay?

Confusion is to be expected, but I promise you a fulfilling HAPPY ending (unlike the first draft of this book that was rather . . . grim, but we don't talk about that).

If you've read *Fairydale* by me, then you know to expect a mindfuck.

Don't lower your guard, or you might find yourself deceived.

That being said, enjoy the wild ride, besties.

This story includes occurrences of: blood and pain play, bullying, demonic pacts and possession, domestic abuse/physical assault, dubious and nonconsensual acts, explicit sexual scenes, fire, gaslighting and possessiveness, graphic murder and mutilation, grief, gun violence, mass death and sacrifice, oppressive religious cult, poisoning, religious and occult themes, revenge porn, self-harm, stalking and manipulation, suicide and suicidal ideation, teen pregnancy, violence and gore.

BREAKING NEWS

Radcliffe Herald

30 YEARS AGO

ST. ANSELM HALL TO REOPEN ITS DOORS AS A HIGH SCHOOL

After almost a century of inactivity, St. Anselm Hall has reopened its doors! The eminent institution, previously a celebrated university, will now welcome high school students from all over the country. With a reported endowment of over $1 billion USD, St. Anselm Hall debuts as one of the most elite private institutions.

St. Anselm will hold its own annual admittance exam, said to be one of the most rigorous of its kind.

A LEGACY OF THE OCCULT

Regarded as one of the most illustrious institutions of higher learning in the nineteenth century, St. Anselm Hall University closed down in 1896, after a series of rituals that resulted in the death of over twenty students. The public is concerned about whether this will affect the reputation of the new high school, but the Board of Trustees confirms that the days of the occult are far behind.

Mrs. Levine, the president, said, "We are happy to live in an age where people do not believe in such nonsense anymore. St. Anselm Hall will regain its reputation as a pinnacle of education."

The townsfolk, however, are still skeptical. Particularly, members of the Reformationist church, whose families were the main contributors to shutting down the university. The town, it seems, is once more divided.

PART ONE

CHAPTER ONE

PETRA

Present Day
Radcliffe, New England

I smell the fire before I see it. Acrid, plasticky, thick—it singes the cold night air as shouts and yells echo around me. In the next few seconds, I see a flaming figure in a mascot costume leap off a balcony, heading straight for the pool underneath the ivy-trailed railings.

Then I hear a loud splash followed by silence.

"What the hell?"

"Was that Benny?"

The kids who have just entered the compound behind me are aptly shocked as well, drawing together and murmuring among themselves.

We all stand rooted to our spots, waiting for whoever the lunatic was to resurface.

"ANSELM HEROES, BITCHES!!" a brash voice shrieks from somewhere inside the mansion as the glowing blue waters of the pool roil and break apart.

Soon after, Benny's shaggy-haired head emerges from the depths, like some dollar-store Poseidon.

Instantly, the music is back on—when had it stopped? I don't think any of us noticed—and people are crowding around the pool, hooting and cheering Benny as he slowly wades out onto the steps and plonks himself into a nearby lounge chair.

"Dude, that was so sick!" says a burly football player, poetically named

Dick or Chad (I don't really care enough to find out), while Benny chugs down beer from a can like it's manna from the heavens.

But the sight of another guy near them halts me in my tracks. He's tall, taller even than most of the football players actually, and athletic. It feels like he's looking straight over Benny's head to where I'm standing, an unreadable expression in his piercing blue eyes.

A warm flush covers my face; I have seen him on campus before. Sin something—

"Benny, what the fuck, man?!" Elias's scream breaks through the swirl of my thoughts. "Why'd you do that? My parents will kill me if they find out!"

"Dude, relax!" Benny rolls his eyes. "Me and the boys were just messing about."

"You were ON FIRE!" Elias's eyes are bulging with dread, while others around them are busy creating looping videos of Benny's jump and posting them to their socials.

And these are my peers, I think with a dejected sigh.

When I look back at the scene, I realize that the blue-eyed guy—Sin—has disappeared.

As I stare back up at the grand façade of the house looming above me, its dark stone exterior softened by the moonlight and the glow from the windows, I realize that coming to Elias Rutherford's party was probably a mistake. I mean, I could have just stayed home and sketched.

On my eighteenth birthday. That even my parents forgot.

Who am I kidding? That last part is the very reason I'm here.

Look, I get that my parents are busy. Their million-dollar tech company wouldn't function without my father, who is the CEO, and my mother, the CTO. The same company whose skyrocketing revenues bought me the vintage Prada Mary Janes on my feet and my Valentino crossbody.

But they could spare *one day,* couldn't they? For their only daughter?

These gloomy thoughts threaten to overtake my mind, even as the bass from the music inside pulses through the air, vibrating in my chest.

I take a deep breath, steeling myself.

Enough of the pity party.

Time for an *actual* party.

Tonight, I need to do something different. Amelia's voice echoes through my errant thoughts: "Celebrate your birthday, Petra. You deserve it."

By now, I have reached the half-open oak doors of the Rutherfords' mansion. The artist in me can't help but admire the building's ornate stonework and looming towers that seem to yawn toward the sky.

As I step up to the door, sounds of the revelry from inside drift into my ears. Someone has put on a Lorde song, and the melody soothes my frazzled nerves.

Hey, maybe this won't be so bad, I tell myself before taking a deep breath and entering.

Once inside, Lorde's husky voice resonates in the air. I look around the rooms, hoping against hope to catch a friendly face, at least one kind glance.

Like most students who go to St. Anselm Hall, the extremely elite, private, co-ed school where I spend the larger part of my days with the sons and daughters of billionaires, Elias Rutherford is rich.

Adding to that, he's the captain of the school football team, the St. Anselm Heroes. Unsurprisingly, his multi-hyphenate status means that any party he throws is sure to blow up into an all-night *event.*

Tonight, the grand foyer is bathed in a warm golden glow from the chandeliers overhead, and somebody's set up a smoke machine in a corner of the living room.

Strobe lights cast colorful patches on the walls, and there are people *everywhere.*

Raucous groups of jocks exchanging lewd jokes, giggling Instagram fashionistas posing in front of the wall-length mirrors in the hallways, stoned punk-rock kids jamming away in the corner of the drawing room . . .

The party has them all in attendance. And in abundance.

Normally, the dense, milling crowd would make me feel suffocated. To be honest, I'm already experiencing a faint sense of claustrophobia from all the smoke and mirrors.

Right, time to find a safe corner, my instincts tell me, so I head for the kitchen and pour myself a much-needed drink.

Thankfully, whatever jungle juice these football bros have mixed together warms me up and calms my nerves, and I lean back against the cool counter, taking a minute to gather myself.

As I try to relax, I again remember my chat with Amelia from earlier today.

I still remember the first time I stumbled into the chatroom on Instafriends. It was late at night, and the house was quiet, except for the AC's soft hum. It was another birthday made memorable by my parents' absence.

My fourteenth, if it matters—it obviously didn't matter to them.

That was the night I had first clicked on the "Misc Midn8 Meets." I had shied away from all forms of social media before then, probably because of my utterly bleak outlook on most human beings, borne out of a special kind of isolation called "homeschooling."

But that night, something about the chatroom called to me. It had been relatively empty, with just a few usernames drifting in and out. I hesitated for a moment, then typed a simple message.

Petrified: Hello, anyone here?

A few moments passed before a reply popped up.

AmeliaEarheart: Yo, love your username! What's up?
Petrified: Thanks! I like yours, too.
AmeliaEarheart: Why you up so late? Can't sleep?
Petrified: Yeah it's been a rough night tbh.
AmeliaEarheart: Sorry to hear that! What happened?

And the rest is history, as they say. That night, I found my soul sister, a girl who lived somewhere in New York while I was in Radcliffe, a few miles away from New Haven. Over the next few weeks, Amelia and I chatted almost every night.

Despite her laconic style, there was a warmth to her messages that made me feel seen, even when she couldn't actually see me.

Petrified: So, what's it like going to school in New York?
AmeliaEarheart: Girl, it's DA BEST! Classes are great, and there's so much to do. Museums, parks, random street performances that could put bloody *Hamilton* to shame. It's like living in a movie sometimes, I kid you not.

Her enthusiasm was infectious. The more she talked about New York, the more I wanted to be there. To walk the same streets and visit the same places with her.

I had long wanted to attend college there, perhaps at the School of Visual Arts or even Parsons, if they'd have me.

And when I met Amelia in that dingy little corner of the internet, it felt like a homecoming in a way. Like I had finally found my people.

My happy musings are rudely interrupted by a sudden onslaught of visitors streaming into the kitchen, so I make my way out into the dining room.

The full-length French windows are draped with expensive fabric. The room is lush with potted plants, but these have been moved to one side to create more space for the party.

As I hesitantly push through the crowd, trying to not poke or prod anyone and draw the least amount of attention possible, I can hear snippets of whispered conversations.

"Isn't that Petra Valentine?" someone says.

"O.M.G. *The* Petra Valentine? Can't believe she deigned to come down among us mortals," a snarky voice responds quite audibly.

The words sting, but I keep my head held high and continue sipping my drink.

"Why's she here, slumming it out with us peasants?" I hear next, and it takes everything in me not to turn around and walk out instantly. "She's so stuck up that even her own parents can't stand to be in the same house."

Ouch, that really, really hurt.

At this point, I'm desperate to be alone, so I turn the knob on the next visible door, step inside, and close it behind me with a loud bang, not caring who heard it.

Turns out I'm in a guest washroom. I splash some water onto my face and stare at the mirror, not even recognizing the brown-haired, dark-eyed girl looking back at me. When did she—I—become so cynical, so aloof from all the other kids my age? Are my parents the only ones to blame here?

Of course, family has always been a sore subject for me. It's not like Mom and Dad don't love me; it's that they don't care enough to show it in ways that make me feel valued.

I think back to our last conversation.

"I don't understand why you're being so stubborn about this, Petra," my mother had said in a sharp voice. "Yale is one of the best universities in the world. It's close to home, and it will give you all the networking opportunities you need."

"Don't you ever listen to me?" I'd snapped back. "I don't *want* to go to Yale. I don't *want* to study law or business or whatever else you think I should do. I want to study graphic design."

My father had stepped forward, his brow furrowed.

"Graphic design is fine as a hobby, Petra, but you can't make a living out of it. Think about what you could do with a degree from Yale! Be realistic, Petra, you can always pursue graphic design on the side."

"A hobby?" I'd repeated, my voice rising. "Can you just . . . It's not a hobby to me, Dad! It's what I love. It's what I want to do with my life. Why can't you just support me for once?"

"We do support you, Petra." My mother's tone was softened with exhaustion, as if we had been at odds long before I had grown a will of my own. "But we want what's best for you. We understand that—"

"No, you don't understand," I'd interrupted her coldly, enraged at the fake display of affection. "You've never understood. You're always too busy with your own lives to even notice what I want or what I'm passionate about."

"That's not fair, Petra," Dad had replied in a low voice simmering with anger. "We've always given you everything you needed."

"Everything except your time and attention," I shot back. "You're never here. You don't know anything about me. You don't know what makes me happy or what I care about because you're never around to find out."

"Petra, behave!" my mother warned. "We're doing this for you. We work hard so you can have a good life, the best life."

"Oh, please, spare me the drama," I was quick to retaliate. "You're doing it for yourselves and because it makes you look good to other people. But it's not what I want. I don't want to be like you. I *never* want to be like you!"

The room had fallen silent as my parents exchanged a look, perhaps of regret, perhaps of resentment . . . I didn't know.

After that, I was back in my room, curled up on the bed, my body racked with sobs.

It looks like tonight might just be another one of those lonely, alienating nights.

As I stare at my reflection in the gilded mirror, Amelia's words come floating back through the haze of sorrow. *"You're a special girl, Petra,"* she had texted this morning; it was her birthday message for me. *"You deserve to be seen and celebrated for being the unique, beautiful soul that you are."*

Like always, even the memory of her words jolts me out of my current funk. I open my eyes and adjust my hair. Light filters through the glass pane on the door, and music creeps in; now they're playing Lil Nas X.

Over the strains of "Industry Baby," I smooth down my pleated Thom Browne skirt. My fingers brush against the soft fabric, grounding me. Tonight, I'm leaving my comfort zone. I'm going to look those bullies in the eye and give them a piece of my mind.

Stepping out of the washroom, I spot a group of girls huddled together and instantly feel my hackles rise up when I recognize them from school.

There's that icy blonde, Daphne, queen bee of the St. Anselm Hive, an IG page reportedly dedicated to the welfare of the student community—if "welfare" meant spreading vicious gossip about whoever has crossed or even slightly irked Daphne.

Next to her is Lenora, a tall brunette with a sleek bob and a perpetually bored expression. And then there's François, the most pretentious guy at school, always preening and showing off because his mother's French.

Their eyes flicker in my direction, and I catch my breath.

Uh oh, here it comes. Brace yourself, Petra.

"Ooh, the devil does wear Prada," François says with a nasal twang that grates on my nerves.

"C'mon, Frankie, be nice! She's probably here to see what normal people do for fun," I hear Daphne say in a faux whisper that carries to the end of the room.

"You guys think she even knows what 'fun' means?" Lenora adds, doing nothing to hide her sneer or lower her voice.

"I do know what words mean, Lenora," a cold voice responds, and I'm half-surprised to discover that it's my own. "See, unlike you, *I* didn't fail English last semester."

The girls look up, startled. For a moment, there's silence, then Daphne smirks and says, "No need to be so dramatic, Petra, we were just wondering... Parties are not really your scene, are they?"

"Well, what can I say? I'm a keen observer of animals in their natural habitats," I say without pausing for breath.

"Excusez-moi?" François spits out.

"Is that what your mother told you when you asked her to hug you last, Frankie?"

Even I'm shocked at the undisguised vitriol in my voice, but I have been suppressing too many big, messy emotions for far too long. And no matter what people say about Daphne and her cronies, they are easy targets for me.

The trio is visibly flustered as scattered laughs follow my last remark.

"Wow, feeling really smug today, aren't we?" Daphne manages to sputter out in the end. "Just so you know, we've placed actual bets on how long you'll last before you bolt back to your cave."

I smile sweetly at her. "Well, I'd simply *hate* for you to lose all that money, wouldn't I? Oh, wait, I wouldn't."

And while the idiots are still scrambling to assemble a witty response between the three of them, I turn around and walk toward the drinks table.

I'm positively parched for a drink. In fact, I could down several shots of that jungle juice doing the rounds.

Not caring to get back into the crowd yet, I'm content to watch from the sidelines for now. If I know anything about Daphne, it's that she won't forget my insults in a hurry. She'll be waiting and watching for any chance to put me down.

Well, her and everyone else, I can't help but tell myself bitterly. I've always been a bit of a loner, but lately, the incessant feeling of not belonging anywhere has dimmed my spirits.

Once more, I remind myself of Amelia's words.

At least I have her.

But though the darkness lightens up, it doesn't recede altogether.

So I do something stupid. I pour myself another shot, my fourth, and let the liquid sear its way down my throat.

With every gulp, I feel mellower as a soft, cottony haze settles over the sharp edges of my righteous fury, and the world seems like a less hurtful place.

For a while, I just drift through the throngs of guys and girls dancing in the halls and drinking in the living room and making out in the myriad corners around the house.

The alcohol seems to have numbed me to any hostile stares or whispers. This is what all the fuss is about, I guess. I could get used to this—

Just then, I collide into something hard. And tall.

"Oh my God!" a deep, velvety voice exclaims while broad, sturdy hands gently hold my shoulders, steadying me. "Are you okay?"

I'm tipsy enough to appreciate the note of concern yet not drunk enough to ignore the fact that now my blouse is wet.

"I'm so sorry," the same pleasant voice is rambling in earnest panic now. "I wasn't looking where I was going, and I spilled my drink! Let me help you with that. It's Petra, right?"

In that moment, I finally recognize the blue-eyed guy I'm speaking to.

"Yes, thasright, I mean." I clear my throat and try to appear more sober. "That's right. And you're . . . Sinclair?" I slur.

"Sin Arnoult, at your service," the tall—I should say "towering"—guy responds with a charming little half-bow.

And when he looks up next, something in his eyes makes my breath hitch in my throat.

CHAPTER TWO

PETRA

Present Day

This can't be happening, says the cynical voice in my head as I look up and my eyes lock with Sin's. This is a moment straight out of a rom-com. The heroine collides with the hero, literally and metaphorically.

If it's your standard Hallmark suckfest, she's either going to be a swooning, clumsy mess or a mildly disgruntled (but *hot*) woman whose entire schedule for the day is thrown off because of this annoying (but *hot*) man who decided to bump into her.

But I am neither. After my encounter with Daphne and Co., I don't have the energy to be visibly vexed. And I also don't fall over myself at the sight of blue-eyed guys with stylishly tousled hair.

Instead, I merely say, "*Oh,*" and keep staring at the rapidly expanding wet patch on my light-teal satin blouse. I had 'borrowed' this one from my mother's enviable collection. She'll probably hire a hitman to kill me; Mom doesn't like to get her hands dirty.

"I'm so sorry!" Sin exclaims again, and though he sounds genuinely apologetic, I can see the lightest of smiles playing on his lips.

Despite the shots I have downed, some remaining shred of dignity forces me to regain my composure and muster up a wry smile. "Well, I guess I'm wearing your drink now. Do you always greet people this way?"

This makes him chuckle.

Hey, he's got a nice laugh, I think, and then chide myself for getting sappy.

"Only the ones who stand in my way," he says, leaning toward me so I can hear him over the music. "Here's a radical idea. Maybe, *just maybe,* you can try watching where you're going the next time?" he whispers in a low, gravelly voice that sends shivers down my spine.

"Me?" I blurt out, shaking away the intrusive thoughts. "You almost managed to blame me for you colliding with me."

Sin grins. "All right, all right, you caught me." He puts up his hand, feigning surrender. "But you were standing right in my path, so I'd say it's a fifty-fifty split."

"Nice try," I reply, laughing despite myself, "but I was minding my own business. Maybe *you* should watch where you're going."

He chuckles again and grabs some napkins from a nearby table for me. "Let's agree on a truce, shall we?" he proposes.

I take the napkins and dab at the wet stain on my shirt.

"Fine, truce. But seriously, you owe me a new shirt. Or even better, when my mom kills me for ruining this one, you could write a eulogy for my tombstone."

"Eulogy? Emo much?" Sin shoots back playfully. "Fine, I'll add, 'write a eulogy for the girl I bumped into at Elias's party' to my to-do list."

This makes me laugh aloud in real time, something that rarely happens. Then, realizing that no matter how hard I try, the blouse is beyond repair, I give up and stand there with a resigned look.

"I've got a solution for your shirt. Elias's mom wouldn't mind if you borrowed something from her closet. She's got plenty of clothes, trust me," Sin adds.

The way he says the last two words, raising his eyebrows and looking around furtively, makes me laugh again.

But then I shake my head and say, "Thanks, but I'm not really in the mood for a wardrobe change. I think I'll just head home."

Perhaps that is what I need after all: a restful, if anticlimactic, end to what has been a turbulent birthday.

"You're leaving already?" Sin asks with a look of mild surprise, which seems somewhat . . . disingenuous. "Come on, the night's still young."

"Yeah, but I've had enough excitement for one night, young man!" I say in my best imitation of a crotchety grandma as Sin lets out an amused snort. "Besides, I don't exactly fit in. Nobody wants me here, in case you didn't notice."

"Wait, so what brought you to this wild party in the first place?"

"Just wanted to see what all the fuss was about. And it's my birthday, so I figured, 'Why not?'" I shrug and avoid his eyes, not knowing what exactly I'm trying to avoid.

Maybe I don't want to make it seem like my birthday is a big deal? Maybe I'm so used to people undermining my special day that I'm starting to wonder if it's anything special to begin with?

But Sin's reaction surprises me. His expression softens as he exclaims, "Your birthday? Happy birthday, Petra! You should have told someone."

"Just didn't seem like a big deal," I respond with a nonchalant expression, even though I feel glad that finally, *finally,* someone other than Amelia has wished me happy birthday.

In the next instant, that cynical, sour voice in my head mutters, *Wow, Petra, two whole people acknowledging you on your eighteenth birthday! Congratulations, girl!*

I'm not sure if Sin can see even the faintest hint of the turmoil raging within me, but his smile turns sympathetic.

"What? It's a big deal. Eighteen, right? That's a milestone. You should be fucking celebrating, pardon my French," he encourages.

"Thanks." I smile again without meaning to. "It's nice of you to say that."

We stand there for a moment, the silence between us charged with all the bleak thoughts I try to dispel from my mind.

His gaze weighs me down in a way. That precise scrutiny of his eyes is a new sensation but . . . not entirely uncomfortable.

Just then, I spot Daphne and her cronies walking, nay, *marching,* toward us. My stomach contracts, and I instantly know that they aren't planning to compliment me on the avant-garde design of my half-wet blouse.

I need to get out of here *ASAP*.

"I should go." I step back, my eyes never leaving the approaching trio. "I don't really want to deal with them right now."

Sin follows my gaze and frowns slightly. "Oh, please, Daphne and her minions? They're all bark and no bite. Don't worry about them."

His words are kind, and a part of me wants to stay and give them another round of sucker punches straight to their stupid faces. But frankly, I'm just tired by now. This has been a *long* evening.

"Maybe next time," I say shortly, hoping that Sin won't press the topic any further. "Thanks for the birthday wish, Sin. And for not plowing me down under your stomping giant's feet."

The comment makes him laugh, but I know he wants to say more. "All right."

He's still standing in front of me, unmoving. He's watching me, his lips spread in a wide smile. There's something odd about his gaze, something that doesn't quite sit right with me.

Perhaps it's just his baby-blue eyes. They're quite pretty.

Just as the thought enters my head, I shake myself.

Here comes the Wicked Witch of the West, I think, as Daphne gets even closer. I'm not a fool to wait around any longer, so I make a beeline for the nearest door before me, ignoring Sin's lazy eyebrow lift.

To my luck, the door opens out into the pool area, and it's that time of the night when most of the party has spilled onto the back patio. The music is in full swing, and I hear a splash every few seconds as people dive and cannonball and trust-fall into the azure depths.

A prickle of awareness travels down my back.

Is Sin following me?

Are Daphne and Lenora and that nauseating François almost at my heels?

I'm too chicken to actually turn around and find out, so I keep trying to push through the pulsing crowds of dancers and drunk jocks.

Looking back, it's hard to pinpoint when it happened. I am picking my way through the crowd near the pool. We are all sandwiched tight enough that I can't see beyond the next body in front of me.

Just as the crowd before me seems to thin out, I hear someone say, "And just where do you think you're going?" I'll never forget how cold the voice sounds, and when I whip around to see who it is, I feel my foot slip over an edge behind me.

In the next instance, *someone shoves me into the pool.*

This time, the loud splash from my own fall seems to stop mid-sound as water engulfs me completely.

A shock of cold takes my breath away.

My mouth is half-open in a frozen scream as I drop down *fast.*

The sounds of the party become a distant, echoing throb, replaced by the gentle, rhythmic lapping of water against my ears.

Everything slows down. In the dim pool, I see legs and feet kicking nearby. The weight of my clothes pulls me down, making it hard to orient myself. My hair fans out around me like a halo. Like I had already drowned.

I open my eyes wider, trying to see through the chlorinated blur.

CHAPTER THREE

PETRA

Present Day

Who pushed me?

Glimpses of faces hover at the edge of the pool, some laughing, some looking concerned, but it's all a murky mix of shapes and forms.

Panic starts to claw at my guts. I kick my legs, struggling to find the surface. My lungs begin to burn as the air supply dwindles to nothing. Just when I think I can't hold my breath any longer, a strong hand grabs my arm, pulling me upward.

I break the surface, gasping for air and desperately blinking water from my eyes.

The next moment, Sin is floating right beside me, his hair plastered rather amusingly to his forehead.

He looks half-concerned and half-pissed. He's saying something, but there's water in my ears. As I try to shake it out, he guides me to the steps leading out of the pool.

Now I can hear him better.

"Are you okay?" he asks again. The music has been paused, it seems, and people are talking among themselves—while looking pointedly at us, of course.

I nod weakly, still trying to catch my breath. "Ye-yeah . . . I th-think so."

"Dude, what the absolute fuck?" Elias is back and panicking again. "Are you okay, bro?" He's looking at Sin with concern and fear.

I mean, I'm the one who got pushed into the pool, but whatever, I guess.

"I'm fine. Petra needs to go inside and warm up," Sin replies curtly, and I'm surprised he takes that tone with the guy who's supposed to be his best friend.

At this point, I'm fully drenched and shivering violently from the cold and the shock.

"Who did that?" Sin demands again, looking around the crowd with a menacing expression.

Many of the guys and girls seem to flinch away from his glare. I'm not the least bit surprised to notice that Daphne and her cult are nowhere to be seen.

"Did you see them, Petra?" Sin asks again.

I shake my head, and my teeth chatter miserably as I say, "N-n-no . . . I-it hap-happened s-s-so fa-fast!"

Sin's jaw tightens as he says, "Let's get you inside and dried off. You're freezing."

"Yeah, man, that's a good idea," Elias chimes in, and from his tone, I can tell that he wants to get on Sin's good side again.

I nod erratically, too cold and too overwhelmed to argue. As Sin leads me back into the mansion, I can't help but feel a mix of humiliation and gratitude—humiliated by the cruel prank, yet grateful for Sin's swift rescue.

The warmth of the house assaults my senses at first as the sudden shift in temperature makes my skin crawl unpleasantly.

Sin's hand is perched firmly on the small of my back, and I'm both discomfited and comforted by it.

I suppose a near-death experience will do that to a girl.

He leads me through the thinning crowd and up a grand staircase as the cold sinks deeper into my bones. We soon reach the third floor, entering a room with an en suite bathroom. I surmise that the washer and dryer are at the end of the hall.

The room itself is spacious, with a large bed draped in rich, dark fabrics and a window that offers a view of the moonlit pool below.

As soon as we enter, I feel something break inside me, and a sob slips past my lips. It's too late to try to stifle it. The tears come rushing down, almost violently.

If one humiliation weren't enough, now I'm about to make a fool of myself in front of a stranger, too.

I don't cry.

I really don't.

So what the hell is wrong with me now?

"Hey, hey, hey," Sin says in a soothing voice. "It's okay, Petra. I mean, it's not okay, someone pushed you into the pool for fuck's sake, but you're okay now. You're safe." His palm traces small circles over my back as I try to stem the sudden flow of tears.

"I don't . . . I don't know why I'm crying," I manage to gasp out in the end.

This is partly true. I have been moping around the whole day, but breaking down into tears seems like an overreaction, even to me.

But if I thought that Sin would judge or pity me, I'm proven wrong when he says nothing and continues to pat my back as I finally calm down and bring my breathing under control.

"Better now?" he asks gently, and I nod, feeling lighter than I've felt the whole day.

The carpet is plush and soft beneath my bare feet. Sin hands me a towel and a velvet robe, both incredibly soft to the touch. It makes me yearn to snuggle inside and never come up for air.

But there's still the issue of my clothes, which are still clinging to me, drenched and cold.

Sin shifts uncomfortably by the door, glancing around the room as if looking for something to focus on other than me.

"So, um, if you don't want to borrow any of Elias's mom's clothes, we could just toss our stuff in the dryer," he suggests. "And while they're drying, we can change into the bathrobes?"

"Yeah, that works," I say, suppressing a smile at the lost-puppy look on his face. "Thanks."

With that, I turn my back to him and start peeling off my wet shirt. He starts taking off his shirt and trousers as well, and for a while, there's just the squelching noise of our clothes coming off—in the most unerotic sense.

If you had told me that this is what I'd be doing on my eighteenth birthday, getting dunked in the swimming pool and then awkwardly shedding my wet clothes in a room with a guy I just met, I would have laughed at you.

Things like these happen to heroines in novels and movies, I would have told you. *I'm just an angsty, rich teenage girl who wants to be seen.*

Funnily enough, at one point, I *do* feel Sin's eyes on me, and even though I know he's trying not to look, it's impossible not to be hyperaware of his presence.

It's not like he's that bad to look at. From the corner of my eye, I catch a glimpse of his corded back muscles and athlete's arms.

Phew, this guy works out, my inner critic mumbles, and I am quick to shush her. As I fumble with the blouse, I catch a glimpse of him looking at me in the mirror.

Just as I see him, his gaze quickly darts away.

"Ahem, Sin?" I say sharply. "Do you mind?"

He flushes a bright shade of red. "I swear I wasn't looking! I mean, not on purpose." He's already shrugged off his attire and is wearing a bathrobe.

"Just turn around, okay?" I say, smiling a little at the sight of his flustered face.

"Right, right. Sorry." He quickly turns his back to me, staring intently at the wall.

Once I'm out of my blouse and skirt, I feel cold again, and goose bumps erupt all over my skin. Standing there in just my bra and panties, I hastily wrap myself in the soft, warm robe, tying the belt tightly around my waist.

Outside, the party sounds somewhat muted now. People may be starting to leave in earnest.

"Okay, you can turn around now," I say at last, gathering my wet clothes into a bundle.

Sin turns back, carefully avoiding my eyes.

"Do you want me to take those to the dryer?" he offers, nodding toward the soggy pile in my arms.

"Yeah, that'd be great," I reply, handing them over. As he takes the clothes from my hands, his eyes meet mine for a moment.

There's a softness there, a genuine concern that makes my heart ache in grief. Am I going to have to rely on the kindness of strangers all the time? And more importantly, would that be so bad?

"No problem," Sin stammers. "I'll be back in a few minutes. Just . . . make yourself comfortable, I guess."

I nod, watching as he leaves the room, and the door clicks shut behind him.

Alone again, I let out a trembling breath. Despite the awkwardness, there's something comforting about Sin's presence, something that makes this chaotic night feel a little less overwhelming.

Who did that? I can't help wondering. The most obvious suspects are Daphne and her followers, but I am somehow not convinced.

Sure, the three of them are notorious bullies who have ruined the lives of many an unsuspecting juvenile pariah, and pushing me into a pool is *just* the kind of petty trick they would play.

But . . . but what? My instincts are telling me something, though I'm not sure what that is.

All I know is that the voice I heard immediately before being pushed into the pool couldn't have come from any of the trio. It sounded far too calculating.

Does that mean I have another enemy? Someone else who wishes me harm? It's a daunting question, but one I have to face if I deny that it was Daphne or Lenora or François who had sent me into the pool's icy depths.

"Great, just great," I mutter. "Could this night get any weirder?"

In hindsight, I shouldn't have posed more rhetorical questions to the universe. It has a funny way of answering them.

CHAPTER FOUR

PETRA

Present Day

How can a girl who just turned eighteen have enemies? Maybe a hater or two, like the St. Anselm Hive admins, but not full-blown adversaries who would actively try to harm me by, let's say, drowning me in a pool?

While Sin is off to the dryer, doing practical, *useful* things, I sit on the edge of the bed and grapple with a fresh round of paranoia.

The room is dimly lit, and shadows dance across the walls, cast by the revelers who are now scattered across the grounds adjoining Rutherford's mansion. The party has moved to the lawn, and it feels like I'm strangely alone inside this sprawling structure.

A couple of minutes later, the door creaks open, and Sin steps back in, looking slightly awkward.

"They're in the dryer now," he says, giving me a small smile. "Shouldn't take too long."

"Thanks," I reply, my voice barely above a whisper. "I really just want to get my clothes back and go home."

"Yeah, I would too if I were you," Sin replies, sitting down on a chair across from me, his posture as stiff as mine.

There's a moment of silence that stretches awkwardly over the next several minutes. Exhaustion and lingering alcoholic tipsiness combine to make me quite lethargic. I simply sit there, fiddling with the sash of my robe.

Sin clears his throat a couple of times, but when I fail to react, he is forced to break the silence.

"So," Sin begins hesitantly, as if flailing around for a safe topic to discuss, "what's your favorite class this year?"

Again, his obvious efforts to put me at ease endear him to me, so I decide to help him out by at least trying to make small talk. "Probably my graphic design class. I get to work on some cool projects."

Sin looks genuinely interested. "That sounds awesome. I've never really hung out with someone from that field. Tell me more?"

And though it feels surreal to talk about mundane stuff like schoolwork after the evening I've had, I say, "Yeah, I designed a poster series for a local art event. Lots of people seemed to like it."

Why did I say that last part out loud? Do I *want* to impress Sin?

"Amazing!" he says, his eyes actually lighting up. "I'd love to see them one day."

"Maybe I'll show you sometime." It would be nice to have someone to talk to about these things. Maybe it was high time I got myself other friends. Well, *other* is an overestimation.

I'd have to have *one* friend first, and though I consider Amelia a member of that—very exclusive—group, she's still just an online person, not a real one.

So when Sin drops the thin thread of our conversation, lapsing into a fidgeting silence, I pick it up.

"What about you? Any favorite classes?"

"Well, practice, *obviously*," he replies with a mischievous grin. "But honestly, I've been enjoying my English classes more than I expected."

"Hey, come on! How was I to know that you weren't just born looking like that?" I reply, nodding to the bulging muscles visible even through the frumpy robe.

He smiles.

"So . . . are you reading anything interesting at the moment?" I ask.

"Right now, we're going through some classic literature. Just finished *The Great Gatsby*."

"Ah, Fitzgerald," I say, nodding. "I like *Tender Is the Night* better. Have you read it?"

"Nope, but now I must," Sin replies with more enthusiasm. "What's it about?"

"It's about an alcoholic man married to a madwoman," I reply drolly before realizing that Sin looks puzzled. "It's a way more poignant book than my description would have you believe. I just . . ." My words taper down into nothingness because this is delicate territory.

How do I convey to this popular, well-mannered, well-liked guy that I'm drawn to morally gray, outright toxic characters like the couple at the center of Fitzgerald's final novel?

"Just what?" Sin chimes in, urging me further on with a nod.

"I guess I just like the idea of two broken people trying—and inevitably failing—to make each other whole, if that makes sense." *There, I said it. Let the judgment begin.*

"Wow, that's . . ." Sin begins, and the look on his face is inscrutable. "That's such a nuanced take, Petra. Now I *really* want to read this book."

I smile and look away, not wanting to show how relieved I feel that he didn't deem me a bigger freak than I'm usually known to be. "So what did you think about *The Great Gatsby*?"

"I actually liked it a lot. The whole idea of chasing a dream that's always just out of reach . . . that was painfully relatable."

"How can you have unattainable dreams?" I blurt out, half-amused and half-incredulous. "You're the poster child for success: popular, athletic—"

"Handsome?" Sin cuts in with a joking wink, and we both end up giggling. When we pause for breath, he sighs and says, "There's a lot you don't know about me, Petra."

It's a cryptic statement, sure, but I won't give him the satisfaction of my curiosity. Even though I *am* curious.

"I guess I'm learning," I reply instead.

He shifts in his chair, his expression turning more serious.

"What is it?" I ask, unable to keep a lid on my nosiness after all.

"Why did you come to the party tonight?" Sin asks seriously, as if he wants to really understand my scattered motives, those I couldn't make sense of myself. "I mean, you don't seem like the party type—and not in a bad way!" he hurries to add, ever-sensitive to how his words could be construed in different ways. Something I find I quite like about him.

I look away, feeling a twinge of regret and other unspeakable feelings. "I don't know. I guess I just wanted to do something different on my birthday. My parents forgot about it, so . . ."

"What? Your biological parents?" Sin asks with an expression of disbelief before looking regretful about his words. "Sorry for that question; it just came out."

"No, I get why you would ask that. And yes, my biological parents, as far as I know. I've even got my father's nose. Famously so." I try to lighten up the conversation that's gotten really serious really fast.

Sin's face softens as he says, "Petra, I'm sorry it hasn't been a great birthday. And about your parents. That sounds really tough."

"It's actually not that bad." Somehow, I feel the need to defend my parents. Or maybe I want to reduce the amount of abjection my life seems to contain.

At any rate, I suddenly feel that I don't want to continue being an object of pity any longer.

"I get to spend a lot of time on my own, and honestly, it's a relief. It's made me really independent and self-reliant, you know."

"That's pretty obvious, but . . ." Sin hesitates, as if trying to summon the kindest words possible. "It must be lonely, right?"

"Yep, it is," I reply without missing a beat. "I thought *that* was pretty obvious, too."

We both chuckle briefly, and then another spell of silence settles between us.

Outside, our peers are playing hide-and-seek among meticulously manicured hedges, while others are probably engaged in more lascivious activities in the manor's many rooms.

Thinking about the latter group makes me blush and become anxious for some reason, so I clear my throat.

"Actually, I almost wouldn't have come tonight. But my friend Amelia convinced me to give it a shot," I admit. I don't want Sin to think that I am a loser with literally no friends, so I continue, "She's my best friend, in case you were wondering. The one person in my life I can rely on without thinking."

"She sounds real cool, Petra. Where do you guys usually hang out?" Sin asks, getting up from his chair and stretching his legs.

My eyes can't help straying toward his sinewy calves, but I train them on his face before he can notice.

"Umm, on Instafriends? I've never actually met her." I have a sheepish expression on my face, but not for long. "It's like we don't even need to see each other to be in tune with each other. I know it sounds corny when I put it like that, but trust me, she's . . . yeah, she's a real one."

Sin has been watching me wax eloquent about my online friend with a faint smile on his face. When I fall silent, he says, "And you've never wondered if you were being catfished or something like that?"

"You mean that Amelia is actually a fifty-year-old creep who likes befriending teenage girls online?" I ask with a throaty chuckle.

"Something like that, yeah." Sin's voice is teasing and gentle, as if he wants me to laugh more, lighten up more.

"Not really, no. And even if it *is* a grown man masquerading as a girl, and a *very* girly girl, then he has never made me feel unsafe or unheard, so that's a win in my book!"

Sin has been grinning and chuckling this whole time, and I don't want him to stop. I want the easy, friendly banter to keep going till it fills up the aching hole in my heart.

But pretty soon, sooner than I'd like, another long stretch of silence unfolds.

Just then, Sin looks around the room, then down at the bed.

"You know," he says, a mischievous glint in his eye, "I think I remember Elias mentioning something about a hidden stash in here."

"A stash of what?"

Sin drops to his knees and peers under the bed. "Yeah, let's see . . ." After a moment of rummaging, he pulls out a small, dusty box. "Bingo!"

He opens the box to reveal several bottles of assorted liquor.

"That's a lot of *expensive* alcohol," I point out.

Sin looks up, his smile widening. "Want some? It might help pass the time."

I hesitate. I probably shouldn't. But the thought of sitting here, awkwardly, waiting for my clothes to dry, feels unbearable.

"Sure," I say, trying to sound casual. "Why not?"

Sin pulls out a bottle of whiskey and two plastic cups. He pours a generous amount into each cup and hands one to me.

"To broken people," he says, raising his cup.

"To broken people," I repeat, clinking my cup against his before taking a sip, the whiskey burning its way down my throat. Soon, my body feels relaxed again.

Sin sits back on the floor, leaning against the bed.

"You know," he begins, as if getting ready to articulate a very deep thought, "I've had my fair share of embarrassing moments, too."

"Yeah, right!" I retort instantly. "What happened? You didn't lift as much at the gym as you wanted to? Got some crap from some gym bro?"

"No, really! I was made a fool for a whole day," Sin says with a voice that's trying hard to sound solemn.

"So, my sister and her friends," he starts, already grinning, "they decided it would be hilarious to play a prank on me. I had this big game, and they snuck into my room and redecorated the back of my jersey."

A real storyteller, this fellow, I think privately, while out loud I ask, "Redecorated?"

"Yeah, they replaced my name with 'Mr. Sparklepants' and added a bunch of glitter. Of course, yours truly didn't notice it until halftime, wondering why everyone was laughing and pointing at me," Sin says, shaking his head.

I burst out laughing. His words had conjured up a scene that was too hilarious to pass up. "Please tell me there are tons of pictures of you from that day!"

"Forget pictures; there are entire videos of it floating around. Besides, the guys on the team won't ever let me forget it."

"Gotta hand it to you, Arnoult," I say, feeling a bit lighter, "you do know how to make a girl laugh."

And forget that she almost drowned an hour ago.

"Yeah, I had to laugh it off," Sin says with a shrug. "I mean, what else can you do? Couldn't drop out of the team, right? I love the game far too much."

"Hmm, I sense a lesson coming on," I say teasingly.

"No lesson, Petra. Just wanted to tell you that..." He struggles to find the right words, even though he doesn't need to. "That I understand, somewhat. What it feels like to be set apart and laughed at, I guess. Of course, that's nothing compared to falling in the pool."

I take a deep breath, feeling more at ease. "Yeah, I suppose. But it's not just tonight. People at school... they don't like me. They think I'm a stuck-up bitch with my nose in the air."

"That's *their* problem, Petra," Sin says in a firm tone as he changes his posture, unfolding and stretching out his legs before him. "I hope you don't agree with them?"

I shrug, staring at the floor.

"I don't know. Maybe I *am* too quiet and standoffish? You gotta admit I don't really fit in with anyone; my people skills are almost nonexistent."

"Sometimes people judge what they don't understand," Sin points out. "But that doesn't mean you have to believe them."

"I try not to," I admit, my voice soft. "But it's hard when you feel like an outsider. All. The. Time!"

He nods empathetically as his expression softens again. "I get how that could quickly become very tiring. But trust me, Petra, you're not as predictable as that. You're more than what they think. If only they could see the side of you that I have seen today, you know?"

"Thanks, Sin. That means a lot." And it does, in ways I still fail to articulate properly. So I take a deep breath, deciding to share more. "It's just . . . I've always felt different. Like there's this wall between me and everyone else. No matter what I do, I can't seem to break through."

He nods. "Yeah, I get what you mean. I feel like I'm putting on an act most of the time. And you know what? I *am* pretending. How else are we supposed to survive high school? It's downright brutal out here."

"Yeah," I say in a choked voice as a lump forms in my throat. "I see people with their tight-knit groups, their inside jokes, and I just . . . I don't have that. I have Amelia, but that's on the internet. Here, I'm always alone." I give a defeated shrug.

"But you're not alone right now," Sin says softly when I stop speaking, too overcome with bitterness to continue. "And I think it's brave of you to even be here tonight."

"Brave?" I scoff lightly. "It doesn't feel like it. You know what it does feel like? Like I'm constantly trying to prove myself. And failing!"

"Hey," he says, leaning forward, his face furrowing with concern for me. He looks pained at the sight of my distress. "You don't have to prove anything to anyone. You're amazing just as you are. And if they can't see that, it's because they are blind idiots."

His words hit me hard, and I blink back tears.

"I wish I could believe that. It's just so exhausting, trying to tailor myself to appeal to others and still not managing to forge genuine connections. It's like, am I defective? Am I a psychopath or something?"

"Well, if you are, then maybe I like psychopaths more than normal people," Sin says with a small chuckle.

"Ah, I wish I was truly abnormal," I continue. "Then I couldn't care less that everyone hates me."

"Hey!" Sin protests. "I don't hate you! In fact, I think you're quite a badass."

I blink, surprised by his words. "Really? A badass? What do you mean?"

Sin assumes a thoughtful expression. "I've noticed you before. You have this air about you, this . . . quiet strength. What you call 'coldness' I call 'discernment.' You can exist without needing others to validate your existence. That's pretty badass."

I feel a warmth spread across my cheeks, and I know I'm blushing again. "You really think so?"

Dammit. I sound like some breathless scullery maid from a Jane Austen novel.

"Absolutely," he says in that signature earnest voice. "You don't let people's opinions define you. You walk through those halls like you own them, even if you don't feel that way inside. That takes guts."

I smile shyly, the compliment making my heart flutter. "I guess I never thought about it like that."

"Well, you should!" Sin says with a grin. "It's inspiring, honestly. Most people can't handle being alone. They need constant validation. But you? You're like . . . like a fortress!"

"A fortress." I turn the word around in my mind like it's a rare gem. "That's a nice way to put it."

Sin's eyes twinkle with amusement. "See? Don't sell yourself short, Petra. You've got more going for you than you realize."

I look down, my heart pounding. "Thanks, Sin. That really means a lot."

He shrugs and grins suddenly.

"Just laying out facts, you know? Besides, anyone who can stand up to Daphne and her crew like you did tonight definitely has my respect."

It is a welcome recollection, so I smile. "Well, they had it coming."

"They did," he agrees with a laugh. "And you handled it like a pro."

The room feels hazy now, the warmth of the alcohol buzzing through my veins.

Who would have thought that I would actually end up connecting with someone today?

And at Elias Rutherford's party, of all places! Sin and I have been talking for hours, and it feels like we've barely begun to scratch the surface.

And I have gotten so comfortable that I haven't even noticed my robe has fallen apart near my neck.

I only see Sin's smiling eyes as he leans closer. Like he has another secret to share with me. There's an edge to the soft lines of his face as he says, "Would you mind terribly if I told you how pretty you are?"

CHAPTER FIVE

PETRA

Present Day

Feeling a little silly and a *lot* flattered, I giggle. "You're just saying that because we're both drunk."

"Maybe I can say it out loud because of liquid courage," he murmurs, slowly tracing the bloom of my cheek with a long, slender finger. "But that doesn't mean it's not true."

At this point, our faces are inches apart, and when I realize this, my heart starts pounding again. Maybe this was all happening too soon, maybe we had both had too much to drink, maybe we should—

His lips brush mine, soft and tentative at first.

I freeze for a second, my mind spinning, and for once, that nagging voice in my head is silenced.

My hands are clasped together in my lap, getting sweatier by the second.

Then Sin's warm, broad palms cup my face and tilt it slightly upward as his lips press and suck on mine, deepening the kiss before I can even get a word in.

His tongue probes at the seam of my lips, and on a soundless moan, I allow him access to my mouth.

At first, I'm not sure what I'm doing exactly.

I've seen movies where people French kiss, but experiencing it for myself is a whole different matter.

He tastes sweet, inviting.

Perhaps this isn't so bad—having my first kiss with a beautiful guy on my eighteenth birthday.

In fact, that's quite a nice present.

I barely start to get used to this kissing business when Sin's lips move to my neck.

I gasp as a shiver goes down my back. Meanwhile, his hands are everywhere, exploring, stroking, cupping.

The taste of alcohol is still strong in my mouth, and behind my closed eyes, the black tapestry seems to be swirling with odd shapes.

Still, I don't ask him to stop when he starts loosening the sash around the robes—both his and mine.

Soon, my back hits the floor, and he hovers over me, dropping butterfly kisses over the length of my body, starting from the tip of my nose to my collarbone and sternum, and then swooping down lower still.

In fact, Sin handles me expertly, as if I were a doll whose parts he had put together.

Despite the earlier chill in my bones, I'm warm and sweaty now. His body is like a blanket, covering every shivering inch of me and turning it into a molten mass of . . . want?

Is that the word?

I'm not sure.

Perhaps it's the alcohol, but *everything* is warm.

My robe falls around my sides and pools on the floor.

Sin, too, shrugs his robe off, throwing it to the side.

A part of me is delighted that I'm throwing caution to the wind, being reckless and wild like this.

But another part of me is somehow set apart, as if I were watching our entangled bodies from a distance.

I blink, a moment of awareness seeping through.

What am I doing? Here? With Sin, a guy I barely know?

I've never given much thought to how my first time would be. Considering my lack of friends, it seemed like something that wasn't even in the cards for me.

But I certainly never imagined it would be like this. With a . . . stranger.

The faint hum of voices drifts up from the party below. Some people are still splashing around in the pool, it seems. Someone turns up the music, and the bass matches the beat of my heart.

Is this fear? Anxiety? Nervousness?

I think I am far too drunk to make sense of what I'm feeling. But one thing is certain. If I were to scream, no one would hear me.

Do I even want to scream?

Confusion swirls in my mind. On the one hand, his touch is pleasant. Warm. Familiar. But on the other hand, I *know* that I am being far too reckless. I may know of him, but I don't *know* him.

"Sin—" I start. But before I can say anything else, Sin swallows my words. His lips are back on mine, his kiss more savage than before. He plunders my mouth until all the previous resistance falls away.

Shifting, he nestles his hips between the cradle of my thighs, rubbing against me.

My eyes widen when I feel him at my center.

Big. Hard. *Ready*.

There's only the thin material of our underwear separating us.

"Oh!" I gasp out loud.

"You're such a good girl, Petra." Sin praises me on a breathless moan. "So beautiful . . ."

One of his hands cups my breast, strumming my nipple between his fingers. The other hand travels lower down my body as he traces the outline of my panties.

No one's touched me there before.

He pulls my panties to the side and swipes his fingers along the seam of my sex, slowly at first, as if he's trying to commit this moment to memory, before going faster.

And when his movements are too obstructed by the material of my panties, he grabs the sides with both hands and tears them. The flimsy cotton falls away easily, giving him unfettered access to me.

My head feels heavy. My throat is parched.

"Sin," I whisper. I'm nowhere near sober enough to be making such a huge decision right now. He isn't either. Yet something about this feels wrong *and* right at the same time.

We should stop. We should—

"Such a pretty pussy," he murmurs appreciatively as he cups my sex. He focuses his attention on my clit, petting it with increasing speed until all potential protests become a mass of moans that I barely recognize as coming from me.

I need to stop this. But I also want more of it. I'm *curious* about what more there is.

But just as I feel close to . . . something, his weight is lifted off me.

The alcohol is making my head spin too fast, and I can't see what he's up to. It's only when he settles back down between my legs that I realize he's fully naked.

"Sin." I open my mouth to tell him to stop, that we've already gone too far and I don't think I'm ready. Or am I? I can no longer tell. It's almost as if I am under a spell.

His fingers probe at my entrance, and he inserts one finger inside me.

The sudden intrusion makes me startle, but he's gentle enough that soon I'm squirming under him as I find myself once more getting close to that elusive peak.

"You're doing so good, Petra," I hear him say dimly. "I need to make you mine so badly . . ."

I frown at his words. But before I can ask him what he means, he lines his cock against my entrance and pushes in.

What follows is a brief, blinding moment of pain.

And then a muffled groan from Sin as I'm fully pulled under a veil of darkness.

CHAPTER SIX

PETRA

The Past
1 March 1896

The doors to the bookshop open, and I set foot inside, my steps faltering with excitement. A handful of girls around my age from the congregation do the same, with Mrs. Jenkins, our chaperone, following suit.

Though she keeps to the back, not engaging with us, her presence is felt at every step, a warning not to stray into the back of the shop where the controversial material is found.

The girls giggle as they grab books from the shelves, loudly flipping through the pages.

Mrs. Jenkins gives them a severe look, but soon her attention is captivated by a new prayer book with gilded pages.

The front of the bookshop is made up entirely of prayer books and treatises on theology, alongside the occasional memoir of some pious person long gone.

But it is in the back where the true treasure lies: science, arts, travel, music, and so much more.

I glance longingly at the shadowed section.

I'd come alone once to pick up a book for my brother. With no Mrs. Jenkins around, I'd wandered off into the back and found myself staring at outrageous titles like *On the Origin of Species* or *The Age of Reason*. But instead of scandalizing me, as no doubt was the notion of my congregation, they had only piqued my interest.

Mrs. Jenkins continues to peruse her golden leaves. The girls are deep in conversation with one another as they compare books, debating which one to buy.

I have pin money. Not a lot, but enough to afford a book. A *religious* book. I would never be able to buy one of the others. But I can . . . look? Just for a moment. Just beyond the titles.

My heart in my throat, I slide backward. Slowly. Quietly.

If I'm caught, my excuse is ready: I was feeling faint and required a place to lie down. Due to my small frame, I have been known to have a frail constitution, particularly during the harsh New England winters, so Mrs. Jenkins should easily accept the explanation.

A few more steps. No one takes note of me.

Finally, I'm in the shadows.

The back of the shop. The *forbidden* area.

With how darkened the rows are here, I must squint to get a good read of the titles through my veil. But as luck would have it, I am in the right section.

The *literature* section.

Our congregation prides itself on being modern, on keeping with the times, but they still frown upon frivolous pursuits, especially for women.

In an age where women have already graduated with medical degrees, I am to resign myself to a lonely fate as a future wife and mother. Even the knowledge that women *can* receive degrees should not be attainable, but I read it in a newspaper once.

For all my education in philology and fluency in Latin and Greek, I am forced to only use those skills when reading religious texts. The church does not even call it education; that would be impossible for someone of my sex. Instead, it is seen as initiation in the religious texts, mandatory for girls and boys alike from the age of four until fourteen.

Why allow me to step into the world of learning, only to cut my wings just as I'm about to soar?

I can read Greek and Latin better than any classics student, yet my father will never allow me to enroll in a college even though I am already twenty years of age.

"They are deeply disturbed places. Women should not be freely walking around men," he'd say. "It would invite temptation."

As if the mere presence of a woman next to a man is enough to turn him into a primal beast.

Alas, the congregation certainly seems to think so. Even the sermons are performed in segregation. A panel separates the men and the women, lest they glance upon one another and fall into sin.

Our side of town is equally as divided. Women must wear a veil in public and cannot be seen consorting with unknown men.

Though I've only traveled a few times outside of Radcliffe, once to Boston and once to New York when I was around fourteen, even I know this is not normal. I've heard whispers of the suffragette movement, of women demanding more of society. They're even aiming to gain a vote in the elections.

Preposterous, I know! If anyone from my congregation heard me mention this, they would brand me a heretic, not that I would mind it overly much. In fact, I would not mind it if I were excommunicated from the church, even if that meant being ostracized by my congregation and my family.

The issue is that I am barely twenty, with nothing to recommend me except my Bible-reading skills in dead languages and drawing, the latter of which I've kept a tight secret my entire life. Yet both of those things are useless in the real world, aren't they?

If only those suffragettes won! If only they started a revolution to allow women to live freely as they like!

As it stands, I am bound by my ties to my community, my religion, and my sex.

That doesn't mean I will conform forever. Only until I have a better alternative. If there is something I know from the depths of my soul, it's that I do not want to become like my mother.

Alone in her world, never acknowledged, always isolated. She speaks, but no one listens. She exists, but no one minds her. And no matter how much I try to interact with her, decades of the same routine have imprinted on her: I am female, too, therefore when I speak, even she does not listen.

My brother, I love to pieces. But at twenty-two he is becoming every day more and more like our father: cold, authoritarian, and self-important.

A fortnight ago, he had taken it upon himself to rebuke me for how I wear my veil. Too loose, he'd said. Too revealing. Boys his age talked about me because of that, and it was in unflattering terms.

The voices in the front of the shop become louder as one of the girls gets into a theological argument with Mrs. Jenkins. I recognize it as a purposeful tactic, no doubt trying to divert her attention while the other girls sneaked a peek at the forbidden books, too.

Farther in the back, I'm no longer visible to anyone. It's just me and the books, and I quickly take advantage of the time I have to browse the titles. There are so many! I wish I could have a library of this size and diversity.

As my eyes scan the spines, I come across an intriguing title: *The Portrait of a Lady*. Curious, I reach forward to grab it at the same time as someone pulls on it from the other side.

Momentarily shocked, I let the book slip from my grasp. It slides out on the other side, leaving a small hole in between the other tomes.

Stark blue eyes stare at me with equal surprise. He looks to be slightly older than my brother. Dark hair curls around his ears, giving him a boyish look. But the strong angle of his jaw and the corded muscles of his neck leave no doubt that this is a man.

A beautiful man. The artist in me rouses to the surface, and my fingers start moving around in the air, tracing his features to commit them to memory.

I've never seen him before in our part of town, which means he must be an outsider. We don't mingle with those of his "ilk" as my father would call them. It is a marvel that our community has survived for as long as it has in both seclusion from and cohabitation with the rest of the world.

We live in the same town, but we are worlds apart.

His lips part on a wordless, "Oh," and immediately my fingers stop.

The pregnant silence from before builds to an unbearable crescendo as I know what he's going to say—what all outsiders say.

"You're one of those. The weird ones who sequester their women." Though my reply would be a dry, *"I am standing here, therefore I am not sequestered."*

"What are you, some new age puritans?" A lot of people are known to call us that, though we reject the appellation. The official name of the Church is the Reformationist Church of Christ and Saints. Puritans, a branch of Protestantism, do not recognize saints. Our religion is derived from Catholicism, or The True Doctrine.

"Fanatic freaks," another crowd favorite. Unfortunately, we are a rather boring group, hence the strict rules.

"They keep their women on a tighter leash than dogs." Now that one is downright offensive. My community might have many faults, but treating animals badly is not one of them. They have souls, like people, and deserve the same type of respect. If only that extended to women too . . .

"My apologies. You may have it," the man says in a low, gravelly voice. He presses the book toward me.

I shake my head, my fingers curling tighter against the folds of my dress.

"I can't," I say, barely above a whisper. My voice is steady, yet I feel my resolve waver as I look at the book he holds out to me.

His brow furrows slightly, the only sign of disappointment.

"Then I might as well have it," he says casually, tucking it under his arm. He isn't mocking me; I know that much. He is simply stating the obvious: If I won't take it, then it is his.

I exhale sharply, willing my feet to move. Disappointment floods me as I realize my little interlude in the shadows has come to an abrupt end.

But when I turn, I find myself face-to-face with him, the beautiful man.

My breath catches in my throat as my eyes trail upward, past the dark fabric of his coat, past his collarbone, his chin, until I meet his gaze. He is tall. Too tall. More than that, he is close. Too close.

And he is a man. A stranger.

My pulse drums in my ears as I take a step back, finding myself even deeper in the shadows. The store suddenly feels too small, too stifling, as if the very air has thickened around us.

I cast a careful glance toward the front counter, barely visible now through the small hole where the book had been. The other girls remain engaged in a heated argument with Mrs. Jenkins about the selection of books we are permitted to buy. No one is looking toward the back. There is no reason, after all—no one would dare go there.

The protective shield of the darkened back row should ease me.

It doesn't.

"I'll buy it for you," he offers.

The words snap my attention back to him. "What?" I stare at him in shock. He might not see my expression, but the cadence of my voice should echo my surprise.

His hand moves, deliberate and unhurried, as he places the book into my gloved one. Its weight is startling, as though I have been handed something far heavier than mere pages. "If you want to read it, you should," he encourages.

My fingers twitch against the cover, an instinctive response to something I desire yet cannot have. I push it back toward him. "I can't."

"Why?"

I swallow. "You know why."

The veil covering my face and neck, the gloves covering my hands, should be answer enough—there is no part of me left uncovered. He must know what that means. Everyone else does.

A flicker of understanding passes through his expression. He tilts his head slightly, studying me. "I know, in theory," he finally says. "But I also know you're interested."

"I shouldn't be," I say quickly.

"Why?"

I open my mouth, then close it again.

Why? What kind of question is that? The answer should be obvious. It has been given to me since childhood. I don't even have to think about it; it is simply truth.

But standing here, with a forbidden book in my hands and a stranger's expectant gaze fixed on me, I find that I don't know how to answer.

He extends his hand again, calm, patient.

I move one step back to avoid his touch. Even through layers of material, it feels far too intimate.

"Let me pay for it," he offers again in the same kind manner.

A flare of irritation rises in my chest, and I clench my jaw.

"No one has to know."

"I will know," I insist.

"Ah, but isn't that precisely what you desire?" His lip curves upward in a daring smile.

My nostrils flare in annoyance.

It isn't just the book. It isn't just the fact that he won't take no for an answer. It's the fact that he likely knows what happens to women who stray in my community—everyone knows.

No, it's more than that.

It is him.

The way he stands there so confidently, so unburdened by rules drilled into me since birth. The way he looks sharp, composed, free.

"You don't understand," I say, my voice clipped. "You never will."

He doesn't argue. That, more than anything, unsettles me.

"No," he agrees. "I don't and likely never will." He lets the words settle, as though acknowledging a truth neither of us can change. "But I do understand one thing—curiosity."

My heart beats faster, that one word settling somewhere deep inside of me: somewhere it seeks to hide, somewhere it seeks to thrive.

"You have that," he continues, his voice quiet but firm. "Enough to stand here and argue with me. Enough to think about it, even though you shouldn't. Enough to want something you know you aren't allowed to have."

He is right. And I hate that he is right.

I flick my gaze back toward Mrs. Jenkins, whose sharp voice still rings through the store, keeping the other girls occupied.

I have little time. If I get caught—if I am seen—

He must notice my hesitation. "Take it," he says again, softer this time.

I hesitate, truly hesitate, for the first time. "Why are you doing this?" I ask, my voice barely above a whisper.

Something flickers in his expression—pity, amusement? The former is more likely. "If only one thing were free in this world, it should be knowledge. Take it, read it, and learn from it."

I glance at the title again. His words seem measured, thoughtful.

"You speak as if you already know everything."

He chuckles, the sound oddly melodious. "Everything? I wish." Another laugh. It's not loud, so as not to draw attention to us. A part of me is grateful for it. "But I do know something about this book." He pauses. "I will pay for it. It is yours to do with as you please now."

Before I can object again, he turns to leave, but not before adding something else: something oddly foreboding.

"Hide it well, Petra. Don't get caught."

His steps echo through the shop as he briefly stops by the counter and exchanges a few short words with the bookseller. His departure is announced by the chiming bell at the door.

I stand there unmoving, holding the book but not thinking about it.

I never told him my name . . .

CHAPTER SEVEN

PETRA

The Past
8 March 1896

I got caught.

The soulful music echoes through the room. Everyone is rooted in the moment, feeling every word sung aloud, surrendering to the melody.

I open my mouth to sing along, though I am not sure if any sound escapes.

My throat is still raw from screaming for mercy. My body aches with the memory of the beating I took just days ago.

I had been foolish to think I could sneak a book into the house and go unnoticed. Foolish to believe I wouldn't be found out. And now, I wear the consequences. Every movement is a reminder—each breath, a searing pain. My split lip, a memento of my father's slap, is caked with dried blood.

Of course, I was forced to attend church. It's Sunday, after all. But at least my veil hides the artwork he painted across my face. No one sees. No one suspects. Around me, the congregation sings on, blissfully unaware.

Every motion sends a ripple of pain through me. Yet, in some twisted way, I am glad no one can see my suffering. I would not want the shame of it to accompany the pain. And yet, part of me wishes they could.

I wish they could look upon my bloodied face, my bruised eyes, my battered ribs. I wish they could see the price we pay for stepping out of line.

This church preaches forgiveness, acceptance. And yet, one mistake, and you are out. There was a moment when I thought that was it—my end. Lying on the floor as my father's foot crashed into my ribs, my stomach, my back.

Dying over a book. Would that have made me a martyr?

I was a mere step away from death for something so small. For curiosity.

Even now, despite the pain, despite knowing that had my brother not interfered, I could be dead—I wonder: Would I have still read it?

The seeds of doubt had long been planted in my mind—sometimes watered, sometimes left to wither. But this book, this forbidden book, fed those seeds, rained upon them, and made them flourish. And now, I am different.

Because now, I understand what it is to truly doubt. To wonder if there is such a thing as right and wrong, or if anyone truly knows the difference.

I glance around at the congregation, all pretending, all going along with the service, even as the hypocrisy in the words they sing and the actions they take is deafening.

The song eventually ends. We all take our seats while the reverend resumes his sermon. I sit with my family, though this is the last place I want to be: next to the man who made me limp in pain, who made me choke on my own blood.

I steal a glance at my father, sitting beside my mother and brother. The three perfect members of our family. The pillars of our congregation. No one would suspect anything, would they? My father, respected, revered. My mother, celebrated as the perfect wife—silent, compliant, always standing by her husband. Even when he beats their child nearly to death.

I looked at her while I writhed on the ground. She was in the room. But it was as if she weren't there. I wonder—does she condone what my father does, or does she simply refuse to see? Most days, she is little more than a ghost, a shell of a person, a woman without a voice.

And then there is my brother. The eldest. The heir. He will inherit my father's position in the congregation. Already respected as a young man of proper manners and a good education.

And then there's me.

Not troublesome, not officially. One cannot have such a reputation here without being excommunicated. But there have been moments, instances, where I have asked the wrong questions, where I have been harshly reprimanded. If people knew my father had taken his fist to my face over a book, they would not be surprised.

Theoretically, it would not be condoned. In practice, it is expected. Every household enforces discipline. I know because this is not the first time I have worn bruises. And it is not the first time I have seen them on others—even through the veils, pain cannot always be hidden.

The scent of incense fills my nostrils. I close my eyes and take a deep breath. I hate this place. And yet, I love it. Or rather, I have been forced to love it.

The sermon finally ends. People rise. The church, once silent, hums with murmured conversations. Niceties. Platitudes.

I almost scoff, but even that would hurt. I stand with my family as they greet person after person. I make the appropriate sounds of approval, ensuring my presence is noted, but I speak as little as possible. The singing has taken everything out of me. I taste blood in my mouth; my lip wound has reopened.

The reverend approaches my father, smiling. "Such a pleasure to have you here."

"I would not be anywhere else," my father replies smoothly. The same pleasantries. The same falsehoods.

As people begin to leave, my father suddenly turns to the reverend.

"Do you need any extra help cleaning up?" he asks.

The reverend raises a brow. "I believe I have a few volunteers for this week."

My father clicks his tongue. "I think we can make an exception this time."

The reverend hesitates but does not refuse. "What do you have in mind?"

I take a slow breath, steadying myself, just as my name is called.

"Petra."

The reverend blinks in surprise. "Your daughter? But it is a large church—"

"She has expressed interest in helping more than usual," my father interjects, voice like velvet. "I believe we should allow her. Wouldn't you agree?"

The reverend shifts uncomfortably. "Of course. But surely one of my volunteers—"

"No," my father cuts him off, and a shudder runs through me. "She can do it alone."

"But it will take her hours."

"She can do it alone," he emphasizes, voice hard.

The reverend, mindful of my father's influence and generosity, relents.

"Very well. Miss Petra will be responsible for cleaning the church this Sunday."

My father smiles, satisfied.

Ah. It wasn't enough for him to beat me. Now, he takes pleasure in knowing that with my sore body, I will toil for hours. Another punishment. Another lesson.

He turns to me. "Do not shame our family, Petra. You will do a good job. You will clean every single part of the church. Isn't that right?"

"Of course, Father," I say stiffly.

"Good."

The reverend leads me to the cleaning supplies—a few tattered cloths, a bucket of murky water, a bar of soap.

"There is more soap if you need it," he says. "And you know where the well is for fresh water."

"Yes, Reverend."

Satisfied, he finally leaves.

Alone in the vast, empty space, I stare at the polished seats, the gleaming icons, the endless religious memorabilia. I stare at it all and ask myself: *What now?* But the question is pointless.

I add soap to the bucket and carry it to the center of the room. Kneeling, I dip a cloth into the water and begin scrubbing. The recent rain has left muddy footprints streaked across the wooden floors, each one a reminder of the many who passed through the church's doors.

There is so much to do. Now I understand why my father refused to let the reverend assign other volunteers. This will take me the entire day. And then, when I arrive home too late, he will punish me again. I take a deep breath and scrub. I scrub and scrub.

Hours pass. Time loses meaning. All I know is that my aching bones are now throbbing, my body teetering on the edge of exhaustion.

My nails have become brittle, and the noxious soap—probably the cheapest they could find, since no one here bothers to make their own anymore—seeps under them, burning my raw skin. The booming industry in the nearby towns has flooded us with chemical-laden products, this soap included. I feel its sting, the slow damage it inflicts, yet I keep cleaning.

I hurry, finishing the floor before moving on to the benches. Thankfully, those require little effort, but the podium—this is where the real dirt lies. Mud and grime, left untouched for far too long, despite the church supposedly being cleaned every week.

Taking a deep breath, I dump the murky water, refill the bucket, add more soap, and begin again. My mind drifts as I scrub, wondering what punishment awaits me. Will it be verbal—preferable, though still humiliating—or will he reopen my wounds? He has a talent for that.

Footsteps echo through the church. Startled, I scramble to my feet. My breath catches. Is it the reverend, checking on my progress? Or worse—my father, telling me my work isn't good enough, ordering me to start over?

I brace myself as a shadowed figure moves down the aisle.

But it is neither.

The sight of a stranger unsettles me. Quickly, I pull my veil into place, ensuring my face is covered. "Who's there?" I call from behind the podium.

A man steps into view. His suit is immaculate—far too fine for someone from our congregation. The fabric is crisp, untouched by wear. My religion preaches humility; even those with wealth must wear their clothes until they are threadbare. This man does not belong here.

I instinctively step back. "Who are you? Why are you here? It's dark outside. No one comes to the church at this hour."

No response. My pulse quickens. I dare to peek over the reverend's stand, trying to see him more clearly.

And then I do.

He stands in the middle of the church, staring at me.

His eyes—light blue, piercing even in the dim lighting—are unmistakable.

I know those eyes.

I press my lips together. I have seen them before. And the last time I did, it led to the worst punishment I have ever endured.

"Why are you here?" I demand sharply.

The corner of his lips lifts slightly as he studies me, his gaze sweeping over my disheveled appearance, my stained gown. Then his eyes shift, locking onto my veil as if his gaze could burn through it.

"Hello, Petra."

"Please leave," I tell him. "You're not allowed to be here."

He steps forward and casually takes a seat on the front bench, leaning back and resting his hand against his temple. All the while, his eyes stay locked on me.

"I'm not allowed here because?"

"You do not belong to our congregation. Outsiders are not allowed here," I repeat, steeling myself, though I can feel my heart racing. Is it terror? Yes, that must be it. If I am found alone with a man inside the church, a beating would be the least of my punishments.

He will kill me.

"Please," I say again, my voice breaking.

He frowns. "What if I want to be part of your congregation? What would I need to do to join?"

I stammer, "You . . . you cannot."

"And why is that? Shouldn't people of God welcome the curious with open arms?"

"Curious?" I scoff at the word. He's called me that before. And look what curiosity has brought me.

"Yes, curious," he repeats with a small smile. "I am curious about this religion of yours."

"You are no more curious about my religion than I am the Queen of England," I tell him sternly.

He chuckles. "Why wouldn't I be? Is it not an interesting place?"

"No, it is not. And you are not curious. You are here to mock me, aren't you?"

"Mock you?" At this, he seems offended. "Why would I mock you?"

"Because you speak of curiosity, and that curiosity"—my voice falters—"brought me nothing but suffering."

His gaze hardens. His posture shifts. No longer the relaxed, amused man from before, he leans forward, his expression dark.

"What do you mean by that?" His voice is slow, deliberate.

"I don't have to tell you. Please, leave."

"No. You will tell me," he commands. "You got caught, didn't you?"

I try to laugh, but it comes out hollow.

"You got caught," he repeats, more certain this time, "and it's my fault, isn't it? If you hadn't had that book . . . if you hadn't been caught with it—"

He suddenly stands and closes the small distance between us. The damp cloth slips from my fingers as I step back, intimidated by the fire in his eyes. Concern.

Why?

Why is he concerned about me? Why would a stranger care? I don't understand. Not after he was the one who gave me the book, knowing how forbidden it was, knowing what would happen if I was caught with it.

He stops just short of me, his hand reaching out as if to touch my veil. Then, he catches himself and lowers it.

"What happened?" he demands. "What did he do to you?

"He hit you, didn't he?" His hand rises again, his thumb hovering near my face. "Where did he hit you?"

I shake my head. "I don't understand you. Why are you here? Why are you talking to me? If you know what is going to happen to me, if you know I will be punished, then why are you here? Why are you putting me in danger?" I cry out.

My voice is raw, my throat burning with every word. I cannot hide it anymore. My voice breaks completely, and tears spill down my cheeks, dripping onto my lips, stinging my reopened wounds. I wince at the pain.

"What's wrong?" he asks quickly, stepping forward. This time, he wastes no time closing the distance. He is just one step away.

I can feel his presence, his warmth—too close. And to my great shame, I don't step away. Why? I cannot say.

Perhaps it is the concern in his voice. Perhaps it is because, no matter how much I suffer at home, no one has ever looked at me with even a shred of compassion. Even as I lay bleeding in my own house, my brother only glanced at me and said, "Next time, I won't stop him."

"Where does it hurt?" the stranger asks, his hand inching closer to my veil.

I swat it aside. "Stop. Get away from me. Leave."

He doesn't move.

"You have no idea what will happen if we're caught together," I hiss.

"We won't be caught. No one knows I'm here."

"No one will know," I scoff. "Just like they didn't know about the book." I glare at him.

"I told you not to get caught, didn't I?" he says, but this time there's no smugness in his voice. This time, he looks guilty.

"Maybe you shouldn't have given me the book in the first place."

"Why did you take it?" he counters.

"I . . ." I stammer. That is a question I've asked myself countless times. Why did I take it?

"Because you *were* curious," he says. "Because you want to know. You want more than this." He gestures to the church. "You're not meant for this life, Petra."

My breath catches. "How do you know my name? How do you know anything about me? What gives you the right to say anything about me?"

"Because I've been watching you."

I freeze. "You—what?"

His lips curve into a sad smile. "I've been watching you for months. From afar, yet so close."

I shake my head, stepping back. "What are you saying?"

I collide with the wall.

I'm trapped.

There's nowhere to run.

Can I scream? My gaze darts around the empty church. My voice would echo, but no one would hear. No one is around at this hour. Even if there were someone, they would blame me, wouldn't they? They would say I invited it.

My hands on the wall, I slide away from him, waiting for the perfect moment to run.

"Stop," he commands.

And I do.

My body trembles with fear, but I hold myself still, eyes locked on him.

"I will not hurt you," he says.

"That's not reassuring," I sneer.

"I give you my word, Petra. I will not harm you."

"Why? Why are you doing this? I don't understand."

"Will you let me help you?" His voice is soft, comforting.

"Help me?" I ask incredulously.

"You're in pain," he states.

My breath catches, but I steel myself.

"You're the reason for that," I retort. "Please let me go. You're too close. We're alone. You could do whatever you want, and I wouldn't be able to stop you."

"And yet, I give you my word that I won't." Holding something in his hand, he extends it toward me. "Will you please let me help you?"

I look down at the small jar he holds out.

"What is this?"

"An ointment. It will help with your injuries."

I stare at the tin jar and gulp down uncomfortably. How many times have I wished for something like that?

My congregation is against medicine and anything that might interfere with the human body as God created it. If you are meant to die, you will die. It is a thing to rejoice, for you will go to the heavenly realm and take your seat next to God.

"Take it," he urges. "Please."

I let out a dry laugh. "You must know this is forbidden, too."

"What should be forbidden is for someone to hurt you, to lay a hand on you." His voice is harsh, an undercurrent of violence behind his calm countenance.

I stiffen, my body once more on alert.

He lets out a sigh. "You don't have to take it home with you. I would not want you to get in trouble again."

I look from his face to the small jar. It's tempting. But I've already seen what temptation does to me—it only brings more pain.

Yet there is another question that plagues my mind.

"How did you know I would be hurt?" I ask suspiciously.

"I did not."

"Then why carry this with you?"

He presses his lips together. "I was aware of the possibility, though I hoped it would not be the case. I know what your kind does to its women," he spits out in disgust.

"My kind?" My brows go up. "If *my kind* is so repulsive to you, then please leave me alone."

"I did not word that right. I apologize."

"Apology not accepted."

The ghost of a smile appears on his lips. "I suppose I deserved that." He lets out a dry chuckle.

This man . . . He is strange.

"You do not have to accept my apology, or even like me." He pauses. "For now," he adds. "But please take this. It will take away some of the pain and prevent infection. Apply it to any open wound."

Laughter bubbles in my throat. "And what about the wounds inside?" My words are weighted, heavy with meaning.

His expression darkens. "I wish I could help with those, too. Maybe someday I will . . ."

He speaks in code, and I am far too weak and in pain to try to understand him.

I bring my gaze back to the jar, my resolve wavering.

After what feels like forever, I reach out and take the ointment, careful so even my gloved hands don't touch his.

"Good," he murmurs.

I place the tin jar in the pocket of my dress. "And what do you want in exchange for this?"

His gaze meets mine, unwavering.

"What do I want?" he repeats, his voice almost a caress. He steps closer. Then shakes his head and steps back. Without another word, he turns and leaves.

When he is almost at the door, the echo of his voice travels to me, low, decisive.

"We will meet again, Petra. Perhaps then I will tell you what I want."

I stumble forward, confused. "W-what? Why? When?"

The door opens, and he steps out. But not without leaving me with more cryptic words.

"Wait for my sign."

CHAPTER EIGHT

PETRA

The Past
15 March 1896

The sign comes a week later on my windowsill.

Just as I open my window to let in the night air, I find a small bundle resting on the sill. Frowning, I take it in my hands. It's the shape of a book, wrapped carefully, and nestled inside is a letter. I hesitate. I live on the second floor. Who could have reached my window to leave this? Certainly no one in my family.

Curiosity gnaws at me. Quickly, I open the letter. The handwriting is crisp, masculine. I don't even need to read past the first sentence to know who it's from.

"Once you read this, burn it. Leave no evidence behind."

Who else could it be but him? He knows the danger. He knows the cost of getting caught. And yet, he still sent this.

Before reading further, I stick my head out the window, scanning the grounds. The air is cold and clean. The silence is unnerving. There's no sign of anyone. We have dogs—big, aggressive beasts trained to attack at the slightest provocation. No one dares to enter our property, not with those dogs, not with the armed guards stationed near the barn protecting us from the sinful outside world.

And yet, the dogs are silent. Asleep or undisturbed. If someone had been here, they would have barked. They would have raised the alarm. But they didn't.

How did he get here? How did he reach my window? More questions pile up the longer I think about it. Not only did he avoid the dogs and the guards, but he knew exactly which window was mine. He knew I didn't share my room. He knew I would be the one to find this.

He knew.

Just as he knew I had a fireplace to burn this letter.

His words from before echo in my mind.

I've been watching you. For a long time, I've been watching you.

I don't know how to feel. Fear prickles at the edges of my thoughts. Someone has been watching me, lurking in the shadows, tracking my every move. It should terrify me. And yet . . . I am curious.

There it is again—that word. Curious.

Why me? What does he want? What is his goal?

Last week, in the church, we were alone. He could have done anything he wanted. He could have hurt me, and I would have been powerless to stop him. Worse, I would have been unable to say anything, for fear of being branded a harlot. A Jezebel.

But he didn't hurt me. On the contrary, he helped me.

The ointment he gave me not only healed my busted lip and the scrapes on my body, but it soothed the pain. I've never had an injury heal so quickly.

For that alone, I don't fear him.

Is that dangerous? Perhaps. Perhaps I am so starved for kindness, for knowledge, for anything beyond the rigid confines of my life, that I am willing to accept that a stranger has been watching me.

I glance at the book and the letter. Taking a deep breath, I continue reading.

I will not let you get caught. Not again. It was a mistake on my part not to foresee what could happen to you. Please accept my apologies. Or better yet—don't. Not yet.

A small smile tugs at my lips as I recall our last meeting.

The letter continues.

I don't want you to give up what you want most—knowledge. I don't want you to abandon your curiosity out of fear.

Every night, I will leave a book on your windowsill. Every morning, I will take it back. Read to your heart's content, and when you are done, return it to the windowsill.

Perhaps, in time, you will find it in your heart to forgive me—little by little.

Perhaps you will start to be curious about . . . me.

There is no signature at the bottom. Just one word.

Yours.

I blink.

Yours?

I know it's just a customary way to end a letter. But here, without a name, it feels more intimate. More meaningful.

What did he mean by it?

Yours.

The word echoes in my mind, over and over again. But it is not my voice I hear—it is his. A whisper looping in my thoughts.

Yours.

I shake my head, forcing the feeling away. I place the book back on the windowsill, the letter with it.

This is unseemly. I should not even be entertaining this. He is taking too many liberties with me. Liberties I never granted.

I should put an end to this now.

Perhaps I won't be caught today. Perhaps not tomorrow. But eventually, I will be. And when that day comes, I do not want to face the consequences.

I return to my bed, pulling the blankets up to my chin. I squeeze my eyes shut, willing myself to sleep.

"Sleep," I command myself.

But no matter how hard I try, my thoughts drift back to the book on the windowsill.

It is the same book as before. The one he bought for me at the bookshop. The one I hid. The one that led to my punishment.

The one I only got halfway through.

If it were another book, I might not care as much. But because it is *that* book, I need to know. I need to know how it ends.

After what feels like an eternity of tossing and turning, I finally make a decision.

Slipping out of bed, I return to the window and pick up the book.

As per his instructions, I go to the fireplace and toss the letter into the flames, watching as the embers flicker and devour the paper, turning it to ash.

Opening a drawer, I retrieve a candle. Our house is powered by gas, but turning on the lights would make noise, and then everyone would know I was awake.

So I settle for the glow of the fire and the soft flicker of candlelight.

I only leave my seat when the first light of morning seeps through the window. Letting out a yawn, I rise, tidy the room, place the book back on the sill, and slip into bed. Exhaustion pulls at my body, yet sleep remains elusive.

Something gnaws at me.

Eventually, I get back up, take a pen, and turn to the last page I read. In the corner, I write a small note: *Thank you.* Satisfied, I return to bed.

When I wake, the book is gone. No sign remains of anyone having been here. Just like before, I have no idea how he managed to get past the dogs, past the guards, and up to my second-floor window.

Yet, despite the mystery, I still find myself checking the window again the next night. And once more, after darkness falls, I find another book—and another letter.

You have lovely handwriting, Petra. Thank you for gracing me with it. I hope I shall be the object of your writing in the future, too. Read on, my beautiful darling, read on.

And once more, it is signed,

Yours.

I stare at the letter. *Yours.* No name. Just that word.

Why won't he write his name?

And yet, I read the letter again and again.

"*My beautiful darling,*" he called me. The words stir something warm inside me. Too warm. I shake my head, trying to dispel the strange heat curling in my chest.

I take the book to the fireplace and start reading.

By the third day, I have finished it. I close the cover, a pang of disappointment settling in my stomach. It's over. And with it, perhaps, this entire exchange. Maybe he will not leave me another book. Maybe this was it—his apology.

And yet, the night after finishing it, I still check the windowsill.

This time, there is another book. A different title. *The Picture of Dorian Gray* by Oscar Wilde.

Tucked within the first page is a letter.

Have I perhaps contributed to that curiosity of yours, my beautiful darling?

Perhaps this will help me put myself in your good graces again. It is a story of appearances that deceive. A story of immortality, but not as one might imagine. Because immortality, though desirable, can be lonely.

I look forward to hearing your thoughts. Just remember one thing—appearances deceive. You are not who you seem to be, and I am not who I seem to be. We are all far different from what the world perceives us to be.

And at the end, again,

Yours.

I trace my fingers over the word before picking up the book and settling in for another long night of reading.

When daylight creeps through my window once more, I return the book to the sill—this time, with my own note.

If appearances deceive, then who are you, stranger?

I don't sign it. I leave it at that. Even though I itch to write the same appellation he uses.

Yours.

But I cannot, can I? I am not his. He is not mine. We are just two strangers playing a game, wondering how long we can continue before we are caught.

The next letter, though, surprises me.

So you are curious about me, my beautiful darling.

If you are curious, then perhaps I should let myself be known. But not now. Not yet. I like the shadows far too much. I like watching you wonder about me.

I continue reading, and when I finish the book, I leave another letter.

Yes. I am curious. I want to know why you are watching me.
How you are doing it. I want to know—why me?

When the next letter comes, I unfold it with bated breath.

Why you?

He writes,

Why not you?

Why not you, the beautiful girl who cares for others far too much and for herself far too little? Why not you, the girl who would rather suffer punishment than silence her curiosity? Why not you, the lost lamb searching for guidance?

I want to be that for you, my beautiful Petra. I want to be the recipient of your kindness. I want to be your guidance, your beacon of light. I want to be everything you think of, from morning until night, and from night until morning. I want to be the sole object of your curiosity.

The letter ends, once more signed,

Yours.

I read it again. And again. Each time more confused, yet more curious at the same time. If he meant to arouse my curiosity, he's certainly achieved it. So now, he should quench it, too.

I take a pen and write just one word.

Why?

When the next letter arrives, the response is just as brief.

Yours.

I frown. What does it mean? Why would he write that? Why would his answer to my question be this word? I don't understand. Perhaps I am not worldly enough to grasp its meaning. Perhaps this is the kind of seduction spoken about in hushed tones.

Perhaps this is what drives women to jeopardize their virtues, all for the attention of one man.

And to my great shame, I can see why.

Because I crave his attention. I crave his next letter as much as I crave my next breath.

Taking a deep breath, I put pen to paper once more, this time with firm resolve.

If you do not tell me the reason why you are so interested in me,
I will stop replying to your letters. I will stop taking your books.
I will stop interacting with you. So please, tell me. Who are you?
And why are you so concerned with me?

I don't sign the letter.

Yet, as I reread my own words, I realize that *concern* is not the right term. It is not *concern*, is it?

It is something else—something far closer to *obsession*.

THE NEXT DAY, I go about my chores, waiting for nightfall. And when it does, I rush to the window, expecting another book, another letter.

But to my surprise, there is nothing.

No book. No letter. No sign of him.

Did I—did I do something wrong? Did my last letter upset him? Was I too direct? Too demanding?

Or was this all just a game to him? Had I simply been an amusement, something to be toyed with and discarded?

The following night, still nothing.

Each evening, I check the windowsill, and each evening, I am met with silence. No words, no stories, no letters.

Day by day, my mood darkens.

I think back on our exchanges, replaying every word he wrote, every word I wrote in return. Now I regret burning those letters. They are gone, reduced to ash, and yet the questions remain.

What went wrong?

Perhaps he has finally realized that I am not so easy a target.

But why does that thought bring no relief? Why does it not make me feel victorious? Why does it only leave me feeling hollow?

Two weeks pass in silence.

And that is when I give up hope of ever hearing from him again.

It is early morning when I prepare to go into town with the other girls from my congregation, under the watchful eye of Mrs. Jenkins. We are heading to the town fair, where vendors have set up their stalls, displaying the bounty of the new season. With spring's arrival, everything feels renewed, fresh—a stark contrast to the heaviness lingering in my heart.

Flowers bloom, and even the trees bear the first tender buds of life.

We wander through the fair, taking in the sights, the chatter, the lively bustle. With the little money I have, I purchase a new pen.

A strange choice, isn't it? Especially given that I have no one left to write to. And yet, the moment I saw it, my mind drifted to *him*.

I shake my head, pushing away the thought. I must stop thinking about him.

The other girls are deep in conversation, sharing the latest church gossip. Mrs. Jenkins haggles over a hairpin, her attention fixed on bartering. Once we've made our purchases, we begin walking through the town square.

That's when the commotion erupts.

A loud noise rings through the air, drawing attention. Mrs. Jenkins immediately tenses.

"Ignore it," she says. "Perhaps it's best we return home."

But the girls are too curious. They point toward the crowd gathering ahead, and after some urging, they take off toward the scene.

Mrs. Jenkins shouts after them, but she doesn't seem particularly determined to stop them.

Perhaps she is curious, too.

So, I follow.

I weave through the growing crowd, pushed forward by the throng of onlookers, until I find myself at the edge of the circle.

In the center, a fight rages. Two men, both finely dressed, locked in struggle. One grips the other by the throat, his expression dark with violence. The other man, equally well-dressed, looks terrified.

And then I see *him*.

The man strangling the other. It's *him*.

My stranger.

A cold wave crashes over me. *He is not mine,* I remind myself. *He never was.*

But he is here.

People shout around me. Their voices blend into a fevered chant.

"The devil." "The devil must be vanquished." "Cast him out." "Cast out the devil!"

A chill creeps down my spine.

I turn to an older woman beside me, her face twisted with concern. "What devil?" I ask, my voice low.

She glances at me, intrigued, then leans in conspiratorially. "You don't know?"

I shake my head.

She scoffs. "He's the new professor at St. Anselm Hall."

Confused, I ask, "Why does that make him a devil?"

She tsks, leaning even closer. "Because he studies demonology and other pagan things. I don't know how someone like that was allowed into an institution like St. Anselm. And in Radcliffe, no less! They should throw him out. They should *stone* him."

I flinch at the vehemence in her voice. *A professor?*

But more than that, I am stunned by another revelation.

Demonology. Pagan things.

Before I can fully process the thought, my gaze lifts to him once more.

He is already looking at me.

His expression shifts. Recognition, yes, but something else. Something deeper.

He didn't want me to see this.

His grip slackens. The other man breaks free, throwing a punch. My stranger stumbles to the side, but his eyes remain locked on me.

Another blow.

His gaze never leaves mine.

The crowd surges forward, throwing stones, objects—whatever they can find.

"Devil."

"Demon."

"Cursed."

A sharp object strikes him, splitting the skin just above his brow. Blood trickles down his face.

And still, his eyes remain on me.

CHAPTER NINE

PETRA

Present Day

Two and a half months have passed since that night at Elias Rutherford's house, and as I sit at my desk, exhaustion seems to press me down ever further into my chair.

I'm always tired these days, no matter how much I sleep. And even that sleep is disturbed by peculiar dreams.

In some of them, I drift through large rooms filled with transparent, fleshless outlines of people. They stand around and hold silent conversations, all dressed in old clothes, as if frozen in time.

It's like watching a period drama where the main character is some weird version of me: a repressed and misunderstood young woman fighting against the confines of society.

Perhaps I've been watching too much of *The Gilded Age.* Perhaps . . .

Yet sometimes, the dreams are vivid scraps of sense-memory from time spent in that room with Sin: the deep colors of the bed coverings and the curtains, the muted glow of the ornate lamps, the music . . . as if by going over those scenes while I slept, my mind is trying to recover some lost memory.

And not to mention my mood swings, which have lately been affecting all personal relationships.

My parents did manage to procure a gift for me when they finally remembered that their daughter was again reaching important milestones in utter isolation.

I had been in a particularly nasty mood at that time, so I made them—well, their assistants, actually—run all around the place so I could have exactly the dress I wanted: a knee-length black and gold brocade dress from Dolce&Gabbana's Fall 2012 collection.

Though the gift did nothing to dispel the bleak clouds of resentment that now hung over all my interactions with my parents, I did look like a scandalous Austrian princess with a reputation for getting widowed in the first year of all her marriages. So I was probably going to forgive my primary caregivers when they, inevitably, forgot my next birthday.

Apart from that little indulgence, the past weeks have felt rather gray.

In the mornings, I try to put together a creative portfolio for my applications to design schools, and by the late afternoons, I am yawning and longing for sleep.

My body feels heavy, and soreness takes root in my limbs and torso.

While I'm being miserable like this, my phone buzzes with a message from Amelia.

Hey, Petra. How you feeling?

I had shared with her a little of what had been happening with me: the tiredness, the odd dreams, the hole in my heart that gaped wider each day.

Like the best friend ever, she kept regular tabs on my moods and physical well-being. Earlier, I would have thought all of this sweet.

In my current state, I feel somewhat irked. As if her concern is forcing me to put on a façade that tells her I'm fine, even though I'm clearly not. And what stops me from being honest with her? I have wondered the same and have come up with no answer.

Truth be told, Amelia has always been my rock, but ever since that night with Sin, I've been holding back.

Because now I had experienced something that couldn't be shared with someone else; I had neither a coherent memory of the whole event nor the suitable words to articulate it.

This thought niggles at me as I start typing a response but stop midway, unsure of what to say.

Just then, another message pops up.

What's up? Everything cool?

Yeah, sure. Why?

Not the most elaborate of responses, but it was better than not responding at all.

Nothing. Just, feels like you've been avoiding me lately.

I can't blame her for feeling this way. But did she have to insist on knowing anyway? Yes, we took pride in how vulnerable we dared to be with each other, how we entrusted each other with our tenderest jealousies, our tiniest perversions.

But did she have the right to demand any confessions when I was in such a mess? It feels like too much; it feels unfair.

Still, I try to remain courteous as I text back:

I'm fine, Ames. Just been feeling off lately.

Almost instantly, she replies:

Off how? Talk to me, Petra.
You know you can, right?

I take a deep breath, trying to stem the burning ire that rises in my throat, blocking my actual passageways. A dull ache persists around my temples as I write back:

I know, Ames. It's just . . . a lot.

A lot how?

She messages back almost immediately. Already the conversation has been taxing, so I almost put the phone away at this point. But it buzzes with another message from her.

Are you shutting me out, Petra?
Was it something I said?

The frustration in her words finally sparks something in me. Or maybe it's one of those unpredictable swings in my disposition, the rapid to-and-fro across the full spectrum of human emotions that has lately affected me.

Whatever the reason, I snap at the most caring person in my life so far.

It's not that simple, Amelia!

There's a pause, and then she writes back:

What's not simple, Petra?

We are using each other's full first names now. That's how bad things have gotten.

Tears prick my eyes as I type back, my anger and guilt finally spilling over.

You wouldn't understand.

Try me!

Her response is instantaneous; it feels like if I did ask her, she would somehow appear in my bedroom in a flash and a twinkle, like some teenage fairy godmother.

And still I hesitate, my fingers suspended midair, contorted and quivering, as if I'm literally grasping at straws.

How can I explain the whirlwind I have been caught in since that night?

How can I tell her about Sin and everything that happened?

I can't say right now.

Why not? You used to tell me everything.

I don't know, Ames, please don't push. Things are difficult.

But we deal with them together, remember?

I remember, Ames. This time . . . it's different.

Different how?

More relentless questioning that I'm not prepared for. How can I explain something I don't fully understand myself?

I don't know how to explain.

Is this about a guy?

The question hits me like an uppercut from nowhere, and I feel my anger rising again.

Why does it always have to be about a guy?

Because you're acting like a girl who's got her heart broken.

That's such a snarky thing to say, Ames. Just FYI, EVERYTHING in my life is difficult right now.

Okay, now you're scaring me, Petra. Just tell me what's going on. Are you sick or something?

I pause and grapple with the sheer force of my instincts to just tell her, just come clean. But I am not sure how.

I need time, Ames. Please, can you just understand that? I'm not doing this to shut you out.

She takes a while to respond this time. I almost expect her to never talk to me again, but my phone buzzes with a final message from her.

It's all right, Petra. Take your time. See you on the other side.

The last line sounds like a farewell message, and I feel a tear slip down my cheek. I don't respond. I can't.

Instead, I throw my phone onto the bed, pick up a pillow, and let out a guttural, winding scream into its soft depths.

Of course, it's because I can't shake off the feeling that I've just pushed Amelia further away. It's also because I have been a hot mess the last few weeks, because after that night with . . . with Sin, I have received exactly *zero messages* from him.

Despite my best efforts, my mind drifts back to that night. The way Sin had looked at me and touched me, how our comfortable chat had turned into something more, something that still felt . . . illicit in a way.

I remember the way everything had felt good and bad at the same time. Was that what sex was supposed to feel like? Or is my experience, like me, an outlier?

Just then, a loud beep from my phone, signaling a health notification. The moment I see that little message, a rush of adrenaline makes me sit up. I realize I've been so caught up in everything that I haven't noticed a crucial development.

I've skipped my periods.

Panic floods away any attempt at rational thought. I do a mental calculation. It's been over two months.

How did I not notice this sooner? My hands start to tremble as I grab my phone and search for the nearest drugstore.

Then I pause and say, "WHAT THE FUCK?" out loud because life has felt so surreal as of late that I wouldn't be surprised if tomorrow I wake up and the whole thing—the fight with Amelia, the odd dreams, my lethargy—has been a dream.

Yet, one look at the cycle tracker on my phone, and I know that I'm in trouble. I take a deep breath, trying to steady myself. *One step at a time, Petra.* First, I need to know for sure. Everything else can wait.

But as I head out the door, my belly does flips, and my knees shake so hard I struggle to descend the steps in front of it. Why does it feel like my life is about to change forever?

Half an hour later, I walk into the drugstore. I had to find a place farther away from home; nobody we knew could see me here.

Already, the feeling of being *wrong,* of doing wrong, is starting to corrode my spirits.

Intellectually, I know that mistakes happen and that such mistakes are in no way a judgment on a girl's moral character.

Yet the larger part of me is already on the lookout for persecution. My senses are on high alert and my footsteps erratic.

Once inside the store, I glance around nervously, trying to avoid eye contact with anyone. The aisle with the pregnancy tests seems miles away, but I force myself to move forward, even though my feet drag on like lead.

I scan the shelves and finally reach for a box. Vaguely, I remember that you're supposed to take a bunch of tests from different brands to ensure that you don't get false positives or false negatives.

I grab a couple more of those discreetly packaged boxes and reach the counter.

The cashier, a pretty older woman with soft green eyes, smiles warmly as I place the boxes in front of her.

"Hi there," she says while scanning my item without really looking at it. "How are you doing today?"

I'm a teenage girl buying at-home pregnancy tests at a drugstore, so take a guess, lady! I think hysterically while trying to muster a smile.

But it comes out as a mangled grimace as I say, "I'm . . . okay."

At this point, she finally registers what I'm buying at the store. When she looks up, her eyes are filled with empathy. "It's going to be all right, sweetheart. Here, take this."

She slips a small brochure into the bag along with the tests.

"I know you're young, so if you need someone to talk to, someone grown up, or even someone *other than your parents*, there are people who can help."

I glance at the brochure. It's for the Planned Parenthood center in Radcliffe.

I feel so numb with terror at this point that I can only whisper, "Thanks," in a barely audible voice.

She squeezes my hand and gives me another reassuring smile that completely fails to comfort me. "You take care of yourself, okay?"

I nod and rush out of the store. The walk home is a blur.

By the time I reach my house, my hands feel chilled to the bone, even though it's warm enough outside.

After stepping in, I head straight to the bathroom, where I take the tests out of the box.

CHAPTER TEN

PETRA

Present Day

I follow the instructions mechanically and lay out two tests on the counter, beginning the most anxious wait of my life.

What to do in the meantime? Nothing holds my attention long enough to stop the rising tides of fear.

I pull out the brochure and try reading some of it.

But the words are generic—"choices," "options," "empowerment"—and I barely register the shape of the sentences, let alone their actual meanings.

I already know the test results. The missed periods, the exhaustion, the mood swings. All the signs are there.

So when the timer on my phone finally goes off, I don't even need to glance at the sticks before the bottom drops out of my belly. As if the timer has marked the beginning of some terrible ordeal.

When I finally bring myself to pick up the tests and look at them, my ears are filled with a loud ringing noise.

Two lines. On both of them.

Positive.

I stare at it, my vision blurring with tears. Hot and urgent, they stream down my face.

I chant, "No, no, no."

I think of the kind woman at the drugstore, her caring smile, and the hope in her eyes.

I think of my parents who must be in some client briefing at a hip tech office with minimalist glass décor.

I think of Amelia, and the distance between us that feels even wider now.

And I think of Sin, and the night that changed everything.

I stare at the positive pregnancy tests in my hands.

How could this happen?

How could I get pregnant from the first and only time I had sex?

Short, panicked gasps burst out of my chest as I try to process the shit-show my life has become. The bathroom suddenly feels too suffocating. I clutch the edge of the sink, trying to steady myself, but my legs feel like jelly.

I sink to the floor, hugging myself tightly and rocking back and forth.

What am I going to do?

My parents will flip out when they find out their perfect daughter is pregnant.

Maybe they'll disown me.

Maybe they'll kick me out.

More panic crashes down on me, and it feels like I have been pushed underwater, all over again.

I need to finish high school. I need to graduate, so I can go to college, get away from this place, start a new life.

But I can't do that without their financial support, no matter how dissatisfied I am with my home life.

I don't know what to do. I don't have anyone to talk to. Amelia is mad at me, and even if she weren't, how could I tell her about any of this? How could I admit that I'm pregnant and can barely remember how it happened?

The woman at the drugstore said I could talk to someone, that there are people who can help. Maybe that's what I need—someone who isn't my parents, who isn't Amelia, someone who can help me come up with a solution without judging me.

Maybe I will eventually come out on the other side.

But right now, I'm in for another spate of sleepless nights till school starts.

WHEN THE ALARM finally goes off on the first day of the next term, I drag myself out of bed like a zombie.

The girl in the mirror wears an ashen face, her eyes lined with dark circles.

I put on the biggest Jimmy Choo sunglasses from my wardrobe and pray to whatever eldritch horror is pulling the strings of my life that I can survive the day without any more terrifying discoveries.

Please don't let me miss out on Art History, I think wryly, coolly, but I'm dying inside; everything feels like the end of the world, and it's not just because I am a moody teenager, but because I'm preg—

No, no, no, not thinking about that, not yet. I know I can't be in denial forever, but I have no idea how to go about doing what needs to be done.

Scratch that, I have no idea what needs to be done!

Instead, I just get inside the car that drives me to school, like I do every day.

When I reach my destination, the school grounds are already bustling with students. They look sprightly and carefree, perhaps glad to be back among their friends.

The air is filled with the chatter of excited teenagers, and groups form and reform here and there. Stories of summer adventures are shared in brash, bragging tones.

In the starkest of contrasts, I make my way through the crowd with my head down, trying to avoid eye contact.

I usually feel like everyone is staring at me, but today, that feeling is amplified. I keep thinking that all of them—including the teachers, the custodians, the lunch lady—know my secret and are judging me for it.

It's probably all in my head, but I can never be sure anymore.

In the hallway, I see Sin talking to his friends, and my heart almost throbs in pain.

How to tell him? *Do* I tell him? What will he say? Will he be angry? At who? Who's at fault here anyways?

Will he blame *me*?

Each of these questions sends pangs of anxiety through my limbs.

Still, I attempt to play it cool. Instead of spying on Sin like a loser, I turn around and walk into the registration office.

Time to bag the art history class. It had been one of my top choices for this semester, the only thing I had been looking forward to all summer.

As usual, the office is abuzz with activity; students shuffle in and out, while advisors tap away at their keyboards.

I approach the counter, clutching my schedule and request forms.

"Hi. I'm here to register for my classes."

"Name?" says the woman behind the counter in a curt voice.

"Petra Valentine."

She types my name into the computer. After a few moments, she looks back at me with an office worker's vacant stare, like she's looking at a spot on the wall behind me.

"Class requests?"

I hand her my forms, my excitement barely contained.

"I'm really excited about Art History with Ms. Matthews. It's my first choice."

She scans the forms and then starts entering the data into the system. The whole time, her expression doesn't budge an inch.

I watch her face, trying to read any hint of a reaction, but it's an exercise in futility. Finally, she looks back at me, and I know something's wrong before she even speaks.

"Yeah, no, Art History's full."

My stomach drops. "What, already? I came here as soon as I could."

"It's a very popular class," she responds in a monotonous drawl, like she has been reciting the same line to other enthusiasts and hopefuls throughout the morning. "I can put you on the waiting list, but there's no guarantee you'll get in."

My shoulders slump, and my heart sinks. "Is there really no way to get in? Maybe I can speak to the professor and-and show her all my preparations for the cou—"

"Can't help, sorry. Gotta stick to the enrollment limits. For the already-registered students." The woman is not even looking at me, a merciful respite because I'm on the verge of tears.

Then she hands me back my forms, along with a revised schedule.

"Here are the other options. Find something else that interests you, and let us know within the week."

I glance down at the list, but it's hard to focus. All I can think about is how much I had been looking forward to this class, and now another thing is slipping out of my control.

"Thanks," I say, forcing a smile. "I'll figure something out."

I walk out of the office, the revised schedule crumpled in my hand.

Great, just great.

First the pregnan—the you-know-what—and now this.

Which of my haters is vengeful enough to make a voodoo doll of me? Will they ever stop sticking pins into it?

Though my inner cynic poses such zany questions, she's also freaking out.

At least a part of me is still making jokes.

But things are always destined to get complicated, right? As I am trudging past the quad, wondering when my life started to spiral so rapidly, so comically, into the bottomless pits of hell, who do I spy with my weary eye?

Sin.

A tight-knit circle of admirers stands around him. Girls laugh at his jokes, touching his arms, vying for his attention, fluttering their eyelashes like debutantes at some Victorian ball.

I feel a pang of jealousy and self-consciousness.

How many of those girls has he been intimate with? Am I just one of many? Did he get any of them pregnant, too? Did he make them get an abortion?

After all, if he was so quick to have unprotected sex with me, who else has he been having it with?

Oh my God. I haven't even thought about STDs.

Fucking hell! That's the last thing I need right now . . .

I turn away quickly, knowing that these thoughts will gnaw at me all day. As he shares jokes and tells amusing stories, Sin seems so far out of my league, so different from the guy who held me in his arms that night.

Should I tell him? What if he doesn't care? I am unable to concentrate in class, my mind replaying the same doubts and fears over and over again.

By lunchtime, I've made up my mind.

I will tell him. He's as responsible for this as I am—maybe more so, considering I can barely remember any of it.

I find a quiet corner in the library, looking around carefully to ensure nobody can see me, and write a note.

I am obviously not going to text him out of nowhere. It's better to do things this way.

Safer.

More . . . impersonal.

By the end, I've rewritten the note a bunch of times. But the one I'm holding now is as good as it's going to get.

I haven't signed it with my name, as if wishing to preserve my privacy, my anonymity, for as long as I can. Or maybe I'm scared that he will not do as the note says once he finds out it's from me.

Furtively, like some two-bit detective from a sitcom, I make my way to Sin's locker, trying to look casual.

The hallway is still crowded with students, but they are all busy chatting. *Probably crowing about bagging a seat in Art History,* I think glumly.

I walk briskly till I reach his locker, and once there, I glance around before slipping the note into the slats.

Even I'm surprised at the smoothness with which the maneuver is executed. After securing the note in place, I simply walk away, but its message lingers in my mind, clear and simple:

Meet me after class in the gardener's shed.

CHAPTER ELEVEN

PETRA

Present Day

I attend the rest of my classes in a dreamless stupor, the incessant exhaustion of my body seeping into every movement. The voices of various teachers merge into a background drone against which I struggle to structure my scattered thoughts.

In a few hours, the final bell rings, and a weight seems to drop on my chest. My stomach is a nervous knot, and I feel like I might be sick—though this could also be attributed to the you-know-what condition of my body.

The walk feels surreal, like I'm moving through a wall of fog. Though the larger streams of outgoing students head for the main gates or the posh café near the fencing area, I turn down a little-trodden path, a shortcut that mostly the janitorial and security staff use.

After a few minutes of walking, the shed comes into view—an arched, single-storied wooden building surrounded by overgrown bushes.

The gardener's shed is at the edge of the school grounds, tucked away behind the old gym. Not like St. Anselm Hall prides itself on the farm-fresh organic fare it feeds its wards.

No, the job of the head gardener and his handful of minions is to maintain the sprawling school grounds that are dotted with flowerbeds and groves of elms, all with the aim of making the place look *tastefully* wild and unmanned.

If for nothing else, at least for the two times a year when alumni walk inside the gates of the school and marvel at the beauty of their alma mater—and bestow large amounts of money as a result, of course.

The shed itself is quiet and secluded, as I had discovered pretty early on when I first started hanging out on my own, years ago.

The tall-ceilinged structure is made of wooden beams and meticulously lined with shelves on which rest the gardeners' tools. Birdsong from the nearby woods weaves between the thin columns of light that fall crisscross on the floor.

I watch dust motes swirl in a lone ray of sunshine, wondering how this spot, which had been a comfortable nook to recede into and catch up on some sketching, has now become the loneliest place in the world.

I can see the figures of other groundsmen walking up and down the narrow path outside, so I find a spot near the back of the shed from where I can still see the door but won't be immediately visible.

My thoughts race through innumerable scenarios. *What will I say?*

"Hey, Sin, remember me? I'm the girl you knocked up at Elias Rutherford's party!"

Or, "Hey, Sin, guess who it is? The mother of your future child!"

I shake my head to dispel the increasingly hysterical visions of the very near future.

At that moment, a creaking sound halts my mental spiral. The door opens, and Sin pokes his head inside, looking around.

"Hello? Anyone there?"

I can't do this. A sense of certainty sends a chill down my arms. I can't face him. *I can't tell him.* Already my feet are rooted to their spot, and I can barely squeak a word to announce my presence.

"Hello?" Sin calls out again, gingerly stepping inside the shed. "Someone put a note in my locker, so here I am."

When he gets no response, Sin starts looking around a bit before running his fingers across the various tools in the shed near the entry door.

"Seriously, was that note supposed to be some kind of bait?" he says to the air. "Are you going to kill me? Please don't kill me! I'm too young and good-looking to die."

He chuckles, and I almost, *almost,* follow suit.

I can see his profile from this angle; the familiar lines of his face look relaxed now that he doesn't have to smile and entertain a crowd of admirers. He looks almost like a little boy, delighted and intrigued by the display of tools, watering cans, and other implements in the shed.

As he moves toward the back area of the room, I am forced to press myself further into the wall, willing myself to disappear.

Looking at his handsome face and full lips, my heart sinks.

What was I thinking? Why did I ever believe this would work? My inner cynic is back in full force, chastising me for assuming Sin would want any part in this charade.

He's the most popular guy in school; everybody wants a chunk of his time.

And me? I'm the most disliked person among our peers, the perpetual grump who has her nose buried in her iPad and headphones in her ears.

One could argue that opposites attract, but from personal experience, that saying only applies to magnets with opposing polarity. Period.

After a minute or two, Sin moves away from where I am trying to vanish inside a patch of darkness. As he walks to the far end of the shed opposite me, I inch toward the front door.

Of course, given my luck, I manage to step on a rake and then skitter away into a small bundle of spades. This results in a loud crash, and Sin's head snaps in my direction.

"Petra?" he exclaims with a dumbfounded look on his face. "Petra!" he repeats while I desperately try to smooth down my mauve-colored school skirt and blazer. When I look up, he's standing right before me, hands on his hips and his eyes twinkling with joy. "It is really you!" he continues. "Wait, did you leave that note in my locker?"

"Umm, note? What note?" I respond, trying to come up with an excuse for being inside the shed at the exact time mentioned on the note. "I usually come here to chill by myself. What brings you here?"

"Oh, come on, Petra!" Sin replies brightly, leaning against a wall with the casual air of a guy who *always* feels comfortable in his skin. "You expect me to believe that?"

"No, really," I shoot back with, I hope, my usual hauteur. "Ask the head gardener, Mr. Jones. He'll tell you."

"Fine, let's agree to disagree, okay?" Sin says before giving me a curious smile and pointedly falling silent, as if waiting for me to fill up the wordless gap between us.

But my mind is already roving ahead of me. I don't know how I'm going to hide the pregnancy. It's only a matter of time before people start noticing.

"So, designed any more posters recently?" Sin asks in a tentative voice, and I'm shocked that he remembers what we talked about.

"Yeah," I reply, seizing the lifeline. "I'm putting together a creative portfolio for my applications to SVA and Parsons."

"Damn, Petra! Do you ever take a break?" Sin's teasing voice shifts into one of interest as he continues, "Will I get to see them if I say 'please' like, a thousand times?"

Despite everything, despite the horrors of my current situation, I can't help but smile a little. "Maybe. Depends on if I like it enough to show it to others."

"Don't be too hard on yourself, okay? I'm sure you'll knock it out of the park." Sin's words sound sincere, like always.

We both laugh, the sound awkward but relieving. It's a fleeting moment of normalcy.

"So, are you looking forward to the fall dance?" Sin asks next, shifting his weight from one foot to the other.

"Not really," I reply, my tone casual. "School dances aren't my thing."

"Yeah, I get that," he says, nodding. "They can be pretty boring."

The conversation stalls again.

We look around, study the floor beneath our school-mandated tan-brown Oxfords, the dents and chips on the wall, the serrated edges of the gardeners' tools.

A few more agonizing minutes pass by before Sin clears his throat.

"Petra," he begins, his voice soft but firm, "do you want to talk about what happened? At the party, I mean."

CHAPTER TWELVE

PETRA

Present Day

My cheeks flush instantly. His words seem to summon up long-buried images and sounds and sensations that I would rather keep suppressed.

I shake my head, my hair falling forward to hide my face.

"No," I whisper in a barely audible voice. "I don't."

"That's okay," Sin replies in a gentle tone. "But I just want you to know . . . I don't regret it."

This makes me look him square in his face. He's looking at me with the same intensity that he had worn on the night of the party.

"You don't?" I ask, a quiver breaking up my voice.

Sin shakes his head, his expression sincere. "Really, I don't, Petra. And I don't think you should either."

I want to respond with something, *anything*, to tell him how conflicted I feel, but the words form a lump in my throat.

Instead, I can only look at him in wordless wonder, searching his face for any mark of insincerity. But all I see is honesty and a hint of concern.

I take a deep breath, gathering my thoughts.

What I say next may have been a matter of instinct or a secret part of my brain playing its tricks without consulting the rest of me.

But the moment the lines leave my mouth, I know there's no taking them back.

"Sin, let's just forget about it," I say with a nonchalance that amazes me. "Everyone has an embarrassing sex story, right? That's all it should be."

His face falls, and for a moment, he looks hurt. But then something shifts in his eyes, an almost . . . sinister glint I've never seen before. "Is that all it was to you?" he asks, tension hardening the edges of his voice.

I swallow, taken aback by the sudden shift in his demeanor. "Wha-what do you mean?"

"Do you have many of those stories, Petra?" he shoots next. "Other guys like me who amused and entertained you before being sent packing?"

The heat in his voice feels like a physical blow at this point.

"No, of course not!" I cry out. "That's not what I meant."

"Then *what did you mean*?" Sin's eyes narrow as he steps closer, and I realize that he has blocked my way to the only door out of the shed.

Can I blame my raw, emotional state for the way my senses now mark him as a source of very real danger?

Am I overthinking it when the gentle guy I had known and befriended is completely replaced by this grim-faced, tight-lipped interloper?

"Of course I have a past, Sin," I eventually manage to say, a slight tremble to my voice. "I bet you have one, too."

"With whom?" he asks without missing a beat, his voice a little too calm. "Names, Petra."

The intense timbre of his words makes me take a whole step back. It's an eerie scene, as if the person before me has just taken off a mask I didn't even notice he had been wearing this entire time.

My frightened face must have cautioned him. Or maybe I have been hallucinating. Because in just another instant, the old Sin is back with a wide, charming smile, and the broody, frowning Sin is nowhere to be seen.

"Sorry, sorry, that was weird," he says, stepping back and giving me a wide berth. "I'll do what you want, Petra. Anything to make you happy."

Again, I'm confused by this swift change from demanding to placating. It leaves me feeling off-balance, unsure of what to say next.

"I just . . . I don't want anyone to know, Sin," I finally manage to say. "I don't want people to gossip. They already dislike me enough, and I don't want to give them more reasons to resent me."

Sin's smile fades, replaced by a look of understanding.

"You won't," he assures me. "I won't say a word. Pinky promise."

He raises his pinky finger so solemnly that I smile again, despite the tension between us just seconds ago.

"Thank you," I reply shakily, not entirely sure what else to say.

Sin steps closer, closing the distance between us.

"We can keep this between us," he says, his voice gentle. "No one else needs to know."

Something about the velvety purr of his words frightens me a little. Is he flaunting his power over me by assuring me he wouldn't misuse it? The thought of being at the mercy of anyone, even a guy like Sin who's supposed to be easygoing and laid-back, makes me see red.

I *have* to convince him that I couldn't be more indifferent, more unaffected, by our fateful tryst that night.

"Besides, God forbid I become a target for your groupies. Those girls can be vicious."

"That is slander, Petra!" he cries out with an exaggerated look of rage. "I don't have any groupies."

"Right, Sin." I roll my eyes. "I see them every day. There's Brittany, that freshman girl whose dad owns an NFL team." I begin counting names off on my fingers. "There's her snooty friend Joanna who has like, a million followers on Instagram, and don't forget that sophomore who allegedly comes from royalty . . . what was her name again? Quirm? Quint?"

"Her name's Quinn," Sin replies between bouts of laughter, "and her mother is a cousin of the Dutch princess. And she is *not* a groupie. None of those girls are!"

"Sure, Sin, whatever you say." I cross my arms and lean back, even though my heartbeat is still pretty high and my fingers are quivering in tension. I will not let him see how unsteady I actually feel.

But what he says next ends up leaving me floored, nevertheless.

"You know, Petra." Sin looks thoughtful, as if carefully choosing his words. "What you see and what might actually be are two completely different things."

I stare at him, trying to read between those cryptic lines. Does he mean that all those girls vying for his attention don't really mean anything to him?

Screw it, I don't have the patience for these fuckboy mind games.

"You got more of those pearls of wisdom?" I straighten up and start gathering my things. "Anyways, just . . ." I can't really look him in the face, so I turn toward the main door as I say, "forget it happened, okay? Let's agree that it was a one-off thing and leave it at that."

What am I doing? What about this ba— this you-know-who? So great is my distress that I don't even care about referring to the new life inside me by a nondescript nickname.

Ha, a Freudian slip! Maybe that's what you really think about this situation?

Before my thoughts can unravel anymore, I say, "I should go." I *need* to get out of here, or I will lose my nerve completely. "I have . . . things to do."

Wow, Petra, that was so smart!

As I turn to leave, his hand shoots out, gently grabbing my wrist.

"Wait, Petra," he says softly, a great yearning in his voice.

"It's okay, Sin. We don't have to talk about it anymore," I reply with the most forced indifference ever displayed by a human. "Let's just forget about it, right?"

Almost at the same time, he says, "What if I don't *want* to forget about it?"

At first, I almost don't hear him. But then, his words seem to rebound in the silent, sun-specked air of the shed.

And I know I will never forget them.

CHAPTER THIRTEEN

PETRA

The Past
20 March 1896

The violence in the square continues. The crowd erupts into chaos. A loud cry rises above the din—constables. Within seconds, the onlookers scatter, panic spreading as people flee in every direction. The constables begin arresting bystanders at random, only intensifying the confusion.

I glance around, searching for my friends, but they're gone. Not a single veiled figure remains. I turn, looking for Mrs. Jenkins, but she, too, has vanished.

Someone slams into me, nearly knocking me over. Another jostles past. I stumble, but then strong arms catch me. A hand grabs mine, steady and firm, pulling me away from the crowd.

Without a word, I'm led into a shadowed alley, tucked into its dark corner, hidden from the chaos outside. Shouts and scuffles echo in the distance, but here it's quiet.

And then I see him.

Him.

Even in the dim light, the blood on his face is stark—dripping down to his mouth, staining the collar of his white shirt.

Instinctively, I reach into my reticle and pull out a handkerchief. He watches me, puzzled, but doesn't resist as I dab gently at the wound. Then he catches my hand and holds it to his cheek.

My arm softens, my gloved palm pressed against his face. He leans into it. And though our skin doesn't touch, the moment is unbearably intimate.

I try to pull away.

"Stop," he says. "Just stay like this . . . for a moment."

I swallow, stunned, as he continues to press his cheek to my hand, breathing slowly, deeply, as if he's memorizing the feel of me.

Then he moves, pressing his lips to my glove, then lower, to the bare skin at my wrist. A kiss.

A sharp inhale escapes me. A shiver ripples down my spine. Every nerve in my body sparks alive.

Frightened by this strange reaction, I yank my hand back.

"I never gave you permission to do that," I say, trying to sound stern despite my shaking voice.

He smiles, unfazed. "I'd be a fool not to take the chance when I had it."

"Why are you smiling? You're bleeding."

He shrugs. "That doesn't matter. You're here. Next to me. That's reason enough."

"Really? If I'm the reason you're smiling, then why haven't you written to me? It's been weeks—"

But I stop myself. *Don't let him see how much it mattered,* I whisper inwardly.

And yet, I can't help it. I need to know if I meant anything, or if it was all a game.

He smirks. "Did you miss me, my beautiful Petra?"

"What?"

"Did you miss me?"

"Was that your goal?" I shoot back. "To make me miss you? To toy with my emotions?"

His smirk fades. "Never. I would never do that."

"Then why didn't you write? Why start something you had no intention of finishing?"

"It wasn't a game," he insists. "Why would you think that?"

"Why wouldn't I? You've admitted to watching me for months. Then you bring me a forbidden book. Then, somehow, you appear at my window, night after night—and then you stop. What else *am* I supposed to think?"

He presses his lips together. "It seems . . . my approach may have been wrong."

"It was," I say flatly.

His expression tightens. "I didn't want to frighten you. I was . . . concerned."

He steps closer, and I stiffen.

"Did I scare you?" he asks gently.

I raise my chin. "You can't scare me."

It's mostly true. I *should* fear him. But I don't.

"But you can annoy me," I add.

He chuckles. "So I've annoyed you."

"Yes. With all your secrets. If you say you care about me, then why keep everything hidden? You're a professor of demonology—"

He smiles. "At least you're curious."

"Tell me who you are," I cut him off. "Or I'll never speak to you again."

"Is that so?" His brow arches. "You'll never speak to me again?"

His tone is amused, but his eyes are serious, dark and sharp. He steps closer. I back away until my spine meets the alley wall.

"What are you doing?" I whisper.

"I thought you weren't afraid of me."

"You're too close. Please—keep your distance."

"Why?"

"Because I said so. And because if you claim to care, then prove it. Step back."

"No," he replies simply. "I will not step away. And I will not let you shut me out."

My breath catches. "What?"

"Don't threaten me again, Petra. Don't threaten to withhold yourself from me. Not again."

Laughter bubbles up in my throat. "So you can withhold yourself from me, but I can't?"

He narrows his eyes. "That's not what I meant."

"Of course it is."

"I didn't do it on purpose," he says. "I was just—"

"Concerned. I know," I cut him off. "Then be concerned now. Tell me who you are."

His lips press into a line. "Yes, you're right. I'm a professor at St. Anselm Hall. But I'm not the pagan monster they make me out to be. My background is in theology. Demonology is simply a branch of it."

"It's blasphemous," I mutter.

"Why? It's knowledge."

"Knowledge made man fall."

He smirks. "Then we've already fallen. Why not learn something on the way down?"

I open my mouth to argue but close it again. He has a point.

"Why study it? And why *here* of all places? You knew this town wouldn't welcome you."

"You're here," he says simply.

"Be serious."

He chuckles. "My mentor invited me. He was my teacher at Harvard and recommended me for the position."

"Harvard?" I blink. "And yet you're here, in Radcliffe?"

"I told you. Because *you* are here."

I roll my eyes, though he can't see it. "You're toying with me. And I don't like it."

"How many times must I say it? I'm not toying with you, Petra. I'm trying to help you."

"Help? I never asked for your help."

"Haven't you?" He steps closer again, his fingers brushing the edge of my veil. "You crave knowledge, just as I do. I see it in you. You're bound by expectation, by what others think you must be. But you're not what they want. You're something else entirely."

"Appearances deceive," I whisper, remembering his letter.

"Exactly. And not just for them—for us, too. I see who you *really* are."

I swallow. "Then let me see you, too. Tell me who you *really* are."

A sad smile tugs at his mouth. "Perhaps I'm afraid. That if you knew, you *would* fear me."

"I told you I'm not scared."

"You think that now. But I've learned that people fear what they don't understand."

"Then let yourself be understood."

"Ah," he says with a soft laugh, "you clever, clever girl. Yes, I should let myself be known. But if you turned your back on me, as so many others have—"

"You mean the townspeople? Because they called you a demon? I don't believe that. You're not a demon."

He raises a wry eyebrow. "Am I not?"

"No. You're a person. Just like me."

"If only that were true," he muses.

"People say many things. That doesn't mean I believe them. I make my own opinions."

He watches me closely. "That's what I saw in you. Your mind is your own. No matter how much your church tries to suppress it."

I open my mouth to argue but stop. Because he's right. From the beginning, the church has done nothing but try to stifle me. My thoughts. My questions. My voice.

"Then tell me," I say. "Tell me who you really are."

"Is it a name you want, Petra? Or is it something more?"

"We can start with a name," I say quietly.

He tilts his head, seemingly considering the request.

"You know mine, and I never even told it to you," I add.

A thoughtful hum leaves his lips. "Perhaps I'll tell you. Quid pro quo—you give me something, and I'll give you my name."

I frown. "You already know everything about me. What more could I possibly give?"

"Oh, there's one thing," he says with a sly smile. "I want to see you."

My breath catches. "What?"

"Your veil. Take it off, and I'll give you my name."

"That . . . I can't," I whisper, shaking my head.

"Why not? Because your church says so?"

"If anyone found out," I murmur, "I'd be . . ."

"Excommunicated?" he finishes the sentence, almost as though he'd welcome the thought.

"No. Not just that. I'd be . . . hurt. Again."

His expression darkens. "I would never let that happen. Not again. You have my vow."

"You can't stop them," I protest. "You can't be everywhere. You can't protect me all hours of the day—"

"Shh." He places a finger gently over my lips. Even with the veil between us, the gesture silences me. "It's just you and me here. No church. No university. No family. No townspeople calling me a demon. Just you and me. And I want to see *you*. The real you. And then—I'll show you who I am."

I stare at him, frozen. Do I dare? Do I commit the ultimate transgression: remove my veil before a man I barely know? My fingers twitch with the temptation. But my mind reels with all the teachings pressed into me since childhood.

Then, gently, his hands rise to the edge of my veil. Slowly, he lifts it.

He pauses when the fabric rests just beneath my chin.

"Show me, Petra," he murmurs. "It's your choice. Show me who you are—and I will show you who I am."

For what feels like forever, I stand frozen, debating. *Should I show him my face?* The thought churns in my mind like a storm. The longer the silence stretches, the more I realize this is dangerous. He is a stranger. Why would I risk everything—my safety, my place in this world—for someone I barely know?

I press my hands to his chest and shove him away.

His eyes widen in surprise, his expression briefly raw. But then it vanishes, replaced by a tight, unreadable mask.

"Perhaps I was wrong about you," he murmurs.

"Perhaps you were," I reply. "I don't owe you anything. If you truly want me to know you, then you'll reveal yourself freely. No games. No expectations. Until then, I shouldn't even entertain your presence."

I turn my back and start walking toward the main square. I've already lingered too long. Mrs. Jenkins is likely searching for me. The others must be wondering where I've gone. Trouble may already be brewing.

Step after step, I move forward. He doesn't follow.

A tightness coils in my chest. Did I mean what I said? Maybe. I'm not sure. I just know I don't like being toyed with. I won't be controlled—not by another arrogant man I barely know. Our only connection is a handful of secret letters passed in the dark.

My heart races. I swallow hard. Am I already regretting this?

No. I can't regret protecting myself. This is about my safety. My survival.

Just as the light breaks through the mouth of the alley, a hand grabs me.

I gasp.

He pulls me back with terrifying swiftness. I never even heard him move.

In an instant, he pushes me against the wall, his body close—too close.

"What did I tell you, Petra?" he says, voice low and dangerous. His expression is no longer gentle. There's something unhinged in his eyes. "You do *not* threaten me with withholding yourself."

Before I can react, before I can scream or protest, his hand rips at my veil. In a single motion, it's torn from my head and falls to the ground.

I suck in a ragged breath. My lungs feel crushed.

He sees me. And yet—he doesn't look surprised. If anything, there's a sick satisfaction curling at the edge of his mouth.

He leans in, his breath warm against my skin. I turn my face away, eyes shut tight.

"Leave me alone," I whisper.

He says nothing, just leans closer. His lips brush the side of my face, traveling up to my ear. Then, teeth—light and sharp—graze my earlobe. A shiver races down my spine.

I should be afraid. I *am* afraid. And yet . . . there's something eerily familiar in his touch.

"Please," I whisper again, weaker this time. "Leave me alone."

"Sin," he breathes. "My name is Sin."

He steps back. He picks up my veil from the ground and gently places it back over my face, securing it.

"Sin," I repeat. The name tastes bitter. "That's . . . blasphemous."

"Yes," he replies, his smile crooked. "It is."

"Why would someone name you that?"

I ask the question before I can stop myself, forgetting—if only for a moment—what he's just done.

"Perhaps that's a lesson for another day."

"Another *quid pro quo,*" I scoff. "How is it an exchange when you take what you want anyway?"

His features darken. "That's the first lesson, Petra. You cannot say no to me."

Laughter bursts from my lips, sharp and bitter.

"Now I understand," I say. "This is why they call you Sin. Because you sin with every word, every deed."

Anger floods me, burning away any remnants of confusion or affection.

I step forward instead of shrinking back. I jab my finger into his chest.

"I see now why you kept your name from me. Because it's as ugly as you are."

I don't wait to see his reaction. I don't want to.

His name might be Sin, but he will not make *me* sin.

Not with him. Not without him.

I END UP finding my way back to Mrs. Jenkins and the girls. They accept my excuse that I got lost in the crowd—and as it turns out, I wasn't the only one. Some of the other girls return even after me. Thankfully, no one suspects a thing.

We all make our way home, and Mrs. Jenkins decides it's best not to mention anything about the commotion in the square to our parents. If you ask me, that's the best decision she could have made. I don't need to be barred from future outings over one chaotic afternoon.

At home, I go through the motions. We eat dinner together, and afterward, everyone retires to their rooms. Once I'm alone, I let out a relieved breath.

And then my mind begins to turn.

From the charming man who sent me letters and books under the veil of night, he became a monster in front of my eyes. I know his name now, but somehow, I feel further from understanding who he is than ever before.

I begin my nightly routine, performing my ablutions and preparing for bed. Out of instinct, I move to the window.

I don't even know what I expect to find.

But there it is. A letter. No book this time, just a single envelope.

For a brief, reckless moment, I consider throwing it out the window. But someone might find it. That would be worse.

I pick it up, intending to burn it. *I won't read it,* I tell myself. *There's nothing left to say.*

He's shown his true colors. He doesn't care about what I think, not really. He's just another man seeking control, another man pretending to care.

I walk to the fireplace, letter in hand, ready to toss it into the flames. But as I lift it, something catches my eye.

The corner is damp—sticky. Red.

"What . . ." I whisper.

Curiosity overtakes dread as I carefully peel the envelope open.

There is no letter inside.

Just a small, raw piece of flesh. Wet, bleeding. It slips from the envelope and hits the floor with a sickening thud.

I recoil, hand over my mouth. I try not to scream.

What is this? *Why* would he send something like this?

Gingerly, I grab the fire poker and nudge it. As I roll it over, I see ink. A message, scrawled in familiar handwriting:

Forgive me.

I gag.

Is it his flesh? Someone else's? The thought makes my stomach churn.

He's mad. That's the only answer. Madder than I'd dared to believe. Sin, he called himself, and now the name makes cruel sense. He doesn't just bear the name. He *is* the embodiment of it.

I grab the piece of flesh and drop it back into the envelope, ready to destroy it. But just as I hold it over the fire, something stops me.

My hand trembles.

Why can't I let go?

I take a step back, open the envelope again, and this time hold the flesh in my hand. It fits perfectly in my palm. The message is unmistakable. The writing is his.

Forgive me.

He asks for forgiveness—with this?

Madness.

And yet . . . perhaps some of that madness has sunk into me as well. Because instead of throwing it into the fire, I carefully wipe the blood from the flesh, preserving the words.

Then, slowly, almost reverently, I slide it into the pages of my Bible and hide it away.

He is mad.

But maybe . . .

Maybe I am, too.

CHAPTER FOURTEEN

PETRA

Present Day

The following days bring no respite from my condition, nor from the eerie dreams. They are all centered around the same character—the other me that lived in a time long since past.

Stranger still is the way the relationship between dream-Petra and dream man develops. He reminds me of Sin far too much at times, even bearing his name.

I have to wonder if this is not my brain telling me something: that he's no good for me, that he is as dangerous as I am morbid for conjuring up dreams of bloodied flesh and forbidden encounters.

I stop myself just as I'm about to go into a Freudian analysis.

I'm sure it's just my pregnancy brain acting out because he is the father of my child.

Ugh.

Waves of morning sickness make me spend a good hour slumped next to the toilet as I will myself to get ready for school.

Yet my mind manages to stray, recalling Sin's chimerical personality shifts from yesterday. How chilly his voice had sounded when he demanded the names of my previous (imaginary) sexual partners.

How he had instantly shifted to Prince Charming mode while saying, "Whatever makes you happy."

Washing my face and taking a warm shower help dispel some of these troubling recollections.

Although the physical toll is manageable right now, this . . . addition to my body seems to have warped my way of thinking.

I can't shake off a nagging suspicion that there's something I know but haven't understood clearly yet.

My SAH-monogrammed skirt and blazers still fit, *thank fuck,* but my face is an accurate depiction of the chaos swirling through my head.

Enough is enough, I decide, and carefully prepare myself for the day.

Thankfully, a touch of concealer and blush make me look human again. I round out the look with a light mauve line over my upper eyelids to match the school uniform.

Hair pulled back in a muted ponytail, a few dabs of my favorite Dior perfume that makes me smell of oud and warm spices, and I am ready.

Well, as ready as I can be under the circumstances.

The drive to school is spent oscillating between warm, positive memories of Sin and my anxiety about facing him again.

Today, I'm more preoccupied, so I pay less attention to any whispers or pointed glances directed at me. Or perhaps I ignore any sly gossipers because, in my absentmindedness, my feet have brought me to the registration office.

There still remains the matter of finalizing my schedule for this semester.

I wait for a few minutes before entering.

The loss of a coveted seat in the art history class has left me feeling even more raw, so I need to gather myself before facing the impassive woman at the desk. I don't want to start sobbing before her like a big pile of mush, so I steel myself before stepping inside.

"Hello," I say briefly, offering a small smile to Ms. Stoneface (her name is written on her desk, but I don't want to learn it).

"Yes, how can I help you today?" she responds with the sunny disposition of a prison warden.

"Just checking if there's any update on my schedule," I ask, trying my hardest to steady my voice and look unfazed while she clicks around on her computer with a perfunctory nod.

My air of forced nonchalance vanishes when her eyes widen.

"Looks like you're in luck," she says, and for once, the monotone of her voice is flecked with notes of surprise. "That art history class you wanted? A spot just opened up."

"Really?" is all I can gasp out at first.

When she keeps looking at me without any response, I manage to stammer something more. "Ho-how did that happen?"

She shrugs. "What always happens: Some other kid dropped out. Now I have to reenter their files."

Even if I actually liked her, I would have thanked the gods in heaven for putting more work on her plate if it meant I got a seat in Art History!

No other words occur to me on the spot, so I mumble a weak, "Thank you," before completing my forms, handing them over, and exiting the office with my updated schedule.

For the first time in months, my heart sings with joy as I almost glide through the buzzing corridors of St. Anselm Hall.

The art history classes are typically scheduled for the afternoon, and I can barely pay attention in English, Economics, and Biology before the lunch bell rings.

I think of stealing away to the gardener's shed and catching up on my portfolio. But the memory of my encounter with Sin yesterday is still too fresh; that place could not possibly help me relax today.

Besides, the cafeteria is usually too packed for me to be a discernible target for any lowlife trolls.

... So that last assumption was incorrect, I think when I catch sight of Daphne and François just as I turn around after collecting my lunch tray.

"Cute eyeliner, Petra!" Daphne calls out while I can muster nothing more than a sigh. "Let me guess, you had 'wannabe Euphoria extra' on your Pinterest vision board when you put *that* look together?"

"Ugh, Daphne, just get a life," I respond, unwilling to even dignify such a cheap jab with anything more eloquent.

"You almost lost yours in that pool, didn't you?" François chimes in next, and I stop in my tracks. "You know you literally don't have to kill yourself for Sin's attention."

"What did you say?" My voice could have chilled hot tea in a second.

"Not that we are sorry to see you unhurt," Daphne says hurriedly. "We were really shocked when that happened, you know."

"So sorry," François repeats with a smirk.

"Daphne, I swear to God I couldn't care less about your pedestrian, everyday taunts," I begin, not caring a rat's ass about who can hear me. "But if I find out that it was *you lot* who pushed me into that pool, I will destroy you. I will make you terribly, *horribly* sorry you ever crossed my path."

Thankfully, my voice doesn't flinch as the heat of the sun seems to power the rage coursing through my veins.

"Ladies, ladies! Relax!" François exclaims in an annoying, piping tone, and both of us take a step back. "We didn't push you into the pool, Petra. We would never do that."

"Yeah, right!" I snap back at him, though my eyes never leave Daphne's face. *C'mon, you little moron, slip up and admit it was you! Give me something to pummel with my bare hands!*

"Really, Petra," Daphne says with an emphatic nod. "It wasn't us."

"Then who was it?"

Just then, the bell rings, and the sounds of people putting away their plates and gathering up their things fill up the tense space between us three.

"I will find out one day, Daphne." I almost hiss out the words at her. "And you will regret that you didn't confess sooner. You will regret *everything* you've ever done."

Daphne and François look too stunned at the relentless fury coloring my face and stiffening my limbs. But they don't know how that unceremonious dive into the pool had triggered an avalanche of life-changing moments, how I'm still dealing with the fallout from that night.

Without waiting for more mediocre jabs from the duo, I walk out of the lunchroom, feeling lighter. Confronting those two makes me feel stronger, more in charge, and less helpless. What compounds my joy further is realizing that it's time for my first art history class.

Art History with Ms. Matthews is one of the most sought-after classes at St. Anselm Hall. Having gotten her MA and PhD from Yale and Stanford, respectively, she is an outright genius when it comes to the subject.

Her office is decked out with photos of her chatting and chumming it up with famous artists like Louise Bourgeois and Olafur Eliasson. She's a rockstar, and I want to be like her when I grow up.

By now, I have reached her classroom, so I stop to smooth my skirt and adjust my hair before entering. Despite my efforts to contain myself, a wide smile settles on my lips when I step in.

And just like that, the grin slips right off my face when I see that Sin is here.

He's lounging against a desk, his blazer draped rather precariously over his chair, and his sleeves rolled up to reveal his muscular forearms.

As usual, a cluster of girls and guys surrounds him. Laughter punctuates their conversation, and his light blue eyes glimmer when he tells—or retells, by the look of it—some inside joke I'm not part of.

He's a magnet, drawing everyone in.

But did he have to take this class, too? I would never have pegged him as someone interested in the evolution of art through the ages, but what do I know?

Just as I am stewing in a complicated mix of bitterness and excitement, he catches my eye and nods ever so slightly.

As if he were hitting pause on the pretense of "popular guy" to be "Petra's friend."

Once again, I'm amazed at the ease with which he steps in and out of the many roles people expect him to fill.

I nod back clumsily as my heart pounds harder. I don't want to think about the shed, about his smile, or what I'm keeping from him. I just want to get through this class.

Why couldn't I have just this one thing for myself?

Further hand-wringing and lamenting will get me nowhere, so I start looking for a vacant seat, moving toward the front of the classroom almost instinctively.

Still, I can feel the weight of his gaze pinned to my body—without even looking directly at him. Of course, I don't want to keep looking at him, so I don't turn around to confirm my suspicions.

In the end, I slide into an empty seat somewhere in the middle row, dropping my bag onto the floor beside my chair. My hands are shaky as I pull out my iPad to take notes.

I don't dare steal a glance back at him. All I can do is focus on the clock on the wall, willing Ms. Matthews to arrive and completely claim my attention. For the moment, I am content to let the murmur of conversations around me seep into my awareness.

"Anyone see the new art installation in the lobby?" a girl near the window is saying to her small group. "I can't believe the school actually invested in something so modern."

It's an original Damien Hirst, I want to add but don't.

"I know, right?" one of the guys in her group replies. "It's like, finally, they're catching up with the times."

Behind me, a deep-voiced guy is grumbling over something. "Man, I just hope this class isn't a total snoozefest. I heard the project is like, half our grade."

"Yeah, but Ms. Matthews is supposed to be really cool," another guy chimes in. "She lets you work on whatever inspires you. I'm thinking of doing something on street art."

It's a comforting feeling, this passive way of listening to the opinions and perspectives of others, and I let their words float around me, a background noise that keeps my mind tethered to reality.

I fidget with my stylus almost instinctively, the motion calming my nerves a bit.

Just then, another conversation catches my ear. "You know that party at Elias's place?" says a girl. "I heard someone fell into the pool."

My blood runs cold.

"Yeah, Sin Arnoult was there," her friend responds in a gloating tone. "He's always where the action is."

I stiffen and try to return my full attention to my screen, but more gossip about that fateful night starts pouring into my ears. Almost immediately, a wave of nausea hits me as I almost pass out from the light buzz at my temples.

Whether it's a reaction to the gossip or the physical remnant from that night that still inhabits my body, I don't care. I have to do something fast.

I'm not *going to hurl in my first-ever art history class!*

With shaky movements, I get up and start moving to the front of the classroom exactly when the door opens and Ms. Matthews walks in.

Dressed in a monochrome red-colored suit and sporting the most stylish little pixie cut, she draws everyone's eyes almost immediately.

"Afternoon, everyone," she says in a brisk, commanding tone. Feeling thankful for her unwitting intervention, I reach my seat and start to pull out my chair.

I hear a snicker.

"Teacher's pet already, huh?" a guy near the back, someone from the football team, says loudly enough for everyone to hear. I am surprised that any of those granite-headed idiots would be interested in Ms. Matthews's class, but before I can say as much, Sin's voice fills the silent air.

"Cut it out, Eric." There it is again, that sudden edge to his voice. "Not everyone needs to hide in the back to coast through class."

Even Ms. Matthews remains silent, watching this entire exchange with an amused look on her face. I can feel all eyes shifting between me and Sin.

At last, even I am forced to glance at him.

He's leaning back in his chair, arms crossed casually and body relaxed as usual, but his eyes glitter with a total lack of mercy.

Eric mutters something under his breath, but he doesn't push back. I sit back in my chair and take deep breaths to calm my heart, stomach, and brain.

Having gained back some of my composure, I finally look at Sin and give him a tentative smile, small and grateful.

He returns it with one of his own, warm and completely disarming.

For a moment, the brooding intensity that has astonished me of late is replaced by something softer, more protective.

Someone clears their throat loudly.

When I see that it's Ms. Matthews, my face turns almost as red as her attire.

"Shall we begin?"

The class settles down as the lesson begins. Ms. Matthews starts with a slide of Renaissance paintings. Soon, I'm completely lost to the world as the rich colors, luxurious fabrics, and intricate details absorb me.

Throughout the first fifteen minutes, I can't help sketching quick impressions on my iPad.

But every so often, I catch movement out of the corner of my eye. It's Sin.

He's not just glancing; he's staring. I can feel the hairs on the back of my neck stand on end, half out of anticipation and half out of curiosity, if I'm being honest.

I am not sure what he sees in me, what he's trying to find by looking at me so frequently.

Just as I steal a sideways glance at him, our gazes brush against each other, and I turn around so suddenly that Ms. Matthews stops mid-speech and peers around.

I try grounding myself in the lesson again.

"Of course, when we're talking about the use of perspective in painting, we have to mention da Vinci and his *Last Supper*," Ms. Matthews carries on. "Can anyone tell me why?"

A veil of silence drops over the classroom. But I raise my hand without even thinking.

"Yes, Miss . . . ?"

Shit, shit, shit, why did I do that? What if I fuck this up?

Ms. Matthews is still waiting for me, one elegant eyebrow arched in question, so I say, "Valentine, err-Petra Valentine. Umm," I fumble around with my iPad before resuming in a firmer voice. "It's the vanishing point. He-he positions Jesus in such a way that the viewer experiences an illusion of depth. Our eyes are sort of guided toward the center. And that was quite unique for his time . . ."

Here, my voice trails away as everybody looks back at Ms. Matthews, waiting to see her reaction. To my greatest relief, she beams at me. "Well put, Ms. Valentine, very well put."

A warm glow of pride flares in my chest. For the first time in a while, I feel competent, like I truly belong here. I catch a glimpse of Sin out of the corner of my eye again, but this time, he offers me a subtle nod of approval.

It's not as unnerving as earlier, but I still can't shake the feeling that his attention is sharper, more directed than anyone else's.

"And this is why it's so important to understand the fundamentals of art history," Ms. Matthews continues, her eyes twinkling. "If you don't understand the rules, you won't be able to break them."

A murmur of agreement ripples through the class, and I relax back into my seat. The lesson transitions into a hands-on analysis, and everyone is tasked with jotting down their interpretation of the different principles of perspective in painting.

As I get lost in my drawing, the class around me feels almost distant. Yet, the times I do glance up, Sin's eyes find mine too easily.

With half an hour to spare before the final bell, Ms. Matthews packs away the projector and turns on the lights.

"All right, everyone, before you go," she calls out over the sudden hum of students stretching their limbs and starting to gather their things. "I'd like to discuss our mid-term project. If you know anything about me, it's that I value continuous testing. You've gotta be *on. Your. Toes.*" She underscores the last three words with three snaps of her fingers. "So, our mid-term assignment will be big. It will be fifty percent of your grade, to be exact. You must choose a topic of interest and research its history and how its historical context has shaped its final form."

Urgent murmurs ripple through the room. The studious ones look smug, while the jocks who had joined thinking that this was going to be an easy class start looking anxious.

Even I feel a pang of apprehension.

Fifty percent of our grade means this project could make or break my grade in this class.

Cool, cool, cool, no pressure at all.

"Now, I've taken the liberty of pairing you up with partners," Ms. Matthews continues, glancing down at a sheet of paper. "And before you come at me, know that I don't change my mind once I've made it up. Cheers!"

My heart sinks a bit. The last thing I need is to be tied up to someone else's work habits and preferences, especially given my current mix of nerves and . . . secrets.

"Let's see . . . Claire and Eric," Ms. Matthews starts reading off the list. I hear the girl called Claire groan a little next to me. Thank God Ms. Matthews didn't partner me with that airhead.

I have celebrated too soon because she reads out, "Petra and Sinclair," next.

My head snaps up so quickly I almost crick my neck.

I must have misheard her.

This can't be happening.

But Sin is already looking at me, a smile playing on his lips, and Ms. Matthews has finished reading from the list.

You've *got* to be kidding me.

"Right then, class dismissed," says Ms. Matthews. "We will be discussing the finer details about the project in the next class. In the meantime, get to know your partners, and feel free to come to me with any questions."

The classroom empties quickly after that. I take my time zipping up my bag so I can compose myself before the inevitable encounter with Sin.

"*Get to know your partners,*" Ms. Matthews had said, and that's what we have to do.

"Hey, Petra," Sin's voice jolts me out of my buzzing thoughts.

I turn to look at him, trying to appear more collected than I felt. "Hey, Sin. Did you want to talk about the project—"

"Meet me after class," he cuts me off rather abruptly, and the way he quotes my own words from the note shocks me into silence. "In the gardener's shed."

As he walks away, leaving me alone in the classroom, the words loop around my head. A strange day made stranger still.

CHAPTER FIFTEEN

PETRA

Present Day

If you ask most people at St. Anselm Hall, "Where can I find Petra Valentine?" they'll reply, "Who?"

And when you describe me to them, the handful who might finally recognize me would probably say something along the lines of "Oh, that weird goth chick? Check the library, I guess."

All this is to say that when I'm not sitting through endless lectures on logistics and supply chain management ("practical" classes mandated by my parents) or stealing away to meet popular playboys in the gardener's shed, I can be found browsing the shelves of the library.

Like any posh school worth its (old) money, St. Anselm Hall has an exquisitely laid out colosseum of books.

Standing tall to the north of campus, it's a multi-columned structure built along Art Deco lines. Inside, you will find shelves of leatherbound first editions as well as the newest texts on almost all subjects. Antique sconce lighting is interspersed with LED-lined wall paneling to create the optimum visibility and reading conditions.

The scent of old books and polished mahogany fills the air—a welcome respite from the stuffy classroom I have just left behind. Walking down the numbered rows, I glide my fingers along the spines of the books and feel rooted, sure of my steps.

But even in this safe space, troubling thoughts trail me. While walking to the far corner of the second floor where books on art and art history are stored, my thoughts rise and ebb like churning tides.

I think about my first class with Ms. Matthews and how much more eventful my life has become since then, as if that were even possible given my you-know-what condition.

Add to that Sin's see-sawing disposition: sunny and soft one instant and broody and intense the next, his smiles disarming and also somewhat . . . darker. And now I have to team up with him on a project that makes up half my grade in my favorite class.

It's all so overwhelming that I find a secluded table by an arched window overlooking the courtyard and slide into the upholstered chair beside it, trying to sink into the cushiony seat and hide away, just for a little while.

The afternoon light filtering through the stained glass casts patches of colors onto the table. Watching them slide across the wooden grain is a strangely soporific pastime. I let my head empty out, and pretty soon, my eyes are fluttering against the heavy press of sleep.

The library is mostly empty, and the silence is occasionally punctuated by the soft rustling of pages turning, distant footsteps, and muffled conversations.

Sounds like these can sometimes make St. Anselm Hall feel like an ancient cathedral: a space where time slows, congeals, grows sticky with daytime reveries and half-baked recollections . . .

"Do you need help?" A soft voice pulls me out of encroaching sleep. It's Mr. Langdon, the turtle-necked librarian. His kind eyes peer at me over round, thin-rimmed spectacles.

"Oh, Mr. Langdon, thank you," I say hastily while simultaneously checking if I had started drooling over my book during my almost-nap. "I was just working on a project." And when he keeps smiling at me in that mild, well-meaning way, I continue, "For Ms. Matthews's class."

"Ah! You are one of the lucky few," he exclaims politely. "Might want to check out rows 700 through 708; we recently received a sizable consignment from one of the most well-curated private collections in America, maybe even the world . . ." He realizes that my eyes have that glazed look people get whenever he starts drifting onto tangents. "Anyways, check out the books in 704. Some rare books there. Very rare indeed," he finishes with a nod.

"That would be wonderful, thank you," I say in a feeble voice as he walks away, still nodding absentmindedly.

The numbers he has given me lead me to the back of the art section.

Quite a few of the books here appear to be single-edition tomes on obscure topics: occult geometry, Bergsonian layouts that mixed temporal and spatial planes in dizzying diagrams, an actual numbered edition of the *Codex Seraphinianus* by Luigi Serafini.

That last book actually arrests my attention, Serafini being one of my favorite surrealist artists from the late '70s.

Finally, I manage to lose myself in the animal-plant phantasms that fill the *Codex,* its mystical anti-language drawing my imagination to the shifting boundaries between perception and illusion and the memory of both—

"Fuck!" I yell out suddenly, having stubbed my toe against the iron claws of a large pot shaped like a gnome. "What the fuck?" I shout again as searing pain blooms through my foot, and I stumble back a couple of steps.

Before I can reel out more expletives, strong hands have grasped my arms and steadied me.

Thinking it's the nice librarian, I say, "Thanks, Mr. Langdon. Would you mind terribly if I set that thing on fire?"

But when I turn around, it's not Mr. Langdon. Instead, I'm looking into the amused face of a guy my age. A medium-built dark-haired guy with eyes the color of stormy clouds, a brilliant satiny gray that immediately gets etched in my memory.

"Are you okay?" the boy's asking me in warm, honeyed tones.

My foot is still throbbing, but it's a dull ache now, and I shake my leg instinctively, trying to encourage more blood flow to that poor appendage.

"You walked right into it before I could stop you," the boy continues with a friendly chuckle.

"Yup!" I say with a brittle chirpiness I don't feel. "Walking into things is my specialty!"

"And so is Italian surrealism?" he asks, motioning to the book in my hand. "I wanted to have a look at the *Codex* as well," he continues, "but you beat me to it."

His face has the open, honest expression I always look for in people and never find. A well-used but obviously expensive leather bag is slung over his shoulder, and pinned to it is a rainbow-colored badge that says "ALLY."

His sleeves are rolled up, as are the hems of his pants, and his Oxfords are stylishly scuffed.

"I'm Harry, by the way."

"Petra," I reply, offering a small smile as I place the *Codex* back on the shelf and half-limp, half-stagger to a nearby chair.

As I flex my toes and rub my foot, Harry inspects me from a polite distance, as if waiting to see if I need any assistance.

"Thanks . . . erm, for helping me back there," I continue in an awkward tone.

"Yeah, about that . . . I was actually saving myself from being stepped on by a pretty girl with her nose buried in a book," Harry says with a poker face. "You won't believe how often that happens to me these days," he continues in a shocked tone, "what with all these *educated* women everywhere."

And I can't help it anymore, so I finally do laugh at his artless but innocent jokes.

"Sorry about that, Harry. It's just . . . I haven't been able to focus on work for a while, so I got carried away when I found the *Codex* . . ."

"That's cool!" Harry replies with a twinkle in his eyes. "What are you working on?"

"Art History project," I reply in an easy tone. "I'm thinking of exploring the liminal perspective in contemporary design for my mid-term assignment."

"Cool, cool, liminal perspective and whatnot, we all know what that is," Harry replies with a self-effacing smile that again puts me at ease.

"Oh, you'll pick it up soon enough. The concepts are really interesting."

The conversation has been such an easeful one that I have completely forgotten about the pain in my toe.

"What brings you to St. Anselm Hall, Harry? Yale aspirant?" I ask with genuine interest.

Harry laughs softly and says, "We have relatives in town. I've heard only great things about St. Anselm Hall, though."

He looks around, taking in the long rows of tables peppered with slanted beams of dusk light streaming through the windows, the neat steps of Mr. Langdon doing his last rounds before the library closes for the day, the huddled groups of teenagers working away on their sleek iPads, and then looks back at me, a subtle unrest in his eyes.

"Really?" I quirk my brow.

"It's cool . . . in a way." He shrugs.

I give him an empathetic nod before replying carefully, "Yeah, it has its moments. It can be a pretty lonely place for a newcomer, right?"

"Yes!" Harry cries out, as if thrilled to be understood.

Sigh, welcome to the club, I think glumly before saying out loud, "Well, if you need help finding your way around, let me know. I need to make up for almost stepping on you."

My openness is surprising but not completely unexpected. Something about Harry feels . . . safe.

"Thanks, Petra. I might take you up on that," he says, his smile widening. "Any chance I could bribe you for a quick tour now? Maybe show me where the best study spots are?"

Too late for that, I think as I realize that it's almost five. "I'd love to, but I actually have to be somewhere right now. Maybe another time?"

"Sure thing," Harry says in the same easy and understanding tone. "But hey, thanks for the offer. And . . . I'll see you around?"

"Definitely," I respond, heading toward the exit. "Good luck, Harry."

"Thanks, Petra. You, too."

The conversation felt nice. Refreshing. But there's no time to dwell on that now.

The shadows are lengthening, and the air is growing cooler. And I must make my way to the gardener's shed. Sin is waiting, and I need to face what's coming.

Dusk is the loveliest time at St. Anselm Hall. The elm groves wear haloes of remnant daylight while around them, evening spreads its inky black lace. I reach the gardener's shed just as the last hints of sunshine disappear under this twilight veil.

The large oak looming over the shed casts shadows over the sprawling structure, adding to the overall eeriness that I find so endearing and romantic. *Usually.*

Right now, I am much too bundled with nerves to appreciate the stunning interplay of light and dark. I'm further flustered when I see Sin leaning against the entrance, his taut yet muscular figure outlined against the cobwebbed beams supporting his weight.

Something feels different about him today—there's a tension in the set of his shoulders, a tightness in his jaw.

He watches me approach, and instantly I am struck by the difference between his and Harry's body language. "Petra," he says offhandedly, pushing himself off the doorframe. "Thanks for coming."

I nod sedately, trying to read his expression. "Of course. We-we need to get started on the project."

Sin puts on a smile that doesn't quite reach his eyes. "Sure, we can do that. Or—and hear me out before you say 'no'—how about we ditch the shed tonight? Let's go out."

"Out? Where?" I ask without thinking.

"Dinner, silly!" he replies with a dazzling smile, like it's the most natural thing in the world. "Why don't we discuss the project over some good food? No distractions, no interruptions."

I hesitate, feeling that familiar wariness creep in. "Sin, we have a lot of work. I'm not sure if—"

"Come on, Petra," he cuts in smoothly, stepping closer in the same fluid movement. His voice softens. Now it's beguiling, coaxing, caramel-sweet as he says, "We'll have plenty of time to go over everything. Besides, you could use a break."

He is right, you know, my inner voice notes. *We need a break. And you need to chill.*

"What the hell, let's go," I reply with a shrug.

How bad can it be?

CHAPTER SIXTEEN

PETRA

Present Day

Crickets and cicadas sing in the tall grass as we walk to his car, a black Porsche Panamera.

He opens the passenger door for me, a gentlemanly gesture completely in line with his persona of the knight in football uniform, and I slide into the plush leather seat.

As we drive away from the school grounds, I keep glancing at Sin, searching for any signs of tension on his face. But he looks utterly relaxed, even whistling a few bars as he lightly steers the car down the paved roads lined with looming oaks and pines.

Finally, Sin clears his throat.

"So, did you have any plans for dinner?"

I shrug, looking out the window. "Not really. What do you have in mind?"

"You'll see," he responds with a small, mysterious smile.

Soon, we pull up to a smartly designed restaurant just a few blocks from St. Anselm Hall.

It's a popular spot called L'Avion and was supposedly built by a retired World War II pilot who had dropped tons of bombs on the Nazis, at least according to local legends.

The well-stocked bar and spacious seating, not to mention the bartender's lazy disregard for the fact that many of the patrons are below the drinking age, make sure that the place is always bustling.

Sin parks, and we step into the vibrant space.

Instantly, I can smell freshly baked bread and garlic frying in butter. My stomach growls, and I realize how scattered my eating habits have become.

While I try to banish intrusive thoughts about how I should be extra careful about my diet given my . . . condition, I look admiringly at the antebellum décor, an eclectic mix of rustic wooden beams and modern art pieces, cozy yet chic.

The hostess greets us, and Sin smoothly arranges a table. We're led to a semi-private corner with a perfect view of the kitchen, where chefs are moving in perfect symphony, sautéing, stirring, and stewing. Sounds of clinking cutlery, soft laughter, and murmured conversations float around me, and I feel much less discomforted than I do at school.

Meanwhile, Sin is studying the menu. "How about some lasagna? Or maybe some shellfish risotto?" he asks warmly. "Wait, you're not allergic, are you?"

"No, I'm not," I reply with a smile. "I actually love shellfish. The risotto sounds great."

As we chat so casually, so effortlessly, I notice how he fits so well into this world. The tension between us seems to have dissipated. I might even say that we are chilling at the moment.

We order some risotto and chicken cacciatore. Over a truly delicious amuse-bouche of Parmesan arancini balls, we lapse into the friendly banter that had instantly sprung up between us the first time we met.

"Never pegged you for someone who likes fish," Sin says jokingly.

"Why? That's some next-level profiling, Arnoult!" I shoot back.

"Not profiling! Just, you seem like an expensive-cuts-of-wagyu-beef kinda girl, you know?"

"That is *so* random, Sin!" I roll my eyes and take a long sip of my berry lemonade. And then he smiles at me with the same kind of intensity as he had shown the night we . . . the night I—

"Actually, I did some research today," I say abruptly, pulling out my notebook and moving my thoughts away from dangerous territory. "I think we can consider working on artists like M. C. Escher and Serafini to-to show how art can blur . . ." I try to fashion a topic from the roiling cauldron of my thoughts, but Sin is staring at me in that silent, broody way that makes my heart beat faster and my mouth stumble over my words.

Nevertheless, I persist, determined to remain unfazed by his obvious attempt (and success) at smoldering.

"How art can-can warp the ways in which we physically interact with the world—"

"Petra," Sin says at this point, gently, reassuringly, as if trying to calm me.

But why? I am calm already, the hysterical voice in my head cuts in.

"I'm really glad you agreed to this. The dinner, I mean." He looks so earnest that I am momentarily stunned.

"That's okay, I-I'm enjoying myself."

"I'm glad to hear that, Petra." Sin moves his hand closer to mine over the table, and our fingers almost brush.

It's an electrifying feeling, as if my skin is suddenly hypersensitive to the lightest of touches.

"I was really sad about how we left things off at the shed."

"Oh, that whole thing?" I sputter in mock surprise. "Water under the bridge, Sin. Don't worry about it."

"But I want to worry about it. In fact, I can't stop thinking about it, about what you said." Sin's voice drops lower as his palm strokes the back of mine. His hand feels warm and soft and all things nice, and his features are suffused with the glow of a man set on courting the lady before him.

"That's-that's not what we came here to discuss, Sin," I begin in a cautioning tone, though a part of me wants to take him up on the offer—indulge in some sweet nothings in this cozy, warm restaurant where we can be away from prying eyes.

Yet I'm acutely aware of the secret growing inside me, and I need to keep myself grounded.

"We really need to outline our approach for the project," I insist. "We haven't even decided on the topic."

Sin waves a hand dismissively, still smiling. "We'll get to it. With your brains and my looks, and also with your looks," he adds teasingly, and I can't help but laugh, "this project is gonna be a breeze. But let's not stress about it tonight. I want you to enjoy yourself."

There's a sincerity in his voice that's hard to ignore, but my mind is restless.

"But this is important, Sin. Fifty percent of our grade is on the line."

"And we'll ace it," he says confidently. "But right now, let's talk about us, Petra. If there can even be an 'us' . . ." Alluring words that I long to sink into, but a sense of discomfort has settled over me now.

I'm not used to this kind of attention, especially from someone like Sin.

But just as I'm about to respond, the waiter arrives with the main course.

The buttery risotto looks divine—but I know something's wrong the instant I smell the shellfish.

My stomach turns, and a wave of nausea washes over me, chilling my limbs and making me dizzy. Panic sets in as I realize I might be sick.

"Excuse me," I mutter and get up, nearly knocking over my chair as I rush toward the restroom.

I completely ignore Sin when he says, "Petra, are you okay? What's wrong?"

As the bile gushes to my throat, his words are drowned out and distorted, eventually fading away when I step into the women's room.

Luckily, I make it to the toilet just in time. The walls around me spin briefly, but I take deep breaths and splash cold water on my face to suppress whatever vile effluvium my hormone-racked body wants to keep spewing out.

Like that possessed girl from *The Exorcist.*

Humor doesn't really help my situation as the room keeps shifting around me.

I just huddle down and bury my head in my knees like I do during the intermittent episodes of morning sickness that have marked my days as of late.

Minutes trickle by, or maybe millennia, before my head and stomach seem to settle down. I fix my hair and face again before plastering on a fake smile and stepping out of the washroom.

But when I return to our table, the sight unfolding before me halts me in my tracks.

Sin is surrounded by a group of his school friends, and loud bouts of laughter and raucous conversation have engulfed the table. And just like that, I feel alienated again, standing on the outside and looking in at the scene of casual camaraderie before me.

"Petra!" Sin calls out the minute he sees me. "What happened? Are you all right?" He strides over to where I am standing, and I can feel the group's attention shifting to me.

"I'm fine," I manage to say with a forced smile. "Just stress and bad sleep catching up to me, I think."

Sin continues to look worried as he guides me to our table, which is now occupied by boys and girls who are surveying me with the same interest as a pack of lions would show on sighting a lone deer.

One of the girls, her hair perfectly styled and her makeup flawless, eyes me curiously.

"Hi, Petra," she says in the same tone in which one might say, "Die, Petra."

"I didn't know you were friends with Sin," she continues, though her tone suggests she's more surprised than impressed.

"We're partners for the Art History project," I clarify.

But Sin adds, "She's the brains of the operation, of course. She knows everything about art." His voice is proud and encouraging, and I smile weakly, grateful for his attempt to include me.

His friends glance at me for a moment more before resuming their conversation. I sit quietly on the side, trying and miserably failing to not feel too excluded.

After a while, Sin turns to me, his expression softening.

"You okay?" he repeats his earlier question in a more covert tone that is only intended for my ears.

"Yeah," I lie, forcing another smile. "Just . . . a little overwhelmed."

"We can leave anytime. Just say the word."

I glance at the cheerful faces around us and then back at Sin. Maybe I was too quick to judge him. Maybe, just maybe, he actually did want to wine and dine and romance me before his stupid friend group showed up.

"We'll see how it goes," I say, trying to keep my tone light. I don't want to be a Yoko to his band. "But about the project—"

"You're relentless, aren't you?" Sin laughs and squeezes my hand. *Be still, my heart. And belly!* "Okay, how about this? We finish dinner, say goodbye to these guys, and then go somewhere quieter to talk about our plans. Deal?"

"Deal," I reply with a tentative smile. Maybe tonight can be salvaged after all.

But soon I'm feeling restless and ignored again, as Sin gets busy with some long-standing argument with his friends. When they start dropping inside jokes and shared anecdotes, I feel even more disengaged and bored.

But I don't want to appear bitter and lonely, so I smile placidly and pretend to show interest in the most pedestrian stories.

"So, remember that time we snuck out to the roof of the gym during Mr. Wallace's class?" Sin is saying.

"Oh yeah, dude. Fuck, that was sick!" chimes in a guy named Chris. "And then, and then you got stuck." He is clutching his stomach and wheezing, like he's about to utter the funniest lines in the history of situational comedy. "Coz you were trying to be all 'Spider-Man.' Dude, Mr. Wallace was *so* mad!"

Another round of laughter follows, and I force a smile, trying to appear interested as well. It's pointless, though, and I might as well not be here at all.

That's fine, I'm a grown girl, and I can suffer through this tedium for a while longer if it means we get to discuss the assignment later and make some real progress.

As Sin and his friends chatter away about their thrilling lives, my thoughts drift off to less juvenile musings.

I know that I just want to get the project done without getting sucked into Sin's complicated personal life, but at some point, I have to deal with my own big news. I think about the Planned Parenthood pamphlet I have hidden in my cavernous closet that only I am allowed to organize.

Of course, my parents can't know, and neither can Amelia, for reasons I'm not sure of yet. I need to figure this out alone, but the more time I spend with Sin, the harder it is to ignore.

"So Petra," says another snobbish-looking girl in the group. "How's it feel to suddenly be hanging with the 'cool' crowd?"

I stiffen, unsure how to respond.

But before I can shoot any clever quips at the snooty bitch who's smirking at me—her name's either Drea or Daisy or something silly like that—Chris snickers.

"Yeah, it must be a change from burying your head in books all the time," he says, like he's thrown the dankest shade of all time.

Okay, that's it. Time to teach these brats some lessons they won't forget in a hurry.

Just as I open my mouth to rain hellfire and brimstone on these morons, Sin says, "Knock it off, guys. Petra's smarter than all of us combined. She doesn't even *need* to be in your group."

All the snickering voices fall silent at the same time, and the stiff-lipped hoe—Deidre? Dodo? Duckface?—stares at Sin in shock.

But the relief is short-lived as her friend, the flawlessly made-up piranha from before, leans forward. "By the way, saw you getting all cozy with Harry in the library earlier. New boyfriend?"

Heat floods my cheeks. "It wasn't like that," I say quickly, but it's already too late. Sin tenses beside me; I can *feel* it.

"Harry?" he repeats the name with instant scorn, eyes narrowing. "What were you doing with Harry?"

"We were just talking, Sin," I reply tersely, irritated beyond measure that I even have to dignify such an intrusive question, and that too in front of a whole bunch of Sin's groupies. "Not that it's anybody's business," I finish in an icy cold tone.

But Sin either doesn't pick up on my haughty voice and the tightness of my expression or he chooses to ignore both, because his eyes glint with jealousy.

"Really?" the horrible girl, the wench who set the ball rolling on this terrible invasion of my privacy, continues. "It didn't look like that. Looked like you were cozying up with him."

"That's ridiculous," I snap back, my patience thinner than the lace dress on that she-wolf. "And again, it's none of your business. Any of you."

Sin frowns, his face sporting a possessive and unsettling expression yet again. "It is my business if people are talking about my project partner."

"Your project partner, not your property," I retort, pushing back my chair. "You know what? I'm done with this. I'm going home."

"Petra, wait—" Sin starts, standing up and grabbing my bag.

"No, Sin. I need some space," I say firmly and turn around to leave.

Tears fill my eyes and almost roll down my face as laughter erupts behind me and the kids start making jokes again, but I will not turn around.

Even when I hear Sin running after me and calling my name, even when I hear a voice say, "Oh, c'mon, Sin, let her go. She's just too stuck-up for the likes of us," I don't stop.

As soon as I'm outside, I frantically wave down a cab. The night air is chilly and stings my cheeks, but I'm in no mood to tarry around.

Right as a cab pulls up to the curb, Sin comes barreling out of the restaurant.

"Petra, stop! Let's just talk about this."

And for a fraction of a second, I hesitate, actually thinking of stopping and hearing him out. But the impulse passes when a mixture of confusion, anger, and the need to be anywhere but here takes over instead. I open the cab door and slide in.

Sin reaches the cab just as it starts to pull away.

His hand slams on the door on my side, and his eyes are desperate and angry. "Petra, please!"

But it's too late. I can't—I won't—deal with this right now. The cab speeds down the street, and I watch Sin's figure grow smaller in the rearview mirror.

At last, I slump back into the seat and let loose the torrent of tears I had tamped down since my mishap in the washroom. My life keeps on whirring into one fateful collision after another. And I let go of the steering wheel a while back.

As the cab maneuvers the bustling streets, I close my eyes, trying to bring my breathing under control.

One thing is clear: My priorities need to shift. I have to find a way forward with my personal and academic trials *without* the distractions that incessantly tag Sin.

For now, I just need to get home and breathe.

CHAPTER SEVENTEEN

PETRA

The Past
26 March 1896

The loud voices coming from inside the house wake me up. I glance at the clock on the mantel—one in the morning. With a yawn, I climb out of bed and make my way to the door to find out who's speaking so loudly at this hour. The voices carry on. One of them is unmistakably my father's.

The other voice, though, I don't recognize. It's another man. From what I can gather, he sounds like a high-ranking member of the church. I'm about to return to bed when a few words catch my attention—*St. Anselm Hall . . . its professors.*

Curious, I crack the door open and tiptoe quietly, slipping around the staircase and creeping toward the source of the voices. They're in the library. The door is shut, but they're speaking so loudly I can hear them clearly from the hallway.

"We must do something about it," my father says, voice low and grave. "They're poisoning society with their eccentric ideas."

I frown. Is he talking about Sin and his demonology studies? Or something else?

"Indeed," the other man replies. "There have been rumors of late-night rituals at the university. Who else could be behind them, if not him?"

Him? I wonder. *Does he mean Sin? That's absurd.*

"It's preposterous to allow such things to happen in our town," my father continues. "Some of the youth in our congregation are already showing interest in these . . . gatherings."

A pause.

"Even my son has mentioned them in passing. I fear he'll soon want to join their ranks. And he's not alone."

"You're right," the other man agrees. "I've heard the same from other young men. They're drawn to this new way of teaching, to the society they've built."

A society? That's new. I've never heard anything about that. My curiosity burns brighter. If Sin won't reveal himself to me, maybe this is how I'll learn more. I edge closer.

"Did you not hear what they're planning in two days?" the man asks. "On the full moon?"

"The full moon?" my father echoes. "That sounds downright pagan."

"It is. I've no doubt," the man agrees. "I believe they're trying to summon something. An entity of some kind. I haven't confirmed it, but the rumors . . . if they're true, we cannot allow it to happen here."

"A summoning?" my father says, aghast. "Of an entity? A demon? On our soil? Absolutely not. But what can we do? They already have so much influence. And if we do nothing, they'll gain even more."

"All the students at the university are part of that society. They praise this new teaching, this so-called 'enlightened' worldview—encouraging questions that were never meant to be asked." His voice lowers. "They even have a map of demonic sigils."

"No," my father gasps. "That's something only the Vatican is supposed to possess."

"The leader of this . . . society . . . he's well-connected. Not just in the Vatican, but beyond. That's how he seized control of the university. Before him, the Theology Department was revered as one of the best in the country. Now look at us. Why would we allow someone like that to desecrate our community?"

There's a silence.

"Are you sure this is what they're planning?" my father asks at last. "A summoning? But why here? Why in our little town?"

The man pauses before replying, "Come now. You must know why."

"What do you mean?"

"This land . . . it's fertile. But not for crops."

"What are you—?"

"Even our church's founder, the great Father Reuben, said this land was sacred. Mystical. It allowed our church to flourish. Perhaps they see the same potential for their society."

My father sighs. "And already we've seen the damage. The divide. It's no longer one town—it's *us* and *them.* A fracture has split this place."

"Yes," the man agrees. "Everyone has seen it. It's been nearly twenty years since that madman arrived. For our children, this divide is all they've ever known."

Twenty years? I think, startled. *That can't be. Sin doesn't look much older than I am. He would've been a child back then.*

"From the beginning," the man continues, "when they created that new department and students flocked to it, we've watched our own church lose influence. People mock us. They turn away from our teachings."

"That's why I keep telling my son to stay away," my father mutters. "I've even pleaded with the reverend to impose stricter rules, to keep us from mingling with the outsiders. But he won't listen. He still lets our children roam the town—visit the shops, attend fairs, go where they'll cross paths with those outsiders. Pagans with a skewed understanding of life."

He falls quiet.

"But no one listens to me."

"I do," the man says gently. "I know the dangers all too well. And I believe this upcoming ritual could affect more than just our church. It could destroy all of Radcliffe."

"If they summon this demon," my father says, his voice tight, "it will be the end of us."

"We must act," the man says. "We must stop them."

There's a long pause.

"We are of the same mind, Jeremiah," he finally says. "It might be a sin . . . but is it, really, if we do it to protect ourselves?"

He lets the words hang for a moment before continuing, almost reverently:

"Think about what our church father, St. Augustine, said: Killing has its place in society as long as it serves a just cause. Sometimes, it is necessary."

I clap a hand over my mouth to keep from gasping.

Killing? Did I hear that right? They're talking about *killing people*?

How could they say something so vile so casually? I understand not agreeing with the people at the university. I even understand not wanting to live alongside them. But *this*? *Murder*? We can't—

"We cannot let them get their way," my father says firmly. "I believe God will forgive us for this transgression."

"This is a just cause. We are protecting innocent people."

My father hums in approval. "We can kill the leader and—"

"The leader won't be enough," the other man replies with a sharp *tsk*. "Not *just* him—his main disciples, too. If he's gone, they'll just carry on his legacy. We must wipe out the core of the movement. Otherwise, everyone in this town will be doomed."

I can't listen to another word. I retreat upstairs on shaking legs, my breath coming fast. Did they really just plot to kill someone?

Someone who merely disagrees with them?

Yes. They did.

And knowing my father, how deep his fanaticism runs, I can see it happening. I can see him doing it, truly believing he's committing a righteous act. They'll call it a necessary evil. They won't even realize they've become worse than the people they claim to condemn.

But it isn't just the murder they're planning—it's *who* they're planning to kill.

They didn't say his name. But it has to be him. He must be one of those "disciples" they mentioned. Why else would people in the square speak of him with such venom? Why else would they call him "cursed," a "demon"?

He's part of that school of thought. Of course he is. It makes sense now.

Oh, Lord. This is bad. This is really, truly bad.

If that ritual, or whatever they're planning, is happening two days from now, then they're going to act *tomorrow.*

Panic grips me. No matter how much I've tried to push Sin out of my mind, no matter how I've tried to forget our strange encounters, the letters, the disturbing gift he left me (God, *a piece of flesh*), that doesn't mean I want to see him *dead,* does it?

No. I don't want to see him hurt. Not in any way.

I think of the moment he was hit in the face, blood running down his cheek, that look of shock and pain when he saw me listening to the cruel things being said about him.

In that moment, he looked so vulnerable, and something about that struck a chord in me. Maybe I'm more sentimental than I want to admit. But one thing is certain: I *cannot* live with myself knowing a crime is about to be committed and doing *nothing*.

But *how*?

I'm watched, day and night.

Since that final, grotesque letter, Sin hasn't reached out. It's been days. I have no way to contact him.

The clock is ticking. The night creeps forward. Soon, the new day will dawn, and my father and that stranger will set their plan in motion.

I have to act. Fast.

I begin to pace, racking my brain for a way to reach Sin—*somehow.* There's only one answer I keep circling back to:

I must go to him.

But where? I don't know where he lives . . . but I know where he spends his time. The university. I could go there. I *must* go there.

But how do I leave without anyone seeing me? How do I get across town without being caught?

The questions swirl, but one thing is louder than all of them—my conviction. I *must* do something before it's too late.

I shed my nightgown, throw on a day dress, and tie a scarf around my head. Instinctively, I reach for my veil—but no. If anyone sees me wearing it, they'll know I'm from the church. Word will spread fast.

I take off the veil and leave only the scarf. I slip on my shoes and move toward the window.

Sin once left a letter for me there. He climbed up the wall. Could I climb *down*?

I peer over the ledge. There are a few protruding stones—places to grip, places to step. But I'm no climber. I've never done anything so physically demanding in my life. What if I fall? What if they hear me?

Still, I have no choice.

Gripping the window frame, I hoist myself onto the sill. My feet dangle in the cold air as I turn, slowly, and search with my toes for the next ledge.

The first step is easy. But when I glance down, fear rises like bile.

I swallow hard. *Good Lord, help me. I know I haven't been too earnest in my prayers lately, but just this once, please, just this once. I'm trying to prevent a murder. That must count for something.*

I stretch my hands out to the next ledge and lower myself again. Dim lights from the outhouse flicker across the courtyard. The guards' lanterns barely light my path. Shadows stretch around me, twisting with the wind—strangely comforting, like they're shielding me.

And then, miraculously, my feet touch the ground.

I blink, startled that I made it without injury, but there's no time to dwell on it. I bolt across the courtyard, skirting the dog pens and praying they don't catch my scent. It might be foolish, but I'm running on instinct now.

When I reach the gates—*outside* the gates—I freeze.

I made it.

And just for a moment, I think maybe fate is on my side tonight.

I'VE BEEN WALKING for what feels like forever, and I've only just reached the town square. The streets are quiet tonight. A few pubs are still open, their windows glowing faintly, but there aren't many people around. The ones I do pass, I avoid by keeping my head down, slipping by unnoticed.

I know the university lies at the far end of town, but I've never ventured that way before. I end up going in circles for a while before I finally find it—and I only recognize it by the sheer grandeur of the place. The building is majestic, its gothic architecture breathtaking, almost otherworldly.

Tall wrought-iron gates, twice my height, line the perimeter—dark and imposing, like sentinels guarding whatever lies within.

I got out of my house, yes. But now what? How am I supposed to scale these fences and get inside? And even if I do, *then what?* It's the middle of the night. Would Sin even be there?

I don't know. I won't know . . . unless I try.

As I search for a way inside, perhaps a narrow nook or a gap in the fence, the mighty gates suddenly creak open before me, beckoning me in.

A little fearful, but resolute, I step through. The university gardens are just as breathtaking as the grand buildings themselves: meticulously groomed and now bursting with springtime blooms.

The air is sweet and fruity, almost intoxicating. It strikes me as strange that a place so beautiful could be the site of such madness—at least, if my father and the rest of the villagers are to be believed. They all say the same thing: that Sin and his mentor are wrapped up in blasphemous practices.

I walk through the gardens, eyes searching for a door, but the windows are dark. No lights, no signs of life. Perhaps this was a mistake. Maybe I should just leave him a note and go.

I'm just about to do that, slip a message by the door, when I hear something. My heart leaps. I swivel toward the sound, scanning the darkness, but no one's there. Or is there? I can't see a soul, and yet . . . someone is breathing.

Close. Too close. I turn again—and gasp.

I stumble back, nearly falling, but strong arms catch me, pulling me upright. Sin.

"Petra," he says, voice low, a touch surprised. "What a surprise to see you here."

"I—I must speak with you," I manage.

"You've decided to accept my apology?" he asks, a hopeful note in his voice.

"I . . . We need to talk. But not here. Is there somewhere more private?"

"Of course. Come in."

He takes my hand and leads me to the main door, opening it with ease. Even in the darkness, I can tell it's forged from the same heavy iron as the gates. Once we're inside, the hallway bursts into light. I flinch.

"What—how did you do that?"

"This building runs on electricity," he replies.

"Electricity?" I echo, stunned. "That's unusual for a small town."

He nods. "My mentor is well-connected. He ensured the university had access the moment it became available."

"This mentor of yours—"

"Enough about him," Sin interrupts gently. "Let's go to my office. We'll have all the time in the world to talk there."

I nod, still dazed, and follow him through a maze of winding staircases until we reach a room on the third floor. It's enormous. The moment he opens the door, I realize it's more than an office; it's where he lives.

"This is your study?" I ask in wonder.

He chuckles. "Ah, I've been caught. Yes, it is. And most nights, I sleep here, too. Can't be too far from my research."

"It is a nice room," I murmur. And it is. Warm, lit, inviting.

"Come, make yourself comfortable. Would you like some tea?" he offers.

"Yes. Thank you. That's . . . very thoughtful."

For a moment, I forget everything—our strange history, the fact that he once sent me a piece of his flesh.

The word erupts in my mind.

Flesh.

I glance at him, scanning quickly. He's turned away, sleeves rolled up as he prepares the tea. Something feels off.

Not just that he lives here, but that he greeted me as if he *knew* I was coming.

"Sin," I call.

He half turns. "So now you can say my name."

I look away. "It *is* your name. What else am I supposed to call you?"

A smile spreads across his face. "I may hate it, but hearing it from your lips . . . perhaps I could start loving it."

"You shouldn't say things like that," I mumble.

"Things like what?"

"Like that. It's not proper."

"Maybe not," he says, "but neither is you being here in the middle of the night. How did you get away?"

"I climbed out of my window," I admit. "Ran across town to get here."

"Without your veil," he adds.

I reach for it instinctively, my fingers brushing bare skin.

"Yes," I whisper. "I thought people would find it strange, a veiled figure walking alone at this hour."

"You did good, Petra," he says gently, bringing over the tea. "Very good indeed. Such a brave girl."

I flush under his praise, ashamed to like it, but I do. I'm just about to tell him why I came when I notice his arm in the light.

His sleeves are pushed up to the elbow, and there, just above his wrist, is a wound. Fresh. Healing. And the exact size of the flesh that had been sent to me.

I gasp.

"Is that . . . ?" I point.

He follows my gaze to the wound and smiles. "I gather you liked my present."

"You're insane," I whisper. "Why would you do that to yourself? Why would you—"

"Yes," he says simply, as if foreknowing my next words. "I hurt myself. I thought . . . only if I suffered as much as I hurt you, would you believe I meant what I said."

"I . . ." My voice catches.

"Petra, I was out of line. I realize now I came across all wrong. It was never my intention to scare you. On the contrary. I don't want you to see me as the monster they say I am. I want you to see me as someone who—"

"Someone who?" I echo.

He presses his lips together. "As *me*. Just myself."

"Giving me a piece of your flesh—that's not normal. That's . . ."

"Perhaps I *am* insane. But are you not insane, too?"

"What do you mean?"

"You kept it. You didn't throw it away."

My breath hitches. "How would you know that?"

"I know everything about you, Petra. Just as I knew you'd come. Just as I knew you'd seek me out."

"But . . . how?"

"You'll understand. Maybe not now, but in time."

He sits beside me, lifts the tea to his lips, and smiles—calmly, as if everything about this moment is perfectly ordinary.

CHAPTER EIGHTEEN

PETRA

The Past
26 March 1896

Sin's gaze on me is unnerving as I try to summon the courage to say what I came here to say. But how does one casually bring up murder? He looks at me, expectant.

I bite my lip. "Can you . . . can you not do that?" I whisper.

"Do what?"

"Look at me like that."

"Like what?"

"*Like that,*" I repeat.

"Why wouldn't I, when you're the most beautiful thing I've ever seen, Petra?" he replies smoothly.

I flush a deep red.

"The fact that you've graced me with your bare face humbles me. That alone . . ." He trails off with a smile. "Has no one ever told you how beautiful you are?"

I shake my head slowly.

"No? Unacceptable!" he exclaims. "You're extraordinary. *So* beautiful." He tilts his head. "My eyes almost hurt from looking at you."

I blush and turn away. I've never been the object of so many praises—of any praises at all. I don't know how to respond, especially when he looks at me like that . . . Like he would like to . . . devour me.

"We should talk about why I came." I clear my throat.

"Yes, please," he says calmly, though I feel anything but calm. Inside, a storm is raging—not just because of how close he is, or the fact that I'm alone with him, unveiled, exposed, but because of what I'm about to say.

"I overheard my father speaking with one of the men from his congregation," I begin slowly.

"About me?" His brows lift slightly.

"Well . . . I think it was about you. And your mentor."

He doesn't speak, just waits.

"They believe you're planning something. In two days. On the night of the full moon."

Still no reaction. Just that steady gaze.

"They want to stop you," I say. "They want to hurt you. Maybe even kill you."

He continues to watch me, unreadable. Not a flicker of surprise.

"You don't seem shocked."

"No," he says simply. "It was only a matter of time before your church tried something drastic."

"Aren't you scared?"

He shrugs. "What I am is . . . grateful. That you would risk so much to come warn me. To try to save me."

"I—I didn't do it just for you," I stammer. "I'd do it for anyone. Killing isn't right, it doesn't—"

He cuts me off gently. "Doesn't matter. You did it for me. That's how I'll remember it."

"But—"

He smiles faintly. "You snuck out of your house, in the middle of the night, knowing what could happen if you were caught, just to come find me. You have no idea what that means to me."

I flush again. "I just don't want to see you get hurt. I don't want *anyone* to get hurt."

"Don't worry," he says. "Now that you've gone through so much to warn me, the least I can do is make sure your effort wasn't in vain."

"What are you going to do?"

"I'll have to speak to my mentor. We'll plan accordingly."

"But is it true? What they're saying? That you're going to perform a ritual to summon . . . something? An entity?"

He hums. "What do you know about demons, Petra?"

"Not much," I admit, shivering slightly. "Only what I've read in the Bible."

"Then you know nothing," he replies. "The demons in the Bible and the demons that exist in our world are not the same."

"Exist in our world?" I echo. "You mean they're already *here*? They're not in hell?"

"Come," he says, beckoning me.

He leads me to a massive wall lined with shelves—hundreds of ancient-looking tomes—and nestled between them, a large section of the wall is devoted entirely to art. One painting in particular dominates the space. It's enormous, violent, the image it depicts resembling some kind of hell on earth.

He stops in front of it and waits until I'm beside him.

"I've met a demon before," he says suddenly.

My eyes widen, but before I can ask anything, he turns to me.

"You once asked about my name."

"Is it short for something else? Like Sinclair?" I inquire, my brows furrowed. I'd spent days thinking over our interaction and his *name,* and I thought he'd said it to shock me—that perhaps it was just a nickname.

He shakes his head. "No. Just *Sin.*"

"I don't understand. Why would anyone name someone that?"

"Because that's what I was to them," he says simply. "A sin. My sin was being born."

"What?" I breathe. "What do you mean?"

He turns away, facing the painting again. The absence of his gaze leaves me feeling strangely hollow. I watch his profile, the tightness of his jaw as he draws in a slow, steady breath.

"I never knew my parents," he begins. "I was abandoned as a baby, left on the steps of an orphanage. They took me in, but that doesn't mean they wanted me there."

He pauses, his voice steady but distant.

"My only stroke of luck was that the orphanage was attached to a church. A church not so different from yours, actually. But that luck didn't last. They couldn't exactly toss out a child into the streets; it wouldn't have looked good. Still, that didn't mean they had to *like* me. And they made their dislike clear from the start."

"But why?" I ask. "Why would they treat a child like that?"

"Ah, Petra," he says with a faint, sad smile. "You're too sweet. You see, in their eyes, I wasn't innocent. Every time I happened to be near someone when misfortune struck—a fall, an illness, an accident—they blamed me.

They remembered only the bad things, and I became the common thread. The bringer of misfortune."

He exhales.

"My birth parents, well, they must have seen the same darkness in me, to abandon me like that. They must have *known* something."

I stare at him, stunned.

"Still," he goes on, "because of the orphanage's reputation, and the need to seem like good Christians, they kept me. Took me in. Raised me. I stayed there until I was old enough to leave and forge my own way in the world."

"That's horrible," I whisper, stepping forward. I reach out, gently placing my hand on his arm.

He flinches, just slightly, but then he relaxes beneath my touch. He glances at me, and in his eyes, I see sadness, yes, but also something deeper. Regret. Shame. And I can't understand why.

"I'm so sorry, Sin," I tell him. "You have to know that it wasn't your fault. You were just a child. Even if bad things happened around you . . . how could anyone blame you for that?"

"And yet they did," he replies softly.

"I can't understand people like that," I murmur. "I don't want to."

"That's because you have a pure heart, Petra. There aren't many like you in this world."

"But still. You *must know* it wasn't your fault."

"Was it not?" he asks quietly. "I don't know. Maybe . . . maybe it was, in part. I was different. Even I can see that now. I didn't act the way a child was expected to. I kept to myself."

"Well, of course you did," I argue. "If they treated you like that—of course you pulled away."

He shakes his head. "Even before that. Something was . . . off. Something was wrong with me. And maybe they saw it. Maybe even my birth parents saw it."

"How can you say that?" I ask, horrified. "How can you believe that?"

"It's kind of you to care, Petra," he says, his voice softening. "You don't know how much it means to me. That you would be angry on my behalf."

He looks away for a moment, then back at me.

"I've made peace with my past. Maybe it *was* as awful as you say. But no matter how terrible it was . . . it made me who I am. And everything that happened, all of it, brought me to this moment. To you."

He turns fully now, facing me. My mouth parts, but no words come. I stare at him, stunned, heart racing.

"What are you saying?" I whisper.

"You don't know, do you?" he murmurs, reaching out for me. "How much . . ." He doesn't finish the sentence. His hand falters midair before he pulls back, shaking his head to himself. "I was fourteen when I came face-to-face with a demon for the first time."

He turns again to the painting, as if he can't bear to look at me while recounting these traumatic experiences.

"First time . . ."

"It seems I have shocked you," he chuckles. "It's no exaggeration to say that my time at the orphanage shaped who I am. I was a pariah—made fun of, avoided. As a child, I didn't understand why. But as time passed and their behavior worsened, I began to doubt myself.

"If I truly was a sin, a blight upon the world . . . why did I even exist? Why go on suffering, and make others suffer just by being near them? I could see it, even as a child—they believed my presence brought misfortune. So one day, I decided to end it all."

I gasp aloud. "You don't mean . . . ?"

He presses his lips together. "Yes. That's exactly what I mean."

"But that's a . . ." I trail off.

"A sin." He lets out a dry laugh. "Yes. I decided that since they named me Sin, I might as well become one."

He moves to a second painting, smaller but equally as striking. It shows a single, solitary column rising from a landscape of ruin—silent, detached, watching it all unfold. Weathered by time, yet unmoving. Still standing. Still strong.

"My room was on the fourth floor. An attic, really. It had been turned into a bedroom because none of the other children would share a room with me. In some ways, that was a blessing; I didn't have to sleep in a crowded dorm. One morning, after enduring more of their ugly words, I opened the window. I stepped onto the sill . . . and I jumped."

My breath catches. The sound startles him.

"My, my, Petra," he says with a faint smile. "From your expression, one would think you actually care for me."

"Stop," I say, voice trembling. "Don't make light of it. You *actually* jumped? You tried to kill yourself?"

"I did," he says simply. "I jumped. And I fell onto the pavement of the main road below."

"But you're . . . alive. You seem whole."

He smiles sadly. "Now, yes. But not then. When I landed, I hit my head hard. My legs were twisted beneath me. My bones were pushing through the skin. I couldn't move. I was bleeding out on the street, but I was conscious. I was aware of everything."

He draws a breath.

"People saw me. Passersby. Some even stopped to look. But no one helped. People from the orphanage saw me, too. And they turned away."

"They *what*?" I whisper, horrified.

"From their perspective, I wasn't dead. But I was dying. And helping me, calling a physician to try to save me, would have cost money they didn't have. Or didn't *want* to spend. So they left me there. They waited for me to die."

"But you didn't," I say softly.

"No. I didn't. Night fell again. The lights at the orphanage went out, and I was still lying there. I heard the sounds of carriages, of people walking past. Some sneered. Some whispered. But none stopped. Not until *he* did."

"He . . . you mean the demon?"

"I didn't know what he was, not then. And maybe he's not a demon in the way we think: horns and fire and damnation. But he was . . . not human. He stopped, looked down at me, and asked, '*Do you want to die*?' I couldn't speak—I could barely make a sound—but he knelt beside me and said, '*Blink once for yes, twice for no*.'

"And in that moment, after all the pain, after being abandoned again and again . . . some part of me still wanted to live. I didn't want to live the life I *had* been living, but I wanted to live. So I blinked twice."

He pauses.

"He asked me why I had done this. I couldn't answer, but somehow—through some kind of magic, or power, he *knew*. He could read my thoughts. He saw that I was of two minds. That I wanted to live but only if my life could mean something. Only if it could matter."

He turns back to me.

"He saw that. He saw that I wanted more. So he offered it."

"Offered what?" I ask, barely able to breathe.

"Before I could think about what he meant, he let a few drops of his blood fall into my mouth. And then . . . the pain vanished. My bones shifted back into place. The wounds closed. By morning, I was completely healed. I was alive. Whole."

He looks down at his hands, as if remembering the moment. Mouth ajar in shock, I glance at him, too, letting my gaze trail all over his body. Save for the fresh wound on his arm, there is no evidence that he might have been hurt in the past.

He sees me staring in shock, so he comments, "If it hadn't happened to me, I wouldn't believe it either."

"And then?" I whisper. "What did you do?"

"I left. I knew I couldn't go back to the orphanage after that."

"But," I say slowly, "if that man—*that thing*—healed you . . . what did he want in return?"

"There it is, that curious mind of yours," he murmurs appreciatively. "What do you think he wanted in return, Petra?"

I gulp down. I'd heard whispers in the congregation of those damned, who accept the lure of the devil in exchange for their immortal soul. It is something often said about witches, that they willingly sell themselves to the devil in exchange for power, beauty, money.

Looking at him, so distinguished, so successful, I can't help but wonder. After all, how could a fourteen-year-old runaway get a degree from Harvard, or a professorship at St. Anselm Hall?

"Your soul?" I dare ask.

His lips curve into a sly smile.

CHAPTER NINETEEN

PETRA

The Past
26 March 1896

"Would you begrudge me my deal, darling Petra? Would you blame me if I sold my soul to a demon in exchange for a better life?" he asks smoothly, his eyes pinned on me.

I don't answer, still reeling in shock from what he revealed.

"Knowing what my life at the orphanage was like, knowing that they left me to rot on that pavement, happy to be rid of me; would you blame me if I sold my soul to escape that?"

"I . . ." I stammer, unable to form a single coherent thought. Do I begrudge him? I don't know. His life, at least as he's told it, was full of pain and rejection.

But still . . . we're talking about a *demon*.

We're talking about something evil. Who knows what it really wanted? Who's to say it didn't deceive him? Isn't that what we're taught from the beginning—that the devil's greatest trick is deception?

When I don't answer, he chuckles.

"Don't worry, sweet Petra. I did not sell my soul. Not yet, anyway."

I slap his shoulder. "That's not funny. Selling your soul isn't something to joke about."

"And yet, there are people who *want* to do exactly that."

"Your mentor . . ." My voice trails off. "The ritual. In two days."

He nods, and my eyes widen.

"You mean they're trying to *summon* a demon to make a deal and sell their souls?"

"People want different things, Petra. Different desires, different dreams. Tell me, if someone offered you what you wanted most in the world, wouldn't you even *consider* it?"

I shake my head. "No. Not for eternal damnation."

"Why do you assume that's the price?" he asks.

"Because they're *demons*," I shoot back. "They're evil."

"And I told you, they're not the demons from your Bible. They're not fire and brimstone. They're something else entirely. Powerful, yes, but not always evil. If anything, I find that *humans* can be far more cruel. More deliberately destructive.

"Just because we don't understand these beings, just because they're different from us, doesn't mean they don't have their own sense of morality."

"Why are you defending them?" I ask.

"Why *wouldn't* I?" he counters. "The one who healed me asked for nothing in return."

"But you said he *offered* something to you."

"Yes. But I never said he *demanded* anything in exchange."

"But if he's a demon, how could he do something like that out of kindness?"

"Maybe," he says quietly, "he pitied a boy so hopeless he was ready to die. A boy who'd spent his life being hated, feared, mocked. Do you really think showing compassion to someone like that is evil?"

"No," I whisper.

"Then there you have it."

I hesitate. "But that still doesn't explain what you're trying to do now. The ritual. Are you being *forced* into this? Is it your mentor? Is he making you do it?"

"I'm not being forced into anything," he says, his tone firm. "Quite the opposite. Back when I was studying at Harvard, during my first year, I started looking into these entities, asking questions others were too afraid or too proud to ask. Some people didn't like it. But there were others, like my mentor, who had been asking the same questions long before I ever did."

He leans back slightly.

"He took me under his wing, and together, we started to study. Who *are* these beings? These powerful entities whose blood, just one drop, can heal a person from the inside out. And if they can do *that,* what else are they capable of? Where do they come from? Why are they here? Wouldn't *you* want to know the answers?"

"Yes," I admit softly. "But . . ."

"I was drawn to your curiosity, Petra. Because I'm curious, too. I want to know more than what we're spoon-fed—by our families, our communities, our schools. We're taught to accept what we're told and never dig deeper. But if we don't ask questions, we'll never know."

"Maybe," I say hesitantly. "But sometimes it's better *not* to know. Knowledge is powerful, sure, but it can also open the door to things we're not ready for. What if you accidentally unleash something terrible?"

"And *that,*" he replies, "that unknown—is exactly what people are looking for." He meets my gaze. "There are dozens of students here, just like me, who want answers. They want to understand what lies beneath the surface."

"They want to sell their souls," I snap.

He shrugs. "Some do. Some want things that feel impossible to get otherwise—and would strike a bargain with something that could give it to them. Others, like me, are driven purely by curiosity."

"But what happens if someone *does* sell their soul? What if you summon something, and it *won't* leave? What if it stays in our town and starts *consuming* it?"

He smiles. "Maybe that's the point."

"Sin, *please* be serious."

"Why do you think I'm not?"

"Because I never know when you are," I huff. "You speak so lightly about everything, as if none of it matters. As if people dying, or sacrificing themselves, is just . . . inevitable."

"And isn't that what your church teaches? That God gave humans free will? Well, they're using it. They're choosing to summon something. And if something goes wrong, they'll bear the consequences."

"But what about *you*?" I press. "What happens if *you* get hurt?"

At that, he smiles wider. "Ah, there it is. So you're not worried about all those other lost souls, just *mine*. And I wonder why."

I flush but don't respond.

"We're talking about something serious," I say instead. "My father mentioned Vatican sigils. He said your mentor has them. If that's true, if the information is really coming from the *Vatican,* then that means the entity you're summoning is incredibly powerful. *Dangerously* powerful."

"And why do you assume the Vatican knows best?" he asks.

"What?" I blink, thrown off. "What do you mean?"

He leans forward slightly, voice calm but unwavering.

"The Vatican, like any institution, protects its own interests. Think about it. If there's something out there, something more powerful than us, something that's *neither* God *nor* the devil, what does that mean for the Church? What does that say about all the teachings, all the centuries of rituals, all the promises of salvation and heaven?"

He pauses, watching me.

"What if there *is* no heaven? No hell? What if everything we've been taught is just a comforting illusion?" he challenges.

I stare at him, heart pounding.

"Just because the Vatican has information," he says quietly, "doesn't mean they *understand* it. And it certainly doesn't mean they're using it in the right way. Come." He motions toward his desk.

He opens a drawer, and I lean over to see what's inside, catching a glimpse of a beautiful rosary wrapped in silk. It's such a strange item for someone who claims to want to summon demons.

He pulls out a heavy, ancient-looking tome and closes the drawer—much to my disappointment. As he flips it open, I see the pages filled with intricate drawings—geometric symbols etched like stamps, made of sharp lines, circles, and strange patterns.

"Are those the sigils?" I ask.

"The Church has been collecting these for thousands of years," he says. "What you saw, those sigils, are just a few my mentor managed to obtain from high-ranking officials in the Vatican."

"Do they correspond to a specific demon or something?" I ask.

"Yes and no," he replies. "From what I understand, they can be used to call upon one of *those* entities. But until now, no one's actually done it."

"What do you mean?"

"We have the drawings, yes. But we don't truly know how to use them. Not yet."

"Then what's the point of the ritual?" I press. "If you don't even know how to activate them?"

He exhales. "I can't tell you more, Petra. I've already said too much."

"You know I'd never tell my father. Or anyone from the church."

"I know," he says, nodding. "But that's not what I'm afraid of."

"Then what are you afraid of?"

He looks at me, a smile flickering at the corners of his mouth. "Let's just say it's better if you don't know."

That makes my blood boil. "So that's it? You're just going to ignore everything I told you? Pretend I didn't warn you? You're going through with it anyway?"

"I am," he says, calm as ever. "Unless you ask me not to."

"Didn't I *just* tell you you're in danger?" I snap.

He shrugs. "I think I could be persuaded to walk away from this particular curiosity if another one of my curiosities were satisfied."

I narrow my eyes. "What are you talking about?"

He closes the tome and slides it back into the drawer. Leaning back in his chair, he tilts his head and fixes his gaze on me.

"One kiss," he says. "Give me one kiss, and I'll vow to stay away from the ritual."

I stare at him, stunned. "*What?*" I blurt. "You can't be serious."

"It's simple," he says, unbothered. "One kiss on the lips. And I promise I won't take part in the ritual."

"You're insane," I gasp, stepping back. "Why would you ever think I'd agree to something like that? I've done my part—I warned you. I told you what my father and his congregation are planning. That is *enough*."

He lifts a brow, and his laid-back expression makes me even more angry. How can he joke about something like this?

"You said it yourself—free will. You choose whether to participate or not, whether to put yourself in danger or not. Why should I sacrifice myself for you?"

Without waiting for a reply, I turn sharply on my heel to leave.

Behind me, his voice follows—soft, almost amused.

"Is that what it would be? A sacrifice?"

I stop in the middle of the room, frozen.

"Would kissing me really be so unbearable, Petra? So unthinkable that it would feel like a *sacrifice*?"

I say nothing.

"You're doing it again," I murmur without turning. "You're trying to make a trade."

"If you won't grant me this little curiosity," he says, "then perhaps I *should* just sell my soul to get it. I'm sure that entity would have no trouble securing me a kiss from you in exchange for my soul."

"You—" I gasp, whipping around to face him. I march forward, stopping in front of him with clenched fists. "You're *impossible*. You're not taking this seriously. How could you—"

"What? Sell my soul for a kiss?" he finishes for me. "But you see, I would. A kiss from you. I'd give up anything. *Everything*."

"Why are you doing this?" I ask, breathless. "Why *me*? How would you even *think* of something like that?"

He grips the arms of his chair and propels himself forward until our faces are nearly touching. His eyes lock on mine, steady and unwavering.

"Because kissing you," he says softly, "is my greatest desire. And I would do anything to have it."

"You're playing dirty," I whisper.

"Maybe," he replies, lips curling faintly. "But look at it this way—give me one kiss, and I'll keep my soul. I won't trade it. I'll keep it safe . . . for *you*." He leans in just a little closer. "What do you say, Petra?"

I blink, suddenly unsteady. He's so close I can feel the warmth of his breath on my lips. A shiver runs down my spine as I inhale sharply.

"If it helps," he murmurs, "think of it as charity. A small sacrifice to save my soul."

"Just . . . one?" I breathe.

"Then you *are* considering it," he says, voice light.

I don't reply. Still frozen in the moment, captive to my thoughts and a hidden desire that makes me want to embrace this madness.

"Tick tock, Petra. Just one kiss. It won't hurt you. You're not losing anything."

I swallow hard. My gaze drifts to his mouth, then back to his eyes. I don't know what's come over me. One kiss. Just one.

I lick my lips, nervous.

"One kiss," I repeat, barely a whisper. It's madness that I'm even considering it. Madness that I'm here at all. And yet, despite everything I know is wrong about this, about *him*, I can't bring myself to walk away.

Not just because he's not part of my congregation. Not just because he's technically still a stranger. It's more than that. He's a contradiction in every possible way—charming and infuriating, magnetic and mysterious. Nothing he does makes logical sense, and yet, there's always a strange reasoning behind it.

He speaks with conviction. He's eloquent, persuasive, and I've never been more confused by someone in my life.

I *should* be running. I *should* never have eavesdropped; I should have never left my house, without my veil of all things.

Yet, here I am.

Slowly, I lift my hands and rest them on his shoulders. I meet his gaze, my voice trembling. "One kiss," I say again. "Just one."

"Just one, Petra," he echoes.

I press my lips together and draw in a deep breath. Leaning in, I close my eyes and gently purse my lips.

He doesn't move. He doesn't reach for me. He doesn't pull me in.

He leaves everything up to me.

So I do it.

I press my lips against his. His mouth is soft, warmer than I expected. A small sigh escapes me as I move my mouth, barely brushing over his, testing, unsure. It's strange—but not unpleasant. There's something oddly comforting in the contact. Something I hadn't anticipated.

Just as I begin to pull away—thinking, perhaps foolishly, that I've done my Christian duty—his hands suddenly grip my waist.

A gasp escapes me.

He uses it. Seizes it.

And in that moment, he takes full possession of the kiss.

His mouth parts against mine, his tongue gently tracing the seam of my lips, seeking entry. I clutch the fabric of his shirt in both fists, trying to anchor myself, trying to stay grounded, but it's useless. A flood of unfamiliar sensations crashes through me, overwhelming and raw.

His grip tightens.

"Open up for me," he breathes against my mouth.

"What—?" I try to ask, but before the words leave me, his tongue slips past my lips, stealing my breath and any sense of control.

The tip of his tongue brushes mine, coaxing it into a slow, deliberate rhythm—seductive, consuming. My knees weaken. A shudder runs through me. He kisses me like he's starving. Like he's trying to drink me in. And I don't know how to explain the way I feel, because I've never felt anything like it before.

He deepens the kiss, and suddenly there is no distinction between where I end and he begins. My breath becomes his breath. My thoughts scatter.

His teeth graze my lower lip before he returns to me again, this time more urgently. Faster. Deeper. He holds me so tightly I couldn't pull away if I wanted to.

But . . . *do* I want to?

What is this madness? What is he doing to me?

He asked for *one* kiss. This—this isn't a kiss. This is possession.

The thought jolts through me like ice. I begin to return to myself, realizing—*this isn't right*. My fingers are still curled into his shirt. Slowly, I loosen them. I press against his chest.

"Please," I whisper. "Let go."

He doesn't.

He swallows my plea, his mouth devouring mine again and again, claiming me with every breath I try to take.

"No," I gasp, louder now. I push against him with everything I have.

He falls back in his chair. I stagger, breathless, eyes wide, lips tingling and swollen. He looks just as wrecked—his shirt rumpled, his lips red, his gaze locked on me in awe.

"You said one kiss," I say, barely above a whisper.

But he only smiles. "Ah, and that, my dear Petra, *that* wasn't even one kiss."

I blink. "What?"

"That was only a *quarter* of a kiss."

"You're insane," I whisper, trembling.

"No, I'm not," he says softly. "You still owe me three-quarters."

"This isn't what we agreed to. I don't even know why I agreed at all. I—" I step back, frantic. "You—"

He rises from the chair. His eyes don't leave me. There's something unhinged in that gaze, yes, but also something vulnerable. Something raw. Desire, maybe. But what do *I* know of desire?

"Don't come any closer," I warn, voice shaking. "I shouldn't have come here. I shouldn't have done *any* of this. I have to go."

He doesn't respond. He just smiles—that infuriating, knowing smile.

"Go back to your safe world, Petra," he says. "But we both know tonight, it's *my* kiss you'll be dreaming about."

"Stop," I whisper.

But to my great shame . . . he's right.

CHAPTER TWENTY

PETRA

Present Day

After a night filled with much heartburn (both the literal kind because of my you-know-what state and more eerie dreams about that stranger also called Sin), I pull myself out of bed with the express intent of requesting Ms. Matthews to assign me a different partner.

Literally *anyone else* will do.

It's not enough that he's haunting my days with his wicked smile and stupid charm, but now he has to invade my dreams, too? How is it that since that fateful night, I haven't been able to dream of anything else *but* him?

Well, it's him and it's not, since apparently my brain found it better to center our *forbidden romance* in the *actual* Gilded Age.

Not to mention him being a dazzling occult professor and me . . . well, I was just a member of a *cult*.

Nice, Petra, you just got yourself the plot of a smutty romance.

I grimace and berate myself: *Those dreams have been quite steamy, all right. Perhaps not full-on, fuck-your-brains-out type, but close enough.*

Good gracious, I'm really starting to lose it if this is what my subconscious is conjuring up.

Yet no matter how decided I am to change my project partner, my resolve falters when I arrive at school. The corridors of St. Anselm Hall buzz with an inscrutable energy, a certain urgency underscored by whispered conversations, furtive glances, and tense faces.

Even in the midst of my inner anguish, I can feel the pervasive sense of doom that's settled over the SAH junta as soon as I step through the front doors.

"Did you hear?" Claire announces as she skids to a halt before me. "Oh my God, Petra, it's just horrible!"

These are the most words I have ever heard Claire utter, as she usually keeps to herself.

So I ask, "Hear what?" almost instinctively. Something must be very amiss if Claire is this unsettled.

"That kid who dropped out of Art History?" Claire begins in a breathless voice.

"Yes? I got his seat when he dropped out," I respond fearfully.

Are they going to tell me that there was some kind of mistake? That I don't have the seat after all?

Of course, the real news is much worse.

"They-they found him dead on the school property," Claire stammers. "They're saying it might be—"

"Wait, what? Claire, did you just say someone's *dead*?"

I grab her shoulders to steady her because her eyes are wide and unfocused. Her hair's all over the place, and frankly, she looks like she's coming apart at the seams.

"Edwin Greenfield!" she cries out. "That red-haired guy who got an early-decision to Harvard, remember? He was your partner in that course last year, right?"

The blood drains from my face as the name finally registers.

Edwin.

We'd worked together on an Econ 101 project, and he'd helped me understand the toughest parts of microeconomic analysis. More importantly, Edwin was a *nice* person, someone who had helped me without judgment or mockery.

"Wha-what happened?" I finally manage to ask in a trembling voice.

"They found him in the woods, Petra. Right past the track-and-field arena. One of the gardeners found him . . . It's all anyone's talking about."

My vision blurs as the thought of someone's *dead body*, that, too, of someone I used to know quite well, floods my mind and overwhelms me completely.

"I can't believe it," I whisper in a weak voice, automatically leaning against the cool metal of my locker.

"Me neither!" Claire cries out before a guy, one of the jocks from Ms. Matthews's class, stops beside her.

"Did you guys hear?" he asks, his expression stricken.

"About Edwin? Yes!" Claire exclaims, as if relieved to find someone else who might offer more words than I am coming up with.

"I heard the police are questioning people," the guy continues, looking at me.

Okay . . . why would he look at me while saying that?

My paranoia is already working overtime, so the tiniest look or gesture can set me off.

"And the teachers are trying to keep a lid on the whole thing," Claire adds, running her fingers through the mass of curls uncoiling atop her head.

"Huh, as if that will work," the guy scoffs back.

"I have to go," I hear myself say as I start walking away. "I left something in the . . ."

But neither Claire nor the guy is listening to me anymore, so I just stroll away without completing my sentence.

How could this happen? And why? Edwin had disappeared so suddenly that I didn't have a chance to ask why he left, but I never imagined anything like this.

"Hey, Petra," I hear someone else call out my name. It's Harry. "You okay?" he asks, and when I don't say anything, he continues, "I guess you heard about Edwin."

I shake my head, unable to find the right words.

"I . . . I knew him, Harry. We did a project together last year."

Harry's eyes widen. "Fuck!" he says in a soft voice.

We stand in painful silence for a few seconds.

"I'm so sorry," Harry begins again in an awkward tone. "This must feel so unreal to you."

"I don't really know, it's all so . . . I just found out that he was the one who dropped out of Art History."

Harry looks puzzled, unsurprisingly because he doesn't know that I had gotten Edwin's spot in the class instead.

Oh God. The reality of it sinks in deeper.

The thought that Edwin's death had inadvertently opened a door for me makes me feel sick and twisted with guilt.

"Do-do they know what happened?" I ask, not knowing what else to say.

"Not yet," Harry replies. "They're still investigating." The bell rings at that moment, and Harry says, "I gotta dash, Petra. But let me know if you need to talk or something."

He looks sincere when he offers to help, but I can only give him a grateful nod in return. After he leaves, I too force myself to move, to put one foot in front of the other, and head to class.

On the way, I get a message from Amelia.

Hey Petra, how you holding up?

Am I holding up? Am I barely managing to keep my head above water? I don't know, so I text back:

I'm fine, just busy with schoolwork.

Her reply is almost immediate.

Ah good, I was hoping to ask you something kinda personal . . .

Sure, what's up?

I text her back. Anything to get my mind off this hellish situation.

Her next message surprises me.

I was just wondering . . . Are you into anyone at school? Any guys? Or girls?

Why do you ask?

I fire back, not knowing how else to respond.

The last time we texted was tense, right? So I thought maybe I touched a nerve with my tactless questions.

Hmm, a plausible explanation. But Amelia and I always ask tactless questions; it's kind of our thing, being able to ask each other about the most personal bits of our lives without offering any explanation or context.

Yet that conversation really had been a bad one, so I text back, trying for a truce.

There's nobody like that, Ames. I just don't have the time for such things these days.

And besides, it's not like people are just lining up to date a grumpy teen mom-to-be. Of course, I don't tell her that last bit.

But you'll tell me? If there's someone special?

I stiffen a bit, thinking of my entanglement with Sin, even though *he* doesn't know about the most solid knot in the thin thread connecting us for now.

Course Ames, you know I will.

I send the text and take a deep breath, trying to center the swirling visions and restive thoughts assailing me.

Edwin's dead. He was around last week, and now he's not.

Harry was right: The whole situation feels more than unreal.

It feels like I'm living my own version of *The Truman Show* and at any moment, the people behind the scenes are going to jump out and tell me it was all scripted. Even the you-know-who and my whole trip to the pharmacy and my conversation with the lady at the counter.

A bitter chuckle escapes my lips as I tuck my phone back into my pocket. Regrettably, my life is all too real at the moment.

Over the course of the day, the whispers and murmurs in the hallways continue to grow and multiply, becoming more frantic and frayed as more gruesome details of Edwin's death begin to surface.

I'm ever-wary of the rumor mill, so instead of dwelling on the hushed exchanges that speculate about alien and mafia involvement, I head to the library.

But I am wrong to assume that the library would be a safe space.

Here, too, students huddle in tense, agitated groups, with the more dramatic ones bursting into tears while live-streaming to their followers.

I sit at one of the far tables, still trying to steady my breathing but failing to temper the growing dread in my chest.

A shadow falls over my table, and I look up to see Harry again. I know something is very, very wrong the moment I see him. His face is pale, and his eyes are darting everywhere.

"What happened?" I ask at almost the same time as he says, "Petra, have you heard the latest?" in a quivering voice.

I shake my head and repeat my question. "What?"

He glances around before sitting down next to me.

"I-I heard some of the faculty talking. Turns out . . . Edwin wasn't just found dead. He was—" He breaks off and wipes his face, as if trying to erase a nightmare that's still unfolding when he's awake.

"Harry, please!" I implore. "You're scaring me now."

"They say he was mutilated, Petra," Harry says at last.

My blood runs cold. "What do you mean?"

Harry runs his hands through his hair, and I notice that they are shaking slightly. "His chest . . . they said it was empty. Someone removed his organs." He finally looks me in the face, and I am stunned at the sheer horror permeating his features. " . . . and filled the cavity with dead rats."

At first, I let out a loud laugh, as if trying to dispel Harry's words with the force of my incredulity. But the sound dies on my lips when he keeps staring at me with unmitigated terror.

"No, that-that sounds fake. Just another messed-up rumor," I say firmly, shaking my head in disbelief.

"I thought so at first. But then the teachers were talking about it, Petra. This is not a rumor. I wouldn't have told you if I wasn't absolutely sure." Harry sits back and puts his face in his hands, like he's trying to rub out the garish, nightmarish images that keep springing up before his eyes.

My hand flies to my mouth as I try to process the enormity of Harry's news. The room seems to tilt, and bile starts crawling up my throat.

"Who . . . who would do something like that?" My voice comes out shaky, barely louder than a whisper.

"Who knows, Petra? This is some . . . sick fucking prank, but it's not a prank even. This is . . . it's beyond anything I could have imagined."

Claire joins us at that moment. Her face is ashen now compared to the hysterical energy that had animated her features when she had first told me of Edwin's death. She must have heard about the latest development.

But the facts are just too horrific to even be discussed out loud.

Instead, she asks, "Do the police have any suspects?"

Harry shakes his head. "Not that I've heard."

"Well, they can't keep a lid on this forever," Claire says indignantly. "Do they really think they can hide the . . . *horrific* things done to our classmate? Who the fuck are they kidding?"

This is her way of coping, I guess. Panic has turned to righteous anger.

As for me, nausea and dread are mixing into a lethal cocktail that sloshes around my insides. The grotesque detail of the rats makes it all the more disturbing.

It seems like the most twisted, neurotic thing to do. As if murdering a minor wasn't bad enough!

"I need some air," I say abruptly, standing up.

Claire just nods in return while Harry stands up quickly, saying, "Do you want me to come with you?"

"No," I reply with a smile that comes out looking like a grimace. "Thank you, but I must have a moment alone."

Harry falls back into the chair and looks almost relieved that he doesn't have to comfort me when clearly he's having a hard time wrapping his head around the horrid affair.

But I can't dwell on his fragile mental condition for much longer because the bile is back in my throat and my vision is getting hazy from tears.

Thankfully, there's a small courtyard in this quadrant of the campus, so I head there.

CHAPTER TWENTY-ONE

PETRA

Present Day

Wordless shock pilots my steps to the shaggy willow tree in the center of the courtyard. A woozy static makes my temples throb, and nausea makes it all so much worse.

Once I reach the tree, I kick off my shoes and dig my feet into the springy grass. It feels like a cool, prickly blanket and helps to finally calm my breathing. I take deep breaths to fight the general queasiness before popping an orange candy into my mouth. The clean citrus tang helps settle my stomach.

Not caring about how absurd or needlessly dramatic I may look, just standing barefoot on grass under a willow tree, I spend the next several minutes breathing deeply.

Just then, my phone pings. It's Amelia again.

So I also want to talk about this date I have tonight, she writes, as if still continuing the same conversation we were having before I had learned about . . . the rats. In Edwin's chest. Which had been hollowed out.

These recollections threaten to send me over the edge, so I force myself to focus on the words on the screen in my hands.

It's happening, Petra! I'm losing my v-card. It's high time.

I stare at the message for a while before the words start to make sense. What do I write back? What would a friend say in this situation?

Wow, Ames, that's a big step. Are you sure you're ready?

There, that sounds like a coherent enough response.

Yup, 100%. But I'm nervous lol.

Again, I surprise myself by reacting appropriately.

Yeah, that's understandable.

Got any advice? What was your first time like?

Again, I'm yanked into another unsettling memory: Blurry images and sensations from that night with Sin flood my mind, and I feel a knot tighten in my stomach. I type slowly, choosing my words carefully.

Tbh, I wish my first time had been better. Just . . . make sure you know what you want. I wish I did.

And still do.

This time, several minutes pass by before she writes back:

Thanks for that, Petra. Was it not good tho? Your first time?

Do I even remember enough of it to answer the question? And what about the result of that encounter, that "first time" that left such an indelible mark on my body?

All these unanswerable questions further swell the growing mass of despair in my heart, and I hold back a fresh stream of tears when I type:

Nothing like that. Just be careful, okay. Promise me you'll be safe.

I promise, Petra. Pinky promise.

She sends a string of heart and hug emojis. I put the phone away and return to my panicking senses.

I just need to breathe. I just need to center myself. I just need to *SCREAM AND SCREAM TILL I GO DEAF OR MUTE OR BOTH.* I just need to breathe. Just breathe.

And so, I keep standing under the willow tree, chanting to myself in a fruitless bid to calm down. Fruitless because in a few minutes, the PA system crackles, and a dull voice resounds in the air.

"Petra Valentine, please report to the principal's office."

My heart drops to my stomach, and my feet freeze in the grass.

What now?

How could a single day be full of so many unexpected incidents? Before I can rage against the universe, the same message blares over the speakers again, so I start putting on my shoes.

By the time I reach the principal's office, I have already been asked to do so thrice. The secretary, Mrs. Grenville, gestures for me to sit on a wooden bench outside the door. Inside, muffled voices are locked in a serious conversation.

I sit and twiddle my sweaty thumbs until the door swings open and Principal Rhodes steps out with a carefully blank face and says, "Petra, please come in. The detectives need to ask you a few questions."

Detectives? Questions? I can barely begin to process these words when I find myself inside Principal Rhodes's office, an old-fashioned affair in green leather and dark mahogany.

Don't panic, Petra, you haven't committed a crime. Unless getting knocked up as a teen is a crime.

The irony of that sentiment is not lost on me, so I almost crack a smile, but the sight of the two detectives in the room ensures it doesn't blossom fully on my face. Not to mention my *parents* and what they will think once they hear about this.

"Hi, Petra, I'm Detective Fiona Bedford, but feel free to call me Fiona," says the wavy-haired woman in a dark blue suit.

Medium in height but well-built with stately proportions, Fiona smells good too—something with vanilla and coffee—and for some reason, it helps me relax.

"And I'm Detective Phil Martinez," says the tall, lean man next to her. He's dressed in a gray suit that's a little too loose around the shoulders. But his face has a boyish charm, and his smile is friendly as he gestures me toward a chair next to Mr. Rhodes's desk.

"H-hi," I begin hesitantly before clearing my throat and using a firmer voice.

I am no criminal, and I have rights!

"Hi, Fiona and Phil. What is this about?" I ask, emulating my mother's tone while talking to the landscapers who regularly mess up her plans for the garden.

Perhaps my tone surprises them because they exchange a look before turning to me. "We won't beat around the bush, Petra," Fiona begins softly. "I trust you already know about Edwin Greenfield?"

This is about Edwin?

My brows furrow. "Yes . . . that he's dead. And . . . the rest. Whatever the rumors say," I finish lamely.

"You had a class with him last semester, right?" Phil continues.

"Yes, we were partners on a project."

Fiona starts making notes on a small pad.

"You two must have spent some time together. Care to tell us more about him?" Her tone has changed into a brisk, interrogative one.

"Sure. He was really smart, so he didn't have to do a lot of work on his half of the assignment. But instead of taking it easy, he—" I break off for a bit as the memory hits a tender spot in my heart. "He helped me with my portion of the project as well. And he never took credit for that either."

The detectives are nodding as I narrate. "And can you tell us about his other friends?" Phil asks when I fall silent. "Did he have any bullies or rivals or . . ."

"Or someone else who wanted him dead?" I blurt out and immediately reprimand myself. Being a smartass with the cops isn't advisable.

"Yeah," Fiona says with a little chuckle. "Something exactly like that."

"Honestly, I don't remember anyone being mean to him," I reply to the best of my recollection. "He was a good guy and had his own friend group.

We barely hung out outside of the project, so I couldn't tell you much about his social life either."

At this point, Principal Rhodes steps forward, clearing his throat. "Petra, sometimes the smallest details can help. So try your best to remember, will you? Even if something seemed insignificant at the time, it could be important now."

"No," I say, shaking my head slowly. "He seemed fine the last time we talked, but that was . . . months ago. I didn't know he had dropped out until this week." I shrug.

"Did you notice anything unusual about him recently?" Phil asks next. "Anything out of the ordinary?"

I rack my brain for anything that might help.

"He did mention once that his parents were strict, and he felt pressured by them to succeed. But I can't imagine how that can be connected to something like this."

Fiona's eyes narrow slightly. "Following up on that, did he ever mention feeling threatened or scared?"

"Not to me, he didn't," I reply with a sigh. "We weren't really that close."

"But just now you said he spoke to you about his parents?" Phil points out.

"So? Doesn't mean he had to confide everything to me," I snap back, feeling testy by now. They could be out talking to the kids Edwin actually hung out with instead of grilling me, but that's how cops work, I guess.

The detectives must have sensed the change in my tone and mood, because Fiona adds, "I know this must be very difficult, Petra, but we want to find the culprit as soon as possible. So, why don't you tell us everything you know?"

She has put on a pleasant expression meant to pacify me, but it's fake as shit, and two can play this game.

"I already told you everything I know," I reply in a cold voice. "And again, I haven't even spoken to him in months, so I fail to see why I have been summoned away from my classes to speak to law enforcement officers. In the absence of a guardian or an attorney, that, too," I address the last barb at Principal Rhodes, who knows the exact figure the school stands to lose if my parents learned how their daughter has been treated today.

Mr. Rhodes looks abashed while the detectives exchange another look before Fiona puts away her writing pad. "We understand how you feel, Petra," Phil begins in a sugary tone that annoys me to no end. "All we ask is that you let us know if you recall anything else that can help."

"We can tell that you admired him, Petra," Fiona adds gently, though my hackles are still raised against her. "And we know you want to help us find whoever did this to him." She stops and looks me in the eye. In that moment, I know I can trust her.

"Yes," I reply shakily. "I do."

"Good, here are my details. Call me if you remember anything." Fiona hands me a small card with her name and number on it.

"I will." I carefully put away the card in my bag and nod at her and Phil.

"Thank you, Petra. You've been very helpful," Phil says in a final-sounding tone, and I know the interrogation is over. For now.

As Principal Rhodes walks me to the door, he says, "Take care, Petra. I hope there are no hard feelings? Please remember that, given the circumstances, I must cooperate with the police."

"It's all right, Mr. Rhodes," I reply in a weary tone.

The day has taken a heavy toll on my mind and body, and I just want to get away for now. But the conversation lingers with me, right alongside the haunting images of Edwin's mangled body.

As I head toward my next class, my classmates' whispers and looks are added to the pile, but I push through. I have one more class until the end of the day, and I am capable enough to survive without having a public meltdown.

I haven't fallen that far.

CHAPTER TWENTY-TWO

PETRA

The Past
27 March 1896

The day before the supposed ritual, I'm consumed by anger, fear, and paralyzing anxiety. My father is nowhere to be found, and I can't stop wondering—where is he? What is he doing?

And while it's still daylight outside, I'm locked inside the house, shut off from the world, clueless about what might be unfolding.

Is my father putting his plan into motion? Is Sin in danger?

And then I catch myself, and I scold myself for even thinking such things.

Why should I care anymore? He treated the entire situation like a game, laughed at my warnings, and demanded something I should've never given. All for what? A promise that he wouldn't take part in that obscene ritual? A vow as flimsy as his morals?

He spoke of free will, didn't he? If he truly wanted to listen, he could have. He didn't need to barter for a kiss. And worse than him, *worse*, is me. I should never have agreed.

And yet . . .

When I got back last night, slipping inside just as easily as I'd slipped out, I tried to sleep, but I couldn't. My thoughts kept spiraling back to that kiss.

He was right: It awakened something inside me. Something I don't have a name for. Something new and frightening and far too consuming.

I can still feel it—his lips, his hands, the heat of it. That kiss. *My first kiss.*

No, my inner voice corrects me, it was only *a quarter* of a kiss.

If *that* was a quarter . . . then what is a full kiss?

He was going to devour me, wasn't he? That deranged man was ready to claim me, body and soul, in the name of a kiss. And perhaps I'm the more unhinged one because I can't stop thinking about it. One taste of something forbidden, and now it's all I can think of.

I pace my room, restless, unable to sit still. I wait, achingly alert, for any sound from below. Any sign that my father has come home. I *need* to know what happened.

But it doesn't come. And so, I spend another night plagued by devilish dreams of a man named Sin and his sinful lips.

The next day, my father fails to return again. As the sun descends in the sky and the cloak of darkness covers everything in sight, my anxiety becomes unbearable.

All pretense of not caring disappears as I keep thinking about Sin, about whether he is all right, about whether he was *there*, summoning that creature. About whether . . . he sold his soul. And whether my father and his cronies fulfilled their macabre plan.

Another dilemma appears in my mind: Do I *want* my father to find them? Prevent them from summoning that entity? Or do I want them to get away and be successful?

I don't know anymore. I only know that I do not *want* to see that infuriating man hurt. No matter how angry I still am at him, I just want him to be safe.

It's not until late that night, long after we've retired, that I hear the front door creak open.

My father heads straight to his study, and a few others follow. I strain to hear and recognize the voices of some congregation members. And then . . . him. The strange man from before. The one who was plotting something alongside my father.

I wait. When the house is quiet enough, I slip out of my room again, my steps careful and silent. I tiptoe down the hallway, getting as close to the study door as I dare. I press myself to the wall and listen.

"They should have been there," my father says, frustration sharp in his voice. "I had it on good authority they would be. One of the students in that seminar told me everything. They *should* have been there."

I hear the sound of his fist slamming against the desk.

"They must have found out about our plan somehow," the other man says. "Either your source lied to you, or someone tipped them off."

"No," my father replies firmly. "He wouldn't lie to me. He's a good friend—I've known him since he was a boy. I trust him. If the plan failed, it wasn't because of him."

"Then someone else must've warned them," the man counters.

"But who?" another voice chimes in. "Only the five of us here knew about it."

"I don't know," the first man says. "But someone must have leaked it. Otherwise, why would they suddenly change the ritual's location at the last minute? It doesn't make sense unless someone gave them a warning."

No. No, no, no . . .

I swallow hard and begin inching away from the door, quiet as I can. Now that they're suspecting an insider, the last thing I need is for them to catch me eavesdropping outside the study. My heart pounds as I slip back upstairs, careful not to make a sound.

Still, I can't help the small rush of relief. Whatever their suspicions, the truth remains—*I* stopped the plan. Sin wasn't harmed. And more importantly, my father and his men didn't commit a grave sin themselves.

Right?

At least, that's what I tell myself as I lie in bed and try to fall asleep.

29 March 1896

ON SUNDAY, EVERYONE gathers for church. As is tradition, the members of our congregation meet at the designated spot to walk in procession toward the chapel. It's a custom older than I am, meant to strengthen our bonds by giving us time to speak before and after the sermon.

But today feels different.

My family walks in silence toward the meeting place. My father is still tense from last night's events. He doesn't speak a word. My brother, too, seems on edge—his jaw tight, his movements rigid.

I say nothing, not daring to break the silence, especially after hearing how furious my father had been about his failed plans.

My mother, of course, remains oblivious.

It's my brother who keeps drawing my attention. I remember my father mentioning that he had shown curiosity about the university students dabbling in the occult. Watching him now—his tight shoulders, clenched hands—I wonder if he might be the "source" of information my father had referred to.

Had he made friends at the university? Had they told him something?

My thoughts scatter when we reach the assembly point.

Something is wrong.

Only about half the usual number of people are there. At this hour, the spot should be full. My father scans the area, his expression darkening.

"Where is everyone?" he snaps at one of the elders.

"I don't know," the man replies, brows furrowed. "I've been wondering the same thing. This isn't like them. These are good, loyal people. They wouldn't just stay home."

Something must have happened.

At those words, I watch the color drain from my father's face. He parts his lips slightly and hurriedly makes the sign of the cross over his chest and forehead.

"Dear Lord," he mutters. "This is what I feared from the beginning. This is the end of our congregation. It's happened."

My brother steps closer to him and whispers something I can't quite catch. But from the way they begin speaking in hushed, urgent tones, I can guess what they're thinking: that the reason half the congregation is missing must be tied to the ritual they believe happened last night.

"We must act," my father says suddenly, turning toward the other elders. "We must not let this stand. This is because of *them*, those pagans, those demons—"

He doesn't get to finish.

A young boy, maybe thirteen or fourteen, comes sprinting toward us. I've seen him at service before. His face is flushed, his breath ragged.

"Oi! Oi!" he shouts. "It's bad. It's really bad!"

"What is it, Michael?" one of the men asks, stepping forward. "Where's your family? Why aren't they here?"

Michael stops in front of us, catching his breath. When he sees my father, his eyes widen.

"Oh my God, Mr. Jeremiah, you're here, too. Come quick. The reverend—he's in the town square!"

"Town square?" My father frowns. "He should be here for the procession."

"No, no." The boy shakes his head, breathless. "You have to see it. You *must* come. It's bad."

"Speak, child, what is it?" my father demands.

"My father said you have to see it for yourself. So you'll believe it."

With a tired sigh, my father starts after the boy. The rest of the congregation follows, so I fall in step, too, along with my mother. We walk for nearly twenty minutes, the mood heavy, silent—until we reach the square.

Just like the last time I was here, there's a crowd gathered at the center, a thick ring of people encircling something. Low murmurs ripple through the air, words like *blasphemy*, *devil's work*, and *sacrilege*.

We press forward.

One by one, those reaching the front drop to their knees, making the sign of the cross, clasping their hands in urgent prayer as they lift their eyes to the sky. I push forward, unable to stop myself, needing to see what has brought everyone to their knees.

But nothing could have prepared me for what I find.

There, beside the obelisk—the long-standing cultural symbol of our town—lie bodies. Corpses. Young men, lined up in neat, deliberate rows.

Dead.

At first glance, there must be over two dozen of them, all no older than thirty. All killed brutally. The breath leaves my lungs in a sharp exhale, and my knees buckle beneath me. My legs tremble with shock.

And I'm not the only one.

All around me, people faint. Women wail. Some try to shield their children's eyes. Others kneel, whispering prayers through tears.

Seeing it in daylight makes it all the more horrifying. The bloodless bodies, the gaping wounds at their throats—clean, deliberate. My first thought is the ritual.

My second: *Did Sin participate?*

Is he among them?

I push forward, trying to get closer, even as my stomach churns. The front rows are filled with men from the congregation—eyes fixed, praying loudly, condemning what they see. I inch forward, scanning the bodies, trying to study each face, even as bile rises in my throat.

One.

Two.

Three . . .

I stop counting at twenty-five.

Twenty-five corpses. All young men. All drained of blood, each with a puncture wound at the jugular—clean, precise, like a ceremonial knife had been used.

The way they're arranged, positioned around the obelisk like spokes of a wheel, feels intentional. Ritualistic. This wasn't chaos. This was *planned.*

But . . . how?

Sin never said anything about death. About *sacrifice.* He never said the ritual would involve this.

Then again . . .

He never told you, a voice whispers inside me. *And you never pressed him about what the ritual would require.*

He told me he couldn't say. And I let that be enough.

Is this why? Because people were going to die?

Because they were going to *kill* themselves?

Who did this?

Did they sacrifice themselves?

Did the entity kill them?

Did someone else?

If they sold their souls for wishes . . . why are they dead? Shouldn't they have gotten what they wanted?

No. Something is *wrong* here. This isn't some university experiment gone wrong.

This is murder.

And the worst part is—

I'm afraid to ask who's responsible.

Afraid to know who is *guilty* of this.

"He's not among the dead," my father's voice reaches my ears.

I quickly gather my bearings and inch closer to where he's standing, keeping my head down, veil covering my eyes in a sign of submission.

"Then there's only one explanation," an elder says, someone whose voice I recognize from my father's study.

"He must have done it. He must have killed them for that demonic sacrifice," he adds.

He? Who? Not Sin, right?

The reverend finds my father, his expression just as grim.

"We must fight back," he says with determination, and a shiver runs down my spine. More violence.

My father grunts. "If you'd have listened to me, it wouldn't have gotten to this."

"When you came to me with your concerns, I thought you were overreacting. Misplaced worry. But now . . ." he shakes his head. "I see

I should have listened. And I'm sorry for that. I can't turn back time. I can't undo what's been done. And seeing these young men lying here like this . . ."

His voice cracks.

"You have no idea how deeply this wounds me. And I carry some of the guilt for letting it come to this."

"We can still act," my father insists, stepping forward. "We have the numbers on our side."

"What are you saying?" the reverend asks.

My father straightens. "Gather the men. All of them. Everyone over the age of fourteen. Bring them to the designated place." There's steel in his voice now. "We're going to drive this evil out of our town. *Now.*"

"But . . . *he* wouldn't still be here, would he? Not after this? Not with the town already suspicious?" the reverend echoes.

I edge closer, straining to catch every word.

Who is this "he" they're talking about?

The implication is heavy—*Sin*. *My* Sin.

The thought hits like a stone to the chest. Could he really be responsible for this? Could he be the hand behind this massacre?

Something breaks inside me at the idea.

The image of his mouth, of his kiss, still lingers in my mind—tender, warm. *Not savage.* And yet . . .

"No, he's still here," my brother says suddenly, cutting through my thoughts. "He's holding a lecture right now."

"That damn Arnoult the First's going to pay," my father growls. "We're taking our town back. And we'll drive those devil worshippers out once and for all."

Arnoult? Who is Arnoult?

BREAKING NEWS

Radcliffe Herald

30 MARCH 1896

ST. ANSELM HALL UNIVERSITY TO CLOSE DOWN INDEFINITELY

After a number of complaints from eminent members of the Radcliffe council, St. Anselm Hall University has been closed down indefinitely. Rumors of involvement in the occult and satanic rituals have plagued the eminent university for decades, but with the latest events, the University's Board has announced it would perform a thorough investigation into its faculty and students.

SATANIC RITUAL GONE WRONG: TWENTY-FIVE MEN DEAD

The corpses of twenty-five students from the illustrious St. Anselm Hall University have been found in Radcliffe's town square, all drained of blood. The evidence points to a satanic ritual. This is not the first time the University has been embroiled in scandals surrounding the teaching of the occult. There is an investigation pending, and more details are expected to emerge when the police catch those responsible.

PROFESSOR OF THEOLOGY OR DEMON WHISPERER?

Three names associated with the Theology Department of St. Anselm Hall have emerged as high interest after the ritualistic murders in the town square. Mr. Arnoult, Mr. Kimaris, and Mr. Haas have not been sighted since the horrific events that occurred on Saturday night. Mr. Arnoult, an eccentric but well-regarded academic in his field, is at the center of this controversy as rumors have started to spread about his peculiar interests in the occult, the monthly soirees he hosted with his students and out-of-town occult enthusiasts, and his claim to be able to speak with the dead. Not much is known about Mr. Kimaris.

CHAPTER TWENTY-THREE

PETRA

Present Day

I must be more traumatized by Edwin's passing than I realized. Hearing the details of his sadistic murder did not help at all, and now I find myself dreaming of the strangest pagan rituals and satanic sacrifices.

Even the prospect of Ms. Matthews's spirited lectures cannot pull me out of the trenches. The very hallways of the school seem darker, and the sky grows more overcast as well.

My conversation with Fiona and Phil sits heavily on my shoulders, and I feel like I'm moving through a fog. Yet my surroundings are as animated as ever. Even as I find my seat and start taking out my things, whispers echo around me, and I catch bits and pieces of conversations that make my skin crawl.

"—some sort of satanic ritual," a girl is saying. "Just trust me. It has to be connected to the Society."

"What's that?" another student asks.

The girl—Sierra's her name, I think—replies, "The Ouroboros Society. Haven't you heard of them? The admins on St. Anselm Hive always post about them close to Halloween."

"Yeah, I heard about that," another voice cuts in. "It's almost Halloween, right? Maybe it's a sacrifice for the Ouroboros Society."

"Excuse me," says the same voice that had responded to Sierra the first time. "Who or what are the Ouroboros Society?"

A secret society, I want to respond, but don't have to because Sierra says as much.

"They were formed in the 1800s, apparently. And get this"—her voice drops lower, as if trying to heighten suspense—"their 150th anniversary is coming up *this year*! And the same year Edwin turns up dead and stuffed with rats? That *cannot* be a coincidence."

Though I'm disgusted by the way she speaks of Edwin, the hairs on my neck stand on end when I realize that the truth will probably be way worse than whatever tale Sierra Nelson cooks up.

"No way," another girl gasps as the blood drains from her face. She actually believes this local legend nonsense. "You mean like those secret cults you see in horror movies?"

Yeah, right, like St. Anselm Hall is cool enough to have its own Midsommar *staged in these hallowed halls.* My annoying inner voice is back in full force, and even outwardly, I don't bother to hide my scorn for all the melodramatic theories. Yet the fact that my mind conjured up something similar in my nightmare gives me pause.

"Exactly," Sierra says with not a shred of irony, bless her. "And get this—there were similar murders exactly a hundred years ago. Bodies found all torn up and missing organs and all their blood."

Well, at least there's that—in my dream, the bodies were *only* drained of blood.

As if that makes it any better.

"Dude, that's fucking *insane*," another guy whispers. "And you're saying it's happening again?"

The talk is getting really cheap at this point, so I try to focus on my iPad instead, jotting down random lines and observations about today's reading material to keep my mind occupied. But the chatter in the classroom is impossible to ignore, each horrific theory gaining wind and swirling around like a dark cloud.

I bury my face in my hands. Edwin's death is becoming a grotesque piece of gossip, and it feels so wrong and disrespectful to the memory of that sweet boy.

I take deep breaths again, trying to block out the voices around me.

At that blessed moment, the teacher finally enters, and the room eventually settles down. The rest of the class passes in a similar subdued vein, and I do my best to pay attention. In another half hour, the lunch bell rings, and I'm happy to put some space between myself and the chatty Sierra.

"And everyone in Radcliffe knows about the Society, too. I've heard my parents talk about them when they think I'm asleep," she's saying to the group gathered around her.

I shake my head and stride toward the cafeteria. Maybe I will feel less homicidal toward that mouthy idiot after I've eaten some bread.

Then again, the cafeteria resounds with its own cacophony of conversation and clattering dishes.

My nerves still on edge, I pile a tray with French toast and fruits, some of the safer foods that my sensitive stomach can handle these days, and scan the room for a familiar face.

That's when I spot Harry near the buffet. He catches my eye and waves me over. I'm only too happy to comply.

"Hey, Petra," he says as I approach. "Want to sit together?"

I nod gratefully. "Yeah, that'd be nice."

We find a table near the back of the cafeteria. There is less noise here, and the ugly gossip doesn't quite reach my ears.

"I heard the announcement yesterday," Harry begins. "What happened?"

"Oh, you know, the usual," I respond in a frustrated voice, finally glad to be asked a normal question. "I got called to the principal's office so the detectives investigating Edwin's death could interrogate me about the time we spent together and if I knew who might have killed him so brutally and if I could just give them the culprit's IG or Twitter handle, that'd be great, too."

Harry's eyes widen, and then his face changes color when he realizes I'm not entirely serious. "Why would they interrogate you, though? You just had *one* class with him."

"I don't know! That's why it was so irritating." I take an angry bite of the fluffy French toast and almost immediately feel better. "It's just been rough," I continue. "All the rumors and then the graphic details . . . it's all just too much."

Not to mention my dreams that are riddled with satanic rituals and charming rakes that want to sell their soul to the devil for a kiss.

I take another bite of my toast, the dream-memory of that kiss suddenly rising in my brain.

"Yeah, no, this whole situation is beyond messed up," Harry replies. Though he has selected an appetizing dish of baked ziti, he's barely eaten any of it. I don't have any bracing words to offer, so we just sit in silence for a while.

But soon I notice a flurry of voices whispering very close to us, and not long after, I see that Sin has just entered the cafeteria with a bunch of his friends.

Even though the girls and guys around him are talking and joking among themselves, his eyes are fixed on me, or rather, on me *with* Harry.

Again, a dark pool—of malice? or anger—glistens in his eyes. I feel my skin prickle at the expression on his face. So singular is his focus, so concentrated is his gaze, that even the crowd can sense its tangible presence.

Though they can't pinpoint the exact source of tension in the room, the senses of this mob, which is composed of incredibly spoiled teenagers with a greater-than-average penchant for casual cruelty, are finely attuned enough to detect an incoming tussle.

The SAH crowd loves nothing more than a messy spectacle.

"Petra, I've been thinking—" Harry begins, but stops abruptly. Because he has also sensed the shift in the general mood.

Following my line of sight, he sees Sin making his way over to our table with purposeful strides. Instantly, Harry tenses beside me.

What the fuck, what the fuck, what the fuck—

"Harry, is it?" Sin's chilly words cut into my inner monologue. "Can I talk to Petra for a sec? Alone?"

Harry turns to me, as if he's trying to show that he only cares about what *I* want in this situation.

"Is something wrong, Petra?" he says in a level voice.

Sin's the one who replies. "I need to speak with her," he says in a crisper tone than before. "*Privately.*"

I see the confusion and underlying fear on Harry's face.

"Sin," I interject here, a barely veiled impatience in my voice, "what's so important that it can't wait?"

When Sin glances at me, his expression softens slightly, but the hard lines on his face don't relax fully.

"Please, Petra. It's important."

Harry hesitates for a second more and then reluctantly stands up. "Okay, Petra, if you're sure. I'll . . . catch you later," he finishes in a sheepish tone, giving me a questioning look.

"Thanks, Harry," I try to reassure him with a small smile.

Sin sits down the moment Harry walks away. His eyes follow Harry like a hawk before turning back to me. The kids around us are furiously whispering among themselves, and Sin's friends look pretty annoyed, but Sin's gaze stays focused on me.

"Sin, what are you doing?" I'm beyond pissed at the scene this man is creating, so I try to infuse each word with the utmost derision I can muster. And why does he have to look so good? With his hair perfectly tousled, and his lips plump and inviting, and—

No, no, we're not going there!

Yet the fact that he looks identical to the man from my dreams makes the situation worse. The memory of our night together at Elias's party is now gaining depth with the addition of these new emotions from my dreams. Where the alcohol-clouded kisses we shared might be a little fuzzy, the dream kiss was *not*. It was . . .

I squeeze my eyes shut. Fuck this and fuck him, and while we're at that, fuck my idiotic brain, too, for conjuring up those dreams.

"Petra," Sin begins in a voice thickened with some ineffable emotion. "Look, I'm really sorry about the other night. I didn't mean for things to escalate like that."

I cross my arms tightly, not giving him an ounce of sympathy. "Sin, you can't just scare off my friends and demand that I talk to you."

Seriously, who the hell does he think he is?

"I know," Sin replies with an agonized expression. "I shouldn't have done that. I know I can be overbearing. And I'm sorry for that. I just really wanted to tell you—"

I guess I will never find out what he wanted to tell me at that moment because his words are drowned out by a loud comment from a nearby table.

"Whoa, Sin Arnoult is wooing Petra Valentine. Isn't he scared his dick will freeze off from her frost?"

The remark is followed by snickers and sharp laughter as St. Anselm Hall's students display their mettle—and taste—for jokes of the lowest possible caliber. Even then, I wince because the cruel words hit home.

But Sin looks positively thunderous, and his jaw tightens. Before I can react, he stands up abruptly. The room falls silent, and the whispering voices are completely cut off.

"Listen up," Sin says, and the edge in his voice could have beheaded a thousand French nobles. "I know you all like to gossip, but if I ever hear *anyone* say *anything* bad about Petra Valentine again, I'll make you pay for it—and *dearly*."

He looks around the cafeteria with fire in his eyes, and I notice some of the students sitting closer to us physically flinch away from his gaze.

"Consider this your only warning," he finishes in the same low voice, which almost sounds like a leonine growl, and sits down. As if he was used to commanding entire roomfuls of people to do his bidding.

Even after he sits down, the silence remains unbroken for a while. The entire cafeteria seems to be holding its breath. The sheer menace in Sin's tone has spooked me, as well. Some people exchange nervous glances. Others are suddenly very interested in their trays, which are mostly clean anyway.

"Sin," I whisper in shock. I'm undeniably stunned and scrambling for words as I sputter, "Sin, you didn't have to—"

"Yes, I did," he cuts me off firmly, but his eyes are softer when he looks at me. "You deserve better than their pettiness."

I am even more bereft of words because nobody, *nobody*, has ever defended me like that. For as long as I can remember, I have always had to come to my own defense—hence my allegedly thick skin and aloof demeanor.

Yet Sin had declared his allegiance toward me so boldly, so fearlessly, that I'm once again captivated by his chivalry.

The murmurs of the cafeteria gradually do restart, but there's a noticeable slump in their flow now, like everyone's too afraid to say anything too loud. I catch a few girls glaring at me, but I lift my chin in open disdain. To hell with the lot of them!

"Thank you," I tell Sin in a soft voice. "Th-that was nice of you."

"You deserve to be treated with respect, Petra," Sin insists again, "and I was only doing what's right. Don't think of it as a favor, please."

The remaining tension in my chest loosens slightly. Still, I can't completely forget how Sin had menaced Harry just a while back. He needs to know that grand gestures don't always absolve him of his occasional tendency to strong-arm others.

Before I can say as much, a wave of nausea hits me out of nowhere. Or maybe my body has been sending me warning signals that have gone unnoticed amidst all the conflicts and confrontations.

Either way, I know I won't be able to hold it in.

"I have to go—" I gasp before bolting down the hallway toward the nearest bathroom. Why must this happen to me in front of Sin? Why must he always catch me in my most vulnerable physical states?

The questions mix with the other bilious swirl surging along my food pipe, and once again, I barely make it to the toilet in time.

Of course, my body being unused to these sudden onslaughts of sickness,

I am overwhelmed enough to not notice when the bathroom door creaks open or when sharp footsteps ricochet against the walls.

When I exit the stall slowly, my legs shaking ever so slightly and my hair disheveled, Daphne is fixing her hair at the mirror.

She glances at me with her usual expression of disgust until she notices how pale my face looks.

"Rough day, huh?" she says, her tone light. "Or maybe you're bulimic?"

I ignore her and start fixing myself. The cold water helps me feel better, but Daphne can't stand anyone looking comfortable in her vicinity, so she says, "Oh, please, don't tell me someone knocked you up! Is Petra prego?"

She starts laughing at her own apparently clever quip.

But I do something stupid. I flinch, unwittingly and *very visibly*, at her last taunt.

Daphne may be obnoxiously oblivious to everyone's feelings, but her sharp eyes widen in realization when she sees my reaction. The laughter stops abruptly. She turns toward me and starts clicking her heels.

"My, my, what do we have here?" Her voice is slippery with poison, and her eyes narrow as she steps closer. "I touched a nerve, didn't I? Little Miss Better-Than-Us has a bun in the oven!"

Before I can tell her to fuck off, the bathroom door flies open with a loud bang. Sin rushes inside, eyes askance with worry.

"Petra! Are you okay?" he demands, rushing to my side.

Daphne takes a step back, her eyes darting between Sin and me. "Whoa, Sin, calm down! She isn't the delicate damsel you think she is."

My heart starts racing as I realize that Daphne is infinitely petty and calculating. If she has indeed understood that her joke is very real to me, she will use that information in the worst way imaginable.

Sin ignores her and steps toward me.

"Hey, what's going on? Why didn't you tell me you were feeling this bad?"

Behind him, Daphne continues to smirk at me, and the ghastliest question presents itself: *Will she tell him right now*?

CHAPTER TWENTY-FOUR

PETRA

Present Day

Daphne is not your typical Mean Girl; she doesn't bully openly or oppress people in ways that can be directly traced back to her. No, she likes to play with her prey and make them second-guess her intentions till the last moment.

I'm no exception, it seems.

"Oh, Sin, I didn't know Petra was sick!" she cries out dramatically as Sin hovers over me, inspecting my body for any signs of distress.

"I am *not* sick," I correct her furiously before turning to Sin. "And you can't be in here."

Behind him, a gaggle of girls loiter near the door of the washroom, some looking interested and enraptured by the whole debacle, while others look uncertain and uncomfortable at Sin's presence.

Perhaps all the eyes boring into him do leave a mark because Sin straightens up and looks around, and I can *see* him put on one of his disarming smiles.

"Sorry, ladies, just checking up on a friend!" he says gallantly. "I'll be out of your lair pretty soon."

"The expression is 'out of your hair,' Sin," I mutter slyly.

He gives me a dazzling smile and a wink.

Then he *finally* acknowledges Daphne's existence. "I need you to leave, Daphne darling," he tells her.

At this turn of events, the group near the restroom door starts murmuring. Daphne looks like she wants to punch someone in the neck.

"I'm not done, Sin," she says with a pout.

"Yes, you are," Sin replies firmly. And that's that.

Daphne throws me a vile look and saunters out of the restroom.

In a few more moments, the small group near the door has also melted away, and I am alone once more with Sin.

The relief of not having the cover blown off my secret is short-lived because Sin is saying something. I force myself to pay attention and hear.

" . . . really sorry about everything. Look, can we have a do-over?"

He's almost pleading now.

"Please, Petra. I know I've been a lot to handle, but I can do better. I want to be a good partner to you." My head snaps up at those last words, so he hurries to add, "A good *project partner* to you. I know I have been delaying our work on Ms. Matthews's assignment—"

"A do-over?" I finally manage to get some words in. "Sin, after everything—"

"Please," he says again, his expression quite earnest. "I know of a place where we can conduct research. It's quiet, secluded, and it honestly might help us get an outright A+. Do you know how rarely Ms. Matthews gives those out?"

"What place? What are you talking about?"

"The crypt of St. Anselm Hall." Sin's eyes glitter with real delight, as if he has pulled the cover off the most original magic trick.

"The crypt," I repeat in a scoffing tone. "Like the crypt where the infamous Ouroboros Society used to meet underneath the school? You expect me to fall for that?"

"I know everyone says it's just a rumor, but the place is real! It dates back to the late 1800s."

Sin's face is as animated now as it had been cold when he warned the entire school against bullying me.

"It's mostly sealed off, but there are ways inside for those who know the Ouroboros Society's true history."

"True history?" I snap back in complete disbelief. "That would apply to an actual cult or secret society."

Sin doesn't say anything in return but just smiles at me.

"No way!" I exclaim. Sin nods excitedly, so I say, "No way the Society is real. Fuck off, Sin!"

"Now, the crypt I'm talking about," Sin continues, as if I did not just express my utter refusal to accept this tall tale, "it's got a secret entry. Well, not really secret because it's splat in the middle of the east wing, in plain sight, actually. But anyways, I stumbled upon it during freshman year. It's an amazing place, Petra. There are old paintings on the walls, all kinds of spooky stuff we could use for our project."

Now, I know that St. Anselm Hall is filled with the children of very wealthy and very immoral people. The campus has been around forever, and there could be secret rooms, walls, and entire floors of the building that have now been sealed off to the general public.

Despite my reservations about the whole thing, I feel a surge of curiosity.

"Okay, Sin. Let's do this," I say, biting my lip. "Show me this crypt."

Sin's tense posture relaxes slightly, and a wider smile breaks through.

"Great. We'll need to go after classes. Don't want to be seen by too many people. Let's meet by the eastern wing at dusk. Do you know the willow tree in the middle of that courtyard?"

"Of course I do!"

"Perfect," Sin says. "Trust me, Petra. This will be worth it."

AFTER I'M DONE with classes, I head for the willow tree. I haven't spent much time in that part of the campus, so I'm genuinely curious about Sin's plan. Yet as I reach the thick canopy of the willow, I can't help wondering whether a part of me also wants to spend more time with Sin.

He's already standing under the thickest part of the arboreal canopy.

"I love this tree," he says, looking up and taking a deep breath. "It's got a very calming presence."

"Right, Sin, where is this crypt you were talking about?" I'm impatient to either get to this secret place or force Sin to confess that he has made up the whole thing.

"Come this way," Sin replies, beckoning me to the spot he's standing on. He looks down, and so do I. "See it yet?" he asks after a couple of minutes.

At first, I don't know what I'm looking for, but then one of the last departing sun rays of the day falls on the ground where we stand, and I catch a faint glint of something under the loose soil near the willow's roots.

"What's that?" I bend down at the same time as Sin.

"Ta da!" He swipes the dirt off the spot to reveal a chipped granite block embedded in the soil.

What had caught my eye was a polished onyx arrow etched into this gray block.

"And when we follow the arrow . . ." Sin says next to me, nudging my gaze along the length of his outstretched arm. I follow his pointing finger to see a small corridor branching off the back of the classroom that opens into this courtyard.

"I thought that corridor ended in a broom closet," I say as we move through the classroom and enter the dusty hallway.

"Yeah, me too," Sin replies with a glimmer of amusement in his eyes.

Soon, he takes me through a series of passages connected through decrepit stairs that have always looked like they lead nowhere.

Yet here we are, turning and climbing down, deeper into the bowels of St. Anselm Hall. After around five such flights of stairs, we finally reach a very unassuming wooden door that looks like it hasn't been touched in decades.

Sin produces a key, and soon the metal scrapes against the lock's ancient mechanisms until it finally clicks open.

"Here we go," he says quietly, pushing the door open.

The air is cooler here, and the scent of damp stone and earth makes it seem like we are underwater. This place looks like a set straight out of an *Indiana Jones* movie.

The walls are made of rough-hewn stone, all of them covered in a thin layer of moisture. It is dark enough that we have to switch on our phone lights. I realize that the space is vast, with alcoves branching off into the shadows.

"This is not real," I whisper in awe at one point. "It can't be."

"Almost there," Sin replies with a delighted voice that sounds strangely out of place in this somber setting.

After a couple more steps, we reach a section of the crypt where the walls look even older. Splashes of color catch my eye, and soon, the faded outlines of intricate scenes start taking shape.

I step closer, squinting to make out the details in the dim light.

"What do you think?" Sin asks, his voice a soft echo.

"It's incredible," I breathe, moving along the wall.

The lines are simple yet disproportionate, while the brush strokes can only be described as frenzied. At first, it looks like the various scenes on the crypt's walls depict events from medieval life.

But when I step closer, and when I look more attentively, I see something else—something very unsettling.

As my eyes adjust to the lighting in the crypt, I notice that certain drawings depict horrendous events. One of them freezes me on the spot: On the wall, the sinister lines curve and straighten to depict a human figure with its chest torn open and the resultant cavity filled with rats.

I gasp and shout, "Sin, look at this!" before I can stop myself.

"What is it?" he asks, stepping closer.

"Look at this! Don't you see? It's exactly like how they found . . . Edwin's body."

"Fuck!" Sin exclaims as his eyes widen in recognition. "Fuck, you're right!"

"What does this mean, Sin? This isn't one of your pranks, right? Or so help me God, Sin, if it's some kind of joke—"

I'm stepping away from him, and I'm rambling because my life has gone topsy-turvy of late, and now I'm in an underground room and there are murderous paintings on the wall.

"Petra, no!" Sin cries out, his face pale and his body shaking. "What are you even saying? I never even looked at the paintings properly before today. This . . . I don't know what the fuck this is!"

"Then tell me what you *do* know!" I demand in a surprisingly firm tone.

"Just that the Ouroboros Society was formed in the 1800s, and that they were initially a theological society searching for answers beyond what the Bible taught," Sin replies hurriedly. "Petra, please, believe me! I just thought these are cool ancient paintings of harvest festivals or something."

"Then why would someone paint something like this?" I ask again. "What are you not telling me?"

Sin takes a deep breath. "Petra, I only know what my family and other adults told me growing up. St. Anselm Hall University—it was a university back then—had one of the most prestigious departments of theology in the country. But at some point, their study veered toward the . . . unorthodox. It's said that a group of professors and students made a deal with a demon."

As he speaks, we continue walking along the dank walls, the meager light from our phones weakly illuminating cloaked figures on the wall. Despite a part of me that's not convinced by even one word uttered by Sin so far, my heart is pounding, and my hands feel cold.

University. Rituals. Department of Theology.

Why is this so similar to my dreams?

"They performed sacrifices," Sin continues, his voice barely more than a whisper, "because they believed—or read somewhere—that it would please the demon they were . . . summoning. It's said that every few decades, these rituals have to be repeated."

"So, what we're seeing on these walls," I begin nervously, "are depictions of those rituals?"

"I suppose so. That's the only explanation. *And* it fits the timeline. This year would mark the 150th anniversary of the society, right?"

When I glance back at the painting of the hollowed-out figure filled with rats, the gnawing feeling in the pit of my stomach intensifies. "Edwin . . . he was part of it, then. A sacrifice?"

"Looks that way," Sin replies grimly. "But the question is—who's continuing these rituals now?"

"But why would anyone even want to continue doing stuff like this?" I ask, my voice trembling. "Aren't we past that kind of superstition?"

"Power, Petra," Sin whispers softly—and is there the slightest hint of longing in his voice?

"Even if the demon wasn't real, some of the people involved with the University did end up becoming quite wealthy. And even now, they are some of the richest, most influential people in Radcliffe."

We have turned a corner to arrive at the left arm of the room's semicircle expanse. Sin stops beside another ebony-rich, Goyaesque painting whose palette of deep blacks and rusty reds suggests a kind of barbarism I can't even imagine but that I can sense quite vividly.

The weak beams of our phone lights fall on a scene of robed figures standing in a circle around a shadowy, spectral form at the center. I'm halted in my tracks at the ghostly figure's face: a smooth orb of a head with large black eyes and a bloody gash for a smile. A smile that will eat into my already thinning sleep and latch on to even more of my dreams now.

"Tha-that's the demon?"

I don't need to look at Sin to know that he's nodding or that he looks spooked out of his brains.

"According to what I heard, the first murder spree began sometime in the 1890s, and although some people were accused of those crimes, people suspect that some got away with it or were never accused in the first place."

"What do you mean?" I frown.

"There were people who were said to be directly involved who disappeared and were never brought to justice. But there were also people who were on the Board of Trustees of the University who, soon after it closed, became extremely rich."

"But that doesn't mean anything," I say, the skeptic in me rising to the surface. "It could all be a coincidence. There could have simply been some deranged serial killer who decided to put a Biblical spin on his murders. Maybe a lunatic like Jack the Ripper."

"Perhaps." He shrugs. "But a lot of the people in this town don't believe that. In fact, they think the people who got away with it are still doing it."

"By doing it, you mean—" I gulp down. "The sacrifices?" I still can't tear my eyes away from the perfectly circular black-eyed face of the abomination.

"While the first sacrifice was meant to summon the demon, once the hellion granted their wishes, they had to keep the . . . tradition alive."

"Wha-what do you mean?"

My eyes shift to the robed and hooded figures surrounding the fiendish form.

"Every couple of decades, those descendants must sacrifice a number of people to appease the demon and keep their wealth," Sin continues.

CHAPTER TWENTY-FIVE

PETRA

Present Day

"What the actual fuck?" I exclaim, taking a step back. "You're telling me they—"

"Kill more people, yes," Sin says. "At least, that's how the story goes."

And now, my perspective on the painting before us is completely changed: Now it's the robed figures that invoke fear. I wonder how they look behind those hoods. Are they twisted in agony, like the sinners burning in Dante's eight circles of hell? Are they triumphant and filled with unslaked bloodlust?

"So you're telling me that Edwin was one of those sacrifices," I murmur. "Meaning there might be more to come."

"*If* we are connecting his death to the paintings here, then yes," Sin says in a tight voice.

"And they do this every few decades?" I know I'm repeating myself, but no matter how hard I try, it's impossible to wrap my mind around the bloodcurdling revelations. He nods, so I quickly continue, "When was the last odd murder? Did anyone else die strangely in town?"

"Yes, I'm pretty sure some people died." He pauses, looking pensive. "Although not as bloody as Edwin, as far as I know. I don't think they were flagged as anything overly suspicious, though there are a lot of townsfolk who claimed the deaths were sacrifices, that it was the third cycle. The police didn't think so, though, and dismissed the claims as myths."

"But they're not myths, Sin!" I cry out. "They're fucking real, aren't they? What happened to Edwin was real. And oh God . . . we're living in the fourth cycle."

Some other fact has been tugging at my attention this whole time, and when we lapse into a frightful silence again and peer at the gruesome scene on the wall, I get an epiphany. My own family had moved to this town when I was fourteen. We're relative newcomers. Does this put us—*me*—more at risk?

"Sin," I begin in a tone laced with pure, cold terror, "my parents and I . . . we moved here when I was fourteen. We're technically new people in this town. We're not connected to any of the old families."

His eyes flicker with guilt as he says, "That's good to know, isn't it, Petra? Looks like your family are not human sacrificers and satanists!"

"Who are the main families, then? The ones people suspect of being the devil worshippers?"

"Ah, I was really hoping you wouldn't ask that question," Sin replies with a nervous smile that turns solemn when he continues. "If you must know, the five families are Arnoult, Underwood, Snowden, Rutherford, and Haas. I know those names sound familiar . . ."

"Wait, Arnoult?" I exclaim again. "*Your* family?"

Sin nods sheepishly and tries to avoid my eyes as he adjusts his phone camera to take a picture of the painting.

"Yeah. My family's apparently related to one of the professors at the University in the 1890s. If it makes you feel any better, I have never heard my mom and dad planning or discussing the semicentennial family jamborees where we worship demons and sacrifice people."

The last sentence is a desperate attempt at jest, and he looks uncomfortable enough that I don't press him further on the topic.

Instead, I say, "And the other families? They're all still around?"

"Yup. And they still wield substantial power over the town," Sin replies. "The Underwood family owns most of the businesses downtown, all those strip malls, bodegas, burger joints, etc. The Snowdens are major stakeholders in the local government—every generation sees at least five Snowdens on the town council. Then the Rutherfords are well-respected and widely feared attorneys, and the Haas family has significant real estate."

"But you're not . . . involved, are you?" I ask hesitantly, the question feeling necessary and ridiculous and dangerous. "With the rituals, I mean."

"No, Petra, of course not!" Sin insists with such an earnest and anguished expression that I turn my attention back to the paintings.

We proceed farther into the crypt, the air growing colder with each step. Yet the complete silence and calm atmosphere make me feel physically fine, a rare event these days.

"These paintings," I whisper. "Do you get the feeling that they're not just ritual depictions or snapshots of the past? Like, they're *instructions* instead?"

Sin pauses to examine the mural more closely as I take a few more photographs. "You know what? I think you're right. These images are showing them *how* to perform the sacrifices."

I turn back to the mural before us, trying to process how intricately the horrors of our present are linked to a long line of evil deeds that have darkened Radcliffe's history.

It's true that I can't help but admire the pure artistry of these paintings: The blending of colors is so skillful, the gradience between blacks, grays, and reds creates such a unique atmosphere of dread. Even the grisly context of the artwork cannot detract from its savage beauty.

Another mural, another macabre depiction of ritual sacrifice, catches my eye. My gaze zeroes in on a specific section, and my stomach twists in recognition.

"Sin," I say quietly. "Look at this."

He steps closer, his eyes following my pointing finger. It's a grim image: a person lying on the ground, obviously dead, with blood pouring from their eyes, nose, mouth, ears—every orifice. The scene makes my skin crawl, but the brushwork makes me hold my breath.

"Jesus!" Sin mutters. "That's just sadistic."

"Now compare it to this one," I say, having moved beyond bowel-churning repulsion and arrived at intrigue. "This is like Edwin's death, right?"

"Yes, and?" Sin looks skeptical and wary, as if bracing for something really bad.

"And this one." I point back to the bleeding figure. "It looks like the second in a sequence. Edwin's was the first death."

"Petra, are you sure? You're saying that the next . . . death will look like that?" Sin points a shaking finger at the painting before us.

My heart pounds as I nod in agreement. We don't know what else to say, so we keep walking. The mastery evident in the drawings keeps me engaged as we pass from one damp wall to the next.

At the same time, I can't help but be impressed by Sin's knowledge about art. He points out small details that I would have missed, even explaining the underlying connotation of various symbols and patterns.

"Look at this symbol here." Sin points to a concentric, looped sigil drawn, or almost branded, onto a ritual scene. "Did you notice that it's repeated in multiple places? Maybe it refers to a seal, as in a sealing of the pact with the demon?"

"Oh, wow, that sounds really cool, Sin," I reply with utmost sincerity. "You really know a lot about this stuff."

"Comes with the territory of being an Arnoult, I guess." After a few more minutes, Sin steps back and stretches his arms. "I don't know about you, but I could really use a break from squinting at all these wonderfully brutal depictions."

"I agree." In fact, my feet have been killing me for a while now.

"Excellent!" Sin says, rifling through his backpack. To my surprise, he pulls out a blanket and some snacks. "Here," he says, spreading the blanket on the cold stone floor. "Time to rest those legs, darling."

I smile gratefully and sit down on the soft fabric.

Sin hands me a small bag of chips and a bottle of water. "Figured we might need some nourishment."

"Thank you, Sin. This was really thoughtful of you."

"Please, it was the least I could do," he says graciously, sitting down beside me—much closer than I expected. But I am not going to complain. The perfumed warmth of his body is a welcome respite from the crypt's relentless chill.

To my continued surprise, Sin takes my hand in his, a casual movement that implies an intimacy between the two of us, alone as we are in this underground chamber of horrors.

I struggle to keep my breath steady at the unexpected contact, but I don't pull away.

There's something undeniably magnetic about him, something that draws me in despite *everything*.

"Petra," he begins softly, his thumb drawing gentle circles on the tender skin at my wrist, "I haven't been able to stop thinking about that night."

"Then why didn't you text me afterward?" I blurt out the one question that has been burning at the tip of my tongue for months now.

He winces, as if I had again asked a question he was hoping I wouldn't voice.

"Because I felt guilty. We were both drunk when we . . . and afterward, I thought you needed some space. But in all honesty, Petra, you've been on my mind. All. The. Time."

How vulnerable he looks, how forlorn! His honesty stirs something within me, thawing out some of the ice that's settled around my heart over the past months.

"I'm . . . I don't know what to say," I admit in a hoarse whisper.

"You don't have to say anything, Petra," Sin replies, his fingers now stroking my palm. "I just wanted you to know how I feel. I really care about you."

Silence stretches between us, and I take deep breaths, the woodsy notes of Sin's cologne helping release the stress held up in my body for Lord knows how long.

Despite all the wrenching discoveries we made today, I find myself leaning into him. As my head reaches his shoulder, his arm automatically drapes over my upper back and draws me closer to him.

We sit like this for some time, and I sink deeper into the sense of security that settles over me like a silken shawl. It's Sin who breaks the silence.

"There's something I wanted to ask you. The fall ball is coming up . . . and I'd like to take you. Would you go with me?"

His fingers twirl the curly ends of my hair, and it's an endlessly cozy feeling. But his words put me on alert, and I hesitate at the thought of attending the fall ball. For one thing, it will be riotously crowded and unbearably noisy.

"I don't know, Sin. Honestly, I'm not really into those kinds of events. Especially not now . . . with everything that's been happening."

"I get it," Sin replies in an even softer voice as he squeezes my hand. "But maybe the dance could be a chance to feel normal for a night? Maybe it will help you forget about all this, just for a few hours?"

For a while, I'm quite torn.

"I'll think about it," I reply eventually. "But right now, I need to focus on the project and just keeping my wits about me, you know?"

"Of course I do, Petra. Know that the offer stands."

His hand has been gently massaging my arm and shoulders this whole time. And as the silence between us ripens and deepens, I feel a fluttering in my belly—one wholly unconnected to the you-know-who floating inside its amniotic dream.

The way Sin sighs into my hair, the way his fingers glide over my limbs like butterflies . . . all of it leaves me bewitched, hazy with desire.

"I'm really glad we're doing this together," Sin whispers, softly tucking a silken strand of hair behind my ear. "I like the feel of you in my arms, Petra. It feels so right."

His fingers have moved to caress the smooth planes of my cheek. I close my eyes and let the feel of his skin over mine lull me further into his embrace.

"It does feel good," I reply just as gently.

Now his finger is lightly tracing the outline of my lips, and his mouth plants small kisses on my forehead. I sigh as he turns me toward him, so gently that it might be a trick of the wind. Now he's cupping my chin and tilting my head up. His lips inch closer to mine.

Suddenly, a loud clatter echoes through the crypt, a sharp, metallic sound that bounces off the stone walls. My eyes snap open, and Sin's head whips around.

"The fuck was that?" I gasp in fear.

Sin grips my hand tighter. "I don't know. Stay close." His voice is calm but edged with caution.

In a few seconds, we have sprung to our feet, forgetting the blanket and snacks in our rush toward the exit. The cozy intimacy of the previous moments vanishes, and the crypt feels like a trap closing in on us.

As we reach the narrow staircase leading up to the first of the five flights that will take us to the surface, the noises grow louder. Now we hear scratches, squeaks, the flapping of wings.

What in the ever-loving hell? my inner voice cries out, but I'm too frightened to pay heed.

"Hurry, Petra!" Sin shouts, looking behind and pulling me forward by the arm.

Finally, we burst through the wooden door and into the dusty, abandoned hallway in the east wing. Slamming the door shut behind us, we just stand there, panting urgently and clutching our hearts.

"Wh-what *was* that?" I say between gasps for air.

Sin leans toward the door, carefully listening to the eerie quiet lurking behind it. Then the blasted guy actually grins!

"You know, I think it might've just been some bats."

"Bats? *Bats?*" I repeat in hysterical incredulity. "You mean we ran out of there because of—because of bats?"

"Yup," Sin replies with a dry chuckle. "Probably just some scared, harmless bats."

Now the adrenaline turns into nervous laughter that leaves my arms and legs shaking. "Well," I manage to say between uncontrollable giggles, "I guess that'll be a story to tell."

Sin's eyes are twinkling with warmth and a certain je ne sais quoi. "Just the first of *many* stories to tell, I hope."

And when I see the expression on his face, I lose any and all clever comebacks in my arsenal.

CHAPTER TWENTY-SIX

PETRA

Present Day

This charming, idyllic scene is not unfolding at a park or a classroom or even a classy restaurant à la L'Avion. Surrounding us are the rough stone walls of the crypt where an occult secret society allegedly met—and is perhaps still meeting—to summon demons and sacrifice humans.

"Okay, your turn," Sin says with a mischievous smirk. When I raise my eyebrows quizzically, he hands me a card from our impromptu trivia game.

I only have to glance at the note before a smile starts dancing on my lips. "Okay, this one's *so* easy! Who painted the ceiling of the Sistine Chapel?"

"I don't know, Bernini?" Sin replies with a goofy grin, and I punch him playfully on the arm.

"Come on! Be serious," I say in the tone of a long-suffering teacher. "And Bernini wasn't even a painter, was he?"

"Okay, okay, the answer's . . ." Sin puts on a serious face and places his hands on his temple, in a hyperbolic imitation of a psychic, before exclaiming, "Michelangelo! The answer is Michelangelo."

I am guffawing by now, so he gives me puppy eyes and says, "Did I get it right?"

"Yes, you did," I reply in a wry tone, "Anyone would, Sin."

Mary Shelley would actually find this all very romantic, I think, while Sin shuffles the remaining cards of our little quiz game.

It's been a few weeks since we first explored the crypt together. In a surprising turn of events, we have entered a tacit understanding: The partnership in Ms. Matthews's class can be further explored, safely, in the dreadful confines of this ancient (and alleged) slaughterhouse.

Here we can enjoy each other's . . . company away from prying, petty eyes and snide remarks. Over the last few weeks, we've been meeting regularly for what we've started calling "study dates."

Corny, I know. But my life has been stranger than fiction for a while now. Some commonplace corniness is *just* what I need.

Tonight, Sin has outdone himself, having procured some choice Camembert, juicy red grapes, and butter crackers.

When I praise his charcuterie skills, he says, "Oh, this is nothing! You should see the spreads my dad arranges for our famous literary soirées."

"Ooh, they sound fun." I dip another cracker into the melting cheese and bite into it with apparent relish.

"Yeah, they're all right," Sin says with a self-effacing gesture. "They'll really like you, Petra."

The food almost catches in my throat at the last sentence, and I cough for a few seconds. "No, it's fine. I'm good," I say when Sin looks alarmed.

Why would he just say something like that? Now he wants me to meet his parents?

Well, you are the mother of their grandchild, so it's not that off base. My annoying inner voice never takes a day off, so my anxiety surges back and perhaps shows on my face, because Sin hurries to add, "Because you're so well read and clever. They love meeting my friends."

"Sure, that sounds . . . nice," I reply with a reassuring smile.

A cozy silence ensues. Only a few weeks ago, I wouldn't have even imagined that such a scene would be possible between me and Sin, but here we are. And he's been such a gentleman, almost *too much* of a gentleman.

Perhaps this is how a body changes while growing another, smaller one inside it. Perhaps my hormones were such a raging mess that every now and then, I catch myself wishing Sin would just . . . lean in and kiss me. And maybe do more than that.

There's an undeniable tension building between us. But he hasn't made a move since that night.

And now I'm more charmed by him, and even hornier.

Sigh.

"All right," Sin says loudly, jolting me from my daydream. "Next question: Who painted *The Starry Night*?"

"Vincent van Gogh. That's like, the easiest one!" I chime back.

"Fair enough," he concedes with a chuckle. "You're getting too good at this."

"And you're not working hard enough!" I offer a delighted smile. "Come on, Arnoult, hit me with your best shot."

"Fine, how about this: Petra Valentine, will you go to the fall ball with me?" he asks with all the somber anticipation of a guy proposing marriage.

But here's the catch: Sin's been asking me to the fall ball for *weeks* now. And every time, I have refused.

"Oh my God, you're like a dog with a bone!" I toss a grape at him, and he smoothly catches it with his mouth. The sight of his Adam's apple bobbing as he swallows the fruit sends a tingle down my spine. "Seriously, what is with you and this fall ball?"

"It's not just another school dance, Petra. It's an exclusive St. Anselm Hall tradition. And the food at these things is to *die* for, trust me."

I roll my eyes playfully and shake my head.

He adds, "Besides, I want to hold you in my arms and dance to a nice song."

The way his voice cracks over the last words affects me more than the words themselves and their yearning for intimacy. I blush and laugh softly.

"You're really not going to give up, are you?"

"Not a chance," he says, sitting back with a coy grin. "So what's your answer?"

His persistence is obviously very endearing, and I find myself considering the offer more seriously than ever before. Honestly, I don't mind getting dolled up and dancing the night away. God knows I need to let down my hair.

But something else is nagging at the back of my mind: a reminder of another guy who had asked me to the ball.

Just last Friday, Harry had shuffled up to me in the library: incidentally, in the art history section where we had first met.

"How's the project going, Petra?" he'd asked, looking over the books I had in my hand with genuine interest.

"Hey, Harry, it's going good!" I had brightly replied. "What have you been up to?"

"Oh, you know, the usual. Classwork and homework and all the many hours of leisure in between," he said with a nervous laugh.

"Of course! How can I forget all this free time we get?" I joked back before realizing that Harry had a sheepish look on his face. "What is it? Something wrong?" I had asked.

"Nothing's wrong . . . I-I was wondering if you'd come to the fall ball with me?" He had sprinted through the words so fast that for a moment, I was confused.

Then it dawned on me. *Ah, this is going to be awkward.*

"That's really sweet, Harry, but umm, I don't really do school dances. Tacky costumes, mediocre food and beverages, even more mediocre music," I was rambling away, internally praying for the earth to open up and swallow me whole. "It's just not for me. Thank you for asking, though, I just—I hope you understand . . ."

"Of course, Petra, no pressure!" Harry had sputtered when I had finally paused for breath. "And no hard feelings at all."

He'd smiled warmly at me.

"You don't have to explain yourself to me. Or anyone."

It had been a bittersweet proposal and a graceful decline (at least I hope so), but now, when Sin asks me to the fall ball for the umpteenth time, I can suddenly not find any of my usual qualms about these dances.

Caught in the moment's erotic drift, I find myself responding to Sin without thinking. "You know what, Arnoult? All right. I'll go to the fall ball with you."

Sin's eyes light up with genuine surprise. "Really? You mean it?"

"Yup, you've convinced me. Let's go. What the hell, right? Let's make it a night to remember."

THE DAYS LEADING up to the fall ball whirl by in a blaze of coursework for Ms. Matthews and putting the final touches on the first draft of my creative portfolio for college applications.

But they are also marked by long sessions of costume selections, styling vision boards, and micro photo shoots, as I fully indulge my guilty pleasure of dressing up to the nines.

Thankfully, it's been a relatively quiet period when it comes to my odd dreams; perhaps it's because I've been spending more time with Sin, and therefore, my mind does not have to make up more absurd scenarios anymore.

Maybe.

I have just put on a demure white and gold Karl Lagerfeld ensemble when my phone pings with a message from Amelia.

Hey, girl! Tell me tell me tell me that you found THE dress?

I'm still trying to decide. My closet feels like a battlefield right now.

And I'm not even exaggerating. My room is now littered with half of my wardrobe. Dresses, skirts, heels, and accessories are strewn across every surface.

Show me! I help!

I snap a few pictures of potential ensembles that I have laid out across the room and send them over to Amelia.

What will it be, Petra? LV or Dior? Or are you going with something new and edgy?

Decisions, decisions.

I don't know yet, Ames!

I text back.

Hopefully I won't go crazy and end up in a boring Chanel two-piece.

Anything *but Chanel.*

All my homies hate Chanel!

She texts back, making me chuckle.

Mama wants more shots,
so keep them coming, baby girl.

I try on a Burberry dress from the 2012 collection and take a few selfies. I haven't had this much fun in ages.

Next, I put on a red and blue dress with an ombre effect, a sleek silhouette from Armani Privé that highlights my collarbone and plunges quite low in the back. I take a mirror selfie and send it to Amelia for approval.

O.M.G. You look hawt!

She texts back immediately, following that up with a string of heart-eye emojis.

But her effusive praise doesn't distract me from the fact that, though the clothes fall over my body in just the right way, I can see and feel a bump forming over my panty line.

Well, fuck, I think. Amelia is sending more messages telling me how ravishing I look, but I have suddenly lost all interest in the whole charade.

My thoughts are again consumed by the fearful realization that it's been almost four months since . . . and neither have I told Sin, nor Amelia, nor any other adult for that matter, nor have I made the much-needed trip to the Planned Parenthood center in New Haven.

Why have I been dragging my feet on this, you ask? Partly because I'm being courted by the dreamiest, most popular guy in school, and it's a heady feeling that's left me ill-disposed to negative rumination. And partly because I don't have the nerve to make a full-fledged *final* decision just when my life has started to get interesting.

So, determined to enjoy whatever time I had left to be a "normal teenage girl," I dress myself carefully on the night of the fall ball.

I have chosen a baby-blue tulle slip dress that softly cascades to my ankles and is loosely belted at the waist with pearls. A thin band of flowers and small pearls sits on my head, and my hair falls to my shoulders in waves.

My parents aren't home, which is both a relief and a bit disheartening. They're always so busy with their own lives, and tonight is no different. The house feels oddly quiet, save for the ticking of the clock and my own racing heartbeat.

A knock comes at the door.

Sin's here.

CHAPTER TWENTY-SEVEN

PETRA

Present Day

I open the door to see him standing there in a sharp suit with a rather fetching handkerchief folded in his breast pocket. His eyes widen when he sees me, and he puts his hand over his heart in a theatrical gesture.

"Stop!" I say, feeling immensely flattered. "You're the better-looking one."

"Are you insane, woman?" Sin counters. "You're the most . . . gorgeous forest nymph who ever drifted out of the woods one day and decided to grace this grateful mere mortal with her presence."

"Shut up, you're so dramatic!"

But inside, my heart is doing flips and somersaults.

"And you're coming to the fall ball with me, right?" Sin asks, making a big show as usual. "You aren't going to just change your mind when we reach the school and just leave me hanging, are you?"

"Oh my God, will you stop it?" I punch his arm again, and he staggers back, holding his heart.

"Okay, okay! I'm done, I'm done," he says, still sighing at me. When I put on a stern face and cross my arms, he offers me his arm. "Shall we?"

I take his arm, and we step out into the cool evening air. The ride to St. Anselm Hall passes pleasantly, too, like all our "study dates" so far: filled with banter and laughter.

When we arrive at the school, the sight of the grandly decorated entrance stuns me. Twinkling lights and beautifully arranged flowers create a magical atmosphere, and for a moment, I allow myself to get lost in it.

Sin parks the car and turns to me, an excited grin on his face.

"Ready to make some jaws drop, Valentine?"

"More than ready, Arnoult," I reply with genuine enthusiasm. After all, my time for such shenanigans is fast running out.

We step out of the car and walk into the large hall set aside for the ball. Music and laughter weave together, passing over fashionable coiffures and whimsical braids.

The SAH populace has truly delivered, it must be noted, with the girls looking bright and colorful and even the guys delivering killer looks from Balmain and Thom Browne.

Sin holds the door open for me, and we step inside, greeted by the ethereal strains of a Mitski song.

I can feel the music reaching all the way down to my soles.

"First dance of the evening?" Sin asks, perhaps sensing my mood. I take up his offer and his outstretched hand, and we head to the dance floor.

The music pulses around us, and I allow myself to get swept up in the rhythm. For the first time in a long while, I feel light and carefree. Sin's eyes never leave mine as we swing our arms and do the silliest moves.

Soon, the crowd has been taken over by a spirit of revelry, and limbs move askance as the music turns from synth pop to techno to trap house and EDM and so on.

"Petra," he yells into my ears as a Claire Laffut song starts playing.

"What do you think?" I yell back into his ears with a huge grin on my face.

Laffut's smoky voice sings of being bespelled by love, and I wonder if this is what it feels like . . . this mad ecstasy, this joyful abandon.

Sin pulls me closer, and I go into his arms willingly. For a while, we just hop and sway to the beats of the song, while other couples also join hands and lean into each other, savoring the heady combination of music and romance.

But the body's crude reality encroaches into this dream bubble of strobe lights, artificial fog, and pulsing music.

My bladder's been getting full more frequently now, for obvious reasons, and it is with the greatest reluctance that I tell Sin.

"Wait, I gotta use the restroom."

"Sure." He nods and kisses me on the forehead. "I'll grab us some drinks in the meantime."

The music grows slightly muffled as I enter the quiet hallway leading to the restrooms. My feet are starting to get sore from the dancing, but my spirits have never been higher.

As I'm done with my business and push open the door to the stall, I hear a couple of girls chatting near the sinks. At first, I automatically filter out their chatter as I wash up and freshen my makeup.

Then one of them, a willowy brunette with perky breasts and long legs, says, "I can tell you that Sin Arnoult the First's an ass man. From personal experience, you know. He was wild this summer."

She winks at her friends, who are giggling loudly.

The mascara in my trembling hand almost slides down my eyes. I blink as water gathers at the edges of my waterline.

The brunette is still bragging.

"On a serious note, he sure knows what he's doing. Man's got moves!"

She makes an obscene gesture to her friends, who laugh even louder. Meanwhile, I barely manage to slip my things into the small purse on my arm.

"Oh, he can be really gentlemanly and reserved," the girl is saying now. "But trust me, when he lets loose . . . ugh, I couldn't keep my voice down; it just felt *so* good. I was surprised he even took Petra to the ball tonight. Must be out of pity or something."

The floor seems to be sliding out from under my feet, but I still manage to pull away from the sink, which is clutched so tight in my hands that my knuckles whiten, and stagger toward the bathroom door.

The girls' laughter follows me all the way out, and the surrounding sounds take on a distorted feel.

A heaviness seems to settle over me. The ballroom's lively atmosphere only emphasizes the discord I feel inside.

For a moment, I just stand there, looking around in utter distress and unsure of what to do.

In the next moment, I spot Sin by the drinks table.

He is joking and chatting with a group of sweaty guys and girls.

He looks relaxed and completely unaware of the hailstorm I plan to rain down on him.

How dare he lie to me? How dare he try to manipulate me by pretending to be this vulnerable, charming guy who was seemingly taken with me?

Blinded by fury and heartbreak, I stride toward him.

Just as I reach him, he turns and smiles at me.

"Petra, there you are. I got us some—"

"You fucking liar," I cut him off in a trembling but sharp voice.

Sin's smile vanishes. "What? Petra, what are you talking about?"

"You-you asshole! You told me you had been thinking about me all summer,' but you had no issue hooking up with other people. What, you thought I'd never find out? That I'm some dumb, naïve—"

"That's not true at all, Petra!" Sin cuts in vehemently at this point. "Who the fuck told you that?"

"Does it matter who told me?" I snap, trying my best not to cry. I will not give him that satisfaction. "I should have known better. Coming here with you . . . it was a mistake. A terrible fucking mistake."

"Petra, please listen to me," he pleads in an urgent tone. "Whatever you heard, it's not true. I haven't been with anyone since . . . since that night we—"

"Liar!" I shout at him and turn around, pushing my way through the crowded dance floor. Over the rising strains of Dua Lipa's "Dance the Night," I can still hear Sin calling after me.

"Petra! Wait, please!" His voice is desperate and loud enough to cut through even the din of the party.

But I keep moving, even when my vision blurs with tears and I am shoved and jostled by the dancers around me. Just as I reach the middle of the dance floor, the music stops, and the lights dim even further.

The sound of a projector whirring draws everyone's attention as a video starts playing on the large screen mounted over the stage.

The sudden change in lighting makes the video too bright for my eyes, and I raise an arm to shield them.

But even before I can see the visuals, the audio makes me gasp.

"Hi there. How are you doing today?" I hear a woman say, and it's the same voice; I know it.

Oh God, what is this?

When my eyes finally adjust to the light, I realize that playing on the screen, before all of St. Anselm Hall, *before Sin,* is a video of me at the pharmacy.

Buying a pregnancy test.

No, no, no, this is not real. But that's clearly me on the screen, looking pale and frightened, handing over boxes of *pregnancy tests* to the cashier.

Murmurs break out around me as my breathing becomes shallow and rapid. I clutch my chest as my heart gallops like a wild horse.

I'm about to be sick.

This can't be happening.

But the hellish experience is not over.

Crude comments shoot out of the crowd.

"Slut!" someone yells.

"Who's the dad?" another chimes in.

Each word causes physical pain as my vision blurs again.

I turn around desperately, searching for Sin, but he's nowhere near me. Instead, I just stand there feeling utterly alone and exposed, surrounded by people who are mercilessly mocking me when I'm at my most vulnerable.

Tears are now streaming down my face, and I struggle to breathe.

"Please, stop," I whisper, but my voice is barely audible over the ruckus. "Just stop . . ."

But the crowd is baying for my blood at this point. Their laughter only grows louder, more pointed, more malicious.

"Aww, look at the poor thing. She's going to cry!" a girl in the crowd exclaims.

My knees buckle, and my hands shake uncontrollably.

I cover my ears with my hands, chanting, "This is not real, this is a dream, this isn't happening," over and over again.

I look around again for Sin, but with all the lights dimmed, only the outlines of faces are visible.

But I do see Daphne's face at the very back of the room.

And when I catch her eye, she gives me a knowing smirk.

Everything feels surreal, like a nightmare I am trapped in forever. The walls seem to close in, and the lights are glaring down on me.

My heart is beating in my ears.

"I can't breathe," I gasp, desperately trying to ground myself. "I can't breathe . . ."

In a blessed moment, I see Sin pushing through the crowd. "Petra!" he calls out, his voice ringing high and clear over the enormous, swelling noise of the malicious crowd. "I'm here."

"Sin . . ." I begin weakly before realizing that he could have just understood that the baby is his. "Sin, I meant to tell you—" I begin, and Sin starts saying something, too.

But our words are drowned out by a thunderous crack. People gasp, and a scream or two rends the air. Another loud crack fills the auditorium.

"What the hell was that?" someone shouts, while some of the faculty have entered the room and are trying to calm the crowd.

A third deafening crack. The room freezes in time for a split second.

Then, the ceiling collapses with an earth-shattering crash, and something long and heavy falls through, hitting the floor with a sickening thud.

"What is that?" a girl screams.

"My God, what is that?" Other shouts and screams fill the room.

But I don't scream. I don't even blink. I only stare at the corpse that fell through the ceiling and whose detached head is now lying near my feet.

It's Harry.

That I can recognize him at all is a miracle because his headless body is badly disfigured. His eyes have been scooped out, and blood spurts forth from his severed neck. A great gush of it sprays over my baby-blue tulle, over the actual baby cocooned in my body.

"NOOOO!" a loud, guttural yell rings through the auditorium, and I realize it's coming from me.

I clutch at my stomach and let out the most terrifying scream I can muster.

I am scared the force of my outburst might hurt the baby, but I can't stop.

Harry is lying before me.

His dead body is lying on the floor right before me. His blood is all over my clothes, and he is *dead*.

The room is spinning, Sin is still shouting something incoherent in the distance, and the sneers and jeers of the crowd have turned into hysterical sobbing and flat-out pandemonium.

I have no idea if that damned video of me is still playing because the lights are flickering in and out of focus.

My head is pulsing with something bright, and bitter, and black . . .

As I crumble to the floor, my last coherent thought is that I could have come to the ball with Harry. He could have been with me.

He could have lived.

PART TWO

BREAKING NEWS

Radcliffe Herald

8 APRIL 1896

OF MAD MEN, GHOSTS, DEMONS AND THE DEVIL

MYSTERIOUS ABSENCES FROM THE THEOLOGICAL FACULTY

In the wake of the horrific ritual slayings that have shaken our quiet township, three prominent figures associated with the Theology Department of St. Anselm Hall have come under grave suspicion. Arnoult, Kimaris, and Haas—once regarded as learned men of high standing—have not been seen since the bloody spectacle that occurred late Saturday last.

Particular attention has turned toward Mr. Arnoult, an eccentric scholar long whispered about in academic and spiritualist circles for his curious predilection for necromantic studies.

Known to host strange monthly gatherings in his private residence—attended by students and reputed occult enthusiasts from afar—Mr. Arnoult has oft claimed an ability to commune with spirits from beyond the veil.

Of Mr. Kimaris, little is yet known, save for his quiet disposition and sudden disappearance.

As for Mr. Haas, no statement has been issued by the University, though his name appears on several rosters of faculty involved in theological instruction.

Authorities remain tight-lipped while the investigation proceeds. Fear and speculation mount, and the townsfolk pray this darkness will soon be brought into the light.

Further developments shall be published as they arise.

TURN THE PAGE FOR DR. BRINKLER'S HEALTH TONIC THAT CURES ALL AILMENTS!

CHAPTER TWENTY-EIGHT

PETRA

The Past
10 April 1896

For a week now, the authorities have been trying to track down the main suspects—several professors connected to St. Anselm Hall University. But I haven't heard any mention of Sin.

My father keeps repeating one name: Arnoult. There were a few others implicated, too, names I don't recognize.

Still, my thoughts can't stay away from Sin.

What if those bodies weren't the only ones?

What if he really *was* involved in the ritual and is now lying dead somewhere, abandoned in a ditch, forgotten?

What if something *happened* to him?

After our so-called bargain, I thought he would at least find a way to let me know he was safe. Some sign. Anything. But there's been nothing.

Easter came and went, but no one celebrated. The town feels too heavy, too shadowed to embrace joy. Everyone's on edge, waiting for something awful to happen again.

The murders still haven't been solved. No arrests. No explanations.

Now, we're not allowed to leave the house alone. Not even with Mrs. Jenkins. No one from the congregation is permitted to go into town, and from what I hear, the same rules apply to the outsiders. They're just as afraid.

People whisper that if they leave their homes, they won't come back alive—that something is lurking out there in the dark, waiting to grab them and offer them up in sacrifice.

No official statement has linked the killings to a ritual, but that hasn't stopped the rumors. What started with our congregation has spread like wildfire. Now the entire town believes the university was hiding some kind of occult group. One that tried to summon the devil himself.

The university gates have been shut ever since. No one knows if or when they'll reopen.

Day after day, I keep asking myself if I could have done more. If I should have tried harder to stop Sin. Tried harder to *save* him. The idea that he might be dead gnaws at me. It doesn't feel right. I *won't* believe it.

And so, slowly, my sanity begins to unravel.

Until one night, I can't take it anymore.

I escaped once. I can do it again.

I just need to *know*, once and for all, if he's alive. If he's safe.

If Sin is still out there.

I wait until the entire household has gone to bed before I begin to seriously consider my plan. Like before, I head straight to the window, unlatching it quietly and peering outside. I can see the security outpost, the sheds where the dogs sleep. The world is still.

I'm about to climb onto the windowsill when I pause.

Is this the right thing to do?

If Sin *wasn't* involved, then someone else out there is responsible for the deaths of twenty-five young men. A killer is still on the loose. And by going out alone, I'd be putting myself in danger.

But the conviction burning inside me is stronger than fear. I *have* to know. I have to see with my own eyes that he's alive. That he's not responsible. I don't know why it matters so much—it just does.

I can't stay suspended in this state of not knowing. Of waiting.

Taking a deep breath, I climb onto the windowsill and begin my descent. Like last time, it's surprisingly easy to make my way outside. Almost too easy. It feels as though the shadows themselves are helping me—wrapping around me, guiding me, shielding me from sight. As if the darkness is on my side.

Once I'm past the gate, I follow the same path I did before, heading toward the university.

But the town feels *different* tonight.

Last time, even at a late hour, there were people drifting between pubs and shops, conversations and laughter spilling into the streets. This time . . . nothing.

The silence is eerie. The streets are deserted. It's as though the whole town is holding its breath.

But at least that means no one is around to notice me.

When I finally reach the university, it's completely dark. Not a single light glows from the windows. Still, when I reach the front gates, they open for me again—just like before.

I step inside cautiously, squinting through the blackness as I move toward the main door. It's shut tight. I reach for the handle, but it doesn't budge. Locked.

Still, I can't shake the feeling that he might be here. Even with the university shut down, he could still be living on the premises. He might still be inside, waiting.

I move around to the back of the building, searching for another entrance. The hedges back here are tall, perfectly sculpted into strange, ornamental shapes that make it difficult to see where I'm going. They twist and wind like a garden maze, and I have to navigate carefully.

Eventually, I manage to find a narrow path through the shrubbery—and just when I think I spot another door ahead, my foot catches.

One wrong step.

I fall.

The breath is knocked clean from my lungs. I hit the ground hard, pain blooming through my side as I struggle to breathe, to orient myself again in the dark.

The fall is steep. As I gather myself, I glance up and realize what happened. I must have stepped on loose stones, and the ground crumbled beneath me. Now I'm somewhere underground, in what looks like a tunnel or an old passageway.

I can see the night sky far above, but there's no way I can climb back up. The drop is too high, the walls too sheer. My only option is to move forward and hope there's another way out.

Fear prickles down my spine. *Good Lord, what have I gotten myself into?*

Considering those pagan rituals originated in the university, the fact that I am here, underground, alone and trapped, terrifies me even more.

What if, in my misguided attempt to find Sin, I find *myself* in the midst of another ritual?

I have no idea where this tunnel leads, and no way out. A nervous laugh bubbles in my throat, quickly chased by the sting of tears. *What was I thinking?*

Still, I'm not one to give up easily. I take a deep breath, steady my nerves, and start moving forward.

The tunnel is cold and silent, but after only a few minutes, I spot something ahead—a flicker of light.

Odd.

Does that mean someone is down here?

Could it be Sin?

The thought brings a rush of hope. I straighten my back, pick up my pace, and am ready to call out his name, to ask him why he disappeared, why he never let me know he was safe. Why he left me in silence.

But the closer I get, the more I realize it's *not* him.

I hear voices. Two. Maybe more. I slow down and stop just before the tunnel opens into a wide, well-lit alcove.

I peer around the corner, and what I see turns my blood cold.

I slap a hand over my mouth to stifle any sound.

The space is aglow with candlelight; there's no electricity here. Candles line the chandelier above, the ledges of the walls, every crevice. The illumination is eerie, casting flickering shadows over the carved stone.

The walls are painted—images drawn directly onto the stone, crude but clear. Some too distant to see in detail, but others close enough for me to make out the crimson hues, the depictions of murder, torture . . . blood.

But even that is not the most horrifying part.

There are four, maybe five figures in the chamber. Most are cloaked in a deep burgundy fabric, their hoods drawn up like monks—like those old drawings of Franciscans I've seen in dusty books. But they aren't praying.

At the center of the room is a massive stone table, easily twice my size.

Lying on it is a woman. Naked. Her wrists and ankles are bound. The cloaked figures circle her slowly, moving in unison, performing some kind of ritual.

My heart hammers in my chest.

Is this a sacrifice? Are they going to kill her?

And if they are, if they *see me*, will they kill me too?

I can't go back. There's no way up. My only hope is to move forward, *deeper* into this place. But how can I move past this? What will happen to me if they realize I'm here?

Fear—no, true horror—grips me as I realize the potential consequences of my actions.

Stupid, Petra! Stupid!

I press myself to the wall, desperate not to be seen.

But then, something unexpected happens.

One of the cloaked figures stops at her side and begins to untie her hands. Another releases her ankles. She rises slowly, her body trembling, breasts heaving as she sits up on the cold stone. But she doesn't speak. Doesn't resist.

Once she's free, she swings her legs off the table and turns, resting her torso against the stone while her feet touch the floor.

I don't understand. What is this?

Then one of the cloaked men moves behind her.

A metallic rattle echoes through the chamber.

A gasp escapes the woman as he presses himself to her from behind, thrusting.

My eyes widen.

What is this?

My stomach turns.

What are they doing to her?

Before I can process it, two more of the cloaked figures step forward, reaching into their robes. The woman's hands rise, as if to receive something.

I never get to see what.

Darkness blinds me.

A hand presses firmly over my face, smothering my sight, muffling my breath.

Someone leans in close, breath warm against my ear.

"Don't make a sound," he whispers.

That voice—

I know that voice.

"Come. We need to get out of here," he whispers, pulling me away from the horrifying scene I had just witnessed.

We move quickly, retracing my steps toward the place where I fell, but instead of helping me climb out, he bypasses the crumbled stones and leads me deeper into the tunnel.

Hidden in the shadows, he opens a concealed door and gently pushes me through it before taking my hand again, guiding me through a series of narrow, winding passages cloaked in darkness.

I can't see where I'm going, have no idea where we're headed—but somehow, the fact that it's *him* leading me fills me with a strange sense of trust.

Foolish, maybe.

But he's alive, and right now, that's all I need.

I don't know how long we walk. Time loses meaning in the dark. Then, at last, he opens another door and pulls me into a small, dimly lit room.

Two candles burn low on a table. There are no windows. One bed, one chest of drawers, and a desk littered with crumpled papers. The place looks like a prison: bare, cold, isolated.

"Is this where you've been hiding?" I ask as he quietly shuts the door behind us.

He locks it, then peeks through a tiny slit in the wood, making sure no one has followed. "What are you doing here, Petra?" he asks without turning around. "Why did you come?"

"To see if you were alive," I murmur, the words coming out awkwardly, uncertain.

"Well," he says, facing me, "you've seen. I'm alive."

His voice is cold. Angry. But why would he be angry at me when he's the one who went missing?

"Why didn't you say anything?" My voice is suddenly stronger. "Why didn't you come to me? After the bodies were found in the square . . . after everything?"

"It's not safe," he replies. "Not for me, and not for you. Please believe me—it wasn't on purpose. If I could have reached out, I would have. But if anyone sees me, it won't end well."

"I know," I whisper. "But I was worried about you."

Something in him softens at my words. His shoulders drop slightly, and I finally take a good look at him.

He's still the most striking man I've ever seen, but he looks . . . worn.

There are dark circles under his eyes, and tension is etched into the lines of his face.

"Is this how you've been living?" I ask, glancing around the room again, my chest tightening as I imagine him closed up in here. No one should live like this. No windows. No light.

"This isn't where I live," he says. "But it's one of the chambers I use when I need to stay at the university."

"In the *tunnels*?" I frown. "I thought you were sleeping in your office."

"Sometimes there. Sometimes here," he says. "It doesn't matter now. What matters is getting you out before someone realizes you're here. Before they realize what you've seen."

"No." I step in front of him. "You need to explain. What was that back there? Who *were* those people? What happened with the ritual? *Did you go?* Did you—"

I choke on the question.

"Did you kill those people?"

He presses his lips together. The silence is astounding.

"Please," I whisper. "Tell me you didn't participate, Sin."

"I wasn't there," he promises.

I let out a harsh breath, relief flooding through me.

"You weren't?" I ask, needing to hear it again.

"No. I wasn't there. I wasn't personally involved in the ritual, or whatever it was. I told you I wouldn't be."

"You mean . . . you kept your end of the bargain?" I whisper.

"If you're asking whether I sold my soul, no, I did not."

"Then what *happened,* Sin?" I ask, voice trembling.

He takes a deep breath.

"Come, sit down. Are you hurt?" he asks, already guiding me gently to the bed. "You must've fallen through the cracks; I saw the debris."

I nod. "My back's a little sore, but I'll be fine. Nothing serious."

He gives a brief nod, as if willing to drop the subject, but then his gaze sharpens.

"What's that?" He gestures toward my hand.

I follow his line of sight and realize two things: one, I'm not wearing my gloves; and two, my palms are scraped and bruised, likely from trying to break my fall.

"Come here," he says, brisk but gentle. "We need to clean those."

Before I can protest, he pulls me toward the bed and sits me down. From the drawer in his desk, he retrieves the same ointment he gave me on our second meeting in the church.

He lowers himself to his knees in front of me, carefully turning my hands palm-up to assess the damage.

"It's not too bad," he mutters. "But I don't want them getting infected."

"I'll be all right," I say lightly. "It doesn't really hurt. It's nothing I'm not used to."

His jaw tightens.

"Nothing you're not used to?" he repeats. "Please don't say that, Petra."

"I didn't mean it like—"

"No," he cuts in softly but firmly. "You *did* mean it. Knowing what your life has been like is one thing, but actually hearing that from your own lips . . . It breaks something inside me."

He pauses, eyes flickering with something deeper.

"I'm sorry. I'm sorry for *that,* and for everything. For whatever pain you've known. Especially for the part I played in it."

"It's fine," I whisper. "It's in the past now."

"It's *not* fine. You were hurt because of me—again. My God, Petra. What were you thinking, coming here in the middle of the night, *after* what happened? After those murders?"

"I wanted to find you," I say quietly. "To make sure you were alive. What else was I supposed to do?"

He sighs. "The ritual happened. The authorities were right: Some of the University's higher-ups were involved. They've fled. No one knows where they are. My entire department is under suspicion now. Some of the staff have vanished. The rest of us . . . the ones with nowhere to go . . . we're still here."

"What about those people I saw? That woman?" I ask, my voice lowering to a whisper. "Was that another ritual?"

He finishes rubbing the ointment into my palms, then looks up, locking eyes with me.

"No. They're from my department, yes. But it wasn't a ritual. That woman, she's a prostitute. She was just doing what they paid her to do."

"A prostitute?" I blink. "You mean they were . . ."

"Fucking, yes."

A sharp gasp escapes me. I glance away.

"That's crude," I whisper.

"No. It's part of life," he counters with a dark chuckle.

I chew on my lip, still looking away.

"Is that . . . Have you ever done that?"

He tilts his head. "Are you asking if I've participated in *that*?"

I nod tentatively.

"No."

Relief washes through me.

"But," I add hesitantly, "have you ever been with a prostitute before?"

"What are you asking me, Petra?" he says, meeting my gaze squarely. "Are you asking if I've paid someone for sex? If I've *fucked* someone?"

I falter, trembling and full of nerves. "I think so. I-I don't know."

The pain in my hands has faded under the balm, but my mind is a whirlwind of uncertainty. He watches me carefully, then a slow, unreadable smile touches the corners of his lips.

"And what if I *had*?" he asks. "Would it change something for you?"

"I . . . I don't know," I admit. "I suppose . . . that's just what men do."

"Even the men in your church?"

"They're still men," I say quietly, the truth bitter. "Maybe not openly, but things happen. Even in our community."

And yet the thought of *him*, my Sin, with someone like the woman from before, with her full curves, her confidence, her worldliness . . . it crushes something inside me. Something tender and unsure.

He sees it. I turn my face away, blinking hard.

"Petra," he says softly. "Look at me."

He touches my chin and gently turns my face toward his. I meet his eyes.

"Would you care?" he asks. "If I had?"

I shake my head faintly. "I don't have a say in what you do. Or what you've done before. Women are supposed to be chaste, pure, for their husbands. But no one expects the same of men. I know that. Even my brother's been to brothels. I've heard him brag about it to his friends."

"Eavesdropping again, huh?" he says gently.

"I'm good at it," I mutter.

"You didn't answer my question. Would you care?"

"Uhm." I swallow. "Can we talk about something else?"

But the thought of him with another woman still echoes inside me. I can't silence it. I picture him kissing her like he kissed me, touching her with the same hands. A sob slips out before I can stop it.

I look away, blinking repeatedly and hoping I won't devolve into a mass of sobs, though I can tell I'm very close to doing so.

Not only have I somehow found my way to a forbidden tunnel where God knows what pagan rituals were performed, but I also witnessed something that will perhaps forever be engraved on my retina. Then to think of Sin doing that, too . . .

"Petra," he says, reaching for me again. "Look at me."

"Please," I beg, eyes shut tight. "Can we talk about anything else?"

"I've never done it," he swears.

I look up slowly. "What?"

"I've never paid for sex. I've never been with a prostitute."

The tightness in my chest eases. "You haven't?"

"I've never been with another woman. *Ever.*"

He holds my gaze.

"Do you understand what I'm saying? That's the truth. Until *you* I'd never even *looked* at anyone else."

CHAPTER TWENTY-NINE

PETRA

The Past

I stare at him in confusion, his words looping in my mind.

"But why me?"

"Why *not* you?" he counters without hesitation.

I take a deep breath, trying to piece it all together.

"I'm trying to understand you, Sin. To understand *this*." I gesture vaguely between us. "Why would you suddenly take an interest in me? Before the bookstore, we'd never met. You said you'd been watching me. But . . . when? How? What could I possibly have done to deserve that kind of attention? What made you interested in *me*?"

He tilts his head, his eyes fixed on mine. "Because you're my person, Petra."

"What?" I whisper, my heart fluttering madly at his words.

"You're the only one who was made for me—and only me. I knew you were out there. I knew I would find you. So I waited. Why would I waste my time on anyone else, when I knew once I found you, I'd finally be happy? That I'd finally belong somewhere?"

"But that doesn't make sense," I protest. "What's so special about me? I'm just a regular girl from a conservative church. I have no freedom, no voice. I'm a prisoner in my own life."

"Maybe *that's* what drew me to you," he says gently. "Maybe I want to be the one who sets you free. The one who opens your cage and lets you fly—far beyond the horizon."

He pauses, his voice low and reverent.

"And if you flew, I'd follow. I'd be tethered to you. Wherever you go, I'd go."

I shake my head. "It just doesn't make sense."

"Not everything has to make sense, Petra," he says. "But this, what's happening between us, you feel it. Don't you?"

He presses his hand over my heart, and I shiver.

"See?" he whispers, taking my hand and guiding it to his chest. "Our hearts . . . they beat together. Because we were made for each other. You for me, and me for you. That's how it's always been. Since the beginning of time."

"You speak in such strange terms," I murmur.

"Perhaps. But what's strange now won't always be strange. Why won't you let yourself *feel*, instead of trying to analyze it away? What's between us is pure feeling."

"Maybe for you," I say. "But how do you know what I'm feeling?"

He places a finger over my lips, quieting me.

"You want to tell me you feel nothing for me? When you risked everything to warn me about your father's plan? When you came here tonight, alone, in the dark? You said it yourself—you were *worried* about me. Be honest, Petra. Am I not in your heart? Even just a little?"

"You are," I whisper, the admission soft and hesitant. "But I don't know if it's right, Sin. I don't know if *we're* right."

He hushes me again. "There is no right or wrong. There's only *you* and *me*. And in this moment, tell me, how could this feel wrong?"

His hand rises to cup my cheek, his thumb tracing slow, reverent circles over my lower lip.

"You have to understand, we're from different worlds," I protest. "I'm from a conservative church. You . . . you're part of something liberal, chaotic. Insane, even."

"And yet, it's that so-called insanity that brought me here. If I hadn't accepted this job, would I have ever found you? Would I have met you?"

"No, but—"

"No more buts, Petra. Just yes or no. Be honest. Do you like me?"

"Yes," I breathe. "Even though I shouldn't. Because—"

"Because of what?"

"Because all of this is madness. The rituals. The skin you gave me. None of this is *normal*."

"Normal is subjective," he says. "This is who I am, Petra. And maybe, just maybe, that madness is part of what draws you to me." He leans closer, his eyes darkening with intensity. "Because I do what no other man would dare."

"What . . . what do you mean?" I ask, my breath catching in my throat.

"I dare to *take* you for myself. I defy all laws—moral, human, divine. I am willing to do *anything* to make you mine."

His words hit me like a wave. A deep, trembling flush blooms under my skin, curling low in my belly. The way he's looking at me, like I'm the only thing in the world that matters, it unravels me.

No one has ever looked at me like that before.

And what he says . . . it *rings* true. He has shown me time and time again that he'll go against anything—rules, tradition, even sanity—to get to me.

And what terrifies me most?

I want him back.

I don't even need to say it. Because when he leans in and kisses me, I don't push him off me. The warmth of his lips is startling at first, but as he draws back, I feel instantly bereft.

He gazes at me with concern and almost apprehension. Unlike before, he's waiting for my cue to continue, and that gives me enough courage to lean forward and press my lips against his. I wrap my arms around his neck, drawing him closer. His scent drifts everywhere around me, earthy and spicy, a combination that makes my head spin.

We slowly fall back until I'm lying on the narrow bed, his big frame looming over me, blanketing my body. And yet, he's surprisingly careful not to crush me.

Resting his forearms on the mattress on either side of my face, he pulls back to look at me.

"Petra," he rasps in a harsh voice. "My Petra."

I stare into his eyes, my heart beating loudly in my chest. I recognize the vulnerable position I find myself in, but there is something oddly calming about it, about the way his presence makes me feel safe and protected.

I raise a hand and press it against his cheek, caressing his skin.

His blue eyes never leave mine, their color deepening with intensity. He lets out a sigh as he nuzzles further into my touch.

"Tell me you want this as much as I do," he murmurs.

"I . . ." I press my lips together, not even knowing what "this" is.

"No more bartering," he whispers. "I only want what is freely given, Petra."

I raise a brow at him, surprised by his words. "I am at your mercy, Sin. You could do anything you want to me, and I would be helpless to fight you."

His features tense, and he shakes his head. "No, no, no," he mutters. "Never."

"Never?" I whisper.

"I want you to want me as badly as I do you, Petra. I realize my past behavior might have been . . . intense. But it was only so because I burn for you. You have no idea . . ." He takes a deep breath. "I want you like I've never wanted anything in my life. *Anything!*"

"Then here I am," I whisper as I continue to caress his cheek. "I—" I gulp down nervously. "I want you, too, though I have no idea what that means."

His first reaction is shock. It spreads across his features like wildfire. But soon his lips spread into a brilliant smile, and he leans in and presses a soft kiss to my lips. Then my nose. Then my eyes. He peppers a flurry of small kisses all over my face, his reaction giddy and unrestrained.

"We can find out together," he says.

I give him a small nod, and he captures my lips again, this time with renewed fire. His tongue brushes against my own. I respond in kind, meeting him stroke for stroke.

I'm not sure where this boldness is coming from, but as I give myself to the kiss, all my worries disappear. I forget about who I am, who he is, and the circumstances surrounding our meeting. There's nothing else but his sensual embrace that makes my head spin.

His lips trail lower down my neck until he reaches the edge of my bodice.

"Can I?" he whispers as he reaches for the buttons.

A flicker of uncertainty crosses over my features, but he's quick to assuage my worries.

"I won't take your virginity tonight, Petra. Not like this. Not until you're absolutely comfortable with me."

"Oh," I whisper.

"I just want to touch you, taste you, learn you . . . will you let me?"

I bite my lip as I gaze at his earnest expression. "All right."

He gives me another quick peck on the lips and gets to work on the buttons of my bodice. He gets a couple of them loose, but it's clear he has a hard time with them, so I offer to help.

He draws back, his cheeks flushed.

"I told you I'm just as much a novice as you are when it comes to these matters."

Somehow that emboldens me, and sitting up, I slowly unbutton the bodice under his watchful gaze. He has an intense expression on his face as he follows my every move.

"Damnation, what you do to me, Petra," he groans when I reach the final button and shrug the garment off.

I'm wearing only my night shift underneath, a white cotton gown with a lace pattern at the neck. His hungry gaze lingers on the exposed skin before going lower to my chest. A shiver runs down my back.

"Perfection," he whispers.

His hand trails down my neck, hovering over my chest as if he can't quite dare to touch me. This is a stark contrast to the man who bargained for a kiss before. But his bashfulness only makes him more appealing in my eyes.

He leans in and presses his lips against my neck, trailing open-mouthed kisses down my chest until he reaches my breasts. He cups them in his hands through my nightgown, opening his mouth over one stiff peak and sucking it into his mouth.

A loud gasp escapes me, and I hold onto his shoulders, though the wetness of his tongue against my sensitive flesh, even through a barrier, makes my head spin.

He's making me feel things I never thought possible, and it's almost as if an entirely new world is opening up in front of me.

His teeth nibble at my flesh, the warmth of his mouth spreading down to my core.

His urgency for me is so great that we find ourselves tumbling around on the small bed, with him on top of me. He lets out a deep chuckle that vibrates into me before he takes my mouth in another intoxicating kiss.

His hands have changed course now. Instead of touching my breasts, he's moving lower.

Gripping the hem of my skirt, he pulls it up to the top of my legs. The cold air hits my bare flesh at once, which only serves to emphasize the hotness of his touch as he trails small caresses along my inner thigh. I'm not sure what he's about to do.

In fact, I'm both curious and terrified. I've seen animals mate, and I have a guess as to how humans might do it, too. But he told me he wouldn't take my virginity.

Was I a fool to believe him?

He's still clothed. To do that, he would need to take off his clothes, no?

He senses my anxiousness, and he glances back at me, the candlelight illuminating his strikingly beautiful face.

"Trust me," he murmurs.

I gulp down.

"Will it . . . hurt?" I whisper.

His eyes widen.

"What? Of course not. I would never do anything to hurt you, sweet Petra. I only want to make you feel good, to give you pleasure."

I blink at him, trying to rack my brain for any notion of pleasure in the intimate act between a man and a woman. Yet there's none. His kisses and caresses on my chest might have felt good, but the shushed rumors I've heard said the act itself is painful and unbearable for the woman.

Seeing his expression, so filled with desire—for me—I end up just nodding.

His hand now rests between my thighs, awfully close to my most intimate place.

I grind my teeth, waiting for what's to come.

Yet when he touches me there, a touch so soft, so gentle, I nearly jump out of my skin. He parts my folds carefully, two fingers sliding down my slit.

It's . . . not painful? But that realization barely registers because another worry takes its place.

There, where he's touching me, drops of moisture spill out from within me, coating his fingers.

"Sin," I whisper in embarrassment.

"Ah, fuck, Petra," he groans. "You're wet." The last word is uttered in reverence. "My woman is wet for me." He squeezes his eyes shut and takes a deep breath.

"Is that . . . good?" I ask tentatively.

"Good? It's all I've ever dreamed about. My sweet, sweet Petra." He removes his hand from under my skirt and brings it to his mouth, licking his fingers clean. "Sweet Petra with an even sweeter pussy."

I redden at his use of such a word, but then I find myself growing even wetter at the gesture.

He grins at me as he touches me there again, this time probing, searching, learning. He presses one finger inside of me, and I instinctively tighten my muscles.

"Easy," he whispers. "I'm not going to hurt you."

I nod.

He pushes his finger in and out of me a few times, his expression one of reverence. "You're so tight. I can't wait to . . ." He trails off and shakes his head.

I wait for him to continue, but he doesn't

Instead, his fingers move slightly higher. I feel a zap of electricity shoot through me, and I lose all train of thought.

"Oh!"

He smiles. "That's perfect. Tell me everything you're feeling."

"It's strange but . . . good?"

His thumb presses on that spot again, and the same spark ignites within me.

Watching my expression carefully, he continues to swirl his thumb around that pressure center. Each time, the spark gains strength. It slowly builds in my lower stomach, like a matchstick striking against a match safe in search of ignition.

His strokes gain speed, and at the same time, he leans in to kiss me again.

Perhaps it's his wicked hand movements, perhaps it's his kiss, or perhaps both. But something erupts within me, my entire body tensing as he swallows my moans.

"What . . ." I whisper, barely able to find my voice. "What was that?"

"The most beautiful thing I've ever seen," he murmurs against my lips. "You're so beautiful when you come undone, Petra."

"I . . ." I blink away tears. My eyes are moist. My entire body is languid and relaxed. I gaze at him, and warmth unfurls inside me. "Sin . . ."

He removes his hand from between my legs and arranges my skirt back into place.

Pulling me into his arms, he cradles my head to his chest and rocks lightly with me.

"Thank you for giving me this," he whispers in my hair. "For allowing me to touch you."

The euphoria from before slowly clears from my mind, and I start to ask myself questions: Why is he suddenly so gentle, so obsequious, when before he would have been fine baring his soul for a kiss?

Yet just as I want to voice my concerns aloud, a knock at the door fills the silence.

He tenses, his arms tightening around me.

Another knock.

He ignores it; or *wants* to ignore it.

But on the third knock it is clear that whoever is at the door has no intention of leaving.

"Stay here. I'll be right back." He deposits me on the bed and goes to the door. I stare at his retreating back as the door closes behind him.

At first, silence is once more my companion.

But a few short moments after, a raised voice echoes through the tunnel.

Sin's voice.

"I told you I would do it," he says. *"B."*

Yet the odd thing is that no voice answers back.

Frowning, I tiptoe to the door and fit my eye against the peephole.

The hallway is dark save for a few candles in the periphery. I can make out Sin's back. He's talking to someone, gesturing with his hands.

"It was just one time," he adds, seemingly in anger.

This close, I can hear him perfectly. Just as I can hear the silence that greets him.

"Don't you dare threaten her!" he shouts.

This time, something knocks into him. He lets out a gasp of surprise and moves to the side, revealing his interlocutor—or lack thereof.

No one. There is no one there save for darkness.

My hand flies to my mouth as I watch Sin's body levitate, as if some invisible force has taken hold of him.

I stumble back in horror.

A bang reverberates outside the room. Then the door opens, and Sin strides inside. His features are tense and tight, so different from the gentle lover from before.

"I will take you home."

"But . . . what was that? Who was that, Sin?"

"I will take you home, Petra," he repeats, this time more emphatic.

So stunned I am by everything that happened, by the intimacy we shared and then the strange occurrence in that dark hallway, that I can only follow along in a trance.

Yet a thought persists.

The devil. He was talking to the devil.

BREAKING NEWS

Radcliffe Herald

15 APRIL 1896

SHOCKING MURDER!

OF PROMINENT PHILANTHROPIST

WIDOW DISCOVERS BODY; SINISTER WHISPERS OF ACADEMIC TIES AND RITUAL ATROCITIES ABOUND

The community was struck with horror and disbelief this morning upon learning of the untimely and brutal demise of Mr. Joseph Rutherford, esteemed industrialist and reputed to be one of the wealthiest gentlemen residing upon the Eastern Seaboard. Mr. Rutherford's lifeless and grievously mutilated remains were discovered within his private residence at dawn by his bereaved widow, Mrs. Eleanor Rutherford.

Authorities have yet to name a suspect, and the circumstances surrounding Mr. Rutherford's death remain murky at best. However, whispers abound regarding the deceased's long-standing affiliation with St. Anselm Hall University, a venerable institution of learning with which Mr. Rutherford was intimately connected. He was, it is known, the most generous patron of the Theology Department, having contributed vast sums over the past two decades.

Of particular note is Mr. Rutherford's much-discussed friendship with the reclusive and enigmatic Professor Arnoult, a figure both revered and feared in equal measure within certain intellectual and esoteric circles. Their association, described by many as "peculiarly devoted," has long been the subject of parlor-room gossip and drawing-room speculation.

Dark clouds further gather over this tragedy in light of the recent, still-unsolved massacre of twenty-five students enrolled at St. Anselm Hall. The killings, which have shaken the foundations of the academic world, were marked by dreadful ritualistic elements, the nature of which this publication shall refrain from detailing out of respect for the sensibilities of our readers.

It is not yet known whether Mr. Rutherford's demise is connected to these earlier atrocities, but speculation grows apace. Whether his murder is the work of a madman, a secret society, or some more unspeakable evil, only time—and Radcliffe—shall reveal.

Funeral arrangements for Mr. Rutherford have not yet been announced. Meanwhile, the local constabulary urges anyone with pertinent information to come forward.

More as this dreadful affair develops.

CHAPTER THIRTY

PETRA

Present Day

"Aaaaaa!" A shrill sound interrupts this vision as I sit up straight in my bed. A few more seconds pass before my throat aches and closes up from the sheer volume and force of my scream. It's the second morning in a row that I wake up from the same nightmare.

Harry's dead, my inner voice—of late uncharacteristically resigned—whispers urgently. *He died. His head came off his body. He fell through the ceiling. And there was just so. Much. Blood.*

Of course, the tears gather and roll down before I can stop them.

Of course, the morning sickness makes me rush to the washroom shortly after.

Of course, today is an overcast, rain-soaked day that's only going to get worse.

It is the day of Harry's funeral, and I am shivering from a mix of nerves, nausea, and numbness. His grief-stricken, devastated family has let it be known that anyone from St. Anselm Hall is welcome to join the service, yet I keep wondering if I can keep my wits about me when they put him in the earth.

Should I be going at all? But no, I *have* to go.

As has been happening of late, I lose track of my surroundings even as I find and put on the most somber black shirt-skirt ensemble in my wardrobe, walk down to the car, get driven to an understated cemetery, and stand amidst a sea of other black-clad figures.

A number of SAH students are also in attendance, and several of them are sporting the same "ALLY" badge that used to adorn Harry's backpack. Sobbing family and friends stand in the front while the priest reads moving Bible passages over a closed casket.

Harry's inside that box.

Do I say this in my head, or do I hear some other kid saying this? It doesn't really matter because the thought itself is so horrific that none of us has managed to fully grasp it.

My eyes are raw from days of crying as I scan the crowd, and that is when it happens, as if almost in a montage from some artsy, A24 movie. My gaze lands on the kids of the five founding families that Sin had told me about in the crypt.

Daphne Underwood, with French braids and disdainful expression. Quinn Haas, donning a small, black, netted face veil covering a pair of cold green eyes. Elias Rutherford, who looks bored and restless, shirt half tucked. Leonidas Snowden, with furrowed, bushy eyebrows over an aquiline nose and an expensive Armani suit in midnight black. And—

My eyes instantly drop when they meet Sin's. He's been looking at me, too, it seems, and I can feel his glance slide over my skin like the hot tip of a burning piece of coal. But he has chosen to stand with the SAH Club, as I have started calling them.

The five of them appear rather formidable as they look on at the moving tableau of mourners with an impassive serenity that leaves me feeling very unsettled. *Who the hell do they think they are?*

At this point, I'm already untethered from the proceedings and riding the waves of my imagination.

What secrets are these five hiding?

Why was Harry's body torn up in such a specific manner?

While I ponder, almost obsessing, over such dark theories, the priest's words turn into a distant, echoing hum under the constant drumming of the rain.

The parents of my dead friend are almost crouching over their son's coffin now, unwilling to let the pallbearers lower it into the ground. Their distress breaks my heart all over again.

In the end, Harry's coffin, dark and glistening with rain, is slowly lowered into the ground, and it really hits home then—he's gone.

He's well and truly *gone.*

As I watch the earth swallow his casket, a hollow sob balloons up in my chest, and I feel a swell of tears forming a lump in my throat.

This can't be happening, oh God, no.

But dirt has been deposited over the departed, and the gathering begins to disperse, mourners retreating under umbrellas, their figures dissolving into the misty landscape.

When my knees start wobbling from the strain of my despair, I, too, turn away from the grave and start to walk back toward the car.

Like other graveyards in the more affluent parts of town, this place is stately and dignified. The burial plots are neatly lined and spacious, and the whole compound spans several acres.

Stone benches line the main pathways. One can often sight a hunched, desolate figure perched on them, though today they stand empty and forlorn. The iron fence surrounding the area is covered by the cursive calligraphy of ivy vines. And the wrought-iron gates at the entrance and exit are similarly rusty.

Even steeped in despair, my senses are on high alert and take in every minute detail around me: the looming, moss-covered obelisks carved from granite, disfigured marble angels guarding the final resting places of doomed men and women (and in the worst cases, children), the crunch of gravel underfoot . . .

I am observing everything with a frantic attention that I haven't known since I stopped taking Adderall a few years ago.

And as I move through the cemetery, I keep feeling that I'm being watched.

No, I'm *certain* of it.

Eyes seem to follow my every step, hidden behind the veil of rain and the silhouette of gravestones. I glance back over my shoulder, but the fog and shadows blur everything into an indistinct, menacing haze.

Am I being followed? I wonder, and a chill trickles down the nape of my neck.

The feeling of being watched intensifies, so I start rushing, trying my best to avoid slipping on the rain-slick ground. I glance back, my pulse echoing in my ears.

The central knot of mourners has thinned, but the SAH Club kids linger at the edge of a ragged crowd made up of St. Anselm Hall students.

Are they watching me? I wonder next, and the idea causes a clattering panic that speeds up my footsteps. Fear tightens its grip on my gut as I hurry, the rain blurs my vision, and the sound of rhythmic squelching just behind me catches my attention for the first time.

Thinking you are being followed is nothing compared to realizing that your suspicions are true before you can reach a safe space. In my case, the waiting car.

At the hurrying sounds behind me, I let out a loud gasp, and my umbrella slips from my hand, busily rattling on the unpaved path. But I don't dare stop and pick it up.

Just then, a firm grip encircles my arm, and before I can say anything more than, "What the fuck?" . . .

I'm tugged into the gloomy fenced-in space inside a mausoleum. While I struggle to free my arm, I look up to see Sin, his clothes soaked and eyes dark with an inscrutable emotion.

"Petra, we need to talk," he insists.

Talk, talk . . . his voice echoes slightly within the stone walls.

"You've been ignoring me," he adds.

"I don't want to talk, Sin. Fucking let me go." I shake off his arm and step backward.

As luck would have it, my feet are almost swiped out from under me as they glide over a mossy patch of ground. Sin catches my flailing arm and pulls me toward him.

Outside, the rain patters down on the mausoleum roof, creating a sonorous mask over our clandestine encounter. Our faces are inches apart in that slightly damp, slightly warm air buffeting around the house of the dead.

In the next moment, I shrug off his grasp on my arm and step away—only this time, keeping my eyes well trained on the ground so I don't slip again.

"Thanks for that," I say in a clipped tone, "but I need to get going."

Sin's face softens, and his eyes are pleading as he says, "Petra, please. You have to believe me. I've never been with anyone else. I have no interest in anyone else."

"I don't know what you're talking about," I reply indifferently, while my stomach flips around in nervous tension. "And even if I did, how am I supposed to believe something like that, Sin? After everything I heard at the . . . the fall ball?"

He shakes wet hair off his face with a decidedly attractive flick of his hand. A shadow of frustration falls over his face, but his voice remains steady.

"Look, I know it sounds corny, but it's God's honest truth. That girl in the bathroom . . . she was lying. I swear to you, Petra. I'm not this cool fuckboy you think I am. I only have eyes for you."

"Well, I-I don't know what to believe anymore, Sin," I shoot back, just as a clap of thunder roars over the windblown trees, and for a moment, a flash of light falls over Sin's face.

What do I see in it that makes me falter and stand rooted to my spot?

His face is contorted with some anguish I can't make out. But whatever I do see makes my heart tighten.

He steps closer. "How can you say that, Petra? What about all the time we spent together? Did you think I was faking then?"

He can't mean what he's saying. He's just trying to derail my thoughts with all the romanticism of our storm-struck isolation.

CHAPTER THIRTY-ONE

PETRA

Present Day

While I mull over these apprehensions, sounds of high wind fill the insides of the mausoleum, and birds ruffle their feathers over our heads, sheltering from the stormy gale by perching on the ledges near the ceiling.

"Petra, did you hear me? What are you thinking of?" Sin's voice seems to be coming from some distant place.

I'm also trapped in another faraway place in the past, in that festively lit washroom at the fall ball . . . and the girl by the sink is wondering aloud if Sin has asked me to the dance out of pity.

"I don't need more of your pity, Sin," I almost hiss at him. "I don't need your interest, charitable or genuine. I'm fine on my own."

"You're more than fine on your own, Petra, but that's beside the point." Sin is speaking in a firmer tone, as if my delayed responses have given him the time to marshal his thoughts together. "What I'm trying to say, and make you believe, is that I've never lied to you about my feelings. That I've been entirely truthful from day one."

The rain has thinned to a drizzle now. Water droplets pool and stream over the stained-glass windows so that their reflections over the stone floor seem to be melting together into a colorful puddle.

Cobwebs hang in the corners, undisturbed by the elements altogether. It's as if we have stepped outside of regular time into our own dusty nook in the fabric of reality.

"I find that hard to believe, for some reason," I reply in a quiet voice.

Sin emits a low growl in frustration, and his eyes bore into mine as he steps ever so close. "Now you're just enjoying me suffer, you lovely, maddening girl."

Next, his eyes have dropped down to my lips, and I can see the desire beading in them.

"If you believe nothing else, Petra, believe this," he whispers.

And then he pulls me in for a kiss.

The warmth of his lips against the chill of the mausoleum empties my mind on the spot, and my body responds almost on autopilot. I'm already leaning into his arms, letting them ring around my waist as I kiss him back, angling my head and parting my lips ever so slightly.

"Petra," he croons as he moves down my neck, his lips tracing out soft lines from the back of my earlobes to the little dip at the base of my throat.

His hands are placed way low over my back, and in a swift movement, he shifts me against the wall, trapping me there with his whole body.

"Fuck, I want you so badly, Petra." His voice is a velvet snarl as he nips and bites at my throat. Heat pools between my legs, and a breathy little moan escapes my lips every now and then.

In the next moment, he has cupped my ass and hoisted my legs around his waist. I clutch at his shoulders as he rubs against my moistened center through layers of clothing.

Now his hands are scrabbling at my clothes. Between fiery, lip-swelling kisses, Sin pauses to suck at the exposed skin under my blouse.

My eyes almost roll back from the sensation.

Over the past weeks, my body has been wrecked most miserably by the unexpected influx of hormones, and it finally feels good to have its incessant needs met.

Great, maybe you should have another baby with this guy, a dry observation, presumably from my annoying inner voice, throws an entire bucketful of water on the fledgling flames in my body.

"Sin, stop!" I gasp. When he keeps fumbling with my panties without pausing, I push him away abruptly and start straightening my clothes. "What the—" I gasp and massage my neck and chest area; they feel sore from all the sucking and biting.

I will probably have golf ball–sized hickeys tomorrow.

"What the fuck are we doing?" I cry out in exasperation, the 'we' alluding to two pairs: Sin and me, and me and my own body. All four of us have a lot to learn about self-restraint.

He stumbles back, eyes wide with surprise that I wanted all the delicious frottage to stop.

"Petra, did I hurt you? I didn't mean to . . ." He's stuffing his shirt back into his pants and trying to pat down his hair into place.

I shake my head, more as an effort to gather my thoughts than to dispel his doubts.

"I'm fine, I just . . . we can't do this. *I* can't do this. I need time, Sin."

"I don't understand, Petra," Sin says, his voice softer now, but there's outright hunger in his eyes as he reaches for me. "I thought you wanted me to . . . I thought you were enjoying it."

"And I was, I'm not denying that," I reply in a flustered, trembling tone. Because Lord knows it had felt good.

At the same time, I have just been to a friend's funeral. My emotions and physical sensations are all over the place. The stuffy atmosphere of the mausoleum has started dampening my spirits, and the thought of being watched by dead people is rather unnerving.

Besides all these abstract considerations is the very real weight of the you-know-who floating in its warm, dreamy cocoon inside me. My life is much too complicated at the moment for me to be cavorting around cemeteries with devastatingly handsome guys.

"It's just too much too soon for me. I'm a bit of a mess right now, Sin, and I need to focus on getting my shit together."

He doesn't say anything, but his eyes visibly harden, as do the lines of his face. There are subtly perceptible changes in his body language as well.

Again, he seems to be undergoing some subtle metamorphosis, as the pleasant, swooning lover from a few seconds before is suddenly replaced by a frowning guy who looms over me.

Nah, I'm not doing this, I mentally decide.

That is all the courage I need to take a step toward the exit, even though the rain outside has picked up again and is now pouring down in broad sheets rippling in the wind.

He doesn't really step aside to make space for me, so I clear my throat and say, "I need to go," in a louder voice that's also supposed to remind him I can always call out for help.

"Very well, Petra," he responds in a strikingly curt tone. "If that's what you really want. But before you go, there's something else we must talk about."

I freeze, somehow knowing what's coming next. My heart pounds in my chest, and I feel my throat tighten.

"Sin, I don't want to do this right now."

"I saw the video, too, Petra," Sin continues, as if he hasn't heard me. "The one from the ball. Is it true? Are you pregnant?"

Okay, okay, calm down, my inner voice says, trying her best to maintain my—our—composure.

"It's not yours, Sin," I blurt out, my voice trembling. "The baby . . . it's not yours."

Why did I say that?

I will think about the reasons later because right now, some hidden impulse runs strong and sure over my tongue and locks it before I can take back the words.

His face falls instantly, and his eyes cloud over with confusion and pain.

"What? Petra, what do you mean?"

"It's getting late, Sin. I have to go," I respond in the most brusque tone I can muster. And while he's still reeling back in shock, I take advantage of his disoriented state to slip past his arms and run out into the rain.

The cold water feels like so many needles poking against my skin, but I don't care. All I want is to get away, so I start pushing against the hefty wind and hurrying toward the exit gate where the car would be waiting for me.

"Petra! Petra, wait, please!" Sin's voice calls after me, desperate and pleading, but I don't turn back.

I run directly into the pebbling curtain of water that covers everything in sight.

CHAPTER THIRTY-TWO

PETRA

Present Day

Does the chauffeur know what just happened? I wonder when the voluptuous violin opening of a Madonna song fills up the car on my way back home. But if he has any inkling of the mess I am in, Ron doesn't show it as he expertly maneuvers the car through the stormy streets.

"*Tsk, tsk, you should have just called me,*" he had said in a doleful tone when I slid into the backseat and implored him to start driving. "*I've got an umbrella and everything.*"

"Do you want to stop by a pharmacy, Miss Valentine?" he says presently, while I stare out the window, glassy-eyed, and occasionally sniffle into my sleeve. "We can pick up something quick if you're catching a cold."

"No thanks, I just want to go home, get into the bathtub, and never come out." I sigh and set my head back, trying to settle my wobbling nerves and queasy stomach. In a couple more minutes, I am dropped home with an "I'll check up on you later, Miss!" from good ol' Ron, who drives away without waiting for a response.

My clothes seem plastered to my skin as I fumble with the keys, my hands shaking from the cold and the remnants of adrenaline.

When I push open the door, there's a familiar quiet draped over everything: the antique pottery huddled over at one corner of the entryway, the plush carpets smothering my lonesome footsteps, the stately piano in the foyer that nobody has the time or inclination to play.

Presently, Mom and Dad are away at some conference in Austin, so here I am again, solitary specter of La Maison Valentine.

I kick off my wet shoes and quickly discard my drenched clothes in a soggy heap by the door.

I have only one goal in mind: a bath in scalding hot water, the hottest water my skin can tolerate before melting, while the *Nouvelle Vague* album plays in the background.

So I put the record on the sleek electric vinyl player my parents have set up in my room and make my way to the bathroom. Soon, the soothing strains of the band's song float into the air, and as I wait for the tub to fill with steaming water, I croon along, singing.

The stringed melody casts a soporific spell over my tired body. I take off my plush bathrobe and step into the sudsy water.

The warmth is a stark contrast to the chill that has settled into my bones, and as I sink into the tub, a shuddering breath escapes my lips.

The water's warmth eases the tension in my muscles, and I gently massage my knees and hips to alleviate some of that perpetual discomfort into which the you-know-who's mass has plunged me.

At the same time, I close my eyes, trying to drown out the heated memories of Sin's hands on my skin, grasping at the same curves that I'm currently massaging. A blush blooms over my face at the steamy recollection.

But I'm far too comfortable in the bathtub to get up immediately.

After what feels like an eternity, the water has become cooler, and I force myself to rise and put on my bathrobe. The record has run out by now, and the house is eerily quiet as I slip into my Gucci loafers and walk to the kitchen.

Rain sputters against the taut glass windows of the living room while I rummage around in the fridge and the cupboards.

Of late, my cravings have gotten particularly esoteric: first there was the experiment of strawberry dipped in melted queso cheese, then there was the adventure of chili lime chips dipped in salted caramel sauce. So I have to look around for a few minutes before an acceptable meal can be plated up.

The cook my parents employ is nobody remarkable, and salads, soups, layered pastas, noodles, and a few choice desserts are all he can reliably stock in the fridge.

In the past, this limited repertoire of dishes was quite acceptable to me because I could just order out if I wanted something more specific.

But none of that seems especially palatable at the moment. My stomach turns at the sight of most meat these days, and the changes in taste because of my you-know-what condition (the teachers didn't tell us about that part in Biology class!) make it hard to stick to a set menu day in and day out.

The staff might gossip if I suddenly start demanding something totally new, so I have stuck to repurposing the meals prepared by the cook.

Today, I find a small casserole of mac and cheese, which I garnish with some fragrant organic kimchi from a jar and a balsamic onion relish that I have just whipped up.

The piquant, tangy notes would pair well with the creamy pasta, I have decided. And in case my carb cravings are still unsatisfied later on, I can always heat up some garlic bread.

Just as I finish putting the plate together, something catches my attention—a faint sound from the living room. It's subtle at first, barely discernible over the storm's relentless drone and crackle.

I stand still for several seconds, and the spoon between my fingers rattles loudly against the delicate bone china laid out over the counter.

"Who . . . ?" I barely manage to whisper into the silence.

Outside, the storm unfolds in an unending dirge, muffling all small sounds and making it hard to trace out the exact outlines of the noise I have just heard. I strain my ears as much as I can without actually leaving the safe confines of the kitchen.

I try to catch any further sounds—do I hear footsteps? Are the curtains rustling in the dark patch behind the slim-necked ceramic pot near the French windows?—but all I hear is the rain.

My instincts are still on high alert, so at last I give in and take a hesitant step toward the living room.

Usually, I don't notice it, but the house feels unnervingly large for just one person; every furnishing and meticulously curated décor item casts a distorted shadow.

Get a grip, Valentine, my inner voice mutters in my head, and I am just starting to relax when I hear it.

Another sound—this time clearer, like something being moved or, more horrifyingly, a door being creaked open with the utmost care.

My imagination runs wild with images of gnarly, homicidal intruders, the kind that make you realize, "*Oh, no, that last frightening, ominous call came from* inside the house!"

"Hello?" I call out, my voice trembling. "Is someone there?"

Real smart, Petra, my inner voice chimes in almost immediately. *What did you expect them to say*? "*Here I am, come and find me*!"?

Of course, my question is answered with silence.

I can't ignore the urge to see for myself. I start tiptoeing toward the living room, praying to whatever occult primeval spirit was now acting in place of my guardian angel that the floorboards wouldn't creak under my weight and give away my position.

I pretty much made a beeline toward the bathtub once I reached home, so there hasn't been time to switch on the lights or start a fire under the antique mantelpiece.

The dim lighting from the small lamps scattered tastefully around the room amplifies the penumbral quality of the space, its simmering menace.

Some movement at the far end of the room catches my eye; it does look like the curtains breathe and sigh in the wind. But is anyone lurking behind them? I pause and turn in that direction, looking out into the well-maintained garden beyond the full-length glass doors.

My heart is hammering away so loudly in my ears that it's a wonder I can hear anything else.

And there it is. Movement near the lush velvet hangings, just at the edge of the sliding doors. My knuckles are now white from the tension of my fists being balled up by my sides.

The wind roars and rages outside, but a pool of unnatural quiet has been spreading within these walls.

Another faint sound, a rustle and swipe as if of feet creeping stealthily across the floor. "Who's there?" I ask in a firmer tone.

No response. I inch closer to the sliding doors, noting how the garden lamps cast haloes on the walls.

This time, the curtains move in a more pronounced way.

Startled, I step back and ask, "Who the fuck is that?"

Of course, there is no answer for this polite query either.

But something more fearful happens: A gust of wind pushes back the heavy cloth over the tall outline behind it.

The scream dies in my throat as my mind races. Thankfully, my legs start moving before my mind can catch up, and I take off running toward the safety of my room.

Fear narrows my focus, and every sound is blown out of proportion as I race down the corridor between the kitchen and the flight of stairs leading to my bedroom on the first floor.

Yet it feels like I'm caught in the sticky maws of some nightmare where I can't run even when I try my hardest. Though I am no slacker and would define my general fitness level as "decent," some lumbering fear seems to slow down my steps.

As I finally manage to reach the first landing at the base of the second flight, I make the critical mistake of glancing back, half-expecting to see the shadow following.

But there's nothing.

Thwack! I turn around and collide with something solid. Staggering back, my heart leaping into my throat, my eyes lock onto the last person I expect to see here.

"Sin!" I cry out loud. "What the fuck? It's really you?"

"Petra, are you okay?" The words nearly escape my notice because there's a prolonged ringing and quivering in my limbs as the adrenaline from a few moments ago charts its departure course through my veins.

"What are you doing here?" I shout at the same time.

How did he get inside? Why is he here?

Sin's eyes are brimming over with concern as usual, but there's a hint of something else too; something that unsettles me even more.

"Petra, relax! You're okay," he says in a soft voice underlined with the tiniest hint of urgency. "Actually, I came to make sure you were okay. I was worried. You just ran out into the rain, and it was so cold . . ."

"Forget all that, Sin," I cut him off impatiently while also taking a step back, my hand reaching for the banister behind me. "How did you get in?" I continue in a shaky voice. "And why the hell didn't you knock?"

The guys who had set up our intruder alarm system had assured my parents that we had the latest, state-of-the-art home security system. Of course, I was too young to remember, but the impenetrable safety of the house was something I had always taken for granted.

"The door was slightly open, Petra. I think you must have forgotten to lock it in your hurry," Sin replies easily enough, in a tone that hides any deception. "And I didn't want to startle you by knocking in the storm. I'm sorry if I scared you."

I swallow hard and take deep breaths as I try to steady my nerves. The house feels colder all of a sudden.

"Sin, that doesn't sound right. Even if I hadn't locked the door, we-we have security. No one can just walk in. There are cameras and . . . and alarms—"

"That's not important right now," he says, his tone sharper than I've ever heard it. Some dark flicker crosses his face, and his eyes narrow. "We have more serious matters to discuss. For starters, you can tell me who the father of your baby is."

His abrupt question stuns me.

"What-what do you mean?" I manage to stammer as I step farther away from him. The landing is big enough for the both of us, but it is also a blocked-off space that I long to flee from.

"Petra, don't you think I deserve the truth?" Sin replies in an entreating voice that completely contrasts with the pointed, frowning expression on his face. "Who is it?"

By now, I can feel my back pressing against the wall behind me.

"Sin, please calm down. Why are you doing this?"

Some sharp pain blazes across his face, and he says, "I-I need to know, Petra. Why have you been avoiding me if the baby is not mine? And if I'm not the father, who is?"

CHAPTER THIRTY-THREE

PETRA

Present Day

"I can't tell you," I reply in a soft tone, trying to defuse the situation. "It's—let's just say it's complicated, Sin."

"Complicated?" he snaps, and the glint in his eyes sets my heart aflutter. It is at once questioning and condemning. "What does that even mean?"

"Sin, I told you, it's not your baby. That's all you need to know." There. That's the ground I'm willing to concede to this pushy, frustratingly attractive young man.

"No, Petra, that's not enough! I need more, Petra. Please, tell me: Who's the father?" His eyes have something unhinged in them now.

The lines of his body are taut, and even in my current state of defiance-laced fear, I can't help but notice how his neck muscles strain against the lapels of his shirt. "Sin, please, you're scaring me. This isn't the way to—"

"Who. Is. The. Father?" Each word uttered with a staccato rhythm that bores into the sides of my head. I just stare back at him with the coldest look I can muster.

Instantly, his expression shifts.

Now he steps back and places his hands on his hips, shaking his head in frustration.

"Damn it, Petra! Don't you see? I *need* to know. You owe me that much."

"How—how dare you say that?" I snap back with fire in my eyes. "I owe you nothing. Nothing at all!"

My words are followed by a dramatic streak of lightning that momentarily illuminates our surroundings in a brilliant flash.

"And you're in no place to make such demands—"

"Fine," Sin cuts me off in a brisk tone that chills me to the bone. "If you're not going to tell me who the father is, then I need a list. A list of everyone you've slept with."

"Wh-what?" I stammer out after a few seconds. "Sin, that's insane!"

"Well, maybe that's because I *am* mad, Petra," Sin says back in a smooth enough tone, but the look in his eyes is fervent and bright. "I'm mad *for you,* Petra. And I need to know."

His words sound somewhat skewed, as if I am hearing them through a shaky tube. I try stepping around him, and my back slides across the wall.

"Sin, you're scaring me," I repeat as I move very, very slowly. "This doesn't sound like you. Please . . . you need to calm down."

And you need to get the fuck away from this guy! my inner voice yells in my head as Sin takes a step closer.

"Don't you understand, Petra?" His voice is much watered with emotion and tears, but his face is . . . frankly terrifying. "Ever since the fall ball, the video . . . I can't think straight. I can't sleep. I can't eat. All I can think about is you and this . . . this baby. I need to know everything, Petra. I need you."

"Sin, please," I murmur back as he lightly tucks a strand of hair behind my ear. "This isn't the way. You're not thinking clearly."

His face contorts with desperation and anger as his palms cup my face. The way they are shaking makes me wonder if he is struggling against a mad, savage impulse to tighten his grip.

"Then make me understand!" he whispers harshly, pressing his forehead against mine. "Give me something to go on. How many others were there? Who else do I need to worry about?"

The last words are uttered in a singsong inflection that will haunt my future dreams.

All this time, my mind has been trying to figure a way out of this nightmare.

Once again, the surrealness of the situation strikes me. Much like the ill-fated Dr. Jekyll, the Sin I know—charming, funny, laid-back—seems to be completely taken over by Mr. Hyde, the obsessive Sin who sees no issue with invading my privacy and asking me uncomfortable questions.

And also proclaiming that he's mad about you! My annoying inner voice chimes in again. *Are we seriously going to move past that part?*

"I don't know what you're talking about, Sin. This is—this is unbelievable." My voice quivers a bit, but I manage to get the words out. "And even if there was anyone else, I wouldn't give you a list. This . . . this isn't normal."

"Normal left the building a while back, Petra." A hollow humor laces his poisoned words. "Look, it's not that complicated. I just need the truth. I need to know who's in your life, who I have to compete with."

"You're scaring me more than anyone right now, Sin. This isn't about competition. What am I saying, you need to *leave*, Sin. Now!"

But he just stands there, drenched and desperate, his face and limbs twitching slightly under some duress.

"I've done everything right," he starts with a snarl. "I've kept all the guys away from you. I've acted like a gentleman. And still, you managed to find someone to sleep with. How in hell did you manage that, Petra? How many guys? How many times?"

There is so much heated hate in his words that I physically recoil from them. Who in the world talks like this? No, who the hell does he think he is to talk to me like this?

"NO!" My voice cracks over him like a whip, and with some satisfaction, I watch him stumble back. "You don't get to control this. You don't get to fucking *demand* these answers from me. And what the hell was that about . . . about keeping guys away from me—"

"I did it because I care about you, Petra," Sin cries out just as I shout, "You think you have the *right* to decide who I date?"

We are both breathing harder now.

"I thought I was doing the right thing," Sin spits out. "But now . . . now this? How many, Petra? How many times did they touch you?"

"There's no 'they,' Sin!" I shout back. "I'm not some fuckboy like you. Stop making this into something it's not."

"I'm *not* a fuckboy!" Sin retorts in a louder, more sonorous tone than he has ever used with me. "I tried. So. Hard. I waited for you, I cared for you! And still it wasn't enough. So tell me, Petra. I need to know."

And though I try hard to appear aloof, the distorted conversation has me spinning around in circles, mentally, as I struggle to reconcile the person standing before me with the same guy who had shared secrets and laughter with me in the dark bowels of St. Anselm Hall.

Are you really surprised? The guy used to take you to a crypt for your "study dates." The sarcasm of my inner voice is hard to ignore, but I keep the rancor out of my voice.

"Sin, clearly, you're not yourself at the moment. This macho alpha personality is impressing nobody. Seriously, whatever you think you're protecting, you're destroying it instead." The last words are delivered with a wince as he lunges at me midway through the utterance.

"I just-I just want you to be mine, Petra. As I will be yours. It's a special thing we have here, don't you see?" His shoulders have slumped down, and there's a broken longing on his face that almost, *almost,* makes my heart ache for him.

I take a shaky breath as a part of my fear morphs into deep sorrow.

Ah, how many sweet dreams had been spun around handsome boys like Sin! How many of those reveries were bitter illusions in the end . . .

"Because love isn't control, Sin," I manage to whisper at last, spurred to urgent response by the rapidly darkening expression on his face. "It's about trust and respect. And you're destroying that with every demand. Like, this is so beyond normal that I can't believe you're not joking right now."

His silence is deafening as he looks at me in pointed observation. As if he were a scientist and I the insect squirming under his magnifying glass.

In this storm-battered moment, any hope for understanding seems like a distant dream. I realize, with mounting panic, that he has taken hold of my arm, his fingers tightening imperceptibly with each passing second.

"Sin, please," I whisper, my voice trembling. "Just let me go."

But he takes a step closer, completely ignoring my words. "Petra, you can't run from this. From us."

The hell I can!

The next second, I push at his chest with all my might. "Petra, wha—" Sin cries out as I brace my shoulder against his shoulder and shove once more. He stumbles back and loses his footing, but I don't stick around to see what he'll do next.

Instead, I bound up the last flight of stairs before the hallway, and once in the corridor, I keep running—even as I hear Sin follow me close behind, yelling something indistinctive, perhaps a wordless shout of frustration.

"Damnation!" I hear him shout just as I reach the door of my room.

I scamper inside and try to slam the door shut—

"Petra, stop!" Sin cuts in, putting his hand between the door and its frame at just the last moment. And I hate that my hand stops automatically, that I can't bring the door crashing down on his stupid, slender fingers. "Petra, stop running away from me!" he says in a loud voice, rushing into the room after me.

"Sin, you're scaring me," I start saying but already the edges of my vision are blurring, the walls of the room slanting and the ceiling dipping. "Just let me be!"

His face softens for a moment, but the wildness remains—a barely disguised streak of madness. "I won't hurt you, Petra. I will *never* hurt you."

But I'm far away now, and his voice is muffled by a cottony layer that's settling around all my senses. My vision is blurring now, and my legs shake uncontrollably; at one point, they fail to support me entirely, and I start slipping.

"Please, Sin," I manage to say before the world turns black. "Please, just leave."

CHAPTER THIRTY-FOUR

PETRA

The Past

There's a new letter on my windowsill.

For eleven days now, he's left one there—every single night without fail.

I opened the first. Then the second.

After that, I stopped reading them. I burned them instead, one after the other, without even breaking the seal.

I know what he wants.

He's asking me to meet him again. Always the same secret place, somewhere on the university property. Always the same promise: Slip away in the dead of night and be with him once more.

He wrote it in the first two letters, and I'm certain he's written the same thing in all eleven.

But I haven't replied. I haven't even glanced at the others.

How could I?

I've been wracked with guilt since that night in the catacombs beneath St. Anselm Hall. I replay our time together and barely recognize myself.

Who was that girl? That wanton creature who allowed him such liberties?

My cheeks flush at the memory, and something sharp twists in my stomach.

I should never have let that happen. Not with him, not with anyone.

Yes, I may not be perfectly faithful to my religion, but that doesn't mean I should've risked my safety for a moment of euphoria.

He must wonder why I haven't come, why I haven't written back.

He's probably been waiting for me, night after night.

But how can I go when I now know the most important thing?

He lied to me.

I may be naïve and untried in the ways of the world, but that doesn't mean he can deceive me in such a blatant way.

He told me he had nothing to do with those rituals, that he'd never invoked anything, never bartered his soul. And yet . . . that thing I saw outside his door?

That thing wasn't human. It was something else. Something dark, powerful . . . frightening. He was one with the shadows, not a corporeal identity. And the way it had easily lifted Sin off the floor? With *inhuman* strength?

Now, in hindsight, there's something unmistakably sinister about Sin. About everything that has happened since I met him in that bookstore.

Yes, I'm drawn to him. Physically.

But beyond that, what do I really know? His name, his profession, what he claimed about his childhood? He could have very well lied about that, and I would be none the wiser.

Twenty-five people are dead. For all I know, he had a hand in it.

And I can't forget what I saw in the catacombs: those men with that woman, their disturbed actions. Sin swore he'd never been part of anything like that, but I don't know if I can believe him anymore.

If he lied to me once, what else has he kept hidden?

I remember the argument he had with that . . . entity. He was speaking of doing something, promising something, shouting when the thing spoke ill of someone.

Maybe that someone was me.

Because I *did* do wrong.

I snuck out. I disobeyed. I was reckless.

I see that now. So let him leave his letters. Let him wait beneath the moonlight. I will not read his words. I will not meet him. Not when I can no longer trust him. Not when I fear he may be involved in something vile and immoral.

But then . . . I shake my head.

I still have the one thing even the devil cannot steal: my will. And I will not be his plaything. I will not be his prey.

Maybe it's too late for some things, but not everything.

At least I never went to bed with him.

For that, I'm grateful.

I pick up the latest letter. Still sealed. Still untouched.

I walk to the hearth and toss it into the fire.

The paper curls, blackens, and burns.

And for just one second, I wonder—did he write something different this time? Did he finally confess and ask for forgiveness? Did he give a new explanation?

Curiosity burns inside me.

Just one second.

I nearly reach into the flames, but I stop myself.

I stay still.

I watch it burn and pray that the fire will carry away the last of my longing. Because yes, to my shame, I *do* feel something for him. And I know if I see him again, he'll use that against me.

"Goodbye, Sin," I whisper to the fire. "I hope we never meet again."

When the last ember dies, I crack open the window to let the smoke escape.

At peace with my decision, I head to the bathroom to take a hot bath before bed. While waiting for the water to fill the porcelain tub, I shed my clothes and arrange them neatly to the side.

The light flickers a few times, the bathroom illuminated by only one bulb.

A shiver runs down my back, but I quickly shove aside any ominous thoughts and lower myself in the tub. The hot water engulfs my skin, and I let out a sigh of contentment.

Yet even that cannot banish the thoughts of Sin out of my head. I glance down at my naked body, my lips pursed in contemplation.

Before, I've never taken notice of my body; never analyzed it. But I would be lying if I said the things he did to me, the things he showed me about my body, didn't make me . . . curious.

It takes me a couple of minutes to gather the courage to slide my hand lower down my stomach until I reach that place between my legs.

But then I stop.

I shouldn't be doing this, right? It's immoral, or so I've been taught.

Yet how can something that feels so good be so bad?

In my mind, the bad is relegated to the church's teachings and my experience with Sin—though the latter is not because I did not enjoy it, but because I was misled into it; because he abused my trust and lied to me.

And yet . . . why would I allow another man to dictate how I *should* feel?

I reach lower, searching for that hidden spot. The first touch startles me. It makes something coil low in my stomach.

I blink, both scared and excited.

Focusing on that spot, I emulate the same movements as Sin had done, hoping I can re-create the same feeling as before.

The anticipation is there. That spark appears the more I rub at it. But ultimately, it fizzles out before I can reach that elusive pinnacle.

I let out a tired sigh and remove my hand from between my legs. That was . . . disappointing.

Submerging deeper under water, my gaze moves to the flickering light on the ceiling. But something there gets my attention. There's a shadow moving over the opposite wall, and another on the same one. Shadows don't work like that . . . no?

Fear brims inside of me, and I cut my bath short, quickly getting out and putting my night robe on.

When I get back to my room, I head to the vanity to braid my hair for the night.

But as I lower myself before the vanity, I catch a shadow moving in the mirror. A chill climbs my spine.

I spin around and gasp.

He's here.

Sin.

He's in my room.

How did he get in?

I just came back from the bathroom. I only turned my back for a moment.

But somehow, he's here.

Quietly. Stealthily. Like a shadow creeping from the darkness.

He's as handsome as I remember. But there's something different now. A coldness in his eyes. Something darker, something . . . sinister.

"What are you doing here?" I breathe, my voice sharp with panic.

That we might be caught together by my family is the last thing on my mind. More urgent is the fact that I now *know* he is not what he seems. I fear for my own well-being, for my safety. Yet I'm not sure if it's bodily harm that I'm afraid of.

I'm scared of the damage he'd wreak on my soul.

"Why haven't you come to meet me, Petra?" His voice is slow. Tense. "Why haven't you answered my letters?"

I stagger backward, my voice rising with fear. "You should've taken the silence for what it was. I don't want to see you again. Please leave." Yet my voice lacks conviction. Even to my ears, the pronouncement sounds weak.

He takes a step forward, his brows furrowed.

"You are scared," he mentions quietly. "Why? I have not done anything to you. I *would* never do anything to you."

Every step he takes brings him closer to me, closer to the light from the candle on my vanity that illuminates his features, his expression.

His features are ravaged by pain.

"Stop. Don't come any closer," I warn.

He pauses, confused. His eyes narrow. "I don't understand you, Petra. What happened?"

And that's the problem, isn't it?

He doesn't understand. He lies and manipulates and calls it love. And maybe he believes it. Maybe that's what frightens me most.

That he thinks this is normal.

That *he* is.

"Please forget about me," I say. "Forget everything and stop looking for me."

"Why?" he asks. "Did something happen? Does your family suspect anything?"

I shake my head. "It was all a mistake," I whisper. "I shouldn't have come to you . . . I shouldn't have left my house in the middle of the night. I shouldn't have let you touch me."

"That doesn't answer my question, Petra," he states slowly, his eyes glinting in the dark as he steps closer.

I swallow hard. There's something dangerous about him—something simmering beneath the surface.

My heart pounds in my chest. I can't tell if what I feel is fear or excitement. Maybe both. But I know one thing: I can't let him see the truth.

I know what he is.

I know he has something to do with that . . . entity. And that makes him dangerous—far too dangerous.

Now it's not *just* my body that is in danger with him, but my immortal soul, too.

So I lie. "I think after what happened between us," I say quickly, "I realized I'm not in love with you."

It hurts, even as I speak the words. But it's the only way to protect myself. To end this.

"What happened between us . . ." I continue. "It was new. I was curious, but—"

"But?" he presses.

"But I see now that it was just physical."

He repeats my words, slowly. "Something new," he echoes. "So it was just *curiosity* that made you let me touch you like that?"

"Please, Sin . . . don't make this harder than it has to be," I plead. "You shouldn't be here. If they catch you—"

"No, Petra. You're going to tell me exactly what you mean."

"I *told* you. It wasn't love."

He stares at me like he's trying to see through the lie.

"Not love, huh?" he says, skeptical. "So . . . you'd let just *anyone* touch you the way I did?"

"I—well, you're the most handsome man I've ever met," I stammer. "And I haven't met that many, so I-I don't know . . ."

"So you'd let another man lift your skirt and *fuck you* with his fingers?"

I gasp, stunned.

I inch toward the door, preparing to run if I have to.

"That's disgusting," I add, my voice shaking. "How can you say that? Please, go."

"No." He steps closer. "Not until you tell me the truth."

"That *is* the truth. What more do you want?"

"Liar," he hisses, tilting his head. "But you're such a *pretty* liar, Petra." He tuts at me, lips curling in something between anger and desire. "I would be furious," he says, "if I didn't want you so badly."

He's a storm of contradictions. I don't know what he wants, and I don't care anymore. I just want him gone.

"Please," I repeat. "Let's not make this worse. Maybe I led you on, and I'm sorry about that, all right? But I've had time to think, and I've come to realize I don't want this. I don't want *you*."

"You don't want . . . me?" he repeats, almost in disbelief.

"No," I say, more firmly. "I don't want to see you again. I don't want you to touch me. I don't want to be anywhere near you."

His face tightens. The warmth drains from it. He steps closer, so close that I can feel his breath on my skin.

"I wonder . . ." he murmurs, voice low and venomous, "what your father would think. About you letting someone lift your skirt and finger you . . . taste your breasts . . ."

I don't let him finish. My hand flies.

Slap.

He staggers, tongue darting out to lick the blood from his lip. For a long moment, he says nothing.

Moments pass as we are at a standstill. He stares at me. I stare back at him, chest heaving.

"You're right," he finally mutters. "I apologize. That was uncalled for."

I press my lips together.

"Fine. Apology accepted. Now go. Leave." I point to the window.

But he doesn't move.

So I do the only thing I can. I grab the poker from the fireplace and aim it at him.

"Come any closer, and I'll hurt you."

He doesn't flinch. Doesn't even blink.

Instead, he smiles.

"My brave, brave Petra," he says, almost laughing. "What will you do, hit me over the head with the poker?"

I push the poker forward until it skirts past his waistcoat.

His eyes flash with something dark, something that makes my stomach twist. He . . .

I gulp down. This doesn't scare him. It only excites him more.

"You're lying," he says. "I *know* you want me. You want my fingers deep inside you, petting your little pearl. You want me because you know you'll never feel the same without me." He pauses and smirks, almost as if he knew about my secret time in the bathroom. "I'll leave. For now. But don't think for one moment that you aren't mine. You'll admit it one day. You *will*."

He moves toward the window, his presence pulling the air with him. Before I can speak, he leaps.

Out the window.

I rush to the ledge, my heart thundering in my chest.

What . . .

It's impossible.

I'm on the second story. No one could jump from this height and just . . . vanish. And yet, he's gone.

Gone.

I scan the street, the shadows, the rooftops.

Nothing.

Not a sound. Not a trace.

I think of all the letters he left on my windowsill. How I never heard him approach, never heard him leave, never heard even one rustle. Not even once.

And now I wonder—

Maybe the way he comes and goes . . .

Maybe it isn't natural at all. Maybe it never was.

What if he told the truth when he said he did not take part in the summoning? Because what if . . .

What if he *is* a demon?

CHAPTER THIRTY-FIVE

PETRA

The Past

It's hot. *Too* hot.

I toss and turn in bed, shoving the sheets off my body in search of some sliver of coolness in the thick, oppressive night. But instead of relief, I'm met with more warmth—arms sliding around my waist, breath hot against the back of my neck.

And there he is. As if haunting my every waking thought wasn't enough, now he's invading my dreams.

"What are you doing?" I murmur, still half-asleep.

"Did you really think you could get rid of me that easily, sweet Petra?" he whispers into my ear.

"We shouldn't . . . this isn't right," I mumble.

"How can something that feels so good be wrong?" he says, his lips ghosting down my neck.

I turn to face him, and suddenly the room glows with a soft, otherworldly light. Everything feels hazy and surreal, like the air itself is soaked in moonlight. And yet I can see him perfectly—his face illuminated, his eyes gleaming a brilliant blue as they meet mine.

"Sin," I whisper.

"My sweet, sweet Petra," he murmurs.

He leans in, lips brushing mine in a kiss so light it barely lands before he's trailing lower, kissing his way down my body. I realize then that

I'm only in my nightgown, the fabric barely shielding me from the heat of him.

He undoes the buttons at my bodice slowly, deliberately, and where his fingers linger, his mouth soon follows—kissing, licking, sucking the skin beneath.

A soft gasp escapes my throat.

I want to tell him to stop. To stop haunting me. To stop living in my thoughts like some lingering fever. But the moment he closes his mouth around one nipple, a wave of sensation pulses through my body—and the words vanish.

This is just a dream, right?

Dreams can't hurt.

It's not real. It's not real.

He continues teasing, touching me with the same hunger that fills my own thoughts. His hands slide down to my ankles, fingers curling around them as he pushes the hem of my nightgown higher, over my hips, until I'm bare to him.

He kisses the inside of my thigh, slow and reverent.

And suddenly, I realize . . . this is my mind reimagining what happened last time. Reconstructing the way he made me feel. Trying to recapture something I haven't been able to reach on my own since. But instead of touching me with his fingers . . .

He does something entirely unexpected.

He puts his mouth on me.

I jerk in surprise, hips lifting off the bed.

He laughs softly against my skin, breath fanning over my most intimate place. "Easy," he breathes, "just one taste. Give me one taste."

I don't know how my mind could dream this. I've never even imagined something like it. But since it *is* a dream, since nothing is real, I let it happen.

I open my legs for him, welcoming him between them. His shoulders press against my thighs, anchoring me as he kisses me again—deeper this time.

And then his tongue slides over me.

I cry out softly, my hands tangling in his hair. The sensations are sharper, deeper than last time. Every soft flick and slow swirl makes my body tremble. He kisses me like he kissed my mouth—hungry, aching, wild.

His tongue presses deeper, finding that sweet, secret place, and then he *sucks*.

I moan loudly.

"Good girl," he whispers, his voice ragged, his lips wet against my flesh. He kisses me again, everywhere, as if worshipping my body. "You feel it, don't you?" he murmurs. "You feel how only *I* can make you feel."

I cling to his hair, trying not to lose myself completely, but every flick of his tongue sends me spiraling. I rise, then fall, crashing into release so hard I gasp for air, knowing in my bones that no one else—not even myself—could ever do this to me.

It's not just the act. It's *him*. His presence. His warmth. The way my body responds to *him*.

He chuckles again. "So sweet," he says. "You're so damn sweet, Petra. Like nothing I ever dreamed before."

My body trembles in the aftermath. Still tangled in the sheets, I feel the aftershocks coursing through me—and yet he doesn't stop. He continues kissing me, giving me everything, until I come undone all over again.

It's startling. And yet . . . I want more.

The more he touches me, the more I crave him. It's as if he knows my body better than I do.

When he finally slows, he kisses a trail up my stomach, sucking the skin just below my navel and leaving a tender red mark in its place. Then he rises over me, looking down with eyes that seem to glow.

"My darling girl," he whispers. "You feel it?"

He takes my hand and places it against the front of his trousers.

"Do you feel what you do to me? What only *you* have ever done to me?"

I make a low sound, unsure of how to respond.

He doesn't wait.

Instead, he leans down and kisses me. Soft, deep, and unrelenting. I'm briefly scandalized by the taste of myself on his tongue, but the heat of it only stokes my anticipation.

What will he do next?

I shouldn't have dared to wonder.

With a final kiss to my lips, he moves down again. This time to my chest. And just above my right breast, he sinks his teeth into me.

Hard.

I gasp, body arching in shock.

There's a flash of pain—but beneath it, something deeper. Something darker. Something that scares me more than the blood or the bite: my own feelings.

He bites down hard enough to break skin. When he lifts his head, I see the evidence—drops of red staining his teeth, trailing down his chin.

"What are you doing?" I ask, my voice dazed.

"What do you *think*, Petra?" he says, smiling. "I'm claiming you. You're it for me. Don't you know that? This"—he gestures to the wound, to the blood, to *us*—"this will make sure we're together. In this life, the next . . . and beyond."

I don't understand what he means. Not really. But I'm too far gone to question it.

He strips off his shirt in one fluid motion, revealing the hard lines of his chest. Then he pulls a knife from his pocket. The silver gleams briefly before he presses the tip just above his right breast—right where he bit me. With one precise movement, he slices. The cut is clean. The blood surfaces immediately.

I frown, confused, but not repulsed.

When he pulls me closer, his hand firm against the back of my neck, guiding my mouth to his wound, I don't resist. I don't even flinch. I press my lips to the cut. I lap at his blood—greedily, instinctively—like he did mine.

And then something strange happens.

A new kind of euphoria overtakes me. It's not unlike what I felt when he kissed me *there*, but it's also more. It's *everything*. My body hums with him, fills with him, as if his blood has become part of me.

We don't need to do anything else. Not even that final act. Because this, this exchange, *this* makes us one.

I drink from him like it's something holy, something forbidden and divine. When the bleeding slows, I watch as his skin knits back together, smooth and unmarked.

And then I feel it.

A sharp cry tears from my throat as pain blooms at the spot where he bit me. A searing heat spreads over my chest, like someone is branding me from the inside out.

He grimaces, too, his features mirroring mine.

We're sharing it. The pain. The transformation. I watch, wide-eyed, as a black stain appears on his chest—and then on mine. But it isn't just a blot of ink.

It's a design.

A symbol.

A swirling, complex array of shapes, intricate and arcane—identical on both of us.

I recognize it. It's just like the sigils he once showed me.

Mysterious. Sacred. Marking us.

"What is this? What's happening to me?" I ask in wonder.

He only smiles. "What *should* have happened all along," he murmurs.

Before I can demand more, he surprises me again. He picks up the knife and presses it directly against the center of the sigil on my chest.

The blade carves a letter—an *S*.

But this time, the pain barely registers. Compared to the burn from before, it's nothing. I can only stare at his face, so focused, so calm.

"There," he says, satisfied. "Now you'll carry me with you. Always."

Then he places the knife in my hand and brings it to his own chest.

"Do it," he urges.

He doesn't have to explain. I already know. The knowledge is inside me now.

I press the tip of the blade into his skin and carve the letter *P*.

It feels ritualistic. Profane. Depraved.

And yet I don't hesitate. I can't. It's like he's feeding a part of me I've always kept hidden. A part I never dared to show anyone else. A part I've tried to *save*.

As the blood wells from the fresh wounds, the letters begin to shift. They don't stay as cuts—they darken, solidify, *transform*. Inked lines take root beneath our skin, fusing with the earlier sigils.

The result is permanent. Binding. Marked.

"You're mine," he says. "And I'm yours."

He kisses me, lips soft, almost reverent.

"You can never run from me, Petra. *Never*."

Suddenly, I jolt awake.

My heart races. My chest heaves with panic. Morning light spills across the room.

I'm alone.

I turn toward the bed.

There's nothing. No trace of anyone else.

No blood. No stains. No knife. No one.

I breathe in—then out. Over and over, trying to steady the tremble in my limbs.

It was a dream.

Just a dream.

So why doesn't it *feel* like one?

There's only one way to know for sure.

I walk to the mirror and pull down the neckline of my dressing gown. I expect to see something. Anything. That twisted, arcane symbol inked into my chest. A mark. A scar. A letter.

But there's nothing.

My skin is smooth. Untouched.

I stare. Waiting for relief to settle in. For my mind to make peace with the idea that it was all in my head.

But it doesn't.

Instead, all I feel is an unexpected pang of disappointment.

A knock at the door startles me out of my reverie.

"Come in," I call out, hastily buttoning up my nightgown.

My mother enters, her expression as cold and unreadable as ever. "Your father says we are expected at someone's house for dinner this evening. You must wear your best ensemble."

"Oh? Who are we going to see?"

She doesn't answer. Instead, her gaze drifts around the room with a vacant, far-off look. Then she mutters, almost to herself, "What are we going to do? Poor thing . . ." And then, more clearly: "Do not put your veil on."

That shocks me into stillness. "What?" I blink. "How am I supposed to leave the house without it? You know I'm not allowed to go anywhere unveiled."

"A carriage will arrive to take us directly to the house. No one will see you," she replies flatly. "Remember—you must not anger your father. This is a very important dinner."

With that, she turns and leaves.

I stare at the closed door, my thoughts a whirlwind of confusion.

What friend? Who are we visiting?

As far as I know, no one in our congregation would allow a woman to enter their home unveiled—unless she were a wife or a daughter. No stranger would be granted such liberties.

And yet, my father, so unyielding about appearances and rules, is the one making this exception?

It's preposterous. Suspicious. Which only raises the question: What purpose does this dinner serve? Why is it so important?

Of course, my mother offers no clues. She has the best poker face I've ever seen. If she weren't trapped in this life, I sometimes think she could have been the best player in the entire nation. No one can read her; if there's anything left to read, that is.

I sit with the unease for a moment, turning the possibilities over in my mind.

What could this dinner mean for me? For our family?

CHAPTER THIRTY-SIX

PETRA

The Past

The entire family gathers in the foyer for dinner. Everyone is dressed in their finest. My mother wears her veil, of course, so I am the only one without mine. My father and brother are impeccably dressed, as well, waiting in composed silence for the carriage to arrive.

And still, the question gnaws at me: *Who are we going to see?*

I've never known my father to have connections outside our insular community. He's famously strict, a devout man with an almost fanatical adherence to rules. And yet now . . . he merely glances at me, studies me from head to toe, and gives a single, curt nod.

Approval. Silent and unexpected.

Not a word about my unveiled face. No rebuke. No lecture. Nothing.

We step outside and into the waiting carriage. The ride is short. I count each second to steady my nerves: exactly eight minutes before we arrive in front of a sprawling estate.

We disembark. A wrought-iron gate swings open for us, manned by a uniformed staff member. We walk through it and then continue for nearly half a mile along a winding, tree-lined road. Whoever this person is, they must be unfathomably rich.

Even with my limited exposure to the world outside, I know this isn't ordinary wealth. It's the kind that makes my own family's fortune look modest.

When we finally reach the house, another servant opens the door, takes our coats, and gestures us inside. We are led down an impossibly long corridor toward the drawing room.

The hallway itself feels like a gallery—lined with paintings on either side. Some are vibrant: fields of flowers, sunlit scenes, genteel moments of daily life. Others are dark, grim, and haunting. It's an odd juxtaposition that makes the air feel heavier with each step.

But one painting in particular stops me in my tracks.

I linger behind to get a better look. In the corner, scrawled in elegant hand, are a signature and a title: *Sinful Desires.*

"Sinful . . ." I whisper.

"Petra, come on."

My father's voice cuts through the silence like a blade. I hurry to catch up. Once I fall into step beside them, he looks down at me, eyes hard.

"Don't you dare embarrass me today," he hisses. "Do you hear me, Petra?"

"Yes, Father," I murmur, lowering my eyes.

"Do not speak unless asked."

"Yes, Father. Of course."

The drawing room is lavish, with gilded walls, rich tapestries, and more paintings, some of which echo the eerie tone of those in the hallway. In the center, two sofas form an L-shape, and already seated are two people.

One of them I recognize immediately: the man from the square on the day of the murders. He's the voice I overheard speaking with my father, the one behind that disturbing plan to purge sin and dismantle the faculty at St. Anselm Hall.

The other must be his daughter. She's young, perhaps two or three years my junior, with golden curls tumbling around her face, the rest pinned neatly at the back of her head. Her cheeks are full and rosy, but her eyes remain fixed to the floor, her hands knotted nervously in her lap.

The downcast expression surprises me. She doesn't even glance up when we enter.

"Jeremiah, welcome," the man says, his voice sending a chill down my spine. Maybe it's because I've already cast him in the role of villain, or maybe it's because I can tell that title fits him far too well.

"Thank you for hosting us, Andrew," my father begins as we step into the center of the room. The introductions follow. "You already know my son."

"Yes, of course. How do you do, young man?" Andrew replies, shaking my brother's hand with a measured nod. "This is my wife Caroline, and this is my daughter, Petra."

I incline my head, as does my mother. We don't speak—because we haven't been given leave.

"This is Mr. Andrew Snowden," my father announces, his voice swelling with admiration. He launches into a stream of compliments—eminent, respected, generous—but I stop listening, distracted by the sudden click in my memory.

Snowden. The name has appeared in the *Radcliffe Herald* countless times. One of the wealthiest men in the region, known for his dominance in textiles and recent investments in railway construction. The papers often mocked his pretentious airs and flamboyant displays of wealth, but what stuns me more than anything is that he and my father are friends.

Snowden isn't a member of our congregation, so when he spoke of "our community" in the square, he must have meant the town, not the church. But how does someone like him know my father?

And why would my father—rigid, devout—defer so readily to a man outside the faith?

A servant enters, announcing that dinner is served. We follow, filing into the grand dining room where our places are already set.

Leah is seated next to my brother. My father takes the spot beside my mother, opposite Mr. Snowden. I find myself across from him, a position that makes me uncomfortable.

There's something about this man—something far more unsettling than anything I've ever felt when it comes to sin or temptation. It's deeper. More dangerous.

"Thank you so much for joining us today," Mr. Snowden begins with a smile. "It's a wonderful occasion for our families to get to know one another."

"Of course. My son and daughter were very excited to be here," my father replies.

Lies. At least on my part. My brother, for all his efforts to impress, is clearly trying to earn favor, eager to seem older, more important.

"We're grateful you made the trip," Snowden says. "Especially with how unpredictable things have become, it's not always safe to travel after dark."

"And whose fault is that?" my father growls. "That damned Arnoult. We must catch him before he does something else to shatter the peace of our city."

Snowden snorts. "Don't worry. I'm making it my personal mission to see that he's caught, and punished, for all he's done."

"Yes, yes, I have no doubt," my father agrees. "You've got your own score to settle with him."

Snowden sighs. "Can you believe he used to rent properties from me? Said he needed spaces for academic use. I had no idea he'd turn them into dens of iniquity."

It's on the tip of my tongue to ask what he means, but I stay quiet. From the corner of my eye, I see Leah stiffen, her shoulders trembling. Strange.

"What properties?" my brother asks, thankfully voicing what I can't.

Snowden waves a hand, as though brushing away something distasteful. "As you may know, I own most of the buildings surrounding St. Anselm University—or what's left of it."

He chuckles darkly.

"Arnoult rented several of them from me. One became his personal residence. The others were used for his . . . seminars." He pauses, then adds with a pointed smile, "At the time, I didn't question it. The university is large, with plenty of rooms. I assumed he wanted privacy. But now I see that he needed somewhere unobserved. Somewhere hidden."

"So you've known Mr. Arnoult for quite a while?" my brother asks.

Mr. Snowden nods. "Seventeen years, maybe more. He arrived in Radcliffe nearly two decades ago. No one suspected anything at first. It's only in the last few years that the rumors started—about his seances, his gatherings. Some say he holds rituals on the full moon. Some even claim he invited Madame Blavatsky."

My father frowns. "Who's that?"

"She was one of those self-proclaimed mystics who alleged to hold all the secrets of the universe," Mr. Snowden explains. "She died five years ago, but there are rumors she came to Radcliffe shortly before her death to meet with Mr. Arnoult."

"You really think he was behind the murders?" my brother inquires.

"Of course. Who else?" my father says curtly.

But Mr. Snowden clicks his tongue. "Now, let's not be hasty, Jeremiah. Arnoult couldn't have acted alone. We already suspect he was in league with that industrialist, Rutherford. After all, those properties he rented from me weren't cheap. And I seriously doubt a professor's salary from a provincial university could've covered the cost. He had to be backed by someone." He leans forward, lowering his voice slightly. "And considering how Rutherford died, I'd say it's obvious he was involved, too."

"Didn't you think it was strange?" I blurt, unable to hold back. "That he could afford them, I mean, when you rented the properties to him?"

The words leave my mouth before I can stop them. Silence falls across the table. My father's jaw tightens, and his fists clench. I brace for the inevitable scolding.

But Mr. Snowden speaks before he can.

"No," he says calmly. "I didn't question it at the time. He told me he'd come into an inheritance—said his financial situation had improved significantly. I took him at his word. I see now I should've looked deeper."

Realizing I've opened the door for more questions, I rush to ask another before my father can shut it.

"Then why would Mr. Arnoult hold a grudge against you? Shouldn't he be grateful, after using your properties for so long?"

Mr. Snowden chuckles. "Smart girl you've got, Jeremiah," he says. "Yes, you'd think he'd be grateful. But vermin like him don't know gratitude. Over the years, I've confronted him several times—questioned the strange goings-on in those buildings. He always had some excuse ready to throw me off. It's only in the last couple of years that I began to push back more forcefully." He exhales and turns to my father. "You already know what's been happening."

"Indeed," my father mutters grimly. "The devil's work."

I frown, waiting for them to elaborate.

Mr. Snowden shifts in his seat. "The first real confrontation we had, when I told him to vacate the property, he claimed his lease was valid for another ten years. Said I couldn't touch him. The more I threatened to sue, to evict him regardless, the stranger things became."

He takes a slow breath, his voice thick with memory.

"It started with my mother. The night I came home after one of my fights with Arnoult, my mother had a seizure."

His voice falters.

"She only lasted three days before she died."

Silence envelops the table as we all stare at Mr. Snowden.

"Then, of course, was the death of the horse stock on my estate. Ten horses died! Barely one month after my fight with that vermin."

Shock and disbelief fills the faces of everyone at the table. Everyone but Leah.

“There were other odd instances; noises late at night that no one could explain, some strange apparitions . . . But by far the worst was the death of my dear wife.”

He lets out a dramatic sigh.

“One day she was completely fine, the next she came down with consumption. She wasted away slowly, and we had to watch her become a shell of herself.”

A collective gasp rises from my mother, my brother, and my father. I, too, am stunned. But when I glance toward Leah, I’m struck by her stillness.

She doesn’t react at all.

“Enough talk of the morbid,” Mr. Snowden says, waving a hand dismissively. “Today is a day of celebration. We should focus on the joy of the present.”

At that, I frown. *Celebration?* What exactly are we celebrating?

My father smiles fondly, straightening his back with pride.

“I’m happy to inform you that the engagement party has been set for later this month,” Mr. Snowden announces.

Engagement party? Who is getting engaged?

CHAPTER THIRTY-SEVEN

PETRA

The Past

Panic tightens in my chest. Is *an engagement* why my father told me not to wear my veil? What is happening here?

Is he serving me to this creepy old man on a platter?

Dread fills me to the brim, and immediately, ideas form in my mind.

I need to find a way out of this. I cannot let this happen.

Of course, I'd known that sooner or later I would be married, but not now and certainly not to this man who's three times my age!

"And of course, I'm very excited about the wedding," my brother adds smoothly. "Leah and I make the perfect couple."

I turn to look at them, my brother and Leah.

First, I feel a deep sense of relief. Then the questions abound.

Leah? But she's so young. Far too young.

The shock doesn't wear off, not even as the conversation continues around me. Everyone begins discussing the engagement—who will be invited, which members of the Radcliffe elite are expected to attend.

My brother preens. My father wears a smug, satisfied smile.

So *this* is what he's been working toward all along: his attempt to climb the social ladder, to secure a place among the powerful. All of it—his pious persona, his strict adherence to the rules—has been a performance, a mask he wears to suit his ambitions.

The more I watch the carefully curated cheerfulness between the families, the more disgusted I become. This entire evening is a transaction dressed as celebration.

And now it makes sense: his willingness to fall in line with Mr. Snowden's plans, his quiet compliance, his eagerness to please. He's not just a friend. He's a would-be in-law. A union with Leah ensures access to her inheritance, her dowry—wealth that would pass to my brother, and by extension, to him.

Looking at small, quiet, painfully meek Leah, I feel a cold fury build in my chest. I can already see how they'll mold her into the same shape they forced upon my mother: voiceless, compliant, used.

The dinner ends, and the men retire to the study for cigars, leaving the women to take tea in the drawing room. Mr. Snowden urges Leah and me to spend time together, to "get to know each other better," since we'll be "family soon."

In the drawing room, my mother sits alone in the far corner, distant and uninterested in the conversation. That leaves Leah and me, side by side in silence.

After a few minutes, I finally ask, softly, "How old are you?"

She startles at the question, flicks her eyes toward me, then quickly looks down again. "I'll be eighteen in two weeks," she murmurs.

Ah. So that's the plan.

They're waiting for her to reach marriageable age—barely. Even in our community, marriages don't happen until nineteen or twenty. Barely eighteen is unheard of. Unthinkable.

I bite my lip, holding back the words I'm not allowed to say—the fury threatening to spill out. Fury not only at my father and brother for going through with this, but at Mr. Snowden, too.

Because it's not just that he's marrying off his too-young daughter; it's that he's *raised* her for this. She's been trained to sit still, to speak softly, to avoid eye contact, to submit. She is a doll. A lifeless, decorative thing.

And suddenly, I wonder if I've been too hard on my own community. Perhaps it's not just our congregation that silences its women. The outside world does it, too—packages them into quiet, compliant forms and calls it virtue.

They are used, displayed, married off . . . but never heard.

The realization makes my blood boil.

"Do you want to marry him?" I ask quietly.

She takes a deep breath but doesn't answer. Instead, I catch the subtle shake of her head.

I don't know if it's meant as a message, a quiet defiance she can't voice, or just an involuntary tremble of her body. But either way, I see it.

I ask Leah what she enjoys doing in her spare time and a few other questions to try to get to know her better, but after several failed attempts to get her to speak, I give up. She only stares at her feet, fidgeting with her hands. Even a simple nod now seems too much. With a quiet sigh, I rise from the sofa and murmur something about finding the ladies' room.

I make my way back toward the sprawling hallway, drawn again to the paintings—especially the one I remember being titled *Sinful* something. But just as I turn the corner, a servant appears in front of me, startling me.

"What is it you're looking for, Miss?" he asks in a somber voice.

"Oh, I was just looking for the ladies' room," I reply awkwardly, my gaze lingering longingly toward the hallway with the paintings. But I know I won't be able to return to it.

"Yes, of course. If you'll follow me," he says, and I trail after him. He leads me through a different section of the house and shows me to the guest bathroom.

"Thank you," I say, stepping inside.

After I finish and wash my hands, I exit—but soon realize I have no idea how to get back to the drawing room. The house is a maze, filled with endless corridors and tucked-away rooms.

I try to retrace the path we took when we first arrived, but instead, I find myself somewhere near the cigar room: the one reserved for the men.

My first instinct is to scurry away before I'm seen. I already know my father is going to reprimand me later for speaking out at dinner, and the last thing I need is to be caught here. But just as I turn to go, the sound of voices inside stops me. Mr. Snowden is speaking.

"There are some things of grave importance we must discuss, and I didn't want to bring it up at the table so as not to disturb the ladies' sensibilities," he says gravely. "I've learned more about that cult that's taken hold of Radcliffe." He pauses, then adds, "A student from the university, someone who was part of the group, came forward—for the right price. He said they call themselves the Ouroboros Society."

"The Ouroboros Society?" my father repeats. "As in the serpent from mythology?"

"Yes. Apparently, we were right about the sigils; Arnoult was the one who acquired them. But they didn't know how to use them. They wanted to test each to see which demon could be summoned. That's as far as the informant would go. He didn't want to get further involved once the stakes got higher."

"Sounds like a man of good sense," my father murmurs.

"Perhaps," Snowden agrees. "But now we're back to square one. We know little more than before, and I'm afraid there's been a new development."

"What kind of development?" my father asks.

"There have been more murders."

"What? I haven't heard anything about this," my father says, shocked.

"The police are keeping it under wraps. They're afraid that if word gets out, the townspeople will panic. Radcliffe has already begun to isolate itself. No one dares go out anymore."

"But who were the victims?" my father presses. "Locals?"

"No. Outsiders. Strangers to Radcliffe. That's how they've managed to keep it quiet. The bodies were discovered in a mausoleum—fifteen adult males."

"Fifteen?" my father repeats, stunned. "And no one knows?"

"Only because the mausoleum kept them hidden. A gravekeeper noticed the smell and alerted authorities."

"And how did they die?" my father asks.

"The same way as the others. A puncture wound to the neck."

My father sighs heavily. "This is outrageous. One man couldn't do all this: first twenty-five, now fifteen. And these were men, not children."

"That's where it becomes more complicated," Snowden says grimly. "The medical examiner believes the wounds were self-inflicted."

"What?" my father exclaims. "How?"

"I don't understand it either. Why would so many kill themselves? Why publicly? And how could anyone convince them?"

"You said they were outsiders. Do we know anything about them?" my father asks.

"Some have been identified. All from reputable families. Men from upstanding homes, the kind you wouldn't expect to dabble in arcane rituals. I've even done business with a few of their families."

"Good Lord," my father breathes. "How many more will die before this ends?"

"I don't know," Snowden says. "But I fear this will continue until they achieve whatever satanic goal they've set. And if these were suicides . . . we must ask what, or who, made them do it."

"Mind control?" my father hedges.

"I've thought of that, too. Everyone who knew Arnoult said he was charismatic. If he had powers, demonic or otherwise, he could've used them to sway minds."

"But for what? A ritual?" my father asks incredulously. "I've never heard of one like this."

"Just because we haven't heard of it doesn't mean it doesn't exist," Snowden amends. "This could be the foundation of something much larger. Something darker."

"Did your informant give you any more names?"

"No," Snowden replies. "But he did say Arnoult wasn't alone. There were four others at the meeting he attended. They wore robes with hoods and introduced themselves only by initials. He couldn't see their faces."

Robes. Like the ones I saw in the tunnels.

A loud, shriek-like sound travels down the hallway. I swivel, my eyes wide and fearful.

Nothing. There's nothing there.

I take a deep breath and turn around.

Another shriek, this time higher-pitched, the ghost of an incomprehensible word echoing in the hall.

A shiver goes down my back as I tell myself there's nothing there, that it's just my imagination playing tricks on me.

"What are you doing here?" a voice hisses behind me.

My heart jumps out of my chest.

I whirl around and come face-to-face with my brother.

"I—I got lost," I stammer. "I was just trying to find my way back."

"You were eavesdropping, weren't you?"

"No! I swear—I was just—"

The crack of a slap cuts through the air. Pain explodes across my cheek. I stare at him in shock.

"Go back. Now. And don't say another word until we leave."

I don't argue. I hurry away, trying to find the drawing room, but my mind is spinning.

The Ouroboros Society. Five hooded figures.

One of them has to be Sin. It has to be. I've seen his unnatural strength. His eerie silences. The way he moved without sound.

Perhaps he didn't sell his soul for a kiss, but he sold it for something. Power. Control.

The visit to the Snowden estate ends less than ten minutes later.

At home, I retreat to my room, expecting a punishment that doesn't come. My father and brother are too consumed by what they've learned to pay me any mind.

It's only the next morning, as I head to breakfast, that I notice the stir in the house.

Two physicians rush toward my brother's room. Curious, I follow quietly.

He's lying on the bed, a strip of cloth stuffed in his mouth to muffle the screams.

His right hand, the one that struck me, is severely disfigured. There is a harsh red mark on the back of his hand, as if someone had taken a hot brand and pressed it into his skin.

A demon sigil.

And I know, without a shadow of a doubt . . .

It was him.

Sin.

But . . . did he do it for me?

CHAPTER THIRTY-EIGHT

PETRA

Present Day

Another day I wake up from a bone-chilling nightmare, while the soft morning light slanting through the curtains casts a warm, wholesome glow around me.

For a moment, this stark contrast between my dream state and physical state disorients me completely, and I have the feeling of existing in some warped dimension, an in-between place between wintry horror and sunshiny joy.

A long while after waking up, I lie still, trying to unsee the images creeping into my brain: Harry's detached head, spurting blood from all orifices, Sin's wild expression as he implored me to . . . to what?

Try as I might to piece together the shocking events of last night, there is a disconnect between all the threads of my recollection.

I remember our tryst at the mausoleum, how the encounter had quickly escalated into a heated, physical entanglement.

My face warms up as I remember how he had cupped my breasts and rubbed against me, how he had left behind a trail of hickeys with his accursed, hot-as-hell mouth . . .

And suddenly, the vision tilts, and my mind's eye is now watching the looming figure of Sin on the landing before my room, how he blocked my way and demanded something from me; what was it now . . .

"Who is the father?" he had asked me. Or had it been part of my dream?

Perhaps the strain of lying to him about the you-know-who not being his—a decision I don't completely understand yet—has made me suspect him of harboring sinister motives.

Perhaps I'm projecting.

There's no use obsessing over these thoughts, so I slowly sit up, while all my bones sing a symphony of pain and discomfort.

My muscles are stiff and tense; they must have been held taut in anticipation or anxiety for what feels like hours.

I look around and realize that I'm alone.

But of course I am. Why would anyone else be here?

Perhaps this is all just the pregnancy hormones. This thought is followed by another fluttering one: *I'm starting to show.*

Yup, that's right. What with all the murders, the crypt dates with Sin, and the disastrous fall balls, the small window for getting rid of the you-know-who has closed for me.

At five months, I am well on my way to delivering, whether I am ready for it or not. So I pull back the covers and look down at my body.

My hand instinctively rests on my belly, a small but unmistakable curve. The skin is stretching over it, and the morning light rings it in a neat halo.

Nearly five months along. What does the you-know-who look like now?

If I remember my lessons, it will have started to resemble a human baby, with the head and torso gaining more definition.

Afloat inside me is another person.

The very thought sends a jolt down my limbs. Whether that's fear or curiosity, I don't know.

I stretch my arms and think of getting out of bed, but a leaden feeling has stilled my legs as last night's events keep replaying in my head, though their memories are disjointed and disconnected at some fundamental level.

I need to talk to someone. There's no way I can find a way out of this mess on my own, so I needed to get some support like, *yesterday*.

My parents have been busy with a spate of conferences, trade shows, and investor meetings as of late, and their travels have taken them to Europe, all the way across the ocean. Not that I would have confided in them had they been around.

My father might have been sympathetic, but I'm sure Mom would have tried to kill me. She is far too proud to have a teenage mom for a daughter.

The thoughts threaten to overwhelm me again, and the bleakness threatens to suck me down like a bottomless quagmire. *I know who I can talk to.*

The next moment, I have opened *Instafriends* and found the Misc Midn8 Meets channel.

There it is, the small green circle next to Amelia's handle, the cheery sign that she's online.

Ames, I really need to talk.

Barely a moment or two passes before her reply comes through.

Petra, of course. What's going on?
Tell me everything, girl.

And over the next several book-sized paragraphs, I proceed to do just that.

I tell Amelia about Elias Rutherford's party, the pool dunking I was subjected to, and how Sin had come to my rescue.

Oooh, knight in football uniform,
swoon!

Amelia texts at this point of my story.

Everybody seems to think of him
that way.

I write back in complete candor.

You should have seen the way he
snapped at Elias. Honestly a bit
scary . . . but anyways . . .

And so, I pick up the thread and move on to the more NSFW parts of my tale: our clandestine conversation in the bedroom, where we lounged around in bathrobes over underwear while our clothes tumbled around in the dryer.

Girl, whaaaaaa.

Amelia follows that up with a string of thirst emojis too crude to be reproduced here. But the gist of it is clear.

That is some bodice-ripper level of hotness right there!

It wasn't like that, Ames. We were actually talking . . . like, I enjoyed talking to him.

Raaaaight, Petra.

She adds several eye-roll emojis in a row.

And now my recounting gets rougher as the story turns into darker corners. I finally arrive at the day I found that I was pregnant.

Holy shit, Petra! Are you okay?

That is her first response, and I love her for it.

What did you decide?

She texts next, and I chuckle out loud, knowing that whatever state I find myself in today was not reached *by choice*. In other words . . .

I never decided what to do. I-I just got swept away.

What do you mean? You . . . didn't abort?

Amelia replies, and I can sense her caution. I still haven't told her how I feel about being pregnant. So far, I've just been a narrator of—it feels—someone else's story.

No. I didn't even go to the Planned Parenthood center. I just didn't have the time.

Petra, this isn't some chore you put off till your schedule frees up.

I know, Ames, I know. Just—so many bad things started happening, and I just couldn't.

But you told Sin?

Again, a dry laugh escapes from my lips, and I tell her about my split-second decision to inform Sin that the baby was not his.

But why???

She replies almost instantly.

Why would you do that?
He would help if he knew, right?

Would he? This question makes me remember the Sin from last night, who had stormed into my room after me, demanding that he be allowed to "help" me.

Things got even worse, Ames. And I couldn't tell him.

I write back hesitantly.

Now I have reached the most traumatic part of my story: first, Edwin's death and then . . . Harry.

My fingers start shaking as I type. Tears stream from my eyes as some strange, choking fear makes my heart clench and I write about the fall ball: my giddy mirth at the start of the evening, dancing with Sin, going to the washroom and overhearing those girls chatting among themselves, confronting Sin, and then finally . . .

The images threaten to overwhelm me completely, but I retain enough gumption to describe the whole ordeal to Amelia.

Petra, what the everloving fuck is happening in that town of yours?

I just *know* that she's pacing across her room now.

I take a deep breath, trying to find the right words to convey the absolutely horrifying chaos of that fateful night. But where will the words come from?

Instead, I tell her the real reason I am confessing all this to her.

I need someone to tell me what to do, Ames. I'm in such a mess . . . about this baby. And about Sin.

A handful of minutes pass before her response reaches me. But it is succinct and direct:

Tell. Him.

You sure?

I text back; perhaps I had hoped that she would side with me, though I don't feel particularly surprised by her advice.

Yes!

It seems to be the popular consensus, all things considered, so I don't poke around for further assurance.

And also, take care, Petra.

She texts before I can reply to her latest message.

The things happening at St. Anselm Hall . . . they're beyond disturbing. I hope you're staying safe.

Am I? It has occurred to me that my behavior over the past few weeks has been anything but cautious.

I have been stealing away to crypts hidden under the school with Mr. Popular, who was prone to the type of personality swings that would put a schizophrenic to shame.

I am harboring secrets that could threaten my living situation with my parents.

I am not making much progress with Ms. Matthews's assignment, either.

Yet I know that confiding in Amelia, *finally telling someone my secret*, was one of the saner decisions I have made as of late. Feeling a bit more composed, I close my eyes for a moment, allowing Amelia's (hopefully) honest advice to sink in.

The road I found myself on was not only the one less traveled but also the most riddled with false steps and deceptive snares.

But at least I'm not walking it alone.

A CLEAR SKY heralds the next day, and the morning light bathes a bleak landscape. Overnight, trees have bent and bowed to the ground, some even getting uprooted entirely and blocking important streets in town.

I wake up to the blare and bustle of roadside equipment and workers sawing off fallen trees up and down the neighborhood. My parents are still not home, and for once, the quiet house feels like a refuge from all the noise.

I've just finished whipping up some French toast grilled cheese—yes, it's exactly as decadent as it sounds; instead of two slices of bread, I use two slices of egg-dipped fried bread—when the doorbell rings.

My heart skips a beat, and my belly flops around in anxiety.

Briefly, I wonder how the butterflies-in-the-stomach thing works when you're pregnant, but before I can meander down that tangent, I have already opened the door.

And what do you know, Sin is standing there, a bouquet of flowers in one hand and a stylishly wrapped present in the other.

He looks apologetic, his eyes soft and gentle when they land on me.

This is such a stark contrast to his intense brooding from last night that I am lost for words at first.

CHAPTER THIRTY-NINE

PETRA

Present Day

"Sin," I finally manage to say. "W-what are you doing here?"

"I came to say sorry," he replies smoothly, holding out the bouquet toward me, and I notice he has taken care to fill it with orchids and poppies, the sly man. "For yesterday. I was way out of line at the funeral, and afterward . . ." Here he pauses to give me a scorching look that almost makes my legs quiver. "I was rude and overbearing. Please forgive me," he finishes simply.

I don't know what to say, so I take the flowers and take in their smell. "Thank you, Sin," I reply after a while. "For the flowers, and the apology. They have been well received."

I stand aside and gesture for him to enter the house.

"And I also brought you this," he adds as he steps into the living room. He's holding out the present. "I remember you mentioned this painter once, the one who trained . . . who was it now? Goya? Anyways, I found this painting and thought of you."

He's kidding, I think in complete disbelief. Sin is referring to an unnamed mentor of the Spanish painter Francisco Goya, widely regarded as one of the first truly modern painters.

On one of our dates, I had mentioned how much I love the artist's brushwork and complex use of light and shadows. Surely, he wasn't really paying attention?

So thinking, I unwrap the package carefully. And a loud gasp slips from my lips when I see the piece Sin has carefully wrapped up: Titled *Sinful Desires,* it's the long-rumored last painting by Goya's brilliant master.

The title evokes something in my mind, a long-lost memory that prods at my consciousness. I've seen this before, haven't I? I've seen it *in the flesh,* no?

But as soon as that memory tries to poke its head, it's gone.

Instead, I continue to marvel at the piece in front of me.

My breath catches. "Sin, I can't believe this! Where did you even find this painting?" I gush.

Sin is beaming at my obvious enthusiasm, yet there is no trace of self-importance.

Instead, he looks genuinely pleased to have elicited such a response from me.

But I can hardly remember to thank him before my attention is completely caught up in the frame before me: the solitary figure of a girl walking down a windy English moor captured in such dramatic, gothic detail that it would put the best landscapists to shame (J. M. W. Turner be damned).

I'm enthralled by the dark, muted colors of the girl's velvet-green dress and her long brown hair and the windblown trees in the background—all of it so deliciously stormy, brimming over with savage intensity.

"No, really," I exclaim aloud as the light from the windows falls on the painting and makes me see details that had previously escaped me. "Where did you find this piece? Tell me you didn't just rob a museum or something!"

"Relax," Sin replies with a wry laugh. "We have all sorts of collectors in my family: Edwardian furniture, Fabergé eggs, antique Chippendales, someone or the other is always pawning or circulating stuff around."

I don't look very convinced, so he sighs.

"Look, that's part of the reason I even knew of Ms. Matthews's class. What, did you think a handsome jock such as myself just happened to have a head for art as well?"

Now he is teasing me using the same wits he had displayed the first night we met.

"I don't know . . ." I begin uncertainly but without much conviction, as my attention returns to the marvelous painting in my hands.

"Trust me, Petra. I have *connections.*" Sin waggles his eyebrows theatrically at the last word and plonks down at the dining table.

"Connections? Like, what kind of connections?" I press gently, perhaps because some part of me was still unimpressed by this grand gesture. "Why won't you tell me?"

"Because it's complicated, Petra," Sin replies in a voice that is starting to get testy. As if sensing this ominous inflection, he rubs the back of his neck, his smile strained. "Look, I just wanted to find something special for you. To show you how sorry I was and . . . and how badly I want to set things right. Can you just accept that?"

A knot tightens in my stomach, and the unease from last night resurfaces.

"Sin, I appreciate the gesture, I really do," I begin cautiously, putting the painting on the table. "But given everything that's—that's been happening, you can understand why I'd want to know more."

He doesn't say anything for a while, so I say, "Right?" to jolt him into responding.

"I guess," he responds in a slightly petulant tone.

"You're right. Maybe I'm overthinking it," I say quietly.

And suddenly he's standing very close to me, his hands cupping my face and his cologne—lemon groves and pine—scenting the private space between our bodies.

"I promise, Petra, I'm not hiding anything that would hurt you," he says in a gentle whisper, like one would adopt while talking to a newborn lamb. "I would never let anyone else hurt you either. Trust me on that."

His palms are warm and slightly calloused against my face; his face is hovering inches away from mine. I try and fail to control my breathing and with it, my errant thoughts.

"I'll try, Sin." I'm weighing out my words as carefully as I can, because by now, I'm weathered enough to be wary of this guy's unpredictable moods. "It's just . . . hard right now. Given all that's happened recently, you know."

Like my friend's head detaching from his body and rolling onto the hem of my dress, my inner voice pipes up, and I try my hardest not to wince at the cynical casualness of her tone.

"Of course, Petra, I understand," Sin says in an amiable enough tone before quickly pecking my forehead and sliding back into the chair he had been sitting on.

I sit down at the table, too, and return my attention to the painting.

The old master has used a peculiar shade of Prussian blue, almost grayish, to outline the woods in the distance, and I love how the girl is positioned in the frame, with just a slim sliver of her side profile turned toward the viewer.

But before I can linger on the deft lines with which the folds of her cape have been sketched, another urgent thought tugs at my attention.

"Sin, can I ask you something?" I try my hardest to keep my tone subtle and noncommittal.

"Of course, anything," he replies, gently patting my arm.

"Did you come by my house last night?" I ask without further dilly-dallying; at the same time, I'm watching his reaction carefully. "Were you here?"

I don't know what I was expecting, but it was certainly not this: Sin's brows furrow with confusion, and he shakes his head. "No, I didn't. Why, what happened?"

"I . . . I thought you might have come around," I respond, thinking fast. "I thought I heard someone call my name . . . I guess it was just the wind." I drop my gaze back at the painting, straining to keep my face neutral.

"Petra, you've been through a lot," Sin says in a kind tone, stroking faint circles on my arm—a gesture that is so familiar to me by now that it makes my throat close up with emotion. "And given your pregnancy . . . it's normal to feel overwhelmed is all I'm saying. I'm just sorry that I added to your stress."

"What about my pregnancy?" I blurt out.

"Petra, I don't care that you're pregnant," Sin says in a steady tone as he looks straight at me. "I also don't care who the father of the baby is; all I care about is your happiness. Do you believe me?"

"I-I think I do," I reply hesitantly. What else can I say? And anyway, he does sound sincere enough.

Perhaps my nightmares had been darkening all other aspects of my life, much like the grayish blue of the skies in the painting made many of the features look slightly ashen.

Maybe everything from last night really was just a product of my over-active imagination and pregnancy hormones mixing with fear.

"Thank you for the flowers and the painting, Sin," I repeat myself from before, but this time I offer the words as a genuine gesture of gratitude. "And thank you for apologizing."

"Of course. I so want to make things right between us." He smiles at me for a moment before his expression turns pensive again.

"What is it?" I can't help but ask.

"I should have been gentler with you at the cemetery," he says, his voice softening. "I let my emotions get the better of me. I don't like that you had to see *that part* of me."

Those last words remind me of my earlier analogy of Dr. Jekyll and Mr. Hyde for Sin's many opposing moods.

I am slightly taken aback by this sudden shift in his demeanor.

"Sin, it's . . . yeah, it was sort of messed up. I understand you were upset, but yesterday was really intense."

"I know," he continues, his tone sincere. "And I am really, really sorry about my behavior. But . . ."

"But what?" I reply, piqued by his expression. He looks reluctant, like he's forming some thought he's afraid of saying out loud.

"There's something that's been weighing on me."

"Which is?" And now my tone is impatient at how he's stretching out this air of suspense. "Tell me!" I demand again.

"Look, Petra, the two deaths, Edwin and Harry. They were both people you knew, and I'm—" He breaks off and gets up from his chair, as if determined to look away from me while conjecturing about my safety. "I'm worried about you, all right? I've been thinking about it a lot, and honestly, I'm scared something might happen to you."

At last, he turns around to look at me, and I can see that his eyes are filled with a kind of fear as well. A shiver runs down my spine when I realize that Sin is being honest, and I hug myself surreptitiously.

"Sin, I'm scared, too," I finally admit in a quiet tone full of unspoken despair. "It's all been a little too much too sudden, right? And I just don't know what to make of it all."

He breaks off his pacing to come and stand beside my chair and rub my shoulders in a comforting gesture.

"Apart from all that madness, how are you handling everything, Petra? Are you doing okay?" he asks softly.

"I'm not entirely sure. For now, I'm just trying to get through each day. The deaths, the pregnancy, the crypt, and all those godawful paintings in there—my head feels like it might just burst one of these days!"

As soon as the words are out of my mouth, I gasp and cover my face with my hands. An image of Harry's mutilated body has just swum past my mind's eye. Sin flinches as well but doesn't stop kneading my shoulders in the same cadence as before.

"I can't even imagine what you're going through," he whispers into the tense air. "But don't think for a second that you've got to go through all of it on your own."

He pulls up a chair and sits next to me, his palms grasping my own in an assuring way that calms me down, despite everything.

But there is still a faint recollection of something wrong in the past. Perhaps my mind still retains scraps from the volley of questions and demands Sin had lobbed at me—in dream or recollection, I don't know.

And now he seems genuinely worried for my safety.

Once again, I get the feeling of being manipulated in some way.

"Why do you care so much, Sin?" I ask in a much quieter voice. "You barely even know me."

"And that's where you're mistaken, Petra," Sin replies with an ineffable look in his eyes. "I already feel like I have known you for a long time."

There's a dreaminess to his face that's almost contagious. He puts his forehead against mine, and I'm thrown off by the endearing, affectionate movement.

"But either way, I need you to promise me that you'll be careful. The fact that the two deaths so far were people you knew—it's too much of a coincidence. Just doesn't sit right with me, you know?"

"Of course I want to be careful, Sin!" I cry out in exasperation. "I'm scared, too, but what can we even do about it? It feels like everything is just spiraling out of control."

"I don't have all the answers," he admits, his voice heavy with frustration. "But we need to stay alert. If there's someone targeting you, we can't take any chances."

"I just want things to go back to normal," I exclaim forcefully, a loud sigh following the wistful words.

"I know," Sin adds. "And I am here for you. I won't let anything happen to you, so there's no need to be all doom and gloom yet, you understand?"

"I guess," I reply uneasily, unwilling to be lulled into a potentially false sense of security.

"Great!" Sin jumps up from his chair and prepares to leave. "I have to get going, but if you need anything . . ." He glances at the painting once more before looking back at me. "Anything at all, you call for me, okay?"

"I will, Sin," I reply as I trail behind him, like a miserable little cloud tailing a ray of sunshine.

He pauses at the door. "Stay safe, Petra. And please, think about what I said."

"I will," I reply.

In the next few moments, the door closes behind him, and I come back to the painting on the table. Its faintly solemn atmosphere seems to have touched a raw string inside me.

The more I look at it, the more puzzled I am at how Sin could have something so precious to gift to me.

CHAPTER FORTY

PETRA

Present Day

I cannot believe this day has come. Sin and I are working together to solve a string of murders at our posh school out in the wilderness of New Haven. But needs must when the devil drives, as they say, and things are so dire that we've decided to pool our efforts.

My feelings toward him are still strained from his antics in the past, but I do my best to push past them. As he had taken some pains to point out, I might be the next victim on the list.

The day after our uneasy truce, I'm called back to the principal's office. Only this time, they don't announce my name over the PA speakers.

Instead, the mousy-faced woman who works as Principal Rhodes's secretary interrupts our art history class to whisper something to Ms. Matthews. The latter beckons me toward them with a worried but concerned look, and my heart shoots up to my throat.

"Your presence is requested at Mr. Rhodes's office, Petra," Ms. Matthews says, briefly placing her hand on my shoulder. The touch is friendly and informal without being too intrusive, and for once, I welcome it.

But soon, I find myself following the principal's secretary down the corridors of St. Anselm Hall.

Dread drops through my stomach like a stone as I trudge down the hall. Once we reach the office, the secretary opens the door and goes back to her desk without a backward glance at me.

I brace myself and enter the Spartan room to be met by the familiar sight of Principal Rhodes, his face looking wooden and impassive, and the detectives, Fiona and Phil, standing behind him.

"Ah, Petra, come in, come in," Fiona says briskly, as if I have just walked into the dining room where she was setting the table. "I'm sure you can guess why we are here."

"Is this about Harry?" The words come out jangled and sputtered before I have managed to clear my throat and assume a more aloof tone.

"Bad business all around, isn't it, Mr. Rhodes?" Phil says in a cordial tone while the principal looks flustered, wiping sweat off his brow in mid-fall.

"Yes, I suppose you could say that. I don't quite know what to make of it myself," the principal replies in a tone shiny with desperation.

I can't even imagine the bureaucratic and PR hell this man is going through, so I focus on the two detectives instead.

"Why don't you take a seat, Petra?" Fiona replies with a small smile, nodding at the chair next to the polished mahogany table.

I sit down clumsily, the leather of the chair feeling cold against my skin.

Fiona's piercing gaze locks onto mine, and this time I struggle to find that cool disdain with which I had spoken to these two previously.

"Petra, we understand this is a difficult time," Phil starts, his voice carefully neutral. "But we need to talk to you about Harry's murder and how it connects to Edwin. Now, you were close to both of them, correct?"

"I wouldn't say 'close,' but I knew them both," I respond in a voice that is only slightly trembling. "Like I told you before, Edwin and I were project partners once, and Harry was a classmate."

"Just that? A classmate?" Fiona cuts in smoothly, and I don't like the business tone with which she asks this personal question.

"Well, he was also a friend. If that's what you're insinuating."

That brief spark of annoyance was just what I needed to pull myself together, and now I channel that same anger into fucking around with them the same way they were fucking around with me.

Three can play at this game, I think nastily.

"We aren't insinuating anything, Petra," Phil jumps in with the *we-are-all-friends-here* tone that adults use when they think they are getting along with kids.

Fiona, for her part, is already jotting down notes. "Can you tell us more about your interactions with Harry? Anything that stands out, anything unusual?" She has abandoned all pretenses of being my friend and has reverted to being a cop instead.

"Harry and I didn't have a lot of classes together, but we did hang out occasionally. We sometimes had lunch together."

As I speak, memories of our shared lunches send pangs of sorrow through my heart, and my resolve to not cry in front of these pricks starts faltering.

"His family moved around a lot." It feels grossly wrong to use the past tense when talking of him, so I start counting my breaths to retain some sort of composure.

Phil leans forward with a keen look on his face. "Can we revisit the last bit? Did Harry ever tell you about people he knew before he moved to Radcliffe?"

"N-no, not really. We chatted about school and work and shared interests. We didn't discuss our home lives, to be honest."

As far as I can remember, he seemed like his home life was more or less stable, like he was the son of a solid, respectable family who fit right into the general milieu in these parts.

"What about religion? Did he speak to you about that?"

"I'm not sure what that has to do with this," I say with a frown. "And the answer is no. We did not talk about religion."

He jots something down.

"And what about the days leading to the fall ball?" Fiona asks this next question. "We were told that Harry asked you to the dance, but you refused. Is that correct?"

"Told by whom?" I snap at her. "And yes, I did turn him down then, but there were no hard feelings. Obviously. Harry wasn't the kind of guy to hold grudges."

Though my voice is still level, inside I'm fuming. *How dare they ask these disrespectful questions about my friend?*

Fiona's eyes narrow at my heated response. "Petra, I know you're frustrated and possibly scared. But you have to understand how this looks. You were seen with both victims shortly before their deaths. So it's in your best interests to provide us with as much information as possible."

"I can't pull new information out of thin air, can I?" I almost snarl at her. "And I was with someone else at the ball. Trust me, enough people must have noticed me."

After all, I had been adorning the arm of Prince Sin Arnoult.

"So I don't understand the point of throwing these questions at me—"

"We're not accusing you, Petra," Fiona cuts in before I can continue my rant.

"But given your connection to both victims, we have to consider all possibilities," adds Phil, and I wonder if this is a standard line they are so used to throwing out that they don't even realize when they are speaking in turns and completing each other's stanzas.

At the same time, I have just remembered the paintings I had seen in the crypt, the ones depicting the alleged sacrifices conducted by the Ouroboros Society.

I remember the painting that had come true most recently: the savagely mutilated body with blood spurting out of all orifices, and how Harry's body was desecrated in the same way.

"Now, you mentioned in your initial statement that there was no discernible difference in Edwin's behavior in the days leading up to his death." Phil's casual question snaps me back to the present. "Would you say the same for Harry?"

"Yes! His death came completely out of the blue. I mean we *couldn't* know something like that would happen. How could anyone know?" There's an almost hysterical edge to my voice, but I'm beyond caring at this point.

This time, both the detectives nod thoughtfully before Fiona says, "All right. If you think of anything, please let us know. You already have my card." Here she pauses, her eyes probing mine. "Anything else you think we should know?"

Why do I have this nagging feeling that they doubt my innocence? How on earth could they think I'm capable of something so brutal?

"Sure, if I think of anything, I'll tell you," I say, trying to steady my voice. "Can I go now?"

Phil gives me a bracing smile, though it doesn't really do much to loosen the tight knot of anxiety in the pit of my stomach.

"Of course, of course!" he exclaims magnanimously, escorting me to the door while Fiona starts looking up something on her phone and Mr. Rhodes stares out the window with a conflicted expression.

"Thank you, Petra," Phil says warmly as I step outside. "We really appreciate your cooperation. Stay safe, and don't forget to reach out if you remember anything else!" With those last words delivered in the high-pitched register of a TV commercial spokesman, he shuts the door behind him.

On my way back to class, Sin accosts me by the lockers.

"How did it go?" His eyes are wide in shock and concern, but the arm he puts on my shoulder is warm.

"They think I know more than I'm letting on," I reply in a shaky voice, though I'm not as spooked by the detectives' questions as I am with the thought of possibly more crimes looming on the horizon.

"I wouldn't worry so much, Petra," Sin responds in an offhand manner, the previous tension vanishing from his face. "Sounds like they are just grasping at straws for now."

"How can you be so sure?" We have fallen in step, and our feet automatically lead us to the east wing—where stands the willow tree guarding the secret path to the crypt.

"Well, they must be under a lot of pressure to find a suspect, right?" Sin says in a reasonable tone, as if we are discussing a simple math problem and not the gruesome deaths of our classmates. "But they don't have anyone in custody yet, so obviously they're freaking out and trying to strong-arm all his friends in the hopes that *somebody* would crack."

"Okay, but that would work only if the killer"—how strange the word sounds—"were one of us. You don't think it's a student, do you?"

"Maybe, maybe not. That's what we're going to find out," Sin replies in a firmer tone, and I can see that he is mulling something over. There is a faraway look in his eyes that I have come to recognize by now.

"What are you thinking?" I ask curiously.

At this point, we have reached the shaggy canopy of the willow, and already I can feel myself relaxing. Birdsong weaves through the air here as starlings, warblers, and larks fly in and out of the tree's knotted enclave.

"Not thinking, just feeling. A sense of guilt, you could say . . ." Sin replies hesitantly, watching the flight of a lone skylark against the solid network of branches around it.

"But why do you feel guilty?" Again, a strange question to ask, but one that sets off something ticking at the base of my throat, as if I am experiencing a sense of fear without knowing where the danger is.

"Think about it, Petra: the bodies of Edwin and Harry? The way they were all brutalized? It can't be a coincidence, right? I mean"—here he looks around and lowers his voice—"you saw the paintings in the crypt. It's that goddamned secret society all over again!"

He's visibly shaken now, as if trying to banish some awful image from his mind.

"And my family is one of those allegedly involved back in the day. What if someone I know . . ." his voice trails away; he's obviously refraining from saying, "*What if someone I know—maybe daddy or mommy themselves—is going around killing and mutilating school kids?*"

For a moment, we stand there in tense silence.

"Well, I don't know, have you noticed anyone in your family behaving suspiciously lately?" I do my best to mimic Phil's tone of pompous joviality. And it works. Sin snorts loudly, and we both break down laughing.

"Wow, that was spot on!" Sin says, pretending to wipe tears of mirth from his face. "You're getting pretty good at this."

"You know what? I think so, too." I had never thought my sense of humor would turn this dark, but here we are, so I might as well have some fun. "That's my backup plan in case I don't make it to design school," I manage to say between bouts of laughter. "I'm gonna enroll at Quantico or something."

We stand around chuckling for a couple more minutes before I speak again.

"For real, though, we need to have another look at those paintings, Sin. I've got this feeling that there's more to see in that horrid cavern. Something that will tell us what's about to happen."

"You're so sure something's about to happen," Sin remarks as we sidle into the secret passageway that leads down to the hidden stairs descending into St. Anselm Hall's hidden crypt.

"Maybe I'm just too paranoid or something," I reply with a casualness I don't actually feel. "Still, it's worth checking out the paintings again."

By now, we have reached the last flight of stairs before the unassuming door that leads to the sprawling underground vault.

The echoes of our footsteps bounce off the stone walls, and the air grows colder and damper as we descend the narrow staircase.

As usual, I'm struck by the eerie quietness draped over the place, its air of dark despair. At the same time, there's something melancholic about its emptiness, how abandoned it feels to be here.

Sin's face tenses up when we reach the main chamber lined with the paintings depicting the founding families summoning the hellion and performing their awful sacrifices.

Taking a deep breath, he turns to me.

"What are we looking for exactly?" he asks in a tight voice, and it's obvious how much these macabre scenes affect him.

I, on the other hand, feel my spirits rising as we stop before the grisly frescoes.

In a twisted way, I had missed being here, amidst these dreadful scenes illustrating mankind's worst instincts.

But how rich the palette! I exclaim mentally, as my eyes trace the demon's round bald visage, *How unique the perspective*!

"Anything that might hint at what's coming next," I reply, moving closer to the walls, brushing my fingers along the weathered stone. "We've already seen the first two murders were exactly like the rituals shown here. There's gotta be more clues, I just know it."

We study the series of paintings from before, the cloaked figures—supposedly the Ouroboros Society—performing grotesque acts under the demon's watchful gaze.

My eyes are drawn to one particular frame: Right in the middle of the composition is a figure bent backward over an altar.

Blood pools beneath them in a bright puddle that reflects the terrified face of the victim.

Goya would have blown a fuse if he ever saw these, my inner voice opines, and I have to agree. The atmospheric horror of these wall murals is just something else.

"This one looks newer," I murmur, pointing to the vivid colors and the detailed lines. "Maybe someone added it later?"

"It's possible," Sin remarks, brow furrowing. "You're right, I think. The paint's not as faded. But this is crazy!" He stands back and gives me a wide-eyed stare. "Do you think whoever's doing this might have left a message?"

"What, in the crypt?" I ask. "When do you think they're snooping around here?"

"Maybe they have after-school access?" Sin points out. "Maybe someone from the janitorial staff?"

"Somehow, I can't see Goldie nipping down here for a quick ritual sacrifice before returning home to his wife and kids," I reply dryly, having been on speaking terms with the head janitor for years now. "Still, you might be on to something."

We continue our inspection, passing carefully from one mural to the next. The lights from our phones flicker and cast eerie shadows on the ancient stone walls. The interplay of light and shadow makes the already gruesome scenes even more horrific.

"If we're going to figure this out," Sin says firmly, "we need to think like them. Understand their motives, their timeline."

I absentmindedly mutter something in agreement. Something seems to be tugging at my eye. The scenes we're looking at now are suitably macabre, fitting into the general theme of the artwork in the crypt.

But there's some pattern here that my brain is trying to pinpoint...

"Sin, look at these!" I whisper hoarsely.

"What? What is it, Petra?" He rushes to my side instantly, as if worried I had sustained some harm.

"There are three paintings here that haven't happened in real life yet," I say, pointing to each one in turn. "For starters, look at this one."

I am pointing at a fire-lit panel that shows a woman impaled on a stake, her lifeless body hanging limply, blood pouring down the wooden pole and forming a puddle at the base.

There is such visceral force in the rendition that I can almost hear her anguished screams.

"Oh God!" Sin shouts and turns away from the wall, spitting out cuss-words by the dozen. "That's fucking brutal."

I swallow hard, and my hand moves to the next painting. "And here, this one..."

In the dim light, we see an even worse scene: a man whose body parts have been violently chopped up and scattered across a grim, isolated landscape.

Each chunk of flesh is precisely, realistically drawn—now you're looking at the exposed muscles of the forearm, while the next moment your eye lands on part of the thigh, which has been similarly hacked away into smaller pieces.

The body parts have been positioned in such a manner that you get the impression of a Zen garden with its smooth boulders and neatly furrowed sand.

"This is sick," Sin is exclaiming somewhere behind me, but ideas are fast pouring into my head, and I almost ignore him.

"But it's detailed, methodical," I reply. "Whoever is doing this is not acting under blind emotion. Anyways, look at this next one."

There's almost a note of excitement in my voice that I'm ashamed of—because the last painting is the most chilling of them all. It is bigger than most of the other murals here and shows more people as well. In fact, the crowd is peppered with such feral faces and expressions of wild abandon that you almost don't notice the figure in the middle: bound and gagged, their body arranged in a way that suggests a painful, prolonged death.

"This . . . this is insane," Sin whispers, shaking his head urgently.

"So the killer must have seen these paintings, right? They're following a script."

"I think we're running out of time," I say at last, the certainty dawning on me with a chill. "We need to find whoever's doing all these before these horrors become a reality."

Sin nods, still staring intently at the painting.

In the next instant, something catches my eye: a hole in the stone wall beside the last mural. It's rectangular in shape and fairly big enough for someone to climb through. There are some discolored scuff marks around the edges of the gap, which makes me think someone might have slipped through it recently.

"Sin, look at this." I call him over and point at the hole. "There's something on the other side."

"You want to clamber through *there*?" he asks in an incredulous voice, but I am already trying to reach for the lower edge of the hole.

"Here, give me a leg up, will you?" I ask absentmindedly, and Sin stares at me for a moment before shaking his head and crouching beside my foot. He forms a step with his palms, and I use it to swing myself up and into the dusty space.

The light from my phone illuminates the other side, revealing another chamber, hidden from view.

"There's a room in here," I cry out, my leg resting precariously in Sin's cupped hands. "We need to go inside."

Soon, Sin and I squeeze through the narrow gap to emerge into a dusty, smaller chamber. The smell of grime and decay is even stronger here. And the walls are lined with even more disturbing carvings.

Instead of feeling unsettled by the fresh hellscapes, I say, "Wow! This place is amazing!" Sin gives me a weird look, so I hurry to add, "Ancient, I meant to say ancient. This place looks even older than the crypt."

The lacy pall of light cast by our phones falls on rusting artifacts scattered across the floor.

"Petra, I don't think we should be here," Sin hisses through gritted teeth, but I barely hear him as I move farther into the room.

"This must have been a place for their darkest ceremonies," I remark in an excited tone.

But in the next moment, my feet are halted in shock—another gruesome mural that looms out of nowhere. I step closer while behind me, Sin is swearing again.

"What the fuck? This is just so fucking sick!"

Before us is a triptych of panels depicting mass deaths: The first painting shows a family dying together in a house, the air thick with smoke. Their faces are contorted in agony as they suffocate, the details so vivid that I can almost hear their last, choking breaths.

"Oh my God." Now, even I'm scared, my heart pounding in my chest. "These are whole families. They're all meant to die together."

Sin places a hand on the small of my back, perhaps to brace me or because he's spooked out. Our eyes move to the second painting: a roaring red fire engulfing five people. The flames leap and twist so realistically that they almost spring out at the viewer. But small details suggest this is not a regular fire, more of a metaphorical type. Each of the bodies has distinct injuries.

Once again, the faces of the victims are frozen in screams of terror, as if they know they're going to burn in hell and can do nothing about it.

And now our eyes swing to the third panel: twenty-five people committing suicide simultaneously, all in the same room, all holding a sharp knife to their carotid arteries.

The interplay of light and shadows on the twisted faces and lifeless eyes creates such an unsettling ambiance that I have to force myself to look away.

Once more, something tugs at my consciousness. Twenty-five people . . . I dreamed about something similar, didn't I? The details are fuzzy, but I remember clearly the mention of suicide; self-inflicted wounds; ritual . . .

"The fuck is all this," Sin cries out as I stumble to the side and start taking deep gulps of air.

"We were wrong," I eventually gasp out. "Edwin's death wasn't the first one."

"Why do you say that?" Sin is beside me, patting my back as I hold my stomach and try not to hurl.

"Do you remember the family that died from a gas leak in their house last year? It was all over the news. The Blackwells, they used to live near the diner, remember? Only the children survived. Everyone else died—the mother, father, and two sets of grandparents."

Sin's eyes widen as he finally processes what I'm saying. "Yes, I remember. It was a huge story. All the more so because no one could figure out how the children miraculously survived. Wait . . . are you saying that was connected to this?"

"It has to be," I reply shakily. "Look at this painting. This is how it happened, right? The family died together in their own home. Don't you see what this painting means? It wasn't an accident!"

"But what about the other two paintings? Have those events happened already?"

"I don't know," I admit anxiously. "The one with the five people on fire, and the mass suicide—they might be 'in the works.' Or they might have happened in the past, but didn't get as much media attention?"

"Sounds like we need to keep digging," Sin says with a grim expression. "Perhaps we can find something in the archives."

To my utter surprise, I reply, "You're right."

CHAPTER FORTY-ONE

PETRA

Present Day

Say what you will about the snobbish student body at St. Anselm Hall, they—*we*—know how to spring back from unspeakable tragedies and get to work.

True to our intent of finding out the twisted homicidal maniac who's responsible for the deaths of our schoolmates, Sin and I reconvene at my house the next day, our laptops and a stack of local newspapers spread out across the table.

"Right, we need to go through these systematically," I say with resolve. "Let's start with major incidents and look for any headline that stands out."

Sin nods, flipping through another newspaper and scanning the headlines for any notably grisly murders and deaths.

Jesus, what a morbid investigation, I think to myself.

Then my attention shifts to Sin and the focused look on his face. It's a chilly day, so he has brought me a warm thermos filled with delicious chicken soup. And the most fetching cashmere throw that matches my sea-green pajamas.

My heart flutters at the sight of him: so serious in his perusal of newspapers just because I have a hunch. It's almost embarrassing to admit how much I have been looking forward to us hanging out together, like we used to do before the fall ball.

"Here's one," Sin says suddenly, and I jump a little.

He doesn't notice, thankfully, because he's pointing to an online article.

"Nineteen years ago, there was a mass suicide in the town square. Twenty-five people, all at the same time."

I can't believe he has found something already, so I go behind him and start reading the article over his shoulder. The details are grisly: how the people—all successful SAH alumni, including some CEOs of large companies—had punctured their carotid artery in the middle of the square, which is barely two blocks away from the SAH compound; how the ambulance had taken forever to reach them because the street had been mysteriously blocked off from all incoming traffic.

By the time emergency personnel reached the scene, all twenty-five were already dead.

"This is it." A cold shiver runs down my spine. "This matches the painting exactly."

Though the situation is chilling, I can't help but feel a modicum of relief that the scene from the painting was not the same as the one in my dream. That would be weird . . . right?

I'm sure it's just the stress getting to me, so I shouldn't mind those dreams or give them too much importance. As it stands, in my dream, the suicide of the twenty-five happened in the nineteenth century, not in modern times.

"Apparently, someone told the news crew that these people were part of a cult," Sin points out. "So does this mean they also met at the crypt?"

"Maybe," I reply, unconvinced.

The crypt wasn't known to that many. And if twenty-five people knew about its existence nineteen years ago, there is a high probability that others besides Sin would know about the crypt's existence and location.

Something doesn't add up.

"It explains why those paintings were hidden away," Sin theorizes with a fervent glint in his eyes. "Maybe they were documenting their actions for others to understand their suicide *after* they were dead."

"Hmm, I'm not entirely sure about that theory. Let's dig around some more," I reply.

We resume our search. The next discovery, regrettably, is mine.

"Sin, I found something!" When he hurries over to my seat, I point to an old newspaper article on my screen. "There was a fire at a house party fifteen years ago. Five people died."

"And that's exactly like the second painting!" Sin exclaims, grasping my shoulder. "The fire . . . the number of victims . . . it's all there."

"Sin, if the first incident happened nineteen years ago and then this one took place fifteen years ago, that means whoever's behind these murders can't be someone our age."

Sin looks thoughtful as he skims through the article on my screen. "Yup, that's what I was thinking, as well. The deaths have to be the work of someone older, someone who's been planning this for a long time.

"And since the murders occurred randomly fifteen and nineteen years ago, I doubt it has anything to do with that nonsense about the semi-centennial sacrifices."

Silence ensues.

He has that look on his face, the one he gets when he's pondering over some unpleasant idea that he's hesitant to vocalize.

So I ask, "What are you thinking?"

"I think we need to dig deeper into my family's history," Sin says after a few more seconds of silence have slid by. "Maybe there are other documents or records we could get our hands on. And my parents, they might know something. I think we should have a chat with them."

"Sin, are you sure that's a good idea?" I rush to ask this question because meeting the Arnoult family is a prospect that fills me with bone-chilling anxiety. "What if your parents don't know anything, or worse, what if they don't like me and—"

"Relax, they're gonna love you!" Sin says in a teasing voice before assuming a more serious expression. "I mean it, Petra, you're everything they adore: lovely, stylish, well-read. They'll be thrilled to meet you, I promise."

When I still look hesitant, he adds, "And you'll like my sister, Marie; she's just great. If you feel awkward around my mom and dad, you can always just hang with her. She will make you feel right at home."

"All right, Sin, we'll see if your parents know something."

I sound reluctant because I am. In fact, I'm so flustered that I almost forget about the morning's discoveries from the old newspaper articles because of the impending visit to *Chez Arnoult*.

What will his parents be like? I know that they are a family of academics and generationally wealthy curators, but are his mom and dad like the other rich families in Radcliffe: politely condescending and bitingly particular about their preferences? What if Sin's parents don't prefer *me*?

As these thoughts race across my mind, my stomach churns all of a sudden.

Lately, I have been feeling increased pressure around my lower stomach, and these pangs are often accompanied by bouts of nausea.

Presently, I take a deep breath, but a sudden kick in my stomach makes me wince.

Sin notices immediately.

"Petra, are you okay?" he rushes to my side and starts stroking my back, as if out of instinct. "You look pale."

"I'm fine," I say dismissively, but he clearly doesn't believe me. And besides, I feel another jolt of pain and the attendant feeling of wooziness. "It's just . . . I've been feeling a bit sick lately."

"Ah shit, I'm an idiot!" Sin exclaims so loudly I almost forget my physical discomfort. "You must be under so much stress—first the deaths and then the detectives nosing around, pulling you out of class. No wonder you're so strung up, Petra."

He swoops in and picks me up before I even know what's happening.

"Sin, what are you doing?" I cry out, but he has already placed me down on the plush couch in the living room.

"What I should have done much sooner!" he replies with a stern expression, but his eyes have a mischievous twinkle in them. "Prepare to be pampered."

And with this declaration, he sits down near my feet and starts massaging my soles.

"Oh, wow, that feels good," I blurt out without thinking. Because *fuck*, does that feel good!

"I'm glad, Petra. Try and relax, okay? We don't want you stressing out too much," Sin replies in a soothing tone while his broad, warm hands squeeze and knead the delicate fault lines along my toes and ankles.

It feels like hours pass as he massages my feet, the sickness finally starting to ebb, and I feel a bit more like myself. When I manage to open my eyes and look around, Sin is still there, ever observant and watchful.

Soon, the feeling of pressure and nausea passes by, and I feel my body sinking deeper into the soft cushions.

"No, Sin. It's not just the stress. There's something I need to tell you." The words are out before I can rethink my decision for the umpteenth time.

And thank God for that because Sin deserves to know the truth. Amelia was right. I need to tell him.

His eyes widen at the firm resolve on my face.

"What is it, Petra?"

"Sin, the baby . . . it's yours."

For a moment, the world seems to stop.

Outside, the sounds of traffic proceed at a serene volume, never too loud to encroach upon the meticulously manicured tranquility of the high-end neighborhood.

Sin's face tightens and slackens with a range of emotions—surprise, confusion, and finally, dawning joy. "But you said—"

"I know, I know," I interrupt him in a quivering voice, because I'm afraid I might lose the guts to tell him the whole truth if I stop now. "I lied because I was scared. I didn't know how you'd react, and everything has been so . . . crazy. But you deserve to know the truth, so here it is: This baby is yours."

"Petra, why didn't you tell me sooner?" Sin is looking at me with an expression of elation and intrigue.

"Please don't be mad at me. I was just clueless about what to do, I suppose? And that's why I lied. In the interest of full disclosure, that night . . . it was my first time, and I don't even remember much of it."

I have started to ramble in my disoriented state, but Sin calms me down by taking my hand in his.

His eyes are mellow and golden in the dusk light as he says, "Petra, you're the only woman I've ever slept with, too."

I blink. "What? But . . . how?"

He chuckles softly, even looking down like a shy schoolboy. Which, admittedly, he is. "I've never been with anyone else because . . . I've had a crush on you forever. I couldn't imagine being with anyone else. *Ever.*"

"Now you're just pulling my leg!" I exclaim, but he just looks at me and shrugs. "Sin, I had no idea. I thought . . . I thought you were way more experienced."

He shakes his head with a bemused smile. "And now you know, Petra. You're the only one I've ever wanted. In fact, I knew you were the only one I wanted from the first moment I saw you."

His words sound new and strange, much like some foreign language, but I am much too flustered with desire to care.

Watching me turn over his words in my mind, he leans in closer, and his breath—minty with just the hint of coffee—feels warm against my lips.

In the next moment, I grab his collar and pull him to me.

The kiss starts cautiously at first, with Sin gingerly placing his arms around me, as if he's afraid of hurting me. But I'm not in any mood for restraint, so I deepen the kiss, sucking on his fuller lower lip with much abandon.

He moans a little before tightening his grip around my hips.

After what feels like forever, we pull away, and Sin rests his forehead against mine, looking flushed with happiness. "This has to be the happiest day of my life, Petra. Thank you for telling me. I really mean it."

It feels good to finally unburden myself of the lie I had initially told, and I feel a sense of peace settle over me.

"And you're not mad at me? For lying?" I clarify.

"Of course not, Petra. I understand why you did it." Sin's eyes are full of good-natured concern and only that. "You were scared and overwhelmed. I don't blame you."

"But we're so young to be parents, Sin."

This thought has been preying on me for months now, so it's even more of a relief to say the words out loud to the father of my child.

"I know we're young," Sin replies in a firm voice, "but I know that as long as I'm with you, I can do *anything*. So don't you worry, Petra—" he pats my nose affectionately— "we'll figure it out together."

"Really? Two young lovers, united against the world?" I respond in a wry tone.

"See, you're already sounding like your old self!" Sin exclaims in a grand voice. "Confession is good for the soul, isn't it, Petra?"

And as we melt into each other's arms for the second time today, I'm much too content to contest him on that point.

CHAPTER FORTY-TWO

PETRA

The Past

I open my eyes and see nothing but darkness around me, thick and suffocating.

Panic flutters in my chest as I grope blindly around, my hands meeting rough, dry stone. I'm somewhere—but where? I have no idea.

The air smells old, like dust and time, and with no light to guide me, I must rely on scent and touch alone.

I continue to move, inching forward through the void, hands pressed to the walls in search of an exit. The longer I remain in this darkness, the more certain I become that I've been trapped, sealed inside some hellish pocket of existence meant to rot me away forever.

But just as I begin to lose hope, I spot it: a faint glimmer of light. Instinct takes over, and I rush toward it.

To my relief, I stumble into a well-lit corridor shaped like a tunnel. Its smooth structure immediately reminds me of the underground passages beneath St. Anselm Hall, though there are differences. Most noticeably, this place is lit by electricity, not candles.

How is that possible?

I glance around. The lighting is soft, even elegant, casting no shadows. Along the corridor are several closed doors, lined up like choices in a dream.

My heart sinks.

Am I trapped in some surreal maze? A nightmare without end?

I step forward and position myself in the center of the hallway, turning in place to study the doors. Letting my intuition guide me, I choose the one on the far right and open it. It leads to another door, and another after that.

I push each open cautiously, expecting endless repetition—more doors, more uncertainty.

But the third door surprises me.

I step inside what looks like the foyer of a lavish underground apartment.

My eyes widen.

The space is expansive, with elegant drawing room furniture arranged tastefully in the center, and tall bookshelves built into the walls.

It's breathtaking . . . and unsettling.

How could something like this exist beneath the earth?

"Ah. There you are." The voice cuts through my thoughts, making me start. I turn quickly—and there he is.

Standing in the doorway, leaning casually against the frame.

Sin.

"I was worried for a moment," he says.

"Worried?" I ask, my voice low.

"I thought maybe you wouldn't find your way back."

I frown. What is he talking about?

In a few strides, he's in front of me, reaching for my hand.

"Where are we?" I whisper. "What is this place?"

"You like it?"

"It's beautiful," I admit. "But I don't understand. Where are we?"

"This is my home," he says with a gentle smile. "Welcome."

His home?

"I have a surprise for you," he adds, lacing his fingers with mine and leading me across the room. We approach a section of the wall that appears solid until he opens a hidden door nestled between the shelves. I gasp.

Inside is a room filled with art supplies.

Canvases. Brushes. Jars of paint. Pencils, charcoal, pastels—everything arranged with obsessive care. A chair sits in the center in front of a blank canvas, waiting.

"What is this?" I breathe.

"You mentioned once that you loved to draw," he says, eyes lighting up. "And I know you can't do it at home. So I made this for you. A space that's yours. A place to make you happy."

He looks proud, almost giddy with anticipation. My eyes shift from the room to his face, and something inside me shifts, too.

A tremor passes through my stomach, and my heart begins to beat faster—but this time, not out of fear. It's something else entirely. Something only *he* can make me feel.

"I . . . don't think I ever told you about that," I whisper.

No. I know I never did. It was too private, too sacred. Drawing was mine. Something I did in secret, with joy and reverence. I never even dared speak of it aloud, the way I never dared speak of reading books.

Too intimate. Too forbidden.

Which means . . . this must be a dream, right?

It has to be. Another dream conjured by my subconscious, where he knows things I've never said aloud.

Because that's what dreams do. They give us what we secretly want.

A part of me knows that if Sin had actually done this for me in real life, I'd be terrified. Cautious.

He is a terrifying man—intense, powerful, otherworldly. Forbidden.

And yet . . .

Despite everything, the lies, the half-truths, the shadows that cling to him, this dream is telling me the truth I don't want to admit: I still want him.

Even knowing the danger. Even knowing he's hiding things. I still want him.

"How long have you been living here?" I ask, still stunned by the room around us.

"A few years," he answers vaguely, offering a small shrug.

"But it's underground," I say, trying to make sense of it. "You actually live down here?"

He chuckles. "These tunnels were here long before me. I just happened to stumble upon them and decided to make them my own. A place where no one could disturb me. And since St. Anselm Hall runs on electricity, I managed to connect it here as well. I've had time—and privacy."

I nod slowly, but another question nags at me. "What about the other room you showed me, the small one, with the single bed and study? That one was in a different part of the tunnels, wasn't it?"

"You're right," he says. "There are many who know about those outer tunnels and have access to them. That room is . . . a decoy of sorts. Something simple, to keep up appearances. But this part?" He gestures around us. "This part is hidden. Only I know how to get here. Well, now you do, too. But I trust you with my life. After all, you're the one who saved it, remember?"

I don't respond to that. Instead, I let my gaze wander across the room, taking in the furniture, the polished wood, the soft lighting, the books and art—everything so intentional, so thoughtful.

"When did you even have the time to furnish all of this? And how did you get it down here?" I wonder in awe.

He offers a half-smile. "Let's just say I've had nothing but time. And this . . . I wanted you to like it."

"What?" I blink, confused. "What do you mean?"

He steps closer, his voice soft. "While I was watching you, waiting for you, I noticed something. You longed for a space that was yours. A quiet, private place you could just . . . *be*. So, as I built this, I kept that in mind. I hoped you'd find it comforting. That you'd want to spend time here."

My cheeks flush, and I quickly look away. "You never actually told me," I whisper. "When did you see me for the first time?"

Out of the corner of my eye, I catch his smile. Then he leans in, his lips brushing close to my ear.

"There's no such thing as a first time," he murmurs. "Not when my soul has known you forever."

He wraps his arms around me, and for a moment, I surrender to it. Without the weight of rituals or secrets, this is the version of him I wish were real—gentle, loyal, kind.

Exactly the way I want him to be.

Ah, but what a nice dream this is. I wish *this* could be my reality. The warmth from his body transfers to mine, and a deep sense of comfort settles inside of me.

"Why don't you paint something?" he suggests, leading me back into the small studio and gesturing for me to sit in the chair at the center.

I glance around, momentarily overwhelmed by the sheer amount of art supplies. "I've only ever done sketches," I admit hesitantly. "I've never used paints. Pencils were easier to hide," I add in a quieter voice. "Paints leave traces. I never had the money—or the freedom."

He says nothing, just walks over and places a box of pencils in my hands. "Then sketch. Start there."

I nod, settling into the chair and clutching the pencil. "But I don't know what I should sketch."

"I have an idea," he says, his eyes glinting. "Sketch me."

Before I can respond, he crosses the room and sits on the sofa, already posing. I take a breath and touch pencil to canvas, focusing on the outline, letting my hand move with careful strokes.

But when I look up for reference, something's off.

His tie is gone.

I blink. I'm sure he was wearing one just a moment ago.

Trying not to overthink it, I return to my sketch and add more detail. The next time I glance up, my pencil stills.

His coat is off.

"What are you doing, Sin?" I ask, my voice wavering.

He smirks. "True artists appreciate the naked form best."

"Um . . . yes, but—" I stammer as he slips out of his waistcoat, then his shirt. Now bare-chested, he sits still, as if this is entirely normal.

My eyes widen when I see it again: that same intricate symbol carved into the skin above his heart, and within it, my initial.

It's the same mark I saw in the other dream.

Without thinking, I pull down the neckline of my own dress to check. And there it is. The same sigil. On me.

"What is this?" I breathe, half in awe, half in fear.

"Our connection," he says softly. "See? We both have it. It ties me to you. And you to me. We'll always be bound—across this life and the next."

His words send a tremor down my spine. I can't tell if this is my mind warning me or indulging me. Am I trying to convince myself that, no matter how much I try to reject him, part of me is still his? That beyond the physical, something in him speaks directly to something in me?

I don't want that to be true. And yet, my heart races. My hands tremble. I pretend to focus on the sketch, trying to distract myself, trying not to feel the heat crawling up my neck.

But then I look again.

He's unbuckling his belt.

I nearly drop the pencil. "You—you shouldn't do that! It's not proper!"

He says nothing. Just smiles. And slowly, deliberately, steps out of his trousers.

Now he stands before me, completely naked.

"Draw me," he commands.

Blushing furiously, I force myself to return to the canvas. My strokes are hesitant at first, but soon the rough outline of his form begins to emerge.

I try not to stare. I really do.

But it's impossible not to be aware of him—the taut lines of his body, the strength in his limbs, the sheer, unapologetic masculinity he radiates.

And then there's that other part of him.

That maleness that commands attention, even when I know I shouldn't look.

But I do.

Just for a second.

And I feel like I've done something terribly wicked . . . and terribly thrilling.

Still blushing, I reach for the array of paints and begin choosing colors. The outline on the canvas is done—rough but passable—so I may as well try my hand at painting. It's not as if reality offers me better prospects. At least Dream-Me gets to live her fantasy.

I settle on a dark brown to start with his hair and grab a tube of paint. But when I try to squeeze some out, nothing happens.

Frowning, I shake it, press harder, try again. Still nothing. Maybe it's dried?

I tilt the tube upward toward my face, peering into the opening as I apply more pressure.

Just then—splatter.

A thick line of dark paint shoots straight into my face and across my dress.

There's a beat of stunned silence.

Then laughter. His laughter, rich and unrestrained, echoes through the room.

He crosses the space in a few easy strides, already offering to help. But as I look at him—his bare chest, the open amusement in his eyes, my face smeared with paint—I don't hesitate. I squeeze the tube again and send another jet of paint straight at him.

It hits his chest, dripping lower.

He stumbles back a step, blinking, but then grins. Instead of scolding me, he grabs a tube from the pile and launches a counterattack. Blue smears across my shoulder, and I gasp.

Then laugh.

Before I know it, we're in the middle of a riot of color—shrieking, dodging, flinging paint across each other like children. I forget everything else. The rules. The fear. Even the fact that he's still naked.

All I can do is laugh and spray a streak of green across his stomach.

But just as I reach for another tube, he lunges.

Paints in hand, he tackles me gently to the ground, sending us tumbling among the scattered brushes and tubes. I expect a new volley of color to hit my face, but instead—he shifts.

He pins me softly beneath him, balancing with one hand, while the other goes to my bodice.

In one swift motion, he tears it open.

Cool air hits my exposed skin.

I suck in a breath, but he's already shaking up a tube of red paint—and then pouring it directly across my stomach, letting it run like liquid silk over my skin.

He watches, transfixed.

Then he lowers his hand, spreading his fingers wide, and presses it against the paint.

A crimson handprint blooms across my body.

"So beautiful," he whispers. His voice is reverent. Almost worshipful. "So beautiful . . . and so mine. You have no idea what you do to me, Petra, do you?" he murmurs, voice low and rough. "You have no idea how much you excite me . . . how damn much you turn me on."

My lips part slightly, breath catching as I stare into his face—into the wild intensity darkening his eyes. But my gaze betrays me.

Slowly, involuntarily, it drifts downward.

There.

It had only been a glimpse before, barely a peek, but now . . . now it's different.

Bigger. Much bigger.

My mind scrambles to comprehend it. *Is that normal*? I think, stunned. *How is that even possible*?

Perhaps he didn't sell his soul for a kiss, but he might have sold it for an inhumanly large . . . appendage.

And then, because the situation is so absurd, so surreal, I let out a breathless little laugh.

He arches a brow. "What are you laughing at?"

I hesitate, then point vaguely in the direction of his lower half. "I was just thinking . . ." I trail off, trying to suppress the grin tugging at my lips. "Did you sell your soul for *that*?"

His expression freezes. "You think I made a deal with the devil for a big cock?" he repeats, blinking in disbelief.

And that only makes me laugh harder.

"You little minx," he says with a chuckle.

"Do you blame me for thinking that? It's alarmingly large."

"It is quite the compliment, I must confess."

"A compliment?" I laugh. "You, sir, need to learn what a compliment is. That was merely an observation."

"Still a compliment." He winks at me. "But have no fear, I won't hurt you, nor will I take you today." He leans forward, his cock nestled between my legs as he thrusts it forward over my mons. A shiver goes down my back.

His skin is hot, soft, and though I might find the size of him alarming, the way my body clenches in anticipation tells me that we would fit just fine.

"Ah, sweet Petra," he murmurs, his eyes fluttering closed. "I need you so badly."

Perhaps it's bold of me to do so, but I grab his cheeks with my paint-stained hands and bring him closer until his lips brush against mine.

"What do you need? Tell me."

Surprise flickers across his features.

"You would give it to me?" he whispers.

"I'm not scared of you, Sin. Despite everything, I'm . . ." I trail off, unable to vocalize the strange array of feelings he inspires in me. And though there might be an echo of fear still within me, it's morphed into something else, something resembling more like excitement than true terror. "I'm here," I say eventually.

He regales me with a gorgeous smile as he places a small kiss on my nose before moving my hands lower, to his cock.

The first touch surprises me. For something that looks so menacing, he's soft, fiery, almost melting in my hand.

"Like that," he rasps as he pushes his hips forward, his member sliding in and out of my hands. "Just like that." His features tighten, and he releases an animalistic sound as he utters a low, "Fuck," before a substance spills over my stomach in white spurts.

It meets the red of the paint, and together they make a mosaic of experience: lust and . . . love?

I gulp down, unable to tear my eyes away from his face. So beautiful, so agonizingly vulnerable in this moment.

I keep my grip on his cock as the last of the tremors subside from his body.

He crashes on top of me, though still keeping most of his weight off me.

It's a strange feeling. He's warmth and comfort where I once thought he was going to be my damnation.

Instead, as I hold him close to my body, basking in his presence, only one word seems to drift through my mind.

Home . . . he feels like home.

I wake up with a start. Immediately, I take note of my surroundings and realize I'm in my room, in my nightgown, with not one hair out of place.

It was a dream after all . . . though sometimes I wonder how I could conjure up things I know nothing about.

A deep chasm opens in my heart as I realize the dream Sin, that tender, funny man from that dream, is just that . . . a figment of my imagination.

CHAPTER FORTY-THREE

PETRA

The Past

A loud noise downstairs draws my attention.

I open the door and peer over the banister just in time to see a flurry of movement in the entryway: footmen coming and going, carrying boxes into the house.

With a small spike of apprehension, I make my way down, only to see that Leah—my brother's fiancé—has arrived with her ever-present chaperone, some distant aunt of no clear relation.

My brother is in the midst of issuing commands to the staff, his scarred hand tucked behind his back as if to hide the evidence of his recent injury.

The wound had kept him bedridden for a full week, the physician checking in daily to stave off infection. But that hadn't swayed my father or him from continuing with plans for the engagement party at the end of the month.

As I step into the drawing room, I offer Leah a quiet greeting. "Hello," I say, and she looks up with a small, tremulous smile.

"Hi, Petra," she whispers.

Though we've only seen each other a few times since that first awkward dinner, there's been a silent understanding between us. I can tell she wants to speak more, that she has something to say—if only she could get out from under the scrutiny of her ever-watchful guardian.

Every time Leah opens her mouth, the aunt's sharp glance shuts her down.

We sit for tea while my brother continues barking orders. Apparently, the footmen have been sent by Mr. Snowden with goods and preparations for the party.

My mother appears a moment later with a lemon cake, her specialty, and offers it around. The aunt eagerly snatches a piece and begins shoveling it into her mouth with unseemly gusto.

Leah, however, hesitates. She stares at the cake with something akin to longing, but her hands remain folded.

"You should have some," I say gently, taking a bite myself to show her it's all right.

"Maybe just a little," she murmurs. She barely finishes two bites before she stiffens in her seat and quietly asks where the restroom is. I point her toward the back hallway and watch her rush from the room, troubled.

"Is she all right?" I ask her aunt.

The older woman snorts. "She's just being fussy. Probably expected something more to her liking—what she's used to. A little spoiled, that one." Her tone is clipped and sharp, clearly meant to remind me of our lower status compared to the Snowdens.

I fight the urge to roll my eyes. Already, I dread the prolonged company of this woman. I wait until Leah returns, making sure she looks all right before I excuse myself and prepare to flee upstairs.

But before I can escape, my mother intercepts me with a box in her arms.

"A new dress," she says, handing it over. "For the party."

"I have one already," I murmur.

"You will wear *this* one," she replies with finality. And just like that, the conversation is over.

Back in my room, I don't even look at the dress. I simply toss the box into the closet and change into my nightclothes. It's barely past noon, and yet I'm exhausted—tired of this house, of this family, of the Snowdens and their constant presence.

Every day now, someone from that house stops by, often Mr. Snowden himself, to meet with my father. I try to stay out of their way, but I'm not always so lucky. And with the engagement party looming ever closer, there are more dinners, more events, more obligations.

It's suffocating.

There is only one escape I can rely on.

I slip into bed, pull the blanket up to my chin, and close my eyes, desperate for sleep. And as I begin to drift off, my thoughts latch onto the one person who has come to mean something else entirely.

Sin.

I want to go back to that dreamworld. Back to him. Because if there's no place for joy in the waking world, perhaps I can find it in the world I've come to crave—the one where he waits for me.

A masculine scent wraps around me, grounding me in the place I know I belong. I turn my head slightly, and our eyes meet. He presses a soft kiss to my brow, arms tightening around my body like he's afraid to let go.

Oh, how I wish I could stay here forever, curled against him, untouched by the world beyond this dream.

"I wish I never had to wake up again," I whisper. "That I could stay like this with you for all eternity."

"You really mean that?" he asks, his voice laced with something between disbelief and hope.

"I do," I say, nuzzling into his chest. "You, books, painting . . . what else could I possibly want from life?"

"Then say the word," he murmurs, brushing his lips against my hair. "Say the word, Petra, and I'll make it happen. I'll give you that life. Because you deserve it. You deserve nothing less than everything."

"You're the only one who thinks so," I reply with a sigh. "Things have been getting more chaotic at home. And I don't know what the future holds."

He pulls back just enough to see my face, his brows drawing together. "What do you mean?"

"My brother's engagement. This new connection with the Snowden family. It makes me uneasy." I pause, unsure how to articulate the dread coiling in my chest. "I can't say for sure why, but there's something about Mr. Snowden that I just don't trust."

"You should stay away from him," he says, his voice low and serious. "Snowden is not a good man."

"You know him?" I blink, startled.

"Unfortunately," he says, jaw tightening.

"How? Besides the fact that he's practically waging war against you and your mentor."

"That's not how I know him," he says, voice growing heavier. "It goes back further. Long before the rumors, before the attacks on the university."

He pauses.

"You might be surprised to learn this, but he was once one of my mentor's closest friends."

I sit up slightly, my heart pounding. "He what?"

He only nods, his expression darkening. "He is the one who sponsored my mentor to come to Radcliffe *because* of his connections within the occult world."

"W-what? You mean Snowden was involved in this occult thing, too?"

"Rutherford, Snowden, and a couple others poured a king's ransom into St. Anselm Hall to establish the Theology Department. But only Rutherford's name was made public. The others remained anonymous."

"But . . . why?"

"Because these are powerful men, Petra, men who've held power all their lives. They are used to getting anything they want. Anything money can buy. But eventually, they realized there were things even their immense wealth couldn't grant them. So they turned to other means."

"Like what?" Dread pools low in my stomach as I ponder his words.

"Take Rutherford, for example. He came from a long line of industrialists. His family's among the most powerful in the world, with wealth beyond measure. He grew up with every comfort imaginable. And yet, there was one thing he couldn't buy."

"What?"

"Love," he says simply. "He became obsessed with a woman who wouldn't even look at him. She was married. So, at first, he had the husband taken care of—not by himself, of course, as he wouldn't get his hands dirty. He hired someone to kill him. Easy enough for a man like him."

I swallow. "That's awful."

He nods. "But killing the husband didn't win her affection. She still wouldn't look his way. That drove him mad. So he came to my mentor, hoping for a different kind of solution."

"A love potion?" I ask with a dry laugh.

"Not exactly," he said. "He didn't want *just* affection—he wanted obsession. He wanted her to love him with the same maddening desperation he felt for her. And so, yes, in a manner of speaking, he was asking for a love potion."

I wet my lips apprehensively, wondering if perhaps what I'm feeling might also be a result of magic. "Did he sell his soul for it?

"In a manner of speaking."

Again, these vague terms. There's never any certainty with Sin, is there?

Although he's started sharing more with me, he still keeps the core information hidden. To what end, I don't know.

"What does that even mean?" I frown.

"He thought he did. And he got what he wanted. Or what he believed he wanted."

His words are cryptic, and they leave me more confused than before.

"And no, Petra. I did *not* sell my soul to have you fall in love with me. I fear that's all of your own making," he says smoothly, as if reading my thoughts.

Shock flickers over my face.

"I happen to be in full possession of my soul," he continues, smirking at me.

"I . . . didn't ask," I murmur and look away.

"But you thought about it," he presses on. He tilts my jaw up so I look into his eyes as he continues. "I would *never* sell my soul, for anything in the world. Because it is yours and yours alone."

I blink, my lips parting in surprise. His words should terrify me, but once more, instead of making me fear him, they only serve to make me more drawn to him.

"You alone have a claim on my soul. And I await the day when I will have a claim on yours, too," he adds in a low voice. "But make no mistake, when that happens, it will be of your own free will. No demon deals, no love potions, nothing but your true, honest feelings."

Heat burns in my cheeks. My heart, too, cannot seem to stand still, thundering in my chest with such velocity, it feels as though it's about to break out of my chest and go to him.

I inhale sharply. His eyes glisten—can he read my mind? Can he guess what I'm thinking?

Before he can say more honeyed words that will undoubtedly make me confront my *real* feelings for him, I choose to change the subject.

"What about Mr. Snowden? What did *he* want?"

He stares at me intently for a second more, as if wanting to say something else. But then he sighs and allows this shift in topic.

"Something just as impossible. Something money couldn't buy."

"Love again?"

He lets out a dry laugh. "Something similar. He wanted his mistress."

My eyes instinctively widen at the word.

"Don't look so shocked, my love. Men like him always have mistresses.

They might marry for politics, power, or connections, but they always have someone on the side."

"But," I whisper, "he claimed to love his wife."

"Perhaps." He shrugs. "But love didn't stop him from keeping another woman."

"Would you also have a mistress?"

"No." The answer is immediate. "Never."

I nod thoughtfully. I might not always believe him and his roundabout ways of speaking, but this? This, I believe. "So he sold his soul for a love potion, too?" I continue.

"No, not quite. As a matter of fact, he didn't. You see, his mistress died a long time ago, and he never managed to move on from her death. It all began with him seeking out my mentor. He wanted him to perform séances—to contact her, to receive a message from beyond the veil. But once he got that, it wasn't enough. He wanted . . ." He trails off, his features grave. "He wanted to bring her back from the dead."

"That's not possible, is it? That can't *be* possible—to bring someone back from the dead."

"It's not *technically* possible," he replies again, carefully. "But that's when his plan unraveled. That's when he got angry at my mentor for not being able to give him what he wanted. After all, Rutherford got his love. Why couldn't he?"

"So you mean he tried to sell his soul to bring someone back from the dead? And it didn't work?" I whisper.

"Yes. You could say so."

"Be more clear. I don't understand. Then why does he have this vendetta against your university and your group?"

"Because he *did* make a deal. And he *did* get what he wanted—but not in the way he wanted it. Afterward, he started to notice the decline of everything around him. The effects of that bargain he made. He's been searching for a way out all this time. And he thinks that by shutting the university down, by exposing everyone and vilifying them, he'll finally be free."

"Wait a moment. You said you cannot bring back the dead. So how is it that he got what he wanted?"

"I only said you cannot bring back the dead in a *certain* way. You cannot restore someone whose body has already decayed, whose flesh has rotted away. You can only conjure a *monstrosity*—something that might look like them, but it's not them. Their soul is gone."

"I don't understand what you're trying to tell me. Didn't you say he was communicating with her soul?"

He shrugs. "He *thought* he was. But once a soul crosses over, it no longer resides in this realm."

Again, his choice of words confuses me. So those séance sessions were a sham?

"You mean heaven or hell?"

"Those are mortal terms. Constructs. We've invented them to make sense of what we don't understand. But what's out there—it's not as simple as that. Her soul was gone the moment she died. I don't know if it moved to the resting place of souls or if she began another cycle of reincarnation. Who knows? But when Snowden made that deal, he didn't specify. He just said, 'I want her back.' And he got her back."

He pauses, then adds quietly, "He got a rotting version. A body with no mind of her own. No memories of their life together. She was just a piece of animated flesh."

I stare at him in shock.

"And of course, the next step was getting rid of it," he continues.

"Did he?" I ask, my voice barely above a whisper.

He looks at me solemnly. "That's the crux of the problem, isn't it? He didn't. He created the monster, and now he has to live with it. Though not for much longer. He sold his soul, so the debt will be collected eventually. And when that time comes, the monstrosity should leave this realm with him."

"But until then . . . where is she?"

"Don't ask questions you don't want the answers to," he replies, smiling without humor.

"I'm sure someone would notice a rotting corpse walking around," I try to joke, forcing a laugh.

His features turn serious. "You think it's a joke? Pray, Petra—*pray* you never come face-to-face with it."

I gulp down hard. "What about his wife? His mother? He said they died. Was that part of the bargain, the curse?"

"Not directly," he said. "But the energies around him, the corruption he brought into his life? It seeps into everything. And everyone."

"Even his daughter?"

He looks at me then, his eyes sharp. "What about her?"

"I've met her a few times now. She's engaged to my brother. And something's wrong. She's always so quiet, nervous. She flinches when people get too close. She looks sick all the time. Just this morning, she ate a bite of cake and ran to the restroom."

His expression darkens. "She's ill?"

"Every time she visits," I explain. "She barely eats. Her chaperone says it's because our food isn't good enough, but I don't buy that. I'm . . . worried about her."

"Don't be!" he declares. "Her fate is her own."

"But—"

"Worry about *your* fate, Petra. Not others."

"Like how you worry about me?"

His lips tug up in a sly smile, and I decide this is the time to confront him.

"I know what you did to my brother."

"You know?" He quirks a brow.

I nod. "Only you would do that. Only you would . . . defend me."

He doesn't deny it. "I couldn't let him get away with it." He shrugs.

"But how did you know? When did you see it happen? You weren't there—"

"I'm always watching you," he adds gently.

"How? Do you have some kind of crystal ball?" I let out a wry laugh.

"No." He leans closer, his voice sultry and dangerous. "I have the shadows, and they're my friends. They tell me everything I need to know."

My blood runs cold.

"Petra," he continues in an ominous tone. "Stay away from Snowden. Don't be alone with him. And don't ever wander the halls of his house alone. Do you understand me?"

His chilling voice resounds in my ears, and I can only nod in agreement. But the question remains . . .

What is Snowden hiding?

CHAPTER FORTY-FOUR

PETRA

Present Day

It's a bright Sunday when Sin and I stop by his house. I have fussed and fretted over what I would wear to the Arnoults' for the whole of last week. Even then, the floral midi skirt I have finally chosen seems too tacky when we arrive at Arnoult Manor.

It's a sprawling affair in teal and silver, with ornate arches and modern lighting, the perfect mix of early seventeenth-century austerity and the decadence of the 1920s.

My parents may be rich, but it's clear these people come from *old* money.

"Jay Gatsby would have loved this house," I murmur under my breath, smoothing the pleats of my skirt over and over again.

My anxiety is at an all-time high.

After more eerie dreams with dreams-ensconced-in-other-dreams like a goddamn matryoshka, I am more confused than ever.

There is the information that I know from my day-to-day life, and there is the information from my dreams.

Everything seems to be related to the same weird occult activity happening in Radcliffe, but I am still unsure if my subconscious is making everything up due to the pregnancy hormones or if there might be some truth to it.

Yet the fact that those suicides happened just a couple of decades ago instead of over a century ago like in my dreams tells me I might be simply . . . going crazy.

And if that wasn't enough, now I have to also face Sin's parents, and I really don't know what scares me more: demon-filled dreams or the parents of the guy I'm falling in love with.

"Relax, you look mind-blowing!" Sin assures me, gently squeezing my hand.

"Are you sure? I can rush back and change into something more flattering—"

"What you're wearing *is* flattering, Petra," Sin repeats himself without any visible signs of irritation.

His whole aura has changed since I told him the truth about the baby.

He looks even more boyish and charming these days, his countenance always sunny and his words always sweet.

"Fine, I'll take your word for it," I reply with a smile and a quick peck on the cheek before Sin opens the front door.

We step inside, and the warmth of the Arnoult household greets us immediately.

The smell of something delicious wafts from the kitchen, and laughter fills the air. What a stark contrast to my own home.

"Mom, Dad, we're here!" Sin calls out.

"About time!" a man's rich baritone issues from the kitchen, shortly followed by Sin's father: a tall, willowy man with dark blond, tousled hair, sporting a pair of horn-rimmed glasses.

"What took you so long?" says a woman's voice, and his mother comes out of the kitchen as well. A svelte blond woman with light-blue eyes, she's dressed in a cozy gray sweater and floor-length Versace skirt.

"Oh, you can blame this one for that," Sin says with a laugh, pointing at me before giving his mother a kiss on her cheek and hugging his father. "She was convinced that she is not dressed up enough for the occasion." I blush at his words.

"Nonsense!" his mother replies, coming up to me and putting her arms around me most naturally. "You look absolutely gorgeous, my dear," she tells me before stepping back. "I'm Lisa, and this is my husband, Tom."

"It's so nice to meet you, Petra," Tom says, reaching out to shake my hand. "My son *won't* stop talking about you." He's wearing a goofy smile, and I instantly know where Sin gets his manic pixie dream boy energy from.

"Thank you for having me," I reply easily, as if I've known them my whole life. "It's wonderful to meet you both."

Before I can say more, a younger girl bounds into the room. "Sin-Sin, the greatest fake!" she hollers before punching Sin's arm with all the strength she can muster.

"Ouch, that hurt!" Sin cries out, doubling up—or pretending to—in pain. "Ma, she hit me!" he shouts, turning to his mother.

"Oh, please, have some backbone, you scum," the green-eyed girl scoffs before turning to me. "Hello, beautiful, you must be Petra! I'm Marie, Sin's sister, and Lisa and Tom Arnoult's favorite child."

"Hey!" says Sin at the same time as Lisa says, "M!"

But I'm laughing away at the girl's infectious energy. "It's so nice to meet you, Marie. Sin tells me you're quite the prankster."

"He has given glowing reports of my daring escapades, I hope?" Marie replies in a curt voice, turning to Sin for confirmation.

"I told her about the Sparklepants incident, M," Sin mutters under his breath, but his sister turns to me with a glowing smile.

"And I have done worse," she says happily. "*Much* worse, bwaahahaha!" Marie flicks back her braid, thick and shiny blond, and cackles like a stone-cold hag.

"Why you little—" Sin swears and starts chasing her around the room. "I'll break your legs, you monkey!" he howls as Marie dashes behind the couch and the filigreed coffee table.

"You'll never catch me, you slowpoke!" she yells back, and I'm beyond amused at this cozy picture of siblinghood.

I like her, says my inner voice, and I'm not surprised.

"Oh, stop it, you two," Lisa cries out, while Tom has already slipped back into the kitchen. "Don't mind them, dear," she says to me casually. "Always running around like wild animals. Anyways, dinner's almost ready." She starts walking, signaling for us to follow her. "We're having lasagna, one of Sin's favorites."

After we sit down around the table, the convivial teasing and good-natured jokes continue.

Plates are passed, and laughter flows easily. With a pang of sorrow, I remember the quiet dinners at my house, and I can't help but feel an intense longing for this kind of closeness.

"So, Petra," Lisa begins, her eyes kind yet curious, "tell us a bit about yourself. How do you and Sin know each other?"

"Well, we go to the same school," I blurt out in panic, and Marie *howls* with joy.

"You're no match for her, dumb-dumb," she tells Sin, and he makes a face at her.

"No, I mean," I hurry to clarify, "I mean we have Art History together, and we're working on a project . . ."

"And she's amazing at it," Sin cuts in smoothly. "Petra's got such a talent for art. You should hear her talk about it." He nods at me bracingly, and I smile back.

"That's wonderful to hear, Petra," compliments Tom. "You know our town has a rich history of folk art. Have you guys been reading about it?"

I wasn't expecting the questions to veer toward our time learning the town's colorful history in the crypt, so I am lost for words at this moment.

"Ugh, Dad, let her eat!" Sin chimes in. "He's always harping on about history and such, Petra. Ignore him."

Tom laughs in a good-humored manner, and the conversation keeps flowing easily. The warmth and camaraderie in the Arnoult household are so, so different from what I'm used to that I feel nostalgic for something I've never even had.

"Ignore them both, Petra," says Lisa. "We're just so glad you could join us tonight. Sin speaks very highly of you."

I blush at the unexpected praise from her. "Thank you, Mrs. Arnoult. It means a lot to hear that."

"Please, call me Lisa," she replies with a warm smile. "Did Sin ever tell you he's our miracle child?"

"How do you mean?"

"No, not this story again," Marie groans with a theatrical sigh while Lisa absentmindedly serves her some more pasta.

"You see, Tom and I couldn't have children for the longest time," she begins. "We tried everything, but nothing worked. We even prayed and donated to the Church—all for a miracle. And then, after so much heartbreak, we finally had our Sin." Here, she looks at her son. "And he's been our miracle ever since." Her eyes glisten with unshed tears and the tenderest of affections.

Sin looks down, slightly embarrassed but clearly touched by his mother's words. "Mom . . ."

I glance at Sin, a warmth spreading in my chest. "That's beautiful, Lisa. You must have been so happy."

"Oh, we were," she continues, her voice filled with emotion. "And we still are. Sin's brought so much joy into our lives. And then there's Marie." She lovingly strokes her daughter's head. "She's a blessing too, even though her circumstances were different."

I look at Marie, who is listening intently, even though she must have heard this story before. "What do you mean?"

Lisa and Tom exchange grave looks, and Tom says, "You see, Marie came into our lives in a different way. She's adopted. Her parents died when she was just one year old."

My heart contracts at the thought of the poor girl being orphaned at such a young age. "Oh, I'm so sorry to hear that," I address the words to Lisa, Tom, *and* Marie. While the adults look faintly sad, Marie shrugs nonchalantly. "What happened, if you don't mind me asking?"

Lisa takes a deep breath, but again it's Tom who answers my question. "They died in the house fire at that party fifteen years ago. You kids must have read or heard about it, I'm sure. Afterward . . ." He looks at Lisa, who squeezes his hand. "We decided to adopt Marie. I mean, can you blame us? Look at her!" He ruffles the girl's hair.

"Dad, don't mess my hair!" she cries out before lapsing into a sulk.

But I'm not even listening because the realization hits me hard. The fire we discovered in our research wasn't just a faceless tragedy; it's intimately connected to the family with whom I'm eating dinner in this cozy house.

"That's . . . that's incredible, Lisa." I look at Sin with wide eyes, wondering why he hasn't made the connection yet, but I can see that he looks just as stunned as me.

Perhaps he hadn't really thought about it before.

"We didn't expect to lose close friends that night," says Lisa with a distant look on her face, as if she has traveled back in time. "But Marie becoming part of our family felt like it was meant to be. She filled a void we didn't think could ever be filled."

Sin squeezes my hand under the table as I sit there, trying to tie it all together.

"And so, we have lived . . . messily ever after!" announces Marie before throwing a fork at Sin. He ducks out of the way as if he had fully expected the attack and tries to pull on her braid again.

"Sin, M! Don't fight at the dinner table!" Tom yells at his children while Lisa just looks at her family with a serene, satisfied smile.

After dinner, Sin and I head upstairs to his room, pretending to study while we wait for his parents to go to bed. The plan is to explore the basement and search for his family's archives once everyone else is asleep and the house has quieted down.

I am disconcerted at the thought of rifling through the belongings of the very nice folks who have welcomed me into their house and fed me a delicious meal, but Sin dismisses all my apprehensions with a wave of his hand.

"Oh, please, it's not like we are robbing them or something."

We have reached his bedroom, and I'm dumbstruck at what I see: The room is neat and sparse, almost obsessively so. The walls are mostly bare, the furniture minimal, and there are very few personal items carefully placed around the room.

No dirty socks under the bed, no crumpled shirts or sweaty shorts piled up in a chair, not even an errant pen rolling around without a cap.

"Sin," I say. "Your room is so . . . tidy. It's almost like a show model."

He chuckles. "Yeah, I guess I'm kind of a neat freak. I like keeping things organized."

"I would not have guessed at all," I reply, sitting at the edge of his bed. "You didn't bring me to dinner with a fake family, did you?" The words are supposed to sound like a joke, but I make them sound like a paranoid fancy.

But there is no answer. Instead, Sin closes the door behind us, turns toward me, and falls to his knees, pressing his face gently against my belly.

"Err, Sin?" I whisper, as the warmth of his breath tickles me through my clothes.

"I can't believe we made a baby, Petra," Sin's muffled voice thrums against my stomach. "It's incredible."

His words make me feel awkward and unprepared for the enormity of parenthood.

But I try to keep my voice steady as I say, "That's so sweet of you."

He looks up at me then, his eyes brimming with such naked wonder that I almost catch my breath. "I just can't believe it. It's overwhelming . . . but in a good way."

When he buries his head back in my lap, I run my fingers through his hair, partly for him and partly for me. How many times had I imagined threading my fingers through his thick locks?

"I'm glad you feel that way. It's been a lot to handle. But knowing you're with me makes it easier."

Regret swells inside me as I remember my lies. I should have been truthful from the start. But I only have my scaredy-self to thank for that particular lie. I was so terrified . . . of him finding out, of everyone finding out, that I preferred to pretend it wasn't happening.

Yet now, looking into his deep blue eyes and the way he regards me with such adoration, I realize my mistake.

"I'm sorry for lying," I tell him again. "I'm sorry for hiding this from you. I know it was bad of me to do so, but truthfully, I was terrified."

"No, don't apologize," he murmurs softly. "I admit I was angry thinking you might be pregnant with someone else's baby at first. But after you told me the truth . . . Ah, Petra, you have no idea how relieved I felt. But I also realized that it could not have been easy on you. You've been carrying this weight this entire time. My sweet, brave girl."

"Thank you," I whisper. "For not holding it against me. For being so sweet, so supportive. I—" I turn my face away so he doesn't see the tears forming in my eyes. "I appreciate this. And you. I appreciate you," I clarify as I clear my throat.

Though it's the best word I can think of to use at this moment, it's not the exact truth; I *more* than appreciate him. I . . . I suppose I haven't fully come to terms with what I really feel for him. But it is *so* much more.

And for someone who's been isolated her entire life, who's never really dealt with these types of emotions, it's overwhelming.

"Petra," Sin says softly, his hand gently caressing mine. "I don't regret anything that happened between us. But I do have one regret."

My heart clenches. "What?"

"I know that night wasn't very good for you," Sin says in a soft tone. "I fumbled it quite badly, didn't I?"

"What, no—"

"Don't bother denying it. I know it wasn't as good for you as it should have been, and I can only blame it on my eagerness. I should have taken better care of you."

"W-what are you saying?"

His fingers slide down my leg with the gentlest of pressures.

"I want to make it better."

A flutter of nerves in my stomach. A wave of heat down my legs where he's touching me.

His fingers slowly trail farther up my legs, and soon he's hiking up my skirt, trailing kisses on the side of my knee.

I gulp down as I realize what he means.

"Sin, you don't have to—"

"I *want* to, Petra, so badly." His voice is hoarse with desire.

His fingers gently stroke the delicate skin of my inner thighs. Anticipation builds inside me, made stronger by the feelings he inspires in me and the echo of those dreams: the way dream-Sin had made me feel with his fingers and mouth and . . .

"Please," he whispers against my legs, and I feel a jolt of desire race through me. "Please let me show you how special you are."

My body trembles uncontrollably at the sound of his voice, so needy, so hungry for me.

I lean backward, falling on my back. He looms over me as he continues to hike up my skirt even higher, so that now it lies pooled around my waist.

His eyes are on me, watching, observing. My mouth parts on a soundless moan as he grabs the band of my panties and slides them slowly down my legs.

He leans in and swallows my gasps in a heart-stopping kiss.

"You're the prettiest thing I've ever seen," he whispers against my lips before going lower, kissing my neck. Once he reaches my cleavage, he unbuttons my shirt and throws it to the side before snapping open my bra.

A shiver goes down my back as the cold air hits my naked skin.

His fingers trail over the top of my right breast, his gaze filled with longing. He traces lines over my skin before leaning down to kiss it. He continues downward until he reaches my nipples, now hard and puckered, and he sucks one into his mouth.

"Oh," I gasp.

He nibbles at it, slowly, methodically. "Mine," he whispers. "You're all mine, aren't you, Petra?"

I bite my lip as I nod.

"No one's ever touched you like this," he states, not a question, an assertion.

"No. Only you."

"Good," he purrs.

He reaches my stomach and places an open-mouthed kiss right above the band of my skirt before going lower.

The anticipation is killing me. I'm wet and needy, and as I squirm under him, I have to wonder: Who is this wanton girl? I've never seen myself as a sexual being, at least not before. Now? All I want is for him to reach that place that's weeping for him.

Sin lowers himself between my legs, his eyes locked with mine as he begins to kiss and caress my thighs, biting and sucking at the skin in turns. He's teasing me with what's to come, and I don't know how much longer I can take it.

And then he touches me *there*.

At first, he places a light kiss over my pussy lips before he drags his tongue through my folds.

"Sin . . ." I gasp out, and my fingers tangle in his hair as his tongue settles on my clit.

Seconds flow into minutes, but I'm outside time itself. Sin uses the flat of his tongue to create pressure at my opening before sucking on my clit in short, concentrated bursts.

With each flick of his tongue, the pleasure seems to build inside me, till I can feel my legs quivering.

"You're doing so good, my love," he murmurs against me. I'm too far gone to notice his use of 'my love.' Instead, I focus on those growing sensations pooling low in my belly. The way the room starts to spin around me and my body becomes a mess of trembling limbs.

"Sin!" I moan loudly, but the next instant his hand is clamped across my mouth, and I remember where we are—in his bedroom, in his parents' house.

But I can't help myself as Sin increases the pace, his tongue doing such wicked things to me that I end up biting on his fingers to keep myself from screaming out.

My clit is swollen from all the licking, and still, I'm only at the cusp of blinding pleasure.

But he takes his mission seriously, using a combination of his tongue and fingers as he presses two digits deep inside of me, curling them until he hits a certain spot.

I nearly jump off the bed.

And then it happens: The orgasm begins deep inside my sex, and my clit starts throbbing as I come, moaning and grunting against Sin's hand.

My eyes roll back fully, and the heated overflow of juices between my legs leaves me breathless and gasping for words. For a few moments, I just lie there, trembling and breathless as Sin peppers kisses all over my belly again.

"Did you like it, Petra?" he asks in a voice thick with post-conjugal bliss.

"Sin . . . that was . . . amazing." The words come out warped and a little slurred, but I'm beyond caring. This wasn't how I had pictured my first real-life orgasm to happen, but I'm happy that I finally know what all the fuss is about.

"I'm glad, Petra," Sin says. "You look so beautiful when you come undone."

I blush as I ask, "Do you . . . do you want me to return the favor?"

I am wholly unsure about what to do but completely willing to do what needs to be done.

Sin chuckles and climbs up to lie beside me.

"You don't have to do anything, Petra. This was about you. And about making you feel special."

He leans in, and I can smell myself on his lips. It's a musky, heady fragrance, and when his lips meet mine, it's all I can do not to pin him under me and have my way with him (whatever that means).

For now, I'm happy to relax in the arms of this dreamy guy who has just given me my first real-life orgasm.

And also, your first baby! my inner voice starts in an objecting tone, but I shush her down.

Right now, there's only space for me and Sin—and the baby—on this bed.

CHAPTER FORTY-FIVE

PETRA

Present Day

For a while, it's hard to form any coherent thoughts as I just lie back and relax in Sin's arms.

Only images swirl in my mind: Sin kneeling between my legs and hitching up my skirt, kissing and licking the throbbing nub of my clit, one hand kneading my breast while the other clamped my mouth shut with surprising force . . .

My cheeks warm at this erotic recollection, and I feel myself getting wet again.

But if Sin can sense the second wave of desire breaking over me, he doesn't acknowledge it. Instead, he plants a chaste kiss on my forehead.

His heart beats steadily under my ear, and his breath is warm against my face. His fingers trail lazily across my shoulders and hips.

It all feels like a dream.

Suddenly, a voice just outside the door announces, "Sin, we're turning in for the night!"

We both almost jump up while Sin hastily shouts, "Goodnight, Mom!" so that Lisa doesn't just come barging in on our intimate scene.

Of course, she doesn't seem like the type of woman who'd do that, and my assumption is proven correct when she says, "All right, you two, don't stay up too late!" and walks away to her bedroom.

In a few more minutes, the other sounds of the house die down, too, and a cozy silence spreads over the rooms.

"I think they're all asleep," Sin says to me while I adjust my hair in the mirror opposite his bed.

Something makes me ask, "Are you sure about Marie?"

"Oh yeah," Sin replies easily. "That baby sleeps like a log." He scrunches up his nose to further underline his disgust at his sister's uncouth ways, but I'm not fooled.

"Okay, I'm ready. Lead the way!" I reply in a bright yet brittle voice. I have never snuck around after dark in someone else's house, so I'm understandably nervous.

But Sin slips ahead of me with purposeful strides, while I struggle to tiptoe quietly enough.

Knowing my luck, there's always the risk of walking into some antique chest of drawers or knocking over a Ming dynasty vase that turns out to be worth millions.

Thankfully, we reach the basement stairs without any such accidents.

"Watch your step," Sin calls out behind him as we start descending the slightly dusty wooden planks. The dimly lit basement of the Arnoult home feels even more daunting than the crypt.

The walls are lit up by burnished lighting that makes the whole space look somewhat . . . ancient.

"Just how old is your house, Sin?"

"It was built sometime in the 1860s but was renovated and expanded in the 1950s. Multiple generations of Arnoults have lived here," he adds with a chuckle.

"That's quite the history," I murmur.

As we step inside, Sin swings his phone's light across the cramped space, illuminating shelves lined neatly with file boxes, leatherbound journals, and faded documents.

"Not only that, but people have been quite dedicated to keeping the history," Sin says casually, pulling out a file box at random and going through its contents. "There are several records here dating back to the nineteenth century."

We start digging through the boxes, sorting papers, and flipping through dusty volumes.

The sheer number of leatherbound titles stowed away in this area makes me think of libraries. Something catches my eye, and I pull out a large, worn journal, its cover embossed with intricate designs.

When I flip through the pages, I realize that this is a book of engravings, a collection of what look to be really rare pictures.

"Oooh, that looks interesting!" Sin chimes in from behind me. He's been peering at the pages over my shoulder.

I pause at an engraving depicting men in dark robes surrounding a tall figure.

Their hands are outstretched toward a swirling wispy mass suspended over this person (is it even a person?) in the center.

Goose bumps spring up all over my arms.

"Who-who are they? Do you know?"

"Here, is there a caption for this image?" Sin asks, squinting at the text written in an elegant Victorian font beside the illustration.

"This says it's from the late 1800s—Sinclair Arnoult the First. He was one of the founding members of the Ouroboros Society."

"Sinclair Arnoult the First?" I echo in shock. "The same name as yours?" I raise a brow.

"Unfortunately," Sin replies in a grim voice. "That's one of my ancestors."

"So what number are you *supposed* to be?" I ask with a laugh.

"Fourth." He smiles sheepishly. "There have been quite a few Sinclairs since."

"Fourth? Your father isn't named that," I mention with a frown. Four would imply four generations, and it's been less than one hundred fifty years since the late 1800s.

"Yes, well, all the others died young," he replies absentmindedly, as if reading the silent question on my face.

"Oh," is all I can say as we both lean forward to examine the pictures more clearly.

"The family resemblance is uncanny," I say, trying to keep my voice steady to show that I'm not nearly as spooked as I look. "He looks very certain of himself," I add when the silence between us becomes uncomfortable. "Very confident."

"Very *arrogant*, more like it," Sin says, his eyes glued to the text surrounding the engravings. "It says here that he was the leader of an occult movement said to communicate with beings beyond the veil."

"What, like ghosts?"

"Yeah, but Arnoult's group was on a whole different level," Sin replies with growing unease in his voice. "Says here that they wanted to call upon demons to fulfill their deepest desires."

An actual shiver runs down my spine at these ominous words. "Summon demons? That sounds like a B-grade horror movie."

"It gets worse," Sin adds in a clipped tone, as if trying to distance himself from the gory details of his ancestry. "Apparently, this society, most definitely the Ouroboros Society, believed they could commit human sacrifices to call upon a demon to fulfill their deepest desires."

"What? Human Sacrifices?!" I exclaim, trying to read the pages he's turning with stiff fingers. "But seriously, Sin, how is it that we never learned about any of this before? They teach the Salem Witch Trials in school, but not this?"

"The Ouroboros Society were all men, Petra. *Powerful* men," Sin replies, pointing to a footnote in another of the rare books from a stack on the table. "That's why they didn't face the mobs and pitchforks like the women accused of witchcraft. At least, not initially."

"This is insane," I blurt out, not knowing what else to say.

"Look." He draws my attention to a number of newspaper clippings. One of them details the murder of twenty-five university students in the town square; a couple others mention the grisly deaths of some wealthy men. But one in particular catches my eye—the one that mentions Arnoult and his seances to call upon otherworldly beings.

The newspapers seem familiar. As if I've seen them before. And perhaps I did, because the information is the *same* as the one in my dreams. The twenty-five students who killed themselves in that so-called sacrifice. Rutherford and Underwood's macabre deaths.

These are *all* like my dreams.

And suddenly, a current of terror grips me.

What does that mean? Are my dreams real? Are they a true window to the past?

But how? Why?

How the hell am I dreaming about things that *actually* happened over a hundred years ago?

But the lingering question is: If those events truly happened, then does that mean dream-Petra and dream-Sin were real people, too?

Were they . . . I glance at Sin from the corner of my eye. He looks the same now as he did in my dreams. Everything is the same.

I squeeze my eyes shut and hug my arms to my chest, more confused than ever.

"Hey, are you all right?" Sin asks when he notices my discomfort.

"Yeah," I lie. "Just a little spooked out, you know?" I offer a forced smile.

"Oh, Petra. Come here, sweetie," he murmurs as he draws me into his arms.

"Do you think it's real? That people could sell their souls to the devil or something like that?"

"Sell their souls?" he asks with a frown. "Nothing mentioned that."

"Uhm," I stammer. "But it's implied, right? Summoning demons to fulfill wishes?"

"I suppose so," he replies. "As to whether it's real or not, some people definitely *believed* it to be real."

"Do you?"

"Do I what?"

"Believe that."

He shrugs. "I think there are a lot of things out there beyond our comprehension," he answers vaguely.

"What would you ask for? If you were to sell your soul to the devil. What is your deepest desire?" I press on. I'm not sure why I ask that question, except the scenes I witnessed in my dreams keep replaying in my mind, and I'm trying to make sense of how everything fits in: me, Sin, that creepy Society.

He snorts. "I would *never* sell my soul, Petra. How could I when it's meant to belong to one person only?"

I blink and draw back to study his features.

His words ring in my mind, a strange familiarity to them.

"Would *you*? Sell your soul?" he asks in a languid voice, his face devoid of any of the previous jocularity.

"I . . . I don't think so."

"Enough about that demonic stuff," he suddenly says, his lighthearted expression back on his face.

"Yeah, we should keep looking," I agree, though I can't help but question everything around me, including Sin—and how he is so deft at switching masks.

"We have a lot more to get through," Sin adds, pointing at the other volumes heaped around us.

Again, we sift through the boxes. Perhaps this time, there's more urgency in my movements. More than ever, I *need* to know.

It's almost as if there's a door in my mind waiting to be opened, for all the information to flow in and for the dots to be connected. But I'm missing the key to it.

"Here's another," I say, my finger tracing the faded ink in the yellowed pages of what looks like an old logbook of sorts.

"Someone's jotted down timings for the meetings. And look here: a meeting near St. Anselm Hall. It's from 1894. Says they were gathering to discuss the continuation of the pact."

"See?" Sin murmurs, excitement bubbling in his voice. "You always dig up the best bits."

"But how do we find out who they are now?" I ask, feeling both exhilarated and anxious.

While we are talking, something is tugging at the corner of my vision, something red . . .

"Sin, look at these!" I pull out a bundle of dusty papers bound together with a faded ribbon. "*Darling love,*" I read out loud before my eyes skim the contents of the missive jotted down on the aging parchment. "Sin, these are love letters!"

He steps closer, asking, "What do they say?"

"These are from Arnoult the First to a lover. But there isn't a name. Just the appellation: 'Darling Love.'"

"That's interesting. Is she my great-great-great whatever grandmother?" he asks in good humor.

"I'm not sure. She's the daughter of some type of religious fanatic, it seems," I reply warily, scanning through page after page, and noting her mentions of her very controlling and abusive father with connections to some type of Christian cult.

Most of the exchanges are romantic, with soapy love declarations and promises of fidelity. The others, though, are bordering on eroticism. I skip most of those since it feels intrusive, and I know *I* would not want anyone else to read my love letters.

"Apparently, they had to meet in secret because her father disapproved of him," I say after I've gone through most of them.

"What else do the letters say? Anything about Arnoult the First's occult group?"

"There's no mention of any deals with the devil, if that's what you're asking," I reply absentmindedly, still staring at the stack of yellowed papers.

For some reason, I find myself captivated by the longing in Arnoult's letters.

"He talks about loving her fiercely and wanting to be with her despite the odds. It's almost heartbreaking."

"Sounds like there's more to the story," Sin says, leaning back and crossing his arms as he considers this new information. "Maybe Arnoult established the secret society to acquire some kind of status for himself, so he would finally be able to marry her."

I read another letter, struck again by the raw yearning in which each line was steeped. "Seems like they were really in love, but the pressure from her father and his peers weighed heavily on them."

"History keeps repeating itself, doesn't it, Petra?" Sin asks in a surprisingly bitter voice.

"Look, it's not all doom and gloom," I hurry to assure him, maybe due to the pang of sorrow that pierces my heart at the sight of a sad Sin.

Dang it, girl! You've got it bad, says my annoying inner voice, but I already know that.

"Perhaps they had a happy ending, and she is your great-great-great-whatever, no?"

"I don't know about that," he adds uneasily and hands me another letter. This one is from April 1896 and mentions some type of danger. After that . . . there are no more mentions of Arnoult's lover.

"Who was she, I wonder?" I mutter.

I had started noticing a pattern in the last few letters, where the lovers had cryptically referred to "the gift" or "the love token" or, in one particularly poetic instance, "the loveling."

What were they referring to? I was desperately curious to find out because I had a hunch about what this "gift" might be.

At the same moment, I feel a flutter in my belly, as if like a sign from the universe.

"This doesn't make any sense," Sin mutters while he rifles through other boxes scattered around us, his movements becoming more frantic by the minute. "If they ended up together, there should be more."

"You're right," I say in a distant voice, as my mind is busy speculating. "There has to be more."

"Maybe something happened." An urgency quickens Sin's words, so they come stumbling out of his mouth. "Maybe Arnoult stopped writing to her because of that 'danger'?"

"Or maybe something worse happened," I whisper, unwilling to alert Sin to my dark ruminations.

Dread coils up deep in my chest as I continue searching, my fingers shaking slightly, until I come across a small slip of newspaper tucked between the pages of one of the journals.

"What's that?" Sin asks instantly, as if he had been expecting me to find this at just the right time.

I pull it out carefully, my heart beating like a gong in my ears as I read the headline aloud: "'Double Murder: Father and Daughter Dead; Community in Terror.'"

Yet it still does not say the names—only that they were esteemed members of Radcliffe society.

"What?" Sin says when he finally understands what the title is implying. "*No way,* Petra! What does it say?"

"Sin, it—it's just too horrible."

By now, I have already skimmed through enough of the article to know what it says.

"It says here that her father . . . killed her because he believed she was pregnant." My voice breaks down at this last bit as my hand automatically moves to shield the you-know-who. "He thought she was—" I break off again to draw in big, gasping breaths.

"Petra, what's wrong? Please, calm down. You're scaring me."

Sin strokes my back and shoulders, trying to calm me. But how can I be calm when I've just read that . . .

"He thought she was carrying the child of the devil! The entire community turned against Arnoult and his disciples." I finally manage to force all the words out.

"Petra, it's okay, all of that happened in the past," Sin says in a voice that's failing to sound calm. "Try and relax, please."

"I'm fine," I reply in a firmer tone. *I have my dignity, after all.*

"It doesn't end there," I continue, trying to keep my voice as steady as possible, even though my fingers are gripping the newspaper tightly. "This says that Arnoult killed Snowden and Leah."

CHAPTER FORTY-SIX

PETRA

Present Day

"The townsfolk thought that Arnoult and the Ouroboros Society had summoned the devil and . . . and gotten the girl pregnant."

My voice starts faltering again, and a part of me is astonished at how personally I'm taking all this. I avoid looking at him directly since this is about his family, who, it turns out, are descended from a homicidal maniac.

"So the town turned against Arnoult and his men. And get this—" I glance at Sin warily. "Arnoult died shortly after."

"What? How?"

"That's the strange part." I answer in an absent-minded tone again because I'm already scanning through the rest of the article. "There's no mention of how he died, and all witness statements are kind of vague. But it says here that before he died, he vowed to return and take revenge on those who had hurt him and his . . . his beloved."

There is a long silence between us while we try to wrap our heads around this long train of tragic deaths.

Parents killing children, entire families dying together . . . there seemed to be some foraging force that swept up these people's spirits into a state of murderous frenzy, into a death-desiring obsession that had to end with self-sacrifice.

Dark thoughts like these chase each other through the eerily silent corridors of my mind. I find a dusty chair and sink into it as my knees buckle and give way under all the information we have unearthed.

"Petra . . ." Sin begins in a tactfully neutral tone. "Did you know that Radcliffe is still home to a big Christian cult?"

The non-sequitur jolts me out of my horror-filled imaginings, and for that I am grateful.

He adds, "Though they don't call themselves that. The official name is The True Doctrine."

"The True Doctrine?" I repeat in a hollow tone, forcing myself to pay attention so I won't dwell on the grisly images that keep flashing across my mind's eye, or the fact that I've heard that term before—in my dreams. "What's that about?"

"They've been around for at least two centuries. They are a puritan branch of the Catholic Church, though most people just call them puritans because they don't drink, party, or do anything that's seen as 'fun.'"

"Yeah, I think I've heard my parents talk about that community," I continue, after a brief spell of silence. "Mom doesn't like them, says they are too secretive and secluded, almost cultlike. I've heard people joke about them at school, too, but I wonder how much of it is actually true."

"I think it's more than just rumors. They're . . . well, they're just odd, aren't they?"

There's a distant look in Sin's eyes, as if he's putting together a jigsaw puzzle without a reference image.

"I've seen them at the local farmers' market, and they are always on guard, somehow. Always in their groups, dressed in plain clothes, and the women wear these lace veils that cover their faces. They don't interact much with the rest of the people around here."

"Do you think they know more about Arnoult and his . . . weird vow? Maybe they know about the rituals."

"I somehow don't think they would take it too well if we just barged into their community and asked questions about devils and demons," Sin adds in a cynical voice.

I bite my lip, deep in thought.

"What if we could find a way to get close to them?" I suggest in a mechanical tone devoid of all conviction. "Maybe if we attended one of their church meetings we can ask them about the identity of the girl Arnoult was in love with and—"

Sin scoffs lightly. "Good luck with that! They're notoriously closed off."

"I get it, but there has to be a way we can gather more information," I reply without thinking why it had to be us doing all the digging. "We can't let it go; too many people are at risk."

Sin nods and starts shuffling through more boxes. I try to suppress a yawn as my body begins slackening under the weight of exhaustion and stress and the you-know-who.

At one point, I sit back and stretch my spine to alleviate some of the pressure from my feet.

"Look at this," Sin says, pointing to a document with a beautiful header in curly loopy lettering. "Sources say that Arnoult's legacy was kept alive by some of his members, his most trusted ones in the inner circle."

Sin chuckles and continues, "Apparently, Arnoult had some otherworldly powers."

"Oooh, sexy," I retort in an impassive voice, and this makes Sin snort out loud.

"No really, this article says that he could talk to supernatural beings. And get this—he apparently had some arcane sigils that he used to summon demons."

"Really, Sin? This all sounds so . . . folklorish. It's like we're in a Dan Brown novel and we're racing against time to save the world." I roll my eyes. Yet the word 'sigil' continues to resound in my mind.

Sigils . . . like those in my dreams? That Arnoult had gotten from the Vatican?

"Hmm, I don't know," Sin mutters doubtfully.

"Here, give me that!" I say suddenly, reaching out for the paper in his hands at the same time as he jerks it away from me.

"Argh!" I yell when the edge of the paper slices through the skin of my thumb, and a few drops of red pearl over the pale nailbed.

"Ah, shit!" Sin exclaims before drawing air through his teeth in a somewhat endearing way. "Let me see."

"It's nothing, really," I start, but he's already gently taking my hand and looking at the cut with intense concentration.

"It's not nothing," he insists, and before I can protest further, he brings my finger to his mouth and sucks the tip gently.

The hairs on the nape of my neck stand up, and I can feel my knees trembling a bit.

"Sin," I murmur, my thoughts scattered at the contrast between this tender moment and the dark history of our surroundings.

"Just . . . let me take care of you," he says quietly, nuzzling my fingers in his palm and kissing them softly.

The sight of his lips moving over my skin makes me flush and lose the thread of my thoughts.

So I gently draw my hand away and clear my throat.

Sin sits back and picks up a slim pamphlet from the box he had been reaching for before I gave myself a stupid paper cut.

"So this looks like some kind of local newspaper from that time," he says in a casual tone, as if he hadn't just been sucking my thumb. "It had quite a few articles on Arnoult, speculating whether he was behind all the murders."

I'm floored by this discovery, but a part of me seems to straighten up in tension. As if there is a foreboding voice that is telling me something in words I cannot hear. But Sin looks unmoved by the latest piece of insight into his family's history.

While we rummage through even more boxes, I wonder if any of Sin's family upstairs can hear us.

What if Marie gets up for a midnight snack and passes by Sin's room on the way to the kitchen?

What if there's a fire, and Lisa and Tom rush in to make sure Sin and I are okay?

The thin thread of my thoughts is broken when Sin says, "Found something!"

"What, what is it now?" I rush over to him, my brow darkening with distress as I wonder what fresh news from hell awaits us this time.

Sin is pulling an old letter from a dark corner of the box. The paper looks fragile, tattered, and yellowed with age.

I lean closer as he carefully unfolds it. "What does it say?" I whisper.

"It's dated just before Arnoult died," Sin replies, his voice low, almost reverent. He begins reading aloud:

To My Purest Knights,

I write these words to lock my legacy in stone. I will not rise with the angels nor sink with the sprites from Beelzebub's den. I will not rot under snow nor ripen with fruit in some mortal's orchard. Anoint me with blood, my vessels, and I will be reborn on the next blood moon. I will walk again on this blasted earth when enough sacrifices have been made; I will smite the heathen throng. I will be reborn. I will be reborn.

My stomach twists with every brutal line, shorn of any abashment and dipped in bloodlust. "Reborn? 'Anoint me with blood'? What the hell is he talking about?"

Sin glances at me with fear-ridden eyes. "It means he plans to come back. If they complete the sacrifices—I think that's what 'anoint me with blood' means, he will . . . he will come back, somehow."

"And h-how many sacrifices do they need to make?" I ask again, even though the question itself is too horrific to be answered.

"Ah, that I don't know," Sin replies with a chagrined expression. "I don't even know where to begin with all this . . ." He waves his arms around, as though trying to encompass the fucked-upness of *everything.*

"Sin, if he's going to be reborn on the next blood moon," I begin, as a dreadful realization dawns on me, "and they—whoever is killing these kids—are still operating under that belief, then . . . then we don't have too long, right?"

"Exactly!" he replies, confirming the date on his phone before I've even finished stating my theory out loud.

"So . . ." We both look at each other, and eventually, I turn out to be the one brave enough to ask.

"What do we do now?"

CHAPTER FORTY-SEVEN

PETRA

Present Day

I love Novembers in New England.

The air is cool and crisp, with bright sunshine melting the morning mists on the polished glass façades of the shops and storefronts. The foliage turns all shades of warm browns and reds, while Halloween hangs on the horizon like a tantalizing treat.

On a slightly chilly Sunday afternoon, Sin and I meet at the local diner near St. Anselm Hall.

Cinnamon and pumpkin spice smells waft around us, and the delicious aroma of croissants and pancakes makes my mouth water.

To my utter delight, Sin has already ordered a bunch of baked goods for our table.

"You can pick what you like," he says indulgently, kissing my forehead again while his strong fingers gently massage the back of my neck.

I blush and smile before leaning into his shoulder. Though I'm not the type for PDA, the baby has been weighing down on my back and hips like a bag of bricks, so it's a nice relief when I lean into Sin's warm, strong body.

Nestled in this cozy cocoon and surrounded by freshly baked tarts and pies, I put together the final draft of our Art History project.

It is a multi-page essay on the use of perspective in the rare painting Sin had gifted me earlier.

Ms. Matthews had launched into rapturous exclamations when we'd first shown the painting to her.

"*Can you see how he uses the impasto effect to highlight the break in the trees here*?" and "*How deft is that brushwork*?"

With how long I'd spent staring at the girl walking down the wild, windswept moors, about to enter a dark, shadowy forest, the paper had more or less written itself.

"I think we're getting an A+ for this," Sin says in a satisfied tone as we finish up the draft and send it to Ms. Matthews.

"Really? I've heard she rarely hands those out," I reply while trying to bite into a blueberry muffin at the same time.

"Trust me, I've got a feeling about this," Sin replies with a sparkling grin as he rereads the paper for the umpteenth time.

Just then, my attention is drawn outside the large diner windows.

A procession of dark-clad figures moves down the street wearing solemn expressions and severe-looking costumes, like they walked out of the set of some documentary on the esoteric ways of some religious community.

I am particularly struck by the harsh lines on the faces of the elderly, how they look fierce and unwelcoming, as if resentful of those who do not walk the righteous road with them. And then there are the women, all wearing a thin veil made of lace that semi-covers their features.

"Sin, what's with those people?" I whisper, patting him on the arm. "What's going on out there?"

"Oh, that's the Sunday service," he answers casually, barely giving the group more than a glance. "They're heading to church. It's the Puritans.

"They're real," Sin continues, leaning back slightly as he observes the group. "They've got their own little enclave. They have self-appointed the guardians of the town's northern part, where they live in their own communities, completely cut off from everyone else. It's probably why you haven't seen much of them."

Now the crowd is passing right outside the diner window where we are sitting. I see some children among the crowd. I know that I haven't seen them in school. Do they even go to school?

"So, they really don't interact with outsiders?" I ask out loud.

"Not much," Sin explains. "They keep to themselves and have their own strict beliefs. My dad told me about this. If they even *suspect* you're not a part of their community, they'll avoid you like the plague."

"I wonder what they think about what's been happening around here. The deaths, mutilations—"

"Probably don't care," Sin cuts in smoothly, his tone remaining wholly unaffected by the news he's delivering. "Or they'd just write it off as the consequences of living a sinful life. That's how they think."

"Gosh, that's bleak," I reply, shaking my head.

"That's the thing about their beliefs," Sin says in a strangely quiet voice. "They think they're holier than everyone else. And that by remaining untouched by the rest of us heathens and barbarians, they can remain 'pure.'"

"That's fucked up," I say, absentmindedly nibbling on an almond cookie.

I glance back toward the window, watching the procession of Puritans, their black umbrellas bobbing in the wind like ominous balloons.

"You know Edwin was part of the church, right?" Sin says after a while.

When I sit up with a jolt and look at him in wide-eyed shock, he continues.

"Yeah, he was. I heard my dad saying something along the same lines the other day. It's hard to accept that he was also a victim."

"Bu-but we had that project together." My words are as unsure as my thoughts. "He didn't seem like . . ."

". . . like he belonged to a doomsday cult that believed in raining hellfire and brimstone on all unbelievers?" Sin asks snappily before giving me a wan smile. "I didn't know him as well as you, but I know that he went to church with these folks on certain Sundays. Seen him with my own two eyes," Sin finishes with a deft little nod as he looks at the crowd outside and takes a sip of his Americano.

"Wait, what about Harry? Was he a . . . a Puritan, too?"

Sin's expression turns serious, and his voice low. "As far as I've heard, he wasn't practicing, but his family has ties to them. His mother's family has been around for generations. So if there's a connection there, I wouldn't be surprised."

"Wow, you think you know somebody," I mutter under my breath as memories of Harry flash across my eyes: how we would crack jokes at the lunch table, how we took turns buying snacks for our library study sessions.

A whole lot of despair threatens to drown me under its bilious cloak, so I put my arms around Sin and bury my face in his neck.

Is it a matter of instinct or will?

Doesn't matter, I tell myself. *For now, I feel safe.*

THE NEXT DAY, we attend a very important appointment together.

Bright golden light spills over the plush interiors of the local OB-GYN office's waiting area.

I fill out some forms, and we sit chatting in a comfy chaise lounge among other clients.

A few minutes later, a woman in a stately navy-blue suit ushers us into the physician's office and requests for me to wait for the doctor.

I sit on the examination table, anxiety buzzing beneath my skin. Sin sits beside me, his fingers interlaced with mine, and the mere touch of his hand is enough to ground me.

Today's the day we get to see our baby. I've been looking forward to this ultrasound, but then the bespectacled, kind-looking technician comes in with a warm greeting, "You folks look awfully young, but we're here to help you, so don't be worried."

I suddenly feel a knot of nerves fraying somewhere inside me and look to Sin in blind panic.

"It's okay," he tells me in a bracing tone, while his hands massage my shoulders gently. "You've got this."

I nod and lie down on the table, while the doctor puts gel on the head of the ultrasound wand and then on my distended belly. I shiver at the cold texture of the gel and squirm around a little as the technician probes my stomach with the wand, pressing and prodding some areas in gentle motions.

"All right, Petra," he says after a while. "You're almost five months along, so let's see how your little one is doing."

I glance at Sin, who is watching the screen with a look of awe. "It's insane to think we're about to see him," he murmurs in a hoarse voice.

"I know," I reply, and my own voice rises barely above a whisper. "I'm nervous but excited."

As the technician guides the transducer over my skin, we finally get a clearer picture—an outline of the baby.

"There he is!" Sin exclaims with joy.

I lean in closer to the screen, trying to make out the features of the tiny figure.

It's hard to discern much in the mass of white and black spots on the screen, but my hawk-eyed stare finally starts to see the lines of the baby's body: the round head, small hands, and feet curled up close to the stomach.

The technician captures the image, and I can't help but smile.

"It's a boy," the technician says.

"I can't believe it."

"Looks like a little champ already," Sin adds, voice swelling with pride.

"Everything seems normal from what I can see. He's in a good position," the technician says. I feel myself relaxing and sinking deeper into the bed under me.

But something in Sin's expression catches my eye. He's staring at the technician's face, so I turn to the man as well.

"What is it?" I demand in a voice quivering in fear.

The man's brow furrows for just a moment as he moves the wand around before stopping and pushing on one spot.

"Nothing to worry about," he says in a carefully modulated voice that immediately makes me worry. "Let me just check a couple of things here."

Unease unfurls within me, but I try my best to brush it aside, focusing instead on Sin's hand in mine.

I can see Sin's reflection on the screen—his face is drawn and despairing.

"Wow, look at those little fingers," I say in an attempt to inject some sense of normalcy into what is starting to feel like a living nightmare. "He's perfect."

Just then, the technician's fingers pause. "Hmm. That's odd," he mutters, leaning in closer to the screen. "There's something here, but I can't see . . ."

Suddenly, the lights flicker, and the power goes out completely, plunging us into near darkness. The only light comes from the small screen, which is still displaying the ultrasound.

"What's happening?" I ask, panic rising in my chest in fast waves.

"It's just a power outage," Sin whispers next to me, squeezing my hand. "We'll be fine."

But as the technician mutters to himself about backup generators, I start to feel a tightness in my stomach—a strange pulling, prickling sensation that makes me inhale sharply.

"Um, I don't feel so good," I say in a shaky voice. "I think I'm—" Before I can finish speaking, a sharp pain ripples through my lower belly, and I moan loudly and clutch at my stomach.

"Petra!" Sin cries out, his eyes darting all over me in urgent panic. "Petra, what's happening? Talk to me! Are you okay?"

"It hurts, Sin. I think—" Another bout of tightening muscles, like my pelvis is trying to expel something . . . and then it hits me. "It feels like—" I begin in a stronger voice, but Sin is already looking to the technician for help.

"Do something!" he yells fearfully.

"Umm, Petra, what are you feeling?" the technician stammers. "Where does it hurt?"

"It feels like contractions!" I finally manage to hiss through gritted teeth. "I swear to God, I'm having contractions."

CHAPTER FORTY-EIGHT

PETRA

Present Day

Before Sin or the incredulous-looking technician can reply, tremors hit the walls around us, and the building starts shaking.

"What's going on? What's happening?" I gasp even as a fresh wave of pain rips through me.

The technician looks up, his face contorted with some unseen fear.

"Let me check the heartbeat," he says in a hard-edged voice. But the display flickers and plunges into darkness while the shaking motions get more intense.

I grip Sin's hand tightly, my breathing becoming erratic. "Sin, I'm scared."

"You're going to be okay. I'm right here." He leans closer, his eyes filled with fear and determination. "Just focus on me, Petra. I won't let anything happen to either of you."

As the tremors in the building grow stronger, I can only cling to his words, my heart racing with fear, my breath caught in my throat.

All around us, physician's tools—scalpels, forceps, scissors, injections—clatter and rattle in their trays while the overhead light flickers uncontrollably. The curtains swish and billow around us, and the windowpanes jangle in their frames.

"Sin, the baby—" I groan.

"The baby's fine, Petra," Sin replies in a steady tone, cupping my face with his hands and whispering sweet nothings into my ear. "You're gonna be just fine, my sweet girl," he croons so lovingly that my pulse starts to slow down despite my rising panic.

In the next few minutes, the tremors stop.

"Phew!" says the technician, who had been cowering next to the examination table. "Been years since we had one of those hefty earthquakes," he says while fussing over the screen and retrieving the ultrasound wand. "Ah, now, where were we?" he continues, turning toward me with the same oblivious smile that he had worn at the beginning.

THE RIDE HOME from the clinic passes by in a blur of exhaustion and discomfort, Sin's hand in mine anchoring my wandering mind. He drives with a focused intensity, brow furrowed and lips pressed into a thin line.

I want to say something to reassure him, but fear still gnaws at my insides, and I end up floundering around for the right words.

When we finally reach my house, Sin practically jumps out of the car to help me inside.

"Take it easy, Petra," he says softly, putting his arm around my waist while he leads me up the stairs. "You need to rest. I won't hear any arguments."

"Good, I wasn't gonna argue anyways," I reply somewhat tartly, but he just gives me a low, throaty chuckle that makes me tingle.

Once inside my bedroom, he helps me into bed, tucking the covers around me, and fluffing up the pillows so I'm tightly wrapped like a cozy burrito.

"Now you just make yourself comfortable. I'll get you some water, okay?"

"Sure, sure," I reply in a teasing voice and send him a flying kiss. He flushes with pleasure and returns the gesture.

My heart feels full from all his thoughtfulness.

The days when I had worried about being too much of a grump for this charming, sunshiny guy seem to be way back in the past.

Today, it seems natural that he should be by my side, attending my OB-GYN appointment with me, and then taking care of me when there's a blackout and the earth starts shaking like it's the second coming of Christ.

The last thoughts send a pang of fear through my heart, and I want him back in the room, even though he has just left.

"Sin," I call softly.

"Coming! Just a minute," he shouts back from the kitchen. And from the way the sound of his voice makes my limbs relax and settles the butterflies fluttering around in my stomach, I know that I have fallen for him. Deeply.

Soon, he returns with a glass of water.

"Drink this. You need to stay hydrated, especially after . . . you know, everything."

As I sip the water, he sits on the edge of the bed, looking slightly hesitant.

"How are you feeling now?" he asks.

"A little better, I think. Just tired and sore."

"Good, just rest. I'll be right here if you need anything." He fusses over the blanket, making sure that I'm as comfortable as I can be.

His face looks so adorable and adoring, so filled with the light of affection, that I feel an overwhelming urge to lean in closer, to plant a kiss on those downturned lips.

"Sin . . ." I begin, but my throat tightens slightly.

"Yes? What do you need?" he asks immediately.

"I want—" I begin uncertainly before clearing my throat and trying again. "Can we . . ." But then I lose my nerve at the last minute. By now, I'm tired of all this politeness, so I reach forward and cup his face in my hands instead.

With slightly more force than usual, I pull him toward me.

His eyes widen as our lips connect, but in the next second, his arms are crossing around my body, and he's pulling me closer, too.

The kiss starts out sweet at first, but then it quickly turns steamy as Sin pulls me into his lap so that my legs are wrapped around his waist. His hardness pushes against my center, and I grind myself against him.

I moan into his mouth as he grips my waist tighter.

When we finally pull back, Sin's eyes are downright glittering. "Wow," he breathes, his tone tinged with wonder. "That was . . . mind-blowing."

"It was," I reply, my heart racing. "Today was quite the day, huh?" I laugh nervously.

Sin nods and pulls me down to the bed, tucking me back under the covers again.

"Just know that I'm here," he says in a voice thick with untold emotions. "For you and the baby. No matter what happens."

The night stretches deep and dark before us, but the snug circle of Sin's arms lulls me into a sleep that comes fretfully but stays awhile.

CHAPTER FORTY-NINE

PETRA

The Past

For some strange reason, the venue for the engagement party has changed. Now, it's being hosted at the Snowden estate.

But the information I've received in my dreams clings to me like a shadow as I make my way through this beautiful, haunting house.

What if that wasn't just a dream? What if Snowden truly is keeping some rotting corpse hidden in his basement? What if it gets out—tonight—and terrorizes the very guests he's hosting?

There are dozens of people here, all the wealthiest in Radcliffe. Unsurprisingly, no one from my congregation is present. This kind of excess doesn't align with our values. Everywhere I look, there's extravagant food, wine, and champagne flowing freely, greedily consumed in every corner.

It's a far cry from the teachings of our church. And yet . . . in the last few months, my father's entire worldview seems to have spun on its axis. It's as though I no longer recognize him.

As for my brother, I can't entirely fault him. He's only following in our father's footsteps, as he's always done. But that doesn't mean I can reconcile this new, gilded version of our family with the strict, pious household I grew up in.

Naturally, today I was instructed once more not to wear my veil. To put on the gifted dress. To look pretty. And, most importantly, not to speak unless spoken to.

My mother, too, has come out tonight without her veil—a first for her. Yet even without the physical evidence of her conditioning, her behavior remains the same. She's quiet, absent, invisible.

If there's one piece of dogma my father has chosen to preserve even as he strays away from our congregation, it's the belief that a woman's role is ornamental.

A decoration. Nothing more.

I walk quietly through the ballroom. I hadn't seen it during my previous visits, but it's every bit as opulent as I imagined—perhaps even more so.

The ceiling is adorned with neoclassical designs, while the walls boast a mix of Renaissance paintings and a few Romantic-era pieces that catch my eye.

Of course, I'm drawn to them. But I am not allowed to stray far from my mother's side. I've been expressly instructed to stay close, remain quiet, and above all, make myself invisible.

The paintings in the ballroom mirror those in the hallway—gory, bloody, and almost ritualistic in their depictions. As I gaze at them from afar, my mind drifts back to the dream . . . and to the unsettling thought that Snowden might have made a deal with the devil, too. That he's just as guilty as the very people he publicly condemns.

The music blares through the ballroom—an orchestra that came in from New York City, no less. People speak loudly over the din, their voices clashing with the music. There's a disorganized frenzy to the room, with everyone moving in a constant swirl, never staying still for even a moment.

My mother, however, chooses a quiet corner and settles there, content to simply observe the chaos. I join her, taking in the spectacle. Across the room, I spot my brother, my father, and Mr. Snowden deep in conversation with a circle of important guests.

Leah hasn't made her appearance yet.

I find myself anxiously scanning the room for her. I want to check on her, make sure she's all right. After all, she's the real victim in all of this. If only I had more power . . . if only I could do something to save her.

"Would you please excuse me for a moment? I need to go to the restroom," I murmur to my mother.

She glances at me out of the corner of her eye, offering only a small, almost imperceptible nod in response.

I slip away, cutting through the crowd and heading for the double French doors that lead into the main hallway. Guests continue to arrive, with some veering off to the cigar room and others lured into the gambling parlor. The entire estate has been designed to mimic the opulence of English aristocracy, complete with lavish ballrooms and indulgent side rooms.

But the farther I walk down the hallway, the thinner the crowd becomes. Eventually, the noise fades behind me, and the house grows quieter.

And once again, my thoughts return to that creature.

The one Mr. Snowden might be hiding in his basement.

It's not real . . . right?

It couldn't possibly be real. It was only a dream.

Or was it?

I remember, with eerie clarity, the sound I heard last time I was here—a shriek, unearthly and chilling, just as I was eavesdropping on my father and Mr. Snowden. Seconds later, my brother had caught me and dragged me away.

But that sound still lingers in my memory.

What had it been?

Perhaps my curiosity is a flaw after all. But I can't stop myself. I move deeper into the darker corridors of the mansion.

And before long, I realize I'm completely lost.

The sound of the party fades into a distant hum. As I try to retrace my steps, I realize I'm facing the same problem I had during my first visit to this place: The hallways all look identical. They twist and curve into endless little corridors, and I no longer know which way I came.

I take a deep breath and turn around—only to freeze when I hear it.

That same shrieking sound from before.

It's faint, barely perceptible. But it's there.

My heart leaps into my throat. I close my eyes and focus. Another shriek, closer this time, comes from my left. So I follow it.

Maybe one day I'll regret this decision, but right now I feel like I'm losing my grip on reality. I don't know what's happening to me anymore. These dreams—are they even dreams at all? They seem so real. And yet, every time I wake up, everything is back in place. It's as if I never left my bedroom.

Still, something in me says it's not just imagination. That something is truly happening to me in those hours of sleep. And the only way to confirm it is to find out if the so-called creature really exists.

So, against my better judgment and all reason, I march forward.

The sound grows louder, no longer a shriek but a wail—low, pained, and strange. Step by step, I follow it until I reach a door. Pressing my ear to the wooden frame, I listen.

A moan, ragged and strained, echoes from behind it, like someone in deep pain.

My fingers tremble as I grip the handle. I open the door.

But it doesn't lead to a room.

It reveals a staircase.

A long, narrow staircase that descends into pitch-black darkness.

There's no light down there. Nothing.

Do I dare?

Sin warned me against this. But if this is all just a product of my imagination, then what harm could come of it?

If it's only my mind conjuring wild, delusional scenarios—born of loneliness and dissatisfaction—then I'll find nothing. And maybe then, I can finally admit that I'm simply going mad.

So, though afraid, I steel myself and descend.

I count the steps. One . . . two . . . ten . . . eleven . . . twenty . . . twenty-five.

At the twenty-fifth step, I reach a landing. The chamber is utterly dark. I take a tentative step forward, trying to make out anything, but I'm surrounded by nothingness.

"Guess it really was just a dream," I whisper aloud, almost relieved.

But then, I feel it.

A gust of wind brushes against the back of my neck—cool, sharp, unnatural. I shiver.

I turn quickly, heart racing.

"Who's there?" I call out, voice wavering.

No answer.

I try again. "Who is it?"

Still nothing.

I stand frozen for a moment, trying to see through the suffocating dark. Another gust of air hits me—this time over my face. My eyes sting, and I raise my hands, reaching blindly for anything solid.

But there's nothing.

"Is there anyone there?" I whisper, barely able to keep the tremor out of my voice.

Then it starts.

A hum, soft and melodic.

A lullaby.

I recognize the tune. Vaguely. It drifts through the space, its source unclear, moving, circling. I turn, trying to track it, but I can't find the origin.

"Are you . . . Are you Mr. Snowden's mistress?" I ask, instantly regretting how ridiculous it sounds aloud.

Just when I decide I've had enough, that I don't need to know anything else, I start back toward the stairs.

And that's when the lights come on.

Every wall ignites in a sudden blaze of electric light, flooding the chamber with clarity.

The room is empty. Bare.

Nothing.

And yet . . . I still feel it. That awful sensation of being watched.

"That's it," I whisper. "I need to get out of here."

I bolt for the stairs.

But as soon as my foot touches the first step, another gust of wind slams into me so powerful that it lifts the hem of my skirt and sends loose strands of hair whipping across my face.

There's still nothing I can see.

But maybe, just maybe, it's not something meant to be seen.

Thoroughly shaken, I flee the chamber, racing up the stairs. I slam the door shut behind me and lock it with trembling hands.

"Good Lord," I whisper, chest heaving. "I really am losing my mind."

It takes me a few moments to find my way back to the party. I follow the sound of music until the soft thrum of the orchestra leads me back to the ballroom.

My mother immediately corners me, demanding to know where I've been and why I took so long. I tell her the truth: I got lost. After a few sharp words about how improper it is to wander in someone else's house, she finally drops the subject.

In the meantime, more guests seem to have arrived. The ballroom is full now, buzzing with conversation and movement. Then the orchestra stops playing.

A sharp clink of a fork against glass cuts through the room. Everyone quiets.

Mr. Snowden is the one holding the glass. "If I could have your attention for a moment, please," he begins. "I'm very pleased to welcome you all into my home today for a most special occasion. My daughter, Leah, is now officially engaged to Mr. Robert Creig."

The room bursts into polite applause.

"The wedding will take place in three weeks," he continues, beaming. "And all of you are invited."

But before the clapping has even subsided, my father steps forward, his voice louder, eager.

"But that is not all," he says. "We have another surprise for you. Another engagement we would like to announce."

I frown, confused. Another engagement?

Then my father's eyes lock with mine.

And everything clicks into place. *No.*

"Besides my son marrying Miss Leah Snowden," he says, pausing to glance at Mr. Snowden, as if seeking confirmation, "I am also pleased to announce that my daughter, Petra, will be marrying—"

No. No.

The blood drains from my face.

Now I understand. The times he told me not to wear my veil when Mr. Snowden was around. The strange looks. The dress. The silence. All of it.

He intends to marry me off to Mr. Snowden.

A widower. A man at least three times my age.

It makes sense why, though. He has no heir, only a daughter. A man like him would *hate* to leave his wealth to his daughter and new son-in-law.

And that's why he wants me.

My father did not just sell my brother; he sold me, too.

But perhaps, just perhaps, the fates are on my side tonight; because as my father begins to name Mr. Snowden as my intended, something strange happens.

Mr. Snowden freezes.

His eyes widen, fixed on something beyond the glass doors leading out to the garden. His face goes pale, like he's seen a ghost.

He abruptly places a hand on my father's arm and whispers something into his ear, shaking his head. My father hesitates, clearly startled, but Mr. Snowden quickly excuses himself and vanishes into the crowd.

Trying to salvage the moment, my father clears his throat.

"Ah, that was . . . a mistake. Please excuse my, uh, rash announcement. Let us celebrate the engagement of my son and Miss Leah. Eat, drink, and enjoy the dances tonight."

The orchestra resumes its playing.

And I finally exhale. *Thank God.*

But I don't walk away. I walk straight up to him.

Without thinking of the consequences. Without caring that I'm not supposed to speak.

I plant myself in front of him and ask, "What did you mean by that?"

He glares down at me with that familiar, condescending look.

"What do you think I meant?" he snaps. "You are to be engaged. That is not up for discussion."

"You can't be serious," I whisper. "You expect me to marry Mr. Snowden?"

"I told you to be quiet," he hisses. "Yes, you will marry Mr. Snowden. Perhaps we didn't announce it tonight, but we will—soon."

"What?" My voice rises, trembling. "He's three times my age, for God's sake!"

"Don't take the Lord's name in vain," he snaps. "You will marry him because I say so. I am your father, your guardian, and I know what's best for you. And what's best for you is Mr. Snowden."

"No," I say. "I won't do it."

"Excuse me?" he sputters.

"I said no." My voice is louder now, firmer. "I will not marry him."

He tries to stare me down, to intimidate me, but I don't budge. I won't let him destroy what little life I have left. I won't exchange one prison for another. One tyrant for a richer one.

"I will not marry Mr. Snowden. In fact, I won't marry anyone."

And before he can say another word, I turn on my heel and run.

I don't know where I'm going. I just know I need to get away—from him, from this place, from all of them.

I slip through the French doors and out into the garden, desperate for air, for space, for freedom. The moment I'm outside, my legs buckle. The weight of the moment crashes into me all at once. I gasp, the air sharp in my lungs.

"Why me?" I whisper. "Why always me?"

"You didn't listen to what I told you," a voice murmurs behind me.

I whirl around and come face-to-face with Sin.

Dashing as always. But is he . . . real?

CHAPTER FIFTY

PETRA

The Past

"What are you doing here?" I whisper.

"You never listen, do you, Petra?" Sin cocks a brow at me.

He's dressed in a white shirt with a black vest over it and black trousers. A few buttons at his neck are undone, revealing a glimpse of skin. He's far too casually dressed for the party, which means he's not here for it.

He's here for *me*.

"I told you not to go looking for the creature," he continues. "Did you?"

"You know I did. But . . . you didn't ever tell me anything. I haven't spoken to you in months."

He snorts. "Do you really believe that?"

I shrug. "I already suspected those dreams weren't really dreams, but this confirms it. Besides, I think the creature saved me in this instance."

"Really?" he drawls.

"Oh, come on." I roll my eyes at him. "It's not like you don't know. You've probably been watching me from the shadows, like always. You know what my father meant to do—what he and Mr. Snowden had planned. They didn't go through with it because Mr. Snowden looked terrified. And why would he be scared . . . if not because he saw something?"

"So smart, my darling Petra."

"Don't patronize me," I snap.

"I'm not. It's a fair compliment. Although I'm still not in agreement with what you did. It was dangerous. Reckless. Why would you do something like that?"

"Because I had to know. I had to know if the dreams were real, or if I was just losing my mind." I take a deep breath. "That's how I've been feeling all this time, Sin. And it's *your* fault. You're the reason I've stopped caring about my life. I keep waiting for night to fall so I can sleep—so I can *see* you again."

"Ah, Petra . . ." he whispers, stepping closer.

"Stop toying with me," I mumble, my voice breaking.

"Have I ever?"

"Yes, you have. How could you think you haven't? And the things that happened in those dreams that weren't even dreams . . ." I'm hysterical at this point as I remember the ways in which he'd touched me, the ways in which *I'd* touched him. "Was it real? Or did you . . . do something to my mind?"

"No. I did not do anything to your mind."

"Then how?"

He presses his lips together, and I can see the answer won't come easily.

"I'm done with you," I say. "I'm done with everyone trying to control me. Just when I thought I'd found some small sliver of peace in my sleep . . . it wasn't even real. *You* weren't even real."

"But that's where you're wrong, Petra. I *was* real. I *am* real. What we shared in those moments—that was the real me. *Is* the real me."

"Then why lie to me? Again and again. When you *know* how much I hate it?" I croak.

"Because I had no other way to be close to you. No other way for you to truly know me. And I wanted you to know that I'm not like your father. Or Mr. Snowden. Or anyone else from your congregation. I don't want you as a trophy. I don't want you as a decoration. I want *you*. I want to know your thoughts. I want to hear your voice. I don't want to silence you."

"But can you not understand my side, too?" I whisper. "It's like I'm suffocating. I don't know what's real anymore. I don't even know *myself*. One part of me just wants to run into your arms and never let go. The other wants to flee."

I take a deep breath, moisture clinging to my lashes.

"And then there's my home. Everything has become unbearable. My father has . . . sold me to the highest bidder. For money. He's abandoned his beliefs, his pride, everything. In the past, even though he was a tyrant, at least he had *principles*. But now? Now he's *just* a tyrant."

"I hope you don't put me in the same category as your father."

"Are you not?" I raise a brow.

"I'm *not*." He grits his teeth. He takes a step closer and extends his arms outward, waiting.

He's waiting for me to go to him.

I bite my lip and stare at him. And before I can think better of it, my feet carry me to him.

His arms wrap around my body, and I collapse into his embrace.

"Oh, my darling Petra . . ."

Tears spill down my cheeks. Sobs wrack my chest, and I can't stop them. I can't stop myself from crying, then wailing. I hold on to him as everything I've been bottling up breaks the surface.

"My darling girl, it hurts my heart to see you like this. But you have to trust me. I would never do anything to hurt you. On the contrary—I have everything planned. I will never let anyone lay a finger on you. I will never let anyone *hurt* you. Or *touch* you. You will not marry him. You will not marry anyone but me."

"But how can you do that? How can you stop them?" I plead.

"Don't worry about that for now. Just know I will never let anything happen to you. You believe me, don't you?"

"I . . ." I manage through my sobs. "I think I do."

Do I? Just moments ago, I was telling him I don't trust him, yet that was a lie, wasn't it? Time and time again, my actions have not matched my words, even as I spoke them to myself.

"I *know* you do," he replies smoothly. "You're far too smart, Petra. You must have known for a long time that those dreams weren't really dreams. And yet you kept coming back to me. You kept calling out for me."

"What are you talking about?" I whisper.

He smiles and lowers his hand to my chest, right above my heart. A pulsing warmth radiates through me.

"Here. This ties us together in ways you can't yet fathom. What you feel—I feel. When you hurt, I hurt. And when you cry . . . my goddamn heart bleeds for you."

"The sigils . . . they're real?"

"They are."

I immediately unbutton my bolero and peer down at my neckline. Sure enough, the mark is there, dark, intense, and *visible*.

"But how come I couldn't see it during the day?"

"I hid it. I didn't want to scare you. Not until I could explain everything. Until I told you the truth."

"Then explain. What is happening, Sin? I want to know everything. No more lies. No more half-truths. Tell me about the creature. About Mr. Snowden. About these rituals and this occult and *your* involvement. I *need* to know."

"I'll show you," he says. "If you think you can handle it, I'll show you."

"Show me what?" I whisper.

He doesn't answer with words.

He turns me around in his arms and pulls me close. And somehow we're *moving*. Not walking. Not even floating. But traveling through shadows that curl and ripple around us like smoke.

The lights from the house and garden flicker, then blur, until we are surrounded by shifting dark.

"Don't speak too loud," he whispers into my hair. "You must be quiet now, Petra. We don't want *them* to hear us."

"Them?" I ask.

He doesn't answer.

Instead, he carries me farther into the depths of the estate until we're close to the woods.

Hidden deep in the foliage of the well-groomed shrubs, we watch as if from above. In the middle of a square-like formation, there are two people. It takes me a moment to acclimate to the darkness of my surroundings.

Then I realize that one of them is Mr. Snowden. He is on his back on the grass, his clothes torn to shreds, pieces of fabric littered all around.

On top of him is . . . something. Or someone.

"What?" I whisper to Sin.

"That," he replies. "That is what you freed from that basement, Petra."

"What is it?"

At that moment, *she*—no, *it*—moves. A creature with the body of a woman, her skin dark and greenish, mottled like a rotting corpse. She undulates her body atop Mr. Snowden, her hands pressed to his chest, her nails elongated into talons as she digs them into his flesh.

From her back, tendrils slither outward, gliding toward Mr. Snowden's head. Two tendrils, one on each side. They find his ears and insert themselves into his ear canals.

"What is that, Sin?" I whisper in shock.

"She's feeding."

"What?"

"See what they're doing?" he says quietly. "They're fornicating."

"They're—" I murmur, horrified. "But she's a creature. A dead corpse. How is that—how is that possible?"

He finishes the thought for me. "There are many things that might seem impossible, Petra, but are entirely too possible in the vastness of the universe. That creature is one of them."

"But how can something alive . . . fornicate with something dead?"

"That is the crux of the issue, isn't it? It goes against nature. And yet, it's happening before our very eyes. Those tendrils you see—she's using them to feed on him, on his essence. That's the only way she can be controlled."

"But doesn't that harm him?"

"It does. But that's his cross to bear."

"I don't understand."

"If he doesn't feed her, she will run berserk. And we don't know how many people she might kill."

"Kill?" I gasp.

"It's a non-sentient creature made from negative energy. It only knows how to destroy, but under Snowden's rule, it's a controlled destruction."

"What—what do you mean?"

"What do you *think* I mean? Do you remember how Rutherford died?"

"I saw in the newspapers that his body had been badly torn apart."

Sin smiles slowly. "Yes. Torn apart by something not human."

"Wait. You mean . . . your society wasn't the one who killed him?"

"No. And I told you, I'm not personally involved in any of this."

"But then I don't understand. So his death wasn't part of a ritual?"

"No. It was not."

"What about that other fellow? Underwood? The newspaper said he was killed quite brutally, too."

"Same as Rutherford."

"But why? Why would Snowden command that creature to kill them? And make it look like it's some kind of ritual?"

"Because it's part of a vengeance plan," he continues. "I told you before—Rutherford, Snowden, Arnoult, Haas, and Underwood were the ones who laid the foundation of the Ouroboros Society. They started all of this."

"*They*?" I raise a brow.

He shrugs. "I merely found myself in their proximity. That doesn't make me guilty by default, does it?"

"No, I suppose not," I whisper.

"See, the thing here is while there *were* indeed some rituals performed, and while there *are* people who chose to give their lives for some higher purpose, I cannot tell you why each individual person did what they did.

"But there are also other deaths—deaths that were not committed in the name of any ritual. Deaths committed with far more insidious motives."

"Snowden."

"Indeed."

"But why?"

"Why do you think, Petra? Because he's trying to erase all traces of his involvement. He wants to be remembered as the one who *vanquished* this so-called satanic cult.

"After all, he has everything he needs now, doesn't he? He doesn't need his dead mistress anymore. Not when he's planning to marry you."

"Don't remind me," I grumble.

"Don't worry about that." He places a kiss on my temple. "I will never allow that."

"You said you have a plan. What is it?"

"All in good time, Petra. I *will* tell you. You have my word. But you must be patient. Every piece of the puzzle must fit in its place."

I turn back to the scene before me, unable to look away. Mr. Snowden, now completely naked, is rolling in the grass with the creature. Her tendrils are still connected to his brain—feeding on him, or whatever that means.

And at the same time . . . they're mating.

She's beneath him now.

And he's pumping into her as if she were a real woman, his hands digging into her flesh. Groans and moans erupt in the air.

"I've seen enough. Please take me away."

"Your wish is my command."

The shadows coil around us once more. I blink, and we're suddenly in a room—a library? Tall bookshelves line the walls. A study is by the window with a chair placed neatly under it. There is nothing out of place, almost as if no one lives here.

"Where are we?"

"My home," he answers casually.

"Your home? The one in the tunnels?"

He nods.

"I assume we will need some privacy for our discussion."

"And you just kidnapped me from the party?"

He shrugs.

"You're infuriating! At least tell me how you brought us here. Those . . ." I point toward the shadows around him. "They're alive?"

"No. They are not. They are just shadows. But I can move within them at will."

"You . . ."

"And before you ask," he adds with a laugh, "I did not sell my soul for this ability. Unfortunately, I was born with it."

I stare at him in shock. He . . . what?

CHAPTER FIFTY-ONE

PETRA

Present Day

I jolt awake to find myself in my bedroom.

What the hell did I see?

Thankfully, Sin is still sleeping next to me, his chest rising and falling softly. I blink rapidly to chase the image away from my mind and draw deep breaths to calm myself further.

What time is it? When I check the bedside clock, it's a little after three in the morning.

The witching hour, my inner voice points out wryly. But I am still too unsettled from the dream to find any solace in her witty quips.

I sit up slowly as a strange tension coils tightly around my chest.

Again, I remember the debacle from the OB-GYN appointment: the tremors, the flickering lights, and most terrifyingly, the technician's worried face when he had seen the ultrasound display on the screen.

What did he see? And what if something is wrong with the baby?

Even now, when my heart cracks in pain at the thought of the slightest harm to the you-know-who inside me, it's hard to accept that he is almost here.

True to the nature of anxious thoughts, one is rapidly followed by a host of others.

I remember how Arnoult the First looks strikingly like Sin's father. What if there's a genetic anomaly on the Arnoults' side? Then I remember the crypt and its grisly murals: If Arnoult and his followers were the members of the

Ouroboros Society, that means *they had drawn* those gruesome images on the cold stone walls of St. Anselm Hall's hidden crypt.

This chilling realization is followed by the most unsettling speculation I have had so far: What if the child I'm carrying is a reincarnation of Arnoult?

At first the thought seems too absurd to even entertain for more than a moment. But gradually, I remember more of the information we had unearthed in the basement of Sin's house.

"Blood moon," I mutter to myself. "When's the next blood moon?" I start searching online, my fingers typing rapidly.

My eyes widen at the answer: four months. That's when I'm due to have the baby.

"Please, no," I whisper, as my heart starts racing. "This can't be happening."

Desperate panic courses through me as I sit down at the edge of the bed, my hands cradling my stomach instinctively.

"Sin . . ." I start to say, but I catch myself just in time. I don't want to burden him with this fear. Not yet. Not when he's been so supportive through everything.

And so, I keep my freshest fears to myself, wondering when my life became so unpredictable that I have to look to the stars and the moon to know where it's headed. Yet it's not just my waking moments that give me stress. My dreams are becoming weirder and weirder, to the point where I'm actually starting to question my sanity.

What the hell was that monster from my dream? That undead creature that was fucking a living person? Does that count as necrophilia, because what the actual fuck?!

If I'd been bingeing horror movies day after day, perhaps I could understand why my subconscious would choose to show me such images. But I haven't.

Is it that deep down I'm still traumatized by Harry's death? From seeing his head roll on the floor right in front of me?

Maybe . . . In the past, I would have relegated everything to just that and my pregnancy hormones. But after the OB-GYN visit and the additional information we found on Arnoult and the Ouroboros Society, I have to start asking myself if . . .

If perhaps the supernatural *is* real, that there is something deeply wrong with this town, and that I may have unwittingly found myself in the midst of it all.

I just want my baby to be fine.

Tears of fear and frustration cling to my lashes. I may have been in denial for months now regarding this baby, but the truth is that I *do* want it.

Perhaps it's because I've never had anyone to love me unconditionally before, and this baby might be the answer; or perhaps it's the fact that I have so deeply fallen in love with Sin, and this baby is something we made together—something to *tie* us together. Forever.

I'm not going to let some creepy, long-dead Victorian man steal my baby. No, no! That isn't going to happen. Not on this blood moon, nor ever.

I'm not going to allow it.

How do you plan on stopping him, though? my inner voice asks.

Careful not to wake Sin, I get out of bed and head to my art room. I turn on the light and rummage for a pen and some paper.

Before I forget, I start tracing the lines of the sigil from my dreams. The image is a little muddy, but I think I get most of it right: at least enough to be able to reverse image search it online.

More images flash in my mind, from the past, from my dreams, now more clear than ever.

Why does my dream-Sin look so much like present-day Sin? Did my mind conjure that because I'm in love with him, or is there something more to it? Then there's the resemblance between his father and Arnoult the First. These can't be mere coincidences.

Dream-Petra had been a part of that puritan community, so I doubt I would be able to find any records on her—if that was even her name. But maybe I can find something about the Snowdens?

They were rich and influential at the time. There should be records on them.

I stare back at the drawing I just made. Though not perfect, the symbol is striking. It's almost hypnotizing in the way those lines flow and coil around each other, all converging in the middle where my initial is.

My body hums with unreleased pressure, and I press my hand to my chest where the dream sigil had been. I rub against that spot, feeling an unusual heat build up inside me.

Why does this symbol seem so familiar and heart-aching at the same time?

With my phone, I quickly snap a picture and upload it online. I wait a couple of seconds for the search to be performed, all the while holding my breath anxiously.

No results found.

I blink. Damn it!

Not one to give up, I try another way. I write up a quick description of the symbol, including the circumstances of its appearance as I remember them from my dream, and I hit search.

There are a few hits from Reddit and other forums, so I start perusing each one of them.

They don't answer any of my questions, though. They're all from tattoo communities. But the symbol on my flesh was *not* tattooed, it just . . . appeared.

"Ugh!" I let out a frustrated sigh and throw the paper aside.

"Petra?" Sin's voice echoes behind me. "What's wrong? Are you not feeling well?"

I turn, and there he is, leaning against the doorframe. As I blink, the image shifts, and instead of seeing him in his present state—dark sweatpants and a shirt—I see him dressed in Victorian garb, with a pair of black trousers, white shirt under a dark vest, and a silk bow tie at his neck.

I rub my eyes.

"Petra?" he calls out again and comes toward me.

Once more, I see him as *before* instead of now, and it only freaks me out more as I scurry away from him.

"What's wrong, sweet girl?" He takes in my wild eyes and disheveled appearance before his eyes move to the side, to where my drawing is. He narrows his eyes and picks up the piece of paper. "What is this?" he asks in a low, dark voice that sends shivers down my spine.

I bite my lip, not knowing *how* to explain it. He might think I'm crazy. *I think I'm crazy!*

"Petra, what is this?" His voice is a stark contrast to the dulcet tones he's used on me in the past; it's commanding, domineering . . . "Where did you find it?"

"I . . . I drew it," I whisper.

"You drew it? Why? How?"

He's still staring at the drawing, a myriad of emotions crossing over his face before he schools them in a bored indifference.

"Do you know it?" I whisper.

His lips tremble as he shakes his head. "It's very pretty, though."

I study his face, a little taken aback by his reaction. "I dreamed about it," I blurt out.

"You what?" He blinks in surprise.

I nod. "I've been having these odd dreams for a while."

Since getting pregnant, more specifically, though I don't mention that.

I'm already too scared to entertain the thought that my unborn baby might end up being that psychotic Arnoult guy.

Sin takes a seat next to me, taking my hand in his and lightly massaging it. "And what did you dream?" he asks.

"I'm still not entirely sure. Sometimes the dreams are very clear, sometimes not as much. But it's . . ." I gulp down. "It's almost as if I'm seeing a version of me from the past."

"From the past?" he echoes. He looks at me intently, waiting for me to continue.

"It's silly, right? It's probably nothing."

"It's not silly, Petra. Tell me more. What did you dream about?"

"I can't remember very well," I lie. "Just bits and pieces, sensations mostly."

I'm not sure why I don't just go ahead and tell him everything. But I'm still in the process of figuring it out. And dream-Sin . . . I still don't know who or *what* he was. And if I'm completely honest, a part of me wonders if the man I keep dreaming about isn't Arnoult.

Dream-Sin *was* associated with that Society. He was involved in all those rituals, one way or another. And the way Snowden and my dream-father were talking about Arnoult . . . What if he *is* Arnoult?

But why would he want to possess your unborn child then?

"I was wondering if I could find this symbol online. But it's not anywhere. I've probably imagined the whole thing," I add with a nervous laugh. "Hormones and all that."

"I'm not so sure about that. Those are some very exact details."

"What else could it be, though?"

"A past life?" he wonders.

"A past . . . life?"

"You wouldn't be the only one to remember bits and pieces from your past life. Here," he says as he grabs his phone and searches up reincarnation. Story after story comes up, of people who remember their past lives with startling details.

It's one thing for my dreams to be mere hallucinations brought on by the many traumatic experiences I've had recently. It's quite another to think of them as real.

"Did you see anyone else in your dreams?" he asks.

"Anyone else? Like who?"

He shrugs. "Anyone else that seemed familiar."

"I'm not sure," I answer slowly, averting my eyes.

"Are you sure? Perhaps—"

"I think we should go back to bed," I declare, thoroughly spooked by yet another complication in my already far too complicated life. "Let's go to sleep."

I get up and head back to the bedroom. But he doesn't follow. Looking back, I see him still staring at my little drawing, his expression a combination of sadness and wistfulness that tugs at my heart.

"Sin?" I call out.

"It's really pretty, Petra," he whispers, but he's still not looking at me.

CHAPTER FIFTY-TWO

PETRA

Present Day

After spending a nearly sleepless night wondering if the you-know-who is the reincarnation of my boyfriend's ancestor—or, even worse, my past-life boyfriend—I wake up blurry-headed and groggy.

In the days following all the unsettling revelations about Arnoult's cult and his maniac deathbed promise to be reborn and smite his enemies, I do my best to convince myself that there's no such thing as reincarnation. That I'm just overreacting to the stress and uncertainty that have been incessantly seeping into my life.

During quiet moments between classes, in the shower, in the tranquil pockets of the school library, I keep repeating the same mantra to myself, hoping it will stick.

"It's not possible. It can't happen."

Yet in the back of my mind, a thread of fear runs unbroken.

Because no matter how we see it, Harry and Edwin were killed, in brutal ways. And their deaths were no random acts of violence; if Arnoult's demonic rituals are resurfacing, no one in St. Anselm Hall or the whole town is truly safe.

On another Friday, Sin and I meet at the diner again.

The smells of cinnamon and hot chocolate make me feel cozy and relaxed, despite the troubling thoughts and visions that have been plaguing my sleep as of late.

Sin's arms around my shoulders, draped over me like a heavy woolen coat, keep my heart beating steadily. The you-know-who feels content, too, from the way he's not shifting around like a fat cat in a backpack.

But all the creaturely comforts in the world can't keep the anxiety at bay. Sin notices the instant my face clouds over with worry.

"What's wrong?" he murmurs in a soft voice, lightly tracing my cheek with his fingers.

"Just thinking," I respond in a faraway tone.

"Thinking, thinking, thinking," Sin teases me gently. "How do you have space for so many thoughts in that dainty little head of yours?"

"Umm, knock-knock, it's the 1950s? They want their sense of humor back?" I reply, but the verbal jousting does make me feel better.

Sin must have seen it on my face as well, because he smiles and says, "There, that's better. Now tell me what's bothering you."

"Do—" I break off, wondering how to word my doubts without sounding like I'm accusing Sin in some way. "Do you think the descendants of the founding families could be behind the murders?"

He looks thoughtful and pushes away the menu. "I mean, it's definitely a possibility. But I think it's unlikely, Petra."

"Why do you say that?" I ask, leaning forward. "They're the most likely to know about all those rituals, right? And all the powerful patriarchs of those families would be in cahoots with Arnoult. I'm telling you, if anyone knows about what's happening, it would be them."

Sin shakes his head slowly, as if he's pondering over my theory and marshaling his arguments together.

"Sure, they've got the history, but even now, people remember Arnoult's antics, I think. I guess what I'm trying to say is . . ." He breaks off and stares out the window, where a fine, wintry mist lies over everything. "If you think about it, the descendants live under the shadow of their families' past," he continues, looking at me intently. "They wouldn't want to draw attention to themselves or risk being tied to any of this. At least I wouldn't."

"I did think of that. But what if they feel pressured to keep the pact going? You know, they could actually think that the demon will come and disembowel them all, women and children included?"

Sin snorts out loud at this, but I keep going.

"No, think about it seriously. Maybe one of them is demented *just enough* to take it into his or her head that they have to, I don't know 'uphold the family legacy'?"

"Trust me, Petra, I have mingled with these folks. Expensive tastes, entitled attitudes, and uncanny instincts for keeping secrets. They're just too twisted. If they were involved, it wouldn't be so straightforward," Sin replies. "Take my own family, for instance. You might think my parents are just your regular Jane and Joe, salt-of-the-earth types and all that. But all branches of Arnoults have a public image like that."

There's a hard glint in his eyes as he looks out the window again.

"Families like mine and the other four don't act impulsively. They're protective of their image and wealth. Whatever's happening now, this feels different. Frankly, it feels like the work of some sick fuck who is trying to re-create Arnoult's glory days. For whatever perverted reason."

"Then who is it?" I respond urgently. "If it's not them, then what's the connection to the crypt and all those paintings we saw? Are you telling me that there was not one Rutherford or Haas among the robed figures circling that bald-headed demon?"

"I don't know, Petra," Sin replies with a frustrated shrug. "But we have to keep digging for clues."

"Then what if . . ." I trail off, shocked at myself for even entertaining this train of thought. But if my dreams might be real, then this could be real, too. "What if it's not a human who's committing the murders?"

He turns to look at me with a surprised expression. "Not human?"

"Well, let's think about this," I begin. "If there really are demons out there, and other supernatural creatures, then maybe it's not so far-fetched to say that these murders weren't caused by a human at all. Maybe they were caused by . . . a creature."

"A creature?" he repeats with a frown. "What are you talking about, Petra?"

I realize how crazy I must sound, but I push forward. "The way Edwin and Harry were killed, it was horrific. They were completely disfigured. That's not just a normal killing. And look at the articles we dug up. They said the students committed mass suicide for a ritual. But what if . . . what if we're looking at it all wrong?"

He studies me, then says, "Fine. Let's say you're right. What kind of creature are you talking about?"

I hesitate. "I had a dream," I admit.

He raises an eyebrow. "Another dream?"

"Yes, but this time it was different. It was about this creature. I think the best way to describe it would be like a zombie. Or some kind of raised dead.

She—" I pause, struggling to find the words. "She was being controlled by someone. Someone who made a deal with the devil to resurrect her. But it wasn't really *her* anymore."

Oh God, I'm doing such a bad job at explaining this.

"Forget about it. Forget I said anything," I say quickly, embarrassed.

"No, no, do tell," he insists. "You're saying it might be something supernatural?"

"Yeah." I nod. "In my dreams, the really grisly murders—they were committed by this creature. And they weren't part of the ritual."

"*Not* part of the ritual?" he echoes. "But what about the paintings?"

"Yeah," I say, thinking back. "Now that I really think about it, it doesn't match, does it? The paintings in the tunnels showed deaths that were brutal, just like what happened to Edwin and Harry." I sigh, rubbing my forehead. "I don't know anymore. Maybe I'm crazy. But . . ."

"I think it's worth considering. At this point, I don't think any idea is too far-fetched." Sin smiles at me, small but genuine.

"Thank you for not thinking I'm crazy," I whisper.

He chuckles softly. "Petra, if you're crazy, then we all are."

"It's just . . . if these dreams I've been having are a window into the past, then maybe I can use them to gather more information. Don't you think?" I suggest.

"You're right," he agrees. "We should try to examine them more thoroughly. Tell me more."

"Well," I begin hesitantly, "remember those newspaper clippings we found in your family's basement? The ones about the wealthy people being murdered?"

"Yes." He nods.

"In my dreams, someone told me that those people weren't murdered as part of the ritual. They were killed to keep things quiet."

"To keep things quiet? What do you mean?"

"So, we know now that there were five families involved—five individuals. We have Snowden, Rutherford, Underwood, Haas, and Arnoult."

"Okay, yes. Go on."

"Well, in the past—or at least in the version of the past that I saw—Snowden wasn't one of them, not really. He wasn't on their side. He was one of the people leading the crusade against Arnoult's group. And he was the one controlling that creature."

My heart races as I try to explain.

"The murders happened because, at some point, Snowden had been in cahoots with them. He was interested in the occult, too. But after . . . some disagreement—or maybe after realizing what they truly planned to do with the ritual—he pulled away. He didn't want to be part of it anymore."

"So," he says slowly, "he turned against them."

"Exactly. He started an offensive, gathering people against Arnoult and his followers, spreading rumors, telling them all sorts of things. And then, one by one, the main players started dying."

I take a shaky breath.

"First was Rutherford. And apparently, his death was very disturbing."

Sin leans in. "And after him?"

"Then it was Underwood," I continue. "Which only left Haas and Arnoult, at least in my dreams. Maybe if we can find out how they died, we'll uncover more of the truth."

A light rain has started in the meantime. Pedestrians scurry across the road, and drivers make a beeline for their cars.

I gaze at the water streaming down the window, my mind racing with all sorts of theories.

Unease festers within me, and I can't shake the feeling that something—or someone—terrible is still lurking just out of sight, waiting for the chance to strike.

"You know what we can do?" Sin says suddenly, as if the idea has just occurred to him. When I give him a wary look, he hurries to say, "No, no, nothing too outlandish. You remember the mausoleum in the cemetery? The one where we . . . on the day of Harry's funeral . . ."

He looks abashed, as if trying to remind me of a delicate matter.

And sure enough, I know which place he's referring to, as a row of images flash across my mind: granite obelisks, mossy tombs, acid-corroded marble angels, the damp-smelling insides of a domed mausoleum, and inside it . . .

Sin and I, my legs locked around his hips, his lips biting and sucking at the curving mounds of my breasts . . .

The thought sends a shiver down my spine, and my legs feel weak. But I don't want Sin to see just how undone I feel even at the memory of our escapade there, so I clear my throat.

"Yeah, I remember, of course. Why?"

"Well, don't freak out, okay?" Sin begins cautiously, and of course, those words freak me out. "But that was the tomb of Arnoult the First. He's buried there."

When my eyes widen in shock, and I open my mouth to protest, he trips over himself to say, "I didn't know before, Petra, I swear!"

"Wow, that's . . . um, I'm gonna need a minute here," I stammer.

"So what I'm suggesting is we go back to the mausoleum and take a look around, perhaps find some clues? *Objectively*, without getting carried away and tearing off each other's clothes."

He's laughing by the end of his sentence, and I punch him on the arm.

"Ow! Easy there, Valentine! Damn, girl, the pregnancy's turning you into Superwoman." He grins.

We fall back giggling and laughing for a bit—a miracle, given the awful topic we're discussing and the macabre plans we're cooking up.

"Fine, I guess we can do that," I say in the end.

CHAPTER FIFTY-THREE

PETRA

Present Day

The following day brings more news of doom. Another body has been found—this time in the town square, just like the students from over a hundred years ago. But this time, it wasn't staged as a suicide.

It was murder, plain and simple.

And the details are even more horrifying than I could have imagined.

His body had been chopped up, and parts of it were strewn around the town square. And because of the level of damage to the body, the police have not been able to ID the victim yet.

It seems one of the street cleaners, working in the early hours of the morning, came across a hand hidden among the autumn foliage.

At first, he thought it was a prank and pushed it aside. But quickly, he realized it was real—a human hand.

A dead body.

More body parts started appearing after that, and so the terror returned to our little town in full force.

And if that wasn't enough, there are whispers of a few more odd deaths happening inside the isolated religious community.

Because of their secrecy, these deaths weren't reported at the proper time; apparently, they happened somewhere between Edwin's and Harry's deaths.

That brings the total to five deaths now.

I haven't been able to find much about the victims from the religious community: who they were, how exactly they died, or whether they were somehow connected to the persecution of Arnoult and his group all those years ago.

I'm still digging for a link, but the more I search, the more conflicting information I find.

So many people have motives. So many reasons to kill.

And then there's the most pressing question of all:

What about dream-Sin?

How does he fit into all of this?

Is he . . . Arnoult the First?

And yet, in all of my dreams, he's never introduced himself that way. Never once hinted at it.

But if he *is* Arnoult, then what does that mean for me?

For my Sin—the one who holds me when I cry, the one who whispers promises in my ear?

Oh God, I'm really starting to lose it.

None of this makes sense.

There's Snowden, who seems to be killing people.

There's Arnoult's old group, who convinced others to commit mass suicide.

There's that creature, roaming the past, and possibly even the present, taking more lives.

Or maybe it's none of that.

Maybe we just have some psychotic murderer on the loose who's using the town's creepy history to confuse townsfolk and the police.

All I know is that every day, I feel more afraid.

And it's not just for myself anymore.

It's for my unborn baby, too.

Because what if these dreams aren't just dreams?

What if they're warnings, trying to keep me safe?

What if I did something wrong in a past life, and because of that . . .

I might be the next one to die?

But I'm not the only one feeling out of sorts today.

A pall of unease seems to have permanently settled on the SAH crowd, perhaps because of the temperature dropping, perhaps because of the ghastly incidents in the town's recent history, or perhaps due to a mix of both.

The school counselor has seen a visible increase in the incoming traffic to his office, and we have had a couple of more-qualified (read "more expensive") therapists come and talk to us in class.

A lot of empty talk about how life is precious and grieving is natural and we have to soldier on regardless and "get those college applications ready!"

The lady who was conducting this particular seminar had looked quite stumped when this crisp statement was met with a couple of dry laughs and mostly impassive faces.

After classes are done, we head to the town cemetery where Harry is buried. Sin's warm hand in mine keeps me from lingering too long on that dreadful, leaden thought.

It's been raining on and off, and a damp afternoon gloom lingers around us as Sin and I stride through the graveled paths heading toward the mausoleum.

The overcast sky has dimmed the world around us, and I can't shake the sense that we're venturing into the heart of darkness, prospecting for that glinting stone of cruelty on which a tradition of savagery has been whetted.

"Are you sure about this?" I can't help but ask, voice wavering slightly.

We pass between rows of headstones crouching over the sleeping dead. Coming to the greener part of the plot now, the wealthier parts where the influential families repose in the lap of luxury, even in death.

"What if we get in trouble?" I insist.

By now, we have reached the angular archway.

The walls are covered in creeping ivy and shadowed by gnarled trees, the stone façade weathered and forgotten. Today I am fascinated by the gothic lines, the sinister design meant to create a sense of foreboding.

Much like Ozymandias' statue, Arnoult's grave is dark with menace, announcing to the world the hateful nature of its entombed inhabitant.

The door creaks lightly as Sin pushes it, and we step inside into stale air thick with the scent of damp stone and decay. Thin columns of light shine through the small chinks in the ceiling, swirling with dust motes.

The faint sounds of dripping water echo from somewhere in the depths of the darkness. Our phone lights flicker against the cold, rough walls.

During our first encounter here, I didn't have the chance to properly look around, but now that I do, engravings adorning the stone arrest my steps.

"I remember this place," I say softly. "It felt different before, less . . . ominous."

"Well, it *is* ominous. But we've come this far: might as well see this through."

We start exploring the small chamber for any hidden clues, our footsteps echoing loudly between the stone walls.

Apart from the engravings that depict shadowy, multi-limbed apparitions with murky faces and sharp smiles, I can also see the hieroglyphic script of some unknown language—not Latin, from what I can tell—whose syntax appears to be rather crude and cruel, in a way.

Lost in my fancies, I inch slowly along the walls, my fingers brushing against the cool stone, tracing the symbols.

"What's that?" Sin cries out suddenly, and I turn so fast I almost slip. "Underneath here," he adds, pointing to a section of the floor that looks slightly raised, almost like it's hiding something.

Sin crouches on the floor and pulls at the floorboards.

They open to reveal a trapdoor.

"Whoa!" I say with a note of excitement in my voice. "Is it just me, or does that floorboard look like someone recently moved it?"

"Perhaps," Sin replies with a loud exhale.

He grasps the rusty wheel at the center of the door and starts turning it.

"Wait, should we be doing this?" I fling my hands to stop him, but he shrugs.

"What's the harm? It's not like we're digging up his body or anything. Stand back!" he cautions before pulling open the door.

We look down to see a staircase spiraling into the depths of the earth—dusty marble steps that nevertheless look like they were walked upon recently.

"Do we go down?" I ask hoarsely.

"What do you want to do?" Sin replies in a casual tone, as if he's asking me if I want to pick a spot for dinner.

"I guess we can take a quick peek . . ." my voice trails off as I step down first.

The initial pang of fear is followed by burning interest and a thrill at the prospect of inspecting a grave; I remain true to my idol Mary Shelley in that aspect, at least.

We watch our step over the chipped stairs and finally reach a space no larger than an anteroom, but somehow opulent in the use of a particularly fine mosaic tiling on the walls. Heavy velvet drapes the color of a bleeding heart are hung overhead, all bearing the same crest: a crown of knives in black.

The ceiling, arched high above us, is adorned with intricate carvings of vines intertwined with what looks like guardians—mythical creatures frozen in distorted postures, their faces worn yet noble, impassive yet somehow grotesque.

I can't help but crane my neck to look for long enough that it starts to hurt, yet there's something disconcerting about the way the figures loom over us.

To the left, an alcove houses a large, intricately carved sarcophagus made from dark marble.

The surface is etched with the same swirling patterns that adorn the walls: the strange sigils of a bygone era steeped in superstition and savage pursuit of power.

"Is that somebody's grave?" I ask in an incredulous tone, clutching at Sin's sleeve.

"Yeah, I think that's where Arnoult, his lover, and their unborn baby are buried," he replies, running his fingers along the etchings on the giant catafalque on which rests the despotic cult leader Sin's lucky enough to call ancestor.

Of course, there are more paintings on the walls around us.

The haunting craftsmanship cannot detract from the horrific content of each mural: the brutal rituals that we had read about in the Arnoults' basement. I am intrigued by some of the expressions on the face of what looks like Arnoult the First, who seems to be leading each of these rituals.

In the paintings, he looks foreboding and sinister, a supernatural power looming over mortal weaklings around him.

There's no mercy in that face, no remorse.

"Look at this," Sin says in a somewhat impressed manner, pointing at one particularly vivid painting that depicts a family with terrified expressions.

"The rictus of horror is still so fresh they could have been murdered yesterday," he says in a marveling voice, yet I can't find fault with that.

Over and over again, the mural artist—it must be the one painter, because of the singular style evident in all the paintings we have seen so far—has proven their keen eye for human despair and desperation in various degrees.

"It's like they're frozen in their last moments forever," I add when Sin falls silent, probably looking for the right words.

Sin nods in vehement agreement, but I'm already walking toward the far wall.

Beside it is an altar, its surface covered in layers of dust and old, crumpled offerings—dried flowers, broken trinkets, pages ripped from books, and what looks like a lock of blond hair.

I shiver without noticing, because the "shrine" is just that creepy. And more importantly, was this altar a part of Arnoult's dark ceremonies? Were wailing, masked victims brought here to be killed?

I shake my head; it seems to physically buzz with a swarm of difficult questions swirling.

"This place feels so spooky, Sin," I whisper hoarsely.

The next instant, hands have settled on my shoulders, and I'm turned around.

"Don't be scared, Petra," Sin tells me in a low voice laced with an overpowering sensuality. "I'm right here, aren't I?"

One of his hands sweeps back my hair and cradles the nape of my neck, while the other slides to my hip, gently clasping it.

As has been happening as of late, my body melts at his touch, and I lean into his palms, taking a deep sniff of his skin, the woodsy, citrusy smell underlined with notes of bitter pine, and he turns my chin toward him.

As we kiss, I sigh loudly, not caring who can hear in this abode of the dead, not caring that we are probably committing some sort of sacrilege.

The kiss deepens, with Sin gently pushing me back against the wall behind me, even as the whispering shadows of the crypt wrap around us like a thick fog.

It's true that we've made rather disturbing discoveries about Arnoult and his followers, but in this moment, the rest of the world fades away, as Sin's hand slides down my body, gently stroking the swell of my breasts and the padded roundness of my hips.

He leans ever closer, taking great care not to jostle me or the baby, and I can feel the hardness of him pushing against me, so I part my legs, *gladly*, because the ache between them has grown urgent and more intense in the last five minutes or so.

Damn, pregnant women must be jumping their husbands all the time, my inner voice cooly remarks in my head, but I'm too distracted to care about her snarky comments just now.

We kiss desperately, our hands roaming all over each other's bodies.

In a daring gesture, I cup the bulge in Sin's pants as he slips his tongue into my mouth.

He groans loudly before pushing his hips into my palm.

His fingers are fumbling with the stockings I have stretched over my inflated belly, and I shimmy out of them to help him.

In the next moment, his fingers are teasing my wet folds while he keeps nibbling and licking my lips. I moan again, my fingers tangling in his hair.

"Petra," he murmurs against my lips, the sound sending a thrill coursing through me. "This feels so good . . . You have no idea."

His voice breaks over that last word as I rub him harder.

"I think I might," I reply breathlessly, feeling bold inside the hushed crypt.

"You're so goddamn sweet, fuck."

His fingers circle my clit, teasingly slipping in and out of my wet opening.

"Do you want me inside you?" Sin groans into my neck. "Do you want me to pleasure you? We could stay in bed the whole day, and I would get to know every inch of you."

His fingers increase their pace, and the ache builds inside me so that I am gasping and moaning wildly. More than anything, his words set loose some feral spirit inside me, because I pull his face close to mine and almost take a bite of his lips.

"Don't stop," I murmur into his mouth, hitching my leg up slightly to whatever angle my rather enlarged belly will let me. "Oh God, don't stop!" There's a note of entreaty in my voice, and maybe it's not even addressed to Sin. Maybe I'm just praying to the universe at this point.

"Not God. There is no god in this room, Petra. Just me. Say my name, sweet thing," he growls in my ear.

"Sin, Sin, Sin," I moan.

"Fuck, you're so hot. So fucking hot and ready for me."

He continues to perform an assault on my senses, his fingers digging so deep inside of me, it borders on painful. I never thought of myself as a masochist, but the bite of pain that accompanies the pleasure only increases my arousal.

"More," I gasp.

Just as I teeter on the cusp of what promises to be an earth-shattering climax, he stops.

"I need to fuck you. I need inside you so badly."

"Yes, yes," I chant, unable to recognize my own lust-filled voice. "Please." Anything to take off this edge, to fill this emptiness inside me.

We both struggle with his belt and then the zipper of his pants. I reach inside and wrap my hand around him, hard, hot, and so ready.

If I'd been in my right mind and not so overwhelmed by desire, I would have slowed things down to study him more, to get to know that part of him that's already been inside of me.

I would have marveled at the sheer size of him, just as daunting as the first time, at the softness that belies that hardness. Now, I only shiver in anticipation, knowing that he will not only fill this aching emptiness inside of me, but his size will bring just the right amount of pain to complement the pleasure.

He's mine. This man is all mine. A wave of possessiveness pierces through me at knowing I'm the only one who's ever touched him like this, who's ever seen this side of him. It's so unlike me that I have a hard time tempering it down.

Somehow, I know instinctively that if he ever strayed, things could get bloody. Am I a violent person? No, not really. But for him, I'll make an exception.

"Don't you ever dare look at another woman, Sin," I warn as I tighten my hold on his cock in a warning.

"Fuck," he groans, his eyes rolling back in his head. It seems I'm not the only one turned on by a bit of pain. "Keep saying that, Petra, and I'll spend right here and now."

"Is that so?" I drawl seductively.

"Never looked at another," he says between gritted teeth. "Never will. Only you. Only ever you."

"Good boy," I murmur against his mouth as he nibbles on my lips.

"I love it when you're jealous. I love it when you lay your claim on me." He drags my lower lip into his mouth as his eyes find mine in the darkness.

I continue to move my hand up and down his cock while his fingers are still inside me, drawing out this torture.

"But make no mistake, Petra. I am just the same, if not worse. You have no idea what I'm capable of. For you. For us. For *this*."

"What?" I ask in a breathless voice.

"I'd sell out the entire universe for you," he whispers.

A sudden noise slices through the night—an eerie, heavy rustling that chills my heated body almost immediately.

I pull back instinctively, withdrawing my hands from Sin's pants and pushing his hands away from between my legs.

"What was that?" I ask in a shaky voice, heart pounding as adrenaline spikes through my system.

Sin's expression shifts from languid lust to alertness, and his brow furrows as he leans away from me and toward the entrance of the mausoleum, straining hard to listen.

"I don't know. Sounds like something moving outside."

More rustling, as if several feet are squelching through wet grass. I follow him back to the surface and glance around the dark chamber, while the shadows stretch and shift in the wind. Only they are not just shadows of the stone angels and marble demons.

Something, or someone, is definitely outside. And they are coming for us.

CHAPTER FIFTY-FOUR

PETRA

Present Day

Sin and I crouch behind the shadows inside Arnoult's mausoleum as a veritable storm of sounds whirls outside.

Sounds like a pack of wolves out to hunt.

"Here!" Sin whispers forcefully and creeps toward the narrow, dusty window of the mausoleum.

I trail behind him and eventually catch sight of a whole galaxy of flickering lights approaching our way.

My blood runs cold when I can finally see who exactly is hunting us: a crowd of dark-clad figures, men with severe expressions walking in a tidy file and women with veils covering their faces.

Some of them are holding torches, some of them are holding batons, and all of them look determined to kill.

"Sin," I whisper urgently in a voice that just won't stop trembling. "W-what's happening?"

"It's them," he whispers back. "The Puritans. Fuck!" He actually *chuckles* in the face of this marauding horde. "Why would they come here?"

"I don't know! But that looks like a very angry mob to me," I say in a panicked tone. "Is it because of those new deaths, maybe? Perhaps they're having funerals and—"

"They don't use this cemetery for their own people," Sin cuts me off. "And they would have buried them a long time ago. No, this is something else."

"Wait, who's that in the front? The leader?"

But as he comes closer, I finally recognize the man, and my toes go cold. It's Edwin's father, and his face is contorted with a dangerous fury.

"Burn the sinners!" a solitary voice cries out, and I glance back through the window—so fast I almost crick my neck.

Outside, more voices pick up the words, and soon we hear the crowd chanting, "Burn the sinners!" and "Cleanse Radcliffe!" Their voices rise together in a fervent hymn, echoing in the darkness of the night.

I watch with bated breath as the crowd comes to a halt right in front of the mausoleum door. "What are they doing?" Sin whispers urgently, but I shush him.

At that moment, Edwin's father steps forward, raising his torch high. "My brothers and sisters, tonight we stand at the house of the devil himself. The same God-flouting, evil-churning, pain-peddling devil who took my son from me!"

His eyes are bulging, and his face is contorted with heart-wrenching anguish.

"We will not take this travesty lying down. We will rain fire and brimstone on the sinners of the world. We will take revenge for our children taken too soon from us!"

Something about the tight-lipped looks on the faces of his listeners alerts me.

"Burn the sinners!" someone else shouts from within the crowd, and the chants restart.

Fear starts closing off my throat.

"Sin, they're going to—"

Almost at the same moment, the first torch is thrown.

As Sin and I watch, open-mouthed in shock, the flying flame lands splat at the base of the mausoleum.

Instantly, flames start licking hungrily at the ancient stone, and as more torches are thrown onto the blazing pyre, the fire starts spreading, climbing the ivy-inked walls and setting the perimeter ablaze.

"They're torching the place!" Sin exclaims—why he sounds surprised, I cannot tell—and grabs my hand. "We need to get out now!"

His words jolt me out of the terror-stricken reverie I had fallen into, but my feet seem rooted to the spot.

"Petra!" I hear Sin shouting, but my eyes are focused on the face of

Edwin's father. The smoldering fire casts flickering shadows across his features, and I can see the hatred glinting in his eyes.

At this moment, even if he knew that Sin and I are trapped inside the mausoleum . . . he might not care.

In fact, knowing that Sin is related to Arnoult the First, this mob might even have come prepared to torch any Arnoults that might get caught in the crossfire.

"Petra, we've got to run!" Sin is shaking my shoulders, and the flames are spreading rapidly; the stone walls seem to be radiating heat now. Outside, the mob's chants grow to a feverish pitch as wild ululations rend the air.

"No more will you desecrate our town with your evil!" Edwin's father shouts in a high-pitched voice. "No more will you tear apart our children, our innocents! Die in this fire, you mongrel hellion!"

"Petra, please." Somehow, I seem to have stepped outside my body, because at this point Sin pulls me away from the window quite easily. "We have to find a way out. Quickly!"

Away from the sight of Edwin's father, who is still demented with sorrow and still shouting, I can finally regain some sense of my surroundings.

Immediately, I start coughing and blinking water away from my eyes as the flames smack us in the face. The smoke begins to fill up the air, and the heat intensifies.

"What the fuck's happening, Sin?" I finally yell out. "And where do we go? The entrance is blocked!"

"There's another way," Sin replies, shouting in my ears while his eyes dart around.

"What way?" I shout back over the sound of stones cracking in heat and flames roaring. I start coughing more because of the thick, acrid smoke filling up the room.

Unbidden, an image flashes across my mind: Benny Truman on fire and cannonballing into Elias Rutherford's swimming pool. The night that everything had changed.

Man, that seems like ages ago, my annoying inner voice says in my head.

"Burn the sinners! Cleanse the darkness!" the mob continues their chant, their voices melding together in an ugly, hateful melody.

"Sin, it's getting too hot. We need to move!"

He nods and grabs me by the arm. "Stay close to me. We will find a way out."

The flames have been eating through the wooden beams, which start cracking and hissing as the last of their sap sizzles in the heat.

Sin holds my hand tightly and starts moving in some direction.

All I know is that I have to put one foot in front of the other—even when the heat seems to morph into a tangible blanket smothering us, and pressing against us, even when I can feel a flame lick my ankle or a small ember graze the sleeve of my Valentino shirt, burning a clean hole through it but thankfully leaving my skin intact.

As the smoke thickens, stinging my eyes and clogging my throat, we keep moving.

"This way!" Sin shouts, dragging me toward the back of the mausoleum, away from the blaze, but the heat always seems to be just one step behind, and always gaining, always getting closer.

My breathing sounds ragged, and my vision starts to blur.

"Sin, stop," I wheeze. "I can't . . . I can't breathe."

Sin's grip on my hand tightens, and he pulls me closer to him, placing his jacket over my head and shoulders, creating a temporary shelter with his whole body.

"Petra, focus on my voice. We're getting out of here!"

I finally realize that he's been leading us back toward the tombs. With a few more steps, we manage to clamber out of the thick smog spreading through the mausoleum, and I see that we have stopped right in front of Arnoult the First's tomb.

"What's—what's happening, Sin?" I cough.

"Just hold on, Petra," Sin replies, planting his feet firmly on the ground and shoving against the ornately carved hunk of stone covering the tomb.

"Sin?" I stand around gasping and panting like an idiot for a moment before throwing my shoulder against the stone as well.

Red and orange tongues of fire have engulfed the entire right side of the mausoleum by now, and the fiery sight before me quickens my arms as I push with all my might.

A few more agonizing moments lapse before the stone grinds open slowly. "Sin, what—" I begin, but he holds up a hand and points down to show a dark, yawning tunnel underneath the slab.

"Down here!" he urges, disappearing into the darkness under the tombstone.

"I thought Arnoult the First and his lover were buried here?" The words slip out of my mouth even as I clamber down behind him. "What . . . what is this? Where does it go?" I repeat when the stairs end at the head of a narrow tunnel.

"It's a tunnel," Sin replies, and I roll my eyes at him, as if to say, "*Yeah, I can see that.*"

He shakes his head with a dry chuckle.

"I meant that it'll lead us somewhere safe," he adds.

I hesitate and look around and then up at the swirling flames burning Arnoult the First's alleged grave.

"Look, Petra, I promise," Sin insists as he dusts off his clothes and pats down a few errant flames on his jacket. "And anyway, what choice do we have?" This last question is uttered in a weird monotone that sparks a feeling of doubt in my mind.

As we duck into the tunnel beneath Arnoult the First's tomb, the temperature drops significantly, and I rub my limbs, trying to orient my body to the cold, damp air, an abrupt contrast to the inferno swirling mere feet above us.

Ha, six feet over us, says my inner voice, but I'm unsettled enough to know that she isn't jesting.

I doubt anyone can joke around in these circumstances.

Or perhaps you *need* to confront such situations—escaping a bloodthirsty mob wielding torches and an actual, literal *fire* by climbing down some secret stairs under the fake tomb of your boyfriend's great-great-great-great-grandfather—with humor.

And yet, that fleeting humor vanishes quickly, replaced by a rush of visions from my dreams: visions of the tunnels I'd seen sprawling beneath St. Anselm Hall, beneath the entire town.

Is this it? I wonder. *Are those tunnels real? And if they are . . . what do they house?*

A fresh wave of fear grips me. In the past, those tunnels served a grim purpose—hosting the rituals performed by the students of the Theology Department.

Even now, they could be the lair of the killer.

Or worse, what if some madman has imprisoned that creature inside these tunnels, keeping it hidden in plain sight, lying dormant beneath the town, just waiting to strike?

My mind spins in a tangle of confusion and dread, but another, colder realization cuts through:

Even if the creature *is* behind the murders, it isn't acting alone.

Not then.

Not now.

Back then, someone controlled it.

And today . . . someone still might.

CHAPTER FIFTY-FIVE

PETRA

Present Day

Ahead of me, the narrow tunnel stretches into a deep, almost profound darkness.

Sin has switched on the light of his phone and is holding it out before him; I do the same.

Upon looking around, I see that the walls are hewn from the same roughly cut stone as the floor of the mausoleum and are slick with centuries of moisture.

The ceiling is low, forcing Sin to stoop slightly as we walk deeper.

A petrichor smell sweetens the air, along with the faint, musty aroma of long-forgotten and rarely used spaces.

The sound of our footsteps eerily bounces off the walls; they are multiplied so cunningly that I keep thinking we are being followed, that some fanatic Puritan foaming at the mouth at the prospect of drawing Arnoult blood has slipped into the tunnels with us.

Imagine if it's Edwin's father, my inner voice adds, and I almost chuckle at the insane idea.

"Stay close," Sin whispers in a steady voice, but some buried instinct in me to doubt him has resurfaced.

Hadn't he told me that the tomb contained the body of Arnoult the First, his lover, and their unborn child? But the tomb had been empty, a façade for the secret exit out of the mausoleum.

So why had he lied to me?

Most importantly, why is he withholding information that could help our investigation?

Yet he had pulled me out of the fire and used his body to shield me. At every turn, he prioritized my safety over his.

For the moment, my doubts are dispelled, and gratitude bubbles up in my heart for this kindhearted, fiercely protective guy who's been snatching me away from the jaws of death—by water and by fire—since the day we met.

I grip his hand tightly, the rough texture of his skin grounding me in the suffocating darkness.

"How much farther do you think it is?" I ask softly.

"Hard to say, Petra," he replies, his tone calm but focused. "You just keep holding on to me, okay? Do you want me to pick you up and carry you?"

"No!" I reply, more forcefully than I had intended, and he almost takes a step back. "I mean, I can walk. You look so tired as well."

He smiles and ruffles my hair affectionately before taking my hand in his again.

As we walk, my fingers trail along the damp walls, feeling the uneven surface of the stones.

The tunnel occasionally narrows further, forcing us to squeeze through tight passages.

"We'll get out of this. We'll get out of this," I keep murmuring to myself, not knowing or caring whether Sin can hear me.

I suppose I'm also talking to the you-know-who inside me, as my hand strokes my stomach and I try to slow down my heartbeat.

"We will," Sin says while squeezing my hand. "We don't have a choice." These last words sound odd, and he has a wistful smile when he says them, but I don't dwell on it too long.

"Watch your step," Sin cautions, glancing back at me. "The last thing we need is a twisted ankle."

"To be honest, I'm more worried about what's ahead," I reply in a tone that, to my delight, sounds aloof and wry.

But I am stunned when a faint glimmer of light reaches us through the end of the tunnel.

"What's that?" I cry out. Sin clears his throat and looks uncomfortable, so I shake his arm and say, "You can see that too, right?"

The light grows stronger as we approach.

He nods, and his pace quickens slightly. "Yeah. I do. It's a sign we're getting somewhere. Just a bit farther."

A few steps later, we walk through a circular opening and into a larger chamber.

My eyes widen.

"What the hell?"

The damp earth of the tunnel gives way to a stone floor, and we pass through an old doorway into a larger space bathed in dim, ambient light. I squint against the sudden brightness and gasp at the stage that unfolds before us.

The chamber is like a time capsule from the 1800s, complete with old, ornate furniture and wooden beams. The ceiling is higher than the tunnels, almost triple in size.

Victorian tables with intricately carved wooden legs, brass knobs gleaming on chests of drawers made from polished walnut wood, even a lovely teak dining table in neoclassical style. The room looks like a mid-nineteenth-century parlor, as if any moment now, the door will open, and a small group will gather for an evening drink.

There's also a grand-looking fireplace with a charred log.

"Sin . . . what in the fresh hell is this place?" I ask in a flat voice.

"Another of Arnoult the First's hiding places, if you can believe it," says Sin in a wry tone that's perhaps supposed to foil the severity of my own. "Think of it as a hidden home," he replies, glancing around.

"Yes, but how do you know about this place?" Even as I ask the question, my eye is drawn to a particularly stately pair of Biedermeier chairs, and I can't help but trace their indulgent frames; the woodwork and graining are so delicate that for a moment, I'm distracted from the nightmare that is our reality.

"I knew you'd like it here," Sin says from behind me, his breath warming my neck.

My shoulders shiver at his touch, and as he draws me into his arms, my back nestled against his sturdy chest, I let out the littlest sob.

"Sweet Petra, you must be so tired," Sin whispers into my neck as his hands encircle my waist and gently caress my bump. "You're safe now," he continues. My shoulders keep shaking long after the tears have stopped rolling down my cheeks.

"Thanks," I manage to say at last. "I feel much better now."

Sin steps back and says, "Come, I'll show you the rest of it."

We look at the leatherbound titles on the shelves and all the pretty knickknacks from the nineteenth century, including antique tables and armoires, more chairs with detailed backrests and fine upholstery, and the Regency-era mantelpiece with animal and bird motifs carved into the wood.

I run my fingers over a slightly dusty table, marveling at how well-curated the collection is, how suited it is to my sensibilities.

Yet something keeps me alert and on the lookout, some faint instinct that cautions me against dropping all my defenses at once. And as Sin and I move deeper into the underground home, I finally start discerning a pattern to the unease knotting my guts.

Despite the overall ancient feel of the place, I can see some unmistakably modern touches scattered around—an old but functional mini-fridge, a microwave, and even a worn-out laptop tucked into a corner.

There's only one person who could have gotten them here.

"Sin," I begin, unsure of how to word the accusation floating up in my mind. "What are all these appliances doing here? Someone's been here before us, right?"

Sin stays quiet, so I turn to look him directly in the face.

"*You* have been here before, right?"

He hesitates for a moment, glancing around the room before finally meeting my eyes.

"I wasn't hiding it on purpose. I found this place a long time ago," he adds as he scratches the back of his head. "I've just been using it as a hiding spot when I needed to be alone."

"So you've been hanging around this place for . . . how long exactly, Sin?" I ask with rising trepidation. "You know how this looks, right?" I press when he just makes a frustrated noise and turns away from me. "You knew about the crypt at the school, and then the secret tunnel under Arnoult the First's tomb, and now this? Doesn't it look rather suspicious?"

"And you're suspecting me of what, Petra?" Sin asks with a low chuckle, but his eyes look serious, as if he's daring me to throw around more accusations.

But I don't have any concrete allegation to level at him.

"Not suspecting, Sin, just wondering. It'd be nice if you weren't so tight-lipped about everything and would just . . . just tell me what's going on." I try to keep the frustration out of my voice, but it's almost impossible at this critical moment.

Sin looks at me with an unreadable expression on his face.

Then a moment later, a blend of concern and earnestness wash over his features.

"No, it's my fault, I should have explained all this." He gestures at the eclectic space around us. "*Before* bringing you here. But trust me—it's not what it seems. I stumbled upon it ages ago, before I joined the football team, before I made any friends. This place became my own secret sanctuary, just like the gardener's shed is for you."

The words hang heavily between us, and I am torn between several emotions—suspicion, understanding, even compassion.

But the former prevails as I scan my surroundings. It's so similar to my dreams, from the big ceiling to the ornate furniture and homely environment. But if I dreamed about this . . . then there's something else I must check.

I take off with single-minded focus, circling the room and examining the bookcase carefully, recalling the hidden rooms from my dreams.

I run my fingers along the edges, pushing and prodding until—sure enough—I find something.

There, concealed within the bookcase, is an entrance.

As I pull it open, I'm met with a smaller, shadowed room.

I stare at it, stunned.

The details from my dreams may have been fuzzy, but the evidence before me is not.

Painting supplies.

All kinds of canvases scattered around—each and every one of them empty.

Yet as I step closer, inspecting the supplies more carefully, I notice how old they are. Some of the paint colors have been discontinued for decades. Others are infamous in art history for containing poisonous compounds.

And yet they're all still here.

It's not that someone bothered to bid on these at auctions or snatch them from estate sales. No—these supplies have been *here* all along.

"Sin, what is this?" I whisper.

"I don't know."

"Don't lie to me." I turn to him sharply. "What is this?"

He exhales slowly. "It seems to be an art room of sorts."

"Yes, but *why* is it here?" I press.

"Petra, I don't know, I swear." And, for once, I believe him.

The air is thick and stale. Dust coats every surface, even the hinges of the door. No one has opened this place in a very, very long time.

"How did you know it was here?" he asks, moving to stand beside me.

I hesitate before answering, the words tasting strange on my tongue. "I dreamed about it."

"You dreamed about it?" He blinks in surprise. "Was this another one of those dreams from the past? Was someone else there?" He asks a barrage of questions that makes my head spin.

"Yes, it was a dream from the past," I answer slowly. "I . . ."

"So you were here before? With whom?"

"I don't know, Sin. It's all a confusing mess in my mind. But somehow, I knew this room would be there."

He opens his mouth as if to ask more before closing it. I don't understand why he's so insistent about me being here with someone else. At the same time, I also don't understand why I don't straight up answer his question and tell him the truth—about dream-Sin and our Victorian love affair.

Yet the more I stare into his eyes, so familiar, so achingly beautiful, I have to confront one of my deepest fears. I don't trust him. Not fully, anyway. If I did, I would have gladly told him everything.

But as it stands, I don't *know* what to believe anymore.

Sure, the Sin before me has never done anything to hurt me. In fact, he's been protective and loving and, at times, nicer and sweeter to me than I deserve.

Yet those dreams continue to haunt me. Dream-Sin continues to haunt me, as does the question: Who is *he*?

Was that Arnoult the First from my dreams? Am I his lover (or rather, my past self)? And if that's the case, then my theory about Arnoult the First trying to reincarnate himself as my baby is moot, because how can that be when he's standing right in front of me? When this man knows things only dream-Sin would?

Another theory appears, and one that I'm almost afraid to consider.

Sin . . . Sin might be the reincarnation of Arnoult the First. But if that's the case . . . Then he might also be the architect of all these murders.

"I apologize for my tone. I'm just curious. No one besides me knew about this place. Until you . . ."

Yes, and that is exactly what dream-Sin said, too.

CHAPTER FIFTY-SIX

PETRA

Present Day

A sliver of fear goes down my spine. Here we are, in some arcane tunnels, away from civilization, in a makeshift home underground. There is no way out, nowhere to run to.

My heart beats faster in my chest as my breathing becomes constricted. It feels suffocating, claustrophobic.

"Petra, are you all right?" Sin comes closer to me, and I take a step back.

I gulp down. "I'm just a little confused," I say with a nervous laugh.

"That is understandable. But you *know* you have nothing to fear from me, right?"

I hesitate to answer, my silence lingering.

He comes closer, taking my hand in his. "I would *never* hurt you, Petra."

"I know. You wouldn't hurt *me*."

But what about other people?

Could it be that he's the one killing people? His surprise at learning about his family's odd history had been genuine. And I just don't see Sin as this sadistic killer.

But . . . all those dreams, all those odd occurrences in real life that mirror the dreams are hard to ignore. He knows far more than he's letting on, and that makes him suspicious.

I pull my hand out of his and slide down into the nearest chair.

My legs and back are sore from all the running to escape a ravaging Puritan mob, so it feels nice just to sit down.

He *could* be Arnoult the First and he doesn't remember. What if he has some split personality disorder like Jekyll and Hyde? Perhaps the soul of his ancestor takes possession of his body when he's not aware and does all those awful things. At this point, anything is plausible.

Mind control. Undead creatures. Demon pacts. It's a whole buffet of messed-up weirdness. And yet . . . the more I think about it, the less it makes sense.

Dream-Sin looked like *my* Sin. The Arnoult I saw in those old photos did not. Unless my mind is playing tricks on me and replacing the unfamiliar with the familiar.

Case in point, my name had been the same in those dreams. Even if by some stretch of imagination (although that is becoming more flexible with each passing day) my dreams are windows into a past life, the chances of both me and past-me being named Petra are slim to none.

And so far, I haven't gotten any ideas about how to find out *more* about past Petra, or whatever her name really was.

"Why didn't you tell me about this place before, Sin?" I ask after a while.

He sighs, running a hand through his thick hair. "I don't know . . . what was I supposed to say? 'Hey, Petra, I have a secret hideout under the tomb of a family ancestor'?"

I chuckle at that preposterous statement, and the tension between us eases a bit.

"At first, it was just my own little secret," Sin continues. "Then, there were the murders, and then *we* got together, but then we had that falling-out at the ball . . . I guess I just didn't want to overwhelm you with more secrets, if that makes sense."

I nod. He seems earnest. And for a moment I feel bad for doubting him in the first place.

We both fall silent, the unease between us starting to fade.

But there are some things around this room that don't make sense, nor do they particularly validate his version of events.

Although there are some newer-ish items lying around, there are also old ones: a broken radio in a corner, a tube TV behind a stack of old records. Sin is not the only one who's been down here.

He follows my line of sight, and I note the tension in his body. His lips are drawn in a tight line, and I'm sure he's trying to think of excuses, or . . . more lies?

"Why do you think they did that?" I ask suddenly, needing to change the subject. I don't know if I can handle more *revelations* at this particular moment—at least not while we're under the fucking ground.

He frowns at my words, so I add, "The Puritans? Why would they torch Arnoult the First's mausoleum?"

"Perhaps they know of his death prophecy as well? That he said he will be reborn on the next blood moon?" Sin replies with a shrug.

"Do you think they blame him for those deaths in their community?"

"It certainly seemed so."

"Would your family be in danger, you think? They might want to take revenge on Arnoult the First's descendants."

"Don't worry about them. They're fine." Sin waves his hand as if a mob of angry people isn't cause for concern. "My father hired some fancy security firm after the last murder, so I doubt anyone can get close enough to my house."

"That's good," I add pensively. He doesn't seem remotely worried about them, so perhaps that security firm is that good. But it's just a little . . . odd, isn't it? Could a security team save them from a crowd of fanatics?

He comes to sit on the floor in front of me. Taking my left foot, he removes my shoe and sock before he starts massaging it softly. He does the same to my right foot, and a wave of relaxation envelops me.

"You have a magic touch," I say on an almost-moan.

"Glad you can recognize my skills." He winks at me. "Don't tell anyone but . . ." He leans in conspiratorially. "This is why I spent all those hours in the gym."

"To spoil me with feet massages?" I laugh aloud.

"To spoil you. Period." His expression is suddenly serious. "To protect you, keep you safe and comfortable. It's all I've ever wanted, Petra."

A shiver goes down my back as I gaze into his earnest expression. And there it is—the reason why, no matter how many doubts I may have, or crazy theories, I will always be partial to him.

Because no one's ever looked at me like that.

No one's ever put me first before.

No one.

"I think you're doing a good job, Sin."

"Am I?" He swallows hard. "Do you think . . ." He suddenly seems unsure of himself. "Do you think I would make a good father?"

His question surprises me. But what surprises me more is my immediate answer.

"Of course. You will make the *best* father." And I mean it. He's so gentle with me, so loving, that I know he's going to offer the same to our child.

A shy smile pulls at his lips.

"I want that. I want him to know I'm going to be there for him. That I will not let anyone hurt him or bully him. That . . ." He trails off as he takes a deep breath. "I never want our baby to feel lonely, Petra."

Somehow, those words hit me right in the heart.

I lean forward and press my hand to his cheek.

"I never want that either, Sin. I won't be like my parents. I want to be present, to live *in the moment*."

"Will you . . . will you accept the baby even if there might be something wrong with it?" he whispers.

I frown. "What do you mean?"

"You know, what happened at the doctor's office. What if he is not . . . normal?"

"Nothing is *normal* anymore, Sin," I say with a dry laugh. But the intense look in his features, shadowed by some elusive sadness, tells me he's serious about this—he needs to know.

"This baby is mine, Sin. *Ours*. I don't care about anything else. No matter what happens, it won't change how I feel about him."

A strange emotion flickers over his features. Getting up, he pulls me into his arms, sitting down on the chair with me in his embrace. He cradles me to his chest, holding me tightly.

"Thank you," he whispers in my ear.

"For?"

"For being you. For being the light in my life, always and forever. For keeping me sane even in my darkest moments."

"What do you mean by that?"

He shakes his head.

"I'm happy," he says. "Holding you like this . . . This is happiness for me, Petra."

"WHAT SHOULD WE do now?" I ask as I yawn softly after a pleasant nap in his lap. His previous words, '*I'm happy*,' somehow imprinted on me because I don't remember ever sleeping so at peace.

In a way, this cozy little underground bunker filled with a mishmash of nineteenth-century furniture and twentieth-century technology has started to feel homely, like we have always lived here.

"How about I give you a small tour of my humble abode?" Sin's excited voice breaks through my dreams of domestic bliss.

"Yeah, I would love that!"

As Sin leads me through the rest of the space, I'm struck by the sheer size and complexity of this hidden world.

Each room we enter is filled with relics and reliquaries, fascinating and eerie at the same time.

Ornate furniture, dusty bookshelves, and old pieces of bric-a-brac; any antique appraiser would kill to get their hands on some, or all, of the items.

"These paintings are incredible," I whisper at one point, even though I don't need to lower my voice.

Somehow the presence of such impressive objects lends the whole space the hushed sanctity of a museum or an art exhibit.

My eyes widen as I take in the rarer paintings adorning the walls: austere still-life artworks and equestrian portraits by Jacques-Louis David, historical paintings by Benjamin West, some of the earlier works by Francisco Goya. Just then, my eyes fall on a particular painting that is immediately recognizable as the product of the same hand that had drawn *Sinful Desires,* Goya's old master.

The same moody lighting over a vast wooded expanse, and the same subject—the brown-haired girl wearing a velvet green gown—looking down the cliff face of an ancient mountain.

The frame before me looks like it could have been part of the same series of artworks as my painting of the girl on the moor.

"So this is where you got the painting you gifted me," I say, trying my best to keep any accusatory note out of my question.

He glances at the painting, a small smile playing on his lips. "Yeah, you got me. This is where I found it. It's not like Goya's master left behind a lot of work as it is. And the painting felt too special to leave buried here. I knew you would give it the appreciation it deserves."

A complex mix of emotions assails me at his words: surprise, apprehension, happiness.

"It's stunning," I say eventually. "And now I kinda like it even more."

We walk down a winding hallway, and I'm surprised that I don't recognize any of the paintings in here, nor do I see any familiarity in the technique. There are three on one side and four on the other, all seemingly painted by the same hand.

"What about these? Who are these by?" I ask as I stop in front of one of them.

It's of a naked man posing like a Greek god, his skin bathed in sunlight coming from behind. He is standing on a gray podium of sorts, his body gleaming, his sinewy muscles painted with such precise rigor.

The painting, however, is unfinished. It stops just above the chest. Pity, it is quite a striking study in anatomy mixed with Romanticism sensibilities.

I move to the next painting. It depicts a lone book in the midst of a sprawling library. The next one shows a wide-open window and a piece of paper fluttering in the wind.

The only painting done by the same artist that seems to be finished depicts a sea of people moving forward while one lone person stays behind, alone with the shadows that coil around her into a protective cocoon.

"I'm not sure." He leans closer to look for a signature. "It's not signed."

"That's a pity. They're beautiful," I add. "Especially this one." I point to the last one.

"That one is my favorite, too."

"I wonder what the name is."

"*Symbiosis,*" he states. My brows go up, and he shows me a small, scribbled script in the corner. No artist name. But there is a title. Strange.

"*Symbiosis*? That is an odd choice for a name. What do you think it means?"

He's staring at the painting, his hands behind his back. He has a wistful expression on his face. "Because this person"—he points to the lone figure—"does not need the world to survive. She only needs her faithful shadow to shield her from everything."

"She? How do you know it's a *she*?"

He shrugs. "That's what it feels like."

I accept his explanation without much thought. But something lingers in my mind, an impression forming that I am unable to properly phrase or make sense of.

We continue our tour, inspecting more of the hidden treasures inside these rooms—wood-paneled walls, more vintage furniture, and elaborate tapestries give the place an air of grandeur, a stark contrast to the cold stone corridor that led us here.

Eventually, we enter a room that leaves me momentarily speechless. It's a bedroom, but one that has been clearly designed with a woman's taste in mind. A delicate canopy bed is placed in the center of the room, and its frame is intricately carved with floral patterns. Soft, opulent linens have been laid over it.

"Wow," I exclaim. "This is such a quaint room, Sin! Did you set it up, or was it this way when you found this place?"

"No, this room was already arranged like this when I stumbled into the underground bunker," Sin replies, his eyes twinkling with pleasure at my excitement. "Wait until you see this!" he says and opens the wardrobe.

Inside is an array of colorful dresses from the 1800s, an eclectic mix of styles, ranging from loose-flowing gowns with empire waistlines and simple silhouettes to corseted gowns with colorful shawls and fitted jackets.

All the costumes are historically accurate, and I'm astounded at how fresh the colors look.

While I scan the row of well-preserved fabrics, Sin fingers a yellow gown with red floral patterns, his eyes roving over me with a hungry expression.

"Would you try this one on? For me?" he asks with a sheepish look on his face.

"You sure? All this looks so expensive, and also quite sensitive," I reply with a sigh of my own. "What if I damage the dress?"

"You wouldn't," Sin replies with a smile. "And even if you did, I don't think anyone will mind. Besides, I think it would look amazing on you. Anything and everything looks amazing on you."

"Oh, stop it," I reply with a blush, but of course, his flattering words please me. I hesitantly take the dress off its rack and feel the soft fabric beneath my fingers. "What if it doesn't fit me? You know, because of . . ." I point to my stomach.

"It has a high waistline. That shouldn't be a problem."

I don't question how he'd know that, and I try not to imagine him rummaging through the closet of a random woman.

But he's right. The waist is high enough that it would not be too tight over my stomach. It doesn't seem to be a Victorian dress, though. Rather, it resembles more mid-1910s Edwardian silhouettes.

I wonder who else has been here between the 1800s and when Sin discovered this place.

"All right. I'll give it a try."

Sin nods toward a privacy screen that's so well made it alone could pay my whole college tuition, and I obligingly head for the secluded spot.

"Or," Sin says, half-jokingly, stretching an arm to block me right as I am about to disappear behind the wooden board—"you could just change here."

His tone is light, but his eyes simmer with desire.

"Thanks, but I think I will use the screen," I reply with a laugh and a light punch to his arm.

He raises his hand and steps out of my way with a wry smile. Though my belly juts out a good deal by now, the fabric of the dress cascades over my body in soft swells, the layers swishing around me as I adjust to its weight.

When I step out from behind the privacy screen, Sin's eyes light up. He lets out a long, low whistle as I twirl before him.

"You look incredible!" he murmurs. "I mean it, Petra. You're the most beautiful thing I've ever seen. This dress was *made* for you."

Pleased at his compliments, I look down at myself, feeling like a character from a historical drama.

The gown is truly exquisite, and for a moment, I wonder what it must have been like to actually live in the time it was made.

"It's very comfortable," I admit, smoothing the fabric. "And it does fit me quite well."

"You look stunning, my love," Sin says with a glint in his eyes that cannot be mistaken for anything other than a deep-seated, insatiable desire for me.

He steps closer, running his hands through the pleats of my dress and across my hips, his fingers intertwining with mine.

"May I have this dance?"

"There's no music, Sin," I reply with a soft chuckle, but inside my heart is literally doing flips.

"We'll make our own," he says with a heated grin.

And just like that, he pulls me close as our bodies start swaying slowly in the dim light of the underground chamber.

The filigreed lanterns mounted on the walls cast long shadows around us, and it feels like we have stepped outside normal time and into a pocket universe of our own.

"You fit in here perfectly, Petra," Sin whispers in my ear as we gently turn on the spot. "This might have been my hiding place, but it's never felt more like home than it does now."

He looks down at me with the most enchanting smile in the world, and it's a good thing his arm is supporting my back because my knees quiver at the sight of that beguiling face, the blue eyes sparkling with desire, the full mouth coming close to mine . . .

Our lips meet and tangle swiftly. Our limbs follow closely behind. Sin pulls me deeper into his arms as my fingers entwine his hair.

My baby bump keeps coming between us, and we laugh freely at the impediment while simultaneously helping each other out of our clothes.

I unbutton Sin's shirt with urgent movements, as if I can't wait to touch his skin. He's much smoother in his movements as he loosens my overgarments and slides them over my shoulders.

In the next few moments, I have taken off his shirt as well, and as I carefully step out of my chemise, he unzips his trousers.

Soon, we stand stark naked.

Sin looks sculpted and sinewy, and I can't help but run my fingers down his chest and defined abs and then the V-shaped dip in his hips leading to . . .

My cheeks flush at the sight of his erect cock, but just as my hand starts to falter, Sin guides it to the base of his manhood, and as I cup him there, where he's hard and tender, velvety and taut, he lets out a low, guttural groan and cups my breasts.

In the next instant, we are writhing and squirming in another heated embrace, where I can feel his cock rubbing across my wet folds. In another swift motion, Sin picks me up, as if I weighed less than a feather, and carries me to the sprawling bed.

As we sink into the plush linens, his cock nestles even deeper into my moist center, and the feel of its hardness makes me arch my back instinctively, a gasp escaping my lips.

"Tell me where to touch you, Petra," Sin says in a hoarse voice as he hovers over me, his fingers stroking my tight nipples before moving between my legs.

He takes utmost care not to jostle my stomach, but otherwise, his caresses are growing frenzied by the minute.

"Tell me where you want to be touched," he repeats against my neck before taking one of my nipples into his mouth and swirling his tongue around it. At the same time, he teases my folds with his fingers, expertly touching me until I'm writhing in his arms.

"This is perfect. It's so good—" My head falls back as my mouth opens on a soundless moan. His thumb is on my clit, rubbing it, pinching in. "Harder. Make it . . . hurt." I'm shocked by my words, but there is something so deeply erotic about mixing pain and pleasure, so carnal and primitive.

He doesn't seem surprised by my request. Or if he does, he doesn't show it. Instead, he trails his lips down my neck, kissing the sensitive area before biting me. Hard.

"Ah," I groan, arching into him. His teeth penetrate my skin until he draws blood, and somehow that only makes me wetter.

"Mine," he murmurs. "You're mine, Petra. My woman. My fucking sanity."

"Y-yes. I'm yours. Only yours." The declaration escapes me instinctively, and as I taste it on my lips, I realize how right it feels.

"And I'm yours. Only ever yours. Don't ever doubt that." He leans back just enough so I can see the sincerity in his eyes. "Never anyone before you, never anyone after you. Only yours," he mutters, his voice dripping with primal lust and . . . something more.

He licks the drops of blood before going lower. Pressing a tender kiss to my stomach, he hikes my legs up onto his shoulders before he buries his face between my thighs.

True to my request, he makes it hurt. Ah, but he makes it hurt so good. He nibbles and bites on my clit until a galaxy explodes before my eyes. I'm so wet and growing wetter, and with each stroke of his tongue followed by a hard bite of pain, I find myself falling over and over, a multitude of mini-orgasms exploding within me in quick succession.

"More?" he asks with a wicked grin as he gives me one more lick.

I dig my nails into his shoulders and grab him forward, smashing my lips against his, tasting myself in the kiss.

"More. Everything. Give me everything," I beg.

The ache in my sex grows more intense as I wrap my legs around him. Instinctively, my hands hold his buttocks and pull him closer, as if to show him how much I want to be penetrated, to be *fucked*.

He smirks at me as he fists his cock, dragging it over my folds and coating it in my wetness. The head of his cock brushes against my too-sensitive clit, and the merciless assault on my senses begins anew.

"Please . . ."

"Patience, my love," he whispers.

"Sin, please. I need you. I need—" I moan out loud, inching my hips even closer to his, eager to be filled, to be completely ravished.

Sin pushes into me in a swift thrust.

My eyes roll back at the feeling of being stretched and filled, his cock throbbing inside me as he starts moving.

Pain and pleasure.

Pleasure and pain.

And everything in between.

I grab and scratch at his lower back, locking my legs over his ass as I tilt my pelvis so he can sink deeper.

He lets out a harsh moan as he wraps one hand around my throat, his thumb slipping inside my mouth just as he retreats and slams into me again.

I suck on his finger, my gaze meeting his rapt one.

His thrusts are harsh, punishing, as if he's exercising some hidden anger on me. And here I am, loving every second of it.

Soon, the air is filled with our breathy moans and gasps.

"So hot," he manages to gasp out between thrusts. "You're so fucking hot. I need you so badly. So fucking badly."

"You have me," I say but somehow the words come out mangled and breathless, scattering away under the heaving grunts issuing from both our mouths.

Just then, Sin shifts position and spreads my legs wider, effectively pushing even deeper inside me.

"Come for me, love. I need to see your beautiful face when you come undone."

By now, I'm close to the edge, and this final thrust sends me over it.

The waves of pleasure thrum over my legs, starting from somewhere deep inside and rippling through my insides. I cry out at the never-ending release, tears flowing down my cheeks. My muscles tighten around his cock as I rotate my hips, needing to pull him over the edge with me.

Sin lets out a harsh groan as his warm release coats my insides.

He collapses next to me, careful not to crush me, and he gathers me in his arms, his hands resting on my belly. I can barely keep my eyes open, but the last thing I hear before a dreamless sleep engulfs me is Sin's voice.

"Oh, Petra, you're so beautiful, so achingly beautiful . . ."

THE NEXT MORNING, I wake up to the soft light of the Victorian lamps mounted over the bed. When I roll around and find the space next to me empty but still warm from Sin's body, I sit up in distress.

But almost immediately, I notice a note left on the pillow beside me:

Petra,

I had to step out for a little to check up on my sister. I'll hopefully be back before you wake up and bring some food. Rest well, sweetheart. You deserve it.

P.S. I can still smell you on my skin. Best perfume I could ever ask for.

Yours,
Sin

And though I'm put out at being left alone the day after our first proper sexual encounter, the message comforts me, and I lie back down, pulling the covers around me.

Memories of last night are forever etched in my mind, and as the images of our entangled bodies flood my inner eye, I feel a shiver run through my limbs.

This *is what all the fuss is about,* I think briefly, pleasantly, before drifting back into a mellow spell of slumber.

Yet the echo of one word resounds in my mind, even as sleep claims me.

Yours.

CHAPTER FIFTY-SEVEN

PETRA

Present Day

"Before you ask," Sin adds with a laugh, "I did not sell my soul for this strange ability. Unfortunately, I was born with it."

"W-what?"

"Why don't I make you some tea, and we can talk more?" he says suddenly, pivoting toward the small kitchen set up in the corner of the room.

He busies himself for a moment, making two cups of tea before returning to the center of the living room. He pats the cushion next to him on the sofa, and I hesitantly sit down.

"Thank you," I murmur as he hands me the cup. I wrap both hands around it, letting the warmth calm my nerves. "Tell me about your powers," I ask directly. "When did you first notice them?"

He exhales, his eyes far away. "I'm not exactly sure. Maybe they've always been there. But I remember odd things starting to happen when I was around three or four years old. Small items would go missing or move without explanation.

"At first, everyone at the orphanage thought it was a prank. But soon the incidents became so widespread, they thought the building was haunted. It wasn't until they saw me unintentionally moving objects with the help of the shadows that they realized it was coming from me."

"Sin . . ." I whisper. I can see this is not easy for him to talk about. He winces every time he remembers something particularly painful, and my heart aches for him.

"Maybe that's when I realized it, too," he continues, trying to keep his voice steady. "In a strange way, maybe that's why my parents abandoned me in the first place. Because they saw I was . . . different. An anomaly."

He pauses, staring down into his tea.

"After that, I was completely isolated. No one dared to talk to me. They were scared. And honestly, I can't blame them. I was so young—I didn't understand what I was or what I was capable of. Maybe . . . maybe I could have hurt someone. I don't know."

He shakes his head and squeezes his eyes shut for a moment.

I want to reach out to him, comfort him, hold him close to my chest and tell him no one's ever going to hurt him again. But I force my hands into my lap and listen to him. This is my opportunity to understand him.

"The moment I realized I had this gift, what everyone else called a curse, I started to explore it. I had to. I had no one to talk to, no one to explain it to. So I learned through trial and error that I could control the shadows around me.

"It was strange at first; I didn't know how it worked. I'd be standing in one area of the orphanage, and the light would cast a shadow beside me. The moment I stepped into it, I'd suddenly be in another part of the building.

"It was terrifying. Confusing. And I don't blame the people who called it unnatural, because back then it felt that way to me, too."

"Is that why they named you Sin?" I ask gently.

"Perhaps. That, and because my parents left me. I was a sin, just for being born."

"How did you cope with all of that?"

He exhales again. "Not well. Once they realized I was behind the strange happenings, they tried everything. Priests. Physicians. Occult experts. People they thought could fix me.

"No one could. Eventually, they gave up. They stopped bothering with me altogether. That's when I was sent to live in the attic. Meals were left at the door. No interaction. No kindness. Just silence."

"Oh, Sin . . ." My heart twists. "I'm so sorry. That must've been awful."

"It was. I won't pretend it wasn't. As a child, I didn't understand why I was being punished, why I was so different. But over time, I've learned to control my abilities. I'm still not sure how or why I have them, but I've come to accept them as part of who I am."

"Can you . . . show me?" I ask hesitantly.

"Of course," he says. "Place your cup on the table."

I do, and immediately the ceiling light casts a soft shadow beside the cup. I blink—and in that blink, the shadow is gone. So is the cup.

Startled, I look around. "Where—?"

He opens his palm, and from the light, he summons another shadow that draws the cup back into his hand. He hands it to me with a quiet smile.

"That's . . . strange," I remark carefully. "Strange, but also fascinating."

He chuckles. "I'm glad you think so. You must be the only one."

"I've never met anyone with powers like yours. This is how you took me from my room at night, isn't it?"

He nods. "You never realized it, because you were asleep. You'd wake up here with me and think it was a dream," he admits.

"But you let me believe it was just a dream."

"You weren't ready," he says softly. "Not then."

"And now?"

"You're not running. You're not recoiling in fear."

"I don't think I could run if I tried," I say with a dry smile.

"But you're not trying," he murmurs, glancing down at our hands with reverence. "More than that, you . . . accept me."

There's a note of wonder in his voice, and I feel a painful tug in my chest imagining the lonely child he once was—cast aside, abandoned, unwanted.

"You're not abnormal to me," I tell him honestly. "It might be strange and a little frightening, yes, but it's still you. And you've never hurt me. On the contrary . . ."

I should be terrified that anyone could wield so much power, but I'm not. In fact, I've never felt safer than I do when I'm with him. Especially now, because somewhere deep inside, I know the truth: He would do anything to protect me.

He looks at me, eyes softening. "You're so sweet, Petra. Do you know that? You make me happy just by saying that."

"You should believe me," I say. "Because it's the truth."

He lifts my hand to his lips, pressing a slow, tender kiss to my knuckles. "I was afraid for nothing."

"What do you mean?"

"You asked why I didn't tell you sooner. It wasn't because I didn't trust you. It's because I've spent my whole life hiding, afraid of being condemned for something I never asked for. Something that isn't my fault. I suppose I just forgot what it was like to hope."

"Oh, Sin," I whisper, heart aching for him. Although he puts on a strong front, I can sense the deep turmoil inside of him, the pain that he tries so hard to mask.

But the more I find out about him, the more I come to admire him and his strength. I cannot imagine what it would be like to be reviled his entire life—so much so that he sought to end his own life.

He not only controls the shadows, but he's *lived* in the shadows his entire life.

"Did you ever find out where your powers come from?" I ask quietly.

"As far as I know, it's something extremely rare. Entities with this kind of power almost never mingle with mortals. I was told it was an anomaly—likely the result of some distant ancestor who once had this ability, and somehow, it was passed down to me."

"Have you ever tried to find your birth parents?" I ask gently.

"No," he says, voice firm. "And I'm not interested. They had me and gave me up. Why would I go looking for them?"

"Maybe just to get some answers. They might know more about your powers, or where they came from."

He lets out a dry, bitter laugh. "Even if they did, I'm not sure I'd want to hear it. What if they looked me in the eye and told me I was a freak of nature?"

"You're not," I insist. "You're not a freak of nature, Sin. I hope you know that."

"It's sweet of you to say that, Petra, but it doesn't change the fact that I am . . . different." He shrugs in defeat.

"Different doesn't have to mean bad. I like that you're different." I give him a tentative smile. "Why, you're like one of those mythological deities from the *Iliad* and the *Odyssey*. I think that is rather capital!"

He surprises me when he pulls me to his chest, his lips finding mine in a swift, hard kiss. The cup of tea disappears from my hand and appears on the table.

"As long as you like me, I like myself, too," he whispers against my lips.

I lean in and give him a kiss of my own before drawing back and smiling mischievously at him. "Then be ready to like yourself a whole lot because I happen to like you tremendously."

His face lights instantly, and it's as if all the sorrow falls away as he gazes into my eyes. My heart skips a beat, and warmth spreads through me. In that moment, he's the most beautiful thing I've ever seen.

And his regard for me only serves to further confirm my own feelings. "Like" is a paltry word for what I feel for him.

I . . . love him.

The sudden realization of my depth of feelings for him rattles me, but it also fills me with so much hope for the future. Perhaps it's bad of me to even consider a future with him when he's involved in some questionable activities.

But I find that the more time I spend in his presence, the more I feel at ease for the first time in my life. And nothing else matters.

"So how did you learn about it? About your abilities?" I ask after a while, hungry for more information about him.

"The one who saved me. The demon, though I don't really see him as a demon. He's . . . something else," he says with a small chuckle. "Not everything is black-and-white, Petra. I've told you that there's a lot in this world, in this universe, that we don't understand. And he's one of those things."

"Did he know about your powers?"

"He was as surprised as I was when he noticed them. But he recognized them for what they were. An anomaly of nature. Something rare. Something that shouldn't be, and yet here I am." He pauses. "Still, he was kind enough to help. To guide me. Without him, I don't think I would have ever fully understood any of this."

"That entity doesn't sound so bad," I note.

"No, he's not. Not at all," he replies. "In fact, he's more humane than most of the people—most of the humans—I've encountered thus far. He has a strong moral compass. He doesn't hurt people for the joy of it. He only acts when it's necessary."

"Necessary?" I frown. "What do you mean by that?"

He presses his lips together. "If he sees an injustice, he will act. There's a lot of discourse around the roots of evil in people, and we tend to picture monsters when we think of true wickedness. But in reality, it's usually the most mundane individuals who do the most harm. They rationalize their actions in ways that absolve them of guilt. Those are the truly dangerous people of the world. I've learned a lot from him, about what's right and what's wrong."

I nod, turning over his words. He's right. I'd never thought of it that way.

We grow up learning about evil through the lens of religion—through the Bible, through stories—but he has a point. In my experience, too, the worst people I've encountered have been ordinary ones, masking their cruelty behind civility.

"Then how did you get involved with these rituals, or whatever they are? Why did those people die by suicide?" I ask.

He makes a displeased sound. "Not everything is as it's made out to be, Petra. I didn't participate in those rituals with any nefarious intent. On the contrary—those people who died, they died as a consequence of their own actions."

He speaks vaguely, but I press on. "Yes, they killed themselves, but why? What would prompt so many people to do that all at once? What was in it for them? What could they possibly gain, considering they ended up dead?"

He chuckles. "Isn't that the most interesting question? What could they have wanted?"

"You're being vague again," I accuse.

"Perhaps," he says. "Perhaps not."

"I just don't understand. First, the students. Then the others, the ones they found in the cemetery. I heard Mr. Snowden mention that they weren't from around here. So why would they come to Radcliffe? Why would anyone come all this way just to kill themselves in a group? It doesn't make sense."

He smiles—a long, lazy smile. "The students weren't from Radcliffe either. They came here from all over the country."

My brows draw together as I stare at him, waiting. After a few quiet moments, he continues.

"None of them were as innocent as you think. Many of the students used theology as a mask for their true desires. Some of them exploited others—the weak, the voiceless. Some preyed on children and women. Some ruined entire families in their pursuit of wealth and influence. None of the people who died were blameless."

"But how would you know that?" I ask, shaken.

He chuckles softly. "One of my responsibilities in the Theology Department was to review applications and admit students. I saw everything. I knew their flaws."

"And the people from outside Radcliffe?" I ask slowly, my thoughts a tangled mess. "Those ones in the cemetery?"

"Let's just say," he replies slowly, "they were invited."

The implication is chilling. He must have done this on purpose—brought them here even if they weren't students. They must have had some ties to the department, or to the university at large.

"Did you only admit people you knew were . . . bad?"

He smiles slightly. "Smart," he praises. "Yes, that's exactly what happened."

"But why?" I press. "Why would you admit people you knew weren't good to a theology program? That goes against everything it's supposed to stand for."

He shrugs. "I was fulfilling a duty."

"You lured them here."

He nods again. "Bravo, Petra. You're very astute."

"But let's say you did invite them, and they came. How could you be sure they'd get involved in rituals or secret societies, or anything like that?"

"That's the easiest part," he says. "Greedy, corrupt people always want more. They're the weakest, because they never know when to stop. When they already have money, power, and impunity, they start seeking the next thrill. And for them, the society was the next thrill."

"I still don't understand how or why they would kill themselves."

"Don't you?" He raises a brow. "What is the one thing a mortal would wish for? What is the one thing humans do not have but always desire?"

I blink. "Immortality?"

"Very good, Petra. Very good indeed. Yes. They didn't think they were killing themselves. They believed they were simply taking the next step toward achieving immortality. Although . . . let's just say it didn't go according to plan."

"You promised them immortality?"

He shrugs. "Did I? I may have implied it. But I didn't kill them. They did it with their own hands."

"But you still engineered it," I argue.

He shrugs again. "As far as I see it, I rid the world of some of the most awful people. And because of that, there are so many others living better lives right now—lives without fear of being attacked, killed, or abused. Trust me when I tell you, very few people are going to miss them."

I stare at him. His words ring true. But still . . . why? Why would he go this far? What would prompt him to take matters into his own hands?

So I ask, "Was it your mentor? Was he the one who put you up to it?"

"No," he answers casually. "It was all of my own making."

"But how? How would you devise this plan? What prompted you to do it?"

He smiles at me, then leans down to kiss my brow.

"I was sincere when I said I would never sell my own soul, Petra," he whispers. "Because that is reserved only for you."

My breath catches.

"But that doesn't mean I haven't sold others'."

CHAPTER FIFTY-EIGHT

PETRA

The Past

"Sold? As in you made a deal with the devil?"

He raises an amused brow. "The devil? No. Let's not go quite so Biblical. I didn't make a deal with the devil. I just made *a* deal."

"But for what?"

"For the one thing I never had but always wished for. A home."

The moment he utters that word, I continue to stare at him. My chest aches. I, too, have longed for the same thing.

I might've had a roof over my head growing up, but it was never a home. Just a house. I was never truly welcomed, never accepted—only used for what I could provide to my family, for what I could bring to my community. But that was never a home.

And given his far worse experiences—always being abandoned by the people who were supposed to love and protect him—I suppose it makes sense. If I were him, I'd do the same. Without hesitation.

"I'm not a good man, Petra," he says quietly, a sigh in his voice. "But trust that I would never hurt you."

"I know you'd never hurt me."

"But . . . ?" he prompts, looking at me expectantly.

"I don't think you should sell yourself so short, Sin. You are a good man. The mere reasoning behind your actions proves it. You're not doing this to destroy; you're doing this to protect. Even if it's only me."

Shock flickers across his face. A flush rises to his cheeks, and he promptly looks away. "I never thought you'd understand me so well," he murmurs, half to himself.

"Perhaps because you never gave me a chance to."

He turns his head toward me, swallowing thickly.

"You're not afraid of me, are you?" he whispers.

"No." I shake my head. "You know I'm not."

His eyes are wet, lashes glistening with unshed tears as he looks at me like he's seeing me for the first time.

Of all the things he could have said, he only whispers, "Thank you, Petra. Thank you for accepting me when no one else has."

His voice cracks on the final syllable, and something inside me shatters.

A fierce protectiveness swells in my chest. I want to wrap him in my arms, shield him from the rejection of the world, keep him safe with me where he is loved and accepted.

I lean in and press a kiss to the tears on his cheek.

I don't know where this boldness comes from. I just know he needs to feel it—that I'm here, and I'm not going anywhere.

"Ah, Petra, you're so sweet, my little darling. What would I do without you?"

"Well, you don't have to wonder about that anymore," I say softly. "I'm here, aren't I?"

"Yes you are . . ." he murmurs, then trails off. "Every day, I have to wonder if this is a dream. If you're actually real."

"I am," I whisper. "I am, and I'm not going anywhere. I'm here with you, Sin."

He groans and pulls me tighter against his chest.

"I never thought telling you the truth would feel like this. I never imagined you'd accept it. That you wouldn't recoil from me. That you wouldn't revile me for what I've done."

My heart aches for him.

He's spent so long being demonized by everyone that he still half-expects me to turn against him. I can feel it in the way he touches me, hesitant and uncertain, as if he's waiting for me to vanish. The way his fingers ghost over my face, as though memorizing the contours before they're gone.

He gazes at me like I'm something fragile and fading, like I'm just a dream he's terrified to wake up from.

And as much as I want to kiss him, to surrender completely to the warmth of his arms and lose myself in this moment, there are still truths I need to uncover.

There are still things I need to know.

"What about the mark on my chest?" I ask quietly. "Why was it not there when I would look for it during the day?"

A slow smile tugs at his lips.

"That was just a small illusion I performed. I've learned over time that I can channel the energy I use to control the shadows into other things. But because it's not the core of my ability, I can only manage it on a small scale—just enough to hide the sigil while you were awake and looking at it. The moment night fell, and you went to sleep, it would reappear."

"That's impressive," I murmur. "But why would you hide it from me?"

"You know why," he says. "Because I didn't want you to be scared." He pauses, then adds more softly, "And because when you started believing that our encounters were just dreams . . . I didn't want to take that away from you. Or from myself. You were freer with me that way—in a way I don't think you would've allowed yourself to be if you knew the truth."

I swallow. "You're right. I let myself be free with you. I felt safe."

He nods. "In those dreams, we were just two people. There was no history, no baggage. Just us."

"I see," I say, and I do. If I had known earlier that those weren't dreams, I might've reacted differently. I might've tried to stop it. I might've feared what it meant—that he could take me from my room without me ever noticing.

But the more I got to know him, the more his presence became the only thing that felt safe.

"You were right to do it," I tell him after a moment. "If you hadn't approached it that way, maybe I would still be trapped in my own misconceptions about you.

"But I'm still curious," I whisper, "about what these symbols mean. Because what happened back then wasn't normal. My skin healed like nothing ever happened, and I remember you piercing it with a knife."

"The answer is simple," he says. "The marks are magical. And this symbol isn't something caused by my own ability."

"Then what caused it?"

He gazes at me and places his hand lightly over my chest, above the mark. "Fate. Because we're meant to be. This happened because, out of everyone in the universe, you and I are the perfect pair. We were destined for each other from the beginning. Your soul is mine. Mine is yours. We're tied together."

He hovers his fingers over the spot. "This isn't just proof of that. It's a tether—binding us. When we shared blood, the bond formed. That was the first step."

"First step?" I ask, furrowing my brows.

"For the bond to become permanent, we would need to consummate it," he answers gently.

I blink. "Consummate? You mean . . . ?"

"Yes," he says. "Exactly that."

"But how do you know this?"

"The entity told me. There are people out there fated to find one another, though not all do so in every lifetime. Sometimes the stars align. Sometimes they don't. But I recognized you, Petra. As mine. And you recognized me, too—I know you did.

"What did you feel when you first saw me?" he asks.

I think back to that moment in the bookstore—how striking he looked to me. The impossible beauty of him, the deep blue of his eyes that seemed to pierce right through me. I hadn't been able to think of anything else afterward. It was unlike anything I'd ever known.

"I see you know what I mean," he murmurs, satisfied.

"What happens after we consummate the bond?" I ask quietly.

"Then we will truly be one. We'll share life and death—in this world and the next. Nothing will ever be able to separate us again. I will find you. Always. No matter what."

I nod. Slowly. Steadily.

The prospect of belonging to this man for all eternity makes me warm and tingly. I *want* that. Perhaps I've wanted it from the first time I saw him. But I know I would have never dared to admit it to myself back then.

Even now, I find myself hesitating. Years of conditioning, of keeping quiet and suppressing my emotions, have taken a toll on me. Yet it's because of *him* that I've started to open up, to go against my fear of being judged and punished for my thoughts.

He became my safe haven the moment he allowed me to be curious, to dare to *know*.

Perhaps I should be scared of being bound to someone until the end of time. Because he's not talking about *just* this lifetime. He's talking of forever.

That is quite the commitment, isn't it?

The logical part of me tells me to take my time, consider things carefully.

But the other part of me? The one that's finally at peace in his presence, the one that yearns for him more than oxygen, that part of me tells me to take the leap. And I choose to listen to it.

"Can we . . ." I wet my lips. "Can we do it?"

His brows go up in surprise. "You want to . . ."

"Consummate the bond," I say with a decisive nod.

"Are you sure? Because once we take that step, there is no going back."

"I know. And I'm ready. As long as it's you, I want everything," I tell him sincerely.

Perhaps I should be more scared of what this means, especially considering the unusual circumstances of our meeting and the rather questionable rumors swirling around him. But it *feels* right.

He *is* right for me. And I want to own him as much as I want to be owned by him. Forever.

He stares at me intently, his eyes darkening with lust. Slowly, his gaze shifts downward to the curve of my neck and the swell of my breasts.

"If you're sure . . ." He swallows hard.

I nod fervently.

"Take off your clothes," he commands.

I blink, a little taken aback by the sudden shift in his demeanor. Where before he'd been shy and reserved, now he is confident and domineering—and somehow, that only makes the heat within me burn fiercer.

"Take off your clothes, Petra, because if I do it, I can't promise I won't rip them off."

My cheeks redden, and I slowly unbutton my bolero and lay it aside. Next is my dress. I struggle with the buttons at the back until I finally slip out of the gown. It pools at my feet, but there's still more.

He watches me closely, barely blinking, taking in every movement. When I reach behind to undo my corset, he lets out a low growl in his throat.

Warmth floods me under his gaze. I wonder what he sees when he looks at me. I wonder if my form is as pleasing to him as his is to me. I pull down the corset, along with my undergarments, until I am fully bare before him.

I have to fight the urge to cover myself. The last time we'd been in a similar situation, I thought it was all a dream. Perhaps that's why I'd been so free then. But now—though I was the one who initiated this—I feel suddenly shy. Not unsure, exactly. Just exposed.

A harsh sound escapes him, and I notice his hands have tightened into fists.

"You're so beautiful," he whispers. "So goddamn beautiful."

I flush even deeper. "I'm glad you think so," I murmur softly.

"Don't hide from me," he says as I instinctively place a hand over my private parts. "I want to see you, Petra. I want to see everything."

Slowly, I move my hand aside and stand tall before him.

"Let me see. Let me see what's mine," he croons.

That one word—*mine*—sends shivers down my spine. Because that's all I want to be. His. Only his.

"Your turn," I tell him in a low voice.

He raises a brow.

"Your clothes," I add, "take them off." I muster the courage to command him back.

He smirks and stands up. Slowly, he removes one garment at a time—first his necktie, then his vest. He unbuttons his shirt and throws it onto the sofa, leaving his chest bare.

I drink in the sight of him, golden and muscular, brimming with vitality. The dark sigil on his chest is a stark contrast to the rest of his body, marking him as mine.

Next are his trousers. He undoes them and pulls them down. Now, he's just as naked as I am. Though I've seen him like this before, it feels as if this is the first time I truly *see* him.

My gaze drops to his abdomen, then lower, until it lands on his erection hardening right before my eyes.

I swallow hard. "I don't remember that being so . . . large?" I mutter before I can stop myself.

He laughs, amused. "Yes, well, it seems I made a deal with the devil to give me a very large cock."

I can't help myself; I burst out laughing, remembering my foolish comment from earlier. The shared laughter eases my nerves and settles my fears.

But then his expression suddenly changes. The good humor from before is replaced with a ravenous look that makes the hair on my body stand up. I wet my lips, waiting for him to fill in the silence.

His body is tense, his jaw locked tight as he stares at me.

"I don't know if I can be gentle, Petra," he admits in a ragged tone. "I want you so much. I've wanted you for far too long."

I swallow hard. "If that is what you want to offer me, then I don't want gentle. I want *you*, Sin. And I want you to show me your truest self. I don't want you to hold back because you think you'll hurt me. You'll hurt me more by doing so. So please, show me. Show me everything you want to do *to* me."

My admission seems to surprise him. At the same time, he looks like he's battling himself, a storm of emotions crossing his features. He doesn't know what to do.

He's still holding back, and I hate that. I hate to see him limit himself just because he's afraid of shocking me—perhaps even of scaring me.

"What do you want me to do?" I ask him.

I'm still rather embarrassed by my naked state, but the more I look into his eyes, the more I lose myself in those stormy blue irises that promise to love and worship me in equal measure, the less I care.

His lips tighten into a line.

"Tell me," I repeat when he makes no move.

He's standing there, gloriously naked, his body rippling with every breath. Broad shoulders. Muscles carved like stone. A chest and abdomen so well-defined, it's like looking at a sculpture brought to life.

And then there's that part of him I'm still hesitant to linger on with my gaze.

By now, he's fully hard, his shaft angled toward his stomach, ready.

He pins me in place with his gaze.

"Run," he says finally. "I want you to run."

CHAPTER FIFTY-NINE

PETRA

The Past

"Run?" I blink in shock. Of all the things he could've said . . . "I don't understand. What do you mean?"

"I want you to run, Petra. Run from me as if I were a monster chasing you. Run from me as if your life depends on it."

"But—"

"And when I catch you," he continues, "I want you to beg me. I want you to beg me not to take you, and I'll take you anyway. I want you to beg me not to touch you with my beastly hands, and I'll touch you anyway. I want you to plead with me to leave you alone, even knowing I never will."

"Sin, that's—" I stammer, blinking rapidly. I don't understand. Why would he want me to run from him, to fight him, to tell him I don't want him . . . when he knows all too well how much I do? How much my body aches for him?

"Don't you see, Petra?" he says, taking a step closer. His hand comes up to my chest and circles my neck, not roughly, but firmly. "I'm fucked up. I am so fucked up. I can't imagine taking you any other way than with you fighting me, hating me. I want you to fight for your life—even while knowing you're at my mercy.

"Does that disgust you? Does it scare you?"

"I just . . . I don't understand."

"Don't you?" he whispers, caressing my cheek with his free hand while tightening the other slightly at my throat. He brings me closer until his lips brush across mine. "You awaken such a wild need in me, Petra. A need so raw, I don't know how to control myself. I don't know how to stop myself from taking and taking. I want to own you, even knowing that I don't deserve you."

I'm still in shock over his demand. I keep wondering what prompted this. We were doing so well—he was opening up to me, being so gentle and comforting. And now he wants me to run away from him?

But as my thoughts continue to churn, it dawns on me that this isn't the first time he's exhibited similar inclinations. The first time he ripped the veil from my face . . . he did it because he wanted me to fight him, didn't he? And the time he bartered for a kiss—he liked my reluctance.

He enjoyed it so much that he pushed the limits as far as he could.

And then there are the dreams—ones that walk a very thin line between consent and coercion. So many things happened between us in those moments that, if they had taken place under normal circumstances, I don't know if they would have happened the same way.

Yet, I find that I don't judge him for his requests. I don't judge him for his behavior, because deep down, I can see where it's coming from.

He still thinks he's undeserving, doesn't he?

He believes nothing will ever be given to him freely—not without something in exchange, not without him forcing the hand. That he's not worthy of being given anything at all, so he can only take.

Well, if this is how he wants it to go, then I'll indulge him—and hope that my submission shows him he can always take from me, and I will always give back.

One last look into his eyes, and I turn on my feet, dashing through the winding hallway of the subterranean home.

I don't know where I'm going. I don't even know how big this house is. Yet it's the sound of sliding footsteps behind me that makes my heart race—and makes me curious to see where this is going.

Immediately, I know he's not using his shadows to move around. He's running after me.

Simply a man chasing his woman.

Am I disturbed for getting a thrill out of this? For loving the way I can't predict what comes next—whether he'll pounce on me in the next second, or whether I'll get another few feet of distance before he does?

I don't know. And that only makes it more exciting.

I run as fast as I can, looking for a place to hide. He's behind me but not running at full speed, taunting me. Just as I turn the corner into what seems to be a bedroom, I find myself tackled to the ground.

He pounces on me, grabbing me midair and turning so that he bears the brunt of the fall as I crash atop him.

His skin is hot against mine, every inch of him pulsing with tension. He holds me tightly, as though letting go would undo him entirely.

Immediately, his mouth goes to my neck, and he bites the sensitive skin. I press my hands against his shoulders, pushing him aside, but that only serves to make him tighten his hold over me.

I struggle to get out and thrash from side to side, not knowing what's going to happen. Yet at the same time, I feel completely safe in his arms.

His bite becomes more painful, and a pang of desire courses through me. I let out a deep moan as I arch under him, inviting him to take more.

He drags his teeth down my collarbone and to my breasts, where he once again wraps his lips against my flesh, biting so hard he draws blood. I shiver, the pain mingling with all those other foreign emotions forming inside me.

"So sweet," he whispers against my skin. "You taste so sweet, my darling Petra. And you're all mine."

He continues his assault down my body until he reaches that private place between my legs.

I open wide for him, not caring about anything else in the world but his touch.

"Please," I whisper. Yet he doesn't do anything. He stares at me, needy and thrashing on the floor, as I wait for him to put me out of my misery.

"Beg," he says. "Beg me, Petra."

"What?" I whisper.

"Beg me to taste you. Beg me to pleasure you."

I blink, a little unsure of myself, yet I see that if I don't say anything, he won't do it. He won't do anything.

"Please, Sin," I start. "Please, touch me. I'm begging you. Please." I thrust my pelvis upward in an attempt to get closer to him, to get some relief from this hunger that's developed inside of me.

He chuckles. "Where do you want me to touch you? Tell me, Petra."

"Right there," I say and point to the spot between my legs. "I need you there."

"How much do you need me there?" he asks with a raised brow.

I can only manage one word: "Please."

He smirks at me. "You need me that much?"

I gulp down and nod fervently. That spot between my legs is already wet and aching, and as I move my pelvis toward him, I try to get some friction to lessen the ache.

"Please, I need you to touch me there. Please," I continue begging.

He smiles sensuously at me as he drags one finger along my folds.

"How do you want me to touch you? With my hands?" he says as he pinches that pleasure spot before going lower and inserting a finger inside me.

The sudden intrusion makes me flinch, but instead of drawing back, I push forward, needing more of him inside.

"Or do you want my mouth?" he asks.

"Both," I whimper. "Mouth, please."

He seems to be having fun at my expense, seeing how much I need him, how much I want him.

So this was his plan all along—he wanted me to be so mindless with pleasure, so needy, that I only care about one thing: his fingers on me, inside of me, his mouth on me.

His cock inside of me.

He pumps his finger into me a couple of times before withdrawing, leaving me bereft.

I clench my muscles, feeling the emptiness already, but it's not for long before he grabs my buttocks with both hands and pushes my pelvis upward toward his waiting mouth.

He throws my legs over his shoulders as he buries his head between my thighs.

I let out a loud moan at the first contact of his mouth with my private part. He licks me thoroughly before wrapping his mouth around that pleasure bud, sucking it deeply, biting and nibbling until I am so far gone that I no longer have control over what I do or say.

I move wildly on the floor, seeking to grab onto something as the pleasure inside me builds and builds. My words, too, are a cacophony of unintelligible sounds as I strain to reach that much-awaited pinnacle.

And then his fingers are inside me again—two of them.

He pushes them all the way in, curling them around a hidden spot while sucking on me until I'm so mindless with pleasure, I cry out loud.

It's an earth-shattering noise as I scream and shout and wail, tears streaming down my cheeks with the power of my release.

Just as I'm about to come down from the high, he lines his cock at my entrance, pushing in.

It's tight, painful, and entirely not what I imagined.

It hurts far too much—though I should have expected it given his monstrous size.

"You're so tight," he groans. "Fuck, you're so fucking tight."

It's so painful, I squirm back to try to get away from him. But there's nowhere for me to run.

Even though everything in me screams to escape the pain, there's also a part of me that wants this, that's curious about it.

He pulls me toward him as he wiggles to get deeper inside, and then, in one swift thrust, he enters me all the way.

I cry out in pain.

He whispers, "Oh, look how good you're taking me, Petra. Shh, my sweet girl. You're mine now. You're mine. Only mine."

"It hurts," I whimper.

"Just for a moment. You can take it, love. You can take me—all of me."

"I—"

"Look," he murmurs. "Look at us joined together. It's me and you, Petra."

I look down where we are joined together. He takes my hand and presses it between my legs. I circle my fingers around the base of his cock, feeling the way he's buried inside of me.

"This is . . ." I gulp down, suddenly overwhelmed with emotion.

"Wondrous," he completes my sentence.

I nod, tears coursing down my cheeks.

"Ah, darling. I know it hurts," he murmurs soothingly, his fingers wiping my tears away. "But there is beauty in pain, because this is something only *I* can give you. Only I can hurt you like this."

"Do you . . . do you like hurting me?" I whisper.

"I only like it when *you* do. And you like it, don't you, darling? You like the kind of pain only I can give you."

As he speaks, he pulls back and thrusts into me again, harsher than before. I cry out, thrashing from side to side.

"Yes, yes, yes," I chant.

My mark vibrates on my chest. There's a searing sensation that spreads through my entire body.

He thrusts inside me again, each time getting deeper.

"Sin . . ." I whimper.

His hand presses on my breast, his fingers grazing over the mark on my chest. And as I gaze upon his own mark, I note an eerie glow. It's a flashing red, glowing in tandem with mine.

It starts out with slow, languid strokes, and when all resistance falls away, he increases his speed.

He groans deep in his throat as he lays kisses all over my face and neck, his arms wrapped around me as he continues to make love to me in a way that is both tender and savage.

I embrace him, squeezing him tight as I hold on to him, pulling him close.

"I love you," I whisper in his ear. "I love you so much, Sin."

He lets out an anguished sound—one that is half disbelief, half wonder.

"Oh, my sweet Petra, I love you, too. I love you so damn much. I've loved you for so long," he says between thrusts. "I never imagined" —he mutters in a ragged voice as he picks up his pace—"never imagined you'd be mine. That we would be like this together."

We're both a mess of limbs, our bodies wrapped together in a tight knot, our hot breaths mingling as he claims me time and time again.

By this point, the pain is just an echo. There is only the feel of him, hot and hard inside me.

It's a completely new sensation as he touches places inside my body I never knew existed. And when I'm so wrapped in his embrace, the world falls away until it's just the two of us.

Love and feeling. So much sensation. I don't know where I begin and where he ends.

His movements grow frantic, and once more, I feel something build inside me—but this time, it's different. A tension coils in my lower belly, yet it's almost as if I don't know how to grasp it, how to reach it.

"Sin," I whisper. "I can't . . . I need—"

"What do you need, Petra?" he asks huskily. "Tell me what you need, darling."

"I don't know—"

He sneaks his hand between our bodies and touches me there, circling that pleasure point once, twice, applying more pressure.

And just when I think I can't take it anymore, the explosion comes—so much more intense than before, so much more powerful that I end up screaming, digging my nails into his back, scratching him and drawing blood.

"That's it. Come with me," he commands. "Come with me, my love."

His movements become out of control as he chases his own high, and then it happens. He nestles his head between my breasts, biting my skin as he convulses around me. I feel his hot release coating my insides just as he lets out another shout of pleasure before going still again.

We're both breathing heavily. I'm dazed, unable to concentrate on anything but the warmth he provides, the feel of his body glued to mine. So much emotion explodes in my chest right where that mark pulses with life—the living proof of our eternal bond.

He licks his way up my breasts, kissing me on the lips again.

Yet just as I think it's over, that we're both finished, I find myself flipped onto my stomach with him behind me, his hand in my hair.

CHAPTER SIXTY

PETRA

The Past

His hardness is between my ass cheeks as he gathers the hair around my nape into a tight fist, pulling me backward so he can bite my neck again.

It's vicious, painful—yet perhaps I am just as deranged as he is because without any other stimulation, I come the moment his teeth pierce the barrier of my skin.

I cry out, sobs making my body tremble as every logical thought flees my head.

He pulls harder on my hair, my scalp tingling from the pain. It's on the tip of my tongue to tell him to stop, that it hurts, but the only things that come out are more pleas.

"Please . . . put me out of my misery," I beg.

I should want him to stop, but all I can do is beg for more. He slowly licks the blood trickling down my back before kissing his way down my spine.

Just as I think he's finally going to thrust into me again, he surprises me with a change of direction. Still clutching my hair with one hand, he reaches between my buttocks with the other, his finger probing at a different hole.

The sensation is so foreign, so unexpected, that I stiffen.

"Sin, what are you doing?" I stammer.

"You're mine, aren't you, Petra?" he murmurs in a lust-clouded voice.

"Yes, but—"

"Then you're wholly mine. Every single thing about you is mine, including this."

His finger pushes against the barrier of my hole, and I react instinctively, trying to get away from him, from this intrusion.

This is odd, I've never heard of anything like this.

What is he doing? This isn't how our consummation should be, right?

But the more I pull away, the more he yanks my hair, keeping me in place while he works his digit inside my bottom.

At first, it's only one, then it's two. It hurts, but there's also something else—

"Sin, what are you doing?" I demand, shocked by my own reaction.

He whispers, "You begged me to take you, remember? So I am. I am taking you."

"I don't understand—" My words are cut off as, before I know it, his fingers are out of my hole.

I think the torture has ended, that he's finally going to claim me again, so my body relaxes in his hold. I no longer try to pull away.

He chuckles at me. "You're such a naughty girl, Petra. Such a naughty girl taking my fingers up her ass."

His cock slides between my ass cheeks. He coats it in my wetness and caresses my sex with it, yet he doesn't enter me.

The anticipation builds inside me. I thought we were done, that this was all there was to this consummation. When animals mate, once the male releases inside the female, it's done.

Not for Sin. He's still hard, ready for more.

Am I ready for more, too? My sex is still sore and swollen from his previous assault, and I'm not sure if I can do it again—at least not now. Yet in spite of the brief moments of pain from before, there was also an entire world of pleasure that I am looking forward to exploring more.

And perhaps, to my great surprise, I am also looking forward to the pain.

It's such a contradiction. Pain and pleasure, two things so diametrically opposite, but together? Why do they sound so appealing?

Am I deranged for thinking that? For craving it?

Sin purrs behind me, a deep, seductive sound that makes me tremble with desire. I did not think I would want him even more after we slept together, but the more he touches me, the more I want him. Every way I can get him.

My arousal, too, grows by the moment, more wetness accumulating at my entrance.

Without being able to see what he's doing, I can only rely on the sensation of him sliding over me, touching me.

I have no way of knowing when he's finally going to put me out of my misery and take me again.

And then it happens. He notches the head of his cock to my opening and pushes in.

But he's not thrusting inside my sex. It's my . . . other hole.

I let out a startled gasp.

It hurts.

Only the tip gets past my ring of muscles before I instinctively try to get away. The pain is even worse than before.

His fist is in my hair as he keeps me in place, pulling me backward just as he pushes inside me. "Shh. Let me in, Petra. Let me in, darling."

"I can't. I—"

"Yes, you can."

He pulls back, his cock still at my entrance.

Glancing back, I watch as he brings his wrist to his mouth and bites his flesh off. Blood pours down in rivulets. Between my ass cheeks. On his cock.

He smirks at me, dark and arrogant.

Lathering his cock in his blood, he pushes it again into that tight hole.

My eyes widen. This time, though my muscles still clamp on him in an attempt to stop his advance, the lubrication from the blood makes it easier for him to go deeper.

Inch by inch, my body becomes accustomed to this type of claiming as he works his cock inside me until he's fully in.

"Oh, fuck," he curses on a ragged moan. "Fucking hell, Petra. So damn tight. You're strangling my damn cock."

I whimper in response, my throat sore from all the screaming.

It's . . . odd. I feel so full, yet it's not an unpleasant sensation.

He keeps his bleeding arm over the place we are joined in, letting more blood pour over his cock as he slowly pulls back only to slam inside me again.

His hand moves from my hair to my hips, holding me in place as he begins a wicked and erotic assault.

There is still an echo of pain, but it slowly morphs into something else. It's different than before. Bolts of pleasure spike through me in quick succession.

I slump onto the floor, clutching at the carpet as my eyes roll back in my head. Ragged moans fill the room—*mine* and his.

"That's it. You're doing so good, darling," he murmurs appreciatively.

He leans over me, his knees planted on each side of my hips as he starts pistoning in and out of me at lightning speed. With each thrust, the pleasure becomes more nuanced, more potent.

I can *feel* it. It's coming. It's the same, but different, and it's coming.

Tears flow down my cheeks as the climax is *wrenched* from me. It's hard, fast, and all-consuming.

I shout his name as I clench around him, and he follows me swiftly in ecstasy, falling on top of me. His release is hot, filling me to the brim, and for moments on end, his cock continues to pulse inside me.

He gathers me in his arms, holding me tight.

"Thank you," he whispers in my ear. "Thank you for giving me this gift. I will treasure it. Always."

"I love you," I reply. "Always."

He nuzzles his face against my nape.

"The bond . . . do you feel it?"

I nod. "The mark burns hot against my skin. It's as if it has a life of its own."

"It does. Our bond is a living thing, Petra. It will follow us everywhere in this universe. *Everywhere.*"

"I'm glad," I say, "that way we can never be parted."

"It is my vow to you that no matter what happens, I will always find you. Not even the devil himself could keep me from you, my sweet Petra."

I sigh happily and burrow deeper in his embrace. I am relaxed, content, and happier than I've ever been.

Unfortunately, nothing this good can last too long, as moments later, I remember the engagement party, the fact that someone *will* notice my absence. And I don't want to think what will happen once my father gets wind of it.

I scramble to my feet, looking around for my clothes.

"I need to go back," I mutter frantically.

"Now?"

I turn to him. He's standing in the middle of the room, stark naked, his body splattered with blood.

"Yes. You know as well as I do that my father cannot notice my absence."

"Then don't go at all. Stay here, with me. Forever."

I gulp down, the prospect of spending an eternity with him, here, is far too appealing.

"I would want nothing else. But we would be confined to an isolated experience. Do you want us to spend an eternity underground?"

"I would not mind it." He shrugs.

"Perhaps I would not mind it either, but there are other considerations."

He raises a brow at me.

"What about children?" I ask tentatively.

Surprise flickers across his face, and I realize he never considered this perspective.

"Me getting with child is a very real possibility, Sin. I would not want a child to only know darkness . . . isolation."

He lets out a loud sigh.

"You are right. I should have thought better of it." He pauses. "What do you want to do then?"

"I think there is only one way to do this," I say carefully as I put on my dress. "We have to discredit the ones who would be against us."

The corner of his mouth lifts up in amusement.

"Do go on, my smart darling," he drawls.

"My father is already losing credibility because it seems he's sold his morals for money. But that's not enough as long as he has Mr. Snowden's backing."

"You want to reveal to the world that Snowden was involved in the rituals, too."

I nod. "With everyone thinking him a hypocrite, the narrative will shift. There will no longer be a right or wrong, one side that is good and the other evil."

"True," he agrees. "It would have been far easier if you'd just accepted to be sequestered with me here," he adds wistfully.

"Perhaps, but nothing easy is truly worth it, is it?"

He chuckles.

"So smart and wise." He lets out a whistle. "All right, Petra. We will do it your way. I will ask my mentor to help us, too. He knows *everything* about Snowden."

"Thank you," I murmur. "There is just one other thing. That . . . creature. If Snowden knows we're after him, he might try to send the creature after us."

"Leave that to me, Petra. Nothing will touch you, I promise." He comes closer to me just as I button the last bit of my dress. He shocks me when he drops to his knees and presses his lips against my stomach. "Not you, nor our future children. You have my vow for it."

SIN USES HIS shadows to transport me back to Snowden's house. The party is still alive, the music louder than ever. It seems there are even more people wandering the halls of the manor. One quick look at the clock on the mantel, and I realize I haven't been gone that long.

I tentatively step inside the grand ballroom, hoping no one has noticed my absence—not with all the chaos surrounding Mr. Snowden's departure.

As I enter, I spot my mother at the other end of the room. I make my way toward her, doing my best to seem inconspicuous. But as I reach her side, I realize I needn't have worried. She's leaning against a column, swaying slightly.

As I get closer, I catch the sharp scent of spirits on her breath. Her eyes are unfocused, and she looks about ready to topple over with the slightest push.

"Petra," she slurs.

"Yes, Mother?"

"I was looking for you," she continues.

"Really? Why?"

"Your father . . . he was looking for you."

She's not making much sense, but I suppose I can use this to my advantage.

"What do you mean? I've been here the entire time. Next to you."

She frowns. "You have?"

"Yes."

"I think you're right," she mutters. "Be a dear and get me another one of those glasses, will you?"

Perhaps I should have said no, that she's had enough. But this is probably the first time she's had spirits—or at least this much. I grab a glass from one of the servers and hand it to her.

At that moment, the crowd parts to reveal my father and brother.

"There," my father says, glaring at me. He has a murderous expression on his face. "Where have you been?" he demands, voice low and menacing.

"What do you mean? I've been right here. Right, Mother?"

"Yes, yes," she says, struggling to keep the slur out of her words. "She's been with me."

He frowns. "I was looking for you and did not see you," he says, his words slow and measured.

"I must have been in the restroom. Did something happen?"

"Your behavior before . . . it is unacceptable. You will find Mr. Snowden, and you will apologize."

Why would I apologize to Mr. Snowden when he wasn't even there to hear my words? I think to myself—but I don't voice it aloud. I won't give my father more reason to be angry, not when we have a plan to put in motion.

"Of course, Father. As you say," I reply dutifully.

He frowns, clearly surprised by how easily I agree, but lets the matter drop. With a loud huff, he turns on his heel and walks away.

I glance around and note that Mr. Snowden has returned to the party. He looks worse for wear, and there are new bruises on his neck, which he's trying very hard to hide with the collar of his shirt. I press my lips into a thin line and shake my head.

Hypocrite. And my father wants me to marry that man? In his dreams. Oh, they'll get a taste of their own medicine soon enough.

Through the crowd of faceless people, I spot someone else—Leah. She's dashing out of the ballroom into the hallway, looking rather upset and slightly green in the face.

"I'm going to the lady's room, Mother."

"Yes, yes," she murmurs, completely out of it.

I follow Leah and see her slip into the ladies' room. I go in after her. The first sound I hear is retching. Then sobbing.

"Leah, are you all right?"

She doesn't answer at first.

"It's just me, Petra. There's no one else in here."

A few moments later, she comes out of the stall, wiping her mouth and heading to the sink to rinse her hands and face. She glances at me, worried.

"Are you all right? Is my brother mistreating you in any way?" I ask, truly concerned for her.

If we manage to unmask Snowden for the devil he is, Leah will face repercussions, too. But maybe, just maybe, we can turn this around. Maybe instead of suffering, she can be freed. She won't be forced to marry my brother.

"Please tell me if there's anything I can do to help."

"No." She shakes her head. "You can't do anything."

"You're wrong. I can help you."

She shakes her head again. A lone tear slides down her cheek.

"You can't," she whispers. "It's far too late."

I frown. "What do you mean? You know . . . you don't have to marry my brother."

"That's the thing. I have to—now more than ever," she says, barely holding in a sob.

"Now more than ever?" I repeat, confused. "What are you talking about?"

"Isn't it obvious?" She lets out a dry laugh, wiping her eyes with the back of her hand. "I'm pregnant."

I stare at her.

"You're pregnant? Did my brother . . . did he do anything to you? Did he force himself?"

For all my brother's faults, I can't imagine him doing something so vile.

"No, no," she says quickly. "It's not that. No."

"Or . . ." I trail off, realization dawning. "It's not his child, is it?"

She swallows hard and gives me a slow nod.

"Who is it? Did someone hurt you?"

"No. On the contrary," she whispers, placing her hand over her stomach. "The father of my child . . . I love him. I love him dearly, but we could never be together."

"Why? Surely, there has to be a way. You could run away and—"

"No. He is my father's sworn enemy."

I pause. "Sworn enemy?" I repeat. "Who is the father of your baby, Leah?"

She bites her lip. "You won't tell, right? You promise you won't tell anyone?"

"I vow it," I say.

She hesitates, still unsure. But at last, she utters two words—two words that shock me to my core.

"Sinclair Arnoult."

PART THREE

CHAPTER SIXTY-ONE

PETRA

Present Day

I startle awake, screaming at the top of my lungs. A searing pain on my chest makes me wince. I scramble out of bed, ripping at my nightshirt as I search for a mirror.

When I finally stand before the reflective glass, what I see shouldn't surprise me, yet it does all the same.

The mark. The one from my dreams.

It's branded on my chest. Intricate lines flowing in a beautiful and complex design, all surrounding one letter.

S

"What . . ." I mutter in shock.

How the hell is this here? How did it suddenly appear?

Panic erupts in my chest. My thoughts turn to my dreams—the only avenue for answers I have. In them, dream-Sin had said he could keep the mark hidden from me.

If so, what else has he done?

Dream-Sin was involved in those grisly murders over a century ago, and while he might not have killed those people with his own hands, he facilitated all the murders.

Does that mean he is involved in the present-day murders, too?

I squeeze my eyes shut and rub my temples against the slowly forming headache.

The conclusion that dream-Sin *must* be present-Sin is self-explanatory. They look the same, they kiss the same, they say the same things. And just like dream-Sin, present-Sin is always there for me, always in the shadows.

Shadows . . . In the past, he'd been able to control them. Can he still do that? Is he some type of superhuman? But if that is the case, then did he reincarnate into his present self, or is he . . . immortal?

Fear accumulates in my breast. In my dreams, he'd talked about people seeking immortality—selling their souls for it. Those students who took their lives did so in hopes they could achieve eternal life.

Is that . . . is that something he did, too?

"You're going crazy, Petra," I whisper to myself. How else can I explain my train of thought?

Despite the similarities between dream-Sin and present-Sin, there are also differences. He doesn't have any of the mannerisms of a Victorian man, nor does he have the vocabulary of one. If anything, he's awfully normal in that regard: a regular teenage boy.

All right, so if he's not immortal, perhaps dream-Sin *was* his past-life self.

Yet that idea brings about other questions: Does he remember the past? Did he approach me on purpose, knowing our history?

In all the time we've known each other, he's never given any indication of that. There have been moments where he'd been rather . . . intense, but I've never sensed that he was lying to me.

In fact, I've known of him since the start of junior year, and our first encounter wasn't until the end of the school year. If he had remembered the past, wouldn't he have approached me sooner?

But then you would have thought him creepy, and a stalker, my inner voice tells me, and I have to agree with her. We're from two different worlds, different crowds, different everything.

I release a loud sigh. My thoughts are running amok, and I don't seem to be getting anywhere conclusive. And if Sin *is* the one murdering those kids, why Edwin? Why Harry? Why those other unnamed individuals? There is no motive for it.

Yet before I jump to his defense, as I'm always doing as of late, another important piece of information comes to mind.

Images flash before my eyes as I remember Leah's words in my dream.

She was pregnant with Sinclair Arnoult's child.

For some reason, I refuse to believe *my* Sin, past or present, would be with another woman. He is, and has been, far too dedicated to me to do that. And despite the inconsistencies in this entire murder-ritual-supernatural debacle, *that* is one thing I am not willing to accept.

Great, Petra, my inner voice adds. *He can be a murderer, but he can't be a cheater.*

Well . . . yes. Because if he *is* a cheater, then he's about to be the next one murdered, by yours truly.

A dry laugh escapes me. I am truly going crazy if this is what I consider morally wrong.

Alas, there is only one way to figure things out. And since I happen to be right here, in dream-Sin's former home, a little snooping is due.

First order of business: Make sure my Sin isn't a cheater. Then I can worry about whether he's a murderous maniac.

Nodding to myself, I quickly put on my clothes from yesterday and start with the obvious place: the massive library.

Books line the shelves, all of them pre-1900s. It's like an entire museum of ancient tomes, and I don't even know where to start. I glance at the first titles, noting they're arranged alphabetically, but as I scan through them, I realize this might be a useless endeavor.

At the same time, the light in the room flickers, and a shiver runs down my back. I have the distinct sensation that someone is watching me.

I turn around, looking left and right—no one. Still, I can't shake the feeling. The hairs on my body stand on end, and goose bumps spread across my skin. I shake my head. I'm probably still rattled by that dream. It's nothing.

After checking one of the shelves, I give up. I'd be here for eternity. Instead, I start searching for other things that might give me a clue about the owner of this home. Surprisingly, everything looks just as it had in my dreams. Very little has changed, except for a few modern appliances. The furniture, the layout—it's all the same.

I move through a dimly lit corridor, checking room after room. Even the art studio is empty of anything useful. But as I walk farther, I find a door I've never tried before. Not even in my dreams. I step forward tentatively and place my hand on the doorknob. It's locked. I sigh in frustration, muttering a curse under my breath as I look around for a key.

Just as I'm about to turn back, a soft click breaks the stillness. I whirl around to see a flicker of light shining from beneath the door. Without thinking much of it, I try the knob again. This time, it turns.

"What?" I whisper to myself.

I push the door open and find myself in a beautiful Baroque-style study. Everything is dusty and covered in spider webs—so much so that it seems no one's stepped inside for over a hundred years. I run my fingers along one of the hardwood shelves, and a thick layer of dust clings to my skin. This room hasn't been touched in ages.

I look back at the door, another shiver running down my spine. That same feeling returns, like someone is here with me, someone I can't see. The door had been locked. I'm sure of it.

Still, this may be my chance to find something. I begin searching immediately for any hidden clue.

Toward the back of the room, there's a massive hardwood desk, the kind you only see in museums. The craftsmanship—hidden compartments, ornate carvings—feels antique, Victorian or earlier.

I allow myself a moment to admire it. It's like stepping back in time, touching a piece of history. But just as I begin opening compartments, a stream of light cuts into the room from the hallway. It's like a beacon, and it lands on a stack of papers in the corner.

I blink, a little unnerved.

"Is anyone there?" I call out.

Nothing.

"Sin? Is that you?" I ask again, thinking maybe he's hiding in the shadows. Still nothing. I'm alone. Alone in this strange, silent room.

I shake off the nerves and kneel on the dusty carpet, pulling the stack of papers toward me.

The first envelope spills open, and several black-and-white photographs slip out, yellowed by time. I pick one up with trembling hands. Two men are in the picture. One of them I recognize immediately. It's the man who held me in his arms just hours ago. Sin.

A shiver passes through me. This is confirmation. If I had ever believed dream-Sin was just my imagination, a superimposition of the present-day Sin onto a fantasy, I was wrong. The man in the picture is him. Exactly him. The same features, the same eyes. There's no mistaking it.

But that's impossible, isn't it? Even if reincarnation were real, how could someone look exactly the same? Scientifically, that's not how it works.

I turn my attention to the second man. He's shorter, with tousled hair and thick-rimmed glasses. I don't recognize him, but something about his posture feels familiar, like a memory I can't quite grasp.

Turning the photo over, I read: *1894 - Sin and Sinclair.*

"What?" I whisper.

Sin and Sinclair. Two people. That means Sinclair must be Arnoult. Right?

I set the picture aside and pick up another. This one shows a group—eight people. Again, I spot both Sin and the man I now know as Sinclair. On the back, written in elegant script: *Theology Department of St. Anselm Hall University, 1895.*

Names are listed left to right. And there it is—Sinclair Arnoult the First. But Sin? His name is listed as Kimaris.

I exhale. Relief floods through me. For all my fears, this is the proof I needed. Sin isn't Arnoult. He's not the father of Leah's child. He never betrayed me.

Still, what is his connection to all this?

The next picture makes my hands tremble. It's a couple. Sin. And me. Or . . . not me. A past version of me. But we look identical. How can that be?

For so long, I've convinced myself that my dreams were just symbolic. That I inserted myself as the main character in someone else's story. But now?

I flip the picture over. *Petra and Sin, 1896.*

"No," I breathe.

It's me. Same face. Same name. And him—same man. Same name.

This is beyond coincidence. There's no logic to explain this. No scientific answer. How can we look the same? How can we be the same?

Desperate for more answers, I dig through the papers. Most are newspaper clippings. One details the murder of Rutherford. Another, Underwood. There's mention of Arnoult's seances and his obsession with the occult.

Then I find a yellowed piece of paper, frayed at the corners. A letter.

Dearest Sin,

We must be on guard. Snowden is preparing something. I do not yet know the details, but I need your help to get my Leah out of that house before the wedding. I can't let her marry another man. I can't let her be hurt again.

Meet me at our designated spot.

Your friend and mentor,
Arnoult.

I set the letter down slowly, heart pounding.

So *he* was Sin's mentor.

Leah was pregnant with Sinclair Arnoult's child. But if Sin and Sinclair were not the same person in the past—why is present-Sin called Sinclair Arnoult?

What exactly is the relationship between Sin and Arnoult the First, and how does that relate to the murders?

I remember the newspaper clipping we found in Sin's parents' house—the one talking about a father-daughter murder-suicide. Now I can't help but wonder: Was the person who died Leah . . . or past-life me?

Because both of us had strange relationships with our fathers.

And although Snowden seemed like quite the character—going as far as using some type of creature to kill his competitors—I cannot see him murdering his own daughter, no matter the circumstances.

My past-life father, on the other hand, was cruel. He was exactly the type of person who *would* do something like that.

So the question is: Who died that night? What happened to past-life me—and past-life Sin?

CHAPTER SIXTY-TWO

PETRA

Present Day

The only way to solve these mysteries is to make sense of the murders—to look for connections, for motives. Because I no longer believe this is simply about sacrifices or some kind of pagan ritual. It's too disorganized, too erratic for that.

Pocketing the photo of past Petra and past Sin, I carefully restack the papers where I found them and slip out of the office.

Back in the living room, I spot the corner where Sin has spread out his school things. I settle onto the sofa, grab a piece of paper and a pen, and begin jotting down everything I can remember about the murders.

If there's a pattern hidden in the chaos, maybe this will help me find it—maybe even figure out who's next. Why it's happening. But more importantly, who's behind it.

The first incident that comes to mind is the obelisk victims: twenty-five students who appeared to have taken their own lives by cutting their jugulars. At the time, it was branded a ritual murder. And according to past-life Sin, it might truly have been just that.

Then, only a few days later, Rutherford was killed. Followed soon after by Underwood.

Those two murders are different; we know they were carried out by Snowden's creature.

At some point, either before or after the obelisk deaths, there were the fifteen mausoleum victims, each bearing the same puncture wounds to the sides of their necks. And lastly, among the known victims from the nineteenth century, there's the still-unnamed father and daughter duo who died together.

I draw a line beneath that list and begin jotting down the more recent murders.

From my discussions with Sin, I remember the mass suicide of the St. Anselm Hall alumni, which took place around nineteen years ago. They died in the same manner—and in the same number—as the obelisk victims: twenty-five.

Then, fifteen years ago, there was the house party where several attendees died in a fire. This incident is eerily preserved in the painting hidden on the walls in the tunnels.

A year ago, the Blackwell family perished from what was ruled a gas leak. I'm still questioning whether this had anything to do with the town's ritualistic history—or if it was just a tragic accident.

And yet, something nags at me.

Children survived in both that incident and the house party fire. In fact, in all these older cases, the innocent were spared.

Until now.

Edwin. Harry. The unidentified dismembered man in the town square. And the unnamed victims from the religious community.

Once I've finished laying out all the facts, I stare at the page, deep in thought.

Sin had mentioned that the town believes a murder must happen every couple of decades—that some sort of ritual is expected. He also suggested that some past deaths might've gone unnoticed, or been explained away as accidents.

And yet, the deaths I've listed . . . they don't follow a pattern. Not clearly, at least.

Next to Rutherford and Underwood's names, I write plainly: *Killed by Snowden*. They're the only two victims for whom we know the murderer, but their deaths are still relevant. They connect to the broader mystery.

For the obelisk and mausoleum victims, I add an asterisk and note that they weren't good people. According to Sin, they were chosen specifically because of their pasts—because of some wrongdoing.

So what about the rest?

The alumni mass suicide from nineteen years ago—did those people also carry dark secrets? I mark that case for further research.

I'll need to find out more about the victims' backgrounds. I'll do the same for the house party attendees and the Blackwell family.

If Sin's account of selective punishment is accurate, they, too, should have had something to hide.

But that brings me back to Edwin and Harry.

Barely eighteen. Children, really. Why them? Why now?

If children had been spared before, why not now? Was an exception made? Or was this something else entirely?

And what about the religious community victims? So much of it still makes no sense.

Frustrated, I put the pen down and let out a long sigh. There's something here, I can feel it, but it's just out of reach.

We know one killer: Snowden. Then there are the nineteenth-century suicides, facilitated by past-life Sin. But the murders from nineteen years ago? Sin wasn't even born then. And fifteen years ago, at the time of the house party, he would have been, what—four? He couldn't have done anything . . . unless . . .

Unless he never died.

Unless Sin sold his soul for immortality.

A shiver works its way through me.

A noise in the back of the apartment draws my attention. A door opens and closes: the one that leads down to the tunnels beneath the cemetery.

Then Sin appears.

I hold myself still, watching him approach with cautious eyes. These recent murders have no explanation . . . unless Sin—*this* Sin—never truly died in the past.

"Hey there," I manage to say. It hurts to speak, but I force a smile, not wanting him to suspect anything. Not until I have something concrete.

"Sweetheart," he starts, setting down a bag of takeout on the table. He looks tense.

"What's wrong?" I ask.

"They identified the body," he says quietly.

"The chopped-up one from the town square?" I ask.

He nods. "It was François."

"What?" I whisper, stunned.

He comes to my side and pulls me into his arms. "This is so fucked up," he mutters.

"But why François? What could he have done?" I whisper.

"I don't know, but everyone is terrified. They think someone's targeting students," he says. "They're even considering canceling classes for the rest of the term."

"What?" I blink. "Canceling classes?"

He nods. "Even if the school doesn't go through with it, I doubt many parents will want their kids coming back. Not with an unknown danger out there."

"You're right," I murmur, shaking my head. "This is . . . I don't understand."

"I don't either. But the students have already gathered in the town square to place candles and flowers where he was found. His parents are already planning the funeral."

"Too many funerals lately," I mutter under my breath.

"And we'll have to go to this one, too."

"Do we have to?"

"Of course. He was our colleague, wasn't he?"

"Was he?" I grumble. "Never liked him anyway."

"Petra!" Sin exclaims, half-shocked.

"What? I feel bad that he's dead, of course. But it's not like I'm going to miss him. I don't think anyone will. All his friendships were surface-level anyway."

He stares at me for a second, stunned. Then chuckles. "My, my. You're so bloodthirsty all of a sudden."

I shrug. François has always been mean to me. Why should I feel sorry for him?

"What do you have there?" he asks, pointing to the piece of paper next to me.

Damn it.

I should have hidden it when I had the chance, before I got distracted by his sudden appearance, his perfect face, and that infuriatingly perfect body.

I mentally berate myself, blaming it on hormones. *Too* many hormones, thanks to you-know-who.

"Oh, that . . ." I trail off as he picks up the paper.

"This is a list of everyone that's been killed so far—or at least the ones we know about," I say quickly, grabbing a pen to add François's name next to the previously unidentified body from the town square.

"This is quite the detective work you've done," Sin murmurs, running a finger over the table I've compiled. "But how would you know about these?" he asks, pointing to the nineteenth-century murders.

It would be so easy to say I saw them in my dreams.

But that would open a whole other can of worms I'm not ready to deal with. I'd have to admit I know about past-life Sin, about his powers, and about his involvement in those deaths. And what if he *is* the same Sin—and never died at all? I'm not ready for that conclusion. Not yet.

I need more proof. More facts. Something undeniable.

More than anything, I can't bear the thought of confronting him only to see disappointment in his eyes. Of being accused of not trusting him . . . of assuming the worst.

So, I lie.

"I found some old papers. Newspaper clippings. They were in one of the locked rooms."

"Really?"

"Yeah. The one at the end of the hallway," I say casually. "There were articles about Rutherford's and Underwood's murders, as well as the mass suicide in the town square."

I conveniently leave out the mausoleum deaths, hoping he won't ask.

"I see. You haven't wasted any time looking around."

I shrug. "This is serious, Sin. We need to figure out who's doing this. Because at this rate . . . I mean, what if *we're* next?"

He sobers instantly. "You're right. You're absolutely right. You did good—really good, Petra."

Momentarily, I find myself lost in his gaze, my cheeks flushing at his words of praise. I've always considered myself a perfectionist, always striving to do well in . . . well, everything really. Unfortunately, praise has never been my parents' strong suit.

"Thank you," I murmur, suddenly bashful.

He leans in to kiss my cheek. "You're so smart," he whispers. "I love that sexy brain of yours."

My heart pounds wildly in my chest. Sexy . . . brain. That must be the best compliment anyone's ever given me.

"Did I make you blush?" he drawls with a grin.

"What? Of course not. Check your sight, Arnoult," I say playfully, hiding my face in the crook of his shoulder.

His chest rumbles with laughter, and for a brief moment, I forget all about my worries, my suspicions, my fears.

How is it that his mere presence has the power to make me feel so safe even when my brain doubts that? It's almost as if my body reacts to his on a cellular level, getting me to lower my guard when logically I should not.

The paper slides to the floor as he pulls me into his arms.

"You smell so good," he murmurs as he trails his nose down my neck.

"Mhm," I say as I pull his face to mine for a deep kiss.

"You drive me crazy, Petra. So fucking crazy . . ." he pulls back just enough to whisper the words against my lips. "Sometimes I'm amazed at my restraint."

I raise a brow at him.

He smirks as he continues. "If I had my way, you'd be on your back, legs spread, my cock inside you twenty-four seven. Alas, perhaps I will indulge in that after our little one is born."

"I think that can be arranged." I wink at him. "*After* my back won't hurt like hell anymore."

"It does?" he suddenly asks, concerned.

I shrug. "Sometimes." *More often than not.*

"Damn it! I should have given it more thought. You have such a small frame; of course, the added weight would affect you."

"It's not really *that* bad. I just get tired more easily."

His lips flatten into a thin line. "And that is unacceptable. From now on, you tell me every time you feel tired or uncomfortable, all right?"

"It's fine, Sin. It's not like you can be with me every hour of the day."

"You think so?" He raises a brow. "Ah, darling girl, I don't think you know me too well."

His words are supposed to be playful, but instead, I find myself frowning. "Meaning?"

"I will make sure you're never out of sight," he replies vaguely.

Once more, my suspicions poke their nasty heads to the surface.

I let out a dry laugh. "So, what, you're going to become my shadow?" I ask pointedly.

"I *am* your shadow, Petra. I'm just waiting for the moment when you will embrace me instead of seeking to get away from me."

My lashes flutter in surprise. Is that an admission? Is he admitting that he *is* past-Sin and he has those shadowy powers? And what does he mean about me trying to get away from him?

Before I react, his hands move to my waist, and he cups the small bump.

"How is our little miracle doing today?" he asks in a gentle voice, a total change from the intensity of his tone before.

"Uhm, good," I mumble.

"Any cravings? I got you some fruit and snacks."

"No, I'm fine for now."

With a tense smile, I wiggle out of his arms and resume my place next to him on the couch. His eyes follow me with exact precision as well as a frightening intensity that seems to disappear whenever I gaze at him head-on.

Odd. Everything is odd. And I am more confused than ever. After spending my entire teenage years daydreaming about morally ambiguous love interests, leave it to me to find a potential murderer/immortal/psycho.

He must see the slight change in my demeanor, but he doesn't comment on it. He simply keeps his arm around my shoulders, holding me close.

I pick up the piece of paper off the ground, and as I look at the random years, another question comes to mind.

"Don't you think something's off about this?" I ask before I can stop myself.

"What do you mean?"

"You said the town believes this so-called Ouroboros Society, or the descendants of those five families, commits ritual murders every couple of decades or so. But there's nothing here that shows any clear timeline. Nothing to suggest a pattern that fits that theory."

"What are you trying to say?"

"Maybe this entire thing, the lore about the society, is just a smokescreen. A convenient story that lets people ignore the things that don't fit. If you expect something to happen every couple of decades, then you dismiss anything that happens in between."

"That makes sense," he says slowly. "But then why blame the five families? Why point the finger at them?"

"Jealousy, maybe? Your families are the most powerful ones in town. Possibly even on the East Coast. People don't like what they can't control—and they hate those who have more.

"More so," I continue, "why would families with that much power *choose* to stay in a place like Radcliffe? A small, insignificant town?"

He nods thoughtfully. "You're right. Something isn't right." He leans forward to look at the list. He's so close, his scent wafts to me. I lick my lips in response.

Get a grip, Petra! my inner voice screams at me—and she's right.

Just seconds ago, I was wondering whether he might be a psychopath, and now I am once more ready to jump on him just because he got a little closer.

Fuck! I am in so much trouble. Worse is that I cannot explain *why* I am so infatuated with him. Sure, I could blame a part of it on hormones, but even before . . .

The night we first slept together, I acted completely out of character. I can blame it on the alcohol all I want, but I *know* there was more to it than that. I liked his attention, the way he listened to me, the way he looked at me. It's almost as if he put me under a spell—one that's only become more potent with every interaction.

Maybe it's my inexperience speaking since he is my first . . . well, everything. But I doubt it. I've seen beautiful people before. I've never once entertained the thought of doing with them what I did with him.

His face is next to mine. He turns slightly and smiles at me before he rubs his cheek against mine affectionately.

My heart almost stops in my chest. My breathing certainly becomes incapacitated as I hold myself still.

Good Lord! Something is seriously wrong with me.

Perhaps it's that mark on my chest. Past-Sin mentioned it's the physical manifestation of our bond. Maybe it does something to my mind?

My eyes suddenly widen in realization.

Wait a moment! If I have the mark *now*, he should have it, too.

"Take your clothes off!" I blurt out.

He blinks in confusion before a slow smirk appears on his face.

"So commanding. I like it," he drawls as he pulls back and starts unbuttoning his shirt.

I wait with bated breath for the confirmation of all my theories, but as he shrugs his shirt off to reveal his muscled chest, there's . . . nothing.

No mark. No blemish.

He could be hiding it from me, though, right?

He starts unzipping his pants, and for a moment, all thoughts leave me.

I gulp down, stirrings of desire taking hold of me.

Slowly, he pulls his pants down until he's only wearing his underwear. The hard outline of his cock is unmistakable. He's ready for me.

I'm ready for him, too . . .

Sweat beads on my brow as indecision gnaws at me.

For once, though, I refuse to let my physical urges cloud my mind—though that's easier said than done.

I force myself to my feet before this can go any further, and with a string of unintelligible mutters, I dash toward the bathroom.

CHAPTER SIXTY-THREE

PETRA

Present Day

I didn't expect to be back home so soon, but after evading Sin one too many times, I realized I needed an excuse to get out of the situation. Not just because it would be so easy to give in, but because the more I think about it, the more suspicions I have—about him, about everything.

I wonder if he noticed something was off with me. Maybe he did. I don't really have a good poker face. Never have, never will. I'm already dreading our next meeting—when he asks me what's wrong, and I'll have to lie.

I release a deep breath and strip off my clothes to hop in the shower. I scrub myself clean, apply some perfume and lotion, and afterward, I realize I'm getting a bit too hungry. Maybe I should've eaten what Sin brought, but that would've given him more time to grill me.

Curious, I check the fridge. Knowing my parents and their sporadic visits, and considering how absent I've also been, I doubt there's much inside.

Sure enough, most of the food is expired.

Damn it.

I guess my only option is to order something. But just as I grab my phone to browse delivery options, the front door clicks open, and my parents strut in, luggage in hand. My mother walks in first, followed by my father—both dressed to the nines despite having just gotten off a flight.

"Petra," my mother intones. "It's so good to see you."

I give her a forced smile. That's not something a parent should say to their child—especially not when they technically live with said child.

"You've been gone a while," I remark dryly.

"Just a couple of weeks, but we have great news! The contract went perfectly. We signed it, and we're moving on to the next stage. Your father was even asking what kind of gift you'd like from the bonus we received. I thought maybe we could check out that new Saint Laurent collection. What do you think?"

I stare at her. "Um, I'm good," I mumble.

They move deeper into the house, leaving their luggage in the hallway. I need to get past them before they get a good look at me. Normally, when they're home, I wear baggy clothes to hide my ever-growing bump. But today, I'm in a tight top and pajama pants.

I cross my arms over my stomach and fidget with my phone, pretending to be busy. As I head for the stairs—almost there, almost free—my mother's high-pitched voice rings out again.

"Petra!" she exclaims, but this time there's no joy in her tone.

"Yes?" I ask, half-turning.

"You've gained weight! She has, hasn't she, dear?" she says, turning to my father.

"Yes," he replies. "You were skinnier before."

I gulp. This is exactly what I didn't want to happen.

"Gee, thanks for telling me I'm fat," I mutter.

"You're not fat, dear, but you're so petite. Too much weight doesn't look good on you," she says sweetly.

"Well, it happened," I shrug.

"But when did it happen? Did you change your diet? Should we hire a new chef? What have you been eating? This is so sudden. I don't remember you being so large."

I glare at her. Because, of course, that's what every teenage girl wants to hear—how large she is.

"Can you please not comment on my weight?" I ask flatly.

"We're not commenting, we're just . . . worried. This isn't like you. You've always been so small and—"

"I'm pregnant," I blurt out.

Maybe it's not the best way to break the news, but her fake concern over my weight pisses me off.

If she's going to act mad, I want her *really* mad. And this will do the trick.

She blinks, stunned. My father's jaw slackens.

Her lips tremble as she tries to find the right words. "But to be pregnant, you have to have sex . . ." she trails off. "And you're too young to have sex."

"That's exactly what got me into this situation."

"But . . . but . . . you're only eighteen. That's so young!" she sputters.

"It might be, but I'm technically an adult," I say, keeping my tone steady.

My mom gasps loudly as if she's just now understanding the implications. My father swallows hard, his Adam's apple bobbing.

"No. This is impossible. This is a prank, isn't it? You're playing a prank on us."

"Do I look like I'm joking?" I ask, deadpan.

"You *do* have a weird sense of humor," she says, forcing a fake laugh. "Ha . . . ha . . ."

"I'm not joking."

"No . . ." Her face falls.

"Yes," I confirm. "And your outrage is a bit late."

I pocket my phone and place my hands on my stomach.

"I'm already five months pregnant. The fact that you're just now noticing should concern you more than the fact that I'm pregnant."

"But Petra—"

"No. Maybe this isn't what you wanted for me. But if you'd been around more, you would've seen the changes in my body long ago."

My mother stares at me, eyes wet, lips trembling. Then she asks in a semi-wailing voice, "Is this an act of rebellion? Are you trying to punish me—punish *us*?"

I glare at her. Of all the things she could've said, she makes it about them.

"Sure, Mom. I got pregnant just to get your attention. I might be desperate, but not that desperate."

Tears stream down her cheeks. "But how could this happen? You've never seemed interested in anyone. You've never even had a boyfriend!"

I roll my eyes. "As if you were ever around enough to know whether I had one or not. Have you *ever* asked me?"

"There, there," my father says, trying to placate us. "Let's not get carried away. Petra, if you're joking, please tell us. This isn't funny."

"I told you. I'm not joking. And not that it's any of your business, since I *am* eighteen, but yes, I have a boyfriend who loves me very much—and he's excited about the pregnancy."

My mother continues to cry. "But you're so young!"

All the while, my father holds her like she just learned the world is ending.

"You weren't much older than me when you had *me*," I retort.

She wails louder. "Exactly! I didn't want this for you. I didn't want you to end up like *me*! That's why I told you to wait. To find someone you love."

"And I *did*," I fire back. "I found someone who loves me, and I love him. Yes, I'm pregnant. But don't worry, I won't end up like you. I actually plan to *be* in my child's life." I've thought about this. A lot. And no matter what's going on, whether this baby is . . . supernatural, or whatever, I'll love him.

Because he's *mine*. I'll love him the way I was never loved. I'll give him the attention I never got.

She gasps audibly, her eyes widening in shock. My father continues to try to calm her down. They're so wrapped up in each other, not even looking at me. And all my old grievances come rushing back.

In a moment that should be about *me*, about the fact that I may actually want this baby—though, it's the first time I've admitted that—they're still talking about *their* feelings. *Their* expectations. *Their* plans.

Pain shoots through my chest.

My eyes sting. I blink quickly, unwilling to cry in front of them. I turn and head up the stairs.

I didn't expect them to be supportive. But I didn't expect *this*.

Disappointment crushes me.

And I don't know if I'm more disappointed in *them* for being who they always were or in *myself* for expecting anything different.

I swallow down the lump in my throat and wipe the tears from my eyes. I try to stay strong, try not to fall apart—but it's cruel, so cruel, that when I need them the most . . . they're still not there.

All I've ever wanted was for them to acknowledge me. Not as a burden, not as an obligation. But as a person.

MY MOTHER KNOCKS at my door and opens it slightly.

She gazes at me for a few moments in silence, her expression tight and uncomfortable.

"I'm sorry," she murmurs at last. And to my shock, she does seem rather apologetic. "May I come in?" she asks.

I give her a small nod and scoot over on the bed, making space for her.

She closes the door and takes a seat next to me. She stares straight ahead, almost as if she doesn't dare look me in the eye.

"I realize now that perhaps I shouldn't have reacted like that," she starts. "You know, we had you when we were very young, and we were poor. We could barely afford the roof over our heads. It was only after you were born that our fortunes changed, and we were able to provide for you.

"Maybe because both your dad and I grew up with nothing, we became too focused on providing. And somewhere along the way, we forgot to actually be there for you. I'm sorry. I realize now that our approach wasn't the best."

She takes a deep breath.

"You never talked about being poor before," I mention with a frown.

"We didn't come from money. Even though we started this company early on, it wasn't a success until after we had you. The company was dying. We were in deep debt—until an investor stepped in and helped us turn things around. He was a godsend, the only one who believed in our vision. If it hadn't been for him, we never would've gotten where we are today.

"I guess I never talked about it because it was such a hard time in our lives. I didn't want you to think about money the way I did growing up: as something that's always slipping through your fingers. I wanted you to always have what you needed. The best things."

My mind is going in circles trying to make sense of everything she's saying—some of it that I'm hearing for the first time. Yet it's one piece of information that gives me pause.

"An investor?" I repeat slowly. Another piece of information I've never heard about before. "Who was this investor?"

"Oh, dear," my mom says, thinking. "He was an alum of St. Anselm Hall, actually. He not only invested in the company but also introduced us to people in the field who helped us expand. He was the one who recommended we move to Radcliffe, so you could attend his old school.

"You know how competitive St. Anselm is. They mostly take legacies. He was the one who vouched for you and sent a letter of recommendation."

I stare at her.

"That's news to me," I say suspiciously. "You never mentioned that before."

"I didn't want you to feel bad. I know how hard you worked, even though you were homeschooled. You were always such a good student, always going above and beyond. When you submitted your art portfolio, I didn't want you to think it wasn't good enough."

"But still," I say, "you should've told me."

"You got in. That's all that matters."

"No. Because *I* didn't get in. *That man* got me in."

"Well, he may have helped, but it was still all you. Your grades have been impeccable—that's all you."

I narrow my eyes.

Before we moved to Radcliffe, I thought I would finish my education being homeschooled and taking my GED. Suddenly, though, my mother pivoted and suggested I might benefit from going to a regular school and making some friends.

She gave me a stack of brochures, encouraging me to consider high schools that offered the best education. She made it seem like I had a choice, but clearly, I didn't. I chose St. Anselm Hall for its art history program and its gorgeous Gothic architecture—but now I learn it was all part of some plan?

Something about this feels too orchestrated. And lately, coincidences have stopped feeling like coincidences.

"Tell me more about this sponsor. Why would he recommend me if the school only takes legacies?"

"His name is Kimaris. We haven't spoken to him in a long time. He's a very successful businessman—reclusive, but kind. He helped us find our house here, introduced us to some very influential people. You know how many important families live in this town. He thought Radcliffe would be perfect for us, and we agreed. After all, he saved the company."

"Kimaris," I echo, my blood running cold. "Did you just say *Kimaris*? What was his full name?"

"Oh, dear, I don't remember," my mom replies. "We haven't heard from him in ages. It was right before we moved here that we last spoke. He helped us get the house and then disappeared."

A shiver runs through me.

The implications are unmistakable. If he's been around long enough to influence my parents, convince them to move here, get me enrolled at St. Anselm . . .

If Kimaris—Sin's name in the past—never died . . .

Then we're talking about someone who's immortal.

And then something else strikes me.

"Mom, I've never asked you this before, but why did you name me Petra?"

It's been bothering me: the fact that I share the name *and* face of past-life Petra. I used to think it was coincidence. But now?

My mom smiles fondly. "Oh, that's quite a story, actually."

She softens, the mood shifting.

"We were visiting Vatican City, and my water broke right there in the crypt under St. Peter's Basilica. We tried to call for an ambulance, but nothing was working as the phone lines were down. The whole tour group was panicking. I wasn't even due yet—only eight and a half months—so we never expected it. We didn't even think we could fly that far along, but the airline said it was all right. That's why we accepted the trip in the first place."

"You accepted the trip? What do you mean?"

"We won it, actually. It was a prize for a random competition your father entered. A very strange chain of events, if you think about it. But it all led to you."

"Right," I say. "So you won a trip to the Vatican and were underground in the crypt."

"Yes." She nods. "And there was this really odd blackout. No way to call for help. We were terrified. No one in our group had medical experience. But coincidentally, *Kimaris* was there."

"Coincidentally," I murmur as the pit in my gut widens to a chasm.

"Yes! Can you believe it?" she exclaims. "He was there alone, visiting. He had some kind of medical training and stepped in to help with the birth. It was easy, shockingly easy. You came into the world wailing in a crypt." She laughs.

"And the name?"

"Oh, yes. Your father and I couldn't agree on a name. We started bickering while I was holding you, and then Kimaris said, 'Why don't you name her Petra—for the place she was born?' Isn't that a lovely story, Petra?"

"Right. Yes. Very . . . nice."

But as I stare at her, as I take in everything she's told me, several things become terrifyingly clear:

One: Sin—*past-life* Sin—is immortal.

Two: He knew I would be reborn.

Three: He orchestrated my birth beneath St. Peter's Basilica to ensure I would be named *Petra*.

Four: He engineered my parents' move to Radcliffe and my enrollment at St. Anselm Hall.

Sin did. *My* Sin.

And yet, even knowing this, it's hard to reconcile the sweet, charming boy I've come to know with this centuries-old manipulator.

"I really am sorry for how I reacted before, Petra," my mother says. "I don't want you to feel alone. I know what it's like to be young and pregnant. You have to be ready—people will judge you."

"I know," I reply almost mechanically.

"But your father and I . . . well, we want to be there for you. We talked, and we're sorting out the business. We'll take some time off. Is it okay if it takes a few days to get things in order? We want to focus on *you* now."

My mouth practically hits the floor. "You want to take time off from the company?"

"Yes. You were right—we haven't been there for you, not like you deserved. And I want to fix that. Before it's too late. Before we become strangers."

"That's very kind of you. Thank you, Mom."

She smiles and moves closer, wrapping her arms around me in a hug, but my bump gets in the way.

"Oh!" she chuckles. "I'll make arrangements to see a doctor, okay? We'll talk about vitamins and supplements and—"

She keeps rambling. I nod along, not really listening.

Though her apology is genuine, and I'm honestly surprised by how well she's handled all this, I don't have the mental bandwidth to deal with both my parents and Sin at the same time.

Because now I know: Sin never died. He is immortal.

And that makes me wonder what truly happened in the past. Did he make a deal with the devil? Is *he* some type of devil?

But more importantly, he survived, and past me did not.

So how did I die?

CHAPTER SIXTY-FOUR

PETRA

Present Day

In a matter of hours, my parents have gone from two people who never gave me much thought to the strangers now preparing dinner for a family meal. I'm a little bit in shock.

After my conversation with my mom, I definitely started seeing things a little differently and began to consider their perspective, but this? This is a complete 180-degree change, and I'm not sure what to think of it.

I put on some nice clothes that won't emphasize my baby bump—no need for awkward conversations over dinner—and head downstairs. The smell of home-cooked food wafts through the air, and I'm immediately salivating.

When was the last time my mom actually cooked? I can't even remember. Not only did she make the effort tonight, but she made my favorite comfort food: mashed potatoes with gravy and steak.

The baby seems to approve, too, tapping lightly against my stomach as my hunger grows into something ravenous.

Eager to dig in, I take a seat at the table. But just as my mom starts plating the food, the doorbell rings.

I frown. "Are we expecting someone?" I ask.

Both my mom and dad look confused. They shake their heads.

"I'll get it," I mumble, getting up to answer the door—only to be greeted by the last person I wanted to see today: Sin.

He's smiling like nothing at all has happened. In his hands, he has a bottle of wine and a bouquet of flowers.

"What are you doing here?" I ask, stunned.

"I thought I'd come over and meet your parents," he says, all casual.

"What?" I demand. "How do you even know they're home?"

"I saw their cars in the driveway," he replies with a shrug.

Before I can say anything—or send him packing—he steps right inside, bypassing me completely and heading straight for the dining room.

"Hello, Mr. and Mrs. Valentine," he greets them cheerfully.

My parents are staring at him, mouths agape.

I close the door quickly and rush in after him.

"This is for you, Mrs. Valentine." Sin hands her the bouquet. "And this is for you," he adds, offering my father the wine. "It's a vintage from the 1980s. I thought you might enjoy it."

"Oh, that's a lovely gift," my mom murmurs, still clearly shocked.

Then Sin moves to my side, slipping his arm around my shoulders and pulling me close.

"I'm Sin Arnoult, Petra's boyfriend and the father of her baby," he says blithely.

We all freeze.

"What are you doing?" I hiss at him in a shushed voice.

"This was bound to happen, Petra. Better now than later," he whispers back.

"You're Petra's boyfriend?" my mother whispers, still trying to process the situation.

"Yes. We go to school together," Sin answers smoothly. "Isn't that right, Petra? We're in the same grade, so there's no awkward age difference. We're both seniors in high school."

"Oh, that's good to know," my mother says, her voice hesitant.

"I've been thinking about coming to meet you for a while now," Sin continues. "But as you can imagine, it's been rather hard to get a hold of you."

I stare at him. The dig is unmistakable. My parents catch it, too.

"But now that we're all here," Sin adds, "I'm overjoyed to finally meet you. I've told Petra many times that now that we'll be a family, I wanted to meet her parents."

No one says a word, so he keeps going.

"And in case you were worried, I just wanted to make sure you know how much I love your daughter and that I'll be there for her every step of the way. We're even planning to get married."

He looks at me. "Isn't that right, Petra? After high school?"

We *never* spoke about that.

I stare at him, trying to keep my face neutral.

But inside, my thoughts are spinning.

"Um," I stammer, not knowing exactly what to say.

He's still smiling at me with that charming smile I've come to expect from him. And to my utter shock, my parents seem to be buying this good-boy persona he's putting on.

"That's very nice of you to take accountability," my mother says. "I must confess, we were shocked when we found out Petra was pregnant, and we had no idea if the father would be involved. But now, meeting you, I can say with absolute certainty that you've put our minds at ease."

"Arnoult, you said?" my father asks. "From the Arnoult family of Radcliffe?"

"Yes, sir," Sin immediately replies.

"Good family. Good stock." My father nods. "We haven't interacted much with them, but we've heard a lot, especially about your father's acumen in business. Your mother, too, she's involved in fashion, isn't she?"

"Yes, she's a fashion designer," Sin replies.

"And you've spoken with your parents about this?" my father asks.

"Of course, sir. I wouldn't have come here without talking to my parents and knowing I had their full support."

"And they're happy about the pregnancy? I mean, you are both so young," my mother gushes.

"They were, like you, a little concerned at first, but they've taken the news in stride. They're very happy. They've already met Petra, and they've both fallen in love with her. They think she's absolutely perfect for me."

"Is that so?" my mother asks, her voice tinged with suspicion.

"Of course. They think she's a charming young lady. They know how well she does in school and that she has big dreams for herself. They think we're the perfect match. Naturally, every parent worries when their child has children too early, but they believe we'll do just fine."

"Oh, I must say that's a relief," my mother adds. "Isn't that so, dear?"

"Yes. Yes, thank you for coming to meet us," my father tells him.

"Of course. Come join us for dinner," my mom offers. "Petra, why don't you put another serving on the table?"

I'm still staring at the three of them, shocked by the direction this evening has taken. Somehow, I feel like I'm living in an alternate reality. What is going on? When did Sin even talk to his parents? He's never mentioned that to me before.

And the marriage? That's . . . We've never spoken about that. Never. How could he bring that up so casually when it's a complete lie?

Still, I keep my thoughts to myself as I head to the kitchen counter, grab an extra plate, and start putting together some food for Sin. My mother is bustling around the kitchen, while my father sits at the table with Sin. From what I can hear, they're currently discussing sports—NFL, NHL, I don't even know. Sports aren't my strong suit, but I know my dad is a big fan.

Knowing that Sin plays on the school team and is a great athlete must make him very happy.

Seeing my mom nearby, I move slowly toward her, trying to see if maybe—just maybe—meeting Sin has jogged her memory a little.

"So, what do you think of him, Mom?" I ask in a low voice, careful that they don't hear me.

"Sin? Oh, Petra. He's wonderful. You should have told us earlier. Not only now, with this situation, but I do understand that teenagers like to have their privacy."

"I'm glad you like him," I say dryly. "But he doesn't remind you of anyone else?"

"Who would he remind me of?"

"I don't know. Don't you think you've seen him before? Doesn't he look like that sponsor you talked about, Kimaris?"

"Oh, but that was so long ago. I don't quite remember what he looked like," she says, frowning slightly. "But I think I would have remembered. Why? Is there a connection between the two?"

"Uh, perhaps . . . Kimaris is a family member of the Arnoult clan," I add under my breath.

"Oh, I see! That makes this even more exciting. I'm so happy for you. And he seems like such a good boy. From the way he looks at you, I can tell he loves you a lot."

"Yeah, he does," I say quietly.

But inside, all I can think is: *He loves me enough to wait for me for over a hundred years, track down my parents, make sure he was at my birth, name me so that I would share the name with my past-life self . . . then he made sure my parents became rich enough to move to Radcliffe so I could attend St. Anselm*

Hall—all so I could meet him again, as the golden boy of Radcliffe: Sinclair Arnoult. Which is probably not even his real name.

And let's not forget the most important detail: He's probably also a murderer. Maybe even in cahoots with the devil. Though I'm still not sure how that particular detail fits into the whole picture.

And now that I think about it . . . how do *his* parents fit into this? If he's some immortal creature, then how did he convince two seemingly normal people to play along with this charade?

Are they being mind-controlled? Does he have that power?

Am I being mind-controlled?

I close my eyes and take a deep breath. Tonight is going to be tough.

But I have to get through it—without signaling any suspicion.

We all sit down to eat, and my father is still deep in conversation with Sin.

My mother, clearly excited and eager to know more about the father of her future grandchild, asks, "So, Sin, tell me—do you have any hobbies?"

"Yes," he answers. "I play sports in my spare time, but to be perfectly honest, the thing I love to do the most is spend time with Petra."

"Oh," my mother murmurs.

I glance at him. What is he trying to do?

"And do you have any plans for the future? For college? A career?" she asks.

"Taking care of Petra, of course. We're going to get married, and we're going to have our kid. I want nothing more than to be there for them—to spoil them and make sure they are the happiest two people in the entire universe."

"So, you don't want to pursue sports at a professional level or something like that?" my father asks.

"No, it's fine as a hobby. But playing professionally would mean taking time away from Petra, and I would never want to do that. But don't worry about it; I have a very sizable trust fund that will last lifetimes. For Petra and me, for our child—or children—and for our children's children. So money won't be a problem. All I want is to be there for them and ensure Petra can pursue her career in art."

"You want her to pursue her career, but you don't want to pursue yours?" my father presses.

"She's such a talented artist. I would never want to see her talent go to waste. In fact, I'm willing to be a stay-at-home dad if it means she can achieve all her dreams."

My parents seem very pleased with these answers, even if they're a little shocked by the vehemence behind them. I mean, to every single question they're asking, his answer is—Petra.

And I'm just staring at him like, *What the hell is going on?*

Hobbies? "*Petra.*"

Plans for the future? "*Petra.*"

I'm surprised they haven't asked his favorite color, because he'd probably say "*Petra.*"

I give him a side-eye, and he notices but only smiles in return. He grabs my hand and places it on the table in full view of everyone.

"I really want nothing else than to love her and be there for her as she deserves. You have a great daughter, Mr. and Mrs. Valentine, and I am the luckiest man in the entire world that I stumbled upon her—and that she decided to give me a chance."

"Oh, she gave you a chance? Doesn't that mean you were the one to pursue her?" my father asks with a raised brow.

My mother chimes in, "Oh, yes!"

"I've had a crush on her forever," Sin admits, "but you know Petra; she's in her own world. It took me a long time to build the courage to speak to her, and even more time to prove to her that I'm earnest."

"Yeah, that would be Petra." My mother chuckles, while my father nods in agreement.

The entire sickeningly sweet exchange makes me so mad, I don't think I'll be able to keep my poker face for much longer.

In a tense voice, I excuse myself to go to the bathroom, pocketing my phone on the way.

Closing the door behind me, I quickly pull up the messaging app and text Amelia.

Ames, help.

It only takes a few seconds for her to reply.

What's up?

I quickly give her the rundown of what's happening.

What do I do, Ames? This is insane.

That boyfriend of yours sounds hella devoted to you.

Don't you find everything a little too . . . much?

Girl! That sounds so romantic.

I'm not sure we have the same definitions of romantic . . .

As if you weren't the one who preferred Spike over Angel.

That's fictional. We're talking about real life here. And this guy just told my parents he wants to marry me!!! We never spoke about it!

So you . . . don't want to?

That's not the issue. But he never spoke to me about it. It feels like an ambush.

You're making him sound like a diabolical mastermind

I think he is . . .

He's your boyfriend! Why are you with him if you think that of him?

I'm not sure what to think anymore. I love him, but something is off about him, and I don't know why.

I haven't told her yet about all the connections I've found about present-day Sin and past-life Sin or the fact that he might be immortal. Not that anyone would believe me about that—not even Ames.

Answer me this then:
Do you feel unsafe with him?

I stare at the message and take a moment to think about it. *Do I? Do I feel unsafe with him*?

No . . .

That's your answer then.

But what if he's a murderer? I want to yell.

A knock at the door startles me.

"Are you all right, Petra?" Sin asks.

I clear my throat and flush the toilet before placing my phone in my pocket and washing my hands.

"I'm good," I say with a smile as I open the door.

He pulls me to his side and leads me back to the dinner table.

The conversation continues with Sin saying all the right things and impressing my parents to the point that they look at him as some god walking among mere mortals.

We're about to be finished with the meal when he suddenly asks my parents, "Mr. and Mrs. Valentine, may I stay over?"

Silence ensues as my parents stare at him.

"Stay over . . . ?" my mother whispers.

Sin places his arm over my shoulders. "In other circumstances, I realize this would not be appropriate, but there isn't anything that could happen between us that hasn't already," he says smoothly.

My mother turns to my father, and they share a look.

"Please? I cannot bear the thought of being away from Petra and the baby," Sin continues.

"I suppose that is all right," my mother eventually says.

All the while, I'm still stunned by the entire exchange.

The shock doesn't wear off while we wash the dishes or while Sin offers to clean the dinner table.

It doesn't wear off as he leads me to my bedroom and rummages through my closet to find something comfortable for me to sleep in.

It doesn't wear off even as he pulls me into bed, holding me from behind, my back flush against his front.

This strange reality only registers when he leans in to kiss my neck, his warm breath fanning against my skin.

"Good night, sweetheart," he whispers.

I hold myself still, eyes wide awake even as the minutes trickle down, turning into hours as sleep eludes me.

Good Lord, I am *trapped*.

CHAPTER SIXTY-FIVE

PETRA

Present Day

A semi-sleepless night later, I wake up and realize everything was real. Sin's arms are tightly wrapped around me.

As I quietly shrug them off and get out of bed, I see he's already wide awake, staring at me.

"Good morning, sweetheart," he murmurs.

"Good morning," I reply, forcing a smile onto my face.

I quickly go take a shower and change my clothes, then return to find him still watching me from the bed.

"You should wear something black," he says.

"Something black?"

"Don't you remember? Today is François's funeral."

I blink. "And we have to go?"

He nods and stands up. He's already dressed—black trousers and a dark gray shirt. "Yes, we do. Everyone's going."

"I'm sure they wouldn't be distressed if we happened to miss it," I add dryly.

"Distressed? No. But there's a reason you must be present, Petra."

I frown at him.

"You know the detectives are already looking at you as a prime suspect. Not going to the funeral would give them more reason for suspicion."

I think for a moment. He does have a point.

"Fine," I mutter, rummaging through my closet for some dark clothes to wear. I end up settling on black tights, a dark gray skirt, and a black turtleneck.

When I'm done, Sin brings me downstairs for breakfast.

"Your parents have already left," he mentions. "They didn't want to wake you, but they told me they needed to take care of something for the business. They'll be back to spend more time with you once they've finished."

I nod absentmindedly. They had said as much the day before. I'm still waiting to see if they'll keep their promise, so I don't put too much weight on their words.

Sin surprises me once more by preparing breakfast before taking me out to his car.

"And how's our little champ doing today?" he asks, patting my belly affectionately.

"Good," I mumble. "He's good."

He smiles at me. And I'm still left wondering—*why are we keeping this charade going?*

Now that we're alone in the car, it takes me a couple of minutes to muster the courage to ask him.

"Why did you do that yesterday?"

He glances at me. "What do you mean?"

"You know what I mean. Why did you come to my house and lie to my parents?"

"I never lied," he replies immediately. "I told them the exact truth. I am the father of your baby, and I'm more than happy to take responsibility. I want to marry you, Petra. You know that."

"But we've never discussed that before."

"Well, what's there to discuss when it's a given?"

"I don't know—perhaps *asking* me? I'm sure girls like to be asked instead of being told they're going to marry someone."

He glances at me from the corner of his eye. "Would it make you feel better if I asked you?"

"Maybe."

"Will you marry me, Petra?" he asks then, that same smile still on his face.

I blink. What am I supposed to say now? I can't very well say no, right?

"See? I've asked you. Now it's all good."

"But I didn't answer."

"You don't have to answer. I know the answer already."

He suddenly stops the car and turns to look at me. The smile is gone. His eyes are intense, his face emotionless.

"You are mine, Petra. You will always be mine. You know it, too. There is no escaping me now."

I stare at him in shock. "That doesn't sound *anything* like what a psychotic murderer would say," I add with dry laughter.

He doesn't share my amusement.

"Psychotic murderer or not, you're not getting away from me. You're mine. You and the baby." Then, suddenly, he breaks into a smile. "But now your parents like me, so that's an added bonus. It would've been hard if they decided to limit my access to you. That wouldn't do. So I had to make sure they were on my side."

"Was that what everything was? Making sure they were on your side? Isn't that a little manipulative?" I hedge nervously.

"No. Just taking care of one extra detail. I want you to be happy, Petra. And that means knowing your parents are happy with you—and with your decisions, too."

I'm even more confused now. One moment, he's declaring I'm his, whether I like it or not. The next, he's saying he wants me to be happy. It's very paradoxical, and I cannot make sense of this constant shift in his personality.

Just who is he?

Is he the intense, no-nonsense guy who only knows how to command? Or is he this sweet angel who listens to everything I have to say?

I no longer know.

He continues driving until we reach the cemetery. There are already several cars parked, and in the distance, I see a line of people heading to the burial site. He parks and we get out, walking toward the funeral location.

As we've come to expect, the weather reflects the emotional charge of the situation—cloudy, windy, and on the verge of rain. A perfect mirror for the grief-ridden expressions of those mourning François.

Everyone from school is there. Some parents. And François's relatives. His mother is holding a black handkerchief to her face, sobbing uncontrollably, while his father tries to console her.

We take our spot in the back of the crowd.

The coffin is still elevated, with the priest standing next to it, reciting a few prayers.

Just as the priest mentions the words *innocent souls*, François's mother wails aloud.

"What did my son do to deserve this? He was always the perfect child, the perfect student. He never did anything to anyone. How could he deserve to be killed in such a manner?"

I note a few classmates also crying—or forcing themselves to cry. There's Daphne and her mother. Her clique of friends, all of them dabbing at almost nonexistent tears.

Yet even though I didn't like François, the question his mother is asking is a valid one. Why *would* he be killed? And why in that vicious manner? He never did anything—except being a posh prick. To my knowledge, he never hurt anyone.

Well, not physically, anyway. He was just an arrogant twat who thought he was better than everyone else. But that's not a crime.

As I scan the crowd, I spot the two detectives in charge of the murders. Sin was right. They were going to be here—and they're looking carefully through the crowd for any odd behavior.

"Isn't it weird that François is the one who died?" I lean in to whisper to Sin. "I mean, yeah, he was an asshole, but . . . why *him*?"

Sin shrugs. "He *was* an asshole, indeed. But Petra, sometimes the real crimes are committed in the privacy of one's life. Just because you might not know what he did, that doesn't mean he's entirely innocent."

"You speak as if you know something."

"Do I?" He shrugs. "But considering the analysis *you* made of the previous crimes, doesn't it raise questions that some random kids—high school students—would be killed in such violent circumstances? No one who died before was innocent. And they all deserved to die."

I stare at him in shock—not only at the nonchalance with which he speaks, which further fans my own suspicions, but also the fact that I never told him the people on the list were bad. That they were chosen *because* they were bad, to be killed or sacrificed.

He wouldn't know that unless *he* was the one who arranged their murders for that exact reason.

I bite my lip uneasily. Yet another piece of confirmation that he's behind all of this.

"And yet . . . why our classmates?" I clear my throat. "Theoretically then, if only bad people are being targeted, what could François have done? I've never known him to be a troublemaker. For all of his big words and loud personality, he never got in trouble at school. Never had an issue with any authority figure."

Sin's lips curl upward. "You really don't listen to gossip, do you, Petra?"

"What do you mean?"

"Do you see the girls in our class who look apathetic?"

I look around and yes, he's right. There are quite a few girls who stare at the coffin with blank expressions on their faces. But that's not unusual. Grief comes in many forms. Even I, who never liked François, can feel a sadness at the loss of life without outwardly expressing it.

"What are you getting at?"

"Those are all his ex-girlfriends," he says, pressing his lips together. "There were rumors that he was filming them without their consent. And then sharing those videos with other people."

"How do you know that?"

He shrugs again. "I know everything that happens around here," he answers with a smile.

"Did you get one of those videos?"

"No. As a matter of fact," he leans in to whisper in my ear, "no one at school has my phone number. No one other than you, Petra."

This is all very strange.

"So?" I ask.

He smiles. "No one could've sent it to me anyway. Not that I would've looked at it." He trails his hand down my back, playing with the ends of my hair. "You're the only woman I've ever seen in a state of undress. And I'm not interested in seeing anyone else."

I don't know how to reply. Mostly because . . . how did this conversation shift *to this*? We were talking about a tragic incident, and now he's telling me I'm the only woman he's ever seen naked.

Not that I don't appreciate that piece of information, but now is not the time nor the place.

I slap his hand aside.

"Behave," I say in a shushed voice. "Tell me more about those videos. He was sharing them around?"

"Yes." He nods. "It was a well-known thing. And those girls were all victims of it. They asked him repeatedly to delete them, to stop sharing them—but he never did."

He smirks.

"Well, until now. Because he's not capable of sharing anything anymore."

The dichotomy between these two personas of Sin is becoming greater and greater.

The priest finishes the prayer, and the gravediggers begin lowering the coffin into the ground. Due to the extreme disfiguration of the body, they had opted for a closed casket.

As people gather to lay flowers on top of the coffin, I notice the two detectives quietly walking toward me. Sin sees them, too, and places an arm across my waist, keeping me at his side.

"Miss Valentine."

"Detectives." I nod in greeting.

"We would like to hold another interview with you. Are you available in the next few days?"

"An interview? About what?" Sin is the one who asks the question.

"And you are?"

"Sinclair Arnoult. I'm Petra's boyfriend."

"I believe Miss Valentine can speak for herself." The detective stares him down.

"No, he is right. Why would you want me to come in for an interview?"

"Of course—to discuss the passing of your classmate."

Sin interjects again. "So you're interviewing all of his classmates?"

"No."

"Then why Petra? She didn't have a close relationship with François. She barely knew him."

"I'm speaking with Miss Valentine, not with you, Mr. Arnoult."

"It's as he said," I reply. "I didn't know François very well, so I'm not sure what you'd like me to say, other than that this is a tragic loss."

"How does Monday at 8 a.m. sound for you? We can meet at the school, or if you'd prefer, at our office."

"She'll be at the school," Sin replies.

The detectives give him a harsh look before nodding and moving along.

I turn to him in confusion. "Why would they want to speak with me again?"

"It's probably just a routine interview, Petra. I'll be there with you."

"I don't think they'll want you present."

"Tough luck. I *am* going to be present. I'm not letting you walk into the lion's den alone."

"All right. I suppose that would help. They've been awfully hostile toward me. I don't know how they can think I had something to do with it. Just because I was on speaking terms with Edwin and Harry. But with François? It's just odd."

"It is," he agrees.

Soon it's our turn to place a flower on top of his coffin, and after both Sin and I do it, we turn around and come face-to-face with Daphne.

Arms crossed over her chest, she stares us down with the typical disdain one would expect from her.

"What are you doing here?" she demands in a loud, high-pitched voice.

"Paying our respects to a classmate," Sin replies in a cold voice.

"He wouldn't have wanted you here," she says pointedly, almost jabbing her finger in my chest.

I grab her hand none too gently and twist.

"Great to hear you can communicate with the dead now, Daph." I roll my eyes. "Because if we're talking about what he would have wanted, I think he would have asked for a little more effort from you. You could have at least bought some eye drops to pretend you're actually crying."

"You bitch . . ." she adds through clenched teeth.

"Sin, would you mind clearing the way for me? I'm not in the mood for an obstacle course," I sneer.

His eyes twinkle mischievously as he more or less shoves Daphne to the side to make room for me to walk.

"A piece of advice, Daphne," I say as I stop a couple feet away from her. "You might want to be on your best behavior in case you're next."

Gasps fly all around me.

"Did you just threaten me?"

"Threat? Oh, no, it was just a friendly tip."

With that, I signal for Sin to keep moving.

But before I can take another step, Daphne reaches for me, her hands going for my hair. I can't say whether I expected that to happen or if my reflexes are just that good, but I half-turn at the right moment. Grabbing her hands before she can grab me, I push her backward.

She wobbles back, her heels catching on a pebble. Her arms begin to flap in an effort to keep her balance and not fall. She's almost recovering, careening forward.

But something inside me—something vengeful and insidious—doesn't want her to get off so easily.

I blow air toward her, muttering under my breath, "Fall."

Eyes wide, body out of control, she stumbles farther backward until a loud thud echoes in the stillness of the cemetery.

Everyone around us gasps in shock.

There, at the bottom of the ditch, and on top of the shiny black coffin, Daphne lies still, her clothes and hair covered in mud.

She's still, unmoving, for moments on end.

"You fucking bitch!" she eventually cries out.

I let out a sigh of relief. She's alive.

Sin takes my arm and leads me away from the commotion. Yet as we put distance between us and Daphne's angry cries, I keep asking myself: *Where did that malice come from*?

CHAPTER SIXTY-SIX

PETRA

Present Day

With my parents gone for the next couple of days, Sin suggests we spend some time at the bunker.

My initial instinct is to say no—because, at this point, I don't know what to think about him anymore. But then I reconsider. This might be the perfect opportunity to search for more clues, and the bunker is the best place to start.

The most urgent thing is to find out whether Sin really is the one who killed the students. Even though I'm almost certain he's the killer, I still have no solid proof.

Once we arrive at the bunker, Sin excuses himself, saying he wants to stop by his house to grab some extra clothes and groceries for the next couple of days.

I nod and encourage him to go, assuring him everything will be fine—because with him gone, I'll finally have the freedom to explore on my own and hopefully uncover something useful.

As soon as he leaves, I return to the map of connections I made the day before, trying again to figure out a possible motive for the murders.

Why would he kill those students?

I've already come to the conclusion that Sin is immortal. And that must mean—at some point—he sold his soul, right?

But then, that theory starts to unravel. If he's been alive for over a hundred years, why would he still need to kill?

Unless . . . maybe in order to maintain his immortality, he has to continue committing these atrocities?

It's the only explanation that makes sense, at least for now.

With a frustrated sigh, I slip on my shoes and head out of the bunker, making my way deeper into the tunnels. Maybe another look at the wall paintings will reveal something I missed. There's also the lingering mystery of who painted them in the first place.

It takes me a few wrong turns before I finally find the tunnel that leads toward the school rather than the cemetery. It's surreal to realize this whole underground system connects the entire city, and yet nobody seems to know it exists.

Well, nobody except Sin.

Armed with the flashlight on my phone, I walk deeper into the shadowed corridors. The walls are slick and speckled with mold. Everything smells musty and damp. The whole atmosphere feels like something out of a horror movie.

But I push the fear aside. I have to.

Somewhere in here, there has to be a clue. Something to point me in the right direction.

I keep walking for what feels like forever. Until eventually, I have no idea where I am anymore. There's nothing but darkness ahead of me and the smell of cold, rotting stone.

The deeper I go into the tunnel, the colder it gets—so cold I can see my breath fog up the beam of light coming from my phone. I walk for what feels like forever, surrounded only by silence and the echo of my footsteps.

Then, out of nowhere, a loud screech erupts ahead of me. Before I can react, a swarm of bats rushes straight at my face.

"Ah!" I scream, stumbling backward and falling hard onto the damp floor.

It takes a moment to catch my breath and gather my thoughts. My chest is heaving. My heart's racing. But when I glance around, I realize the bats are gone. They've moved on—none of them are around me, and more importantly, not *on* me.

The last thing I need is to get bitten and contract rabies or some other horror my panic-fueled brain keeps conjuring up. I close my eyes, trying to breathe through it.

Come on, Petra. You can do this, I encourage myself.

I grab my phone, get back on my feet, and raise the flashlight in front of me. One step at a time.

A few minutes later, something catches my eye—bits of color breaking through the monotony of moss-covered stone. I quicken my pace until I'm standing in front of another cave painting. But this one I don't recognize.

"What?" I whisper, sweeping the light across it.

A pool of vivid red blood is painted on the ground, with severed body parts scattered within it. Head. Hands. Feet cut clean at the ankles.

Is this supposed to be François?

It doesn't match exactly. In the real murder, his entire body had been mutilated. This seems more focused on the disembodiment of the victim. Could this be a *different* murder? One that hasn't happened yet?

As I scan the wall further, I notice another painting—this one even more disturbing. A wraith-like figure bleeds from every orifice. A torrent of blood pours from it, flowing like a river until it merges with the red puddle in the first scene.

Two deaths, one river of blood.

Are they connected? Are these two victims somehow linked?

I move to another part of the wall, where yet another painting waits. This one is different. It's not a depiction of death; it's of someone kneeling in prayer.

The figure is shadowy, bowed before what appears to be an altar. And atop the altar is the same demon-like creature I've seen before.

Worship. Devotion. Sacrifice.

It almost looks like this figure is *praying* to the monster.

Is this meant to be Sin?

Is this a record of his deeds? Or a prophecy of what's to come?

I reach forward and press my fingers to the cold, damp wall. The paint, if it even is paint, is unlike anything I've ever seen. Whatever was used, it's immune to water, humidity, and even touch.

I scratch at one of the boldest lines with my fingernail—nothing comes off. I know my pigments, even historical ones, and nothing should be this *permanent*. Not in this environment.

It shouldn't have survived this long.

I push harder, leaning into the wall—and suddenly, there's a soft *click*.

Then a low, grinding sound starts, like ancient stone shifting. I stumble back just in time to see part of the wall begin to move. Slowly, two slabs of stone shift and roll apart, revealing a narrow opening.

There's something hidden behind the painting.

A little spooked, but already too far in to back out, I squeeze through the narrow gap in the stone and step into what appears to be a hidden room.

I swallow hard.

This isn't what I expected. But I wanted clues. And this, well, this is a clue.

Waving my phone around for light, I take in the space. It's eerily similar to the room from my dreams—the one where Sin first took me after I wandered into the tunnel. The layout is the same: a small bed, a single table, and little else.

But this isn't the same place. It's different.

Everything is covered in dust and cobwebs. The air is thick with neglect. The wood of the bed frame has rotted through in places, and at the first flash of light, cockroaches skitter across the floorboards.

I choke down a wave of revulsion and take a careful step inside. Who lived here? The walls are bare—no paintings, no carvings. Just stone and silence. It's a modest space, stark, empty. Who would live like this, underground?

The mattress is damp and rotting, the smell of mold so strong it hits the back of my throat. I gag, turning my attention to the table instead.

There's a single drawer.

I pull it open.

More bugs. Termites, beetles—tiny creatures that make my skin crawl—but nothing else.

Whoever lived here either owned nothing or took everything with them when they left. I'm about to turn around and leave, already queasy from the mold and the crawling things, when the beam of my flashlight catches a glint of something beneath the bed.

I freeze.

Of course it's under the bed. Just like in every childhood nightmare. My brain flickers back to all the sleepless nights I once spent convinced there was something monstrous hiding beneath me.

And now, in a world where monsters *do* exist, I'm kneeling on a dirty, infested floor, about to see what lies beneath an abandoned bed in a hidden tunnel.

Come on, Petra. I steel myself, pushing through the nausea, and crouch down, aiming the flashlight underneath.

Not a monster. Though in some ways, it might have been simpler if it were.

It's a suitcase. A very old one.

I reach for the wooden handle and pull it out. It's heavy, worn. The design is old—Georgian, maybe even older. I can't date it exactly, but it certainly predates the Victorian era. I search for a lock and, surprisingly, it pops open with ease.

With slow, deliberate movements, I lift the lid, dreading what I might find and yet driven by a hunger to *know*.

To my surprise, the contents inside are almost perfectly preserved. Despite the humidity of the room, the damp, and the decay everywhere else, the suitcase seems untouched. Untouched by time. Untouched by nature.

I wedge my phone between the lid and the case, letting the light shine inside so I can sort through its contents with both hands.

There isn't much.

The first item is a folded piece of dark fabric. I turn it over in my hands, confused—until the light catches on the collar.

A nun's habit.

Next, a heavy silver cross. A worn Bible with yellowed, crinkled pages. A rosary.

And at the bottom, a journal.

With these tangible clues in my hands, I realize two things.

One: This belonged to a nun.

Two: There's no way these items are from the 1800s.

No—scratch that. There's no way they're from the *Victorian* era.

The Bible alone proves it. The quality of the binding, the richness of the pages—this wasn't made with cheap pulp paper like most nineteenth-century editions. This was carefully crafted to last.

And the journal . . . the journal feels just as old.

I carefully open the journal to its first page. The date jumps out at me: 1760.

I blink. Shock settles in. I expected something old, yes, but not *this* old. This is more than a hundred years before the first murders began.

So what is this journal doing here?

Why is there a secret room in these tunnels with belongings from someone who lived over 250 years ago? Are the tunnels really that ancient?

Before I can process it further, a loud noise from outside startles me, and the journal slips from my hands. Footsteps echo through the tunnel.

Heart pounding, I snatch up the journal and tuck it under my shirt.

I shut the suitcase and slide it back beneath the bed, then hurry out of the room.

Pressing both palms to the wall, I push against the stone. After a few tense seconds, the hidden door seals itself shut.

The footsteps grow louder.

"Who's there?" I call out, tone wavering from my nerves.

"Petra?" Sin's voice echoes back. "Where are you?"

Making sure the journal is still hidden, I walk toward him.

"What were you doing here?" he asks, his face tight with concern.

"I was just wandering around. Curious if there was anything else hidden down here."

"You shouldn't be alone. It could be dangerous."

"What kind of danger?" I ask.

He only shrugs. "You never know. Come on," he says with a smile, "I brought food. You must be starving."

I nod and follow him back into the bunker.

The table is already set. While he's distracted arranging things, I slip the journal behind the sofa cushion, between the frame and the armrest. Then I give him a quick smile and start eating.

He tells me he swung by his house, let his parents know he'd be staying at a friend's for a while, and that they weren't worried. He also called *my* parents to reassure them he'd take care of me.

"You have their number?" I ask, surprised.

"Of course I do, silly. It was the first thing I did after we talked. I needed an emergency contact—you never know."

It's strange. Or maybe it's just me, seeing everything he does as strange.

After we finish eating, he tosses the containers and starts tidying up. He's in a surprisingly good mood. Maybe that's why I decide to finally bring it up.

"Sin, can I show you something?" I ask warily.

"Sure," he says.

I take his hand and lead him to the study I found yesterday. This time, the door isn't locked. It opens easily.

"Whoa," he says, stepping inside. "I didn't know this room was here."

"I found it the other day," I tell him.

"This is cool," he says, glancing around.

"Come here. There's something I want to show you."

I bring him to the stack of documents and slowly begin laying them out. Photographs. Files.

"What's all this?" he asks, frowning.

"Look at this one." I hand him the photo of Arnoult and Sin Kimaris. "This man—it looks like you."

He takes it, eyes narrowing as he inspects it. "You're right. It *does* look like me."

"Why do you think that is?"

He shrugs. "Maybe he's an ancestor?"

"Look at the back. It says the man on the left is Arnoult the First. The one next to him is Kimaris."

He flinches slightly at the name.

"So?"

"What do you mean, *so*? The man on the left is your ancestor. The one next to him—the one who looks exactly like you—is not. You don't think that's strange?"

"Maybe I just have a historical doppelgänger." He laughs nervously. "Is that what you wanted to show me?"

"No," I say. "Sin . . . tell me the truth."

"What truth?" he says, voice tightening. "I don't know what you're talking about."

I show him another photo, this time with the entire Theology Department. "Look again. Arnoult the First. Sinclair Arnoult. And next to him, Sin Kimaris." I pause. "He has your name. And your face."

He doesn't respond.

"Don't you think that's strange?"

"Petra . . ."

"And look at these." I shuffle through old newspaper clippings. "All these murders. Don't they mean anything to you?"

"What are you trying to say?"

I meet his gaze, my voice quiet but steady. "Tell me the truth, Sin. Is this you?"

He looks at me, eyes unreadable. There's something there, something I can't quite place.

"You've been reading too many paranormal novels," he says lightly. "How could it be me? This photo is over a hundred years old."

"That's exactly why I find it weird," I say. "This isn't just someone who looks like you. It *is* you."

"Petra, no."

"Sin, please. Tell me."

"I don't know what you want me to say. It's someone who looks like me, but I was born nineteen years ago. Not in the nineteenth century."

"You're lying."

"I'm not."

"You are. I *know* you are."

"Maybe you've been overthinking things—between the funeral, the detectives, all of it. Of course, you're stressed. And wandering through the tunnels . . . it's madness."

"Is it?" I whisper. "Because I've *dreamed* of this. Of Kimaris. Of this place. Of the murders."

He sighs. "Petra . . ."

"What?" I snap.

"I'm worried about you. Come on, you should rest."

"You're not listening—"

"Please."

Frustrated, I storm out of the study. I won't get anything out of him. Not tonight. Even with the evidence—*that* photograph—he won't admit anything.

So how do I find out the truth?

The answer comes to me then.

The only way to understand the past is to *see* it. To *dream* it.

Maybe, in some twisted way, Sin is right. What I need to do is sleep. Sleep, and dream. See how past-life Sin became *this* Sin.

He calls my name behind me, but I ignore him.

I change into clean pajamas and get into bed. Yet even as I close my eyes, a thought keeps needling at me: the journal. The nun's habit. The silver cross.

So I pull out my phone and search for the history of St. Anselm Hall.

Founded in the nineteenth century . . . but before that?

I scroll down. There, a small entry on the university's Wikipedia page. Built on top of an old convent. The land had been gifted to the state by the church.

Just then, Sin slides into bed beside me.

"I'm sorry," he whispers. "I behaved badly."

I tuck my phone under my pillow. "You did. You implied there's something wrong with me."

"No. It's not you. It's me."

I turn to face him. "Then tell me, Sin. What's going on?"

"I can't. Not yet."

"Why?"

"Because it's not my story to tell. Not fully. But when you need to know . . . you'll know."

He leans in and kisses my brow.

"Sleep, my darling. Sleep. Know that you're safe with me. And that no matter what you discover, no matter what happened in the past, I love you. I have always loved you. I always will."

His words are ominous.

But still, my eyelids grow heavy. My body relaxes.

And I sleep.

CHAPTER SIXTY-SEVEN

PETRA

The Past

As I'm getting ready to retire for the night, one of our servants intercepts me on the staircase.

"This came for you, Miss."

I frown as I take in the nondescript brown package. "Who is it from?"

"It is from the Snowden House, Miss," she replies.

"But . . . I'm not allowed to receive anything."

"The Master has specifically said that if anything comes from the Snowden House, you may receive it."

Of course, Father would deem that to be acceptable; he is still planning to sell me to that odious man, after all.

Pursing my lips, I stare at the package. On the one hand, I don't want anything to do with Snowden, but on the other . . . I am far too curious to refuse it.

"Thank you."

With the small package in my hand, I go to my room, oddly curious to see what hides inside. If it's something lewd or inappropriate, then that's all the more reason to encourage Sin to dispatch him in a painful way.

Closing the door behind me, I go to my desk and light my candle. I tear through the packaging, and I'm surprised to see . . . a Bible?

I frown. That is *not* something Snowden would send me. Not only is he the furthest thing from a man of God, but I doubt the man has ever held a Bible in his hands without burning.

I almost dismiss it as a bad joke, but for some reason, I end up rifling through the pages of the book.

There is a natural bend to the spine, and as I reach the midway of the book, I find a small piece of paper inside.

Petra,

You said you could help me leave my house. Does your offer still stand? I fear my father has caught wind of my relationship with Sinclair, and I don't know what he's capable of. I'm scared for myself, for my child, and for my beloved Sinclair.

If you meant what you said, I can meet you tomorrow night outside the south gates of my house.

Thank you.
Leah

I stare at the note for moments on end. For Leah to have done this, to reach out to me for help when she was so hesitant before, speaks volumes. She must truly think she has no other recourse, and knowing what I do about Snowden, I'm terrified for her.

I wait until nightfall, when the entire house has gone to sleep, before opening my window. One moment I'm alone, the next, Sin is behind me.

"You startled me," I gasp aloud.

He smiles that beguiling smile of his and opens his arms for me to nestle within his embrace.

"I thought night would not come soon enough. I missed you, sweet Petra."

"I missed you, too." I sigh dreamily against him, letting his warmth seep through me. We stay like that for what feels like an eternity, neither of us wanting to take the first step and break apart.

With great difficulty, I pull back.

"We need to talk."

His features immediately contort with worry.

I show him the note from Leah, and his lips flatten into a thin line.

"I will speak with my mentor. We will go to her house tomorrow night."

"I'm coming with you," I declare.

He raises a brow at me, and I can tell he's ready to challenge me.

"She asked *me* to help. I must be there. That way, she will be more at ease."

He still doesn't speak, merely staring me down as if that would make me reconsider.

"I am coming, Sin."

He exhales roughly. "All right."

I reward him with a warm smile.

"But that is tomorrow, not tonight. Come here, sweet thing, let me feel you."

Before he can mention it, I shrug my clothes off and move closer to him. His own clothes vanish at some point, and we end up together on the bed between the tangled sheets.

IT'S CLOSE TO midnight when Sin comes to get me from my home.

"Close your eyes," he whispers as he envelops me in his shadows.

Dizziness overtakes me as everything around me spins. When I next open my eyes, we're at the gates of the Snowden estate.

There is another man there, one I have not seen before. It's dark out, so I cannot entirely make out his features save for the thickly rimmed glasses he's wearing.

"Petra, meet my mentor."

"You're Arnoult?" I blurt out.

He inclines his head.

"Pleased to meet the woman of Sin's heart."

I blush at that mention. "Is that how you described me?" I whisper to Sin.

He nods proudly. "Although I should have been more precise: You are *my* heart."

"You may continue your sweet talk after we have saved my *own* heart," Arnoult mentions dryly.

As we wait for the clock to strike midnight, the designated meeting time, I can't help but keep glancing at Arnoult, trying to make sense of it all. He looks to be in his mid-to-late thirties, which already puts me on edge, because Leah is probably half his age.

Sin notices my scrutiny and comes closer. "Are you all right? Do you want to go?"

"No. No, I'm fine. I want to see Leah safe."

"Okay. But if anything happens, know that I'm taking you away from here."

"Sin, I'll be fine," I assure him.

He follows my line of sight toward his mentor.

"How old is he?"

"I'm thirty-six, Miss," Arnoult answers.

Right. Double Leah's age. But at least he's not pushing fifty like Snowden.

"Isn't it a bit of an age difference between you and Leah? How did you two even meet?" I can't help but ask.

His brows go up, and it's a wonder I can even see them behind those thickly rimmed glasses.

Sin's hand brushes my waist, a light touch. Maybe a signal for me to stop pressing. But I continue.

"Did you take advantage of her?" I ask him squarely.

"What? Me? Never," he says vehemently. "Do you think I *wanted* to fall in love with a girl half my age? At first, it was just stolen glances and furtive smiles. But eventually we started talking when no one was watching. I would come to her home to talk with her father, and before I left, she would always give me a little treat for the road, she'd say. But those small gestures became all I could look forward to."

He looks at Sin. "If you doubt my intentions, ask your lover. He knows exactly how I feel about Leah. That I would never hurt her."

"You're hurting her right now. Don't you realize? You and her father are enemies. You got her pregnant while she's still living with her father. Don't you think that puts her at risk?"

"I . . ." he trails off. "I didn't know about the pregnancy until very recently."

"Doesn't matter. You exposed her to the risk. Do you not realize what these men are capable of—her father, my father? They don't care about who they hurt as long as they fulfill whatever sinister purpose they have in mind. And if Snowden believes that she's valuable to you, don't you think he's going to use that? That he's going to use *her* to get to you?"

"Petra, let's not do this now," Sin whispers.

"You're right. We can talk about this later—after Leah is safe. But don't think for a moment that I'm not watching you. I don't care what your relationship is with Sin. I don't care how much he esteems you. Leah is a young girl. A young, impressionable girl who is currently in danger. And half of it is your fault."

He has no reply to that. He just stares at me.

I turn my back to him, not wanting to engage further. On the one hand, I can empathize with the fact that they're two star-crossed lovers, defying all odds to be together, including age-related odds. But at the same time, I don't know what the circumstances of their relationship are.

And Leah, poor girl . . . whenever I saw her, she was always so moody, so sad and depressed. I can't be sure he didn't take advantage of that, can I?

I expect Sin to chastise me for my harsh words toward his mentor, but instead, I catch him smiling at me.

"You're amazing, you know that?"

"Hmm?"

"This is why I love you—because you fight for what you think is right."

"You're not angry that I'm fighting with your mentor?"

He shrugs. "My mentor and I have our own relationship. I don't need you to have the same views about him, especially in this situation." He pauses. "And just for the record," he adds a little louder, "I did not agree with the relationship either. I told him she was too young."

Arnoult shakes his head and sighs in exasperation.

"Alas, this is neither the time nor the place for this," Sin then says. He pulls out his pocket watch and watches the hands move slowly into place. "Five more minutes."

So, we wait.

And then the clock strikes twelve. Midnight.

There's no sign of Leah.

Not only that—but there's no sound coming from the house.

Nothing.

"I should go after her," Arnoult says.

"No," Sin interrupts. "I'll go. You stay here with Petra. It's better if I'm in and out, taking her out of there without alerting anyone. And it's especially better if no one sees you."

Arnoult presses his lips together. "You're right. Thank you."

Just as Sin is about to head inside the house in search of Leah, footsteps echo from that direction. There's a thumping on the ground, a rustling of leaves.

"Someone's coming," Sin whispers.

The sounds grow louder and closer.

The steps become more frantic until a lone figure swishes through the night. I catch a flash of blue muslin against the stark darkness of the environment.

"Sin . . . there she is."

She comes into view, stopping just as she reaches the gate.

Without a word, Sin uses his shadows to teleport to the other side of the gate, grabbing her and moving her seamlessly to our side.

The moment she sees Arnoult, her expression transforms into one of pure joy, and for a brief moment, I forget my complaints from before as I watch her run into his arms, sobbing with happiness and relief.

Arnoult hugs her tightly to his chest, kissing the top of her hair, her cheeks, and then her mouth.

"You're safe. You're with me," he whispers.

"I can't believe you're here, too. I didn't think I would ever see you again."

"Ah, my love, nothing would stop me from coming for you. I told you, I will *always* come for you."

Tears flow down her cheeks.

"I love you," she murmurs in a soft voice.

"I love you, too. So damn much. Now we can be together. The two of us and . . ." he trails off as he places his hand on her stomach. "And our baby." He takes a deep breath. "I can't believe we made a baby," he whispers.

"We did," she replies. "We're going to be a family."

They continue to hold each other tightly. Despite my reservations about Arnoult, he seems to really care about her. I suppose that is enough for me—for now.

As they break apart, Leah turns to me, her eyes misty. "Thank you, Petra. Thank you for everything," she murmurs in a low, broken voice.

"Of course. I told you I would help. I just want to see you happy, Leah."

She smiles and glances at Arnoult. "I will be now. That I vow to you. He's all I need to be happy."

The sight of the two lovers, so clearly in love, warms my heart and, in turn, makes *me* happy.

"We should leave," Sin says, but no sooner does he speak than a low, malevolent laughter reverberates through the stillness of the night.

We all freeze in place.

A slow clap follows, then another bout of laughter.

"Thank you, my dear Leah, for finally bringing me face-to-face with this snake," Snowden reveals, stepping forward.

We watch, stunned.

Had he been here the entire time?

No. That's not possible . . . is it?

Was this all a ruse? Her note? Was it all a trap?

Arnoult's expression is one of shock. Leah's is one of disbelief. Whatever this is, I don't think it's of her doing.

The gates swing open, and Snowden casually struts toward us. Behind him trails a shadowy figure.

My breath leaves my body as I realize who it is.

The creature. The undead creature.

Arnoult pushes Leah behind him, ready to protect her with his body.

"So naughty of you to get my daughter pregnant, Sinclair. That's not what old friends do, is it?"

"Sin, take Leah and Petra and get out of here. This is between me and Snowden."

"No, no," Snowden replies in a singsong voice. "I'm afraid I can't let you do that. You're not going *anywhere* with my property."

His gaze goes from Leah to me, implying we both belong to him.

He is insane!

"I should have realized there was something amiss with you, Petra. Your presence always gave me a headache."

"I'm glad," I grumble under my breath.

"You're not the docile little thing your father advertised. Too bad. I suppose I shall have to recommence my search for another bride. After I get rid of you, of course."

"You really think you're going to get away with it?" Sin challenges, brow raised. "Without Arnoult, you are nothing."

"Perhaps. But I still have *this*," he says as he holds up his hand, and the walking corpse moves next to him.

Her eyes are dead, empty. She's just a vessel for violence.

Sin smiles. "I've always loved a good challenge."

He urges me to get back while he takes off his coat, folding it and placing it in my arms. "Take care of this for me. It's a rather rare model," he adds with a wink.

A wink?

I stare in shock at him. Does he think this is a game?

"Sin . . ."

"Ah, I see now who you are," Snowden laughs. "That odd one, what was your name? Kimar something." He wrinkles his nose in disgust. "Bad energy, both of you."

Sin chuckles. "As if you could recognize *any* type of energy."

Snowden reddens in anger; it seems this is a sore spot.

"I will deal with you later. But first..." He gives Sin a harsh look before turning to Leah and Arnoult. He casually checks his pocket watch and... waits?

I frown. The others seem just as confused about what's going on.

It's not until...

"S-Sinclair," Leah speaks in a low, trembling voice. "S-something is w-w-wrong."

"What? What are you talking about?" he asks, his voice full of concern.

Snowden, meanwhile, continues to smirk as he watches the unfolding scene.

"I—" Leah starts, but on the next breath, she starts coughing blood. She wraps her arms around her abdomen as she continues to throw up a brownish-red liquid.

"What did you do?" Arnoult demands. He's holding tightly onto Leah, but even in the dim lighting coming from a faraway streetlight, I can see her paleness.

"No blood of mine will mingle with yours," Snowden spits out, malice dripping from his words.

"You... You... No..." Arnoult mutters, now utterly panicked as he crouches next to Leah on the grass. She can no longer speak. Every breath is labored and accompanied by bouts of bloody cough.

"You poisoned your own daughter?" I ask in shock.

Snowden shrugs. "She brought this onto herself for dallying with that devil. Now, she will suffer the consequences. And you—" he glances at Arnoult— "you will suffer all the same knowing it's because of *you* that she died."

"Leah, please," Arnoult tries to get her to react, but it's too late.

Her entire body has gone slack, her eyes empty.

I press my hand to my mouth in shock. She falls against Arnoult's chest like a lifeless doll. She's dead. Her own father killed her.

"Now that that's out of the way, I believe you and I have some unfinished business, Arnoult," Snowden adds nonchalantly.

CHAPTER SIXTY-EIGHT

PETRA

The Past

Arnoult is still for moments on end, cradling Leah's head, tears streaming down his cheeks. A loud, earth-shattering wail erupts from him before he carefully lays her down and directs his attention toward Snowden.

"How could you? She was your daughter!" he snarls in anguish.

"And she went and got pregnant with your child. I daresay she is just a casualty. The real target was your unborn child," Snowden scoffs.

"I cannot believe there was a time I called you a friend. You . . ."

Arnoult launches himself at Snowden, pulling a hidden knife from his boot and brandishing it toward Leah's killer. Snowden doesn't seem surprised; in fact, he looks like he was expecting it. Before Arnoult can reach him, Snowden withdraws a pistol from his vest and takes aim.

"No!" I yell, just as Sin uses his shadows to teleport in front of Arnoult, opening a shadow-like void for the bullet to pass through—redirecting it so it doesn't strike his mentor. Snowden stares in disbelief.

"You never said he was capable of that," he mutters with skepticism. He's clearly shocked, but still exudes that same smug self-assurance, convinced he's going to win. "My love, finish that man for me, will you?" he murmurs sweetly to the corpse beside him.

The creature wobbles from side to side, barely balanced on rotting legs. Her flesh is tinged yellow and green with decay. One eye is completely gone, and the other is half-eaten. Her cheeks are sunken—partially consumed by maggots now crawling into the bone.

She walks toward Sin with mechanical movements, ready to attack.

Sin teleports behind her, grabs her neck, and snaps it. She drops like dead weight. But no sooner does she fall than she rises again.

I remember what Sin told me: No matter what you do, she will rise again. The only way to end her is to destroy her maker.

Yet there's something else. Each time Sin kills her, she comes back stronger. Faster. The first time, she could barely stand.

Now, her spine is straight, and her steps are certain as she charges toward him.

"Be careful!" I call out, fear rising in my throat.

"Don't worry about me, Petra," he shouts back. "I can handle this. Trust me."

"Yes, but—"

"Trust me," he repeats, punching through the creature's gut, his fist emerging through her back. I turn away, revolted by the grotesque sight. It's not just disturbing—it's inhuman.

Meanwhile, Snowden is closing in on Arnoult, a smirk on his face. He thinks he's already won. He's killed his own daughter; who knows what else he's capable of?

He raises the gun again, aiming at Arnoult. But his arrogance won't let him act without delivering a final line.

"You cost me everything. And now you'll pay."

I spot a second knife concealed behind Arnoult's back. He wields it deftly, keeping it hidden.

Just as Snowden squeezes the trigger, Arnoult throws the blade—it hits Snowden in the upper arm.

The gun falls to the ground. Snowden groans in pain.

"You coward!" Arnoult growls. "How could you poison your own daughter? You'll pay for this!"

He charges, grabbing the knife still lodged in Snowden's arm.

First, he pushes it deeper to cause more pain, then tries to yank it free. Snowden counters, slamming his other arm down on Arnoult's grip and shoving him away.

I watch from behind, caught between two battles.

On one side, Arnoult and Snowden are locked in hand-to-hand combat. They fall to the ground, rolling, grappling, each trying to seize the knife. It's a blur of limbs and fury. I can't even tell who's winning—until someone is stabbed. But who?

On the other side, Sin continues his fight with the undead creature. There are holes punched through her body—one in her chest, one in her lower stomach, another through her cheek.

I can tell he's trying to destroy her brain, trying to find a weakness. But she's not like other beings. She has no heart. The gaping cavity in her chest proves it. No brain that functions.

She's just a weapon. A body that moves. Obeys. Kills.

My heart hammers in my chest. Sin is covered in scratches and bite marks. His shirt is shredded, blood soaking through the fabric.

"Sin," I whisper. "Please be okay."

Somehow, he hears me.

But the moment his eyes flick to mine, the creature strikes. She mimics his earlier move, punching toward his chest and digging her claws into his skin.

"No!" I scream.

But just in time, Sin teleports again—vanishing before she can do more harm. He reappears behind her and immobilizes her, though he's clearly in pain. His face is pale, blood still trickling from his wounds. But he pushes through it.

"You have to kill him! Kill Snowden, or the creature cannot die!"

The only response from Arnoult is a groan of pain, some guttural, unintelligible sound.

"The only ones dying tonight . . ." Snowden growls, gritting his teeth, "are you."

He straddles Arnoult, who is lying on his back in the grass, and raises the knife high, gaining momentum to stab him in the heart.

Sin notices and quickly teleports to help him, but just as he reaches Arnoult's side, the creature tackles him to the ground. They both roll onto the grass and the knife rolls away.

Arnoult is still pinned under Snowden's body, and both of them search through the grass for the knife.

Once again, Snowden finds it first. Arnoult grabs for it, trying to wrest it away, but the blade is now lodged between their two bodies. Snowden pushes it toward Arnoult's chest while Arnoult desperately tries to stop it from breaking his skin.

Sin struggles to get away from the creature long enough to help his mentor, but by now, she's too fast. She won't give him any opening—any window to intervene.

As I watch, heart pounding, wondering whether Snowden will finally plunge the knife into Arnoult's chest, something catches my eye—a glint of light in the grass just a few feet away from me.

The gun.

It's the same one from before.

I move in slow, methodical steps and pick it up with trembling hands. Just as the tip of the blade breaks Arnoult's skin and blood seeps through his shirt, I raise the gun and aim it at Snowden.

I've never fired a gun before. I've never even held one. But I understand how it works. I think I can do this.

In that moment, I don't hesitate. Maybe I should have stopped to consider what it means to take a life to save another.

But the truth is, I don't care about Arnoult. I don't care about Snowden.

I only care about my Sin.

And if the only way to make that creature stop hurting him is to kill Snowden, then that's exactly what I'll do.

I swallow hard, eyes fixed on my target. My fingers find the cold trigger.

I fire.

The first bullet strikes him in the arm, but I'm already committed.

I take a step forward, then another step, reloading as I go.

Snowden turns to look at me, his face a mask of shock. While he was so focused on the man, he forgot about the girl he called docile.

I shoot again.

This time, the bullet hits his chest. He teeters off Arnoult and collapses in the grass, groaning.

I take another step forward, reload once more.

When I reach him, when I'm standing right over him, I aim at his head.

The only way Sin is safe is if this man dies.

I shoot.

The force of it knocks me back. The bullet enters Snowden's skull and shatters it from within—brain matter, bone fragments, blood—all scattered in the grass. Arnoult stares at me in shock from the sidelines.

I throw the gun aside and turn to find Sin.

A loud, unnatural scream splits the air.

The creature stumbles backward. Her entire body goes slack—frozen in place. Only her mouth remains open, her voice shrieking like a siren, like an alarm echoing in the still night.

She screams and screams until her skin starts to melt off her bones.

Her bones are next, shattering under my very gaze . . . until there's nothing left but ash. Even that is eventually swept away in the wind.

I blink. Adrenaline still floods my veins. I can't fully process what I've just seen—or what I've done.

All I know is that I need Sin to be okay.

I run to him.

He's injured—his chest torn with claw marks, blood seeping from his wounds.

"Sin," I whisper, "please tell me you're okay. Please."

"Petra . . . you . . . you killed him," he murmurs.

"I did," I whisper, nodding. Then I frown. "Did I?"

He pulls me into his arms as I glance back at Snowden's ruined skull.

Arnoult slowly rises to his feet and stumbles toward where Leah's body lies. He's wounded, too, but I know the pain in his heart is far deeper than anything physical. He doesn't look at us. He just pulls her into his arms and mourns in silence.

I stand frozen, still staring at the bloody mess on the grass. "Snowden . . . I did that," I say again, stunned.

"Are you all right?" Sin asks softly.

I look at him, unable to answer. I don't know what to feel, if I *should* feel anything.

"I will be," I eventually say.

He kisses the top of my head, and I note the strain in his features. He's in pain, and he's asking *me* if I'm all right.

"We need to tend to your injuries."

"Not now." He shakes his head. "First, we must take care of the bodies."

"What?"

"We can't leave them here to be found by constables."

With slow, tentative steps, he walks toward Arnoult.

"Sinclair . . ."

"Don't ask me that. Don't ask me to leave her."

"You *must*."

"I can't." He holds her tighter in his arms. His voice is broken and rough. "How can she be gone . . ." he whispers. "She was fine just moments ago. Both her and the baby. And now . . ." He breaks into a harsh sob. "They can't be gone."

"Sinclair, I'm sorry for your loss. But we *must* move along."

"No," he states resolutely. Still holding her in his arms, he rises to his feet and starts walking toward the house.

Sin's lips are flattened into a thin line of concern as he nods for me to come to him. He also grabs what's left of Snowden's body and the gun and carries them toward the house.

"Why . . ."

"You will see," he merely answers.

Once we enter the house, there's a trail of blood that leads toward the hallway. We make our way carefully there, and instead of finding other victims of Snowden, we encounter Arnoult holding a bloody knife in his hand.

Leah is carefully seated on a chair. And on the floor, one of the servants is bleeding profusely.

"What the hell, Sinclair?" Sin demands.

"I can't leave her. Not again. I'm taking her with me," he replies mechanically.

"What is this for then?"

Sin dumps the body of Snowden to the ground next to the dead servant.

"You wanted to arrange the scene. Be my guest. I'm leaving," Arnoult adds.

Pocketing his knife, he takes Leah again in his arms and leaves.

Both Sin and I stare at each other in shock.

"Now what?" I whisper.

"We arrange the scene, I suppose."

"Uhm, in case you did not realize, one person is stabbed, and the other is missing the better part of the skull. No matter how much you arrange it, there *will* be concerns."

"Not if they consider it a murder-suicide."

"Sin. He's missing his brain!" I point out, trying to forget I was the one who did that damage in the first place.

He purses his lips, then sighs. "A little harder to achieve but not impossible."

"What do you want to do?"

He disappears in the blink of an eye, then appears with a canister. The smell reaches me immediately—kerosene.

"A fire it is, I suppose." He doesn't seem too thrilled at the prospect.

"And how will anyone infer that it was a murder-suicide from a fire?" I roll my eyes at him.

"The butler. He must be still sleeping. I will find him."

"And—"

"Pay him." He shrugs.

Then he disappears again. I don't see him for minutes on end while he is no doubt bribing the butler and dousing the house in kerosene.

I let out a weary sigh. I am tired, and angry, and as I look down at the dead bodies, a little disgusted.

I'm not entirely sure if I should be angry *about* killing Snowden—he deserved it more than anyone. But Leah's death? She was pregnant!

Sadness fills me to the brim as I remember the short moments she had with Arnoult, how even *I* had been convinced by their romance, despite my reservations.

And now? She's gone. Just like that.

"I'm sorry," I whisper. "I'm sorry I couldn't do more."

Hopefully, wherever she is, she knows she *was* avenged, and that Arnoult will likely carry her memory with him for the rest of his life.

A flash of color enters my sight.

"Oh, you scared me," I burst out when I see Sin has returned.

"The butler needed a little more convincing. He's out of the house now, though. The only thing left is . . ." He looks around. "We should probably move the bodies to a location that makes more sense."

"They'll find charred bodies, Sin."

He shrugs. "It needs to be believable."

"Well, I'm not touching either of them, so go do your thing."

He gives me a charming smile. "I would have never asked you to." He winks.

He carries Snowden first, then the lady servant. I don't ask him where he decided to put them; I don't think I care that much.

When he's back for me, he merely teleports me outside the house before going in one last time. "The fire has to come from within, from Snowden's own lighter."

So I wait for him while he lays the first spark of the fire. When he's finally back, he just nods at me and pulls me into his arms.

"Close your eyes," he whispers before teleporting us to his underground home. "We should probably take a bath," he says. I would have readily agreed if it weren't for his almost slurred speech and pale countenance.

"Sin?" I ask tentatively.

He's still bleeding from the deeper wounds. At this point, I don't even know how many of those are there. It feels as though the creature ripped through his flesh from head to toe.

He sways a little on his feet, at which point I quickly react, shouldering his weight and helping him to the couch.

"I'll be fine."

Except he's not. He's out cold.

CHAPTER SIXTY-NINE

PETRA

The Past

"Sin? Sin, are you all right?" I call out to him, touching his cheeks. He groans in pain, uttering a string of unintelligible words. "I'll take care of you," I whisper.

He doesn't respond. I hop back up and rush to the washroom, grabbing a clean cloth and filling a bowl with water.

Returning to the couch, I rip the shirt off his chest, my heart in my throat as I take in the myriad wounds and scratches.

"You have to be all right," I murmur, dipping the cloth into the water and starting to clean him. Some of the cuts are light and superficial, but the deeper ones bleed heavily, and I'm not sure how to help him.

The water quickly turns a muddy red. I change it and begin again, wiping the blood from his chest with a wince.

"Sin," I whisper, leaning in and cradling his face.

He murmurs something, eyes fluttering open.

"Medicine . . . do you have any medicine?" I ask. "Something I can use for your wounds?"

"The back cabinet," he mutters, barely audible.

I hurry over and open the cabinet he mentioned, finding iodine, bandages, and a few jars—one of which I assume is a salve tincture. I bring them over and, seeing that the deeper wounds are still bleeding, apply pressure with the cloth.

"I think I might need to suture this for you."

He makes a low sound in his throat.

"Do you want me to do that?"

"Do it," he finally says. "There're thread and needles in the art room."

Once more, I dash around the house, looking for anything useful. I find a spool of thread—even though I don't know the first thing about sewing flesh—and a few needles. I choose the thickest, realizing that human skin will be much harder to pierce than fabric. Then I quickly sanitize them.

Back at his side, I dab iodine onto the wounds, cleaning the fresh blood before pinching the two sides of flesh together and trying to thread the needle through. He hisses in pain.

"It hurts, doesn't it?"

"Alcohol," he grumbles. "There's some on the table."

I turn and spot a decanter with two glasses. Grabbing it, I pour a copious amount of alcohol over his wounds, vaguely recalling its disinfectant properties. Then I lift the decanter to his lips and make him drink.

He gulps greedily, coughing as it burns down his throat. When he's finished, he slumps back on the couch.

I get to work again, cleaning the wound.

The blood just keeps coming.

I pull the edges of the flesh together and make my first attempt at a stitch.

As expected, it's incredibly hard to pierce the skin. I assume surgical needles are not only sharper and thicker but also easier to handle. Still, I can't give up.

No matter how hard it is, I have to do this, otherwise he'll keep bleeding.

Biting my lip in concentration, I push the needle through one side of the wound, then the other, and repeat. Thankfully, though deep, the cut isn't long; it only requires six or seven stitches.

I tie off the thread and pour a bit more alcohol over the wound before rubbing on some of the salve from the tincture jar.

I repeat the process on the other four deeper wounds. Some are larger, some smaller, but eventually I manage to stitch all of them, apply the salve, and wrap a bandage tightly around his torso.

There are still some scrapes and scratches on his face, but I'm out of bandages at this point.

I dab alcohol onto them, followed by more salve, hoping it will be enough for now.

His breathing evens out. He's asleep.

I let out a long sigh of relief. At least he's no longer in pain.

Good Lord, what happened tonight?

The weight of everything finally hits me. Everything I saw. Everything I did.

It's too much. I take a long swig of the alcohol.

Ew, I think with a grimace. *This is terrible.* But if it helped Sin manage his pain, maybe it'll help me, too. Maybe it will numb the thoughts, the guilt, the anger . . . because I can't stop thinking—*if I hadn't gone there, would he still have poisoned her? Or was it always meant to happen*?

Was she going to die whether I was there or not?

I take another swig. I'm not used to drinking spirits, and I feel the effects of it quickly—the spinning in my head, the fog settling in my vision.

I rest my head on the sofa next to Sin, taking deep gulps of air.

"It's fine. Everything is fine. We'll be fine," I whisper to myself.

But then, from the corner of my eye, I see something. A shadowy figure, moving too fast to track.

One moment, it's there—the outline of a man. The next, through hooded eyes, I see a presence standing right in front of us.

My body is too sluggish from the alcohol to react. I just sit there and wait as the hairs raise on my skin.

Is this a hallucination? I wonder. I've never been drunk before. I can't tell what's real. Is the alcohol feeding my paranoia?

My limbs feel locked, frozen. I can't move a muscle. I can't even look up; I can only see the lower half of this figure.

It's a man. He stops in front of Sin, crouching slightly, inspecting his wounds.

No matter how hard I try, I can't speak. I want to yell, to scream at him to leave Sin alone, to not touch him—but I'm a prisoner in my own body.

Is this what alcohol does to you? I wonder again as fear grips me.

All I can see is the man's wrist as he splits it open and then leans toward Sin. I don't see exactly what he's doing, but the next time I blink . . . he's gone.

Did I imagine it?

I must have. My body is too exhausted. My mind, even more so.

Before I know it, I fall into a deep sleep.

It's through the haze of slumber that I think I hear two voices arguing around me. I hear the words, but I can't quite grasp them.

"What did you do, Sinclair?"

Is that Sin's voice? I think it is.

"What did you do with the body?" he presses.

"It's safe," the other man answers, who I presume to be Arnoult.

"Safe? She's dead! She needs to be buried."

"Not yet."

"What the hell do you mean, not yet?"

"I won't allow it. She can't be dead. She will *not* die."

"Sinclair, this is going too far. She is already dead. You cannot do anything else for her. Please, for God's sake, don't. Give me the body, and I'll give her a proper burial. Somewhere safe, where you can visit her tomb whenever you want."

"No," the man argues. "I won't do it. She's mine."

"She's *dead,*" Sin repeats.

"In our world, that doesn't mean anything, does it? Nothing truly dies," Arnoult challenges.

Sin sighs.

"What you're trying to tell me now is . . . what? You want to use her body and turn her into a grotesque creature like the one Snowden created? Is that what you're saying? Do you hear it yourself? That was not a person. Her soul is long gone."

"You don't know that."

"Yes, I do. That was a soulless person. A creature. Do you want to defile her body in that manner? Turn her into an undead creature just to satisfy some insidious desire?"

"She would have wanted to be with me," Sinclair answers.

"Not like this."

Somewhere in the back of my head, I think I know what they're talking about. Is Arnoult trying to raise Leah from the dead? But how could that be possible? We've seen what the creature was.

It wasn't a person—it was just a body. No memories. No conscience. Nothing.

"You're going too far, Sinclair. This is not the way. You can still find her again in another life. But this? Don't do this. Don't put a blemish on your soul. That, more than anything, is going to stop you from finding her again."

"And how would you know that?"

"I know. No, I know far too well, because you would not be the first to think to do something like that."

"What?"

"There was someone else who tried to raise their beloved from the dead. Someone other than Snowden. A long time ago. They almost did it. But the only reason they stopped is because of what I'm telling you now.

"If you go through with it, if you do it, you will damn yourself forever. And that's not just your soul that's in danger. By doing something so forbidden, something that even the gods frown upon, you would be effectively cutting your own thread of fate that connects you with her."

"What the hell are you talking about?"

"I know what I'm talking about. And the fact that I am here today is proof."

"I don't follow."

"Don't do it, my friend. Don't."

There's movement. Loud noises. Raised voices. I struggle to open my eyes, and when I do, there's only Sin in the room with me. He's on the couch next to me, his head in his hands.

"What happened?" I croak, my mouth parched and dry.

He takes a deep breath. I'm so confused about everything that's going on that I barely register the fact that there are no more injuries on his body. Not on his face. Not on his neck.

And though he's wearing a clean shirt, I don't think I'd find any underneath it either.

The memory from earlier comes to mind. What had he said?

The entity came to him when he was fourteen years old and on the verge of death, and with a few drops of blood, that entity—demon, whatever he was—had healed him.

Did this happen now, too? Was it all real, and not just a figment of my imagination?

I move closer to him, pressing my hand to his chest. He doesn't wince. He doesn't startle. No sign that he's in pain.

"What happened?" I ask again, this time my question aimed at his lack of injuries.

He doesn't answer that. Instead, he lets out a deep sigh and pulls me closer into his arms.

"He stole it," he finally says, not making much sense.

"What?"

"The book with the sigils. Arnoult stole it. And he's going to use it." He takes another deep breath. "He's going to try to raise Leah from the dead."

"W-what?"

"I must stop him before he does it. Because if he goes through with this . . ." He swallows hard. "He's going to be damned. Forever."

"What do you mean?" I frown.

"The ritual Snowden did to bring his mistress back from the dead is a forbidden one. Not only for mortals, but for divine beings as well because it screws with the natural order."

"If it's so forbidden, how did he manage to do it?"

"The sigils. There are some demonic entities that thrive on messing with the natural order. He might not know exactly which one to summon to do so, but he will try each and every one of those sigils until he finds an entity to help him."

"When you say he's going to be damned, what exactly does that mean?"

"He will get her back—not as herself, but as that creature. But the act itself will have to be paid for. He will have to sell his soul for it. Just like Snowden. And upon his death, the demon will consume the soul. It will be like he never existed in the first place. No chance for reincarnation. Nothing."

"But if it's his choice . . ."

"No!" he bursts out. "I cannot let him make this mistake. He can still be with her; maybe not in this lifetime, but in the next. If he goes through with this, he will be just . . . gone."

"If he knows the price he has to pay, and he's still willing to do it, who are you to stop him?" I say gently.

"He's my friend! My mentor. I cannot let him." He breaks down in a sob. "He's the closest thing I've ever had to a family. I cannot let him throw away his soul."

"All right." I take a deep breath. "What can we do?"

His brows go up in surprise at my words. "I won't ask anything of you. Not when it can be this dangerous."

"But—"

"I will feel better if you're safe, Petra. I will take you home for the time being, and I will go in search of him. There are a few places where he might perform the ritual."

"If you're sure . . ." I murmur.

He leans in and places a kiss on my forehead. "It will put my mind more at ease knowing you are safe."

It's on the tip of my tongue to remind him who killed Snowden, and that I'm not quite the damsel in distress he makes me out to be. But seeing him so anguished about his friend, I don't want to stress him further.

He ends up taking me back to my room, and for some reason, I find it hard to part ways with him. I'm not sure why, but all I want is to keep him by my side, in my arms—though I can see how selfish that is.

Instead, I say, "Go save your friend."

"I'll be back," he promises. Then he's gone.

Still staring at the open window, it takes me a few moments to gather my bearings and get ready for bed. It's almost four in the morning, and I won't have too long to get some rest before the entire house awakens.

I'm about to unbutton my bolero when the door to my room bursts open, startling me.

CHAPTER SEVENTY

PETRA

The Past

My father bursts into the room holding a gas lamp, my brother and a few men I don't recognize behind him.

"He was right," he spits out at me. "You've been cavorting with the devil himself!"

"What is happening, Father? Why are you here—"

"Shut up! We've caught you red-handed."

"I don't understand . . ." I say and take a step back. "*Who* was right?"

He smirks at me, a mocking smile that sends shivers down my spine.

"Snowden sent word the other day. He told me all about Leah's pregnancy—the fact that she's been spoiled by the devil. He implied you were involved in this monstrous business, too. I did not believe it at first. But you *have* been acting strange, talking back when you haven't before."

He shakes his head in disgust.

"He proposed that I allow Leah to send a message to you asking for help and see what happens. He warned me not to intervene and let things play out. And oh, how they've played out."

Was the entire thing a trap? I should have been more suspicious of that message considering my father *never* allows me to receive any type of packages directly. I should have questioned it more. It seems Snowden had more information about Arnoult and Sin than previously thought.

But how could he have suspected me of being involved with either of them?

"I don't know what you're talking about," I add in a low voice.

"Snowden is dead. His house is on fire as we speak. And you . . ." His nose wrinkles in disgust as he pushes the gas lamp farther into the room, illuminating my figure. "Blood spatters."

I look down, my eyes widening as I note that there are, indeed, blood stains on my dress.

"Son, grab her," he commands.

My brother comes forward, grabbing my arm and dragging me toward the door. I try to fight him off, but he secures both my hands behind my back as if I were a goddamn convict.

"This is madness, Father. Surely you realize this—" Before the words are out of my mouth, he backhands me.

My head reels to the side, and I taste blood from my lower lip.

"Shut up, you whore!" he snarls.

"Father—"

"Take her!"

My brother pulls me into the hallway, following my father and the other men.

Good Lord, this is really happening!

"Sin," I whisper, though it's in vain. I know he cannot hear me. He's probably busy looking for Arnoult. But once he's done, he will come for me, right?

That means I must hold out until he finds me. I must—

The other men are a small distance behind us when we reach the top of the stairs. Seeing a small opening, I push into my brother. His back hits the balustrade, and he winces in pain, momentarily letting go of me.

If I run fast enough, perhaps I can get away.

I pivot toward the stairs at the same time as my brother grabs my skirt, holding on to me. I slap his hands aside, but then he reaches for my sleeves, at which point I bite his hand. Hard.

He lets out a loud yelp, and instinctively, he slaps me. I don't think he realizes his own strength because I momentarily see stars. My feet teeter at the top of the stairs, and my sense of balance becomes nonexistent.

His eyes widen in realization—or I think they do. I cannot be sure what happens in that split second after he slaps me except that I'm falling.

My body hits the first steps, the hard wood digging into my flesh and bones. My mouth opens on a soundless moan of pain.

I roll over, and the pain multiplies as my body hits the steps again and again. My breath is knocked out of me. I can no longer tell what's happening around me except for the fact that at one point, I've stopped moving.

I'm on the ground, at the bottom of the stairs, my body broken and bent out of place. My neck feels stiff, and I cannot move it. But it's my legs that are the worst. One of them is broken beneath me, and every little movement makes me want to howl in pain.

I've been wailing, I realize. For moments on end, I've been crying out in pain from my injuries, until my throat is too sore to make any more sound.

"Fucking hell, boy! What did you do?" Father sputters.

"I didn't, Father! She bit me!"

"Is she dead? She's not crying anymore."

The voices are getting closer, followed by thudding footsteps on the stairs.

"She's not dead. Not yet."

"Good."

What does he mean *good*? Wasn't that his goal? Kill me for cavorting with the devil?

"Get her to the horse."

"She's bleeding, Father."

Am I bleeding? I can't feel it. Everything hurts so badly I can't pinpoint one exact spot that might be worse off than the rest. But given the position of my body, the fact that I cannot seem to move well, I can infer that the damage is great.

Even if they don't kill me tonight . . .

I choke on a sob.

Even if I don't die tonight, I don't think I will ever be the same.

"I don't care. Move her," my father says flippantly.

From the corner of my eye, I see the lot of them gathered around me like it's a sick spectacle. They're watching over me, bleeding on the floor, body broken, with no compassion.

There is only a malicious glint in their eyes.

"She might die on the way. I think we should call a physician," my brother mentions in a low voice.

"And say what? That you threw your sister down the stairs? You'd be branded a murderer!"

"But—"

"Even if she dies on the way, we can still use her."

Use me? Terror engulfs me at my father's words. And somehow the notion that he might *use* me is more terrifying than this gut-wrenching pain I'm feeling right now.

I blink. Tears gather around my eyes, but I still cannot move my neck. I can only stare at these figures looming over me, casually debating what to do with my dying body.

"But she won't be able to stand straight." The voice is unknown—another of the men present.

Why would they need me to stand straight?

"We will manage once we get there. By now, everyone must know about Snowden's passing. The people of this town must be terrified that the devil is out and about, lurking in the shadows, ready to murder the best of us. We cannot allow that," my father intones. "We need to let them know they are safe."

More confusion clouds my mind. What is he talking about? What does he want to do?

My father turns with a harsh stare toward my brother.

"Grab her. Take her to the horse. The crowd is awaiting."

Crowd? What crowd?

I've never felt so helpless in my life. My fate seems to be decided; I won't have much longer. But the thought that they will *use* me for something . . . to prove a *point*, scares me more than anything.

And then there's the thought of Sin.

Does he know? Can he feel my anguish, my pain? Why is he not here?

He's helping his friend, I tell myself. It's not his fault that this happened. It's only my fault for not agreeing to flee with him when he asked.

I gulp down. There is a metallic taste in the back of my throat—blood.

What does that mean? Am I worse than I previously thought?

If I taste blood, it means there is bleeding somewhere *inside* of me. Fear spears through me. Perhaps if it were just my body, I could at some point heal and mend, though not to who I was before.

But if I'm bleeding on the inside? Doesn't that mean death is near?

"I don't want to move her," my brother comments. "It's gross."

"If I tell you to grab her, you will grab her," my father raises his voice.

A few moments pass as my brother walks in circles around me, trying to find something to grab onto. At first, he pulls on my legs, and a strangled sound erupts from my throat.

It *hurts*.

It hurts so badly.

He shakes his head. I can't see his expression, or the state of my lower body, but I hear a string of curses and a few mutters of disgust.

He moves to my arms, then jumps back and curses aloud.

"The bone's sticking out," he cries out.

That confirms more of my suspicions. I am in a bad, bad shape.

"Oh, be a man," my father snickers.

My brother, trembling with revulsion, decides that the best way to *grab* me is by my hair. He wraps his fist into the back of my head, pulling me toward the door.

My mouth parts, and I let out a few barely audible moans of pain. He turns his back to me as if looking at my face while he's dragging me by the hair offends him.

There are a few bumps as he drags me out of the house, all of which only amplify my pain. At some point, my mind becomes foggy. The next time I recover consciousness is while I'm strapped onto a horse.

The horse starts with a slow walk, though each step sends a fresh new wave of pain through my body. But then it goes into a full gallop, and the pain intensifies to such an extent, I struggle to keep myself awake.

I'm in and out of consciousness, though I force myself to bear it as much as I can, fight against the weakness of my body while I count down the minutes.

Please be fast, Sin. I'm waiting for you.

He's going to come. I *know* it. I *trust* him.

We walk for what seems like forever through the dead silence of the night. Yet at some point, something changes. I hear voices—many of them.

Some are louder than others. Some are shouting. From my position on the horse, I cannot quite see far ahead, but as the noises intensify, I realize we've reached an area of town that is very poor.

The horses trot on, slowing down as a crowd of people parts to let them through. I only see some of them. Though it is dark, I recognize faces—people from our congregation, from our church.

But why would they be here at this late hour of the night? Why would they be gathered?

My train of thought is stopped by the sudden halt of the horse. My brother gets off and, not too carefully, pulls me down. I fall to the ground. Pain unlike any I've ever known shoots through me, and I teeter on the edge of blacking out.

The crowd cheers.

What is happening?

Once more, he grabs hold of my hair and drags me forward, this time through the harsh, uneven, and pebbled road. More pain. So much pain that I think I've become numb to it. I just lie there, conscious enough to know it's happening, but far too helpless to do anything about it.

I can only watch as more people arrive, forming a circle around us. And once my brother pulls me up onto a marble structure, I realize where we are: the town square.

The place where everything began.

With the help of a few other men, they pull me into an upright position so they can all look at me—with clear disgust on their faces. Tying a rope around me, they secure me against the obelisk.

One piece of rope around my arms, one around my waist, one around my thighs, and one around my ankles. I'm fully secured. I cannot even slump down from my injuries. My neck is still bent at an odd angle, and I find that even in this position, I cannot move it. But at least now I can watch.

I can see people stepping closer, whispering about me, whispering about the devil's harlot.

Is that what my father told them? Is that why he engineered this spectacle?

My questions are soon answered as my father steps forward and takes his place beside me. I see him from the corner of my eye, puffing out his chest and straightening his back like a peacock.

"Fear not, my townsmen," he begins in a booming voice.

Everyone stops speaking.

"I am here to tell you that I lead the good fight against the devil. I do not care whether evil has penetrated my own family—I will eradicate it all the same. My daughter, Petra: She is and has been the devil's minion. The devil's whore. And I can prove it to you."

Coming toward me, he pulls on my already ripped clothes until the upper part of my chest is revealed, right above my breasts.

"Look! The mark of the devil!" he exclaims.

Gasps erupt through the crowd. People step forward to take a closer look, before crying out in outrage, in fear, in condemnation.

And they all start chanting: *The devil's whore! She's marked! Kill her! Kill her!*

I can only stare in silence at the violent mob threatening to kill me. But as my father smirks at me, I realize that this is just a way for him to get back his reputation, isn't it?

With Snowden dead, he has no more advantages to gain. But he can still redeem his virtue. By eliminating the evil in his own household, he will be seen as a morally upright martyr who decided to sacrifice his own daughter for the greater good.

A bitter laugh bubbles in my throat. Everyone is pointing at me, accusing me, calling me names I've never heard before, but no one tries to stop it.

Even when someone grabs a pebble off the ground and throws it at me, no one says stop. On the contrary, other people follow suit. They imitate what they see, and one stone turns into five, then ten.

I no longer feel the pain. Or at least I cannot distinguish between old pain and new pain. What is pain, even? I'm hanging on by a thread, and I know it. It will only take one more push for me to succumb to my injuries.

And still . . . I keep hoping he will come.

That he will come for me.

I might be beyond saving, but I want to see him one last time.

"Sin . . ." I whisper, barely able to form the word, yet it vanishes in the air with no response forthcoming.

Where are you? I think to myself. *Where are you when I need you the most?*

Why are you not here?

I know I shouldn't blame him, but at the same time, hasn't he always spoken about this greater-than-life love? About this fate that ties us together? And yet here I am, on the brink of death, and he is nowhere to be found.

Here I am, enduring in pain, and he is absent. I don't know why I am so disappointed, but somehow, those feelings are more powerful than any physical pain.

Then I whisper again—

Just as one stone hits my temple. Blood pours down and into my eye until I cannot see anymore. I only have my other eye. But because of the position of my neck, I can only see the ground and a little bit above it.

"I will keep this community safe, I promise you," my father continues, "and that promise will start tonight. I want you to know that I will eradicate all evil from Radcliffe—starting with my own family."

There are some steps around me before a foul-smelling liquid envelops me. It takes me a moment to realize it's gasoline. Isn't it?

"The devil's whore dies tonight," my father intones.

And then the crowd goes mad, chanting the words ad nauseam: *The devil's whore dies tonight! The devil's whore dies tonight!*

It's a chorus of condemnation. Of glee at my suffering.

And then the match is lit and dropped at my feet.

My mouth opens on another soundless moan. I cannot even vocalize anything anymore.

And yet I can feel it—first, my shoes, but then the heat continues, eating at my flesh, going quickly upward, burning through the first layer, reaching the second, the flames burning through my lower limbs and growing taller and taller, threatening to engulf me whole.

If the pain I felt before was bad, this is a thousand times worse. I'm screaming on the inside, even though I cannot on the outside.

I scream and scream.

And all I can think of is him.

Where are you, Sin? Where are you when I need you the most?

The fire continues. It stings and burns and eats at everything it encounters until I simply become numb to it. And that numbness slowly takes over my entire being. My feelings, too, become so numb until I don't even realize what I am anymore—or if I am at all.

It's like the more the fire on the outside burns, the more the flame inside of me is extinguished. Until only the smoke remains.

And the echo of one word: *Sin.*

I don't know when the end begins, or when being turns into not being.

But I do know this: He was never here.

He abandoned me when I needed him the most.

BREAKING NEWS

Radcliffe Herald

10 June 1896

REVEREND'S OWN CHILD BURNED AT THE STAKE.

MYSTERY CORPSE BESIDE HER!

Citizens! The devil walks among us, and yesterday, he claimed his prize in the very heart of our town.

At the stroke of midnight, under a full moon blackened by billowing smoke, the daughter of our most venerable man of God was put to death before a throng so vast it choked the square from one end to the other. Her name is yet withheld, though every soul in town knows it and whispers it behind closed shutters. To speak it aloud is to invite a shudder.

Her crime? Not witchcraft itself, but the most insidious sin—she was the Devil's own harlot. It is said she was in cahoots with the Devil and his flock.

Bound to the stake, the girl stood straight and unflinching, her hair hanging loose about her shoulders. The mark of the Devil is said to have been imprinted on her chest.

Yet she was not alone in her dreadful fate. Another body was turned to ash beside her, though no one knows its identity. Was it man, woman, or some unholy thing? None could tell.

Those with an ear for rumor insist that this second victim was the true leader of the Devil's disciples. Others claim it was no human at all, but a familiar spirit, bound to her through wicked rites.

The Reverend himself was nowhere to be seen. Some say hidden away in prayer, others that he fled in disgrace before the torch was put to the pyre.

As the flames leapt high, the crowd's roar rose with them, half in horror, half in triumph. Mothers clutched their children; men crossed themselves.

What is certain is this: The air in our town is thick with dread, and the Devil's work is not yet done.

Lock your doors, keep to the lamplight, and pray, dear reader. Evil lingers still.

More as details of this dreadful affair come to light.

CHAPTER SEVENTY-ONE

PETRA

Present Day

I wake up screaming. The pain still lingers in my mind, in my skin, my bones. I'm shaking from the residual adrenaline as the images from my dream loop in my mind.

"Petra? What's wrong?" Sin asks, his expression filled with worry.

I continue crying out. He grabs me by the shoulders and shakes me.

"Petra, what's wrong? Did you have a nightmare?" he keeps asking.

I stare at him through tear-rimmed eyes, seeing him—Sin. My Sin. But now I have the knowledge of the past. I know what he did. I know that he . . .

"You left me," I whisper in a broken voice. "You left me!" I cry out, sobs wracking my body.

He frowns and shakes his head. "What are you talking about? I'm here. I never left you."

"Liar!" I shout and push him off me. "Liar!"

I continue backing away from him until I almost fall off the bed. On shaky legs, I get up, still staring at him—at his familiar face that now feels so strange.

Because this person in front of me is the same person from over a hundred years ago.

He's the same person who never came for me when I called for him. The same person who abandoned me to live the most painful moments of my life. The same person who was never there when I needed him the most.

"You . . ." My voice trembles, my body high on adrenaline. I can still feel the lick of the fire from before, that penetrating pain that doesn't seem to go away no matter how hard I try.

And now, there's also the heartbreak.

"You left me," I say again, brokenly.

"Petra, please talk to me. Tell me what this is about, and we'll fix it, okay? I never left you," he swears.

I shake my head at him.

"Please, Petra, calm down. It can't be good for the baby."

"Now you're worrying about me?" I burst out.

Unable to face him for a moment longer, I dash out of the room. And yet, the only place I can run to is the old study. I race across the corridor, reach the door, open and close it behind me, and lock it.

I hear his steps following me, then the bangs at the door.

"Petra! Tell me what's going on, please!"

"No. I can't talk right now. Please, let me be."

"Petra, I'm not going anywhere."

"Suit yourself," I mutter and step away from the door.

I hear him slide to the floor, his back against the frame. Just as he said—he's not leaving.

And yet, there is another reason why I came here. Because if there were newspaper clippings about those other events, then there has to be one about what happened that night in the town square at the obelisk.

I start looking around. I go straight for the stack of papers from before, but this time I know they're not there anymore.

"What?" I murmur to myself.

But now I know—it was him.

He must have been the one to put them there in the first place, and now he's hidden them somewhere for some unknown reason.

So, I start searching.

Like a madwoman, I tear all the books from the shelves. Everything in my path, I fling to the floor when I see it doesn't serve any purpose.

There are so many items in here. A treasure trove of antiques he must have collected throughout time.

And then another question: If he is immortal now, what about then? Was he not immortal back then, too? How long has he been alive? How many other women has he preyed on?

Even though, logically, I know that someone as devoted as Sin would probably not look at another woman, my feelings—my emotions—are running so hot that I cannot think rationally.

I can only look for the things he's hidden from me.

The manipulation, everything he's done from the past until now.

Because no matter how much I love him, I have to admit to myself that I don't know him. I don't know a thing about him.

I didn't know him in the past, either. He might have given me pieces of information, he might have said a thing or two about who he is and where he came from, but even then, the most important things he always hid from me.

I once asked him what deal he made with that entity who saved him when he was fourteen, and he never gave me a straight answer.

Perhaps because *this* is the answer. The fact that he is immortal. The fact that he's engineered the deaths of dozens of people—maybe even hundreds I don't know about.

But that's not all.

He claims to love me, but all he's done so far is take advantage of me, of my insecurities, my situation, time and time again.

I close my eyes and take a deep breath. All around me, books are flung across the room. Some of them are torn from my reckless need for answers.

Now, looking down at the ripped pages, I feel a hole in my stomach.

I caused this. And even I don't recognize myself anymore.

I sink to the floor on my knees. I place my palms on the ground and take big gulps of air in an attempt to calm my wild heartbeat.

Think, Petra. Think. It's not like you to get worked up so easily.

I let out a dry laugh.

How could anyone *not* get worked up over this? Over *everything*?

I was just a regular high school student a few months ago. Just a normal human.

And now?

Now the father of my baby is some type of immortal entity who maniacally murders people. And I have to contend with the fact that I don't know what to trust anymore—about him, about this world, about the evil I've witnessed, about the fact that there might be some type of evil festering inside of me.

I just . . . I don't know anymore.

For minutes, I try to calm myself. And that's when, from the corner of my eye, I see it. The same yellowed paper as the newspaper clips from before. It's not a fixed stack, just a few pages tucked inside the middle of a book.

I crawl toward it on my knees, pick up the book, open it, and remove the slips of newspaper with trembling hands.

The first one is another report on Snowden and Leah's deaths. It details more about the fire at his house and includes the testimony of his butler, who was the one to imply that Snowden had gone mad at finding out his daughter was pregnant out of wedlock and had killed her before killing himself.

No doubt—the narrative that Sin paid him to espouse.

I look at the next file, and horror clamps down on me. It's a photograph of the obelisk in the aftermath of the fire.

There's no body, but I can see the burnt ashes and the pieces of rope that had been around my limbs.

I feel another panic attack incoming—my throat closing up, my vision spinning—yet I push myself to keep going. I read the text:

PUBLIC EXECUTION.

> The daughter of a prominent religious leader was killed in the town square by her father and a zealous mob. She was reputed to be in cahoots with the pagan society from St. Anselm Hall. Some even claimed she might have been the devil's whore.

The article details the symbol on my chest and how its presence confirmed, in the eyes of both my father and the crowd, that I must be marked by the devil.

Nowhere does the article condemn the actions of the townspeople. Nowhere does it express remorse for what happened.

For the fact that an innocent woman was burned alive.

No—it just says these "drastic actions" reflect the townspeople's fear. Their conviction that something evil lingers in Radcliffe.

"Petra . . ." Sin's voice echoes.

I don't answer.

Instead, I grab my phone and text the only person who's still on my side.

I need help.

I type to Amelia, waiting with bated breath, hoping she has her phone on her. That she'll answer. That she'll give me *something*—guidance, support, *anything*.

Please, Ames. Respond.
I need you.

I quickly type again. But then my whole body freezes.

My eyes widen just as the phone slips from my hand.

What was that?

Two low sounds. In quick succession.

Text messages—from behind the door.

No. No, no. Anything but this.

Ames . . .

I send again. Another sound.

Where are you?

Another sound.

Finally, I type:

Sin?

Another ping comes from the other side of the door, followed by:

"I'm sorry, Petra," Sin's voice rings out.

I throw my phone to the ground, tears streaming down my face.

And still, I hold on to some belief that maybe I have it all wrong. That maybe it's just my thinking that is skewed.

So I ask, "What did you do to her? Did you steal her phone? Where is she?

"What did you do to her?" I call out, my voice full of venom and vehemence.

Yet his answer is still the same.

"I'm sorry, sweetheart. I did it for you. For us."

CHAPTER SEVENTY-TWO

PETRA

Present Day

"What did you do?" I ask, already thinking the worst. "What happened to Amelia? What did you do, Sin?" The last question comes out in a frustrated scream.

He exhales loudly. "I did not do anything to Amelia. There was never any Amelia in the first place."

"W-what do you mean?"

He doesn't answer.

"What do you mean she never existed, Sin?"

"I—" He takes a deep breath. "I promised myself I would wait for you; that I would wait until you were old enough. But the truth is, I missed you. Knowing you were out there, within reach . . . I have no excuse for what I did. I know that. But I needed a way to talk to you. Even if it meant . . ."

"Even if it meant pretending to be a teenage girl?"

"I'm sorry."

"You're sorry? She was my *only* friend! And now I realize she wasn't even real?"

"Everything else was real, Petra. I just wanted to talk to you."

"Real? I told you my deepest thoughts and fears under false pretense. You . . . oh God . . ." I choke up as I realize the sly ways in which Amelia would probe about my love life; how she would encourage me to give Sin a chance and find excuses for him even when the situation did not make any sense.

"Petra, darling—"

"Don't you *darling* me! You have no right after what you've done. And it's not even the worst of it, is it? Since we're putting the cards on the table, you might as well admit the truth—you're not human."

"I am not," he answers quietly.

I blink, stunned by the sudden declaration. For some reason, I thought I would have to pry the admission out of him.

"What are you then?" I demand.

"I reckon you have already seen what happened in the past," he starts.

"Don't avoid my question, Sin."

"I am not," he sighs. "But tell me this, you saw what happened? How you . . ."

"How I died?"

"Yes."

"I did. And I know you were not there," I burst out, tears falling down my cheeks again.

He taps his head against the wooden frame of the door a few times. "Except I was."

"W-what?"

"I would not expect you to remember that. You were far too hurt, in pain . . ." His voice is strained as he speaks. "It is my fault for arriving there too late. That, I accept, and trust me, I have beaten myself up over it time and time again over the last hundred years. I should have been there for you when you needed me the most. I failed you, Petra, and you have no idea how sorry I am for it."

"That doesn't erase the fact that I *died*!"

"No, it does not." He pauses. "Now that you've seen with your own eyes what happened in the past, I can finally give you my side of the story—fill in the gaps."

I let out a dry laugh. "Really? So kind of you," I say ironically.

"Petra . . ." His voice sounds weary, old. Not at all the cheery, jocular voice I've gotten used to. But I suppose that is to be expected since this is *not* teenager Sin.

This is immortal Sin, the one over a hundred years old.

"You think I did not want to tell you everything sooner? You think I wasn't dying on the inside seeing you try to make sense of everything and knowing I had the answers—or, at least, most of the answers?"

"Why didn't you, then?"

"There are a few reasons why I did not—why I *could* not."

"I'm waiting," I reply flippantly.

"The first is the most obvious one. You would not have believed me. If you had not experienced the past for yourself, if you had not seen that things are not as they seem, that the normal most people take for granted is just an illusion, you would have never believed me."

I bite my lip as I consider his point. It is true that I would have never believed him if he came up to me and said, *"Hey Petra, I'm Sin, your past life-lover. Oh, and I'm also immortal, and I kill people."*

I would have likely thought him insane and never spoken to him again; perhaps I would have gotten a restraining order against him.

"I will accede to that point."

"In addition to that, I wanted you to fall for me as myself. Before you knew about the past, about our connection. I did not want you to feel compelled to be with me under any other circumstance but the fact that *you* wanted me."

"Really? Are we forgetting the fact that you manipulated my entire life? That you basically ensured my parents moved to Radcliffe, that I attended St. Anselm Hall . . . that I was *named* Petra?"

"I may have engineered the circumstances, but that was only to gain proximity to you. Perhaps I did a thing or two to bring you by my side, but the fact that you came to me, of your own volition, that is all you."

Once more, I roll my eyes.

"And the night at Elias's party? You got me drunk and slept with me! How is that me coming to you? That's you taking advantage of me in a vulnerable position."

He makes a tsk sound.

"Perhaps I did do . . . some underhanded things to be close to you, to touch you, feel you again. I can only blame that on my own eagerness and the fact that I've missed you so damn much. And then there you were, so beautiful, so comfortable with me. I did take advantage. I admit that. But I am not sorry about it."

"You got me pregnant!"

"Another reason to not feel sorry about it," he adds casually. "Although I will say, I did not even think that was a possibility. It was not on purpose. But I am *very* happy it happened."

There isn't much I can say to that since I am quite happy it happened, too. I press my hand to my stomach, caressing it lightly.

From the scared teenager anxiously buying pregnancy tests in a pharmacy to the expecting mother I am today . . . I feel like I am an entirely different person. And the realization that there is another life growing inside of me has had a lot to do with my growth.

"But how can you still say you wanted me to fall for *you* when you manipulated everything to make it happen?"

"Because I never manipulated your feelings, Petra. They are your own."

Another thing I can't quite argue with. There might have been an insane attraction between the two of us from the beginning, but I only started to fall for him after we spent more time together, after we talked, after he listened to me and cared about me and my dreams and passions.

He *listened*. That's what truly made me fall for him. Not only now, but in the past, too. He saw me for myself, something no one else had ever tried to do before.

Moments of silence later, although I wish I had a clever comeback to deny his claims, he continues.

"The other reason why I could not tell you everything is because it's not entirely my story to tell."

"You mean Leah and Arnoult?"

"Yes. You've seen how their relationship has been misconstrued in some articles, how Arnoult himself has been vilified throughout history."

"You did repeat some of the same stories," I add wryly.

"I did, and I did not. I told you what was common knowledge, something any native person in Radcliffe would know, but I've also given you small enough clues so you could question the narrative, to investigate and get to your own conclusions. The most vital part of this equation was your dreams."

"How did you even know I would dream of it?" I shoot back.

"Because that night at Elias's party, alcohol was not the only thing we drank."

I frown. "What are you talking about?"

"The bottle was infused with Jí, a potion that helps a person remember their past life."

"Y-You gave me a magical potion?"

"Fret not, Petra. It did not harm you in any way."

Thinking back, now I realize that the dreams began after the party. And he was the one who engineered this, too? At this point, what hasn't he done?

"You remembering everything was key to understanding how everything fit in together. Although I did not know when or how long it would take for you to remember everything. You weren't exactly forthcoming to me about your dreams—"

"Because I thought I was going insane!" I cry out. "I was seeing this other version of myself living in the eighteen hundreds and this person who looked exactly like you, and I did not know what to make of it."

"I'm sorry. If I could have made things easier for you, I would have. But I did not know how either. I am sorry for my shortcomings. I am sorry that my actions have confused and hurt you. I did the best I could with the resources I had."

"Back up a little. You gave me a magical potion without my consent!"

"I think that's the least bad thing I've done, all things considered," he replies drily.

"Right. I suppose so. But why would you be so concerned as to whether I found out about Arnoult and Leah from you or by seeing it in my dreams? They're dead. It's not like—" I stop. "They *are* dead, aren't they?"

He chuckles. "In a way?"

"Sin . . . What are you talking about? Explain yourself!"

"Well, you've met them."

I blink, shocked.

"What?"

"My current parents," he says. "Leah was reincarnated as Lisa, and Arnoult as Tom. My sister, too, happens to be the reincarnation of the baby that died with Leah."

I stare at the door, shock reverberating through me.

"But . . . how? How is that possible? And they know about you? How did you trick them into accepting this farce?" A barrage of questions comes out of my mouth as I try to wrap my head around this.

It's just so ludicrous.

"Yes, they know. They've always known. One of the promises I made Arnoult before I killed him was that when he was reincarnated, I would help him get back his memories.

"So that is what I did. But before I found him, he was already inseparable from Lisa. I only returned his memories after he turned eighteen. But he and Lisa had been neighbors, best friends growing up, and then lovers in high school. They recognized each other even without those memories. Fate is such a beautiful thing, isn't it, Petra?"

"You gave Lisa her memories, too?"

"Yes."

"And they also remember me?"

"They do."

"B-but . . . what about the fact that you're an adult male and you have been one for the past hundred years or so. How the hell did you fool people? How did you pretend to be a child, a teenager . . ."

"Ah, that? It's called glamour. I can change the perception people have of me. My sister was told everything when she was old enough to understand. As for my presence at school, I only joined when you did."

"Glamour?" I echo.

"Open the door, Petra, and see for yourself."

I shouldn't, should I?

I'm mad at him, I don't want to see him. But I'm also curious, and that particular trait has always been stronger than my will.

With slow but steady steps, I walk toward the door and open it.

He's in front of me, dressed in just a shirt and a pair of sweatpants. His hair is messy and tousled, and for a moment, I don't see much of a difference.

But then I focus on his face. His jaw is more angular, his cheekbones more pronounced. Some of the baby fat has melted away to reveal a more sculpted version of Sin—one that mirrors the version from my dreams.

I gulp down. Is he taller? I'm not sure. But as I stare up at him, I feel suddenly small, defenseless.

"It's you . . ." I mutter, mostly to myself.

"There isn't much of a change now, but I have had to shift my appearance over the ages to match that of a boy going through puberty."

"Going through . . . oh, Lord, Sin! You're a hundred-year-old man, and you've been going to school with teenagers!" I cry out. "That's so wrong!"

"Is it?" He shrugs. "I do admit it was rather odd. But I never had any nefarious intentions, never paid much attention to those around me—except you."

"As if that makes me feel better! I was still fourteen when I started at St. Anselm Hall."

"And I waited until you were eighteen. You can't say I was not a gentleman."

My mouth drops open in shock.

"You're insane."

"Perhaps. But I am insane for you. And I slogged through boring high school courses just to be near you. I had to withstand all those annoying little bastards just so I could cultivate a sense of normality. It wasn't easy. But I did it. For you."

"And that doesn't make it any less weird." I scrunch my nose in disgust.

He shrugs. "I did what I had to do."

"Right. So you've said. But you still haven't told me what you are. You're not human. So what are you?"

He takes a deep breath.

"I suppose I should start with the beginning. You might want to sit down for this."

Against my better judgment, I allow him to take me back to the living room, make me some food and a cup of tea. Perhaps I should be more wary now knowing he fed me some magical potion so I would recover my past life memories.

But no matter how much I want to rage at him, to hate him, there is a part of me that just wants to understand.

"Tell me," I say.

And so, he does.

CHAPTER SEVENTY-THREE

PETRA

Present Day

"For the most part, my childhood was exactly as I told you. I was an orphan, and they named me Sin because they thought I came from sin—and my entire existence was a sin. But they also named me Kimaris, which I later found out means one without a home.

"So I was technically the Sin without a home. When I was fourteen and decided to jump from that window, it was because I didn't think there was anything left for me in this world. I didn't think I would ever find peace, that I would ever find someone to accept me for who I was.

"And as I lay dying on the ground, that entity came to me. You asked me numerous times if I sold my soul, and it was the truth—I told you then, and I'll tell you now: I did not sell my soul. But I did sell something.

"As I was waiting for death to claim me, he asked me what I wanted most in the world. Do you know what my answer was?"

I shake my head.

"I wanted a home. Sin. Kimaris. The one without a home wanted somewhere to belong. Someone to belong to. And then he gave me a choice. I could continue living, or I could die. But I would die knowing that there is a home out there for me. That there is someone I could call home.

"You. He showed me a vision of you. You were out there in the world. The Fates had decided you were to be the only one for me—in this lifetime, the next, forever. When I saw those images, I couldn't believe it. I was still so deep in denial that I couldn't possibly deserve anything better. I thought it must be a trick. That perhaps he was playing with my mind. Or perhaps, because death was so close, I was hallucinating.

"But then he told me: If I chose to die, he could do nothing about it. I would die. And at some point, I might get reincarnated. But because of my—ironically—sin of taking my own life, my time in the afterlife would not be short. It could be centuries before I gained a new incarnation. Centuries in which not only would I have lost you, but there was no certainty I would meet you again in the next life. No guarantee our incarnations would align.

"But if I chose to live, he would make a deal with me. He would ensure I get what I want most: a home. A person to belong to. In exchange for serving him."

"Serving him? What do you mean?" I ask.

"He wanted me to find evil people and kill them—in his name, for him. It's still not clear to me exactly why he required those services. I later thought that, perhaps, while I did not personally sell my soul to him, I was selling other people's souls."

"That's how you started it? St. Anselm Hall University?" I ask.

"That came later."

My eyes widen. "What do you mean, later?"

"As you know, he healed me with his blood. And afterward, for a short time, he took me under his wing. I was still young, and although I'd worked since childhood, I didn't have the skills to make it out in the world. Or at least, I didn't have the skills to do what he asked of me. So, he taught me.

"He taught me everything I know. It was through his guidance that I got accepted into Harvard College, that I completed my studies. It was his teachings that showed me how to identify the people who deserved to die—and those who didn't.

"It was also around this time that I started having more questions. Although we had entered into a contract, it had never been specific enough. To be honest, at that young age, I didn't think to ask for more information. I didn't know how many souls I was supposed to supply him with. I didn't know whether my mission was indefinite, or if there was an expiration date.

"And it's only because I met Arnoult that I started questioning those things. As you already know, Arnoult was interested in the occult, in what separates this world from others—those things we cannot see with the naked eye. And it was through him that I started to realize souls are actually a source of energy. I was effectively giving this entity the energy of the souls I was harvesting in his name.

"After I finished my degree, I had already found ten people whom I led to their deaths as part of our agreement. And that's when I asked him: How many more?"

"What did he say?"

"Fifty in total. I had done ten, so I had forty left."

I mentally go over the sheet I'd made with the murders. There had been the twenty-five people in the square and the fifteen at the mausoleum. Forty.

"And you did that."

He nods.

"And? What happened after you did it? Did anything change?"

"Something did change." He lets out a dry laugh. "You died. Then I died."

I stare at him. Then stare some more.

"What?"

"Don't look so shocked, sweet Petra. I told you I would never leave you, and I meant it. Perhaps I was a little late, but I was never going to leave you to face that alone."

I blink in shock.

"Explain."

He looks slightly uncomfortable as he fidgets in his seat.

"I went to find my mentor because I *knew* he was trying to perform that wretched ritual. It took me a few tries to find the location. Luckily, when I did, he had not gotten too far along with it. I managed to stop it just in time, but he was so mad at me . . ."

He takes a deep breath.

"He tried to fight me, telling me I ruined everything, that life had no meaning without Leah by his side. And as much as I wanted to argue with him, I could not. Because I would have felt the same way if it had been you in that situation. Retrospectively, I can see I had the wisdom of an outsider, and not someone who was deeply suffering.

"That was affecting his judgment, and I cannot blame him for it. But I also knew that if I allowed him to do it . . . everything he yearned for would be forever lost."

"What happened?"

"He eventually realized that the only way for him to ever be with her again, her and not some paltry substitute, was to give up the ritual. But that did not mean he wanted to live on. So the next challenge was stopping him from killing himself."

Sin gulps down uncomfortably.

"I told him what the entity told me, that the act of killing oneself would interfere with the timeline of his future incarnation and that he might not be able to find her again."

He presses his lips together. "So instead, he asked *me* to kill him."

I gasp. "And you . . ."

"I did. It was that, or he would find a way to kill himself. At least that way, I could help him."

"You . . . killed . . . him."

He nods, not meeting my eyes.

"Did it hurt?"

"I tried to make it as painless as possible."

"No, I mean did it hurt *you*?"

He gives me a sad smile. "It did."

A few seconds of silence pass, and he clears his throat.

"I was trying to find a way to bury both of them when I heard the commotion in town. I rushed over there, but . . ." He chokes up. "You were tied up, on fire."

The memory of the pain flashes through me with stunning swiftness, and I physically wince.

"I went straight to you. Caught you in my arms. Cut the ropes. But no matter how much I tried to get you to react, you were . . . gone."

His breath catches, and I note the moisture clinging to his lashes.

"The flames spread to my body, too."

My eyes widen.

"W-what?"

"I held on to you, even as they tore through my clothes, even as they reached my flesh. I couldn't let go of you. I couldn't . . ." He chokes up. "You were gone, and I was not there to save you. I was not there for you when you needed me the most. You have no idea how sorry I am about that, Petra."

"Wait a moment. You're saying you . . . that you burned *with* me?"

He gives me a tight nod. "How could I abandon you?"

"B-but . . . I don't understand. You're clearly alive, and well, immortal."

"By the time I arrived, your soul had already left the mortal plane. I couldn't get to you in physical form, nor in spiritual." He pauses. "As I held on to you, my consciousness slipped from me. One moment I was screaming at the top of my lungs, in pain at having lost you, in pain from the assault from the fire, the next, the pain disappeared.

"I opened my eyes and saw my body—*our* bodies wrapped together—from the perspective of an outsider. I was confused at first, but quickly realized I had died.

"A being appeared to escort me toward the afterlife, as no doubt you had been just moments before. But I couldn't go. If I did, it would mean all of our memories would be gone. I would forget you. I would forget the only home I've ever had."

"What did you do?"

"I was angry. So angry, I could manifest that emotion into the power to refuse to move on. And as that entity, that messenger, left, I saw a familiar face in the crowd."

"A familiar face?" I echo.

"The entity who'd healed me. He was there. Watching. He could see me in my spiritual form. And as he turned his back to leave, I followed.

"It was in a dark alleyway that he stopped, waiting for me. His first words were that I should not have done this, that I should have followed the messenger to the afterlife. But he acknowledged that he would have done the same in my position. He told me that as a wandering spirit, I was vulnerable—even more so because of the innate spiritual energy that gave me my shadow abilities. Demons would prey on me, seeking to consume my essence. Or . . ."

"Or?"

"I could become a demon myself and consume other essences to survive—to gain more power, to regain a corporeal form."

I stare at him in shock.

"So you *are* a demon?" I whisper.

"I am what they call a made-demon: a soul who becomes corrupted in search of power, immortality."

"What have you done, Sin?" I croak.

"What I had to. I did what I thought was right in that moment, and to be honest with you, I do not regret it. Not for a moment."

"But if you're a demon . . . what does it mean, that you consume other essences? Do you make deals with people for their souls, or . . . ?"

"No. I do not engage in that sort of thing, although I *have* consumed souls. The entity told me that there are levels to being a made-demon. The first and lowest is when a made-demon is amorphous. But with each soul consumed, it can become more powerful and regain physical shape.

"The last and most powerful level is level twelve—after which a made-demon attains powers similar to low-level natural-born demons."

"What level are you?"

"Twelve. I ascended to my twelfth level nineteen years ago."

"Nineteen years ago? Those murders . . ."

He nods.

"I fulfilled my contract with the entity when I delivered fifty souls to him. Every other murder after was for the sole purpose of gaining power, to consume more souls, to ascend so I could be once more myself. So I could be with you. In fact, the first soul I ever consumed was that of your father."

"My father?"

"And your brother. And everyone who had a hand in your suffering."

The breath leaves my lungs. "You killed them for me?"

"As I would *always* do. My only regret is that I did not kill them earlier, before they hurt you."

I swallow hard as I try to make sense of the information. This is all too much, too fantastical—though I should not be surprised at anything anymore. "And the students at school?"

He shakes his head. "I did not kill them. At my current level, I only require one soul per year to maintain my power. And I no longer kill for it. I simply watch and wait for an evil person to die and consume the soul before they can cross over."

"But if you did not kill them, who did?"

"I cannot say, Petra. But I did not."

"How do I know you're not lying to me again?" I counter.

"I've already told you this much; why would I lie about something like that? Yes, I am a killer. Yes, I am a demon, though I do not consider myself particularly evil, nor satanic. I am simply a man who has done everything he could to return to the only home he's ever known—you."

He leans toward me, but I pull back. The disappointment on his face is clear, but I am still so confused.

"What about the baby? If you're a demon, then . . ."

"I do not know," he answers sincerely. "I was told made-demons are infertile. The pregnancy shocked me as much as it did you."

"That's why you believed my lie?"

"Yes. Even though I've been watching you, monitoring you all your life, when I found out you were pregnant, I was so sure it couldn't be mine just because biologically it did not make sense. I was so damn angry, so jealous. Just thinking of you with another man . . ." He takes a deep breath. "It destroyed me."

"If you thought it was biologically impossible, then what will happen to the baby? Will he be all right?" I press my hands to my stomach defensively. Just thinking that something might go wrong fills me with so much anguish and desperation.

"He will be fine. He *must* be fine," he states vehemently. "And no matter what he ends up being, if he's not wholly human, he will be loved."

I nod mechanically. "I just want him to be safe and healthy."

"I will do everything in my power to ensure that."

"Thank you."

He tries to reach for my hand, and though my body yearns for his touch, I push it away. Not now. I cannot think with him touching me.

I take a deep breath.

"I don't know what to think anymore, Sin," I whisper. "This is too much."

His face falls. "I understand. I know you probably think I am a bastard, and to a certain degree, I am. I did questionable things to bring you to me again. But *everything* I've done has been for you, Petra. I traded my humanity for immortality just so I could wait for you, so I would never forget you."

"I—" I don't know how to reply to that. My mind is telling me to run, that this is insanity at its highest degree. But my heart keeps skipping beats every time he tells me how he murdered people *for* me.

If he's sick, perhaps I am just as sick for knowing he got revenge in my name, that he made those people pay with blood for what they did. Yet I cannot deny that he's a killer—that he's killed dozens if not hundreds of people over the centuries to gain more power.

He did it for you, silly, my inner voice amends. *Why can't you see how romantic this is?*

Romantic? Did I just think that this entire . . . murderous, demonic business is romantic?

Yes, I must be just as sick as he is.

"I need time," I say instead—a normal reply, if I do say so myself. Although, running screaming would have been preferred. "I need to think, Sin."

He doesn't seem pleased.

"All right. Time . . . all I have *is* time," he says on a dry chuckle.

CHAPTER SEVENTY-FOUR

PETRA

Present Day

What I thought would be a couple's retreat in an underground bunker with lots of lovemaking and *maybe* some detective work ended up with me back at my house.

Alone.

My parents are still away, which gives me some time to think about everything.

Although I'd already suspected a great deal of what Sin told me, some things truly shocked me.

He made a deal with a demon. He sold human souls in exchange for a home. For me.

When I woke up and remembered all the details, I was ready to hate him for abandoning me. But then he told me he did come—that he might have been late, but he never abandoned me. Instead, he embraced death *with* me.

Except death was not the end for him.

I am confused on how to feel about it. The logical thing would be to be horrified. To shun him and forget about him—forever.

But I am far from logical, especially when it comes to him.

He chose to damn himself just so he would not forget about me. He waited years for me to come back. He suffered in silence, all alone.

No matter how much I want to condemn him for all the manipulation, for everything he did to orchestrate my life and our encounters, I find that I cannot. Because if it were me instead of him, if I had been the one to survive, I would have done the same.

I would have done the same to ensure he returns to me, that he remains mine, that he cannot see or meet any other woman.

He might have taken advantage of me, and that does sting a little since I was so oblivious to it all along. But if the roles were reversed, I would have done exactly the same.

Perhaps we're not so different after all—sans the murderous history, of course. But even accounting for the people he killed, he never harmed an innocent. From the beginning, he only went after evil souls.

And despite my previous misgivings, after hearing him out, I *do* believe him when he says he did not kill the students.

But the question remains: Who did?

Could it be Arnoult as Tom? Maybe Leah as Lisa? An attempt to get revenge on those who wronged them in the past? But it still doesn't make sense: Why choose some high school students for that revenge? Unless they were also reincarnations of people from the past.

I exhale loudly as I slouch in my seat at the desk. My brain is fried from trying to make sense of everything, and I can feel the emotional fatigue starting to claim me.

I turn on my computer and note a text from Sin.

Are you all right?

I'm fine. Taking a nap. Talk to you later.

Please let me know if you feel off in any way. I'll be there in a second.

Right, a second, because he has supernatural powers.

Good Lord, what has my life become if this is the new normal?

I'm about to tell him we agreed on some distance when another icon catches my sight. It's the school chat, and there are hundreds of unread messages.

I don't know what makes me open it—chalk it up to curiosity. Although

I've never been active in the chat, it usually is the place for the latest gossip and other announcements.

With the death of François, it's no doubt teeming with terrified teenagers trying to make sense of a potential serial killer in our midst.

As I open the chat, it scrolls up to the last read message. I look curiously through the messages, noting the increased anxiety among my peers.

But then I reach the messages from a couple of days ago, after François's funeral.

"Petra has some gall to go against Daphne at the funeral."

"She has some gall to show her face at all. I can't believe Sin continues to hang out with her when she's so pregnant."

"Who do you think the baby daddy is?"

"I doubt she even knows it."

That message was sent by Daphne.

I ball my hands into fists as I scan through the many messages debating on who the father of my baby is.

"My money's on Harry," someone says.

"If that's true, she's going to end up a single mom. 😂

"She's gonna end up a single mom regardless. Who wants to take care of a baby in high school?"

"I have some info." Daphne, again.

"What?"

"Tell us."

"What is it, Daph?"

"Rumor has it she's been sleeping with Edwin, Harry, and François."

What? What rumor? And François of all people? Ew!

If you're going to lie about something, Daphne, at least make it believable.

"François?" It seems my classmates are also reluctant to believe that.

Yet the next message is a picture. A *nude* picture of me—or, at least, it has my face on a naked body. My mouth drops open in shock as I stare at how realistic it is. It must have been made with some AI software, one of those deepfakes I've heard about.

If I didn't know I've *never* taken any nude photos before, even I would have believed that is me.

A barrage of shocked messages from the other classmates, followed by a few more pictures in different positions. But the pièce de résistance is a video. Of fake me and . . . François?

What the fuck?

Rage bubbles inside of me as I stare at my likeness being used in such a lurid fashion.

"Waaa, slut!"

"She's such a whore. No wonder she has no idea who the baby daddy is."

"Skank."

The insults continue, and Daphne seems to derive great enjoyment from convincing everyone that I must have had some secret affair with François.

Did *she* doctor the pictures and the video? Because I'm pretty sure that has to be a criminal offense. Not only is it a deepfake of me, but it *should* also qualify as revenge porn.

I scroll down to the last messages. After a full afternoon of chats calling me all names on the planet and making fun of my pregnancy, the conversation died down and shifted to questions about school.

My hands are balled into fists, still in disbelief at what I saw.

Fuck you, Daphne!

She *knows* I'm in that chat. She did this intentionally so I could see it. But what did she think she would gain from it?

My embarrassment.

Even if I deny that's me, I doubt I will convince too many people.

Itching to respond, I click on the video and hit reply.

"Ha-ha-ha, nice try with the deepfake. I've never touched that slimy François. My lawyer will be in touch."

The text is immediately seen by person after person. Yet no one comes to my defense. Instead, the replies are calling me out for saying François is slimy.

"How can you speak ill of the dead?" one message reads.

The conversation I had with Sin about François at the funeral comes to mind. What had he said? That he was known to take pictures and videos of girls without consent and spread them around.

Daphne must have gotten that video from his stash and superimposed my face on it.

Bitch.

"Agh!" I cry out loud, frustrated, annoyed, and most of all, angry.

Fucking bitch. Next time I see her, I'm going to mop the floor with her.

Or perhaps I should ask Sin to get rid of her for me. Which, at the moment, is rather tempting.

More messages call me out, and I'm already too annoyed to read on.

I close my computer and plop myself on the bed, kicking at my pillow and screaming at the top of my lungs.

"Fuck you, Daphne!"

Alas, even my vocal exercises don't seem to help too much.

My heart is erratic, and adrenaline pumps through my veins. If I weren't so pregnant, perhaps I would have already gone in search of Daphne to punch her in the face.

As I lie in bed, I continue to make up scenarios in which I confront Daphne and give her a sound beating. It's only when I'm out of ideas and a little bit calmer that I glance at the luggage I'd returned with and remember the odd journal I'd found.

Grabbing it from a hidden sleeve, I prop my pillows up and start reading.

I riffle through the first pages and read the name.

Agatha Marchand. 1760.

The script, though cursive, is neat and clear, so much so that I have no trouble reading it.

I flip to the next page.

The journal starts when she is sixteen.

Agatha talks about growing up with her neighbor's son, Elroy, who was the same age as her. They had known each other since they were babies, and they were always inseparable. He was a playful and daring boy, and though she was always the more cautious one, she somehow ended up roped into his grandiose yet crazy plans—like sneaking out at night to explore a supposedly haunted mansion nearby, climbing up trees to make a tree house, and even swimming naked in the river.

Their parents indulged their friendship and even encouraged it. They were the only children of similar age in the area, and they only had each other.

But after puberty, things started to change. For both of them.

Agatha noticed her feelings shift from friendship to love.

One day, on the cusp of her seventeenth birthday, she decided to confess her feelings to Elroy and hoped he felt the same. She was sure that when they reached maturity, their parents would support them getting married.

It was a hot spring day when Agatha and Elroy went to the river. This time, as they slowly undressed to get into the water, she noticed a reticence in Elroy's movements, and an odd expression on his face as he was watching her.

He seemed to blush when she went to remove her dress. Even though she was only in her shift, he was too flustered to look at her.

Agatha then decided to be the daring one, and she called out to him.

"Look at me," she said, grabbing his chin and turning his face so she could look into his eyes.

He did so, but his entire face was flushed red.

"I love you," she told him then.

"I love you, too," he replied casually.

Agatha felt annoyed at this, thinking he wasn't understanding she meant a different type of love, not merely that of friends.

"I am *in* love with you," she clarified.

Elroy's eyes widened, and he stared at her in shock for moments on end. The boy who'd never stuttered a day in his life was now suddenly at a loss for words.

Agatha felt a stab of disappointment at realizing he might not feel the same way. But slowly, he offered her a reply.

"I-I'm in love with you, too. I've been in love with you forever."

That day, they shared their first kiss.

Their parents welcomed the relationship, and they were soon engaged to be married.

A wedding date was set for spring 1762.

Both Agatha and Elroy were excited to start their life as newlyweds. Perhaps a little *too* excited.

My eyes widen when I get to a certain passage that recounts their first night together. It was winter, months before the wedding, and they'd snuck around at night in the stables.

Agatha doesn't spare too many details when she writes about their first time together, how awkward and painful it was at first, but how lovely and fulfilling it ended up being after their second attempt.

She writes that her mother would have her head if she knew she'd anticipated her vows, but that she cannot find it in herself to regret it because it was Elroy, her sweet, beloved Elroy.

But the happiness did not last.

My heart is in my throat as I read on about the soldiers who arrived at their home, looking to draft young men into the British Army. The war against France was raging, and they needed more manpower. Any man over the age of sixteen was to be conscripted into the army.

Agatha begged Elroy not to go but soon understood that if he defied the orders, he would be arrested and executed.

So, Elroy went to war.

At first, he wrote to her as often as he could.

But a few months after he'd gone, the letters stopped.

It was early 1763 when the war officially ended, and still, there was no word of him.

She assumed the worst. His family suggested he might have found himself another girl and run away, but Agatha knew better. Her dear Elroy would never do that.

In March 1763, word finally reached them.

Elroy was dead. He'd died some months prior, shot in the head.

Agatha was inconsolable. Everyone went into mourning.

Months passed. Her family tried to cheer her up. She wouldn't go out, would barely eat or drink.

Eventually, they surprised her with an announcement—their one last attempt at reaching her. They'd arranged another marriage for her with some lawyer from Boston.

Agatha was aghast that her parents would even try that.

She was still lost to grief, but as her new wedding day approached, she realized she must do something to get herself out of the situation, which she saw as a betrayal to Elroy.

So she did the only thing she could.

She took the veil.

She joined St. Anselm Convent, and she became Sister Agatha.

But she never forgot about Elroy. She never forgot about her beloved, nor did she give up hope that one day they would be reunited.

Except the opportunity came to her much sooner than expected.

CHAPTER SEVENTY-FIVE

THE NUN

The Past
St. Anselm Convent, 1778

"Sister Agatha!"

A knock interrupts my evening prayers. I get up and open the door. Sister Mary gives me a tight nod.

"We have another one," she says in a low voice.

"Have you called for the priest?"

"He sent word he is on his way."

"Good. Let us make preparations then."

I exit my room and expect her to follow me, but she doesn't. She has a worried expression on her face.

"What is wrong?" I frown.

"This case . . . It is different," she says warily.

"Different how?"

She swallows hard. "Fifteen-year-old girl. She's dirty and covered in cuts and bruises. Her parents insist she is possessed, but I . . . I fear it might be a case of abuse."

I click my tongue against my teeth as I consider her words. It would not be the first time this has happened. Our convent is known all over the thirteen colonies for dealing with possession cases, so over the years we've seen all types of individuals who claim to be possessed—or whose families claim they might be possessed.

When I first started at the convent, I did not know how to differentiate between them, but once you've seen enough cases, you get a better grasp of it.

I've been dealing with this for fifteen years now, and most times, the cases end up being either hoaxes or mental illness confused for possession.

The nuns are all trained to deal with such cases, too, and if Sister Mary suspects this might be a case of abuse rather than possession, then I trust her judgment; she's experienced enough to tell them apart.

"The Father will know best," I reply succinctly, and we proceed toward the room.

Father Benedict O'Roark is an Irish-born Jesuit priest who's been serving in the colonies for over twenty-five years. Though his order was technically dissolved, he continues to serve as an exorcist, citing it as his divine calling.

We've been working with him for as long as I can remember, and though he is a firm believer in demonic possession, he is also skeptical of most cases.

Due to his caution, we have not had any casualty in a ritual, and that is the main reason why many people all along the coastline travel days, if not weeks, to come to us for help. And as is our duty, we do our best to help.

I light a candle and walk down the dark corridor that leads to the quarters reserved for outsider guests.

Sister Mary shows me to the room in which the young girl has been placed. Inside, her family is with her, but they keep a cautious distance.

I place the candle on a desk and assess the situation.

"Why is she chained?" I demand.

"Her family asked for it," Sister Mary whispers.

The father, a bald gentleman of about forty, steps forward.

"She's been hurting herself," he mentions. "We've been keeping her like this since she started exhibiting the symptoms."

I nod and go to her side. "What is her name?"

"Claire."

"Hello, Claire," I say softly. She doesn't react.

She's wearing a dirty gown, once white but now a grayish hue. There are specks of blood all over. Her hair is flat and oily atop her head, as if she hasn't washed it in weeks.

I move my gaze to her face. There are bruises under her eyes. Around her mouth, there are oozing sores that continue down her neck. She's staring at the ceiling, her eyes dark, her pupils dilated.

I purse my lips. That is concerning.

Her arms are full of scratches. Long, deep lines that go from her shoulder to her wrist. They are a dark color, the skin around them red and swollen.

I grab her hand and look at her nails. They're dark with dirt and caked blood as well as some pieces of flesh. She's done this to herself.

"Has anyone cleaned her wounds?" I look at her family.

They shake their heads.

"Sister Mary, bring me a bowl of water and a clean cloth."

She leaves the room and returns with what I asked. I pull a chair near the bed and start cleaning some of the girl's wounds, though from what I can see, they've begun festering.

As I clean the deeper injuries around her wrists, she slowly turns her head toward me. Her eyes are empty . . . soulless.

Her lips slowly twist into a grin.

"Te exspectābam," she says in a low, thick voice.

My lashes flutter at the sudden use of Latin.

Her parents gasp loudly and take a step back.

"Does Claire speak Latin?" I ask calmly.

"N-No. She barely knows how to read English," her mother answers.

"I see."

"Malelī 'emi," Claire growls and pushes against her chains to reach me.

I pull back. "I do not suppose she speaks Aramaic either."

"N-no . . ."

"I see. Please step outside." Turning to Sister Mary, I ask her to accompany them to another room and serve them supper.

The door closes behind them, and I am left alone with Claire . . . or the entity possessing her. I am still not certain it *is* a possession case. We once had a boy pretend to speak Latin, too. He'd found an old Bible and had memorized lines.

His parents had been sure he was possessed, but after a closer examination, it was clear he was just trying to gain their attention.

"We are alone now. I will talk to you, Claire."

Father Benedict lives at the outskirts of the town. It shouldn't take him more than twenty minutes to reach the convent via horseback. Until then, I can continue with my assessment to give him the information he needs on how to proceed.

Claire stares at me for a moment before she starts laughing. It starts off as a chuckle that turns into a full-bodied mocking laugh.

"Is everything all right at home? How are your parents treating you?"

I ask as I continue to clean her up. I avoid looking into her eyes. Even though this might prove *not* to be a possession case, there is something quite unsettling about her.

"I don't want to talk about them," she answers in a fluid, self-assured English. "I would much rather talk about *you*." Her accent is odd.

Based on the appearance of her parents, I would think them low to middle class, and as such, I would expect the language to match that. From the brief interaction I had with them, I could tell they were not exactly learned people.

But the way Claire speaks? Completely different. Something you would expect to hear from a noble, not a teenage girl from the colonies.

"And why do you want to talk about me?" I smile.

"Plum misses you," she says with a huge grin on her face.

My hand falters. My heart stops in my chest as I stare at her in shock. "W-What?"

"He says hello."

I back away, bumping into the bowl of water. It crashes onto the floor with a thud. "How do you know that?"

No one knows that. No one.

Plum was the nickname I'd given to my stillborn child. He'd been born dead, his face purple like a plum. He'd looked so beautiful, so peaceful. And although I'd already been at the convent, I had not been allowed to get him baptized.

Some of the sisters who helped me give birth know about him, but they do not know the nickname I gave him.

"I know a lot more." She laughs. "Just as I know your beloved Elroy is in hell."

"W-what?" I whisper.

"They're both in hell. Waiting for you. And I will be the one to personally drag you there."

I keep backing away. Her chains jiggle as Claire strains against them. Her face becomes mottled with anger as she screams at me.

When she sees how spooked I am, she bursts out in laughter again.

I reach for the door, scrambling to open it and get out.

"Run! Run! RUN!" she yells at me as I hurry into the hall.

Sister Mary meets me outside. "I heard—"

"We need to wait for Father Benedict. No one is to go inside until he comes here."

"But—"

"No one, Sister Mary. Not even her parents."

"All right."

I go into the main hallway, pacing around restlessly as I replay her words in my head.

Every morning, I wake up thinking of Plum and Elroy. And every day, I fight against the urge to end it all and join them.

Now, though? I feel as if my chest is being split open, and someone is squeezing my heart in their fist.

Good God . . . Elroy in hell? No, I cannot let her words get in my head. This is what demons do, they lie and cheat, trying to get under your skin until they can manipulate you with your fears.

And yet . . .

A sob escapes me as I bury my face in my hands, the tears flowing freely.

My dear Elroy, how I miss you. If only you hadn't left me. If only you had not died . . . Perhaps Plum would have survived, too.

We'd be together and . . .

The door to the convent opens, and Father Benedict steps inside. He has a worn leather bag slung over his shoulder.

"I got your message," he states matter-of-factly. But as he notices my red nose and tear-stained eyes, his expression turns to one of concern. "What happened?"

"The girl . . . she speaks in tongues, and she . . . knows things."

He purses his lips. "Show me the way."

I take a deep breath, steeling myself for another encounter with her—with that demon.

As we get to the chamber, Father Benedict enters first. I follow, as is the custom.

Claire takes one look at him and guffaws.

"Fools! All of you! You are fools if you think you can win against me."

More rattling of chains as she pulls forward, straining to reach Father Benedict.

He doesn't pay her any mind. Instead, he opens his bag and starts lining up his items: a wooden crucifix, the *Rituale Romanum,* Saint Benedict medal, a bottle of holy water, chrism oil, and lastly, his purple stole.

He places the purple stole around his shoulders, and as he gets ready to begin the ritual, a strange sound erupts in the room.

It's a low screech that becomes louder and louder with each passing second. The whites of Claire's eyes become black, and as she opens her mouth, she reveals a bloody tongue as she spits out a handful of teeth.

"We shall begin," Father Benedict speaks. I nod, though a shudder racks my body.

We both kneel around the bed and make the sign of the cross before chanting.

Sancta Maria, ora pro nobis
Sancte Michael Archangele, ora pro nobis
Omnes sancti et sanctae Dei, orate pro nobis

Claire begins writhing in pain, spasms taking over her body.

Father Benedict rises and goes to her side. Making the sign of the cross over her, he begins chanting.

In nomine Patris, et Filii, et Spiritus Sancti.

He sprinkles holy water on top of her, and the liquid burns her skin. Steam rises from her flesh before the entire surface becomes a deep red. She opens her mouth and screams so loud, the walls of the building start shaking.

Asperges me, Domine, hyssopo, et mundabor; lavabis me, et super nivem dealbabor.

More screams. But this time, the feet of the bed tremble, slowly rising off the ground. My eyes widen. I . . . I've never seen anything like this before. Father Benedict appears concerned, too.

"You whore! I know all your secrets!" Claire shouts, and with Herculean strength, she breaks one of the chains.

"Sister Agatha, leave us, please."

"But—"

"It is not safe for you."

I blink. I've always assisted Father Benedict in his exorcisms before. Yet I also cannot lie and say I am not relieved that I can sit this one out.

There is something about Claire that terrifies me.

"All right. Call if you need anything."

"Whore!" Her shouts follow me as I exit the room.

Three other sisters are in the hallway, their faces marred with worry.

"We felt the tremors. It is dire, is it not?" Sister Theresa asks.

I nod grimly. "Father Benedict will handle it. All we can do is pray."

From outside, I can hear Father Benedict's voice as he continues the ritual. Just as loud, Claire screams at him, calling him all sorts of names and baiting him to stop the chanting. Every time Father Benedict invokes the Lord's name, I can hear Claire's cry of pain.

At some point, though, silence envelops the convent. The sisters all look at each other in concern.

"Father Benedict?" I ask tentatively as I get closer to the door.

Nothing. No reply.

"Father Benedict?" I repeat.

He doesn't answer.

Taking a deep breath, I push the door open.

A gasp flies past my lips as I see the body of Father Benedict lying in the middle of the floor, all his limbs contorted in different directions, his neck snapped.

Claire is no longer chained to the bed. She's nowhere in sight. Except . . .

I slowly look up, horror taking hold of me.

She's on the ceiling, watching me with a manic smile on her face.

"You cannot get rid of me!" she sneers.

I quickly close the door and fumble through my pockets for the key, locking it.

"What happened?" the sisters ask me in horror.

I turn to them, white as a sheet of paper.

"Father Benedict . . . he's . . . dead. The demon . . . killed him."

CHAPTER SEVENTY-SIX

THE NUN

The Past

The clock strikes midnight.

Claire's parents are demanding to see their daughter, while Sister Mary tries to appease them and get them to wait.

The other sisters are all in shock. A few have fainted at the news that Father Benedict is dead, while the others are in a corner, on their knees, praying.

I pace around trying to think of a solution. Claire—or, rather, the demon—is a danger to us all. I have no idea how to go about the exorcism without Father Benedict. Worse, I don't know of any other priest with experience in exorcisms anywhere in the vicinity of Radcliffe.

And if Father Benedict could not finish the exorcism, I doubt an inexperienced priest could.

So where does that leave us?

In an attempt to keep the demon inside, I'd put crosses all over the door and windows, hoping that would at least keep it contained. But for how long? If the entity escapes, none of us are safe.

As I continue to think of a possible solution, loud screams come out of the room, followed by a low, demonic voice that beckons the sisters to open the door.

Worse, the demon seems to know *everyone's* past.

It did not just know mine. It is now calling each sister by name, whispering long-buried secrets and luring them in with wicked promises.

I catch sight of one of the sisters listening in at the door, her ear against the wooden frame, her hand hovering over the knob.

"Stop!" I tell her and pull her away. "Leave."

She regards me with scared eyes before she scurries away.

"Agatha, we meet again," the demon purrs. Its voice is thick and hoarse, and though I know it to be evil, there is a compelling quality to it. "Wouldn't you want your baby back? Your fiancé? I can give them to you. You only have to open the door."

I squeeze my eyes shut. As much as I wish I could say I was beyond temptation, I am not. For just a moment, I imagine what it would be like to have my beloved back by my side, to be together with our baby.

But then I open my eyes and realize that this is all a game to this demon.

Elroy and Plum are long dead, and nothing can bring them back.

I take a deep breath and step away.

A loud noise at the end of the hallway startles me. It's followed by the slamming of a door.

I hurry toward the noise. Claire's father has burst out of the room, his wife behind him. In their wake, Sister Mary is on the floor, her lip busted open.

"I will see my daughter now!" he shouts.

I glance between the spouses and Sister Mary, and a red haze covers my sight.

"You will not!" I tell him sternly. "You will go back into that room and wait."

"I'm not going anywhere without my daughter."

"Your daughter is possessed, and she is a danger to us all."

"I must see her for myself."

"No!" I shout. Grabbing one of the metal candle holders off the wall, I aim it toward him. "You will go inside the other room, now!"

His eyes widen in fear at the sight of the heavy item. But somehow, he thinks a frail nun wouldn't hit him, so he charges at me. Before he can get too close, I raise the candle holder and hit him over the head.

He drops down to the floor. His wife screams in shock.

"Sister Mary, come here," I tell her. She raises herself off the ground and slowly comes to my side. The blow must have affected her quite a bit because her steps are wobbly. "Check his pulse."

She does as told while I give the wife a look. She understands my meaning and backs away into their room.

"He's alive," Sister Mary whispers.

"Good. Now help me drag him into the room."

We manage to get his body inside, after which I close the door and lock the spouses in. This should buy us some time, though I am aware I can't keep two people hostage forever.

"What about the girl?" Sister Mary asks in a small voice.

I tell her the situation and that the entire convent, potentially the entire town, might be in danger.

"Good Lord," she mutters, making the sign of the cross. "What will we do?"

"I . . ." I sigh. "I don't know."

Another scream thunders through the halls of the convent, followed by an unnatural shake of the walls. Sister Mary regards me with trepidation.

Just then, someone knocks at the main door—three loud knocks in slow, measured succession.

"Should we . . ."

"I'll go," I say, marching toward the front entrance.

I raise myself on the tips of my toes to look through the peephole. It's dark out, but I can somehow make out the outline of a man.

"Who is it?"

"I am a friend of Father Benedict," the stranger replies.

I frown. "Father Benedict never mentioned a friend coming."

"Perhaps he did not have the time."

"What are you—"

"You are dealing with something beyond your control. You require help."

His words startle me. It's almost as if he *knows* something happened to Father Benedict. But . . . how?

Against all common sense, I creep the door open just enough to look at the newcomer.

He's young. In his mid-to late twenties at most. He has dark hair that curls around his ears, and a pair of startling green eyes that seem to be staring straight into my soul. He has faint scars on one side of his face.

"Who are you?"

"I can help you," he insists.

I narrow my eyes at him. "How?"

"You have a very limited time until that demon ascends and takes on a physical form. Since it consumed Father Benedict's soul, I reckon it will be only a few hours before that happens."

I blink. "Ascends? What do you mean? And how do you know Father Benedict is dead?"

"I can help you, Sister Agatha."

"How do I know this is not the demon's hand, and he is not using you to get free?"

"You do not. But I think you are smart enough to realize that, regardless of whether the demon is using me or not, you are in danger. The *town* is in danger."

I purse my lips as I regard him carefully. He's right about that. Whether he is just another instrument of the demon or not, it is clear that we might not survive the night if things continue like this.

But if he can help . . . I would rather take the risk.

Pulling the door open, I motion for him to enter.

He gives me a nod and a small smile.

"You may call me Valerion," the stranger says. He takes off his long leather coat and hangs it on a chair near the entrance. "Show me to the demon."

I nod. We walk down the hallway, and as we encounter the other sisters, I advise them to gather in the chapel, quite a distance away from the room, in case the situation worsens.

"Should I stay in case Claire's parents cause trouble?" Sister Mary asks, lingering behind.

"That will not be necessary," Valerion answers. "You may leave."

She glances at me for confirmation, and I give her a silent nod, after which she departs.

Alone with Valerion, I show him to the room where the demon is.

He stops in front of the door.

"Could you please remove the crosses?"

Odd, but I don't question it. I simply take off the crosses before unlocking the door for him.

He steps inside, and I follow suit, wanting to see with my own eyes how he plans on getting rid of the demon when even Father Benedict could not.

Poor Father Benedict, his corpse is in the middle of the room, his eyes bloodshot. I avert my gaze and say a small prayer for him.

Valerion notes the grisly murder but does not mention it. Instead, his attention is on the possessed young girl currently sitting in a corner and crying. She looks . . . normal.

"You may leave if you should wish to," he suddenly mentions.

"What?"

"It appears the demon has not ascended yet, but that does not mean it is not dangerous. You may leave."

"I . . ." I take a deep breath and straighten my spine. "I will stay."

"Suit yourself. Keep to the back, please."

"All right." I take a step back and press myself against the wall.

Valerion walks casually toward the girl—demon. He has none of the tools Father Benedict used for exorcisms, nor does he seem inclined to borrow the late father's items. He's empty-handed as he stops in front of her.

"Claire, is it not?" he says.

The girl slowly raises her head to look at him. No longer does she have the bloodshot eyes from before, nor the rash around her mouth. She looks . . . completely healthy. *Not* possessed.

"Yes," she whispers. "Please help me." Her voice is light and soft.

Valerion sighs. "You do not need to play those games with me," he says. "You can sense who I am, can you not?"

I frown. What does he mean by that?

The girl's eyes glaze over until they become fully black.

"You will not control me," the demon shouts in a thick, monstrous voice.

It jumps back against the wall, climbing backward toward the ceiling.

Valerion shakes his head. "Alas, I do not want to control you. I merely want you gone."

A deafening shriek erupts in the air. I press my hands to my ears. Valerion seems unperturbed.

He doesn't move. He merely watches, almost amused.

The demon shrieks again, and this time, the walls of the convent shake.

"Done with your tantrum?" Valerion asks in a bored voice.

"I will not be your thrall!" the demon continues in what seems like a frantic voice, almost as if it's . . . afraid?

My ears are still ringing from earlier. But even with my focus shaken, I can see there is a strange dynamic between Valerion and the demon.

"Come out now. There's no point in staying there any longer. You will not be able to ascend."

"No!" the demon shouts.

"Yes. Come out while I'm still being nice to you."

"You will not win. I will consume one last soul and—"

Before I can blink, Valerion has the girl in his grasp. W-what? When did that happen? *How*?

He holds Claire by the neck with his right hand while pressing his left one over her chest.

A gray mist oozes out of her chest. It's barely visible at first, but it soon grows in intensity. Claire flails her arms around as she keeps on screaming as if in pain—or rather, the demon does.

What is Valerion doing? And how is he drawing that gray mist *out* of Claire?

I don't understand. I've witnessed dozens of exorcisms in the past, and none have been like this.

The mist becomes a dark smoke, an amorphous blob. Claire's body goes limp.

Still holding onto the blob of smoke, though I do not know how he manages to do it, Valerion carefully lays Claire's body on the bed.

"She's dead. I'm sorry. The demon has been inside her too long and has already consumed her soul," Valerion tells me with a sad expression.

"B-but . . . what is that?" I point to the dark mist.

"What's left of the demon. *Was*," he corrects as the black cloud starts to dissipate toward his open palm. Valerion wrinkles his nose in distaste. "Level one only," he mutters under his breath.

"What are you talking about?"

He gazes at me as if he forgot I was there.

"It was a low-level demon." He shrugs. "I was hoping he'd be stronger."

I gawk at him. "You . . . what?"

"It is of no consequence now. Your demon problem is gone." He dusts off his clothes and makes to leave. But before he does, he stops by the corpse of Father Benedict. "I'll help you bury them," he states.

"But Claire . . . Her family will—"

"They should not see her like this. Her body will rot quicker than an average one because the negative energy from the demon has already eaten at it from within. If you wait much longer, you will not like what you see."

"All right. I suppose we will find a way to break the news to her parents. Poor girl . . ." I say as I take one last look at her body. So young, and now she's forever gone.

"I will ensure the parents do not trouble you."

True to his word, Valerion does all the work: from digging two makeshift graves to carrying the bodies and burying them. Then he somehow convinces her parents that Claire's death was natural.

Not only are they not belligerent with us, but they leave at dawn without asking any questions.

Odd. Truly odd.

So as Valerion turns to leave, too, I can't help but ask.

"Just who . . . *what* are you?"

He pauses in the doorway, his lips curling upward.

"This is not the last you will see of me, Sister Agatha."

Then he's gone. But not for long.

CHAPTER SEVENTY-SEVEN

THE NUN

The Past
St. Anselm Convent, 1790

Valerion has been a constant presence at the convent every time we have a case of demonic possession. Yet in all the years I've known him, he has never changed. No wrinkles or new lines on his face. No gray hairs. Nothing. He still has the youthful appearance of a twenty-something-year-old even though, by my calculations, he should be over fifty—at least as far as I've known him.

But given his experience and the ease with which he deals with those demons, I have come to wonder whether he is at all human.

Perhaps he is an angel sent from above to help us fight this plight that's taken over the land.

Over the years, the cases of possession have multiplied. Whereas before most of them would turn out to be hoaxes, now almost *every* case is real. And Valerion appears, doing his duty of getting rid of that evil.

Tonight, however, is unlike *any* case we've had before. Perhaps because it did not start as a case at all.

When an entourage of three Franciscan friars showed up on our doorstep, all the sisters were curious. It was a first, and while we've heard of the existence of some in nearby towns, they'd never come to our convent before.

Immediately, Sister Prudence arranged for a rich meal, and we all welcomed them to the dining hall as best we could.

Franciscans are known for their repudiation of all material goods, and they live solely from the charity and goodwill of others. The other sisters and I were very curious about the tales they could tell us.

Yet what started as a rather normal dinner with plenty of stories and anecdotes soon turned into something far more sinister.

"Sister Prudence, was it not?" Frey Antonio intones as he gazes at the assortment of food she'd laid out on the table for him.

"Yes." She smiles. She busies herself, moving a bread basket closer to him. But just as she lays it by his plate, his hand brushes over hers ever so gently. She's startled. He merely looks intently at her.

"Your mother is ill, yes?" he asks in a low voice.

Silence descends in the dining hall. All the nuns turn to stare at the exchange. The other two friars don't seem very surprised. In fact, each one turns to the nun next to them and engages in conversation.

What's a little uncomfortable is the way they do it. They all lightly touch the nuns' hands.

Perhaps I am reading far too much into it, but surely that touch is not required, nor is it something a friar would do?

"H-how did you know?" Sister Prudence asks.

He smiles softly. "I know a great many things."

"Oh."

"Sit. Tell me about her," he advises.

Surprised, but not at all displeased, Sister Prudence takes a seat next to Frey Antonio and proceeds to tell him about her mother.

I watch stupefied as she recounts details no one else has heard in the convent—with an unnatural ease and lack of discomfort. As if Frey Antonio were not a stranger who does *not* need to know this about her.

I turn to the other friars and note similar conversations happening around the table.

Frey Miguel engages Sister Mary about the difficult birth of her niece just a few months ago. The little girl has been sickly since birth, and the midwife does not believe she will make it through the winter.

Tears flow down Sister Mary's cheeks as she tells him the many times she's tried to pray to God, to appeal to him to save the little girl, but instead her situation has just gotten worse.

In this short exchange between the two of them, the friar has managed to get Sister Mary to admit to having doubts about God, about her faith, and even about her calling as a nun.

On the other side of the table, Frey Pedro probes at Sister Celine's insecurities, too, getting her to confess she misses her family and that she might have made a wrong choice in taking the veil. Sister Celine is young, only twenty-two, so it makes sense why she would have doubts.

But the way Frey Pedro coaxes the confession out of her is . . . odd.

"Why did you take the veil, Sister Celine?" Frey Pedro asks, his hand atop hers.

She's staring into his eyes, almost hypnotized. She doesn't blink as she responds, "I married at eighteen. But my husband turned out to be a bigamist. He had another family before he married me. Our marriage was annulled, and his wife made it her mission to destroy my reputation back home."

"Do you still love that man?"

She releases a low sob. "Yes."

"If he had not been already married, a bigamist, you would not have taken your vows, would you?"

"No," she chokes out.

"Would you like him back? Would you like him to be yours and only yours?"

"Frey Pedro, I do not think this is a proper conversation," I interject.

"No one asked you," he counters in a rough voice before turning to Sister Celine and being all smiles.

My mouth opens in shock. He continues to press her with the questions until he has what he wants.

"Yes, I would like him back if only he were mine and mine alone . . ."

"What would you do to make that a reality?" he asks smoothly.

"Anything," she whispers. "I would do anything."

"Even give up your soul?"

There's a split second of silence as I think she's not going to answer that. But then she does.

"Yes."

One word. The air becomes thick and suffocating. Frey Pedro's lips curl in a malicious smile.

"As you wish," he mentions. Using a knife, he makes a cut diagonally on his palm. He hands it to Sister Celine to do the same, and she does, without question.

As Frey Pedro extends his hand toward her, I get a strong feeling of fear in the pit of my stomach.

"Sister Celine," I say as I reach for her. But she shies away from me.

She has her back to me, her attention wholly focused on Frey Pedro. And slowly, she shakes his hand, their blood mingling together.

And they are not the only ones.

Around the table, the other two friars do the same with Sister Mary and Sister Prudence before smiling sweetly and engaging the other sisters in conversation.

"What is going on here?" I demand, shooting to my feet.

Frey Antonio's expression changes from a pleasant one to one filled with malice. He gets up from his place at the dinner table and comes to my side, taking a seat next to me.

"Sister Agatha, was it not?" There is a strange lull to his voice. The words are suspicious—the same questions have been posed to the other nuns before they gave in to this madness.

And yet, I cannot stop myself from replying.

"Yes, it is."

"Lovely convent you have here," he continues, and with each spoken word, my body relaxes more. My mind, too, stops questioning *why* this is wrong.

"Yes, very lovely," I reply mechanically.

My mind is screaming at me that it is *not* lovely, that I should leave, but I cannot seem to do so.

"Ah, I see. You lost someone."

I blink. H-how does he know?

"Yes," I reply—once more without truly meaning to.

"Your child and your . . ." he pauses, "lover."

"Yes."

"You can get them back, you know."

Fighting this maddening pull he has on me, I manage to say something that goes against what I *should* say, what he *wants* me to say.

"But they're dead. I cannot get them back."

He narrows his eyes.

"I can bring them back for you."

"W-what? Impossible."

He smiles and shakes his head. "Nothing is impossible for me. They"—he motions toward the other two friars—"can solve matters of the heart, cure illnesses, but only *I* can bring the dead back."

"Surely that is against Christian doctrine."

"Naïve child," he laughs. "Did the Bible not speak of resurrection? I am merely precipitating the timeline."

Something inside me tells me to shut this conversation down, to tell him I am not interested, that he and his strange friends need to go. But even as I open my mouth to demand that they leave, no sound comes out.

I keep staring at him, and suddenly, my head is inundated with images. Me, Elroy, our child. I can see us caring for the baby, loving him. I can see Plum growing up . . .

I gulp down. What is this? What is happening?

"We can make a deal," the friar continues. "And all those dreams will come true."

He grabs the knife from my side and makes an incision across his palm. Belatedly, I note that the previous wound had healed—*unnaturally fast*.

He gives me the knife to do the same.

"Do it. Say yes. Your soul for your dreams," he murmurs in a low, seductive voice.

I feel the pull of his words. The yearning inside of me rises to the surface with such an astounding force it becomes my reigning emotion. There's nothing else but this deep longing—for my beloved, for our child, for the life we never had.

I can no longer think rationally. I am driven only by feeling.

Grabbing the knife, I press the blade into my flesh until blood pools to the surface.

Frey Antonio stares at me expectantly, silently willing me to continue.

"Say the word," he murmurs. "Say it."

I open my mouth to speak just as I extend my hand forward to clasp his. But before our hands can touch, before our blood can mingle, someone grabs my arm and wrenches it back.

The jolt is enough to bring some sense into me. I glance back and note it's Valerion.

When had he come here?

"Do not," he states in a harsh voice. "He will consume your soul."

I stare at him. I can hear the words, but I have a hard time registering the meaning behind them.

"I need it," I whisper. "I need Elroy and Plum back."

"Sister Agatha, if you take the deal, your soul will forever be obliterated. It will become a part of this demon."

"What are *you* doing here?" Frey Antonio asks as he stares Valerion down. "This is not your territory."

Valerion cursorily glances at the friar, an icy gaze that instantly shuts him up.

"He cannot bring your fiancé and baby back. Their souls are already in the afterlife. The *only* way for you to meet them again is in another incarnation."

"Another incarnation . . . ?" I whisper.

He nods. "When you die, your soul will be measured based on your deeds, good and bad, and you will serve time accordingly in the afterlife before the Fates decide if you're worthy of another incarnation."

"But how would I meet Elroy and Plum again then? What if we never get reincarnated at the same time? What if they don't remember me? What if—" The question dies on my tongue as I glance back at Frey Antonio.

Wrenching my arm from Valerion's hold, I tentatively reach forward toward the friar.

"Sister Agatha," Valerion calls my name.

"You cannot stop her, Vitry. You know as well as I do that even *we* cannot interfere with free will. It is her decision to make." The friar smiles triumphantly.

"Perhaps I cannot do anything now, but I can still ensure you won't see another day," Valerion declares.

I gulp down, thoroughly confused by what's happening. I don't know *what* I should do. I only know that there's this gaping hole inside my chest, that my entire being yearns to be reunited with my loved ones.

"I will ensure you are reunited with your beloved in the next life," Valerion suddenly says. "I will ensure he remembers you."

"But you will still require something in exchange for your help, so is this not the same?" the friar drawls. "At least I can bring back your beloved *now*, not in any future life."

"I will not require your soul in exchange for it, Sister Agatha. If you agree to his deal, you will be forever damned. This way, your soul will be saved, and you *will* meet your beloved again. I vow it," Valerion intervenes.

I glance between the two of them.

One promises immediate results in exchange for my soul.

The other promises future results, but in exchange for what?

"And what will you require of me?" I ask in a soft voice.

"Yes, Vitry. Tell the nun what you'll require of her," Frey Antonio says with a laugh.

Valerion takes a deep breath. "Five evil souls of your choosing. Deliver them to me, and our deal will be fulfilled."

Frey Antonio snorts. "Five souls. I'm asking for *one*."

He's right. What Valerion is saying . . . he's asking me to kill people, isn't he? I don't think I am capable of that.

I'm about to shake Frey Antonio's hand when Valerion speaks again.

"He is asking for one soul. Yours. And if you give it to him now, what will you give your beloved? He will be all alone in the universe, going through incarnation after incarnation without ever finding his person. Is that what you want for him?"

My lashes flutter in surprise. Something within me resonates with his words, and before I can make a conscious decision, I pivot and grasp Valerion's hand.

"I accept the terms."

He closes his eyes, pressing his lips together as if in pain.

"So be it. A deal is a deal."

"You cannot do this!" Frey Antonio bursts out. The other friars join him as they confront Valerion. "You cannot steal our prey just like that."

"Free will, is it not, Desmond?" Valerion raises a brow at him.

Pulling me behind him, he creates a sword from dark particles of energy. Before the other friars can attack him, he cuts each of them in two.

Right in front of my eyes, the friars disintegrate, their bodies becoming beacons of dark energy that funnel straight into Valerion's palm. As he looks around the room, he snaps his fingers, and the other nuns enter a deep sleep.

I exhale loudly, a sense of relief overwhelming me. My mind instantly clears. My feelings are no longer in control, but I fear it is too late.

I glance warily at Valerion as I realize what I should have known all along. He is not human. He is a demon, too?

I just made a deal with a demon.

"I am sorry for everything, Sister Agatha. I should have known they would wander in here," he says gravely.

"W-what were they?"

"Mid-level demons. They have their own physical form and different gifts. These three in particular had the gift of uncovering a person's deepest desire, and they used that to exploit it and buy themselves souls."

"But if they're demons, what are you?"

He smiles sadly. "I did not want to introduce myself this way. I am not human, you are correct. But I am not a demon either."

My eyes widen. *He's reading my mind?*

"Correct." He chuckles. "I go by different names. Some people call me a demon, others a god. My mother comes from a long line of purebred demons, but my father is a primordial god of nether. In a way, you could say I am neutral."

"And we made a . . . deal?"

"Yes," he answers grimly. "I do not usually engage in these types of deals, but I like you, Sister Agatha. I would have hated to see your soul consumed by a puny demon. As per our terms, you will meet Elroy and Plum again in another life. Elroy will remember you, too. I will make sure of it."

"I just have to give you five evil souls?"

He nods.

"But how?"

CHAPTER SEVENTY-EIGHT

PETRA

Present Day

"Ahh," I mutter groggily as I turn on my back. Coldness seeps into my skin. My eyes snap open, my heart beating wildly in my chest.

There is nothing but darkness around me.

I am . . . not in my room.

Trying to regulate my breathing so that I don't devolve into a panicky mess, I slowly rise to my feet and feel around my surroundings.

The smell of damp stone and mold immediately hits me like a punch to the gut.

"Hello? Anyone here?" I call out, tone wavering slightly.

My voice reverberates in an echo.

All right, so this is a big space, likely the underground tunnel.

But how the hell did I get here?

The last thing I remember is reading Sister Agatha's journal. I was so close to getting more clues into the murders, too.

Sister Agatha made a deal with Valerion to meet her beloved again in a future life in exchange for five evil souls.

Five . . . like the five paintings depicting the murders. Could they be connected? Could Sister Agatha be the one responsible for them?

But *how*? She lived more than two hundred years ago. It's unlikely she's still around. Unless . . . she's like Sin, immortal. I frown as I think on it.

Although this could be the case, I feel that something is missing—that

I am missing something. Surely in over two hundred years she would have had plenty of time to kill five people instead of waiting around for some angsty high schoolers.

What is clear, however, is that these murders are different from the ones committed by Sin, and they are *not* part of his deal.

So he was telling the truth.

That somehow makes me feel a little better; at least Sin is not going around killing high school kids.

But does that mean that the entity Sister Agatha made a deal with is the same as the one Sin did?

He's never mentioned a name in conjunction with the entity before, but the details of the contract are too eerily similar not to think they might be the same: kill evil souls to get their beloved.

Five evil souls. But there have only been three murders so far.

Unless . . .

Fear accumulates in my gut.

What if *I* am next?

I somehow ended up in the tunnels without any recollection of how I got here. It's dark. I don't have my phone or any means to contact Sin.

I am helpless.

But I'm not evil!

The deal was for Agatha to deliver five evil souls. Although I don't know what Edwin or Harry did, it's clear François did have some skeletons in his closet. It makes sense why he was chosen.

But me?

I've never done anything bad in my life—or at least nothing I would categorize as evil.

Maybe it's something I did in my past life? Is that it? Perhaps because I *did* kill Snowden in the past. That technically makes me a murderer, but is it enough to brand my soul as evil?

Anxiety spears through me until I find it hard to breathe.

Oh God, I'm going to die, aren't I? I'm going to die in these goddamn tunnels, and I never even told Sin that I forgive him, that I love him regardless of everything he's done—perhaps I love him *in spite* of it.

Because no matter what happened, he always put me first. He made sacrifice after sacrifice to get to me, to be with me. He *killed* people to get me back.

And what have I done?

Nothing.

I've just been on the receiving end of everything.

Guilt slams into me as I realize how unfair I've been to him. Not only with my harsh words but also in my thoughts.

My last words to him were that I needed time. Seeing how I am now trapped in these dark, dank tunnels, time is exactly what I may *not* have.

"Sin, I'm so sorry," I whisper, though I know he cannot hear me. Hopefully, he will disregard my request for space and will try to see me anyway. Then, when he notices I'm missing, he will look for me.

Oh, the irony. Just the day before, I was complaining that he was crossing my boundaries, and now I'm *praying* he does.

Until he comes for me, though, I can at least *try* to save myself.

A little wary of the darkness surrounding me, I place one foot in front of the other, feeling my way forward slowly.

So far, so good. But not for long.

"Fuck!" I curse aloud as I trip over something and fall. Immediately, I place my hands over my belly to protect it.

Yet instead of falling onto the cold ground, something breaks my fall. Still cold, but soft, and a little wet.

"What . . ." I mutter.

I move my hands around, trying to make sense of what I'm sitting on top of. But oh, how I wish I didn't know.

At first I feel some soft material, silky and cool to the touch. But as I move my hands upward, the material becomes soaked in a sticky liquid.

"Ew!"

But that is the least disgusting thing. Already, a thought is starting to form in my mind that perhaps the thing I fell on—the thing I'm *sitting* on—might be a human body. That idea solidifies when I feel the shoulders of the body.

Moving my hands up, I note the tapering of the neck and then the jaw and . . .

My hands are now pressed into what is supposed to be the cheeks, but there's a deep gap in between. The tips of my fingers dip inside until they're covered fully in this viscous liquid—blood. And it's still lukewarm.

"Dear God . . ."

It's a dead body. I'm sitting on a goddamn corpse. And it has *no* face.

There's brittle bone and blood, sticky, gooey blood.

Fucking hell. Whoever this is has had their face bashed in.

I scurry away from the body, though the blood follows. I plop down onto the ground and feel the way my pajama bottoms are getting soaked. I squeeze my eyes shut and instinctively start reciting a prayer, though I've never been religious in *this* life.

Nausea rolls in my stomach, and bitter bile makes its way up my throat. I lean forward and retch, emptying the contents of my stomach. Still, the sickness won't leave me.

I may not be able to see the dead body, but I can imagine it has been disfigured—just like the others. And it hasn't been *too* long since this person has been killed. There is no smell of death or decomposition. The body is cool to the touch, but the head area still retained *some* warmth. It's likely only been here for a few hours.

Another murder. The fourth one.

And me being here means I am next.

If before the idea had terrified me, now, being confronted with what is going to happen to me makes me lose my goddamn mind.

"Why me?" I call out. "I never did anything wrong."

Tears stream down my cheeks, my throat clogging with a myriad of emotions.

"I didn't do anything wrong," I continue on a hiccup.

No one answers me. Only the echo of my own voice.

With how big these tunnels are and how they feed throughout the city, there's no way of knowing where exactly I am. The idea of *trying* to save myself goes out the window because no matter how much I'd like to try to do it, I simply cannot.

And there's the other fact to consider. I'm pregnant.

This isn't just about me being the potential next victim of this deranged killer, who more likely than not is Sister Agatha in some form or another, but there's also my baby to consider.

He's innocent. He never did anything wrong.

"Agatha . . . if you can hear me," I start, fighting against my sobs. "I'm pregnant. I'll have a baby soon. I know you understand what that's like. You had your own little one, and you lost him. Please . . . I beg you . . ." I gulp down. "Spare us."

No answer—not that I expected one.

"If you *must* kill me, please do it in four more months, after the baby is born. You can take me then, and I promise I will not fight you. Just let my baby have a chance at life. Please."

This time, I expect there to be no answer, too. But a sudden noise startles me.

A loud thud followed by footsteps against the damp floor.

I draw my knees to my chest and sway from side to side, knowing my end is near. And if I *am* marked to die, perhaps I do deserve it for some unknown sin. But my son . . . he's innocent. He's the only innocent one.

Sin . . . if only you could hear my voice. I don't even want you to save me. But our child . . . he deserves to be born, to live.

If there's any god out there, any deity at all, please spare my child.

The sound of the steps intensifies. Whoever is out there is getting closer.

My heart rams against my rib cage, my breathing out of control. I press my hands to my stomach, holding onto my baby tightly.

Someone is definitely coming.

Each second feels like an eternity until a small beacon of light appears somewhere in the distance.

I squint my eyes. The light intensifies, blinding me. I shield my eyes with the back of my hand.

"Who's there?" I demand.

More steps. The light has now enveloped the entire area. The person carrying the light is close to me, perhaps a few feet away.

A gasp echoes in the tunnel.

It takes me a few moments to acclimate to the change in lighting. But as I do, a few things start to take shape around me.

First is the space I—we're—in. It's a round vestibule at the junction of two narrow passageways. The walls are damp and moldy, with water dripping from somewhere above. A water source nearby?

The second thing I see, however, is the body.

The *dead* body.

My mouth opens and closes, and no sound comes out.

"Daphne . . ." I whisper in shock.

I only recognize her from her blond hair and the *D* pendant around her neck. Her face has been so completely disfigured that no one would be able to tell her identity.

There's blood everywhere. All over her clothes. All over *my* clothes. On my hands.

I stare down at my palms, my eyes wide with horror.

But there's a third thing that catches my eye: a medium-sized boulder, not too far from Daphne's body, covered in blood. The murder weapon?

"Hands where I can see them!" a familiar voice rings out.

I blink. It's Detective Fiona. She's flashing a light toward me, toward Daphne's body. But what is she doing here? How would she know to come to the tunnels?

That question can wait, though, because this looks *bad*.

I'm in a tunnel, alone with a dead body. I'm covered in blood, and the potential murder weapon is right there.

"Detective Bedford. This is not what it looks like," I stammer.

"Do not move, Miss Valentine. Hands where I can see them."

She takes a few steps forward, and I note she has a gun next to her flashlight, aimed straight at me.

Oh, no.

She must think *I* killed Daphne. And to be honest, I don't blame her. It does look like I did it. And the fact that I woke up next to Daphne's body right before the detective showed up makes everything even more suspicious.

Is someone trying to frame me? But why? And how would that fit into Sister Agatha's murderous plan?

Unless . . .

My eyes widen in slow realization.

"It's *you*," I whisper.

"You're coming with me, Miss Valentine. Get up. Slowly."

The barrel of the gun is now just inches away from my face as she orders me to my feet.

I rise up on trembling legs. She has a look of disgust on her face as she gazes down at my blood-covered self.

"Hands behind your back," she commands as she jiggles a pair of handcuffs.

I don't move. I cannot. If she cuffs me, I will not have any way to get out of this situation. It will be akin to signing my death warrant.

Adrenaline rushes through me, and in a moment of pure madness, I butt her in the head. The hit momentarily stuns her, and it gives me enough time to snatch the flashlight from her and sprint down the passageway.

I'm barely a few feet away when a gunshot rings out.

CHAPTER SEVENTY-NINE

PETRA

Present Day

The bullet narrowly misses me, but I lose my footing and end up on the floor. I try to get my bearings, but Fiona is right behind me.

Damn it! I've never been the most athletic individual, but pregnancy has made me a *lot* more sluggish. It takes me twice as long to get up and run again, and by that time, the detective is only a few steps behind.

She shoots another shot, this time a warning one seeing how it's not aimed at me. "Stop, Miss Valentine!"

I'd be crazy to.

"Petra! Stop before you make this more difficult."

"Why? So you can kill me easier? No way!"

I run faster, fueled by the sheer need to survive. But Fiona has had training in chasing criminals, and in just a few moments, she's on me. She grabs my shirt, pulling me backward.

"Stop! Or I will be forced to hurt you."

"Right," I snort. "No, thank you." I elbow her in the gut, but she pulls back in time so I only graze her stomach.

She grits her teeth and grabs my arm, fiddling with her cuffs so she can detain me.

Hell no!

"Stop fighting, or it won't end up too well for you."

There it is—she's clearly stating her intentions now. And unless I act fast, I will be dead like Daphne.

Mustering strength I did not know I possessed, I swivel toward her and punch her straight in the face. She's taken aback by the blow. Hell, even I am shocked by my strength as blood pools down her face.

But this is my moment to act. As she teeters on her heels, I make a run for it.

I'm no match for a trained detective, though. Blood still pouring down her face, she quickly follows after me.

She shoots another bullet that narrowly misses me.

Fuck. At this rate, she *will* shoot me. I don't remember how the last murder was supposed to occur, but I am sure she's skilled enough to aim for a non-vital spot, then keep me alive long enough to torture me to death.

Good Lord! How the hell did I end up here?

I still don't know what I did to deserve this. I'm *not* evil! And Snowden's murder—in a past life, no less—should not qualify as a sin when I was saving someone else's life.

But seeing how I am now running for my life, I must concede that there is something I must not be aware of.

Out of nowhere, I'm falling.

"Agh," I cry out as Fiona tackles me to the ground. "My baby. Please, my baby," I mutter incoherently as I angle my body so I don't hurt my belly.

Fiona appears surprised by my words, but that doesn't stop her from handling me roughly.

"You should have thought about your baby before this," she snarls. "You're done for, Valentine."

She tightens her grip over my arms, and I start believing that perhaps I really *am* done for—that this is the end. My mind feels foggy and tight, my vision dimming by the second, and yet there's still this instinct to survive.

I push back with my leg. I don't know where my blow lands, but judging by the *ow* sound she makes, I think it did land somewhere.

The handcuffs brush against my wrist. I draw my leg back and kick again, this time hitting her in the stomach. It works, just enough for me to shake off the cuffs, throw them to the side, and get on my hands and knees so I can propel myself upward and run again.

But she reaches for me, her hands circling my ankle, and I cannot move.

"Let go!" I cry out. Using my other leg, I try to hit her in the face.

"I won't allow you to get away," she tells me.

"I haven't done anything! I'm not evil," I grit out.

I'm out of breath, tired and aching. The ground is cold. Fiona's grip on my ankle is tight and relentless. I don't know how much longer I can hold on since my strength is waning by the second.

Soon, my body will betray me, and I'll . . .

No, I *can't* die.

Fiona snorts at me. "You're not evil?" she chuckles at me. "Of course you'd think that."

"What the hell are you talking about?"

"I've been watching you from the beginning, Petra. I know everything about you."

I blink.

"E-everything?" I whisper.

"Everything," she confirms in a smug tone. "Martinez didn't believe me, but I knew. Call it a woman's intuition, but I was so sure of you."

Martinez? I rack my brain until I remember that's the name of her partner. But . . . does that mean they're in this together? Have they been killing people in fucked-up satanic rituals as a team?

At first, it seems ludicrous to even consider—two detectives, people of the law, going on a murder spree. But the more I think about it, the more I realize that the way the murders occurred, it seems impossible only *one* person would be behind them.

Especially a woman—not feminist of me, I know. But Fiona is not a large woman. She might have FBI training, but there's just no way she would have the strength to chop a body up into pieces.

"If it hadn't been for that boyfriend of yours, I would have got to you faster."

"W-what? What are you talking about?"

She rolls her eyes. "As if you don't know. Every single time I tried to look into you, your boyfriend would *coincidentally* show up. Don't think I don't know you asked him to threaten me."

"Threaten you?" I stare at her in shock. "What the hell are you on? I never did that."

She narrows her eyes at me.

"For weeks, I've been trying to come to your house for a meeting. Every single time, your boyfriend answered the door to tell me you were not home."

What? But . . . weeks? Sin and I weren't even together at that point, were we? Although granted, with his abilities, he would be able to intervene at the drop of a hat, more so considering he's been watching me constantly.

Then where the hell is he now?

If he's such an expert at watching me, then how could he miss my absence? Did he blink, and suddenly I was gone? For fuck's sake, if he wants to call himself a stalker, he'd better stalk better.

If—*when*—I survive this, I will have some words with him.

"And last time I tried to intercept your parents, he conveniently showed up again to tell me that, without any evidence, my presence could be considered harassment, and he could very easily make it so I won't *ever* have a job again."

My brows go up. He did that? Well, at least he only threatened her and didn't kill her.

No!

He *should* have killed her. If he had, I wouldn't be here, in this precarious situation.

Good Lord, I can't believe that for once I wish Sin had *killed* someone. I guess that's another thing I'll need to have words with him about. Less sparing and more killing—especially when someone is suspicious.

"I did not know about any of that," I say in a small voice. Perhaps I can't fight her off, but I can try to win her over? She's a woman, after all, and I'm pregnant. Perhaps she will show me some mercy.

As if womanly solidarity is more important than whatever deal she has with that Valerion.

"Right. You don't need to act anymore, Petra. I know everything. I *saw* everything."

"You saw what?" My eyes widen.

If she *is* Sister Agatha, does that mean she's immortal? Has she been watching me all this time, past-life me, too? Or is she only a reincarnation like me?

"Every single vile thing you've done. I will make sure you can never hurt anyone again."

"But I *never* hurt anyone," I cry out. Well, technically, anyone minus Snowden, but he doesn't *really* count—he was damned anyway.

"Whatever you say," she says flippantly. "You're not getting away from me now. I have everything I need to finish you off." She has a self-assured smirk on her face that only serves to make the panic inside my chest grow stronger.

Although my body is sore and tired, I will *not* die like this. So I try to think differently. If physically I cannot best her, I need to be smarter than her.

Her gun is a small distance away. There's only the subtle glint of light in the otherwise dark tunnel.

Do I know how to shoot a gun? No. Do I intend to shoot it? And potentially *kill* her? I don't know.

You're only defending yourself, my inner voice tells me. *It's kill or be killed. Get it together, Valentine*!

Fiona follows my gaze—and the decision is made for me.

Either she grabs it first, or I do. And there is only one option in which I prevail.

She runs over to get the gun at the same time that I launch for it.

I grab the hilt, she grabs the barrel. I pull on it with all my might, using my legs to kick at her and make her lose her balance. She does the same with me, but compared to her, I need to protect my belly.

That means I pull back to avoid getting hit, and my hand slips over the handle. I dig my nails into the metal, feeling them snap at the tips. She swivels to the side and brings my arm over her shoulder, hitting the inside of my elbow in an attempt to get me to release the gun.

I won't do it. I *can't* do it.

One hit. Two hits. The pain travels through me at lightning speed. My hand becomes slack. But just as I feel as though I am about to drop the gun, I press my foot on the back of her knee with enough strength, and her hold weakens.

"Fuck," she curses as her knee gives out. I wrench my hand away, pulling on the gun, but Fiona isn't letting go.

She backhands me across the face so hard I see stars.

"Let go!" she demands. "Take your hands off my goddamn gun."

"No chance in hell," I grit out, pulling on it even harder.

In our struggle, the gun has nestled between our chests. We're facing each other at close range, each pulling on one half of the gun. Although I'm afraid the gun could go off at any point, I don't give up—I'm doomed either way. I could gamble, or I could let her kill me. I will always choose the former.

Fiona's features are drawn tight, sweat trickling down her face.

"You'd harm a pregnant woman?" I rasp out. "Do you think Valerion will give you some extra points if you give him the soul of a baby?"

She frowns. "What are you talking about?"

"You don't have to pretend you don't know. *Agatha*," I say pointedly.

Her brows go up. What is that I see in her eyes, recognition, surprise? She probably didn't think I would find out.

"W—" her words are drowned out by the loud bang of a gun.

I freeze. That was a shot, a *gunshot.* But I didn't squeeze the trigger, did I? At least I think I didn't.

Did I . . . did I get shot? I've heard sometimes the onslaught of adrenaline can lead to a delayed pain response.

My thoughts are interrupted by a low moan. It's coming from her.

She draws back, relinquishing her hold on the weapon.

Her hands go to her abdomen, where a red stain is soaking the material of her shirt, growing larger by the second.

"You shot me," she says in disbelief.

"As if you wouldn't have done the same," I counter, though I'm just as shocked by what happened.

Good Lord! That could have been me! The gun could have gone off in my direction—in the direction of my baby.

Fiona breathes hard as she holds tightly onto her wound. She staggers back, and as she hits the wall, she slowly sinks to the floor.

"You shot me," she repeats, more to herself.

I stare at her. Do I run away now? Do I leave her here?

"Call 911," she rasps, her voice tinged with pain. "Call—"

"No," I reply suddenly, shocking even myself.

"You would let me bleed out here?"

Old Petra would have never even entertained this. But this Petra has her baby to consider. Fiona might be hurt, but she's still alive. As long as she lives, she's a danger to us. She might not sacrifice me today to that devil, but she will at some point. And I cannot allow that to happen.

But that means . . .

I glance at the gun in my hands, feeling the foreign metal against my fingers.

If I leave her like this, she might get help, she might survive, she might try to hurt us again.

But if I . . .

Fiona's gaze goes to the gun in my hands, too, somehow knowing exactly what I'm thinking about.

"Don't do this, Petra. You will only make the situation worse for yourself."

Will I? Perhaps I will truly become an evil soul then, and in her next incarnation, she might come after me again.

Maybe. At least for the time being, we will be safe. My baby will be safe.

I raise the gun and point it at her. My hand trembles, but my resolve is unshakable.

I take one step. Finger on the trigger. I squeeze.

The bullet hits her shoulder. She cries out in pain, begs me again to stop.

I get closer. Perhaps this is the frenzy of killing—why this becomes so addictive to serial killers. Perhaps it's just the relief at being alive. But there's this bubbly feeling inside of me that only intensifies with every shot.

Once I'm closer, with better aim, I shoot again.

Face hit. Right in the middle of her nose.

She stops moving.

Another shot. This time her forehead. Head shot, I think they call it. Now I'm certain she will never move.

And yet, I don't stop. I shoot again and again until there are no more bullets in the gun. Only then do I throw it to the ground.

I inhale and exhale. Her face is a mess. Skull exploded, flesh mangled.

I did that.

I stare in shock at my handiwork, and I can barely recognize myself. At least I'm alive, or at least that's what I tell myself. The reality is that this might have been survival—could have been. But if it was, it should have never gotten to this.

She's dead. Fiona—*Agatha* is dead. She failed to fulfill her bargain.

I'm still breathing hard when a slow, methodical clap of hands reverberates in the tunnel.

From the stark darkness, two distinct sets of footsteps emerge. I'm immediately on guard, thinking it's her partner.

Instead, my mouth hangs open in shock when I see two men. The first, I don't know. Tall, muscled, with stark green eyes. He looks a few years older than me, but there's a lethal aura to him that speaks of a lifetime of experience. The second man, I know far too well.

Sin.

Sin? Why is he here? Why now, *after* I was attacked?

Why wouldn't he come in time to save me?

More weird, he doesn't seem at all shocked or surprised to see me like this, with blood-stained clothes and two dead people around me. If anything, he looks . . . pleased.

"Congratulations, Sister Agatha," the first man starts speaking. "You have fulfilled your part of the bargain."

CHAPTER EIGHTY

PETRA

Present Day

"What's happening, Sin? Why are you here? Why didn't you come earlier?" My voice trembles as I speak, and I barely stop myself from adding—why didn't you come in time, like before?

But that would be low of me, especially now knowing what he went through: how long he's waited for me and everything that he's done to get me back.

"Petra, calm down," he says in a low, entirely too unbothered voice.

"Calm down? How can I calm down? I killed someone!" I burst out. "I killed someone and . . ." I trail off as I look around.

Fiona's body is a mess, and as my eyes zero in on her shattered skull, a sliver of shame consumes me. Yet even as I look away from her, there's still Daphne. Equally as disfigured, equally as viciously killed. Could it be that . . . ?

"Fiona wasn't Sister Agatha," I whisper, more to myself.

"Petra, please," Sin adds, moving to come toward me. But the stranger with him extends his arm to the side to stop him.

"Not yet," he says.

"What's happening? What's going on?" I demand as I glance from Sin to the stranger.

"You have fulfilled your bargain. It is time I fulfill mine," the stranger says as he steps forward.

I back away until I hit the cold wall, at which point he touches my forehead with two fingers.

A burst of light explodes behind my retina, and a whirlpool of lost information fills my brain. At first, it's haphazard pieces, but soon the puzzle gains contour.

My lips part, and a harsh gasp escapes me.

Images roll in my mind. What I'd read in that journal had been mere tidbits of information compared with the images I see.

It's like a video playing right before my eyes.

I see him—Elroy. But it's not him, is it? It's . . . Sin. My Sin.

I see everything, us growing up together and falling in love before tragedy struck. Then the images become bleak and hopeless, marred by my own lost sense of self. Slowly, my—*is it really mine?*—life at the convent takes shape.

All the exorcisms, all the caring for the sick.

Until *he* appeared. Valerion. The stranger standing in front of me right now.

We made a deal. Five souls in exchange for meeting Elroy and my baby again in a future life, all the while having the memories of the previous.

Yet something else happened.

I . . . couldn't fulfill my side of the deal.

Soon after, I fell ill. Consumption.

I became so weak I could barely leave my room. Yet I wouldn't give up. So instead, I trudged my way to the tunnels, and with the last of my strength, I painted.

Because those terms I agreed to were . . . tricky.

I, *Agatha,* would have to deliver those souls. I, *Agatha,* would have to find evil souls and devise their demise. Yet if I, *Agatha,* died, then everything changed.

I might get reincarnated in the future, but without my memories. I would still have a pending bargain, but I would be unable to remember the terms, or why I committed to them in the first place.

So I did the only thing I could.

I tried to tell my story through my journal and through paintings, as much as my frail body would allow me to.

For days on end, I toiled in the tunnels, adding as much detail to those paintings as I could—for the future.

But before I could finish, I gave my last breath.

My next life, just like I anticipated, I could not remember anything.

I saw those paintings in the tunnels, and they moved me in strange ways, but without my memories, I could not fulfill my bargain—not even when I shot and killed Snowden. His soul was already damned, so it would not count.

Without being able to remember the past, I would forever be locked in a vicious cycle of being reborn, with no memories, going through life without knowing what I was meant to do.

But there was one thing that changed that.

Sin. His bargain.

While my bargain asked for a reunion with my baby and my beloved as well as our past memories, he simply asked for his person, his fated one.

Me.

His choice to sacrifice dozens of people just to meet me brought me closer to the fulfillment of my own bargain. Because when I died as Petra in 1896, when Sin had fulfilled his bargain yet had still lost me, he gained another boon from Valerion—the opportunity to be with me again; for me to relive the past, to remember it.

When he slipped a drop of Jí in my drink, it wasn't just the memories of past Petra that were awakened. It was also the memories of Agatha. The former took on the shape of dreams, but the latter manifested as a split personality.

Or, as I see snippets of everything that happened, that is the only way I could describe it.

Perhaps it's because present-day Petra was far too innocent of the evil in the world. Perhaps because Agatha's twisted bargain could not coexist inside my mind—yet.

But as the Jí worked in my mind, the consciousness of Agatha became stronger and stronger. And she—*I*—knew what she had to do.

Deliver five souls. Five evil souls.

What is perhaps even more surprising than the fact that I developed a split personality of my past-life self is that Sin has known about it all along.

If I had any question about how I, five-foot-three, one-hundred-twenty-pounds Petra could have killed guys twice my size, now I know—I see it.

Sin facilitated every single murder.

The first one was Edwin.

Present-day Petra had felt so sad about him, had pitied him for the way he'd been killed. Because that Petra did not know the depth of his depravity.

Days before his death, he'd been planning a massacre at the school. He had everything ready. Hunting rifles stolen from his father. Makeshift bombs to create mayhem and confusion. And a list of victims, most of them professors and a few students who'd made fun of him.

Was he evil, or just traumatized? the still-normal part of me asks. He must have been evil, since his death counted as one.

The next was Harry.

Present-day Petra had mourned him, too, without realizing that at the very ball at which he died, he'd planned to spike her drink, bring her to his car, and do . . . unspeakable things to her.

She's felt sad for the poor kid while he was planning to assault her.

My features harden as I realize just how naïve I'd been, how easily I'd been misled by seemingly nice people who were in fact evil. Because Harry's death counted. He was number two.

François had terrorized half the female population at St. Anselm Hall. Present-day Petra had been far too asocial and secluded to know that he'd been taking pictures and videos of girls, sharing them without their consent, blackmailing them.

He was evil! He deserved to die, and he more than earned his place as the third.

That Daphne was truly evil is not a surprise.

Present-day Petra had not been the only victim of her bullying. She'd driven at least one girl to suicide and bullied a few others to the point of self-harm and mental breakdown.

She deserved to die, and so she was fourth.

Now, Fiona was a bit more tricky.

As Fiona had tried to find evidence to pin the murders on me, Sin had done his best to sidetrack her. But in his research, he'd discovered some things that did not make sense.

Complex murders seemingly solved overnight. Rushed convictions. Lives ruined.

Fiona was in the business of planting evidence—all to get a conviction.

For her stellar record, she'd been sent to Radcliffe to investigate the murders. Even if she were correct that I was the murderer, she developed her theory without much evidence at first, based solely on her hunch.

Then, she became single-minded in her focus, which allowed Sin to question her true motives; after all, with his assistance, I had left no evidence at any of the crime scenes.

All the information solidifies in my mind until the shock I felt earlier at having killed Fiona vanishes. In its place, a sense of fulfillment and gratitude appears.

The past and present merge until there is only one Petra—*me*. The sum of all past selves and the convergence of only one desire: to be reunited with her loved ones.

I open my eyes.

I ignore Valerion's presence. My gaze is drawn to Sin—my darling Sin, who's suffered so, so much to get me, who sacrificed the world for me.

My feet move before my mind can register it. And once I'm in front of him, I drop to my knees, my head bent. Tears drip down my cheeks as shame eats at me from inside.

"I'm sorry I ever doubted you," I whisper.

The way I'd been so suspicious of him, how I thought the worst of him, physically hurts me. Yes, I can blame it on the fact that I did not have all the information. But still, I should have known better.

If all else failed, I should have trusted his devotion.

"Petra—" His eyes widen in shock, and before I can blink, he's on the ground, kneeling next to me. "Don't. Don't you dare kneel before me."

"I am so sorry, Sin," I repeat. "I said words I regret. I blamed you for things I did not understand . . . oh, how you must have felt when you saw me back away from you."

He pulls me tightly in his arms, his hand stroking my back in slow, languid movements.

"Don't. I was prepared for it—for all of it. In fact, you reacted to everything *far* better than I expected you to. You think in all the time I've been waiting for you to be reborn I did not entertain scenarios in which you shunned me? I was aware you would have no memory of me in the beginning. I knew you would not see me as I see you. And I was prepared for all that."

He lifts my chin to gaze into my eyes.

"And once more, you proved to me why I love you so much; why all the sacrifices were worth it. Because even when all the circumstances told you I was the bad guy, that you should run away from me, you still stayed."

"I almost did," I whisper.

"But you did not. You had your suspicions about me, but deep down, there was still a part of you that trusted me enough to allow me to explain myself. I could have never asked for more."

I swallow a sob. "Thank you. For everything."

Valerion clears his throat behind us. We both turn to look at him.

"I believe I still have to fulfill *my* side of the bargain."

I frown, not understanding at first. But then Valerion produces a small glass vial and extends it toward Sin.

"She has all her memories. It is time you recover yours, too."

"You mean . . . ?"

"A deal is a deal. I promised you that you would be reunited with your beloved, and he would retain his memories."

Sin glances upon the vial with trepidation. Slowly, he accepts it, and popping off the lid, he brings the drop of liquid to his lips.

I stare at him, waiting.

He blinks, slowly, and a different type of awareness seems to penetrate his gaze.

"I remember."

Two words, and I finally exhale in relief. He smiles at me, that warm smile that I missed with all my might.

He is now, just like me, the sum of all his personas—Elroy, my original lover, past-Sin, and present-Sin. All the pain I endured, all the lonely years spent thinking about him, were not in vain.

Both of us made sacrifices to get to this point, and all of our actions completed each other, working in tandem for the same ultimate goal.

We glance at each other, and a silent current of acknowledgment passes between us.

I'd made the first deal, but I'd forgotten about it before I fulfilled it. He'd made the second deal, but fate had intervened, so he'd made a third deal that put all the wheels in motion so I could finally fulfill *my* deal.

Although he was the one to bear the brunt of the suffering, for which I will be eternally grateful, we would not be here without each other—without both of our efforts.

Even when we lacked the knowledge of the past, we were so in sync that we still completed each other.

Finally, we are once more together, and this time, I plan on *never* letting him go.

But there are still things I need clarification on, so I turn to Valerion.

"How did Sin's powers in his second life come about? Elroy did not have any."

Valerion's lips curl up.

"That question would be best asked of my father. He is the one who granted him his gifts.

I raise a brow. "Your father?"

"He is a primordial deity and has the power to bestow spiritual energy upon whoever he wishes. He's grown rather bored as of late, so he's acquired a few side projects, so to speak."

"He gave Sin powers because he's bored?" I ask in outrage. But then I notice Sin chuckling beside me. "You knew about this?"

He nods. "Valerion and I have had conversations about this. And though I never met his father, I am grateful for the gift he's given me."

"But what about the demon part? Because *you* are a demon now."

"He is a made-demon in the sense that his grief over your death caused him to morph into one. But because of his already existing spiritual energy, he is . . . something else."

"Something else?"

"He exists in a state between a born-demon and a natural one. I have not encountered someone like this before, so I cannot properly define *what* he is."

"But he is immortal, right?"

"Yes, that is correct."

I had assumed as much, which is what makes me a little uneasy.

"If he's immortal, then what about me? I'll grow old, and he . . ." I look back at Sin. He will remain as young and handsome as he is now.

"I have already asked about this," Sin says. "You don't have to worry about that. I would have never become this . . . thing if it meant living on without you."

"Sin is correct. Since he is technically in-between a born demon and a natural one, his spiritual energy is high enough that he can lend it to you, too. Every time he feeds—"

"Feeds?" I blink.

"Every time he consumes a soul."

I glance back at Sin warily. "Evil ones, right?"

He nods, smiling. "That was part of my second deal with Valerion. I would become a demon, but I would only feed off corrupted souls."

I breathe out in relief. "That's good."

Valerion rolls his eyes and continues. "Every time he feeds, if you drink from him, you will get the same benefits."

"By drink from him, you mean . . . ?"

"Blood," he says unflinchingly.

"Oh . . ."

"If you drink straight from the vein, after he consumes a soul, you will receive some of his life force and, as such, you will also not grow old, nor will you die. Of course, Sin must feed more often to accommodate two people, but I do not think that will be an issue."

"That's weird, but pretty cool," I mumble, though I'm slightly relieved.

As long as I get to live forever *with* Sin, I suppose a little blood doesn't hurt. It's not as if I'd *ever* leave him so he could find someone else. Uhm, nope. Absolutely no. Never!

"There is one last thing we'd like to know," Sin adds.

I already anticipate his question, so I say, "The baby. Will he be fine? If Sin is not human, then—"

"The baby will be fine. He will be unique, and perhaps the only of his kind in the entire universe, but he will be fine," Valerion states.

"How do you know for sure? If he's so unique, then how can you be certain about that?"

"Because I know someone who can see all potential threads of the future, and I have confirmed it with her."

"Who?" I ask through narrowed eyes.

Valerion smiles. "Someone *very* powerful."

"Your lover or something?" I continue to probe, needing all the confirmation I can get that my baby will be fine.

He shakes his head and chuckles. "She is family, but she is not my lover."

"I see." I nod. "I suppose that's as good of an assurance as we'll get."

"I will vow to you that should anything happen to your child, I will come to help."

"We will hold you to that," Sin replies solemnly.

I continue to assess this Valerion skeptically. Although I remember him from my past life as Agatha, and I could even say we were . . . friendly, there is still so much I don't know about him. He was a mystery then and is a mystery now.

"You're immortal, too. Don't you get lonely all by yourself?"

He seems startled by my question. A slow smile curves at his lips. "I am not by myself."

"I did not realize you had someone." This time, Sin is the one who comments.

"I do technically have someone, though not in this timeline."

We both stare at him.

"What?" I blurt out.

"It's complicated," he chuckles. "But in the meanwhile, I enjoy seeing others find happiness. Let's just say it's my way of accumulating good karma so I can get my own happy ending . . . at some point."

"That's rather sad," I say without thinking.

He appears stricken by my words, but he quickly composes himself. "I suppose it is. All the more reason for you two to cherish what you have. It's priceless."

He looks upon us with a longing gaze before he takes a deep breath.

"My task here is done. Should your son ever need my help, I will return."

Sin and I nod.

"Farewell, Sin, Petra." He vanishes from sight, as do the bodies of Fiona and Daphne and any trace of blood or biological waste.

I blink. "I suppose that means we don't have to clean up the scene of the crime?"

Sin laughs. "That's Valerion for you. He always thinks of everything."

"Yes, but . . ." I bite my lip. "He seemed rather sad, did he not?"

"He's held a certain sadness to him for as long as I've known him. But despite his odd manner, he is a good person," he assures me.

"We owe everything to him. Which is why I hope he gets his own happy ending eventually."

"I think we should be concerned with our own for now." He waggles his brows suggestively.

I crack a smile. "And what did you have in mind?"

He pulls me into his arms, and in the blink of an eye, we're back at the underground bunker. We tumble together into bed, him on his back, with me on top of him.

I stare into his eyes, unable to believe that after everything, we're here, together, with no more secrets between us.

It's just me and him, as we were always meant to be. And . . . our little plum.

"I love you so much, Petra," he rasps, his eyes glistening with unshed tears. "I will always love you."

"I love you, too, but you should start putting your words into actions. Have you forgotten pregnant women can be *very* horny?"

He laughs and leans in to kiss my nose. "I don't care about any other pregnant woman except you. And if my lady is horny, then I shall do my utmost to satisfy her."

"I'm waiting."

Except I do not have to wait long at all.

CHAPTER EIGHTY-ONE

EPILOGUE I

Four Months Later

"My parents are getting suspicious," I whisper into the phone.

We're at a restaurant celebrating my mother's birthday, and they've been closely monitoring me since I'm way past the due date to give birth.

To my surprise, my parents have made good on their promise and have delegated most of their tasks to other people in order to dedicate more time to the family. My mother has been to all my ultrasound appointments and has taken courses on child-rearing to get up-to-date with all the new tips and tricks. To say she's devoted to the cause would be an understatement.

My father, too. Though always a little bit more stoic, he's tried his best to be more vocal about his feelings and let me know how much he loves me and his future grandson.

That being said, I think the fact that this pregnancy *and* this baby might not be entirely normal is catching on. I'm almost one month over the due date at this point, which my parents find highly irregular.

Yet the doctor, having examined everything carefully, has said that in his professional opinion, the baby still needs time in my belly.

Odd? Yes. Did Sin pay him to say that? Also, yes.

Alas, it seemed to work for my parents, who don't have enough medical knowledge to realize that might not be . . . normal.

But the fact that the pregnancy has progressed somewhat *not* normally worries me. How will the birth proceed? How different will it be than normal, regular births? Are there even doctors equipped to deal with this?

Although I am very happy to meet our little plum, I can't say I'm not terrified of giving birth. I've even suggested to Sin that I'd like to do a C-section since I don't want some non-human baby to tear up my lady bits. But that brought more concerns, too.

Who would perform the surgery? And if the baby is not exactly normal, what then? What if there are complications?

Sin has assured me that in any eventuality, his blood should heal me.

"What do you mean?" Sin asks from the other end of the phone, though he is secretly across the restaurant, hiding in the shadows.

He couldn't very well stay away from me, no? He wouldn't be much of a stalker if he did that.

"They want a second medical opinion."

"That's fine. I'll handle them."

"Not everyone can be bought off," I hiss, placing my hand over my mouth so my parents don't hear me. They're busy researching the micros and macros of the dishes on the menu.

"Petra, is that Sin on the phone?" my mother inquires, noticing me.

I smile guiltily and end the call, placing my phone screen-down on the table. "He wanted to join us," I admit.

She gives me a wry look. "And we love him, but we almost *never* have time just with you. I hope he can understand that."

"He's just overprotective," I mumble. Now *that's* the understatement of the century. Or, erm, centuries. Not that they need to know that.

"A good quality to have." My father nods. "Although sometimes he can be too clingy."

"You think?" I raise a brow.

"I don't know how you youngsters do it anymore." He shrugs. "Perhaps it's perfectly normal, and I'm worrying for nothing."

It's far from normal, but I'm not going to admit that to my father.

"He is a good man."

"That he is. You chose a good one," he agrees. "But you're sure you want to marry so young? You can wait a few more years. You don't have to do it right after graduation."

As if anyone could stop Sin, but I'm not going to tell him that either. Besides, I happen to want that just as much. We've already had one failed engagement in the eighteenth century. I'm not going to let him slip through my fingers again. I want to make that as official as possible.

So what if it technically will not *matter* as much in the future, when we will have to move around, change identities to keep people from finding out we don't age? It's for me. I *want* it.

Sin demands it, too. He wants to see me as a bride, in grand gowns and lace, and I happen to be just as excited for it.

As soon as I give birth and return to my regular weight, that is.

I bite my lip as I feel a little tap against the walls of my stomach.

"No, it's fine, Dad. I'd like us to marry as soon as possible, too," I mention, a little absentmindedly.

"If you say so. It's not as if we can change your mind since you are technically an adult—"

Their voices drown out as I feel a pressure around my midriff.

I've never felt anything like this before. It's not pain per se, it's more like a tension that will not fade.

"I'm going to the restroom," I stammer as I stand up. On shaky legs, I head toward the bathroom. Sin notices me from his spot in the back and meets me in the hallway that leads to the bathroom.

"What's wrong?" His brows knit together in worry.

"I don't know," I answer on a low groan of pain. My hand goes to my bulging stomach, and I let out a harsh gasp.

"Contractions? Is the baby coming?" he asks eagerly, already circling around me and studying me from every angle.

"I—" I don't even get to answer him before I feel wetness between my legs. I look down to the puddle forming under my feet. "Shit," I whisper.

"Shit," Sin echoes.

Grabbing me by the hand, he uses his shadows to take me to a private clinic. I'm so wrapped up in the fact that water pours out of me that I barely register him ordering people around.

Like a trained army, several nurses and two female doctors rush me into an operating room.

Wait! Operating room? What's happening?

"Sin?" I croak.

I'm thirsty. And hungry. That's not normal, is it? I'm also feeling increasingly euphoric as the baby rolls around in my stomach. Wait. Is *that* normal?

"What's happening?"

"I think the baby's coming," he tells me with a serious expression on his face.

"Now? Right now?"

"It will all be fine. I've arranged for some trusted people to take care of you. They've been on standby until now," he assures me.

"But . . . how will they know what to do? He's not human."

"He's still a baby. There *must* be some similarities."

"Right . . ." I mutter dryly.

"Try not to stress and—"

I grab his arm and squeeze, my nails digging into his flesh as agony courses through me. "Fuck! Sin! What the fuck?!"

"What's wrong?" He blinks. "Someone help her!"

The nurses move around me haphazardly, trying to get me hooked to an IV. Someone is pressing on my belly, lifting my shirt and . . .

I let out a loud, earth-shattering scream as I feel pain unlike any other tear through my body. No one has time to do anything to help me. Everything happens in less than a minute.

I feel pressure at my vaginal opening, and somehow, I *know*. Flinging the nurses aside, I pull my pants and underwear down my body, tearing some of the material in my hasty attempt.

My lower half is drenched, and a shiver goes down my back when the air hits my damp skin. But even that sensation is ephemeral as in the next moment, a loud *pop* erupts in the air, followed by a high-pitched scream.

I take a deep breath, the adrenaline masking most of the pain. Shocked, I lean forward to look between my legs. With unsurprising speed, Sin has caught the baby in time and is currently nestling him against his chest.

"What—" I swallow. "How the hell—"

I forget all of my disbelief as I take in the sweet face of the crying baby. He's . . . perfect.

The nurses are just as shocked by what happened, but some laugh it off, praising me and saying how lucky I am, especially when the placenta follows swiftly after.

"Here," Sin whispers, coming to my side and placing the baby on my chest.

The nurse suggests I remove my top entirely in case he might try to suckle. I mechanically do it, though I must confess, I've never even thought about *that* part of motherhood.

Hell, before seeing this sweet little creature—quite normal-looking, by the way—I don't think it truly registered to me that I was growing another life inside of me. That Sin and I created this.

"He's so cute," I whisper.

"He is," Sin agrees, a big smile on his face.

The baby is a bit red, but I'd seen some birthing videos before, and that seems to be normal. He has a tuft of dark hair and the cutest little button nose. And when he finally sits on my chest, he opens his eyes and looks up toward me.

My lips part in awe.

"Sin . . ." I start, a little unsure.

"What?"

"His eyes . . ."

Sin moves behind me to be able to see the baby's face better, and going by his speechless reaction, I don't think he noticed it before.

Red. His eyes are a deep, vivid red that would normally only be achieved with some of those Halloween-type contacts.

It's creepy. It's incredibly cute. But it's also something that will raise *many* question marks. And one thing I've vowed since finding out that our baby would be unique was that he would *never* be persecuted for his differences.

I will do everything in my power to keep him safe. The world can be such a daunting place, and unfortunately, sometimes words are worse than actual physical violence.

"I'll keep you safe, little one," I whisper as I lay a kiss on his forehead. "No one will harm you."

Sin caresses the baby's little head, his expression one of pure, unconditional love that mirrors my own. "Aimarren. His name will be Aimarren, Rren."

"Aimarren," I repeat. "I love it."

We're so lost in our little wonder that it takes us a moment to realize the nurses need to weigh and measure the baby. But that would mean examining him and realizing he has . . . unusual eyes.

"Can you do something about them, so they don't check him? We might also need to move to a more private place," I tell him in a low voice.

"I'll get on it."

Sin ushers the medical staff out of the room and convinces them to move me to a nice, private salon where no one will bother us—at least for a while.

"He's so beautiful," I murmur as I continue to gaze upon his sweet face.

Since we're finally alone, Sin offers me some of his blood to help with my healing. He cuts his wrist and places it to my mouth.

I gulp down until I feel my body start mending, until the pain disappears, as does the remainder of my bulging belly.

I look down at myself in shock.

Well, I guess I won't have to diet to fit into that wedding dress after all.

"Thank you." I blow a kiss to Sin as he wipes the remaining blood off his hand. But a few drops made their way onto my chest. Just as he is about to wipe those off, too, with a cloth, the baby stirs.

Almost instinctively, he crawls on my chest until he reaches the drops of blood, licking them.

I stare at him, then at Sin.

"Maybe it's a one-off," I say weakly. But not a second later, the baby moves on my chest again, this time searching for my breast. "See? He knows where to find food." I smile.

Sin, however, doesn't share the optimism.

Just as the baby's mouth latches onto my breast, instead of the regular pull I've heard happens when you first breastfeed a child, something sharp makes me wince in pain.

He doesn't have teeth—he *shouldn't* have teeth. And yet . . . he's using something *very* sharp to pierce my skin and . . .

"I think he knows *exactly* how to find food," Sin adds jokingly as some drops of blood flow down my breast.

I stare at this cute little baby who has no teeth but has some type of fangs, and I cannot believe what's happening.

"Valerion said he would be unique," Sin continues, as if explaining himself. Well, he'd better; after all, if my son has vampiric tendencies, he certainly takes after *him* not me.

"I think this is a bit more than unique," I retort dryly. "He's sucking my blood!"

"Well, *our* blood," he corrects. "And I suppose now I need to work to feed both of you."

"This is not the time to joke about this! We need to talk to Valerion. This is—"

"It will all be fine, Petra. Look at him. Look how happy he is."

He's finished his feed, and to my surprise, the small incisions he'd made disappear the moment he's done. I'm not sure if this is a result of me still having Sin's blood in my system, which facilitates the healing, or perhaps this is yet another . . . peculiarity.

But I find that I don't care about any of that anymore. Sin is right. He is so happy. He's all red around the mouth and smiling at us, those red eyes sparkling with joy.

"Oh, Sin! He's so perfect!" I gush.

"That he is," he agrees. "Thank you," he whispers as he lays a kiss on top of my head. "Thank you for welcoming me home."

CHAPTER EIGHTY-TWO

EPILOGUE II

Eighteen Years Later

"Do we really have to do this?" Sin asks me with a roll of his eyes.

"Why not? It's fun!" I retort as I pull him closer by his tie so I can arrange it properly.

"I would have thought you would *never* want to wear your school uniform again."

"Under any other circumstances, no, I would not want to wear it again. But this is fun! Think about it as role-playing."

"Role-playing as high school students?" He chuckles.

"I mean, we look the part. And it's not like we can go there as Rren's parents. No one would believe us."

"We could still go as his siblings. We don't have to wear *this*."

"We're going to blend in," I say. "Come on, Sin. For me?" I bat my lashes at him.

With a loud sigh, he ends up agreeing to my request. We finish putting on our uniforms and head out the door toward the graduation ceremony at St. Anselm Hall.

The ceremony is being held on the football field. Upon entering, there are rows and rows of parents, relatives, and other students in the bleachers, while on the actual field, all the graduates are seated together in alphabetical order.

With Arnoult as his last name, Rren is among the first ones. He senses us arriving immediately and turns around, looking toward the entrances until he sees us.

A big smile appears on his face as he winks at us.

I send him a flying kiss, and he pretends to catch it before sending one of his own back—our usual routine. He might be an adult now, having turned eighteen just a few weeks ago, but he'll always be my baby boy.

I note more than a few girls look at the exchange with frowns on their faces. Some start whispering, and it's worse that I can *hear* all that—thanks to Sin's potent blood.

She's so cringe, one of them says.

Cringe? I'm . . . cringe? What the hell!

Can't a mother show her affection to her son? What's with all those disgusted expressions?

I glare at them until they quickly look away, though they continue to whisper about my *cringy* performance.

Fucking twats! Who raised them?

Sin shakes his head in amusement. "You do realize how this looks, right?"

"Huh?" I frown.

"You're wearing the school uniform. And you do look young."

I blink. My mouth parts as I realize why those girls had looked at me like that. They thought . . .

"They are jealous," he confirms my thoughts. "They're now whispering about Rren, how hot he looks."

"Of course he does. He's my handsome baby, and he does take after his father." I bat my lashes at Sin.

He pulls me into his arms and gives me a long, rather passionate kiss. As he pulls back, I'm all flushed and flustered, and my brain is mush. It takes me a moment to realize that now the *parents* are gasping and whispering about *teenagers these days* and criticizing our PDA.

"Perhaps we shouldn't have worn the uniforms after all," I mutter.

Sin smirks. I know what he's thinking: *I told you so.*

I grab him by the hand and lead him to our section in the bleachers, hoping we will not attract any more attention. Goodness mine, I only wanted a fun little adventure. I did not realize the optics of it.

We take our seats while the school principal comes onto the stage and starts his speech.

"How do you feel being here again?" I ask Sin as I snuggle closer to him.

"Can't say I missed it much. The only bright side of high school was *you.*"

I laugh. "Who told you to pretend to be a high school student at your advanced age?"

He glances at me and raises a brow. "And allow you to experience high school *without* me? No way in hell. I had firsthand experience at how horny and debauched high school students are. I wasn't about to risk you finding some fucker to *experiment* with."

He wrinkles his nose in disgust, and I can already tell he's remembering that time, quite long ago, when I'd lied to him about other guys. He'd been beside himself thinking his stalking had failed. Although I don't even know how he could *ever* think that, when I later found out that he was watching me almost *all* the time.

It would be quite creepy, really, if it weren't so romantic.

Alas, I happen to like his stalker-ish tendencies since I have some myself. Now, almost two decades later, I'm more than sure I would have done the same—hell, I think he had more restraint than I would have had in some situations.

"You did well," I praise him gently, laying my head on his shoulder as we watch the rest of the speech.

When the principal is finally done, it's time for the graduates to receive their diplomas.

I take out my phone while Sin prepares his camera to take pictures of our darling boy.

The names are called. Rren is the third one.

My chest is full of emotion as I watch my boy, all grown up, finishing school and ready to go out into the world. Oh, Lord, I mustn't tear up.

I snap picture after picture to make sure I capture every single second of the event.

Rren shakes hands with the principal, takes his diploma, and prepares to walk off the stage. I take another picture.

But . . . something is wrong. He's a bit too pale.

"Sin," I whisper, my voice full of horror.

He's noticed the same thing I did. Quickly rising to his feet, he takes my hand and leads me away from the bleachers. He makes eye contact with Rren and signals for him to meet us outside.

We quickly get away from all the commotion, and I'm surprised to see Sin taking me to a very familiar place—the gardener's shed.

We get there first, with Rren coming inside a couple of minutes later.

He is pale, his lips a little blue.

"You overexerted yourself," I say in a chiding motherly voice.

"No," he shakes his head. "It's something else."

"What do you mean?"

He pulls up his sleeve and reveals his lower arm—it's red and full of blisters.

"What—"

Sin is on him, pulling on his graduation gown to look for any other injuries. There are more red spots, some worse than others.

Rren gulps down and looks at us uneasily. "It's been getting progressively worse since my birthday. I think . . ." He bites his lip. "I think it's the sun. It's burning me."

"But . . . your face?" I frown. But as I get closer to him and touch his cheek, I note a thick layer of sunscreen and foundation.

I rub at it with my sleeve only to reveal the same type of redness.

"Why didn't you tell us before?" Sin asks, his expression grave.

"I didn't want you guys to worry about me." He shrugs.

"Do you know what this could be?" I ask Sin.

He shakes his head. "My mentor said he would be something different . . . unique." He sighs. "We need to research more."

"But how, if there's no one else like him?"

"Maybe there is, and my mentor doesn't know. It won't hurt to look."

"It's fine. I'll just stay out of the sun," he says blithely.

"You can't do that forever." I gasp. "We'll figure something out, I promise."

"It's fine, Mom. I've always known I was different, and I've adapted to all the challenges that came my way."

I purse my lips. That is true. From the moment he could talk, we'd started to introduce him to our special but odd world. He's always known we are not the same as other people, although he only truly grasped it when he went to kindergarten and realized no one else drank blood like him. But that wasn't the only difference between him and other boys. His strength and speed were astronomically different from his peers. His sight, hearing, and smell as well. Everything was heightened.

When he'd been in primary school, he'd wished so badly to try different sports, and we didn't allow him because it would not be fair to other kids.

Yet as he matured, he started to understand why we were so strict with him—after all, we had to make sacrifices to ensure he wasn't isolated, that he grew up as normal as possible.

"In the meantime, let's heal those nasty blisters," Sin added. He manifests a bottle of blood and hands it to Rren, who downs it all at once.

Some of the redness heals. Not all of it.

Sin frowns. He manifests another bottle of blood. After drinking until the last drop, everything heals.

I glance back at Sin. He has the same expression on his face. One way or another, we have to get to the bottom of this. We knew he was going to be different, but I don't know how to feel about him spending his entire life in the shadows.

After a few moments of heavy silence, Sin clears his throat.

"Now that you have your diploma, perhaps we should go out and celebrate."

"Yes but—" Rren wrinkles his nose. "Please change out of those uniforms. It's cringe."

I blink. "Cringe?" I echo.

"We will *definitely* change." Sin laughs.

Although still a little worried about Rren, I tell myself there's time to explore this more in depth later. Now it's his moment to shine.

I plaster a smile on my face and hook my arms through Rren's, then through my husband's.

"Sin, work your magic," I whisper. He teleports us back home so we can change, after which we go out to celebrate Rren's graduation.

Goodness mine, I have an adult son—a high school *graduate*.

What's next, I wonder?

ACKNOWLEDGMENTS

This book wouldn't have been possible without the talented human artists who lent me their skills throughout the writing process. Thank you especially to Sofia and Brian, whose incredible artwork fueled my creativity.

To my amazing friends and family—thank you for being with me every step of the way as I worked through the quirks of this story until it reached its final form.

My gratitude also goes to the team at Atria, who believed in this book and gave me the space to bring my vision to life—thank you.

And finally, to my readers: thank you for your patience and for eagerly awaiting this new story from me.

ABOUT THE AUTHOR

Veronica Lancet is the *USA Today* bestselling author of *Fairydale.* She's a doctoral student by day and an author of dark, epic love stories by night. She loves to tread the line between right and wrong, exploring the many shades of morality through flawed heroes, forbidden desires, and the razor-thin edge between love and obsession.

Atria Books, an imprint of Simon & Schuster, fosters an open environment where ideas flourish, bestselling authors soar to new heights, and tomorrow's finest voices are discovered and nurtured. Since its launch in 2002, Atria has published hundreds of bestsellers and extraordinary books, which would not have been possible without the invaluable support and expertise of its team and publishing partners. Thank you to the Atria Books colleagues who collaborated on *Sinister*, as well as to the hundreds of professionals in the Simon & Schuster advertising, audio, communications, design, ebook, finance, human resources, legal, marketing, operations, production, sales, supply chain, subsidiary rights, and warehouse departments who help Atria bring great books to light.

EDITORIAL
Emilia Rhodes
Elizabeth Hitti Musicant
Natalie Argentina

JACKET DESIGN
Emma Van Deun
James Iacobelli

MARKETING
Zakiya N. Jamal

MANAGING EDITORIAL
Paige Lytle
Shelby Pumphrey
Sofia Echeverry
Abby Borchers

PRODUCTION
Allison Har-zvi
Katie Rizzo
Angel Butts
Davina Mock-Maniscalco

PUBLICITY
Megan Rudloff

PUBLISHING OFFICE
Dana Trocker
Suzanne Donahue
Abby Velasco

SUBSIDIARY RIGHTS
Nicole Bond
Sara Bowne
Rebecca Justiniano